THE COLLECTED FANTASY
OF GEORGE MACDONALD

ILLUSTRATED EDITION

GEORGE MACDONALD

THE CASTANEA GROUP

CONTENTS

PHANTASTES A FAERIE ROMANCE FOR MEN AND WOMEN

THE LIGHT PRINCESS

THE GIANT'S HEART

THE GOLDEN KEY

AT THE BACK OF THE NORTH WIND

THE PRINCESS AND THE GOBLIN

THE PRINCESS AND CURDIE

LILITH

THE FANTASTIC IMAGINATION

An introduction to imaginative fiction by the author originally from The Light Princess *and other Fairy Tales, also reprinted in a* Dish of Orts

That we have in English no word corresponding to the German Märchen, drives us to use the word *Fairytale*, regardless of the fact that the tale may have nothing to do with any sort of fairy. The old use of the word *Fairy*, by Spenser at least, might, however, well be adduced, were justification or excuse necessary where *need must*.

Were I asked, what is a fairytale? I should reply, *Read Undine: that is a fairytale; then read this and that as well, and you will see what is a fairytale.* Were I further begged to describe the *fairytale*, or define what it is, I would make answer, that I should as soon think of describing the abstract human face, or stating what must go to constitute a human being. A fairytale is just a fairytale, as a face is just a face; and of all fairytales I know, I think *Undine* the most beautiful.

Many a man, however, who would not attempt to define *a man*, might venture to say something as to what a man ought to be: even so much I will not in this place venture with regard to the fairytale, for my long past work in that kind might but poorly instance or illustrate my now more matured judgment. I will but say some things helpful to the reading, in right-minded fashion, of such fairytales as I would wish to write, or care to read.

Some thinkers would feel sorely hampered if at liberty to use no forms but such as existed in nature, or to invent nothing save in accordance with the laws of the world of the senses; but it must not therefore be imagined that they desire escape from the region of law. Nothing lawless can show the least reason why it should exist, or could at best have more than an appearance of life.

The natural world has its laws, and no man must interfere with them in the way of presentment any more than in the way of use; but they themselves may suggest laws of other kinds, and man may, if he pleases, invent a little world of his own, with its own laws; for there is that in him which delights in calling up new forms--which is the nearest, perhaps, he can come to creation. When such forms are new embodiments of old truths, we call them products of the Imagination; when they are mere inventions, however lovely, I should call them the work of the Fancy: in either case, Law has been diligently at work.

His world once invented, the highest law that comes next into play is, that there shall be harmony between the laws by which the new world has begun to exist; and in the process of his creation, the inventor must hold by those laws. The moment he forgets one of them, he makes the story, by its own postulates, incredible. To be able to live a moment in an imagined world, we must see the laws of its existence obeyed. Those broken, we fall out of it. The imagination in us, whose exercise is essential to the most temporary submission to the imagination of another, immediately, with the disappearance of Law, ceases to act. Suppose the gracious creatures of some childlike region of Fairyland talking either cockney or Gascon! Would not the tale, however lovelily begun, sink once to the level of the Burlesque--of all forms of literature the least worthy? A man's inventions may be stupid or clever, but if he does not hold by the laws of them, or if he makes one law jar with another, he contradicts himself as an inventor, he is no artist. He does not rightly consort his instruments, or he tunes them in different keys. The mind of man is the product of live Law; it thinks by law, it dwells in the midst of law, it gathers from law its growth; with law, therefore, can it alone work to any result. Inharmonious, unconsorting ideas will come to a man, but if he try to use one of such, his work will grow dull, and he will drop it from mere lack of interest. Law is the soil in which alone beauty will grow; beauty is the only stuff in which Truth can be clothed; and you may, if you will, call Imagination the tailor that cuts her garments to fit her, and Fancy his journeyman that puts the pieces of them together, or perhaps at most embroiders their button-holes. Obeying law, the maker works like his creator; not obeying law, he is such a fool as heaps a pile of stones and calls it a church.

In the moral world it is different: there a man may clothe in new forms, and for this employ his imagination freely, but he must invent nothing. He may not, for any purpose, turn its laws upside down. He must not meddle with the relations of live souls. The laws of the spirit of man must hold, alike in this world and in any world he may invent. It were no offence to suppose a world in which everything repelled instead of attracted the things around it; it would be wicked to write a tale representing a man it called good as always doing bad things, or a man it called bad as always doing good things: the notion itself is absolutely lawless. In physical things a man may invent; in moral things he must obey--and take their laws with him into his invented world as well.

"You write as if a fairytale were a thing of importance: must it have meaning?"

It cannot help having some meaning; if it have proportion and harmony it has vitality, and vitality is truth. The beauty may be plainer in it than the truth, but without the truth the beauty could not be, and the fairytale would give no delight. Everyone, however, who feels the story, will read its meaning after his own nature and development: one man will read one meaning in it, another will read another.

"If so, how am I to assure myself that I am not reading my own meaning into it, but yours out of it?"

Why should you be so assured? It may be better that you should read your meaning into it. That may be a higher operation of your intellect than the mere reading of mine out of it: your meaning may be superior to mine.

"Suppose my child ask me what the fairytale means, what am I to say?"

If you do not know what it means, what is easier than to say so? If you do see a meaning in it, there it is for you to give him. A genuine work of art must mean many things; the truer its art, the more things it will mean. If my drawing, on the other hand, is so far from being a work of art that it needs THIS IS A HORSE written under it, what can it matter that neither you nor your child should know what it means? It is there not so much to convey a meaning as to wake a meaning. If it do not even wake an interest, throw it aside. A meaning may be there, but it is not for you. If, again, you do not know a horse when you see it, the name written under it will not serve you much. At all events, the business of the painter is not to teach zoology.

But indeed your children are not likely to trouble you about the meaning. They find what they are capable of finding, and more would be too much. For my part, I do not write for children, but for the childlike, whether of five, or fifty, or seventy-five.

A fairytale is not an allegory. There may be allegory in it, but it not an allegory. He must be an artist indeed who can, in any mode, produce a strict allegory that is not a weariness to the spirit. An allegory must be Mastery or Moorditch.

A fairytale, like a butterfly or a bee, helps itself on all sides, sips every wholesome flower, and spoils not one. The true fairytale is, to my mind, very like the sonata. We all know that a sonata means something; and where there is the faculty of talking with suitable vagueness, and choosing metaphor sufficiently loose, mind may approach mind, in the interpretation of a sonata, with the result of a more or less contenting consciousness of sympathy. But if two or three men sat down to write each what the sonata meant to him, what approximation to definite idea would be the result? Little enough--and that little more than needful. We should find it had roused related, if not identical, feelings, but probably not one common thought. Has the sonata therefore failed? Had it undertaken to convey, or ought it to be expected to impart anything defined, anything notionally recognisable?

"But words are not music; words at least are meant and fitted to carry a precise meaning!"

It is very seldom indeed that they carry the exact meaning of any user of them! And if they can be so used as to convey definite meaning, it does not follow that they ought never to carry anything else. Words are live things that may be variously employed to various ends. They can convey a scientific fact, or throw a shadow of her child's dream on the heart of a mother. They are things to put together like the pieces of dissected map, or to arrange like the notes on a stave. Is the music in them to go for nothing? It can hardly help the definiteness of a meaning: is it therefore to be disregarded? They have length, and breadth, and outline: have they nothing to do with depth? Have they only to describe, never to impress? Has nothing any claim to their use but definite? The cause of a child's tears may be altogether undefinable: has the mother therefore no antidote for his vague misery? That may be strong in colour which has no evident outline. A fairytale, a sonata, a gathering storm, a limitless night, seizes you and sweeps you away: do you begin at once to wrestle with it and ask whence its power over you, whither it is carrying you? The law of each is in the mind of its composer; that law makes one man feel this way, another man feel that way. To one the sonata is a world of odour and beauty, to another of soothing only and sweetness. To one, the cloudy rendezvous is a wild dance, with a terror at its heart; to another, a majestic march of heavenly hosts, with Truth in their centre pointing their course, but as yet restraining her voice. The greatest forces lie in the region of the uncomprehended.

I will go farther.--The best thing you can do for your fellow, next to rousing his conscience, is--not to give him things to think about, but to wake things up that are in him; or say, to make him think things for himself. The best Nature does for us is to work in us such moods in which thoughts of high import arise. Does any aspect of Nature wake but one thought? Does she ever suggest only one definite thing? Does she make any two men in the same place at the same moment think the same thing? Is she therefore a failure, because she is not definite? Is it nothing that she rouses the something deeper than the understanding--the power that underlies thoughts? Does she not set feeling, and so thinking at work? Would it be better that she did this after one fashion and not after many fashions? Nature is mood-engendering, thought-provoking: such ought the sonata, such ought the fairytale to be.

"But a man may then imagine in your work what he pleases, what you never meant!"

Not what he pleases, but what he can. If he be not a true man, he will draw evil out of the best; we need not mind how he treats any work of art! If he be a true man, he will imagine true things; what matter whether I meant them or not? They are there none the less that I cannot claim putting them there! One difference between God's work and man's is, that, while God's work cannot mean more than he meant, man's must mean more than he meant. For in everything that God has made, there is a layer upon layer of ascending significance; also he expresses the same thought in higher and higher kinds of that thought: it is God's things, his embodied thoughts, which alone a man has to use, modified and adapted to his own purposes, for the expression of his thoughts; therefore he cannot help his words and figures falling into such combinations in the mind of another as he had himself not foreseen, so many are the thoughts allied to every other thought, so many are the relations involved in every figure, so many the facts hinted in every symbol. A man may well himself discover truth in what he wrote; for he was dealing all the time things that came from thoughts beyond his own.

"But surely you would explain your idea to one who asked you?"

I say again, if I cannot draw a horse, I will not write THIS IS A HORSE under what I foolishly meant for one. Any key to a work of imagination would be nearly, if not quite, as absurd. The tale is there not to hide, but to show: if it show nothing at your window, do not open your door to it; leave it out in the cold. To ask me to explain, is to say, "Roses! Boil them, or we won't have them!" My tales may not be roses but I will not boil them.

So long as I think my dog can bark, I will not sit up to bark for him.

If a writer's aim be logical conviction, he must spare no logical pains, not merely to be understood, but to escape being misunderstood; where his object is to move by suggestion, to cause to imagine, then let him assail the soul of his reader as the wind assails an aeolian harp. If there be music in my reader, I would gladly wake it. Let fairytale of mine go for a firefly that now flashes, now is dark, but may flash again. Caught in a hand which does not love its kind, it will turn to an insignificant ugly thing, that can neither flash nor fly.

The best way with music, I imagine, is not to bring the forces of our intellect to bear upon it, but to be still and let it work on that part of us for whose sake it exists. We spoil countless precious things by intellectual greed. He who will be a man, and will not be a child, must--he cannot help himself--become a little man, that is, a dwarf. He will, however need no consolation, for he is sure to think himself a very large creature indeed.

If any strain of my "broken music" make a child's eyes flash, or his mother's grow for a moment dim, my labour will not have been in vain.

PHANTASTES A FAERIE ROMANCE FOR MEN AND WOMEN

BY
GEORGE MACDONALD

Edited by Greville MacDonald

"In good sooth, my masters, this is no door.

Yet is it a little window, that looketh upon a great world."

PREFACE

For offering this new edition of my father's Phantastes, my reasons are three. The first is to rescue the work from an edition illustrated without the author's sanction, and so unsuitably that all lovers of the book must have experienced some real grief in turning its pages. With the copyright I secured also the whole of that edition and turned it into pulp.

My second reason is to pay a small tribute to my father by way of personal gratitude for this, his first prose work, which was published nearly fifty years ago. Though unknown to many lovers of his greater writings, none of these has exceeded it in imaginative insight and power of expression. To me it rings with the dominant chord of his life's purpose and work.

My third reason is that wider knowledge and love of the book should be made possible. To this end I have been most happy in the help of my father's old friend, who has illustrated the book. I know of no other living artist who is capable of portraying the spirit of Phantastes; and every reader of this edition will, I believe, feel that the illustrations are a part of the romance, and will gain through them some perception of the brotherhood between George MacDonald and Arthur Hughes.

GREVILLE MACDONALD.
September 1905.

PHANTASTES A FAERIE ROMANCE

"Phantastes from 'their fount' all shapes deriving,
In new habiliments can quickly dight."
FLETCHER'S Purple Island

Es lassen sich Erzählungen ohne Zusammenhang, jedoch mit
Association, wie Träume, denken; Gedichte, die bloss
wohlklingend und voll schöner Worte sind, aber auch ohne
allen Sinn und Zusammenhang, höchstens einzelne Strophen
verständlich, wie Bruchstücke aus den verschiedenartigsten
Dingen. Diese wahre Poesie kann höchstens einen
allegorischen Sinn in Grossen, und eine indirecte Wirkung,
wie Musik, haben. Darum ist die Natur so rein poetisch, wie
die Stube eines Zauberers, eines Physikers, eine
Kinderstube, eine Polter- und Vorrathskammer.

Ein Märchen ist wie ein Traumbild ohne Zusammenhang. Ein
Ensemble wunderbarer Dinge und Begebenheiten, z. B. eine
musikalische Phantasie, die harmonischen Folgen einer
Aeolsharfe, die Natur selbst...

In einem echten Märchen muss alles wunderbar, geheimnissvoll
und zusammenhängend sein; alles belebt, jeder auf eine
andere Art. Die ganze Natur muss wunderlich mit der ganzen
Geisterwelt gemischt sein; hier tritt die Zeit der Anarchie,

*der Gesetzlosigkeit, Freiheit, der Naturstand der Natur, die
Zeit von der Welt ein . . . Die Welt des Märchens ist die,
der Welt der Wahrheit durchaus entgegengesetzte, und eben
darum ihr so durchaus ähnlich, wie das Chaos der vollendeten
Schöpfung ähnlich ist.--NOVALIS.*

CHAPTER 1

"A spirit . . .
. . . . . .
The undulating and silent well,
And rippling rivulet, and evening gloom,
Now deepening the dark shades, for speech assuming,
Held commune with him; as if he and it
Were all that was."
SHELLEY'S *Alastor.*

I awoke one morning with the usual perplexity of mind which accompanies the return of consciousness. As I lay and looked through the eastern window of my room, a faint streak of peach-colour, dividing a cloud that just rose above the low swell of the horizon, announced the approach of the sun. As my thoughts, which a deep and apparently dreamless sleep had dissolved, began again to assume crystalline forms, the strange events of the foregoing night presented themselves anew to my wondering consciousness. The day before had been my one-and-twentieth birthday. Among other ceremonies investing me with my legal rights, the keys of an old secretary, in which my father had kept his private papers, had been delivered up to me. As soon as I was left alone, I ordered lights in the chamber where the secretary stood, the first lights that had been there for many a year; for, since my father's death, the room had been left undisturbed. But, as if the darkness had been too long an inmate to be easily expelled, and had dyed with blackness the walls to which, bat-like, it had clung, these tapers served but ill to light up the gloomy hangings, and seemed to throw yet darker shadows into the hollows of the deep-wrought cornice. All the further portions of the room lay shrouded in a mystery whose deepest folds were gathered around the dark oak cabinet which I now approached with a strange mingling of reverence and curiosity. Perhaps, like a geologist, I was about to turn up to the light some of the buried strata of the human world, with its fossil remains charred by passion and petrified by tears. Perhaps I was to learn how my father, whose personal history was unknown to me, had woven his web of story; how he had found the world, and how the world had left him. Perhaps I was to find only the records of lands and moneys, how gotten and how secured; coming down from strange men, and through troublous times, to me, who knew little or nothing of them all. To solve my speculations, and to dispel the awe which was fast gathering around me as if the dead were drawing near, I approached the secretary; and having found the key that fitted the upper portion, I opened it with some difficulty, drew near it a heavy high-backed chair, and sat down before a multitude of little drawers and slides and pigeon-holes. But the door of a little cupboard in the centre especially attracted my interest, as if there lay the secret of this long-hidden world. Its key I found.

One of the rusty hinges cracked and broke as I opened the door: it revealed a number of small pigeon-holes. These, however, being but shallow compared with the depth of those around the little cupboard, the outer ones reaching to the back of the desk, I concluded that there must be some accessible space behind; and found, indeed, that they were formed in a separate framework, which admitted of the whole being pulled out in one piece. Behind, I found a sort of flexible portcullis of small bars of wood laid close together horizontally. After long search, and trying many ways to move it, I discovered at last a scarcely projecting point of steel on one side. I pressed this repeatedly and hard with the point of an old tool that was lying near, till at length it yielded inwards; and the little slide, flying up suddenly, disclosed a chamber—empty, except that in one corner lay a little heap of withered rose-leaves, whose long-lived scent had long since departed; and, in another, a small packet of papers, tied with a bit of ribbon, whose colour had gone with the rose-scent. Almost fearing to touch them, they witnessed so mutely to the law of oblivion, I leaned back in my chair, and regarded them for a moment; when suddenly there stood on the threshold of the little chamber, as though she had just emerged from its depth, a tiny woman-form, as perfect in shape as if she had been a small Greek statuette roused to life and motion. Her dress was of a kind that could never grow old-fashioned, because it was simply natural: a robe plaited in a band around the neck, and confined by a belt about the waist, descended to her feet. It was only afterwards, however, that I took notice of her dress, although my surprise was by no means of so overpowering a degree as such an apparition might naturally be expected to excite. Seeing, however, as I suppose, some astonishment in my countenance, she came forward within a yard of me, and said, in a voice that strangely recalled a sensation of twilight, and reedy river banks, and a low wind, even in this deathly room:—

"Anodos, you never saw such a little creature before, did you?"

"No," said I; "and indeed I hardly believe I do now."

"Ah! That is always the way with you men; you believe nothing the first time; and it is foolish enough to let mere repetition convince you of what you consider in itself unbelievable. I am not going to argue with you, however, but to grant you a wish."

Here I could not help interrupting her with the foolish speech, of which, however, I had no cause to repent—

"How can such a very little creature as you grant or refuse anything?"

"Is that all the philosophy you have gained in one-and-twenty years?" said she. "Form is much, but size is nothing. It is a mere matter of relation. I suppose your six-foot lordship does not feel altogether insignificant, though to others you do look small beside your old Uncle Ralph, who rises above you a great half-foot at least. But size is of so little consequence with old me, that I may as well accommodate myself to your foolish prejudices."

So saying, she leapt from the desk upon the floor, where she stood a tall, gracious lady, with pale face and large blue eyes. Her dark hair flowed behind, wavy but uncurled, down to her waist, and against it her form stood clear in its robe of white.

"Now," said she, "you will believe me."

Overcome with the presence of a beauty which I could now perceive, and drawn towards her by an attraction irresistible as incomprehensible, I suppose I stretched out my arms towards her, for she drew back a step or two, and said—

"Foolish boy, if you could touch me, I should hurt you. Besides, I was two hundred and thirty-seven years old, last Midsummer eve; and a man must not fall in love with his grandmother, you know."

"But you are not my grandmother," said I.

"How do you know that?" she retorted. "I dare say you know something of your great-grandfathers a good deal further back than that; but you know very little about your great-grandmothers on either side. Now, to the point. Your little sister was reading a fairy-tale to you last night."

"She was."

"When she had finished, she said, as she closed the book, 'Is there a fairy-country, brother?' You replied with a sigh, 'I suppose there is, if one could find the way into it.'"

"I did; but I meant something quite different from what you seem to think."

"Never mind what I seem to think. You shall find the way into Fairy Land to-morrow. Now look in my eyes."

Eagerly I did so. They filled me with an unknown longing. I remembered somehow that my mother died when I was a baby. I looked deeper and deeper, till they spread around me like seas, and I sank in their waters. I forgot all the rest, till I found myself at the window, whose gloomy curtains were withdrawn, and where I stood gazing on a whole heaven of stars, small and sparkling in the moonlight. Below lay a sea, still as death and hoary in the moon, sweeping into bays and around capes and islands, away, away, I knew not whither. Alas! It was no sea, but a low bog burnished by the moon. "Surely there is such a sea somewhere!" said I to myself. A low sweet voice beside me replied—

"In Fairy Land, Anodos."

I turned, but saw no one. I closed the secretary, and went to my own room, and to bed.

All this I recalled as I lay with half-closed eyes. I was soon to find the truth of the lady's promise, that this day I should discover the road into Fairy Land.

CHAPTER 2

"'Where is the stream?' cried he, with tears. 'Seest thou
its not in blue waves above us?' He looked up, and lo! the
blue stream was flowing gently over their heads."
—NOVALIS, *Heinrich von Ofterdingen.*

While these strange events were passing through my mind, I suddenly, as one awakes to the consciousness that the sea has been moaning by him for hours, or that the storm has been howling about his window all night, became aware of the sound of running water near me; and, looking out of bed, I saw that a large green marble basin, in which I was wont to wash, and which stood on a low pedestal of the same material in a corner of my room, was overflowing like a spring; and that a stream of clear water was running over the carpet, all the length of the room, finding its outlet I knew not where. And, stranger still, where this carpet, which I had myself designed to imitate a field of grass and daisies, bordered the course of the little stream, the grass-blades and daisies seemed to wave in a tiny breeze that followed the water's flow; while under the rivulet they bent and swayed with every motion of the changeful current, as if they were about to dissolve with it, and, forsaking their fixed form, become fluent as the waters.

My dressing-table was an old-fashioned piece of furniture of black oak, with drawers all down the front. These were elaborately carved in foliage, of which ivy formed the chief part. The nearer end of this table remained just as it had been, but on the further end a singular change had commenced. I happened to fix my eye on a little cluster of ivy-leaves. The first of these was evidently the work of the carver; the next looked curious; the third was unmistakable ivy; and just beyond it a tendril of clematis had twined itself about the gilt handle of one of the drawers. Hearing next a slight motion above me, I looked up, and saw that the branches and leaves designed upon the curtains of my bed were slightly in motion. Not knowing what change might follow next, I thought it high time to get up; and, springing from the bed, my bare feet alighted upon a cool green sward; and although I dressed in all haste, I found myself completing my toilet under the boughs of a great tree, whose top waved in the golden stream of the sunrise with many interchanging lights, and with shadows of leaf and branch gliding over leaf and branch, as the cool morning wind swung it to and fro, like a sinking sea-wave.

After washing as well as I could in the clear stream, I rose and looked around me. The tree under which I seemed to have lain all night was one of the advanced guard of a dense forest, towards which the rivulet ran. Faint traces of a footpath, much overgrown with grass and moss, and with here and there a pimpernel even, were discernible along the right bank. "This," thought I, "must surely be the path into Fairy Land, which the lady of last night promised I should so soon find." I crossed the rivulet, and accompanied it, keeping the footpath on its right bank, until it led me, as I expected, into the wood. Here I left it, without any good reason: and with a vague feeling that I ought to have followed its course, I took a more southerly direction.

CHAPTER 3

"Man doth usurp all space,
   Stares thee, in rock, bush, river, in
   the face.
   Never thine eyes behold a tree;
   'Tis no sea thou seest in the sea,
   'Tis but a disguised humanity.
   To avoid thy fellow, vain thy plan;
   All that interests a man, is man."
HENRY SUTTON.

The trees, which were far apart where I entered, giving free passage to the level rays of the sun, closed rapidly as I advanced, so that ere long their crowded stems barred the sunlight out, forming as it were a thick grating between me and the East. I seemed to be advancing towards a second midnight. In the midst of the intervening twilight, however, before I entered what appeared to be the darkest portion of the forest, I saw a country maiden coming towards me from its very depths. She did not seem to observe me, for she was apparently intent upon a bunch of wild flowers which she carried in her hand. I could hardly see her face; for, though she came direct towards me, she never looked up. But when we met, instead of passing, she turned and walked alongside of me for a few yards, still keeping her face downwards, and busied with her flowers. She spoke rapidly, however, all the time, in a low tone, as if talking to herself, but evidently addressing the purport of her words to me.

She seemed afraid of being observed by some lurking foe. "Trust the Oak," said she; "trust the Oak, and the Elm, and the great Beech. Take care of the Birch, for though she is honest, she is too young not to be changeable. But shun the Ash and the Alder; for the Ash is an ogre,—you will know him by his thick fingers; and the Alder will smother you with her web of hair, if you let her near you at night." All this was uttered without pause or alteration of tone. Then she turned suddenly and left me, walking still with the same unchanging gait. I could not conjecture what she meant, but satisfied myself with thinking that it would be time enough to find out her meaning when there was need to make use of her warning, and that the occasion would reveal the admonition. I concluded from the flowers that she carried, that the forest could not be everywhere so dense as it appeared from where I was now walking; and I was right in this conclusion. For soon I came to a more open part, and by-and-by crossed a wide grassy glade, on which were several circles of brighter green. But even here I was struck with the utter stillness. No bird sang. No insect hummed. Not a living creature crossed my way. Yet somehow the whole environment seemed only asleep, and to wear even in sleep an air of expectation. The trees seemed all to have an expression of conscious mystery, as if they said to themselves, "We could, an' if we would." They had all a meaning look about them. Then I remembered that night is the fairies' day, and the moon their sun; and I thought—Everything sleeps and dreams now: when the night comes, it will be different. At the same time I, being a man and a child of the day, felt some anxiety as to how I should fare among the elves and other children of the night who wake when mortals dream, and find their common life in those wondrous hours that flow noiselessly over the moveless death-like forms of men and women and children, lying strewn and parted beneath the weight of the heavy waves of night, which flow on and beat them down, and hold them drowned and senseless, until the ebb tide comes, and the waves sink away, back into the ocean of the dark. But I took courage and went on. Soon, however, I became again anxious, though from another cause. I had eaten nothing that day, and for an hour past had been feeling the want of food. So I grew afraid lest I should find nothing to meet my human necessities in this strange place; but once more I comforted myself with hope and went on.

Before noon, I fancied I saw a thin blue smoke rising amongst the stems of larger trees in front of me; and soon I came to an open spot of ground in which stood a little cottage, so built that the stems of four great trees formed its corners, while their branches met and intertwined over its roof, heaping a great cloud of leaves over it, up towards the heavens. I wondered at finding a human dwelling in this neighbourhood; and yet it did not look altogether human, though sufficiently so to encourage me to expect to find some sort of food. Seeing no door, I went round to the other side, and there I found one, wide open. A woman sat beside it, preparing some vegetables for dinner. This was homely and comforting. As I came near, she looked up, and seeing me, showed no surprise, but bent her head again over her work, and said in a low tone:

"Did you see my daughter?"

"I believe I did," said I. "Can you give me something to eat, for I am very hungry?" "With pleasure," she replied, in the same tone; "but do not say anything more, till you come into the house, for the Ash is watching us."

Having said this, she rose and led the way into the cottage; which, I now saw, was built of the stems of small trees set closely together, and was furnished with rough chairs and tables, from which even the bark had not been removed. As soon as she had shut the door and set a chair—

"You have fairy blood in you," said she, looking hard at me.

"How do you know that?"

"You could not have got so far into this wood if it were not so; and I am trying to find out some trace of it in your countenance. I think I see it."

"What do you see?"

"Oh, never mind: I may be mistaken in that."

"But how then do you come to live here?"

"Because I too have fairy blood in me."

Here I, in my turn, looked hard at her, and thought I could perceive, notwithstanding the coarseness of her features, and especially the heaviness of her eyebrows, a something unusual—I could hardly call it grace, and yet it was an expression that strangely contrasted with the form of her features. I noticed too that her hands were delicately formed, though brown with work and exposure.

"I should be ill," she continued, "if I did not live on the borders of the fairies' country, and now and then eat of their food. And I see by your eyes that you are not quite free of the same need; though, from your education and the activity of your mind, you have felt it less than I. You may be further removed too from the fairy race."

I remembered what the lady had said about my grandmothers.

Here she placed some bread and some milk before me, with a kindly apology for the homeliness of the fare, with which, however, I was in no humour to quarrel. I now thought it time to try to get some explanation of the strange words both of her daughter and herself.

"What did you mean by speaking so about the Ash?"

She rose and looked out of the little window. My eyes followed her; but as the window was too small to allow anything to be seen from where I was sitting, I rose and looked over her shoulder. I had just time to see, across the open space, on the edge of the denser forest, a single large ash-tree, whose foliage showed bluish, amidst the truer green of the other trees around it; when she pushed me back with an expression of impatience and terror, and then almost shut out the light from the window by setting up a large old book in it.

"In general," said she, recovering her composure, "there is no danger in the daytime, for then he is sound asleep; but there is something unusual going on in the woods; there must be some solemnity among the fairies to-night, for all the trees are restless, and although they cannot come awake, they see and hear in their sleep."

"But what danger is to be dreaded from him?"

Instead of answering the question, she went again to the window and looked out, saying she feared the fairies would be interrupted by foul weather, for a storm was brewing in the west.

"And the sooner it grows dark, the sooner the Ash will be awake," added she.

I asked her how she knew that there was any unusual excitement in the woods. She replied—

"Besides the look of the trees, the dog there is unhappy; and the eyes and ears of the white rabbit are redder than usual, and he frisks about as if he expected some fun. If the cat were at home, she would have her back up; for the young fairies pull the sparks out of her tail with bramble thorns, and she knows when they are coming. So do I, in another way."

At this instant, a grey cat rushed in like a demon, and disappeared in a hole in the wall.

"There, I told you!" said the woman.

"But what of the ash-tree?" said I, returning once more to the subject. Here, however, the young woman, whom I had met in the morning, entered. A smile passed between the mother and daughter; and then the latter began to help her mother in little household duties.

"I should like to stay here till the evening," I said; "and then go on my journey, if you will allow me."

"You are welcome to do as you please; only it might be better to stay all night, than risk the dangers of the wood then. Where are you going?"

"Nay, that I do not know," I replied, "but I wish to see all that is to be seen, and therefore I should like to start just at sundown." "You are a bold youth, if you have any idea of what you are daring; but a rash one, if you know nothing about it; and, excuse me, you do not seem very well informed about the country and its manners. However, no one comes here but for some reason, either known to himself or to those who have charge of him; so you shall do just as you wish."

Accordingly I sat down, and feeling rather tired, and disinclined for further talk, I asked leave to look at the old book which still screened the window. The woman brought it to me directly, but not before taking another look towards the forest, and then drawing a white blind over the window. I sat down opposite to it by the table, on which I laid the great old volume, and read. It contained many wondrous tales of Fairy Land, and olden times, and the Knights of King Arthur's table. I read on and on, till the shades of the afternoon began to deepen; for in the midst of the forest it gloomed earlier than in the open country. At length I came to this passage—

"Here it chanced, that upon their quest, Sir Galahad and Sir Percivale rencountered in the depths of a great forest. Now, Sir Galahad was dight all in harness of silver, clear and shining; the which is a delight to look upon, but full hasty to tarnish, and withouten the labour of a ready squire, uneath to be kept fair and clean. And yet withouten squire or page, Sir Galahad's armour shone like the moon. And he rode a great white mare, whose bases and other housings were black, but all besprent with fair lilys of silver sheen. Whereas Sir Percivale bestrode a red horse, with a tawny mane and tail; whose trappings were all to-smirched with mud and mire; and his armour was wondrous rosty to behold, ne could he by any art furbish it again; so that as the sun in his going down shone twixt the bare trunks of the trees, full upon the knights twain, the one did seem all shining with light, and the other all to glow with ruddy fire. Now it came about in this wise. For Sir Percivale, after his escape from the demon lady, whenas the cross on the handle of his sword smote him to the heart, and he rove himself through the thigh, and escaped away, he came to a great wood; and, in nowise cured of his fault, yet bemoaning the same, the damosel of the alder tree encountered him, right fair to see; and with her fair words and false countenance she comforted him and beguiled him, until he followed her where she led him to a—"

Here a low hurried cry from my hostess caused me to look up from the book, and I read no more.

"Look there!" she said; "look at his fingers!"

Just as I had been reading in the book, the setting sun was shining through a cleft in the clouds piled up in the west; and a shadow as of a large distorted hand, with thick knobs and humps on the fingers, so that it was much wider across the fingers than across the undivided part of the hand, passed slowly over the little blind, and then as slowly returned in the opposite direction.

"He is almost awake, mother; and greedier than usual to-night."

"Hush, child; you need not make him more angry with us than he is; for you do not know how soon something may happen to oblige us to be in the forest after nightfall."

"But you are in the forest," said I; "how is it that you are safe here?"

"He dares not come nearer than he is now," she replied; "for any of those four oaks, at the corners of our cottage, would tear him to pieces; they are our friends. But he stands there and makes awful faces at us sometimes, and stretches out his long arms and fingers, and tries to kill us with fright; for, indeed, that is his favourite way of doing. Pray, keep out of his way to-night."

"Shall I be able to see these things?" said I.

"That I cannot tell yet, not knowing how much of the fairy nature there is in you. But we shall soon see whether you can discern the fairies in my little garden, and that will be some guide to us."

"Are the trees fairies too, as well as the flowers?" I asked.

"They are of the same race," she replied; "though those you call fairies in your country are chiefly the young children of the flower fairies. They are very fond of having fun with the thick people, as they call you; for, like most children, they like fun better than anything else."

"Why do you have flowers so near you then? Do they not annoy you?"

"Oh, no, they are very amusing, with their mimicries of grown people, and mock solemnities. Sometimes they will act a whole play through before my eyes, with perfect composure and assurance, for they are not afraid of me. Only, as soon as they have done, they burst into peals of tiny laughter, as if it was such a joke to have been serious over anything. These I speak of, however, are the fairies of the garden. They are more staid and educated than those of the fields and woods. Of course they have near relations amongst the wild flowers, but they patronise them, and treat them as country cousins, who know nothing of life, and very little of manners. Now and then, however, they are compelled to envy the grace and simplicity of the natural flowers."

"Do they live *in* the flowers?" I said.

"I cannot tell," she replied. "There is something in it I do not understand. Sometimes they disappear altogether, even from me, though I know they are near. They seem to die always with the flowers they resemble, and by whose names they are called; but whether they return to life with the fresh flowers, or, whether it be new flowers, new fairies, I cannot tell. They have as many sorts of dispositions as men and women, while their moods are yet more variable; twenty different expressions will cross their little faces in half a minute. I often amuse myself with watching them, but I have never been able to make personal acquaintance with any of them. If I speak to one, he or she looks up in my face, as if I were not worth heeding, gives a little laugh, and runs away." Here the woman started, as if suddenly recollecting herself, and said in a low voice to her daughter, "Make haste—go and watch him, and see in what direction he goes."

I may as well mention here, that the conclusion I arrived at from the observations I was afterwards able to make, was, that the flowers die because the fairies go away; not that the fairies disappear because the flowers die. The flowers seem a sort of houses for them, or outer bodies, which they can put on or off when they please. Just as you could form some idea of the nature of a man from the kind of house he built, if he followed his own taste, so you could, without seeing the fairies, tell what any one of them is like, by looking at the flower till you feel that you understand it. For just what the flower says to you, would the face and form of the fairy say; only so much more plainly as a face and human figure can express more than a flower. For the house or the clothes, though like the inhabitant or the wearer, cannot be wrought into an equal power of utterance. Yet you would see a strange resemblance, almost oneness, between the flower and the fairy, which you could not describe, but which described itself to you. Whether all the flowers have fairies, I cannot determine, any more than I can be sure whether all men and women have souls.

The woman and I continued the conversation for a few minutes longer. I was much interested by the information she gave me, and astonished at the language in which she was able to convey it. It seemed that intercourse with the fairies was no bad education in itself. But now the daughter returned with the news, that the Ash had just gone away in a south-westerly direction; and, as my course seemed to lie eastward, she hoped I should be in no danger of meeting him if I departed at once. I looked out of the little window, and there stood the ash-tree, to my eyes the same as before; but I believed that they knew better than I did, and prepared to go. I pulled out my purse, but to my dismay there was nothing in it. The woman with a smile begged me not to trouble myself, for money was not of the slightest use there; and as I might meet with people in my journeys whom I could not recognise to be fairies, it was well I had no money to offer, for nothing offended them so much.

"They would think," she added, "that you were making game of them; and that is their peculiar privilege with regard to us." So we went together into the little garden which sloped down towards a lower part of the wood.

Here, to my great pleasure, all was life and bustle. There was still light enough from the day to see a little; and the pale half-moon, halfway to the zenith, was reviving every moment. The whole garden was like a carnival, with tiny, gaily decorated forms, in groups, assemblies, processions, pairs or trios, moving stately on, running about wildly, or sauntering hither or thither. From the cups or bells of tall flowers, as from balconies, some looked down on the masses below, now bursting with laughter, now grave as owls; but even in their deepest solemnity, seeming only to be waiting for the arrival of the next laugh. Some were launched on a little marshy stream at the bottom, in boats chosen from the heaps of last year's leaves that lay about, curled and withered. These soon sank with them; whereupon they swam ashore and got others. Those who took fresh rose-leaves for their boats floated the longest; but for these they had to fight; for the fairy of the rose-tree complained bitterly that they were stealing her clothes, and defended her property bravely.

"You can't wear half you've got," said some.

"Never you mind; I don't choose you to have them: they are my property."

"All for the good of the community!" said one, and ran off with a great hollow leaf. But the rose-fairy sprang after him (what a beauty she was! only too like a drawing-room young lady), knocked him heels-over-head as he ran, and recovered her great red leaf. But in the meantime twenty had hurried off in different directions with others just as good; and the little creature sat down and cried, and then, in a pet, sent a perfect pink snowstorm of petals from her tree, leaping from branch to branch, and stamping and shaking and pulling. At last, after another good cry, she chose the biggest she could find, and ran away laughing, to launch her boat amongst the rest.

But my attention was first and chiefly attracted by a group of fairies near the cottage, who were talking together around what seemed a last dying primrose. They talked singing, and their talk made a song, something like this:

"Sister Snowdrop died
    Before we were born."
    "She came like a bride
    In a snowy morn."
    "What's a bride?"
    "What is snow?
    "Never tried."
    "Do not know."
    "Who told you about her?"
    "Little Primrose there
    Cannot do without her."
    "Oh, so sweetly fair!"
    "Never fear,
    She will come,
    Primrose dear."
    "Is she dumb?"

"She'll come by-and-by."
    "You will never see her."
    "She went home to dies,
    "Till the new year."
    "Snowdrop!" "'Tis no good
    To invite her."
    "Primrose is very rude,
    "I will bite her."

"Oh, you naughty Pocket!
    "Look, she drops her head."
    "She deserved it, Rocket,
    "And she was nearly dead."
    "To your hammock—off with you!"
    "And swing alone."
    "No one will laugh with you."
    "No, not one."

"Now let us moan."
  "And cover her o'er."
  "Primrose is gone."
  "All but the flower."
  "Here is a leaf."
  "Lay her upon it."
  "Follow in grief."
  "Pocket has done it."

"Deeper, poor creature!
  Winter may come."
  "He cannot reach her —
  That is a hum."
  "She is buried, the beauty!"
  "Now she is done."
  "That was the duty."
  "Now for the fun."

And with a wild laugh they sprang away, most of them towards the cottage. During the latter part of the song-talk, they had formed themselves into a funeral procession, two of them bearing poor Primrose, whose death Pocket had hastened by biting her stalk, upon one of her own great leaves. They bore her solemnly along some distance, and then buried her under a tree. Although I say *her* I saw nothing but the withered primrose-flower on its long stalk. Pocket, who had been expelled from the company by common consent, went sulkily away towards her hammock, for she was the fairy of the calceolaria, and looked rather wicked. When she reached its stem, she stopped and looked round. I could not help speaking to her, for I stood near her. I said, "Pocket, how could you be so naughty?"

"I am never naughty," she said, half-crossly, half-defiantly; "only if you come near my hammock, I will bite you, and then you will go away."

"Why did you bite poor Primrose?"

"Because she said we should never see Snowdrop; as if we were not good enough to look at her, and she was, the proud thing!—served her right!"

"Oh, Pocket, Pocket," said I; but by this time the party which had gone towards the house, rushed out again, shouting and screaming with laughter. Half of them were on the cat's back, and half held on by her fur and tail, or ran beside her; till, more coming to their help, the furious cat was held fast; and they proceeded to pick the sparks out of her with thorns and pins, which they handled like harpoons. Indeed, there were more instruments at work about her than there could have been sparks in her. One little fellow who held on hard by the tip of the tail, with his feet planted on the ground at an angle of forty-five degrees, helping to keep her fast, administered a continuous flow of admonitions to Pussy.

"Now, Pussy, be patient. You know quite well it is all for your good. You cannot be comfortable with all those sparks in you; and, indeed, I am charitably disposed to believe" (here he became very pompous) "that they are the cause of all your bad temper; so we must have them all out, every one; else we shall be reduced to the painful necessity of cutting your claws, and pulling out your eye-teeth. Quiet! Pussy, quiet!"

But with a perfect hurricane of feline curses, the poor animal broke loose, and dashed across the garden and through the hedge, faster than even the fairies could follow. "Never mind, never mind, we shall find her again; and by that time she will have laid in a fresh stock of sparks. Hooray!" And off they set, after some new mischief.

But I will not linger to enlarge on the amusing display of these frolicsome creatures. Their manners and habits are now so well known to the world, having been so often described by eyewitnesses, that it would be only indulging self-conceit, to add my account in full to the rest. I cannot help wishing, however, that my readers could see them for themselves. Especially do I desire that they should see the fairy of the daisy; a little, chubby, round-eyed child, with such innocent trust in his look! Even the most mischievous of the fairies would not tease him, although he did not belong to their set at all, but was quite a little country bumpkin. He wandered about alone, and looked at everything, with his hands in his little pockets, and a white night-cap on, the darling! He was not so beautiful as many other wild flowers I saw afterwards, but so dear and loving in his looks and little confident ways.

CHAPTER 4

"When bale is att hyest, boote is nyest."
  Ballad of Sir Aldingar.

By this time, my hostess was quite anxious that I should be gone. So, with warm thanks for their hospitality, I took my leave, and went my way through the little garden towards the forest. Some of the garden flowers had wandered into the wood, and were growing here and there along the path, but the trees soon became too thick and shadowy for them. I particularly noticed some tall lilies, which grew on both sides of the way, with large dazzlingly white flowers, set off by the universal green. It was now dark enough for me to see that every flower was shining with a light of its own. Indeed it was by this light that I saw them, an internal, peculiar light, proceeding from each, and not reflected from a common source of light as in the daytime. This light sufficed only for the plant itself, and was not strong enough to cast any but the faintest shadows around it, or to illuminate any of the neighbouring objects with other than the faintest tinge of its own individual hue. From the lilies above mentioned, from the campanulas, from the foxgloves, and every bell-shaped flower, curious little figures shot up their heads, peeped at me, and drew back. They seemed to inhabit them, as snails their shells but I was sure some of them were intruders, and belonged to the gnomes or goblin-fairies, who inhabit the ground and earthy creeping plants. From the cups of Arum lilies, creatures with great heads and grotesque faces shot up like Jack-in-the-box, and made grimaces at me; or rose slowly and slily over the edge of the cup, and spouted water at me, slipping suddenly back, like those little soldier-crabs that inhabit the shells of sea-snails. Passing a row of tall thistles, I saw them crowded with little faces, which peeped every one from behind its flower, and drew back as quickly; and I heard them saying to each other, evidently intending me to hear, but the speaker always hiding behind his tuft, when I looked in his direction, "Look at him! Look at him! He has begun a story without a beginning, and it will never have any end. He! he! he! Look at him!"

But as I went further into the wood, these sights and sounds became fewer, giving way to others of a different character. A little forest of wild hyacinths was alive with exquisite creatures, who stood nearly motionless, with drooping necks, holding each by the stem of her flower, and swaying gently with it, whenever a low breath of wind swung the crowded floral belfry. In like manner, though differing of course in form and meaning, stood a group of harebells, like little angels waiting, ready, till they were wanted to go on some yet unknown message. In darker nooks, by the mossy roots of the trees, or in little tufts of grass, each dwelling in a globe of its own green light, weaving a network of grass and its shadows, glowed the glowworms.

They were just like the glowworms of our own land, for they are fairies everywhere; worms in the day, and glowworms at night, when their own can appear, and they can be themselves to others as well as themselves. But they had their enemies here. For I saw great strong-armed beetles, hurrying about with most unwieldy haste, awkward as elephant-calves, looking apparently for glowworms; for the moment a beetle espied one, through what to it was a forest of grass, or an underwood of moss, it pounced upon it, and bore it away, in spite of its feeble resistance. Wondering what their object could be, I watched one of the beetles, and then I discovered a thing I could not account for. But it is no use trying to account for things in Fairy Land; and one who travels there soon learns to forget the very idea of doing so, and takes everything as it comes; like a child, who, being in a chronic condition of wonder, is surprised at nothing. What I saw was this. Everywhere, here and there over the ground, lay little, dark-looking lumps of something more like earth than anything else, and about the size of a chestnut. The beetles hunted in couples for these; and having found one, one of them stayed to watch it, while the other hurried to find a glowworm. By signals, I presume, between them, the latter soon found his companion again: they then took the glowworm and held its luminous tail to the dark earthly pellet; when lo, it shot up into the air like a sky-rocket, seldom, however, reaching the height of the highest tree. Just like a rocket too, it burst in the air, and fell in a shower of the most gorgeously coloured sparks of every variety of hue; golden and red, and purple and green, and blue and rosy fires crossed and inter-crossed each other, beneath the shadowy heads, and between the columnar stems of the forest trees. They never used the same glowworm twice, I observed; but let him go, apparently uninjured by the use they had made of him.

In other parts, the whole of the immediately surrounding foliage was illuminated by the interwoven dances in the air of splendidly coloured fire-flies, which sped hither and thither, turned, twisted, crossed, and recrossed, entwining every complexity of intervolved motion. Here and there, whole mighty trees glowed with an emitted phosphorescent light. You could trace the very course of the great roots in the earth by the faint light that came through; and every twig, and every vein on every leaf was a streak of pale fire.

All this time, as I went through the wood, I was haunted with the feeling that other shapes, more like my own size and mien, were moving about at a little distance on all sides of me. But as yet I could discern none of them, although the moon was high enough to send a great many of her rays down between the trees, and these rays were unusually bright, and sight-giving, notwithstanding she was only a half-moon. I constantly imagined, however, that forms were visible in all directions except that to which my gaze was turned; and that they only became invisible, or resolved themselves into other woodland shapes, the moment my looks were directed towards them. However this may have been, except for this feeling of presence, the woods seemed utterly bare of anything like human companionship, although my glance often fell on some object which I fancied to be a human form; for I soon found that I was quite deceived; as, the moment I fixed my regard on it, it showed plainly that it was a bush, or a tree, or a rock.

Soon a vague sense of discomfort possessed me. With variations of relief, this gradually increased; as if some evil thing were wandering about in my neighbour-hood, sometimes nearer and sometimes further off, but still approaching. The feeling continued and deepened, until all my pleasure in the shows of various kinds that everywhere betokened the presence of the merry fairies vanished by degrees, and left me full of anxiety and fear, which I was unable to associate with any definite object whatever. At length the thought crossed my mind with horror: "Can it be possible that the Ash is looking for me? or that, in his nightly wander-ings, his path is gradually verging towards mine?" I comforted myself, however, by remembering that he had started quite in another direction; one that would lead him, if he kept it, far apart from me; especially as, for the last two or three hours, I had been diligently journeying eastward. I kept on my way, therefore, striving by direct effort of the will against the encroaching fear; and to this end occupying my mind, as much as I could, with other thoughts. I was so far successful that, although I was conscious, if I yielded for a moment, I should be almost over-whelmed with horror, I was yet able to walk right on for an hour or more. What I feared I could not tell. Indeed, I was left in a state of the vaguest uncertainty as regarded the nature of my enemy, and knew not the mode or object of his attacks; for, somehow or other, none of my questions had succeeded in drawing a definite answer from the dame in the cottage. How then to defend myself I knew not; nor even by what sign I might with certainty recognise the presence of my foe; for as yet this vague though powerful fear was all the indication of danger I had. To add to my distress, the clouds in the west had risen nearly to the top of the skies, and they and the moon were travelling slowly towards each other. Indeed, some of their advanced guard had already met her, and she had begun to wade through a filmy vapour that gradually deepened.

At length she was for a moment almost entirely obscured. When she shone out again, with a brilliancy increased by the contrast, I saw plainly on the path before me—from around which at this spot the trees receded, leaving a small space of green sward—the shadow of a large hand, with knotty joints and protuberances here and there. Especially I remarked, even in the midst of my fear, the bulbous points of the fingers. I looked hurriedly all around, but could see nothing from which such a shadow should fall. Now, however, that I had a direction, however undetermined, in which to project my apprehension, the very sense of danger and need of action overcame that stifling which is the worst property of fear. I reflected in a moment, that if this were indeed a shadow, it was useless to look for the object that cast it in any other direction than between the shadow and the moon. I looked, and peered, and intensified my vision, all to no purpose. I could see nothing of that kind, not even an ash-tree in the neighbourhood. Still the shadow remained; not steady, but moving to and fro, and once I saw the fingers close, and grind them-selves close, like the claws of a wild animal, as if in uncontrollable longing for some anticipated prey. There seemed but one mode left of discovering the substance of this shadow. I went forward boldly, though with an inward shudder which I would not heed, to the spot where the shadow lay, threw myself on the ground, laid my head within the form of the hand, and turned my eyes towards the moon Good heavens! What did I see? I wonder that ever I arose, and that the very shadow of the hand did not hold me where I lay until fear had frozen my brain. I saw the strangest figure; vague, shadowy, almost transparent, in the central parts, and grad-ually deepening in substance towards the outside, until it ended in extremities capable of casting such a shadow as fell from the hand, through the awful fingers of which I now saw the moon. The hand was uplifted in the attitude of a paw about to strike its prey. But the face, which throbbed with fluctuating and pulsatory visibility —not from changes in the light it reflected, but from changes in its own conditions of reflecting power, the alterations being from within, not from without—it was horrible. I do not know how to describe it. It caused a new sensation. Just as one cannot translate a horrible odour, or a ghastly pain, or a fearful sound, into words, so I cannot describe this new form of awful hideousness. I can only try to describe something that is not it, but seems somewhat parallel to it; or at least is suggested by it. It reminded me of what I had heard of vampires; for the face resembled that of a corpse more than anything else I can think of; especially when I can conceive such a face in motion, but not suggesting any life as the source of the motion. The features were rather handsome than otherwise, except the mouth, which had scarcely a curve in it. The lips were of equal thickness; but the thickness was not at all remarkable, even although they looked slightly swollen. They seemed fixedly open, but were not wide apart. Of course I did not *remark* these lineaments at the time: I was too horrified for that. I noted them afterwards, when the form returned on my inward sight with a vividness too intense to admit of my doubting the accu-racy of the reflex. But the most awful of the features were the eyes. These were alive, yet not with life.

They seemed lighted up with an infinite greed. A gnawing voracity, which devoured the devourer, seemed to be the indwelling and propelling power of the whole ghostly apparition. I lay for a few moments simply imbruted with terror; when another cloud, obscuring the moon, delivered me from the immediately paralysing effects of the presence to the vision of the object of horror, while it added the force of imagination to the power of fear within me; inasmuch as, knowing far worse cause for apprehension than before, I remained equally ignorant from what I had to defend myself, or how to take any precautions: he might be upon me in the darkness any moment. I sprang to my feet, and sped I knew not whither, only away from the spectre. I thought no longer of the path, and often narrowly escaped dashing myself against a tree, in my headlong flight of fear.

Great drops of rain began to patter on the leaves. Thunder began to mutter, then growl in the distance. I ran on. The rain fell heavier. At length the thick leaves could hold it up no longer; and, like a second firmament, they poured their torrents on the earth. I was soon drenched, but that was nothing. I came to a small swollen stream that rushed through the woods. I had a vague hope that if I crossed this stream, I should be in safety from my pursuer; but I soon found that my hope was as false as it was vague. I dashed across the stream, ascended a rising ground, and reached a more open space, where stood only great trees. Through them I directed my way, holding eastward as nearly as I could guess, but not at all certain that I was not moving in an opposite direction. My mind was just reviving a little from its extreme terror, when, suddenly, a flash of lightning, or rather a cataract of successive flashes, behind me, seemed to throw on the ground in front of me, but far more faintly than before, from the extent of the source of the light, the shadow of the same horrible hand. I sprang forward, stung to yet wilder speed; but had not run many steps before my foot slipped, and, vainly attempting to recover myself, I fell at the foot of one of the large trees. Half-stunned, I yet raised myself, and almost involuntarily looked back. All I saw was the hand within three feet of my face. But, at the same moment, I felt two large soft arms thrown round me from behind; and a voice like a woman's said: "Do not fear the goblin; he dares not hurt you now." With that, the hand was suddenly withdrawn as from a fire, and disappeared in the darkness and the rain. Overcome with the mingling of terror and joy, I lay for some time almost insensible. The first thing I remember is the sound of a voice above me, full and low, and strangely reminding me of the sound of a gentle wind amidst the leaves of a great tree. It murmured over and over again: "I may love him, I may love him; for he is a man, and I am only a beech-tree." I found I was seated on the ground, leaning against a human form, and supported still by the arms around me, which I knew to be those of a woman who must be rather above the human size, and largely proportioned. I turned my head, but without moving otherwise, for I feared lest the arms should untwine themselves; and clear, somewhat mournful eyes met mine. At least that is how they impressed me; but I could see very little of colour or outline as we sat in the dark and rainy shadow of the tree. The face seemed very lovely, and solemn from its stillness; with the aspect of one who is quite content, but waiting for something. I saw my conjecture from her arms was correct: she was above the human scale throughout, but not greatly.

"Why do you call yourself a beech-tree?" I said.

"Because I am one," she replied, in the same low, musical, murmuring voice.

"You are a woman," I returned.

"Do you think so? Am I very like a woman then?"

"You are a very beautiful woman. Is it possible you should not know it?"

"I am very glad you think so. I fancy I feel like a woman sometimes. I do so to-night—and always when the rain drips from my hair. For there is an old prophecy in our woods that one day we shall all be men and women like you. Do you know anything about it in your region? Shall I be very happy when I am a woman? I fear not, for it is always in nights like these that I feel like one. But I long to be a woman for all that."

I had let her talk on, for her voice was like a solution of all musical sounds. I now told her that I could hardly say whether women were happy or not. I knew one who had not been happy; and for my part, I had often longed for Fairy Land, as she now longed for the world of men. But then neither of us had lived long, and perhaps people grew happier as they grew older. Only I doubted it.

I could not help sighing. She felt the sigh, for her arms were still round me. She asked me how old I was.

"Twenty-one," said I.

"Why, you baby!" said she, and kissed me with the sweetest kiss of winds and odours. There was a cool faithfulness in the kiss that revived my heart wonderfully. I felt that I feared the dreadful Ash no more.

"What did the horrible Ash want with me?" I said.

"I am not quite sure, but I think he wants to bury you at the foot of his tree. But he shall not touch you, my child."

"Are all the ash-trees as dreadful as he?"

"Oh, no. They are all disagreeable selfish creatures—(what horrid men they will make, if it be true!)—but this one has a hole in his heart that nobody knows of but one or two; and he is always trying to fill it up, but he cannot. That must be what he wanted you for. I wonder if he will ever be a man. If he is, I hope they will kill him."

"How kind of you to save me from him!"

"I will take care that he shall not come near you again. But there are some in the wood more like me, from whom, alas! I cannot protect you. Only if you see any of them very beautiful, try to walk round them."

"What then?"

"I cannot tell you more. But now I must tie some of my hair about you, and then the Ash will not touch you. Here, cut some off. You men have strange cutting things about you."

She shook her long hair loose over me, never moving her arms.

"I cannot cut your beautiful hair. It would be a shame."

"Not cut my hair! It will have grown long enough before any is wanted again in this wild forest. Perhaps it may never be of any use again—not till I am a woman." And she sighed.

As gently as I could, I cut with a knife a long tress of flowing, dark hair, she hanging her beautiful head over me. When I had finished, she shuddered and breathed deep, as one does when an acute pain, steadfastly endured without sign of suffering, is at length relaxed. She then took the hair and tied it round me, singing a strange, sweet song, which I could not understand, but which left in me a feeling like this—

"I saw thee ne'er before;
I see thee never more;
But love, and help, and pain, beautiful one,
Have made thee mine, till all my years are done."

I cannot put more of it into words. She closed her arms about me again, and went on singing. The rain in the leaves, and a light wind that had arisen, kept her song company. I was wrapt in a trance of still delight. It told me the secret of the woods, and the flowers, and the birds. At one time I felt as if I was wandering in childhood through sunny spring forests, over carpets of primroses, anemones, and little white starry things—I had almost said creatures, and finding new wonderful flowers at every turn. At another, I lay half dreaming in the hot summer noon, with a book of old tales beside me, beneath a great beech; or, in autumn, grew sad because I trod on the leaves that had sheltered me, and received their last blessing in the sweet odours of decay; or, in a winter evening, frozen still, looked up, as I went home to a warm fireside, through the netted boughs and twigs to the cold, snowy moon, with her opal zone around her. At last I had fallen asleep; for I know nothing more that passed till I found myself lying under a superb beech-tree, in the clear light of the morning, just before sunrise. Around me was a girdle of fresh beech-leaves. Alas! I brought nothing with me out of Fairy Land, but memories—memories. The great boughs of the beech hung drooping around me. At my head rose its smooth stem, with its great sweeps of curving surface that swelled like undeveloped limbs. The leaves and branches above kept on the song which had sung me asleep; only now, to my mind, it sounded like a farewell and a speedwell. I sat a long time, unwilling to go; but my unfinished story urged me on. I must act and wander. With the sun well risen, I rose, and put my arms as far as they would reach around the beech-tree, and kissed it, and said good-bye. A trembling went through the leaves; a few of the last drops of the night's rain fell from off them at my feet; and as I walked slowly away, I seemed to hear in a whisper once more the words: "I may love him, I may love him; for he is a man, and I am only a beech-tree."

CHAPTER 5

"*And she was smooth and full, as if one gush*
  Of life had washed her, or as if a sleep
  Lay on her eyelid, easier to sweep
  Than bee from daisy."
BEDDOIS' *Pygmalion.*

"*Sche was as whyt as lylye yn May,*
  Or snow that sneweth yn wynterys day."
Romance of Sir Launfal.

I walked on, in the fresh morning air, as if new-born. The only thing that damped my pleasure was a cloud of something between sorrow and delight that crossed my mind with the frequently returning thought of my last night's hostess. "But then," thought I, "if she is sorry, I could not help it; and she has all the pleasures she ever had. Such a day as this is surely a joy to her, as much at least as to me. And her life will perhaps be the richer, for holding now within it the memory of what came, but could not stay. And if ever she is a woman, who knows but we may meet somewhere? There is plenty of room for meeting in the universe." Comforting myself thus, yet with a vague compunction, as if I ought not to have left her, I went on. There was little to distinguish the woods to-day from those of my own land; except that all the wild things, rabbits, birds, squirrels, mice, and the numberless other inhabitants, were very tame; that is, they did not run away from me, but gazed at me as I passed, frequently coming nearer, as if to examine me more closely. Whether this came from utter ignorance, or from familiarity with the human appearance of beings who never hurt them, I could not tell. As I stood once, looking up to the splendid flower of a parasite, which hung from the branch of a tree over my head, a large white rabbit cantered slowly up, put one of its little feet on one of mine, and looked up at me with its red eyes, just as I had been looking up at the flower above me. I stooped and stroked it; but when I attempted to lift it, it banged the ground with its hind feet and scampered off at a great rate, turning, however, to look at me several times before I lost sight of it. Now and then, too, a dim human figure would appear and disappear, at some distance, amongst the trees, moving like a sleep-walker. But no one ever came near me.

This day I found plenty of food in the forest—strange nuts and fruits I had never seen before. I hesitated to eat them; but argued that, if I could live on the air of Fairy Land, I could live on its food also. I found my reasoning correct, and the result was better than I had hoped; for it not only satisfied my hunger, but operated in such a way upon my senses that I was brought into far more complete relationship with the things around me. The human forms appeared much more dense and defined; more tangibly visible, if I may say so. I seemed to know better which direction to choose when any doubt arose. I began to feel in some degree what the birds meant in their songs, though I could not express it in words, any more than you can some landscapes. At times, to my surprise, I found myself listening attentively, and as if it were no unusual thing with me, to a conversation between two squirrels or monkeys. The subjects were not very interesting, except as associated with the individual life and necessities of the little creatures: where the best nuts were to be found in the neighbourhood, and who could crack them best, or who had most laid up for the winter, and such like; only they never said where the store was. There was no great difference in kind between their talk and our ordinary human conversation. Some of the creatures I never heard speak at all, and believe they never do so, except under the impulse of some great excitement. The mice talked; but the hedgehogs seemed very phlegmatic; and though I met a couple of moles above ground several times, they never said a word to each other in my hearing. There were no wild beasts in the forest; at least, I did not see one larger than a wild cat. There were plenty of snakes, however, and I do not think they were all harmless; but none ever bit me.

Soon after mid-day I arrived at a bare rocky hill, of no great size, but very steep; and having no trees—scarcely even a bush—upon it, entirely exposed to the heat of the sun. Over this my way seemed to lie, and I immediately began the ascent. On reaching the top, hot and weary, I looked around me, and saw that the forest still stretched as far as the sight could reach on every side of me. I observed that the trees, in the direction in which I was about to descend, did not come so near the foot of the hill as on the other side, and was especially regretting the unexpected postponement of shelter, because this side of the hill seemed more difficult to descend than the other had been to climb, when my eye caught the appearance of a natural path, winding down through broken rocks and along the course of a tiny stream, which I hoped would lead me more easily to the foot. I tried it, and found the descent not at all laborious; nevertheless, when I reached the bottom, I was very tired and exhausted with the heat. But just where the path seemed to end, rose a great rock, quite overgrown with shrubs and creeping plants, some of them in full and splendid blossom: these almost concealed an opening in the rock, into which the path appeared to lead. I entered, thirsting for the shade which it promised. What was my delight to find a rocky cell, all the angles rounded away with rich moss, and every ledge and projection crowded with lovely ferns, the variety of whose forms, and groupings, and shades wrought in me like a poem; for such a harmony could not exist, except they all consented to some one end! A little well of the clearest water filled a mossy hollow in one corner. I drank, and felt as if I knew what the elixir of life must be; then threw myself on a mossy mound that lay like a couch along the inner end. Here I lay in a delicious reverie for some time; during which all lovely forms, and colours, and sounds seemed to use my brain as a common hall, where they could come and go, unbidden and unexcused. I had never imagined that such capacity for simple happiness lay in me, as was now awakened by this assembly of forms and spiritual sensations, which yet were far too vague to admit of being translated into any shape common to my own and another mind. I had lain for an hour, I should suppose, though it may have been far longer, when, the harmonious tumult in my mind having somewhat relaxed, I became aware that my eyes were fixed on a strange, time-worn bas-relief on the rock opposite to me. This, after some pondering, I concluded to represent Pygmalion, as he awaited the quickening of his statue. The sculptor sat more rigid than the figure to which his eyes were turned. That seemed about to step from its pedestal and embrace the man, who waited rather than expected.

"A lovely story," I said to myself. "This cave, now, with the bushes cut away from the entrance to let the light in, might be such a place as he would choose, withdrawn from the notice of men, to set up his block of marble, and mould into a visible body the thought already clothed with form in the unseen hall of the sculptor's brain. And, indeed, if I mistake not," I said, starting up, as a sudden ray of light arrived at that moment through a crevice in the roof, and lighted up a small portion of the rock, bare of vegetation, "this very rock is marble, white enough and delicate enough for any statue, even if destined to become an ideal woman in the arms of the sculptor."

I took my knife and removed the moss from a part of the block on which I had been lying; when, to my surprise, I found it more like alabaster than ordinary marble, and soft to the edge of the knife. In fact, it was alabaster. By an inexplicable, though by no means unusual kind of impulse, I went on removing the moss from the surface of the stone; and soon saw that it was polished, or at least smooth, throughout. I continued my labour; and after clearing a space of about a couple of square feet, I observed what caused me to prosecute the work with more interest and care than before. For the ray of sunlight had now reached the spot I had cleared, and under its lustre the alabaster revealed its usual slight transparency when polished, except where my knife had scratched the surface; and I observed that the transparency seemed to have a definite limit, and to end upon an opaque body like the more solid, white marble. I was careful to scratch no more. And first, a vague anticipation gave way to a startling sense of possibility; then, as I proceeded, one revelation after another produced the entrancing conviction, that under the crust of alabaster lay a dimly visible form in marble, but whether of man or woman I could not yet tell. I worked on as rapidly as the necessary care would permit; and when I had uncovered the whole mass, and rising from my knees, had retreated a little way, so that the effect of the whole might fall on me, I saw before me with sufficient plainness—though at the same time with considerable indistinctness, arising from the limited amount of light the place admitted, as well as from the nature of the object itself—a block of pure alabaster enclosing the form, apparently in marble, of a reposing woman. She lay on one side, with her hand under her cheek, and her face towards me; but her hair had fallen partly over her face, so that I could not see the expression of the whole. What I did see appeared to me perfectly lovely; more near the face that had been born with me in my soul, than anything I had seen before in nature or art. The actual outlines of the rest of the form were so indistinct, that the more than semi-opacity of the alabaster seemed insufficient to account for the fact; and I conjectured that a light robe added its obscurity. Number-less histories passed through my mind of change of substance from enchantment and other causes, and of imprisonments such as this before me. I thought of the Prince of the Enchanted City, half marble and half a man; of Ariel; of Niobe; of the Sleeping Beauty in the Wood; of the bleeding trees; and many other histories. Even my adventure of the preceding evening with the lady of the beech-tree contributed to arouse the wild hope, that by some means life might be given to this form also, and that, breaking from her alabaster tomb, she might glorify my eyes with her presence. "For," I argued, "who can tell but this cave may be the home of Marble, and this, essential Marble—that spirit of marble which, present throughout, makes it capable of being moulded into any form? Then if she should awake! But how to awake her? A kiss awoke the Sleeping Beauty! A kiss cannot reach her through the incrusting alabaster." I kneeled, however, and kissed the pale coffin; but she slept on. I bethought me of Orpheus, and the following stones—that trees should follow his music seemed nothing surprising now. Might not a song awake this form, that the glory of motion might for a time displace the loveliness of rest? Sweet sounds can go where kisses may not enter. I sat and thought. Now, although always delighting in music, I had never been gifted with the power of song, until I entered the fairy forest. I had a voice, and I had a true sense of sound; but when I tried to sing, the one would not content the other, and so I remained silent. This morning, however, I had found myself, ere I was aware, rejoicing in a song; but whether it was before or after I had eaten of the fruits of the forest, I could not satisfy myself. I concluded it was after, however; and that the increased impulse to sing I now felt, was in part owing to having drunk of the little well, which shone like a brilliant eye in a corner of the cave. I sat down on the ground by the "antenatal tomb," leaned upon it with my face towards the head of the figure within, and sang—the words and tones coming together, and inseparably connected, as if word and tone formed one thing; or, as if each word could be uttered only in that tone, and was incapable of distinction from it, except in idea, by an acute analysis. I sang something like this: but the words are only a dull representation of a state whose very elevation precluded the possibility of remembrance; and in which I presume the words really employed were as far above these, as that state transcended this wherein I recall it:

"*Marble woman, vainly sleeping*
  In the very death of dreams!
  Wilt thou—slumber from thee sweeping,
  All but what with vision teems—
  Hear my voice come through the golden
  Mist of memory and hope;
  And with shadowy smile embolden
  Me with primal Death to cope?

"Thee the sculptors all pursuing,
Have embodied but their own;
Round their visions, form enduring,
Marble vestments thou hast thrown;
But thyself, in silence winding,
Thou hast kept eternally;
Thee they found not, many finding—
I have found thee: wake for me."

As I sang, I looked earnestly at the face so vaguely revealed before me. I fancied, yet believed it to be but fancy, that through the dim veil of the alabaster, I saw a motion of the head as if caused by a sinking sigh. I gazed more earnestly, and concluded that it was but fancy. Nevertheless I could not help singing again—

"Rest is now filled full of beauty,
And can give thee up, I ween;
Come thou forth, for other duty
Motion pineth for her queen.

"Or, if needing years to wake thee
From thy slumbrous solitudes,
Come, sleep-walking, and betake thee
To the friendly, sleeping woods.

Sweeter dreams are in the forest,
Round thee storms would never rave;
And when need of rest is sorest,
Glide thou then into thy cave.

"Or, if still thou choosest rather
Marble, be its spell on me;
Let thy slumber round me gather,
Let another dream with thee!"

Again I paused, and gazed through the stony shroud, as if, by very force of penetrative sight, I would clear every lineament of the lovely face. And now I thought the hand that had lain under the cheek, had slipped a little downward. But then I could not be sure that I had at first observed its position accurately. So I sang again; for the longing had grown into a passionate need of seeing her alive—

"Or art thou Death, O woman? for since I
    Have set me singing by thy side,
    Life hath forsook the upper sky,
    And all the outer world hath died.

"Yea, I am dead; for thou hast drawn
    My life all downward unto thee.
    Dead moon of love! let twilight dawn:
    Awake! and let the darkness flee.

"Cold lady of the lovely stone!
    Awake! or I shall perish here;
    And thou be never more alone,
    My form and I for ages near.

"But words are vain; reject them all —
    They utter but a feeble part:
    Hear thou the depths from which they call,
    The voiceless longing of my heart."

There arose a slightly crashing sound. Like a sudden apparition that comes and is gone, a white form, veiled in a light robe of whiteness, burst upwards from the stone, stood, glided forth, and gleamed away towards the woods. For I followed to the mouth of the cave, as soon as the amazement and concentration of delight permitted the nerves of motion again to act; and saw the white form amidst the trees, as it crossed a little glade on the edge of the forest where the sunlight fell full, seeming to gather with intenser radiance on the one object that floated rather than flitted through its lake of beams. I gazed after her in a kind of despair; found, freed, lost! It seemed useless to follow, yet follow I must. I marked the direction she took; and without once looking round to the forsaken cave, I hastened towards the forest.

CHAPTER 6

"*Ah, let a man beware, when his wishes, fulfilled, rain down*
upon him, and his happiness is unbounded."
—*FOUQUE, Der Zauberring.*

"*Thy red lips, like worms,*
Travel over my cheek."
—*MOTHERWELL.*

But as I crossed the space between the foot of the hill and the forest, a vision of
another kind delayed my steps. Through an opening to the westward flowed, like a
stream, the rays of the setting sun, and overflowed with a ruddy splendour the
open space where I was. And riding as it were down this stream towards me, came
a horseman in what appeared red armour. From frontlet to tail, the horse likewise
shone red in the sunset. I felt as if I must have seen the knight before; but as he
drew near, I could recall no feature of his countenance. Ere he came up to me,
however, I remembered the legend of Sir Percival in the rusty armour, which I had
left unfinished in the old book in the cottage: it was of Sir Percival that he reminded
me. And no wonder; for when he came close up to me, I saw that, from crest to
heel, the whole surface of his armour was covered with a light rust. The golden
spurs shone, but the iron greaves glowed in the sunlight. The *morning star*, which
hung from his wrist, glittered and glowed with its silver and bronze. His whole
appearance was terrible; but his face did not answer to this appearance. It was sad,
even to gloominess; and something of shame seemed to cover it. Yet it was noble
and high, though thus beclouded; and the form looked lofty, although the head
drooped, and the whole frame was bowed as with an inward grief. The horse

seemed to share in his master's dejection, and walked spiritless and slow. I noticed, too, that the white plume on his helmet was discoloured and drooping. "He has fallen in a joust with spears," I said to myself; "yet it becomes not a noble knight to be conquered in spirit because his body hath fallen." He appeared not to observe me, for he was riding past without looking up, and started into a warlike attitude the moment the first sound of my voice reached him. Then a flush, as of shame, covered all of his face that the lifted beaver disclosed. He returned my greeting with distant courtesy, and passed on. But suddenly, he reined up, sat a moment still, and then turning his horse, rode back to where I stood looking after him.

"I am ashamed," he said, "to appear a knight, and in such a guise; but it behoves me to tell you to take warning from me, lest the same evil, in his kind, overtake the singer that has befallen the knight. Hast thou ever read the story of Sir Percival and the"—(here he shuddered, that his armour rang)—"Maiden of the Alder-tree?"

"In part, I have," said I; "for yesterday, at the entrance of this forest, I found in a cottage the volume wherein it is recorded." "Then take heed," he rejoined; "for, see my armour—I put it off; and as it befell to him, so has it befallen to me. I that was proud am humble now. Yet is she terribly beautiful—beware. Never," he added, raising his head, "shall this armour be furbished, but by the blows of knightly encounter, until the last speck has disappeared from every spot where the battle-axe and sword of evil-doers, or noble foes, might fall; when I shall again lift my head, and say to my squire, 'Do thy duty once more, and make this armour shine.'"

Before I could inquire further, he had struck spurs into his horse and galloped away, shrouded from my voice in the noise of his armour. For I called after him, anxious to know more about this fearful enchantress; but in vain—he heard me not. "Yet," I said to myself, "I have now been often warned; surely I shall be well on my guard; and I am fully resolved I shall not be ensnared by any beauty, however beautiful. Doubtless, some one man may escape, and I shall be he." So I went on into the wood, still hoping to find, in some one of its mysterious recesses, my lost lady of the marble. The sunny afternoon died into the loveliest twilight. Great bats began to flit about with their own noiseless flight, seemingly purpose-less, because its objects are unseen. The monotonous music of the owl issued from all unexpected quarters in the half-darkness around me. The glow-worm was alight here and there, burning out into the great universe. The night-hawk height-ened all the harmony and stillness with his oft-recurring, discordant jar. Number-less unknown sounds came out of the unknown dusk; but all were of twilight-kind, oppressing the heart as with a condensed atmosphere of dreamy undefined love and longing. The odours of night arose, and bathed me in that luxurious mournfulness peculiar to them, as if the plants whence they floated had been watered with bygone tears. Earth drew me towards her bosom; I felt as if I could fall down and kiss her. I forgot I was in Fairy Land, and seemed to be walking in a perfect night of our own old nursing earth. Great stems rose about me, uplifting a thick multitudinous roof above me of branches, and twigs, and leaves—the bird and insect world uplifted over mine, with its own landscapes, its own thickets, and paths, and glades, and dwellings; its own bird-ways and insect-delights. Great boughs crossed my path; great roots based the tree-columns, and mightily clasped the earth, strong to lift and strong to uphold. It seemed an old, old forest, perfect in forest ways and pleasures. And when, in the midst of this ecstasy, I remembered that under some close canopy of leaves, by some giant stem, or in some mossy cave, or beside some leafy well, sat the lady of the marble, whom my songs had called forth into the outer world, waiting (might it not be?) to meet and thank her deliverer in a twilight which would veil her confusion, the whole night became one dream-realm of joy, the central form of which was everywhere present, although unbeheld. Then, remembering how my songs seemed to have called her from the marble, piercing through the pearly shroud of alabaster —"Why," thought I, "should not my voice reach her now, through the ebon night that inwraps her." My voice burst into song so spontaneously that it seemed involuntarily.

"Not a sound
    But, echoing in me,
    Vibrates all around
    With a blind delight,
    Till it breaks on Thee,
    Queen of Night!

Every tree,
    O'ershadowing with gloom,
    Seems to cover thee
    Secret, dark, love-still'd,
    In a holy room
    Silence-filled.

"Let no moon
    Creep up the heaven to-night;
    I in darksome noon
    Walking hopefully,
    Seek my shrouded light—
    Grope for thee!

"Darker grow
    The borders of the dark!
    Through the branches glow,
    From the roof above,
    Star and diamond-sparks
    Light for love."

Scarcely had the last sounds floated away from the hearing of my own ears, when I heard instead a low delicious laugh near me. It was not the laugh of one who would not be heard, but the laugh of one who has just received something long and patiently desired—a laugh that ends in a low musical moan. I started, and, turning sideways, saw a dim white figure seated beside an intertwining thicket of smaller trees and underwood.

"It is my white lady!" I said, and flung myself on the ground beside her; striving, through the gathering darkness, to get a glimpse of the form which had broken its marble prison at my call.

"It is your white lady!" said the sweetest voice, in reply, sending a thrill of speechless delight through a heart which all the love-charms of the preceding day and evening had been tempering for this culminating hour. Yet, if I would have confessed it, there was something either in the sound of the voice, although it seemed sweetness itself, or else in this yielding which awaited no gradation of gentle approaches, that did not vibrate harmoniously with the beat of my inward music. And likewise, when, taking her hand in mine, I drew closer to her, looking for the beauty of her face, which, indeed, I found too plenteously, a cold shiver ran through me; but "it is the marble," I said to myself, and heeded it not.

She withdrew her hand from mine, and after that would scarce allow me to touch her. It seemed strange, after the fulness of her first greeting, that she could not trust me to come close to her. Though her words were those of a lover, she kept herself withdrawn as if a mile of space interposed between us.

"Why did you run away from me when you woke in the cave?" I said.

"Did I?" she returned. "That was very unkind of me; but I did not know better."

"I wish I could see you. The night is very dark."

"So it is. Come to my grotto. There is light there."

"Have you another cave, then?"

"Come and see."

But she did not move until I rose first, and then she was on her feet before I could offer my hand to help her. She came close to my side, and conducted me through the wood. But once or twice, when, involuntarily almost, I was about to put my arm around her as we walked on through the warm gloom, she sprang away several paces, always keeping her face full towards me, and then stood looking at me, slightly stooping, in the attitude of one who fears some half-seen enemy. It was too dark to discern the expression of her face. Then she would return and walk close beside me again, as if nothing had happened. I thought this strange; but, besides that I had almost, as I said before, given up the attempt to account for appearances in Fairy Land, I judged that it would be very unfair to expect from one who had slept so long and had been so suddenly awakened, a behaviour correspondent to what I might unreflectingly look for. I knew not what she might have been dreaming about. Besides, it was possible that, while her words were free, her sense of touch might be exquisitely delicate.

At length, after walking a long way in the woods, we arrived at another thicket, through the intertexture of which was glimmering a pale rosy light.

"Push aside the branches," she said, "and make room for us to enter."

I did as she told me.

"Go in," she said; "I will follow you."

I did as she desired, and found myself in a little cave, not very unlike the marble cave. It was festooned and draperied with all kinds of green that cling to shady rocks. In the furthest corner, half-hidden in leaves, through which it glowed, mingling lovely shadows between them, burned a bright rosy flame on a little earthen lamp. The lady glided round by the wall from behind me, still keeping her face towards me, and seated herself in the furthest corner, with her back to the lamp, which she hid completely from my view. I then saw indeed a form of perfect loveliness before me. Almost it seemed as if the light of the rose-lamp shone through her (for it could not be reflected from her); such a delicate shade of pink seemed to shadow what in itself must be a marbly whiteness of hue. I discovered afterwards, however, that there was one thing in it I did not like; which was, that the white part of the eye was tinged with the same slight roseate hue as the rest of the form. It is strange that I cannot recall her features; but they, as well as her some-what girlish figure, left on me simply and only the impression of intense loveliness. I lay down at her feet, and gazed up into her face as I lay. She began, and told me a strange tale, which, likewise, I cannot recollect; but which, at every turn and every pause, somehow or other fixed my eyes and thoughts upon her extreme beauty; seeming always to culminate in something that had a relation, revealed or hidden, but always operative, with her own loveliness. I lay entranced. It was a tale which brings back a feeling as of snows and tempests; torrents and water-sprites; lovers parted for long, and meeting at last; with a gorgeous summer night to close up the whole. I listened till she and I were blended with the tale; till she and I were the whole history. And we had met at last in this same cave of greenery, while the summer night hung round us heavy with love, and the odours that crept through the silence from the sleeping woods were the only signs of an outer world that invaded our solitude. What followed I cannot clearly remember. The succeeding horror almost obliterated it. I woke as a grey dawn stole into the cave. The damsel had disappeared; but in the shrubbery, at the mouth of the cave, stood a strange horrible object. It looked like an open coffin set up on one end; only that the part for the head and neck was defined from the shoulder-part. In fact, it was a rough repre-sentation of the human frame, only hollow, as if made of decaying bark torn from a tree.

It had arms, which were only slightly seamed, down from the shoulder-blade by the elbow, as if the bark had healed again from the cut of a knife. But the arms moved, and the hand and the fingers were tearing asunder a long silky tress of hair. The thing turned round—it had for a face and front those of my enchantress, but now of a pale greenish hue in the light of the morning, and with dead lustreless eyes. In the horror of the moment, another fear invaded me. I put my hand to my waist, and found indeed that my girdle of beech-leaves was gone. Hair again in her hands, she was tearing it fiercely. Once more, as she turned, she laughed a low laugh, but now full of scorn and derision; and then she said, as if to a companion with whom she had been talking while I slept, "There he is; you can take him now." I lay still, petrified with dismay and fear; for I now saw another figure beside her, which, although vague and indistinct, I yet recognised but too well. It was the Ash-tree. My beauty was the Maid of the Alder! and she was giving me, spoiled of my only availing defence, into the hands of my awful foe. The Ash bent his Gorgon-head, and entered the cave. I could not stir. He drew near me. His ghoul-eyes and his ghastly face fascinated me. He came stooping, with the hideous hand outstretched, like a beast of prey. I had given myself up to a death of unfathomable horror, when, suddenly, and just as he was on the point of seizing me, the dull, heavy blow of an axe echoed through the wood, followed by others in quick repeti-tion. The Ash shuddered and groaned, withdrew the outstretched hand, retreated backwards to the mouth of the cave, then turned and disappeared amongst the trees. The other walking Death looked at me once, with a careless dislike on her beautifully moulded features; then, heedless any more to conceal her hollow deformity, turned her frightful back and likewise vanished amid the green obscurity without. I lay and wept. The Maid of the Alder-tree had befooled me—nearly slain me—in spite of all the warnings I had received from those who knew my danger.

CHAPTER 7

"Fight on, my men, Sir Andrew sayes,
  A little I am hurt, but yett not slaine;
  I'le but lye downe and bleede awhile,
  And then I'le rise and fight againe."
Ballad of Sir Andrew Barton.

But I could not remain where I was any longer, though the daylight was hateful to me, and the thought of the great, innocent, bold sunrise unendurable. Here there was no well to cool my face, smarting with the bitterness of my own tears. Nor would I have washed in the well of that grotto, had it flowed clear as the rivers of Paradise. I rose, and feebly left the sepulchral cave. I took my way I knew not whither, but still towards the sunrise. The birds were singing; but not for me. All the creatures spoke a language of their own, with which I had nothing to do, and to which I cared not to find the key any more.

I walked listlessly along. What distressed me most—more even than my own folly—was the perplexing question, How can beauty and ugliness dwell so near? Even with her altered complexion and her face of dislike; disenchanted of the belief that clung around her; known for a living, walking sepulchre, faithless, deluding, traitorous; I felt notwithstanding all this, that she was beautiful. Upon this I pondered with undiminished perplexity, though not without some gain. Then I began to make surmises as to the mode of my deliverance; and concluded that some hero, wandering in search of adventure, had heard how the forest was infested; and, knowing it was useless to attack the evil thing in person, had assailed with his battle-axe the body in which he dwelt, and on which he was dependent for his power of mischief in the wood. "Very likely," I thought, "the repentant-knight, who warned me of the evil which has befallen me, was busy retrieving his lost honour, while I was sinking into the same sorrow with himself; and, hearing of the dangerous and mysterious being, arrived at his tree in time to save me from being dragged to its roots, and buried like carrion, to nourish him for yet deeper insatiableness." I found afterwards that my conjecture was correct. I wondered how he had fared when his blows recalled the Ash himself, and that too I learned afterwards.

I walked on the whole day, with intervals of rest, but without food; for I could not have eaten, had any been offered me; till, in the afternoon, I seemed to approach the outskirts of the forest, and at length arrived at a farm-house. An unspeakable joy arose in my heart at beholding an abode of human beings once more, and I hastened up to the door, and knocked. A kind-looking, matronly woman, still handsome, made her appearance; who, as soon as she saw me, said kindly, "Ah, my poor boy, you have come from the wood! Were you in it last night?"

I should have ill endured, the day before, to be called *boy*; but now the motherly kindness of the word went to my heart; and, like a boy indeed, I burst into tears. She soothed me right gently; and, leading me into a room, made me lie down on a settle, while she went to find me some refreshment. She soon returned with food, but I could not eat. She almost compelled me to swallow some wine, when I revived sufficiently to be able to answer some of her questions. I told her the whole story.

"It is just as I feared," she said; "but you are now for the night beyond the reach of any of these dreadful creatures. It is no wonder they could delude a child like you. But I must beg you, when my husband comes in, not to say a word about these things; for he thinks me even half crazy for believing anything of the sort. But I must believe my senses, as he cannot believe beyond his, which give him no intimations of this kind. I think he could spend the whole of Midsummer-eve in the wood and come back with the report that he saw nothing worse than himself. Indeed, good man, he would hardly find anything better than himself, if he had seven more senses given him."

"But tell me how it is that she could be so beautiful without any heart at all—without any place even for a heart to live in."

"I cannot quite tell," she said; "but I am sure she would not look so beautiful if she did not take means to make herself look more beautiful than she is. And then, you know, you began by being in love with her before you saw her beauty, mistaking her for the lady of the marble—another kind altogether, I should think. But the chief thing that makes her beautiful is this: that, although she loves no man, she loves the love of any man; and when she finds one in her power, her desire to bewitch him and gain his love (not for the sake of his love either, but that she may be conscious anew of her own beauty, through the admiration he manifests), makes her very lovely—with a self-destructive beauty, though; for it is that which is constantly wearing her away within, till, at last, the decay will reach her face, and her whole front, when all the lovely mask of nothing will fall to pieces, and she be vanished for ever. So a wise man, whom she met in the wood some years ago, and who, I think, for all his wisdom, fared no better than you, told me, when, like you, he spent the next night here, and recounted to me his adventures."

I thanked her very warmly for her solution, though it was but partial; wondering much that in her, as in woman I met on my first entering the forest, there should be such superiority to her apparent condition. Here she left me to take some rest; though, indeed, I was too much agitated to rest in any other way than by simply ceasing to move.

In half an hour, I heard a heavy step approach and enter the house. A jolly voice, whose slight huskiness appeared to proceed from overmuch laughter, called out "Betsy, the pigs' trough is quite empty, and that is a pity. Let them swill, lass! They're of no use but to get fat. Ha! ha! ha! Gluttony is not forbidden in their commandments. Ha! ha! ha!" The very voice, kind and jovial, seemed to disrobe the room of the strange look which all new places wear—to disenchant it out of the realm of the ideal into that of the actual. It began to look as if I had known every corner of it for twenty years; and when, soon after, the dame came and fetched me to partake of their early supper, the grasp of his great hand, and the harvest-moon of his benevolent face, which was needed to light up the rotundity of the globe beneath it, produced such a reaction in me, that, for a moment, I could hardly believe that there was a Fairy Land; and that all I had passed through since I left home, had not been the wandering dream of a diseased imagination, operating on a too mobile frame, not merely causing me indeed to travel, but peopling for me with vague phantoms the regions through which my actual steps had led me. But the next moment my eye fell upon a little girl who was sitting in the chimney-corner, with a little book open on her knee, from which she had apparently just looked up to fix great inquiring eyes upon me. I believed in Fairy Land again. She went on with her reading, as soon as she saw that I observed her looking at me. I went near, and peeping over her shoulder, saw that she was reading *The History of Graciosa and Percinet*.

"Very improving book, sir," remarked the old farmer, with a good-humoured laugh. "We are in the very hottest corner of Fairy Land here. Ha! ha! Stormy night, last night, sir."

"Was it, indeed?" I rejoined. "It was not so with me. A lovelier night I never saw." "Indeed! Where were you last night?"

"I spent it in the forest. I had lost my way."

"Ah! Then, perhaps, you will be able to convince my good woman, that there is nothing very remarkable about the forest; for, to tell the truth, it bears but a bad name in these parts. I dare say you saw nothing worse than yourself there?"

"I hope I did," was my inward reply; but, for an audible one, I contented myself with saying, "Why, I certainly did see some appearances I could hardly account for; but that is nothing to be wondered at in an unknown wild forest, and with the uncertain light of the moon alone to go by."

"Very true! You speak like a sensible man, sir. We have but few sensible folks round about us. Now, you would hardly credit it, but my wife believes every fairy-tale that ever was written. I cannot account for it. She is a most sensible woman in everything else."

"But should not that make you treat her belief with something of respect, though you cannot share in it yourself?"

"Yes, that is all very well in theory; but when you come to live every day in the midst of absurdity, it is far less easy to behave respectfully to it. Why, my wife actually believes the story of the 'White Cat.' You know it, I dare say."

"I read all these tales when a child, and know that one especially well."

"But, father," interposed the little girl in the chimney-corner, "you know quite well that mother is descended from that very princess who was changed by the wicked fairy into a white cat. Mother has told me so a many times, and you ought to believe everything she says."

"I can easily believe that," rejoined the farmer, with another fit of laughter; "for, the other night, a mouse came gnawing and scratching beneath the floor, and would not let us go to sleep. Your mother sprang out of bed, and going as near it as she could, mewed so infernally like a great cat, that the noise ceased instantly. I believe the poor mouse died of the fright, for we have never heard it again. Ha! ha! ha!"

The son, an ill-looking youth, who had entered during the conversation, joined in his father's laugh; but his laugh was very different from the old man's: it was polluted with a sneer. I watched him, and saw that, as soon as it was over, he looked scared, as if he dreaded some evil consequences to follow his presumption. The woman stood near, waiting till we should seat ourselves at the table, and listening to it all with an amused air, which had something in it of the look with which one listens to the sententious remarks of a pompous child. We sat down to supper, and I ate heartily. My bygone distresses began already to look far off.

"In what direction are you going?" asked the old man.

"Eastward," I replied; nor could I have given a more definite answer. "Does the forest extend much further in that direction?"

"Oh! for miles and miles; I do not know how far. For although I have lived on the borders of it all my life, I have been too busy to make journeys of discovery into it. Nor do I see what I could discover. It is only trees and trees, till one is sick of them. By the way, if you follow the eastward track from here, you will pass close to what the children say is the very house of the ogre that Hop-o'-my-Thumb visited, and ate his little daughters with the crowns of gold."

"Oh, father! ate his little daughters! No; he only changed their gold crowns for nightcaps; and the great long-toothed ogre killed them in mistake; but I do not think even he ate them, for you know they were his own little ogresses."

"Well, well, child; you know all about it a great deal better than I do. However, the house has, of course, in such a foolish neighbourhood as this, a bad enough name; and I must confess there is a woman living in it, with teeth long enough, and white enough too, for the lineal descendant of the greatest ogre that ever was made. I think you had better not go near her."

In such talk as this the night wore on. When supper was finished, which lasted some time, my hostess conducted me to my chamber.

"If you had not had enough of it already," she said, "I would have put you in another room, which looks towards the forest; and where you would most likely have seen something more of its inhabitants. For they frequently pass the window, and even enter the room sometimes. Strange creatures spend whole nights in it, at certain seasons of the year. I am used to it, and do not mind it. No more does my little girl, who sleeps in it always. But this room looks southward towards the open country, and they never show themselves here; at least I never saw any."

I was somewhat sorry not to gather any experience that I might have, of the inhabitants of Fairy Land; but the effect of the farmer's company, and of my own later adventures, was such, that I chose rather an undisturbed night in my more human quarters; which, with their clean white curtains and white linen, were very inviting to my weariness.

In the morning I awoke refreshed, after a profound and dreamless sleep. The sun was high, when I looked out of the window, shining over a wide, undulating, cultivated country. Various garden-vegetables were growing beneath my window. Everything was radiant with clear sunlight. The dew-drops were sparkling their busiest; the cows in a near-by field were eating as if they had not been at it all day yesterday; the maids were singing at their work as they passed to and fro between the out-houses: I did not believe in Fairy Land. I went down, and found the family already at breakfast. But before I entered the room where they sat, the little girl came to me, and looked up in my face, as though she wanted to say something to me. I stooped towards her; she put her arms round my neck, and her mouth to my ear, and whispered—

"A white lady has been flitting about the house all night."

"No whispering behind doors!" cried the farmer; and we entered together. "Well, how have you slept? No bogies, eh?"

"Not one, thank you; I slept uncommonly well."

"I am glad to hear it. Come and breakfast."

After breakfast, the farmer and his son went out; and I was left alone with the mother and daughter.

"When I looked out of the window this morning," I said, "I felt almost certain that Fairy Land was all a delusion of my brain; but whenever I come near you or your little daughter, I feel differently. Yet I could persuade myself, after my last adventures, to go back, and have nothing more to do with such strange beings."

"How will you go back?" said the woman.

"Nay, that I do not know."

"Because I have heard, that, for those who enter Fairy Land, there is no way of going back. They must go on, and go through it. How, I do not in the least know."

"That is quite the impression on my own mind. Something compels me to go on, as if my only path was onward, but I feel less inclined this morning to continue my adventures."

"Will you come and see my little child's room? She sleeps in the one I told you of, looking towards the forest."

"Willingly," I said.

So we went together, the little girl running before to open the door for us. It was a large room, full of old-fashioned furniture, that seemed to have once belonged to some great house.

The window was built with a low arch, and filled with lozenge-shaped panes. The wall was very thick, and built of solid stone. I could see that part of the house had been erected against the remains of some old castle or abbey, or other great building; the fallen stones of which had probably served to complete it. But as soon as I looked out of the window, a gush of wonderment and longing flowed over my soul like the tide of a great sea. Fairy Land lay before me, and drew me towards it with an irresistible attraction. The trees bathed their great heads in the waves of the morning, while their roots were planted deep in gloom; save where on the borders the sunshine broke against their stems, or swept in long streams through their avenues, washing with brighter hue all the leaves over which it flowed; revealing the rich brown of the decayed leaves and fallen pine-cones, and the delicate greens of the long grasses and tiny forests of moss that covered the channel over which it passed in motionless rivers of light. I turned hurriedly to bid my hostess farewell without further delay. She smiled at my haste, but with an anxious look.

"You had better not go near the house of the ogre, I think. My son will show you into another path, which will join the first beyond it."

Not wishing to be headstrong or too confident any more, I agreed; and having taken leave of my kind entertainers, went into the wood, accompanied by the youth. He scarcely spoke as we went along; but he led me through the trees till we struck upon a path. He told me to follow it, and, with a muttered "good morning" left me.

CHAPTER 8

"I am a part of the part, which at first was the whole."
    GOETHE. — *Mephistopheles in Faust.*

My spirits rose as I went deeper; into the forest; but I could not regain my former elasticity of mind. I found cheerfulness to be like life itself—not to be created by any argument. Afterwards I learned, that the best way to manage some kinds of pain filled thoughts, is to dare them to do their worst; to let them lie and gnaw at your heart till they are tired; and you find you still have a residue of life they cannot kill. So, better and worse, I went on, till I came to a little clearing in the forest. In the middle of this clearing stood a long, low hut, built with one end against a single tall cypress, which rose like a spire to the building. A vague misgiving crossed my mind when I saw it; but I must needs go closer, and look through a little half-open door, near the opposite end from the cypress. Window I saw none. On peeping in, and looking towards the further end, I saw a lamp burning, with a dim, reddish flame, and the head of a woman, bent downwards, as if reading by its light. I could see nothing more for a few moments. At length, as my eyes got used to the dimness of the place, I saw that the part of the rude building near me was used for household purposes; for several rough utensils lay here and there, and a bed stood in the corner.

An irresistible attraction caused me to enter. The woman never raised her face, the upper part of which alone I could see distinctly; but, as soon as I stepped within the threshold, she began to read aloud, in a low and not altogether unpleasing voice, from an ancient little volume which she held open with one hand on the table upon which stood the lamp. What she read was something like this:

"So, then, as darkness had no beginning, neither will it ever have an end. So, then, is it eternal. The negation of aught else, is its affirmation. Where the light

46

cannot come, there abideth the darkness. The light doth but hollow a mine out of the infinite extension of the darkness. And ever upon the steps of the light treadeth the darkness; yea, springeth in fountains and wells amidst it, from the secret channels of its mighty sea. Truly, man is but a passing flame, moving unquietly amid the surrounding rest of night; without which he yet could not be, and whereof he is in part compounded."

As I drew nearer, and she read on, she moved a little to turn a leaf of the dark old volume, and I saw that her face was sallow and slightly forbidding. Her forehead was high, and her black eyes repressedly quiet. But she took no notice of me. This end of the cottage, if cottage it could be called, was destitute of furniture, except the table with the lamp, and the chair on which the woman sat. In one corner was a door, apparently of a cupboard in the wall, but which might lead to a room beyond. Still the irresistible desire which had made me enter the building urged me: I must open that door, and see what was beyond it. I approached, and laid my hand on the rude latch. Then the woman spoke, but without lifting her head or looking at me: "You had better not open that door." This was uttered quite quietly; and she went on with her reading, partly in silence, partly aloud; but both modes seemed equally intended for herself alone. The prohibition, however, only increased my desire to see; and as she took no further notice, I gently opened the door to its full width, and looked in. At first, I saw nothing worthy of attention. It seemed a common closet, with shelves on each hand, on which stood various little necessaries for the humble uses of a cottage. In one corner stood one or two brooms, in another a hatchet and other common tools; showing that it was in use every hour of the day for household purposes. But, as I looked, I saw that there were no shelves at the back, and that an empty space went in further; its termination appearing to be a faintly glimmering wall or curtain, somewhat less, however, than the width and height of the doorway where I stood. But, as I continued looking, for a few seconds, towards this faintly luminous limit, my eyes came into true relation with their object. All at once, with such a shiver as when one is suddenly conscious of the presence of another in a room where he has, for hours, considered himself alone, I saw that the seemingly luminous extremity was a sky, as of night, beheld through the long perspective of a narrow, dark passage, through what, or built of what, I could not tell. As I gazed, I clearly discerned two or three stars glimmering faintly in the distant blue. But, suddenly, and as if it had been running fast from a far distance for this very point, and had turned the corner without abating its swiftness, a dark figure sped into and along the passage from the blue opening at the remote end. I started back and shuddered, but kept looking, for I could not help it. On and on it came, with a speedy approach but delayed arrival; till, at last, through the many gradations of approach, it seemed to come within the sphere of myself, rushed up to me, and passed me into the cottage. All I could tell of its appearance was, that it seemed to be a dark human figure. Its motion was entirely noiseless, and might be called a gliding, were it not that it appeared that of a runner, but with ghostly feet. I had moved back yet a little to let him pass me, and looked round after him instantly. I could not see him.

"Where is he?" I said, in some alarm, to the woman, who still sat reading.

"There, on the floor, behind you," she said, pointing with her arm half-outstretched, but not lifting her eyes. I turned and looked, but saw nothing. Then with a feeling that there was yet something behind me, I looked round over my shoulder; and there, on the ground, lay a black shadow, the size of a man. It was so dark, that I could see it in the dim light of the lamp, which shone full upon it, apparently without thinning at all the intensity of its hue.

"I told you," said the woman, "you had better not look into that closet."

"What is it?" I said, with a growing sense of horror.

"It is only your shadow that has found you," she replied. "Everybody's shadow is ranging up and down looking for him. I believe you call it by a different name in your world: yours has found you, as every person's is almost certain to do who looks into that closet, especially after meeting one in the forest, whom I dare say you have met."

Here, for the first time, she lifted her head, and looked full at me: her mouth was full of long, white, shining teeth; and I knew that I was in the house of the ogre. I could not speak, but turned and left the house, with the shadow at my heels. "A nice sort of valet to have," I said to myself bitterly, as I stepped into the sunshine, and, looking over my shoulder, saw that it lay yet blacker in the full blaze of the sunlight. Indeed, only when I stood between it and the sun, was the blackness at all diminished. I was so bewildered—stunned—both by the event itself and its suddenness, that I could not at all realise to myself what it would be to have such a constant and strange attendance; but with a dim conviction that my present dislike would soon grow to loathing, I took my dreary way through the wood.

CHAPTER 9

From this time, until I arrived at the palace of Fairy Land, I can attempt no consecutive account of my wanderings and adventures. Everything, henceforward, existed for me in its relation to my attendant. What influence he exercised upon everything into contact with which I was brought, may be understood from a few detached instances. To begin with this very day on which he first joined me: after I had walked heartlessly along for two or three hours, I was very weary, and lay down to rest in a most delightful part of the forest, carpeted with wild flowers. I lay for half an hour in a dull repose, and then got up to pursue my way. The flowers on the spot where I had lain were crushed to the earth: but I saw that they would soon lift their heads and rejoice again in the sun and air. Not so those on which my shadow had lain. The very outline of it could be traced in the withered lifeless grass, and the scorched and shrivelled flowers which stood there, dead, and hopeless of any resurrection. I shuddered, and hastened away with sad forebodings.

In a few days, I had reason to dread an extension of its baleful influences from the fact, that it was no longer confined to one position in regard to myself. Hitherto, when seized with an irresistible desire to look on my evil demon (which longing would unaccountably seize me at any moment, returning at longer or shorter intervals, sometimes every minute), I had to turn my head backwards, and look over my shoulder; in which position, as long as I could retain it, I was fascinated. But one day, having come out on a clear grassy hill, which commanded a glorious prospect, though of what I cannot now tell, my shadow moved round, and came in front of me. And, presently, a new manifestation increased my distress. For it began to coruscate, and shoot out on all sides a radiation of dim shadow. These rays of gloom issued from the central shadow as from a black sun, lengthening and shortening with continual change. But wherever a ray struck, that part of earth, or sea, or sky, became void, and desert, and sad to my heart. On this, the first development of its new power, one ray shot out beyond the rest, seeming to lengthen infinitely, until it smote the great sun on the face, which withered and darkened beneath the blow. I turned away and went on. The shadow retreated to its former position; and when I looked again, it had drawn in all its spears of darkness, and followed like a dog at my heels.

Once, as I passed by a cottage, there came out a lovely fairy child, with two wondrous toys, one in each hand. The one was the tube through which the fairy-gifted poet looks when he beholds the same thing everywhere; the other that through which he looks when he combines into new forms of loveliness those images of beauty which his own choice has gathered from all regions wherein he has travelled. Round the child's head was an aureole of emanating rays. As I looked at him in wonder and delight, round crept from behind me the something dark, and the child stood in my shadow. Straightway he was a commonplace boy, with a rough broad-brimmed straw hat, through which brim the sun shone from behind. The toys he carried were a multiplying-glass and a kaleidoscope. I sighed and departed.

One evening, as a great silent flood of western gold flowed through an avenue in the woods, down the stream, just as when I saw him first, came the sad knight, riding on his chestnut steed.

But his armour did not shine half so red as when I saw him first.

Many a blow of mighty sword and axe, turned aside by the strength of his mail, and glancing adown the surface, had swept from its path the fretted rust, and the glorious steel had answered the kindly blow with the thanks of returning light. These streaks and spots made his armour look like the floor of a forest in the sunlight. His forehead was higher than before, for the contracting wrinkles were nearly gone; and the sadness that remained on his face was the sadness of a dewy summer twilight, not that of a frosty autumn morn. He, too, had met the Alder-maiden as I, but he had plunged into the torrent of mighty deeds, and the stain was nearly washed away. No shadow followed him. He had not entered the dark house; he had not had time to open the closet door. "Will he ever look in?" I said to myself. "*Must* his shadow find him some day?" But I could not answer my own questions.

We travelled together for two days, and I began to love him. It was plain that he suspected my story in some degree; and I saw him once or twice looking curiously and anxiously at my attendant gloom, which all this time had remained very obsequiously behind me; but I offered no explanation, and he asked none. Shame at my neglect of his warning, and a horror which shrunk from even alluding to its cause, kept me silent; till, on the evening of the second day, some noble words from my companion roused all my heart; and I was at the point of falling on his neck, and telling him the whole story; seeking, if not for helpful advice, for of that I was hopeless, yet for the comfort of sympathy—when round slid the shadow and inwrapt my friend; and I could not trust him.

The glory of his brow vanished; the light of his eye grew cold; and I held my peace. The next morning we parted.

But the most dreadful thing of all was, that I now began to feel something like satisfaction in the presence of the shadow. I began to be rather vain of my attendant, saying to myself, "In a land like this, with so many illusions everywhere, I need his aid to disenchant the things around me. He does away with all appearances, and shows me things in their true colour and form. And I am not one to be fooled with the vanities of the common crowd. I will not see beauty where there is none. I will dare to behold things as they are. And if I live in a waste instead of a paradise, I will live knowing where I live." But of this a certain exercise of his power which soon followed quite cured me, turning my feelings towards him once more into loathing and distrust. It was thus:

One bright noon, a little maiden joined me, coming through the wood in a direction at right angles to my path. She came along singing and dancing, happy as a child, though she seemed almost a woman. In her hands—now in one, now in another—she carried a small globe, bright and clear as the purest crystal. This seemed at once her plaything and her greatest treasure. At one moment, you would have thought her utterly careless of it, and at another, overwhelmed with anxiety for its safety. But I believe she was taking care of it all the time, perhaps not least when least occupied about it. She stopped by me with a smile, and bade me good day with the sweetest voice. I felt a wonderful liking to the child—for she produced on me more the impression of a child, though my understanding told me differently. We talked a little, and then walked on together in the direction I had been pursuing. I asked her about the globe she carried, but getting no definite answer, I held out my hand to take it. She drew back, and said, but smiling almost invitingly the while, "You must not touch it;"—then, after a moment's pause—"Or if you do, it must be very gently." I touched it with a finger. A slight vibratory motion arose in it, accompanied, or perhaps manifested, by a faint sweet sound. I touched it again, and the sound increased. I touched it the third time: a tiny torrent of harmony rolled out of the little globe. She would not let me touch it any more.

We travelled on together all that day. She left me when twilight came on; but next day, at noon, she met me as before, and again we travelled till evening. The third day she came once more at noon, and we walked on together. Now, though we had talked about a great many things connected with Fairy Land, and the life she had led hitherto, I had never been able to learn anything about the globe. This day, however, as we went on, the shadow glided round and inwrapt the maiden. It could not change her. But my desire to know about the globe, which in his gloom began to waver as with an inward light, and to shoot out flashes of many-coloured flame, grew irresistible. I put out both my hands and laid hold of it. It began to sound as before. The sound rapidly increased, till it grew a low tempest of harmony, and the globe trembled, and quivered, and throbbed between my hands. I had not the heart to pull it away from the maiden, though I held it in spite of her attempts to take it from me; yes, I shame to say, in spite of her prayers, and, at last, her tears. The music went on growing in, intensity and complication of tones, and the globe vibrated and heaved; till at last it burst in our hands, and a black vapour broke upwards from out of it; then turned, as if blown sideways, and enveloped the maiden, hiding even the shadow in its blackness. She held fast the fragments, which I abandoned, and fled from me into the forest in the direction whence she had come, wailing like a child, and crying, "You have broken my globe; my globe is broken—my globe is broken!" I followed her, in the hope of comforting her; but had not pursued her far, before a sudden cold gust of wind bowed the tree-tops above us, and swept through their stems around us; a great cloud overspread the day, and a fierce tempest came on, in which I lost sight of her. It lies heavy on my heart to this hour. At night, ere I fall asleep, often, whatever I may be thinking about, I suddenly hear her voice, crying out, "You have broken my globe; my globe is broken; ah, my globe!"

Here I will mention one more strange thing; but whether this peculiarity was owing to my shadow at all, I am not able to assure myself. I came to a village, the inhabitants of which could not at first sight be distinguished from the dwellers in our land. They rather avoided than sought my company, though they were very pleasant when I addressed them. But at last I observed, that whenever I came within a certain distance of any one of them, which distance, however, varied with different individuals, the whole appearance of the person began to change; and this change increased in degree as I approached. When I receded to the former distance, the former appearance was restored. The nature of the change was grotesque, following no fixed rule. The nearest resemblance to it that I know, is the distortion produced in your countenance when you look at it as reflected in a concave or convex surface—say, either side of a bright spoon. Of this phenomenon I first became aware in rather a ludicrous way. My host's daughter was a very pleasant pretty girl, who made herself more agreeable to me than most of those about me. For some days my companion-shadow had been less obtrusive than usual; and such was the reaction of spirits occasioned by the simple mitigation of torment, that, although I had cause enough besides to be gloomy, I felt light and comparatively happy. My impression is, that she was quite aware of the law of appearances that existed between the people of the place and myself, and had resolved to amuse herself at my expense; for one evening, after some jesting and raillery, she, somehow or other, provoked me to attempt to kiss her. But she was well defended from any assault of the kind. Her countenance became, of a sudden, absurdly hideous; the pretty mouth was elongated and otherwise amplified sufficiently to have allowed of six simultaneous kisses. I started back in bewildered dismay; she burst into the merriest fit of laughter, and ran from the room. I soon found that the same undefinable law of change operated between me and all the other villagers; and that, to feel I was in pleasant company, it was absolutely necessary for me to discover and observe the right focal distance between myself and each one with whom I had to do. This done, all went pleasantly enough. Whether, when I happened to neglect this precaution, I presented to them an equally ridiculous appearance, I did not ascertain; but I presume that the alteration was common to the approximating parties. I was likewise unable to determine whether I was a necessary party to the production of this strange transformation, or whether it took place as well, under the given circumstances, between the inhabitants themselves.

CHAPTER 10

"From Eden's bowers the full-fed rivers flow,
To guide the outcasts to the land of woe:
Our Earth one little toiling streamlet yields.
To guide the wanderers to the happy fields."

After leaving this village, where I had rested for nearly a week, I travelled through a desert region of dry sand and glittering rocks, peopled principally by goblin-fairies. When I first entered their domains, and, indeed, whenever I fell in with another tribe of them, they began mocking me with offered handfuls of gold and jewels, making hideous grimaces at me, and performing the most antic homage, as if they thought I expected reverence, and meant to humour me like a maniac. But ever, as soon as one cast his eyes on the shadow behind me, he made a wry face, partly of pity, partly of contempt, and looked ashamed, as if he had been caught doing something inhuman; then, throwing down his handful of gold, and ceasing all his grimaces, he stood aside to let me pass in peace, and made signs to his companions to do the like. I had no inclination to observe them much, for the shadow was in my heart as well as at my heels. I walked listlessly and almost hope-lessly along, till I arrived one day at a small spring; which, bursting cool from the heart of a sun-heated rock, flowed somewhat southwards from the direction I had been taking. I drank of this spring, and found myself wonderfully refreshed. A kind of love to the cheerful little stream arose in my heart. It was born in a desert; but it seemed to say to itself, "I will flow, and sing, and lave my banks, till I make my desert a paradise." I thought I could not do better than follow it, and see what it made of it. So down with the stream I went, over rocky lands, burning with sunbeams. But the rivulet flowed not far, before a few blades of grass appeared on its banks, and then, here and there, a stunted bush. Sometimes it disappeared alto-

53

gether under ground; and after I had wandered some distance, as near as I could guess, in the direction it seemed to take, I would suddenly hear it again, singing, sometimes far away to my right or left, amongst new rocks, over which it made new cataracts of watery melodies. The verdure on its banks increased as it flowed; other streams joined it; and at last, after many days' travel, I found myself, one gorgeous summer evening, resting by the side of a broad river, with a glorious horse-chestnut tree towering above me, and dropping its blossoms, milk-white and rosy-red, all about me. As I sat, a gush of joy sprang forth in my heart, and over flowed at my eyes.

Through my tears, the whole landscape glimmered in such bewildering loveli-ness, that I felt as if I were entering Fairy Land for the first time, and some loving hand were waiting to cool my head, and a loving word to warm my heart. Roses, wild roses, everywhere! So plentiful were they, they not only perfumed the air, they seemed to dye it a faint rose-hue. The colour floated abroad with the scent, and clomb, and spread, until the whole west blushed and glowed with the gathered incense of roses. And my heart fainted with longing in my bosom.

Could I but see the Spirit of the Earth, as I saw once the in dwelling woman of the beech-tree, and my beauty of the pale marble, I should be content. Content!— Oh, how gladly would I die of the light of her eyes! Yea, I would cease to be, if that would bring me one word of love from the one mouth. The twilight sank around, and infolded me with sleep. I slept as I had not slept for months. I did not awake till late in the morning; when, refreshed in body and mind, I rose as from the death that wipes out the sadness of life, and then dies itself in the new morrow. Again I followed the stream; now climbing a steep rocky bank that hemmed it in; now wading through long grasses and wild flowers in its path; now through meadows; and anon through woods that crowded down to the very lip of the water.

At length, in a nook of the river, gloomy with the weight of overhanging foliage, and still and deep as a soul in which the torrent eddies of pain have hollowed a great gulf, and then, subsiding in violence, have left it full of a motionless, fathom-less sorrow—I saw a little boat lying. So still was the water here, that the boat needed no fastening. It lay as if some one had just stepped ashore, and would in a moment return. But as there were no signs of presence, and no track through the thick bushes; and, moreover, as I was in Fairy Land where one does very much as he pleases, I forced my way to the brink, stepped into the boat, pushed it, with the help of the tree-branches, out into the stream, lay down in the bottom, and let my boat and me float whither the stream would carry us. I seemed to lose myself in the great flow of sky above me unbroken in its infinitude, except when now and then, coming nearer the shore at a bend in the river, a tree would sweep its mighty head silently above mine, and glide away back into the past, never more to fling its shadow over me. I fell asleep in this cradle, in which mother Nature was rocking her weary child; and while I slept, the sun slept not, but went round his arched way. When I awoke, he slept in the waters, and I went on my silent path beneath a round silvery moon. And a pale moon looked up from the floor of the great blue cave that lay in the abysmal silence beneath.

Why are all reflections lovelier than what we call the reality?—not so grand or so strong, it may be, but always lovelier? Fair as is the gliding sloop on the shining sea, the wavering, trembling, unresting sail below is fairer still. Yea, the reflecting ocean itself, reflected in the mirror, has a wondrousness about its waters that somewhat vanishes when I turn towards itself. All mirrors are magic mirrors. The commonest room is a room in a poem when I turn to the glass. (And this reminds me, while I write, of a strange story which I read in the fairy palace, and of which I will try to make a feeble memorial in its place.) In whatever way it may be accounted for, of one thing we may be sure, that this feeling is no cheat; for there is no cheating in nature and the simple unsought feelings of the soul. There must be a truth involved in it, though we may but in part lay hold of the meaning. Even the memories of past pain are beautiful; and past delights, though beheld only through clefts in the grey clouds of sorrow, are lovely as Fairy Land. But how have I wandered into the deeper fairyland of the soul, while as yet I only float towards the fairy palace of Fairy Land! The moon, which is the lovelier memory or reflex of the down-gone sun, the joyous day seen in the faint mirror of the brooding night, had rapt me away.

I sat up in the boat. Gigantic forest trees were about me; through which, like a silver snake, twisted and twined the great river. The little waves, when I moved in the boat, heaved and fell with a plash as of molten silver, breaking the image of the moon into a thousand morsels, fusing again into one, as the ripples of laughter die into the still face of joy. The sleeping woods, in undefined massiveness; the water that flowed in its sleep; and, above all, the enchantress moon, which had cast them all, with her pale eye, into the charmed slumber, sank into my soul, and I felt as if I had died in a dream, and should never more awake.

From this I was partly aroused by a glimmering of white, that, through the trees on the left, vaguely crossed my vision, as I gazed upwards. But the trees again hid the object; and at the moment, some strange melodious bird took up its song, and sang, not an ordinary bird-song, with constant repetitions of the same melody, but what sounded like a continuous strain, in which one thought was expressed, deepening in intensity as evolved in progress. It sounded like a welcome already overshadowed with the coming farewell. As in all sweetest music, a tinge of sadness was in every note. Nor do we know how much of the pleasures even of life we owe to the intermingled sorrows. Joy cannot unfold the deepest truths, although deepest truth must be deepest joy. Cometh white-robed Sorrow, stooping and wan, and flingeth wide the doors she may not enter. Almost we linger with Sorrow for very love.

As the song concluded the stream bore my little boat with a gentle sweep round a bend of the river; and lo! on a broad lawn, which rose from the water's edge with a long green slope to a clear elevation from which the trees receded on all sides, stood a stately palace glimmering ghostly in the moonshine: it seemed to be built throughout of the whitest marble. There was no reflection of moonlight from windows—there seemed to be none; so there was no cold glitter; only, as I said, a ghostly shimmer. Numberless shadows tempered the shine, from column and balcony and tower. For everywhere galleries ran along the face of the buildings; wings were extended in many directions; and numberless openings, through which the moonbeams vanished into the interior, and which served both for doors and windows, had their separate balconies in front, communicating with a common gallery that rose on its own pillars. Of course, I did not discover all this from the river, and in the moonlight. But, though I was there for many days, I did not succeed in mastering the inner topography of the building, so extensive and complicated was it.

Here I wished to land, but the boat had no oars on board. However, I found that a plank, serving for a seat, was unfastened, and with that I brought the boat to the bank and scrambled on shore. Deep soft turf sank beneath my feet, as I went up the ascent towards the palace.

When I reached it, I saw that it stood on a great platform of marble, with an ascent, by broad stairs of the same, all round it. Arrived on the platform, I found there was an extensive outlook over the forest, which, however, was rather veiled than revealed by the moonlight.

Entering by a wide gateway, but without gates, into an inner court, surrounded on all sides by great marble pillars supporting galleries above, I saw a large fountain of porphyry in the middle, throwing up a lofty column of water, which fell, with a noise as of the fusion of all sweet sounds, into a basin beneath; overflowing which, it ran into a single channel towards the interior of the building. Although the moon was by this time so low in the west, that not a ray of her light fell into the court, over the height of the surrounding buildings; yet was the court lighted by a second reflex from the sun of other lands. For the top of the column of water, just as it spread to fall, caught the moonbeams, and like a great pale lamp, hung high in the night air, threw a dim memory of light (as it were) over the court below. This court was paved in diamonds of white and red marble. According to my custom since I entered Fairy Land, of taking for a guide whatever I first found moving in any direction, I followed the stream from the basin of the fountain. It led me to a great open door, beneath the ascending steps of which it ran through a low arch and disappeared. Entering here, I found myself in a great hall, surrounded with white pillars, and paved with black and white. This I could see by the moonlight, which, from the other side, streamed through open windows into the hall.

Its height I could not distinctly see. As soon as I entered, I had the feeling so common to me in the woods, that there were others there besides myself, though I could see no one, and heard no sound to indicate a presence. Since my visit to the Church of Darkness, my power of seeing the fairies of the higher orders had gradually diminished, until it had almost ceased. But I could frequently believe in their presence while unable to see them. Still, although I had company, and doubtless of a safe kind, it seemed rather dreary to spend the night in an empty marble hall, however beautiful, especially as the moon was near the going down, and it would soon be dark. So I began at the place where I entered, and walked round the hall, looking for some door or passage that might lead me to a more hospitable chamber. As I walked, I was deliciously haunted with the feeling that behind some one of the seemingly innumerable pillars, one who loved me was waiting for me. Then I thought she was following me from pillar to pillar as I went along; but no arms came out of the faint moonlight, and no sigh assured me of her presence.

At length I came to an open corridor, into which I turned; notwithstanding that, in doing so, I left the light behind. Along this I walked with outstretched hands, groping my way, till, arriving at another corridor, which seemed to strike off at right angles to that in which I was, I saw at the end a faintly glimmering light, too pale even for moonshine, resembling rather a stray phosphorescence. However, where everything was white, a little light went a great way. So I walked on to the end, and a long corridor it was. When I came up to the light, I found that it proceeded from what looked like silver letters upon a door of ebony; and, to my surprise even in the home of wonder itself, the letters formed the words, *The*

Chamber of Sir Anodos. Although I had as yet no right to the honours of a knight, I ventured to conclude that the chamber was indeed intended for me; and, opening the door without hesitation, I entered. Any doubt as to whether I was right in so doing, was soon dispelled. What to my dark eyes seemed a blaze of light, burst upon me. A fire of large pieces of some sweet-scented wood, supported by dogs of silver, was burning on the hearth, and a bright lamp stood on a table, in the midst of a plentiful meal, apparently awaiting my arrival. But what surprised me more than all, was, that the room was in every respect a copy of my own room, the room whence the little stream from my basin had led me into Fairy Land. There was the very carpet of grass and moss and daisies, which I had myself designed; the curtains of pale blue silk, that fell like a cataract over the windows; the old-fash-ioned bed, with the chintz furniture, on which I had slept from boyhood. "Now I shall sleep," I said to myself. "My shadow dares not come here."

I sat down to the table, and began to help myself to the good things before me with confidence. And now I found, as in many instances before, how true the fairy tales are; for I was waited on, all the time of my meal, by invisible hands. I had scarcely to do more than look towards anything I wanted, when it was brought me, just as if it had come to me of itself. My glass was kept filled with the wine I had chosen, until I looked towards another bottle or decanter; when a fresh glass was substituted, and the other wine supplied. When I had eaten and drank more heartily and joyfully than ever since I entered Fairy Land, the whole was removed by several attendants, of whom some were male and some female, as I thought I could distinguish from the way the dishes were lifted from the table, and the motion with which they were carried out of the room. As soon as they were all taken away, I heard a sound as of the shutting of a door, and knew that I was left alone. I sat long by the fire, meditating, and wondering how it would all end; and when at length, wearied with thinking, I betook myself to my own bed, it was half with a hope that, when I awoke in the morning, I should awake not only in my own room, but in my own castle also; and that I should walk, out upon my own native soil, and find that Fairy Land was, after all, only a vision of the night. The sound of the falling waters of the fountain floated me into oblivion.

CHAPTER 11

"A wilderness of building, sinking far
And self-withdrawn into a wondrous depth,
Far sinking into splendour — without end:
Fabric it seemed of diamond and of gold,
With alabaster domes, and silver spires,
And blazing terrace upon terrace, high
Uplifted."
WORDSWORTH.

But when, after a sleep, which, although dreamless, yet left behind it a sense of past blessedness, I awoke in the full morning, I found, indeed, that the room was still my own; but that it looked abroad upon an unknown landscape of forest and hill and dale on the one side—and on the other, upon the marble court, with the great fountain, the crest of which now flashed glorious in the sun, and cast on the pavement beneath a shower of faint shadows from the waters that fell from it into the marble basin below.

Agreeably to all authentic accounts of the treatment of travellers in Fairy Land, I found by my bedside a complete suit of fresh clothing, just such as I was in the habit of wearing; for, though varied sufficiently from the one removed, it was yet in complete accordance with my tastes. I dressed myself in this, and went out. The whole palace shone like silver in the sun. The marble was partly dull and partly polished; and every pinnacle, dome, and turret ended in a ball, or cone, or cusp of silver. It was like frost-work, and too dazzling, in the sun, for earthly eyes like mine.

I will not attempt to describe the environs, save by saying, that all the pleasures to be found in the most varied and artistic arrangement of wood and river, lawn and wild forest, garden and shrubbery, rocky hill and luxurious vale; in living creatures wild and tame, in gorgeous birds, scattered fountains, little streams, and reedy lakes—all were here. Some parts of the palace itself I shall have occasion to describe more minutely.

For this whole morning I never thought of my demon shadow; and not till the weariness which supervened on delight brought it again to my memory, did I look round to see if it was behind me: it was scarcely discernible. But its presence, however faintly revealed, sent a pang to my heart, for the pain of which, not all the beauties around me could compensate. It was followed, however, by the comforting reflection that, peradventure, I might here find the magic word of power to banish the demon and set me free, so that I should no longer be a man beside myself. The Queen of Fairy Land, thought I, must dwell here: surely she will put forth her power to deliver me, and send me singing through the further gates of her country back to my own land. "Shadow of me!" I said; "which art not me, but which representest thyself to me as me; here I may find a shadow of light which will devour thee, the shadow of darkness! Here I may find a blessing which will fall on thee as a curse, and damn thee to the blackness whence thou hast emerged unbidden." I said this, stretched at length on the slope of the lawn above the river; and as the hope arose within me, the sun came forth from a light fleecy cloud that swept across his face; and hill and dale, and the great river winding on through the still mysterious forest, flashed back his rays as with a silent shout of joy; all nature lived and glowed; the very earth grew warm beneath me; a magnificent dragon-fly went past me like an arrow from a bow, and a whole concert of birds burst into choral song.

The heat of the sun soon became too intense even for passive support. I therefore rose, and sought the shelter of one of the arcades. Wandering along from one to another of these, wherever my heedless steps led me, and wondering everywhere at the simple magnificence of the building, I arrived at another hall, the roof of which was of a pale blue, spangled with constellations of silver stars, and supported by porphyry pillars of a paler red than ordinary.—In this house (I may remark in passing), silver seemed everywhere preferred to gold; and such was the purity of the air, that it showed nowhere signs of tarnishing.—The whole of the floor of this hall, except a narrow path behind the pillars, paved with black, was hollowed into a huge basin, many feet deep, and filled with the purest, most liquid and radiant water. The sides of the basin were white marble, and the bottom was paved with all kinds of refulgent stones, of every shape and hue.

In their arrangement, you would have supposed, at first sight, that there was no design, for they seemed to lie as if cast there from careless and playful hands; but it was a most harmonious confusion; and as I looked at the play of their colours, especially when the waters were in motion, I came at last to feel as if not one little pebble could be displaced, without injuring the effect of the whole. Beneath this floor of the water, lay the reflection of the blue inverted roof, fretted with its silver stars, like a second deeper sea, clasping and upholding the first. The fairy bath was probably fed from the fountain in the court. Led by an irresistible desire, I undressed, and plunged into the water. It clothed me as with a new sense and its object both in one. The waters lay so close to me, they seemed to enter and revive my heart. I rose to the surface, shook the water from my hair, and swam as in a rainbow, amid the coruscations of the gems below seen through the agitation caused by my motion. Then, with open eyes, I dived, and swam beneath the surface. And here was a new wonder. For the basin, thus beheld, appeared to extend on all sides like a sea, with here and there groups as of ocean rocks, hollowed by ceaseless billows into wondrous caves and grotesque pinnacles. Around the caves grew sea-weeds of all hues, and the corals glowed between; while far off, I saw the glimmer of what seemed to be creatures of human form at home in the waters. I thought I had been enchanted; and that when I rose to the surface, I should find myself miles from land, swimming alone upon a heaving sea; but when my eyes emerged from the waters, I saw above me the blue spangled vault, and the red pillars around. I dived again, and found myself once more in the heart of a great sea. I then arose, and swam to the edge, where I got out easily, for the water reached the very brim, and, as I drew near washed in tiny waves over the black marble border. I dressed, and went out, deeply refreshed.

And now I began to discern faint, gracious forms, here and there throughout the building. Some walked together in earnest conversation. Others strayed alone. Some stood in groups, as if looking at and talking about a picture or a statue. None of them heeded me. Nor were they plainly visible to my eyes. Sometimes a group, or single individual, would fade entirely out of the realm of my vision as I gazed. When evening came, and the moon arose, clear as a round of a horizon-sea when the sun hangs over it in the west, I began to see them all more plainly; especially when they came between me and the moon; and yet more especially, when I myself was in the shade. But, even then, I sometimes saw only the passing wave of a white robe; or a lovely arm or neck gleamed by in the moonshine; or white feet went walking alone over the moony sward. Nor, I grieve to say, did I ever come much nearer to these glorious beings, or ever look upon the Queen of the Fairies herself. My destiny ordered otherwise.

In this palace of marble and silver, and fountains and moonshine, I spent many days; waited upon constantly in my room with everything desirable, and bathing daily in the fairy bath. All this time I was little troubled with my demon shadow I had a vague feeling that he was somewhere about the palace; but it seemed as if the hope that I should in this place be finally freed from his hated presence, had sufficed to banish him for a time. How and where I found him, I shall soon have to relate.

The third day after my arrival, I found the library of the palace; and here, all the time I remained, I spent most of the middle of the day. For it was, not to mention far greater attractions, a luxurious retreat from the noontide sun. During the mornings and afternoons, I wandered about the lovely neighbourhood, or lay, lost in delicious day-dreams, beneath some mighty tree on the open lawn. My evenings were by-and-by spent in a part of the palace, the account of which, and of my adventures in connection with it, I must yet postpone for a little.

The library was a mighty hall, lighted from the roof, which was formed of something like glass, vaulted over in a single piece, and stained throughout with a great mysterious picture in gorgeous colouring.

The walls were lined from floor to roof with books and books: most of them in ancient bindings, but some in strange new fashions which I had never seen, and which, were I to make the attempt, I could ill describe. All around the walls, in front of the books, ran galleries in rows, communicating by stairs. These galleries were built of all kinds of coloured stones; all sorts of marble and granite, with porphyry, jasper, lapis lazuli, agate, and various others, were ranged in wonderful melody of successive colours. Although the material, then, of which these galleries and stairs were built, rendered necessary a certain degree of massiveness in the construction, yet such was the size of the place, that they seemed to run along the walls like cords.

Over some parts of the library, descended curtains of silk of various dyes, none of which I ever saw lifted while I was there; and I felt somehow that it would be presumptuous in me to venture to look within them. But the use of the other books seemed free; and day after day I came to the library, threw myself on one of the many sumptuous eastern carpets, which lay here and there on the floor, and read, and read, until weary; if that can be designated as weariness, which was rather the faintness of rapturous delight; or until, sometimes, the failing of the light invited me to go abroad, in the hope that a cool gentle breeze might have arisen to bathe, with an airy invigorating bath, the limbs which the glow of the burning spirit within had withered no less than the glow of the blazing sun without.

One peculiarity of these books, or at least most of those I looked into, I must make a somewhat vain attempt to describe.

If, for instance, it was a book of metaphysics I opened, I had scarcely read two pages before I seemed to myself to be pondering over discovered truth, and constructing the intellectual machine whereby to communicate the discovery to my fellow men. With some books, however, of this nature, it seemed rather as if the process was removed yet a great way further back; and I was trying to find the root of a manifestation, the spiritual truth whence a material vision sprang; or to combine two propositions, both apparently true, either at once or in different remembered moods, and to find the point in which their invisibly converging lines would unite in one, revealing a truth higher than either and differing from both; though so far from being opposed to either, that it was that whence each derived its life and power. Or if the book was one of travels, I found myself the traveller. New lands, fresh experiences, novel customs, rose around me. I walked, I discovered, I fought, I suffered, I rejoiced in my success. Was it a history? I was the chief actor therein. I suffered my own blame; I was glad in my own praise. With a fiction it was the same. Mine was the whole story. For I took the place of the character who was most like myself, and his story was mine; until, grown weary with the life of years condensed in an hour, or arrived at my deathbed, or the end of the volume, I would awake, with a sudden bewilderment, to the consciousness of my present life, recognising the walls and roof around me, and finding I joyed or sorrowed only in a book. If the book was a poem, the words disappeared, or took the subordinate position of an accompaniment to the succession of forms and images that rose and vanished with a soundless rhythm, and a hidden rime.

In one, with a mystical title, which I cannot recall, I read of a world that is not like ours. The wondrous account, in such a feeble, fragmentary way as is possible to me, I would willingly impart. Whether or not it was all a poem, I cannot tell; but, from the impulse I felt, when I first contemplated writing it, to break into rime, to which impulse I shall give way if it comes upon me again, I think it must have been, partly at least, in verse.

CHAPTER 12

"Chained is the Spring. The night-wind bold
  Blows over the hard earth;
  Time is not more confused and cold,
  Nor keeps more wintry mirth.

"Yet blow, and roll the world about;
  Blow, Time—blow, winter's Wind!
  Through chinks of Time, heaven peepeth out,
  And Spring the frost behind."
G. E. M.

They who believe in the influences of the stars over the fates of men, are, in feeling at least, nearer the truth than they who regard the heavenly bodies as related to them merely by a common obedience to an external law. All that man sees has to do with man. Worlds cannot be without an intermundane relationship. The community of the centre of all creation suggests an interradiating connection and dependence of the parts. Else a grander idea is conceivable than that which is already imbodied. The blank, which is only a forgotten life, lying behind the consciousness, and the misty splendour, which is an undeveloped life, lying before it, may be full of mysterious revelations of other connexions with the worlds around us, than those of science and poetry. No shining belt or gleaming moon, no red and green glory in a self-encircling twin-star, but has a relation with the hidden things of a man's soul, and, it may be, with the secret history of his body as well. They are portions of the living house wherein he abides.

Through the realms of the monarch Sun
Creeps a world, whose course had begun,
On a weary path with a weary pace,
Before the Earth sprang forth on her race:
But many a time the Earth had sped
Around the path she still must tread,
Ere the elder planet, on leaden wing,
Once circled the court of the planet's king.

There, in that lonely and distant star,
The seasons are not as our seasons are;
But many a year hath Autumn to dress
The trees in their matron loveliness;
As long hath old Winter in triumph to go
O'er beauties dead in his vaults below;
And many a year the Spring doth wear
Combing the icicles from her hair;
And Summer, dear Summer, hath years of June,
With large white clouds, and cool showers at noon:
And a beauty that grows to a weight like grief,
Till a burst of tears is the heart's relief.

Children, born when Winter is king,
May never rejoice in the hoping Spring;
Though their own heart-buds are bursting with joy,
And the child hath grown to the girl or boy;
But may die with cold and icy hours
Watching them ever in place of flowers.
And some who awake from their primal sleep,
When the sighs of Summer through forests creep,
Live, and love, and are loved again;
Seek for pleasure, and find its pain;
Sink to their last, their forsaken sleeping,
With the same sweet odours around them creeping.

Now the children, there, are not born as the children are born in worlds nearer to the sun. For they arrive no one knows how. A maiden, walking alone, hears a cry: for even there a cry is the first utterance; and searching about, she findeth, under an overhanging rock, or within a clump of bushes, or, it may be, betwixt gray stones on the side of a hill, or in any other sheltered and unexpected spot, a little child. This she taketh tenderly, and beareth home with joy, calling out, "Mother, mother"—if so be that her mother lives—"I have got a baby—I have found a child!" All the household gathers round to see;—"*Where is it? What is it like? Where did you find it?*" and such-like questions, abounding. And thereupon she relates the whole story of the discovery; for by the circumstances, such as season of the year, time of the day, condition of the air, and such like, and, especially, the peculiar and never-repeated aspect of the heavens and earth at the time, and the nature of the place of shelter wherein it is found, is determined, or at least indicated, the nature of the child thus discovered. Therefore, at certain seasons, and in certain states of the weather, according, in part, to their own fancy, the young women go out to look for children. They generally avoid seeking them, though they cannot help sometimes finding them, in places and with circumstances uncongenial to their peculiar likings. But no sooner is a child found, than its claim for protection and nurture obliterates all feeling of choice in the matter. Chiefly, however, in the season of summer, which lasts so long, coming as it does after such long intervals; and mostly in the warm evenings, about the middle of twilight; and principally in the woods and along the river banks, do the maidens go looking for children just as children look for flowers. And ever as the child grows, yea, more and more as he advances in years, will his face indicate to those who understand the spirit of Nature, and her utterances in the face of the world, the nature of the place of his birth, and the other circumstances thereof; whether a clear morning sun guided his mother to the nook whence issued the boy's low cry; or at eve the lonely maiden (for the same woman never finds a second, at least while the first lives) discovers the girl by the glimmer of her white skin, lying in a nest like that of the lark, amid long encircling grasses, and the upward-gazing eyes of the lowly daisies; whether the storm bowed the forest trees around, or the still frost fixed in silence the else flowing and babbling stream.

After they grow up, the men and women are but little together. There is this peculiar difference between them, which likewise distinguishes the women from those of the earth. The men alone have arms; the women have only wings. Resplendent wings are they, wherein they can shroud themselves from head to foot in a panoply of glistering glory. By these wings alone, it may frequently be judged in what seasons, and under what aspects, they were born. From those that came in winter, go great white wings, white as snow; the edge of every feather shining like the sheen of silver, so that they flash and glitter like frost in the sun. But underneath, they are tinged with a faint pink or rose-colour. Those born in spring have wings of a brilliant green, green as grass; and towards the edges the feathers are enamelled like the surface of the grass-blades. These again are white within. Those that are born in summer have wings of a deep rose-colour, lined with pale gold. And those born in autumn have purple wings, with a rich brown on the inside. But these colours are modified and altered in all varieties, corresponding to the mood of the day and hour, as well as the season of the year; and sometimes I found the various colours so intermingled, that I could not determine even the season, though doubtless the hieroglyphic could be deciphered by more experienced eyes. One splendour, in particular, I remember—wings of deep carmine, with an inner down of warm gray, around a form of brilliant whiteness.

She had been found as the sun went down through a low sea-fog, casting crimson along a broad sea-path into a little cave on the shore, where a bathing maiden saw her lying.

But though I speak of sun and fog, and sea and shore, the world there is in some respects very different from the earth whereon men live. For instance, the waters reflect no forms. To the unaccustomed eye they appear, if undisturbed, like the surface of a dark metal, only that the latter would reflect indistinctly, whereas they reflect not at all, except light which falls immediately upon them. This has a great effect in causing the landscapes to differ from those on the earth. On the stillest evening, no tall ship on the sea sends a long wavering reflection almost to the feet of him on shore; the face of no maiden brightens at its own beauty in a still forest-well. The sun and moon alone make a glitter on the surface. The sea is like a sea of death, ready to ingulf and never to reveal: a visible shadow of oblivion. Yet the women sport in its waters like gorgeous sea-birds. The men more rarely enter them. But, on the contrary, the sky reflects everything beneath it, as if it were built of water like ours. Of course, from its concavity there is some distortion of the reflected objects; yet wondrous combinations of form are often to be seen in the overhanging depth. And then it is not shaped so much like a round dome as the sky of the earth, but, more of an egg-shape, rises to a great towering height in the middle, appearing far more lofty than the other. When the stars come out at night, it shows a mighty cupola, "fretted with golden fires," wherein there is room for all tempests to rush and rave.

One evening in early summer, I stood with a group of men and women on a steep rock that overhung the sea. They were all questioning me about my world and the ways thereof. In making reply to one of their questions, I was compelled to say that children are not born in the Earth as with them. Upon this I was assailed with a whole battery of inquiries, which at first I tried to avoid; but, at last, I was compelled, in the vaguest manner I could invent, to make some approach to the subject in question. Immediately a dim notion of what I meant, seemed to dawn in the minds of most of the women. Some of them folded their great wings all around them, as they generally do when in the least offended, and stood erect and motion-less. One spread out her rosy pinions, and flashed from the promontory into the gulf at its foot. A great light shone in the eyes of one maiden, who turned and walked slowly away, with her purple and white wings half dispread behind her. She was found, the next morning, dead beneath a withered tree on a bare hill-side, some miles inland. They buried her where she lay, as is their custom; for, before they die, they instinctively search for a spot like the place of their birth, and having found one that satisfies them, they lie down, fold their wings around them, if they be women, or cross their arms over their breasts, if they are men, just as if they were going to sleep; and so sleep indeed. The sign or cause of coming death is an inde-scribable longing for something, they know not what, which seizes them, and drives them into solitude, consuming them within, till the body fails. When a youth and a maiden look too deep into each other's eyes, this longing seizes and possesses them; but instead of drawing nearer to each other, they wander away, each alone, into solitary places, and die of their desire. But it seems to me, that thereafter they are born babes upon our earth: where, if, when grown, they find each other, it goes well with them; if not, it will seem to go ill. But of this I know nothing. When I told them that the women on the Earth had not wings like them, but arms, they stared, and said how bold and masculine they must look; not knowing that their wings, glorious as they are, are but undeveloped arms.

But see the power of this book, that, while recounting what I can recall of its contents, I write as if myself had visited the far-off planet, learned its ways and appearances, and conversed with its men and women. And so, while writing, it seemed to me that I had.

The book goes on with the story of a maiden, who, born at the close of autumn, and living in a long, to her endless winter, set out at last to find the regions of spring; for, as in our earth, the seasons are divided over the globe. It begins something like this:

She watched them dying for many a day,
  Dropping from off the old trees away,
  One by one; or else in a shower
  Crowding over the withered flower
  For as if they had done some grievous wrong,
  The sun, that had nursed them and loved them so long,
  Grew weary of loving, and, turning back,
  Hastened away on his southern track;
  And helplessly hung each shrivelled leaf,
  Faded away with an idle grief.
  And the gusts of wind, sad Autumn's sighs,
  Mournfully swept through their families;
  Casting away with a helpless moan
  All that he yet might call his own,
  As the child, when his bird is gone for ever,
  Flingeth the cage on the wandering river.
  And the giant trees, as bare as Death,
  Slowly bowed to the great Wind's breath;
  And groaned with trying to keep from groaning
  Amidst the young trees bending and moaning.
  And the ancient planet's mighty sea
  Was heaving and falling most restlessly,
  And the tops of the waves were broken and white,
  Tossing about to ease their might;
  And the river was striving to reach the main,
  And the ripple was hurrying back again.
  Nature lived in sadness now;
  Sadness lived on the maiden's brow,
  As she watched, with a fixed, half-conscious eye,
  One lonely leaf that trembled on high,
  Till it dropped at last from the desolate bough —
  Sorrow, oh, sorrow! 'tis winter now.
  And her tears gushed forth, though it was but a leaf,
  For little will loose the swollen fountain of grief:
  When up to the lip the water goes,
  It needs but a drop, and it overflows.

Oh! many and many a dreary year
  Must pass away ere the buds appear:
  Many a night of darksome sorrow
  Yield to the light of a joyless morrow,
  Ere birds again, on the clothed trees,

Shall fill the branches with melodies.
She will dream of meadows with wakeful streams;
Of wavy grass in the sunny beams;
Of hidden wells that soundless spring,
Hoarding their joy as a holy thing;
Of founts that tell it all day long
To the listening woods, with exultant song;
She will dream of evenings that die into nights,
Where each sense is filled with its own delights,
And the soul is still as the vaulted sky,
Lulled with an inner harmony;

And the flowers give out to the dewy night,
Changed into perfume, the gathered light;
And the darkness sinks upon all their host,
Till the sun sail up on the eastern coast —
She will wake and see the branches bare,
Weaving a net in the frozen air.

The story goes on to tell how, at last, weary with wintriness, she travelled towards the southern regions of her globe, to meet the spring on its slow way northwards; and how, after many sad adventures, many disappointed hopes, and many tears, bitter and fruitless, she found at last, one stormy afternoon, in a leafless forest, a single snowdrop growing betwixt the borders of the winter and spring. She lay down beside it and died. I almost believe that a child, pale and peaceful as a snow-drop, was born in the Earth within a fixed season from that stormy afternoon.

CHAPTER 13

"I saw a ship sailing upon the sea
  Deeply laden as ship could be;
  But not so deep as in love I am
  For I care not whether I sink or swim."
  Old Ballad.

"But Love is such a Mystery
  I cannot find it out:
  For when I think I'm best resolv'd,
  I then am in most doubt."
  SIR JOHN SUCKLING.

One story I will try to reproduce. But, alas! it is like trying to reconstruct a forest out of broken branches and withered leaves. In the fairy book, everything was just as it should be, though whether in words or something else, I cannot tell. It glowed and flashed the thoughts upon the soul, with such a power that the medium disappeared from the consciousness, and it was occupied only with the things themselves. My representation of it must resemble a translation from a rich and powerful language, capable of embodying the thoughts of a splendidly developed people, into the meagre and half-articulate speech of a savage tribe. Of course, while I read it, I was Cosmo, and his history was mine. Yet, all the time, I seemed to have a kind of double consciousness, and the story a double meaning. Sometimes it seemed only to represent a simple story of ordinary life, perhaps almost of universal life; wherein two souls, loving each other and longing to come nearer, do, after all, but behold each other as in a glass darkly.

As through the hard rock go the branching silver veins; as into the solid land run the creeks and gulfs from the unresting sea; as the lights and influences of the upper worlds sink silently through the earth's atmosphere; so doth Faerie invade the world of men, and sometimes startle the common eye with an association as of cause and effect, when between the two no connecting links can be traced.

Cosmo von Wehrstahl was a student at the University of Prague. Though of a noble family, he was poor, and prided himself upon the independence that poverty gives; for what will not a man pride himself upon, when he cannot get rid of it? A favourite with his fellow students, he yet had no companions; and none of them had ever crossed the threshold of his lodging in the top of one of the highest houses in the old town. Indeed, the secret of much of that complaisance which recommended him to his fellows, was the thought of his unknown retreat, whither in the evening he could betake himself and indulge undisturbed in his own studies and reveries. These studies, besides those subjects necessary to his course at the University, embraced some less commonly known and approved; for in a secret drawer lay the works of Albertus Magnus and Cornelius Agrippa, along with others less read and more abstruse. As yet, however, he had followed these researches only from curiosity, and had turned them to no practical purpose.

His lodging consisted of one large low-ceiled room, singularly bare of furniture; for besides a couple of wooden chairs, a couch which served for dreaming on both by day and night, and a great press of black oak, there was very little in the room that could be called furniture.

But curious instruments were heaped in the corners; and in one stood a skeleton, half-leaning against the wall, half-supported by a string about its neck. One of its hands, all of fingers, rested on the heavy pommel of a great sword that stood beside it.

Various weapons were scattered about over the floor. The walls were utterly bare of adornment; for the few strange things, such as a large dried bat with wings dispread, the skin of a porcupine, and a stuffed sea-mouse, could hardly be reckoned as such. But although his fancy delighted in vagaries like these, he indulged his imagination with far different fare. His mind had never yet been filled with an absorbing passion; but it lay like a still twilight open to any wind, whether the low breath that wafts but odours, or the storm that bows the great trees till they strain and creak. He saw everything as through a rose-coloured glass. When he looked from his window on the street below, not a maiden passed but she moved as in a story, and drew his thoughts after her till she disappeared in the vista. When he walked in the streets, he always felt as if reading a tale, into which he sought to weave every face of interest that went by; and every sweet voice swept his soul as with the wing of a passing angel. He was in fact a poet without words; the more absorbed and endangered, that the springing-waters were dammed back into his soul, where, finding no utterance, they grew, and swelled, and undermined. He used to lie on his hard couch, and read a tale or a poem, till the book dropped from his hand; but he dreamed on, he knew not whether awake or asleep, until the opposite roof grew upon his sense, and turned golden in the sunrise. Then he arose too; and the impulses of vigorous youth kept him ever active, either in study or in sport, until again the close of the day left him free; and the world of night, which had lain drowned in the cataract of the day, rose up in his soul, with all its stars, and dim-seen phantom shapes. But this could hardly last long. Some one form must sooner or later step within the charmed circle, enter the house of life, and compel the bewildered magician to kneel and worship.

One afternoon, towards dusk, he was wandering dreamily in one of the principal streets, when a fellow student roused him by a slap on the shoulder, and asked him to accompany him into a little back alley to look at some old armour which he had taken a fancy to possess. Cosmo was considered an authority in every matter pertaining to arms, ancient or modern. In the use of weapons, none of the students could come near him; and his practical acquaintance with some had principally contributed to establish his authority in reference to all. He accompanied him willingly.

They entered a narrow alley, and thence a dirty little court, where a low arched door admitted them into a heterogeneous assemblage of everything musty, and dusty, and old, that could well be imagined. His verdict on the armour was satisfactory, and his companion at once concluded the purchase. As they were leaving the place, Cosmo's eye was attracted by an old mirror of an elliptical shape, which leaned against the wall, covered with dust. Around it was some curious carving, which he could see but very indistinctly by the glimmering light which the owner of the shop carried in his hand. It was this carving that attracted his attention; at least so it appeared to him. He left the place, however, with his friend, taking no further notice of it. They walked together to the main street, where they parted and took opposite directions.

No sooner was Cosmo left alone, than the thought of the curious old mirror returned to him. A strong desire to see it more plainly arose within him, and he directed his steps once more towards the shop. The owner opened the door when he knocked, as if he had expected him. He was a little, old, withered man, with a hooked nose, and burning eyes constantly in a slow restless motion, and looking here and there as if after something that eluded them. Pretending to examine several other articles, Cosmo at last approached the mirror, and requested to have it taken down.

"Take it down yourself, master; I cannot reach it," said the old man.

Cosmo took it down carefully, when he saw that the carving was indeed delicate and costly, being both of admirable design and execution; containing withal many devices which seemed to embody some meaning to which he had no clue. This, naturally, in one of his tastes and temperament, increased the interest he felt in the old mirror; so much, indeed, that he now longed to possess it, in order to study its frame at his leisure. He pretended, however, to want it only for use; and saying he feared the plate could be of little service, as it was rather old, he brushed away a little of the dust from its face, expecting to see a dull reflection within. His surprise was great when he found the reflection brilliant, revealing a glass not only uninjured by age, but wondrously clear and perfect (should the whole correspond to this part) even for one newly from the hands of the maker. He asked carelessly what the owner wanted for the thing. The old man replied by mentioning a sum of money far beyond the reach of poor Cosmo, who proceeded to replace the mirror where it had stood before.

"You think the price too high?" said the old man.

"I do not know that it is too much for you to ask," replied Cosmo; "but it is far too much for me to give."

The old man held up his light towards Cosmo's face. "I like your look," said he.

70

Cosmo could not return the compliment. In fact, now he looked closely at him for the first time, he felt a kind of repugnance to him, mingled with a strange feeling of doubt whether a man or a woman stood before him.

"What is your name?" he continued.

"Cosmo von Wehrstahl."

"Ah, ah! I thought as much. I see your father in you. I knew your father very well, young sir. I dare say in some odd corners of my house, you might find some old things with his crest and cipher upon them still. Well, I like you: you shall have the mirror at the fourth part of what I asked for it; but upon one condition."

"What is that?" said Cosmo; for, although the price was still a great deal for him to give, he could just manage it; and the desire to possess the mirror had increased to an altogether unaccountable degree, since it had seemed beyond his reach.

"That if you should ever want to get rid of it again, you will let me have the first offer."

"Certainly," replied Cosmo, with a smile; adding, "a moderate condition indeed."

"On your honour?" insisted the seller.

"On my honour," said the buyer; and the bargain was concluded.

"I will carry it home for you," said the old man, as Cosmo took it in his hands.

"No, no; I will carry it myself," said he; for he had a peculiar dislike to revealing his residence to any one, and more especially to this person, to whom he felt every moment a greater antipathy. "Just as you please," said the old creature, and muttered to himself as he held his light at the door to show him out of the court: "Sold for the sixth time! I wonder what will be the upshot of it this time. I should think my lady had enough of it by now!"

Cosmo carried his prize carefully home. But all the way he had an uncomfortable feeling that he was watched and dogged. Repeatedly he looked about, but saw nothing to justify his suspicions. Indeed, the streets were too crowded and too ill lighted to expose very readily a careful spy, if such there should be at his heels. He reached his lodging in safety, and leaned his purchase against the wall, rather relieved, strong as he was, to be rid of its weight; then, lighting his pipe, threw himself on the couch, and was soon lapt in the folds of one of his haunting dreams.

He returned home earlier than usual the next day, and fixed the mirror to the wall, over the hearth, at one end of his long room.

He then carefully wiped away the dust from its face, and, clear as the water of a sunny spring, the mirror shone out from beneath the envious covering. But his interest was chiefly occupied with the curious carving of the frame. This he cleaned as well as he could with a brush; and then he proceeded to a minute examination of its various parts, in the hope of discovering some index to the intention of the carver. In this, however, he was unsuccessful; and, at length, pausing with some weariness and disappointment, he gazed vacantly for a few moments into the depth of the reflected room. But ere long he said, half aloud: "What a strange thing a mirror is! And what a wondrous affinity exists between it and a man's imagination! For this room of mine, as I behold it in the glass, is the same, and yet not the same. It is not the mere representation of the room I live in, but it looks just as if I were reading about it in a story I like. All its commonness has disappeared. The mirror has lifted it out of the region of fact into the realm of art; and the very representing of it to me has clothed with interest that which was otherwise hard and bare; just as one sees with delight upon the stage the representation of a character from which one would escape in life as from something unendurably wearisome. But is it not rather that art rescues nature from the weary and sated regards of our senses, and the degrading injustice of our anxious everyday life, and, appealing to the imagination, which dwells apart, reveals Nature in some degree as she really is, and as she represents herself to the eye of the child, whose every-day life, fearless and unambitious, meets the true import of the wonder-teeming world around him, and rejoices therein without questioning? That skeleton, now—I almost fear it, standing there so still, with eyes only for the unseen, like a watch-tower looking across all the waste of this busy world into the quiet regions of rest beyond. And yet I know every bone and every joint in it as well as my own fist. And that old battle-axe looks as if any moment it might be caught up by a mailed hand, and, borne forth by the mighty arm, go crashing through casque, and skull, and brain, invading the Unknown with yet another bewildered ghost. I should like to live in *that* room if I could only get into it."

Scarcely had the half-moulded words floated from him, as he stood gazing into the mirror, when, striking him as with a flash of amazement that fixed him in his posture, noiseless and unannounced, glided suddenly through the door into the reflected room, with stately motion, yet reluctant and faltering step, the graceful form of a woman, clothed all in white. Her back only was visible as she walked slowly up to the couch in the further end of the room, on which she laid herself wearily, turning towards him a face of unutterable loveliness, in which suffering, and dislike, and a sense of compulsion, strangely mingled with the beauty. He stood without the power of motion for some moments, with his eyes irrecoverably fixed upon her; and even after he was conscious of the ability to move, he could not summon up courage to turn and look on her, face to face, in the veritable chamber in which he stood. At length, with a sudden effort, in which the exercise of the will was so pure, that it seemed involuntary, he turned his face to the couch. It was vacant. In bewilderment, mingled with terror, he turned again to the mirror: there, on the reflected couch, lay the exquisite lady-form. She lay with closed eyes, whence two large tears were just welling from beneath the veiling lids; still as death, save for the convulsive motion of her bosom.

Cosmo himself could not have described what he felt. His emotions were of a kind that destroyed consciousness, and could never be clearly recalled. He could not help standing yet by the mirror, and keeping his eyes fixed on the lady, though he was painfully aware of his rudeness, and feared every moment that she would open hers, and meet his fixed regard. But he was, ere long, a little relieved; for, after a while, her eyelids slowly rose, and her eyes remained uncovered, but unemployed for a time; and when, at length, they began to wander about the room, as if languidly seeking to make some acquaintance with her environment, they were never directed towards him: it seemed nothing but what was in the mirror could affect her vision; and, therefore, if she saw him at all, it could only be his back, which, of necessity, was turned towards her in the glass. The two figures in the mirror could not meet face to face, except he turned and looked at her, present in his room; and, as she was not there, he concluded that if he were to turn towards the part in his room corresponding to that in which she lay, his reflection would either be invisible to her altogether, or at least it must appear to her to gaze vacantly towards her, and no meeting of the eyes would produce the impression of spiritual proximity. By-and-by her eyes fell upon the skeleton, and he saw her shudder and close them. She did not open them again, but signs of repugnance continued evident on her countenance. Cosmo would have removed the obnoxious thing at once, but he feared to discompose her yet more by the assertion of his presence which the act would involve. So he stood and watched her. The eyelids yet shrouded the eyes, as a costly case the jewels within; the troubled expression gradually faded from the countenance, leaving only a faint sorrow behind; the features settled into an unchanging expression of rest; and by these signs, and the slow regular motion of her breathing, Cosmo knew that she slept. He could now gaze on her without embarrassment. He saw that her figure, dressed in the simplest robe of white, was worthy of her face; and so harmonious, that either the delicately moulded foot, or any finger of the equally delicate hand, was an index to the whole. As she lay, her whole form manifested the relaxation of perfect repose. He gazed till he was weary, and at last seated himself near the new-found shrine, and mechanically took up a book, like one who watches by a sick-bed. But his eyes gathered no thoughts from the page before him. His intellect had been stunned by the bold contradiction, to its face, of all its experience, and now lay passive, without assertion, or speculation, or even conscious astonishment; while his imagination sent one wild dream of blessedness after another coursing through his soul. How long he sat he knew not; but at length he roused himself, rose, and, trembling in every portion of his frame, looked again into the mirror. She was gone. The mirror reflected faithfully what his room presented, and nothing more. It stood there like a golden setting whence the central jewel has been stolen away—like a night-sky without the glory of its stars. She had carried with her all the strangeness of the reflected room. It had sunk to the level of the one without.

But when the first pangs of his disappointment had passed, Cosmo began to comfort himself with the hope that she might return, perhaps the next evening, at the same hour. Resolving that if she did, she should not at least be scared by the hateful skeleton, he removed that and several other articles of questionable appearance into a recess by the side of the hearth, whence they could not possibly cast any reflection into the mirror; and having made his poor room as tidy as he could, sought the solace of the open sky and of a night wind that had begun to blow, for he could not rest where he was. When he returned, somewhat composed, he could hardly prevail with himself to lie down on his bed; for he could not help feeling as if she had lain upon it; and for him to lie there now would be something like sacrilege. However, weariness prevailed; and laying himself on the couch, dressed as he was, he slept till day.

With a beating heart, beating till he could hardly breathe, he stood in dumb hope before the mirror, on the following evening. Again the reflected room shone as through a purple vapour in the gathering twilight. Everything seemed waiting like himself for a coming splendour to glorify its poor earthliness with the presence of a heavenly joy. And just as the room vibrated with the strokes of the neighbouring church bell, announcing the hour of six, in glided the pale beauty, and again laid herself on the couch. Poor Cosmo nearly lost his senses with delight. She was there once more! Her eyes sought the corner where the skeleton had stood, and a faint gleam of satisfaction crossed her face, apparently at seeing it empty. She looked suffering still, but there was less of discomfort expressed in her countenance than there had been the night before. She took more notice of the things about her, and seemed to gaze with some curiosity on the strange apparatus standing here and there in her room. At length, however, drowsiness seemed to overtake her, and again she fell asleep. Resolved not to lose sight of her this time, Cosmo watched the sleeping form. Her slumber was so deep and absorbing that a fascinating repose seemed to pass contagiously from her to him as he gazed upon her; and he started as if from a dream, when the lady moved, and, without opening her eyes, rose, and passed from the room with the gait of a somnambulist.

Cosmo was now in a state of extravagant delight. Most men have a secret treasure somewhere. The miser has his golden hoard; the virtuoso his pet ring; the student his rare book; the poet his favourite haunt; the lover his secret drawer; but Cosmo had a mirror with a lovely lady in it. And now that he knew by the skeleton, that she was affected by the things around her, he had a new object in life: he would turn the bare chamber in the mirror into a room such as no lady need disdain to call her own. This he could effect only by furnishing and adorning his. And Cosmo was poor. Yet he possessed accomplishments that could be turned to account; although, hitherto, he had preferred living on his slender allowance, to increasing his means by what his pride considered unworthy of his rank. He was the best swordsman in the University; and now he offered to give lessons in fencing and similar exercises, to such as chose to pay him well for the trouble. His proposal was heard with surprise by the students; but it was eagerly accepted by many; and soon his instructions were not confined to the richer students, but were anxiously sought by many of the young nobility of Prague and its neighbourhood. So that very soon he had a good deal of money at his command. The first thing he did was to remove his apparatus and oddities into a closet in the room. Then he placed his bed and a few other necessaries on each side of the hearth, and parted them from the rest of the room by two screens of Indian fabric. Then he put an elegant couch for the lady to lie upon, in the corner where his bed had formerly stood; and, by degrees, every day adding some article of luxury, converted it, at length, into a rich boudoir.

Every night, about the same time, the lady entered. The first time she saw the new couch, she started with a half-smile; then her face grew very sad, the tears came to her eyes, and she laid herself upon the couch, and pressed her face into the silken cushions, as if to hide from everything. She took notice of each addition and each change as the work proceeded; and a look of acknowledgment, as if she knew that some one was ministering to her, and was grateful for it, mingled with the constant look of suffering. At length, after she had lain down as usual one evening, her eyes fell upon some paintings with which Cosmo had just finished adorning the walls. She rose, and to his great delight, walked across the room, and proceeded to examine them carefully, testifying much pleasure in her looks as she did so. But again the sorrowful, tearful expression returned, and again she buried her face in the pillows of her couch. Gradually, however, her countenance had grown more composed; much of the suffering manifest on her first appearance had vanished, and a kind of quiet, hopeful expression had taken its place; which, however, frequently gave way to an anxious, troubled look, mingled with something of sympathetic pity.

Meantime, how fared Cosmo? As might be expected in one of his temperament, his interest had blossomed into love, and his love—shall I call it *ripened*, or—*withered* into passion. But, alas! he loved a shadow. He could not come near her, could

not speak to her, could not hear a sound from those sweet lips, to which his longing eyes would cling like bees to their honey-founts. Ever and anon he sang to himself:
"I shall die for love of the maiden;"

and ever he looked again, and died not, though his heart seemed ready to break with intensity of life and longing. And the more he did for her, the more he loved her; and he hoped that, although she never appeared to see him, yet she was pleased to think that one unknown would give his life to her. He tried to comfort himself over his separation from her, by thinking that perhaps some day she would see him and make signs to him, and that would satisfy him; "for," thought he, "is not this all that a loving soul can do to enter into communion with another? Nay, how many who love never come nearer than to behold each other as in a mirror; seem to know and yet never know the inward life; never enter the other soul; and part at last, with but the vaguest notion of the universe on the borders of which they have been hovering for years? If I could but speak to her, and knew that she heard me, I should be satisfied." Once he contemplated painting a picture on the wall, which should, of necessity, convey to the lady a thought of himself; but, though he had some skill with the pencil, he found his hand tremble so much when he began the attempt, that he was forced to give it up. . . . . .
"Who lives, he dies; who dies, he is alive."
One evening, as he stood gazing on his treasure, he thought he saw a faint expression of self-consciousness on her countenance, as if she surmised that passionate eyes were fixed upon her. This grew; till at last the red blood rose over her neck, and cheek, and brow. Cosmo's longing to approach her became almost delirious. This night she was dressed in an evening costume, resplendent with diamonds. This could add nothing to her beauty, but it presented it in a new aspect; enabled her loveliness to make a new manifestation of itself in a new embodiment. For essential beauty is infinite; and, as the soul of Nature needs an endless succession of varied forms to embody her loveliness, countless faces of beauty springing forth, not any two the same, at any one of her heart-throbs; so the individual form needs an infinite change of its environments, to enable it to uncover all the phases of its loveliness. Diamonds glittered from amidst her hair, half hidden in its luxuriance, like stars through dark rain-clouds; and the bracelets on her white arms flashed all the colours of a rainbow of lightnings, as she lifted her snowy hands to cover her burning face. But her beauty shone down all its adornment. "If I might have but one of her feet to kiss," thought Cosmo, "I should be content." Alas! he deceived himself, for passion is never content. Nor did he know that there are *two* ways out of her enchanted house. But, suddenly, as if the pang had been driven into his heart from without, revealing itself first in pain, and afterwards in definite form, the thought darted into his mind, "She has a lover somewhere. Remembered words of his bring the colour on her face now. I am nowhere to her. She lives in another world all day, and all night, after she leaves me. Why does she come and make me love her, till I, a strong man, am too faint to look upon her more?" He looked again, and her face was pale as a lily. A sorrowful compassion seemed to rebuke the glitter of the restless jewels, and the slow tears rose in her eyes. She left her room sooner this evening than was her wont. Cosmo remained alone, with a feeling as if his bosom had been suddenly left empty and hollow, and the weight of the whole

world was crushing in its walls. The next evening, for the first time since she began to come, she came not.

And now Cosmo was in wretched plight. Since the thought of a rival had occurred to him, he could not rest for a moment. More than ever he longed to see the lady face to face. He persuaded himself that if he but knew the worst he would be satisfied; for then he could abandon Prague, and find that relief in constant motion, which is the hope of all active minds when invaded by distress. Meantime, he waited with unspeakable anxiety for the next night, hoping she would return: but she did not appear. And now he fell really ill. Rallied by his fellow students on his wretched looks, he ceased to attend the lectures. His engagements were neglected. He cared for nothing. The sky, with the great sun in it, was to him a heartless, burning desert. The men and women in the streets were mere puppets, without motives in themselves, or interest to him. He saw them all as on the ever-changing field of a *camera obscura*. She—she alone and altogether—was his universe, his well of life, his incarnate good. For six evenings she came not. Let his absorbing passion, and the slow fever that was consuming his brain, be his excuse for the resolution which he had taken and begun to execute, before that time had expired.

Reasoning with himself, that it must be by some enchantment connected with the mirror, that the form of the lady was to be seen in it, he determined to attempt to turn to account what he had hitherto studied principally from curiosity. "For," said he to himself, "if a spell can force her presence in that glass (and she came unwillingly at first), may not a stronger spell, such as I know, especially with the aid of her half-presence in the mirror, if ever she appears again, compel her living form to come to me here? If I do her wrong, let love be my excuse. I want only to know my doom from her own lips." He never doubted, all the time, that she was a real earthly woman; or, rather, that there was a woman, who, somehow or other, threw this reflection of her form into the magic mirror.

He opened his secret drawer, took out his books of magic, lighted his lamp, and read and made notes from midnight till three in the morning, for three successive nights. Then he replaced his books; and the next night went out in quest of the materials necessary for the conjuration. These were not easy to find; for, in love-charms and all incantations of this nature, ingredients are employed scarcely fit to be mentioned, and for the thought even of which, in connexion with her, he could only excuse himself on the score of his bitter need. At length he succeeded in procuring all he required; and on the seventh evening from that on which she had last appeared, he found himself prepared for the exercise of unlawful and tyrannical power.

He cleared the centre of the room; stooped and drew a circle of red on the floor, around the spot where he stood; wrote in the four quarters mystical signs, and numbers which were all powers of seven or nine; examined the whole ring carefully, to see that no smallest break had occurred in the circumference; and then rose from his bending posture. As he rose, the church clock struck seven; and, just as she had appeared the first time, reluctant, slow, and stately, glided in the lady. Cosmo trembled; and when, turning, she revealed a countenance worn and wan, as with sickness or inward trouble, he grew faint, and felt as if he dared not proceed. But as he gazed on the face and form, which now possessed his whole soul, to the exclusion of all other joys and griefs, the longing to speak to her, to know that she heard him, to hear from her one word in return, became so unendurable, that he suddenly and hastily resumed his preparations. Stepping carefully from the circle, he put a small brazier into its centre. He then set fire to its contents of charcoal, and while it burned up, opened his window and seated himself, waiting, beside it.

It was a sultry evening. The air was full of thunder. A sense of luxurious depression filled the brain. The sky seemed to have grown heavy, and to compress the air beneath it. A kind of purplish tinge pervaded the atmosphere, and through the open window came the scents of the distant fields, which all the vapours of the city could not quench. Soon the charcoal glowed. Cosmo sprinkled upon it the incense and other substances which he had compounded, and, stepping within the circle, turned his face from the brazier and towards the mirror. Then, fixing his eyes upon the face of the lady, he began with a trembling voice to repeat a powerful incantation. He had not gone far, before the lady grew pale; and then, like a returning wave, the blood washed all its banks with its crimson tide, and she hid her face in her hands. Then he passed to a conjuration stronger yet.

The lady rose and walked uneasily to and fro in her room. Another spell; and she seemed seeking with her eyes for some object on which they wished to rest. At length it seemed as if she suddenly espied him; for her eyes fixed themselves full and wide upon his, and she drew gradually, and somewhat unwillingly, close to her side of the mirror, just as if his eyes had fascinated her. Cosmo had never seen her so near before. Now at least, eyes met eyes; but he could not quite understand the expression of hers. They were full of tender entreaty, but there was something more that he could not interpret. Though his heart seemed to labour in his throat, he would allow no delight or agitation to turn him from his task. Looking still in her face, he passed on to the mightiest charm he knew. Suddenly the lady turned and walked out of the door of her reflected chamber. A moment after she entered his room with veritable presence; and, forgetting all his precautions, he sprang from the charmed circle, and knelt before her. There she stood, the living lady of his passionate visions, alone beside him, in a thundery twilight, and the glow of a magic fire.

"Why," said the lady, with a trembling voice, "didst thou bring a poor maiden through the rainy streets alone?"

"Because I am dying for love of thee; but I only brought thee from the mirror there."

"Ah, the mirror!" and she looked up at it, and shuddered. "Alas! I am but a slave, while that mirror exists. But do not think it was the power of thy spells that drew me; it was thy longing desire to see me, that beat at the door of my heart, till I was forced to yield."

"Canst thou love me then?" said Cosmo, in a voice calm as death, but almost inarticulate with emotion.

"I do not know," she replied sadly; "that I cannot tell, so long as I am bewildered with enchantments. It were indeed a joy too great, to lay my head on thy bosom and weep to death; for I think thou lovest me, though I do not know;—but——"

Cosmo rose from his knees.

"I love thee as—nay, I know not what—for since I have loved thee, there is nothing else."

He seized her hand: she withdrew it.

"No, better not; I am in thy power, and therefore I may not."

She burst into tears, and kneeling before him in her turn, said—

"Cosmo, if thou lovest me, set me free, even from thyself; break the mirror."

"And shall I see thyself instead?"

"That I cannot tell, I will not deceive thee; we may never meet again."

A fierce struggle arose in Cosmo's bosom. Now she was in his power. She did not dislike him at least; and he could see her when he would. To break the mirror would be to destroy his very life to banish out of his universe the only glory it possessed. The whole world would be but a prison, if he annihilated the one window that looked into the paradise of love. Not yet pure in love, he hesitated.

With a wail of sorrow the lady rose to her feet. "Ah! he loves me not; he loves me not even as I love him; and alas! I care more for his love than even for the freedom I ask."

"I will not wait to be willing," cried Cosmo; and sprang to the corner where the great sword stood.

Meantime it had grown very dark; only the embers cast a red glow through the room. He seized the sword by the steel scabbard, and stood before the mirror; but as he heaved a great blow at it with the heavy pommel, the blade slipped half-way out of the scabbard, and the pommel struck the wall above the mirror. At that moment, a terrible clap of thunder seemed to burst in the very room beside them; and ere Cosmo could repeat the blow, he fell senseless on the hearth. When he came to himself, he found that the lady and the mirror had both disappeared. He was seized with a brain fever, which kept him to his couch for weeks.

When he recovered his reason, he began to think what could have become of the mirror. For the lady, he hoped she had found her way back as she came; but as the mirror involved her fate with its own, he was more immediately anxious about that. He could not think she had carried it away. It was much too heavy, even if it had not been too firmly fixed in the wall, for her to remove it. Then again, he remembered the thunder; which made him believe that it was not the lightning, but some other blow that had struck him down. He concluded that, either by supernatural agency, he having exposed himself to the vengeance of the demons in leaving the circle of safety, or in some other mode, the mirror had probably found its way back to its former owner; and, horrible to think of, might have been by this time once more disposed of, delivering up the lady into the power of another man; who, if he used his power no worse than he himself had done, might yet give Cosmo abundant cause to curse the selfish indecision which prevented him from shattering the mirror at once. Indeed, to think that she whom he loved, and who had prayed to him for freedom, should be still at the mercy, in some degree, of the possessor of the mirror, and was at least exposed to his constant observation, was in itself enough to madden a chary lover.

Anxiety to be well retarded his recovery; but at length he was able to creep abroad. He first made his way to the old broker's, pretending to be in search of something else. A laughing sneer on the creature's face convinced him that he knew all about it; but he could not see it amongst his furniture, or get any information out of him as to what had become of it. He expressed the utmost surprise at hearing it had been stolen, a surprise which Cosmo saw at once to be counterfeited; while, at the same time, he fancied that the old wretch was not at all anxious to have it mistaken for genuine. Full of distress, which he concealed as well as he could, he made many searches, but with no avail. Of course he could ask no questions; but he kept his ears awake for any remotest hint that might set him in a direction of search. He never went out without a short heavy hammer of steel about him, that he might shatter the mirror the moment he was made happy by the sight of his lost treasure, if ever that blessed moment should arrive. Whether he should see the lady again, was now a thought altogether secondary, and postponed to the achievement of her freedom. He wandered here and there, like an anxious ghost, pale and haggard; gnawed ever at the heart, by the thought of what she might be suffering— all from his fault.

One night, he mingled with a crowd that filled the rooms of one of the most distinguished mansions in the city; for he accepted every invitation, that he might lose no chance, however poor, of obtaining some information that might expedite his discovery. Here he wandered about, listening to every stray word that he could catch, in the hope of a revelation. As he approached some ladies who were talking quietly in a corner, one said to another:

"Have you heard of the strange illness of the Princess von Hohenweiss?"

"Yes; she has been ill for more than a year now. It is very sad for so fine a creature to have such a terrible malady. She was better for some weeks lately, but within the last few days the same attacks have returned, apparently accompanied with more suffering than ever. It is altogether an inexplicable story."

"Is there a story connected with her illness?"

"I have only heard imperfect reports of it; but it is said that she gave offence some eighteen months ago to an old woman who had held an office of trust in the family, and who, after some incoherent threats, disappeared. This peculiar affection followed soon after. But the strangest part of the story is its association with the loss of an antique mirror, which stood in her dressing-room, and of which she constantly made use."

Here the speaker's voice sank to a whisper; and Cosmo, although his very soul sat listening in his ears, could hear no more. He trembled too much to dare to address the ladies, even if it had been advisable to expose himself to their curiosity. The name of the Princess was well known to him, but he had never seen her; except indeed it was she, which now he hardly doubted, who had knelt before him on that dreadful night. Fearful of attracting attention, for, from the weak state of his health, he could not recover an appearance of calmness, he made his way to the open air, and reached his lodgings; glad in this, that he at least knew where she lived, although he never dreamed of approaching her openly, even if he should be happy enough to free her from her hateful bondage. He hoped, too, that as he had unexpectedly learned so much, the other and far more important part might be revealed to him ere long.

"Have you seen Steinwald lately?"

"No, I have not seen him for some time. He is almost a match for me at the rapier, and I suppose he thinks he needs no more lessons."

"I wonder what has become of him. I want to see him very much. Let me see; the last time I saw him he was coming out of that old broker's den, to which, if you remember, you accompanied me once, to look at some armour. That is fully three weeks ago."

This hint was enough for Cosmo. Von Steinwald was a man of influence in the court, well known for his reckless habits and fierce passions. The very possibility that the mirror should be in his possession was hell itself to Cosmo. But violent or hasty measures of any sort were most unlikely to succeed. All that he wanted was an opportunity of breaking the fatal glass; and to obtain this he must bide his time. He revolved many plans in his mind, but without being able to fix upon any.

At length, one evening, as he was passing the house of Von Steinwald, he saw the windows more than usually brilliant. He watched for a while, and seeing that company began to arrive, hastened home, and dressed as richly as he could, in the hope of mingling with the guests unquestioned: in effecting which, there could be no difficulty for a man of his carriage.

In a lofty, silent chamber, in another part of the city, lay a form more like marble than a living woman. The loveliness of death seemed frozen upon her face, for her lips were rigid, and her eyelids closed. Her long white hands were crossed over her breast, and no breathing disturbed their repose. Beside the dead, men speak in whispers, as if the deepest rest of all could be broken by the sound of a living voice. Just so, though the soul was evidently beyond the reach of all intimations from the senses, the two ladies, who sat beside her, spoke in the gentlest tones of subdued sorrow. "She has lain so for an hour."

"This cannot last long, I fear."

"How much thinner she has grown within the last few weeks! If she would only speak, and explain what she suffers, it would be better for her. I think she has visions in her trances, but nothing can induce her to refer to them when she is awake."

"Does she ever speak in these trances?"

"I have never heard her; but they say she walks sometimes, and once put the whole household in a terrible fright by disappearing for a whole hour, and returning drenched with rain, and almost dead with exhaustion and fright. But even then she would give no account of what had happened."

A scarce audible murmur from the yet motionless lips of the lady here startled her attendants. After several ineffectual attempts at articulation, the word "*Cosmo!*" burst from her. Then she lay still as before; but only for a moment. With a wild cry, she sprang from the couch erect on the floor, flung her arms above her head, with clasped and straining hands, and, her wide eyes flashing with light, called aloud, with a voice exultant as that of a spirit bursting from a sepulchre, "I am free! I am free! I thank thee!" Then she flung herself on the couch, and sobbed; then rose, and paced wildly up and down the room, with gestures of mingled delight and anxiety. Then turning to her motionless attendants—"Quick, Lisa, my cloak and hood!" Then lower—"I must go to him. Make haste, Lisa! You may come with me, if you will."

In another moment they were in the street, hurrying along towards one of the bridges over the Moldau. The moon was near the zenith, and the streets were almost empty. The Princess soon outstripped her attendant, and was half-way over the bridge, before the other reached it.

"Are you free, lady? The mirror is broken: are you free?"

The words were spoken close beside her, as she hurried on. She turned; and there, leaning on the parapet in a recess of the bridge, stood Cosmo, in a splendid dress, but with a white and quivering face.

"Cosmo!—I am free—and thy servant for ever. I was coming to you now."

"And I to you, for Death made me bold; but I could get no further. Have I atoned at all? Do I love you a little—truly?"

"Ah, I know now that you love me, my Cosmo; but what do you say about death?"

He did not reply. His hand was pressed against his side. She looked more closely: the blood was welling from between the fingers. She flung her arms around him with a faint bitter wail.

When Lisa came up, she found her mistress kneeling above a wan dead face, which smiled on in the spectral moonbeams.

And now I will say no more about these wondrous volumes; though I could tell many a tale out of them, and could, perhaps, vaguely represent some entrancing thoughts of a deeper kind which I found within them. From many a sultry noon till twilight, did I sit in that grand hall, buried and risen again in these old books. And I trust I have carried away in my soul some of the exhalations of their undying leaves. In after hours of deserved or needful sorrow, portions of what I read there have often come to me again, with an unexpected comforting; which was not fruitless, even though the comfort might seem in itself groundless and vain.

CHAPTER 14

"Your gallery
Ha we pass'd through, not without much content
In many singularities; but we saw not
That which my daughter came to look upon,
The state of her mother."
Winter's Tale.

It seemed to me strange, that all this time I had heard no music in the fairy palace. I was convinced there must be music in it, but that my sense was as yet too gross to receive the influence of those mysterious motions that beget sound. Sometimes I felt sure, from the way the few figures of which I got such transitory glimpses passed me, or glided into vacancy before me, that they were moving to the law of music; and, in fact, several times I fancied for a moment that I heard a few wondrous tones coming I knew not whence. But they did not last long enough to convince me that I had heard them with the bodily sense. Such as they were, however, they took strange liberties with me, causing me to burst suddenly into tears, of which there was no presence to make me ashamed, or casting me into a kind of trance of speechless delight, which, passing as suddenly, left me faint and longing for more.

Now, on an evening, before I had been a week in the palace, I was wandering through one lighted arcade and corridor after another. At length I arrived, through a door that closed behind me, in another vast hall of the palace. It was filled with a subdued crimson light; by which I saw that slender pillars of black, built close to walls of white marble, rose to a great height, and then, dividing into innumerable divergent arches, supported a roof, like the walls, of white marble, upon which the arches intersected intricately, forming a fretting of black upon the white, like the network of a skeleton-leaf. The floor was black.

Between several pairs of the pillars upon every side, the place of the wall behind was occupied by a crimson curtain of thick silk, hanging in heavy and rich folds. Behind each of these curtains burned a powerful light, and these were the sources of the glow that filled the hall. A peculiar delicious odour pervaded the place. As soon as I entered, the old inspiration seemed to return to me, for I felt a strong impulse to sing; or rather, it seemed as if some one else was singing a song in my soul, which wanted to come forth at my lips, imbodied in my breath. But I kept silence; and feeling somewhat overcome by the red light and the perfume, as well as by the emotion within me, and seeing at one end of the hall a great crimson chair, more like a throne than a chair, beside a table of white marble, I went to it, and, throwing myself in it, gave myself up to a succession of images of bewildering beauty, which passed before my inward eye, in a long and occasionally crowded train. Here I sat for hours, I suppose; till, returning somewhat to myself, I saw that the red light had paled away, and felt a cool gentle breath gliding over my fore-head. I rose and left the hall with unsteady steps, finding my way with some diffi-culty to my own chamber, and faintly remembering, as I went, that only in the marble cave, before I found the sleeping statue, had I ever had a similar experience.

After this, I repaired every morning to the same hall; where I sometimes sat in the chair and dreamed deliciously, and sometimes walked up and down over the black floor. Sometimes I acted within myself a whole drama, during one of these perambula-tions; sometimes walked deliberately through the whole epic of a tale; sometimes ventured to sing a song, though with a shrinking fear of I knew not what. I was aston-ished at the beauty of my own voice as it rang through the place, or rather crept undu-lating, like a serpent of sound, along the walls and roof of this superb music-hall. Entrancing verses arose within me as of their own accord, chanting themselves to their own melodies, and requiring no addition of music to satisfy the inward sense. But, ever in the pauses of these, when the singing mood was upon me, I seemed to hear some-thing like the distant sound of multitudes of dancers, and felt as if it was the unheard music, moving their rhythmic motion, that within me blossomed in verse and song. I felt, too, that could I but see the dance, I should, from the harmony of complicated movements, not of the dancers in relation to each other merely, but of each dancer indi-vidually in the manifested plastic power that moved the consenting harmonious form, understand the whole of the music on the billows of which they floated and swung.

At length, one night, suddenly, when this feeling of dancing came upon me, I bethought me of lifting one of the crimson curtains, and looking if, perchance, behind it there might not be hid some other mystery, which might at least remove a step further the bewilderment of the present one. Nor was I altogether disap-pointed. I walked to one of the magnificent draperies, lifted a corner, and peeped in. There, burned a great, crimson, globe-shaped light, high in the cubical centre of another hall, which might be larger or less than that in which I stood, for its dimen-sions were not easily perceived, seeing that floor and roof and walls were entirely of black marble.

The roof was supported by the same arrangement of pillars radiating in arches, as that of the first hall; only, here, the pillars and arches were of dark red. But what absorbed my delighted gaze, was an innumerable assembly of white marble stat-

ues, of every form, and in multitudinous posture, filling the hall throughout. These stood, in the ruddy glow of the great lamp, upon pedestals of jet black. Around the lamp shone in golden letters, plainly legible from where I stood, the two words—
TOUCH NOT!

There was in all this, however, no solution to the sound of dancing; and now I was aware that the influence on my mind had ceased. I did not go in that evening, for I was weary and faint, but I hoarded up the expectation of entering, as of a great coming joy.

Next night I walked, as on the preceding, through the hall. My mind was filled with pictures and songs, and therewith so much absorbed, that I did not for some time think of looking within the curtain I had last night lifted. When the thought of doing so occurred to me first, I happened to be within a few yards of it. I became conscious, at the same moment, that the sound of dancing had been for some time in my ears. I approached the curtain quickly, and, lifting it, entered the black hall. Everything was still as death. I should have concluded that the sound must have proceeded from some other more distant quarter, which conclusion its faintness would, in ordinary circumstances, have necessitated from the first; but there was a something about the statues that caused me still to remain in doubt. As I said, each stood perfectly still upon its black pedestal: but there was about every one a certain air, not of motion, but as if it had just ceased from movement; as if the rest were not altogether of the marbly stillness of thousands of years. It was as if the peculiar atmosphere of each had yet a kind of invisible tremulousness; as if its agitated wavelets had not yet subsided into a perfect calm. I had the suspicion that they had anticipated my appearance, and had sprung, each, from the living joy of the dance, to the death-silence and blackness of its isolated pedestal, just before I entered. I walked across the central hall to the curtain opposite the one I had lifted, and, entering there, found all the appearances similar; only that the statues were different, and differently grouped. Neither did they produce on my mind that impression—of motion just expired, which I had experienced from the others. I found that behind every one of the crimson curtains was a similar hall, similarly lighted, and similarly occupied.

The next night, I did not allow my thoughts to be absorbed as before with inward images, but crept stealthily along to the furthest curtain in the hall, from behind which, likewise, I had formerly seemed to hear the sound of dancing. I drew aside its edge as suddenly as I could, and, looking in, saw that the utmost stillness pervaded the vast place. I walked in, and passed through it to the other end.

There I found that it communicated with a circular corridor, divided from it only by two rows of red columns. This corridor, which was black, with red niches holding statues, ran entirely about the statue-halls, forming a communication between the further ends of them all; further, that is, as regards the central hall of white whence they all diverged like radii, finding their circumference in the corridor.

Round this corridor I now went, entering all the halls, of which there were twelve, and finding them all similarly constructed, but filled with quite various statues, of what seemed both ancient and modern sculpture. After I had simply walked through them, I found myself sufficiently tired to long for rest, and went to my own room.

In the night I dreamed that, walking close by one of the curtains, I was suddenly seized with the desire to enter, and darted in. This time I was too quick for them. All the statues were in motion, statues no longer, but men and women—all shapes of beauty that ever sprang from the brain of the sculptor, mingled in the convolutions of a complicated dance. Passing through them to the further end, I almost started from my sleep on beholding, not taking part in the dance with the others, nor seemingly endued with life like them, but standing in marble coldness and rigidity upon a black pedestal in the extreme left corner—my lady of the cave; the marble beauty who sprang from her tomb or her cradle at the call of my songs. While I gazed in speechless astonishment and admiration, a dark shadow, descending from above like the curtain of a stage, gradually hid her entirely from my view. I felt with a shudder that this shadow was perchance my missing demon, whom I had not seen for days. I awoke with a stifled cry.

Of course, the next evening I began my journey through the halls (for I knew not to which my dream had carried me), in the hope of proving the dream to be a true one, by discovering my marble beauty upon her black pedestal. At length, on reaching the tenth hall, I thought I recognised some of the forms I had seen dancing in my dream; and to my bewilderment, when I arrived at the extreme corner on the left, there stood, the only one I had yet seen, a vacant pedestal. It was exactly in the position occupied, in my dream, by the pedestal on which the white lady stood. Hope beat violently in my heart.

"Now," said I to myself, "if yet another part of the dream would but come true, and I should succeed in surprising these forms in their nightly dance; it might be the rest would follow, and I should see on the pedestal my marble queen. Then surely if my songs sufficed to give her life before, when she lay in the bonds of alabaster, much more would they be sufficient then to give her volition and motion, when she alone of assembled crowds of marble forms, would be standing rigid and cold."

But the difficulty was, to surprise the dancers. I had found that a premeditated attempt at surprise, though executed with the utmost care and rapidity, was of no avail. And, in my dream, it was effected by a sudden thought suddenly executed. I saw, therefore, that there was no plan of operation offering any probability of success, but this: to allow my mind to be occupied with other thoughts, as I wandered around the great centre-hall; and so wait till the impulse to enter one of the others should happen to arise in me just at the moment when I was close to one of the crimson curtains. For I hoped that if I entered any one of the twelve halls at the right moment, that would as it were give me the right of entrance to all the others, seeing they all had communication behind. I would not diminish the hope of the right chance, by supposing it necessary that a desire to enter should awake within me, precisely when I was close to the curtains of the tenth hall.

At first the impulses to see recurred so continually, in spite of the crowded imagery that kept passing through my mind, that they formed too nearly a continuous chain, for the hope that any one of them would succeed as a surprise. But as I persisted in banishing them, they recurred less and less often; and after two or three, at considerable intervals, had come when the spot where I happened to be was unsuitable, the hope strengthened, that soon one might arise just at the right moment; namely, when, in walking round the hall, I should be close to one of the curtains.

At length the right moment and the impulse coincided. I darted into the ninth hall. It was full of the most exquisite moving forms. The whole space wavered and swam with the involutions of an intricate dance. It seemed to break suddenly as I entered, and all made one or two bounds towards their pedestals; but, apparently on finding that they were thoroughly overtaken, they returned to their employment (for it seemed with them earnest enough to be called such) without further heeding me. Somewhat impeded by the floating crowd, I made what haste I could towards the bottom of the hall; whence, entering the corridor, I turned towards the tenth. I soon arrived at the corner I wanted to reach, for the corridor was comparatively empty; but, although the dancers here, after a little confusion, altogether disregarded my presence, I was dismayed at beholding, even yet, a vacant pedestal. But I had a conviction that she was near me. And as I looked at the pedestal, I thought I saw upon it, vaguely revealed as if through overlapping folds of drapery, the indistinct outlines of white feet. Yet there was no sign of drapery or concealing shadow whatever. But I remembered the descending shadow in my dream. And I hoped still in the power of my songs; thinking that what could dispel alabaster, might likewise be capable of dispelling what concealed my beauty now, even if it were the demon whose darkness had overshadowed all my life.

CHAPTER 15

"Alexander. 'When will you finish Campaspe?'
  Apelles. 'Never finish: for always in absolute
  beauty there is somewhat above art.'"
  LYLY'S Campaspe.

And now, what song should I sing to unveil my Isis, if indeed she was present unseen? I hurried away to the white hall of Phantasy, heedless of the innumerable forms of beauty that crowded my way: these might cross my eyes, but the unseen filled my brain. I wandered long, up and down the silent space: no songs came. My soul was not still enough for songs. Only in the silence and darkness of the soul's night, do those stars of the inward firmament sink to its lower surface from the singing realms beyond, and shine upon the conscious spirit. Here all effort was unavailing. If they came not, they could not be found.

Next night, it was just the same. I walked through the red glimmer of the silent hall; but lonely as there I walked, as lonely trod my soul up and down the halls of the brain. At last I entered one of the statue-halls. The dance had just commenced, and I was delighted to find that I was free of their assembly. I walked on till I came to the sacred corner. There I found the pedestal just as I had left it, with the faint glimmer as of white feet still resting on the dead black. As soon as I saw it, I seemed to feel a presence which longed to become visible; and, as it were, called to me to gift it with self-manifestation, that it might shine on me. The power of song came to me. But the moment my voice, though I sang low and soft, stirred the air of the hall, the dancers started; the quick interweaving crowd shook, lost its form, divided; each figure sprang to its pedestal, and stood, a self-evolving life no more, but a rigid, life-like, marble shape, with the whole form composed into the expression of a single state or act. Silence rolled like a spiritual thunder through the grand space.

My song had ceased, scared at its own influences. But I saw in the hand of one of the statues close by me, a harp whose chords yet quivered. I remembered that as she bounded past me, her harp had brushed against my arm; so the spell of the marble had not infolded it. I sprang to her, and with a gesture of entreaty, laid my hand on the harp. The marble hand, probably from its contact with the uncharmed harp, had strength enough to relax its hold, and yield the harp to me. No other motion indicated life. Instinctively I struck the chords and sang. And not to break upon the record of my song, I mention here, that as I sang the first four lines, the loveliest feet became clear upon the black pedestal; and ever as I sang, it was as if a veil were being lifted up from before the form, but an invisible veil, so that the statue appeared to grow before me, not so much by evolution, as by infinitesimal degrees of added height. And, while I sang, I did not feel that I stood by a statue, as indeed it appeared to be, but that a real woman-soul was revealing itself by successive stages of imbodiment, and consequent manifestation and expression.

Feet of beauty, firmly planting
    Arches white on rosy heel!
    Whence the life-spring, throbbing, panting,
    Pulses upward to reveal!
    Fairest things know least despising;
    Foot and earth meet tenderly:
    'Tis the woman, resting, rising
    Upward to sublimity,
    Rise the limbs, sedately sloping,
    Strong and gentle, full and free;
    Soft and slow, like certain hoping,
    Drawing nigh the broad firm knee.
    Up to speech! As up to roses
    Pants the life from leaf to flower,
    So each blending change discloses,
    Nearer still, expression's power.

Lo! fair sweeps, white surges, twining
    Up and outward fearlessly!
    Temple columns, close combining,
    Lift a holy mystery.
    Heart of mine! what strange surprises
    Mount aloft on such a stair!
    Some great vision upward rises,
    Curving, bending, floating fair.

Bands and sweeps, and hill and hollow
    Lead my fascinated eye;
    Some apocalypse will follow,
    Some new world of deity.

Zoned unseen, and outward swelling,
With new thoughts and wonders rife,
Queenly majesty foretelling,
See the expanding house of life!

Sudden heaving, unforbidden
Sighs eternal, still the same —
Mounts of snow have summits hidden
In the mists of uttered flame.
But the spirit, dawning nearly
Finds no speech for earnest pain;
Finds a soundless sighing merely —
Builds its stairs, and mounts again.

Heart, the queen, with secret hoping,
Sendeth out her waiting pair;
Hands, blind hands, half blindly groping,
Half inclasping visions rare;
And the great arms, heartways bending;
Might of Beauty, drawing home
There returning, and re-blending,
Where from roots of love they roam.

Build thy slopes of radiance beamy
Spirit, fair with womanhood!
Tower thy precipice, white-gleamy,
Climb unto the hour of good.
Dumb space will be rent asunder,
Now the shining column stands
Ready to be crowned with wonder
By the builder's joyous hands.

All the lines abroad are spreading,
Like a fountain's falling race.
Lo, the chin, first feature, treading,
Airy foot to rest the face!
Speech is nigh; oh, see the blushing,
Sweet approach of lip and breath!
Round the mouth dim silence, hushing,
Waits to die ecstatic death.

Span across in treble curving,
Bow of promise, upper lip!

GEORGE MACDONALD

Set them free, with gracious swerving;
Let the wing-words float and dip.
Dumb art thou? O Love immortal,
More than words thy speech must be;
Childless yet the tender portal
Of the home of melody.

Now the nostrils open fearless,
Proud in calm unconsciousness,
Sure it must be something peerless
That the great Pan would express!
Deepens, crowds some meaning tender,
In the pure, dear lady-face.
Lo, a blinding burst of splendour! —
'Tis the free soul's issuing grace.

Two calm lakes of molten glory
Circling round unfathomed deeps!
Lightning-flashes, transitory,
Cross the gulfs where darkness sleeps.
This the gate, at last, of gladness,
To the outward striving me:
In a rain of light and sadness,
Out its loves and longings flee!

With a presence I am smitten
Dumb, with a foreknown surprise;
Presence greater yet than written
Even in the glorious eyes.
Through the gulfs, with inward gazes,
I may look till I am lost;
Wandering deep in spirit-mazes,
In a sea without a coast.

Windows open to the glorious!
Time and space, oh, far beyond!
Woman, ah! thou art victorious,
And I perish, overfond.
Springs aloft the yet Unspoken
In the forehead's endless grace,
Full of silences unbroken;
Infinite, unfeatured face.

Domes above, the mount of wonder;
  Height and hollow wrapt in night;
  Hiding in its caverns under
  Woman-nations in their might.
  Passing forms, the highest Human
  Faints away to the Divine
  Features none, of man or woman,
  Can unveil the holiest shine.

Sideways, grooved porches only
  Visible to passing eye,
  Stand the silent, doorless, lonely
  Entrance-gates of melody.
  But all sounds fly in as boldly,
  Groan and song, and kiss and cry
  At their galleries, lifted coldly,
  Darkly, 'twixt the earth and sky.

Beauty, thou art spent, thou knowest
  So, in faint, half-glad despair,
  From the summit thou o'erflowest
  In a fall of torrent hair;
  Hiding what thou hast created
  In a half-transparent shroud:
  Thus, with glory soft-abated,
  Shines the moon through vapoury cloud.

CHAPTER 16

"Ev'n the Styx, which ninefold her infoldeth
  Hems not Ceres' daughter in its flow;
  But she grasps the apple—ever holdeth
  Her, sad Orcus, down below."
SCHILLER, *Das Ideal und das Leben.*

Ever as I sang, the veil was uplifted; ever as I sang, the signs of life grew; till, when the eyes dawned upon me, it was with that sunrise of splendour which my feeble song attempted to re-imbody.

The wonder is, that I was not altogether overcome, but was able to complete my song as the unseen veil continued to rise. This ability came solely from the state of mental elevation in which I found myself. Only because uplifted in song, was I able to endure the blaze of the dawn. But I cannot tell whether she looked more of statue or more of woman; she seemed removed into that region of phantasy where all is intensely vivid, but nothing clearly defined. At last, as I sang of her descending hair, the glow of soul faded away, like a dying sunset. A lamp within had been extinguished, and the house of life shone blank in a winter morn. She was a statue once more—but visible, and that was much gained. Yet the revulsion from hope and fruition was such, that, unable to restrain myself, I sprang to her, and, in defiance of the law of the place, flung my arms around her, as if I would tear her from the grasp of a visible Death, and lifted her from the pedestal down to my heart. But no sooner had her feet ceased to be in contact with the black pedestal, than she shuddered and trembled all over; then, writhing from my arms, before I could tighten their hold, she sprang into the corridor, with the reproachful cry, "You should not have touched me!" darted behind one of the exterior pillars of the circle, and disappeared. I followed almost as fast; but ere I could reach the pillar, the sound of a closing door, the saddest of all sounds sometimes, fell on my ear; and, arriving at the spot where she had vanished, I saw, lighted by a pale yellow lamp which hung above it, a heavy, rough door, altogether unlike any others I had seen in the palace; for they were all of ebony, or ivory, or covered with silver-plates, or of some odorous wood, and very ornate; whereas this seemed of old oak, with heavy nails and iron studs. Notwithstanding the precipitation of my pursuit, I could not help reading, in silver letters beneath the lamp: *"No one enters here without the leave of the Queen."* But what was the Queen to me, when I followed my white lady? I dashed the door to the wall and sprang through. Lo! I stood on a waste windy hill. Great stones like tombstones stood all about me. No door, no palace was to be seen. A white figure gleamed past me, wringing her hands, and crying, "Ah! you should have sung to me; you should have sung to me!" and disappeared behind one of the stones. I followed. A cold gust of wind met me from behind the stone; and when I looked, I saw nothing but a great hole in the earth, into which I could find no way of entering. Had she fallen in? I could not tell. I must wait for the daylight. I sat down and wept, for there was no help.

CHAPTER 17

"First, I thought, almost despairing,
  This must crush my spirit now;
  Yet I bore it, and am bearing—
  Only do not ask me how."
  HEINE.

When the daylight came, it brought the possibility of action, but with it little of consolation. With the first visible increase of light, I gazed into the chasm, but could not, for more than an hour, see sufficiently well to discover its nature. At last I saw it was almost a perpendicular opening, like a roughly excavated well, only very large. I could perceive no bottom; and it was not till the sun actually rose, that I discovered a sort of natural staircase, in many parts little more than suggested, which led round and round the gulf, descending spirally into its abyss. I saw at once that this was my path; and without a moment's hesitation, glad to quit the sunlight, which stared at me most heartlessly, I commenced my tortuous descent. It was very difficult. In some parts I had to cling to the rocks like a bat. In one place, I dropped from the track down upon the next returning spire of the stair; which being broad in this particular portion, and standing out from the wall at right angles, received me upon my feet safe, though somewhat stupefied by the shock. After descending a great way, I found the stair ended at a narrow opening which entered the rock horizontally. Into this I crept, and, having entered, had just room to turn round. I put my head out into the shaft by which I had come down, and surveyed the course of my descent. Looking up, I saw the stars; although the sun must by this time have been high in the heavens. Looking below, I saw that the sides of the shaft went sheer down, smooth as glass; and far beneath me, I saw the reflection of the same stars I had seen in the heavens when I looked up. I turned again, and crept inwards some distance, when the passage widened, and I was at length able to stand and walk upright. Wider and loftier grew the way; new paths branched off on every side; great open halls appeared; till at last I found myself wandering on through an underground country, in which the sky was of rock, and instead of trees and flowers, there were only fantastic rocks and stones. And ever as I went, darker grew my thoughts, till at last I had no hope whatever of finding the white lady: I no longer called her to myself *my* white lady. Whenever a choice was necessary, I always chose the path which seemed to lead downwards.

At length I began to find that these regions were inhabited. From behind a rock a peal of harsh grating laughter, full of evil humour, rang through my ears, and, looking round, I saw a queer, goblin creature, with a great head and ridiculous features, just such as those described, in German histories and travels, as Kobolds. "What do you want with me?" I said. He pointed at me with a long forefinger, very thick at the root, and sharpened to a point, and answered, "He! he! he! What do *you* want here?" Then, changing his tone, he continued, with mock humility—"Honoured sir, vouchsafe to withdraw from thy slaves the lustre of thy august presence, for thy slaves cannot support its brightness." A second appeared, and struck in: "You are so big, you keep the sun from us. We can't see for you, and we're so cold." Thereupon arose, on all sides, the most terrific uproar of laughter, from voices like those of children in volume, but scrannel and harsh as those of decrepit age, though, unfortunately, without its weakness. The whole pandemonium of fairy devils, of all varieties of fantastic ugliness, both in form and feature, and of all sizes from one to four feet, seemed to have suddenly assembled about me. At length, after a great babble of talk among themselves, in a language unknown to me, and after seemingly endless gesticulation, consultation, elbow-nudging, and unmitigated peals of laughter, they formed into a circle about one of their number, who scrambled upon a stone, and, much to my surprise, and somewhat to my dismay, began to sing, in a voice corresponding in its nature to his talking one, from beginning to end, the song with which I had brought the light into the eyes of the white lady. He sang the same air too; and, all the time, maintained a face of mock entreaty and worship; accompanying the song with the travestied gestures of one playing on the lute. The whole assembly kept silence, except at the close of every verse, when they roared, and danced, and shouted with laughter, and flung themselves on the ground, in real or pretended convulsions of delight. When he had finished, the singer threw himself from the top of the stone, turning heels over head several times in his descent; and when he did alight, it was on the top of his head, on which he hopped about, making the most grotesque gesticulations with his legs in the air. Inexpressible laughter followed, which broke up in a shower of tiny stones from innumerable hands. They could not materially injure me, although they cut me on the head and face. I attempted to run away, but they all rushed upon me, and, laying hold of every part that afforded a grasp, held me tight. Crowding about me like bees, they shouted an insect-swarm of exasperating speeches up into my face, among which the most frequently recurring were—"You shan't have her; you shan't have her; he! he! he! She's for a better man; how he'll kiss her! how he'll kiss her!"

The galvanic torrent of this battery of malevolence stung to life within me a spark of nobleness, and I said aloud, "Well, if he is a better man, let him have her."

They instantly let go their hold of me, and fell back a step or two, with a whole broadside of grunts and humphs, as of unexpected and disappointed approbation. I made a step or two forward, and a lane was instantly opened for me through the midst of the grinning little antics, who bowed most politely to me on every side as I passed. After I had gone a few yards, I looked back, and saw them all standing quite still, looking after me, like a great school of boys; till suddenly one turned round, and with a loud whoop, rushed into the midst of the others. In an instant, the whole was one writhing and tumbling heap of contortion, reminding me of the live pyramids of intertwined snakes of which travellers make report. As soon as one was worked out of the mass, he bounded off a few paces, and then, with a somersault and a run, threw himself gyrating into the air, and descended with all his weight on the summit of the heaving and struggling chaos of fantastic figures. I left them still busy at this fierce and apparently aimless amusement. And as I went, I sang—

If a nobler waits for thee,
I will weep aside;
It is well that thou should'st be,
Of the nobler, bride.

For if love builds up the home,
Where the heart is free,
Homeless yet the heart must roam,
That has not found thee.

One must suffer: I, for her
Yield in her my part
Take her, thou art worthier —
Still I be still, my heart!

Gift ungotten! largess high
Of a frustrate will!
But to yield it lovingly
Is a something still.

Then a little song arose of itself in my soul; and I felt for the moment, while it sank sadly within me, as if I was once more walking up and down the white hall of Phantasy in the Fairy Palace. But this lasted no longer than the song; as will be seen.

Do not vex thy violet
Perfume to afford:
Else no odour thou wilt get

From its little hoard.

In thy lady's gracious eyes
Look not thou too long;
Else from them the glory flies,
And thou dost her wrong.

Come not thou too near the maid,
Clasp her not too wild;
Else the splendour is allayed,
And thy heart beguiled.

A crash of laughter, more discordant and deriding than any I had yet heard, invaded my ears. Looking on in the direction of the sound, I saw a little elderly woman, much taller, however, than the goblins I had just left, seated upon a stone by the side of the path. She rose, as I drew near, and came forward to meet me.

She was very plain and commonplace in appearance, without being hideously ugly. Looking up in my face with a stupid sneer, she said: "Isn't it a pity you haven't a pretty girl to walk all alone with you through this sweet country? How different everything would look? Wouldn't it? Strange that one can never have what one would like best! How the roses would bloom and all that, even in this infernal hole! wouldn't they, Anodos? Her eyes would light up the old cave, wouldn't they?"

"That depends on who the pretty girl should be," replied I.

"Not so very much matter that," she answered; "look here."

I had turned to go away as I gave my reply, but now I stopped and looked at her. As a rough unsightly bud might suddenly blossom into the most lovely flower; or rather, as a sunbeam bursts through a shapeless cloud, and transfigures the earth; so burst a face of resplendent beauty, as it were *through* the unsightly visage of the woman, destroying it with light as it dawned through it. A summer sky rose above me, gray with heat; across a shining slumberous landscape, looked from afar the peaks of snow-capped mountains; and down from a great rock beside me fell a sheet of water mad with its own delight.

"Stay with me," she said, lifting up her exquisite face, and looking full in mine.

I drew back. Again the infernal laugh grated upon my ears; again the rocks closed in around me, and the ugly woman looked at me with wicked, mocking hazel eyes.

"You shall have your reward," said she. "You shall see your white lady again."

"That lies not with you," I replied, and turned and left her.

She followed me with shriek upon shriek of laughter, as I went on my way.

I may mention here, that although there was always light enough to see my path and a few yards on every side of me, I never could find out the source of this sad sepulchral illumination.

CHAPTER 18

"In the wind's uproar, the sea's raging grim,
  And the sighs that are born in him."
  HEINE.
  "From dreams of bliss shall men awake
  One day, but not to weep:
  The dreams remain; they only break
  The mirror of the sleep."
  JEAN PAUL, Hesperus.

How I got through this dreary part of my travels, I do not know. I do not think I was upheld by the hope that any moment the light might break in upon me; for I scarcely thought about that. I went on with a dull endurance, varied by moments of uncontrollable sadness; for more and more the conviction grew upon me that I should never see the white lady again. It may seem strange that one with whom I had held so little communion should have so engrossed my thoughts; but benefits conferred awaken love in some minds, as surely as benefits received in others. Besides being delighted and proud that *my* songs had called the beautiful creature to life, the same fact caused me to feel a tenderness unspeakable for her, accompanied with a kind of feeling of property in her; for so the goblin Selfishness would reward the angel Love. When to all this is added, an overpowering sense of her beauty, and an unquestioning conviction that this was a true index to inward loveliness, it may be understood how it came to pass that my imagination filled my whole soul with the play of its own multitudinous colours and harmonies around the form which yet stood, a gracious marble radiance, in the midst of *its* white hall of phantasy. The time passed by unheeded; for my thoughts were busy. Perhaps this was also in part the cause of my needing no food, and never thinking how I should find any, during this subterraneous part of my travels. How long they endured I could not tell, for I had no means of measuring time; and when I looked back, there was such a discrepancy between the decisions of my imagination and my judgment, as to the length of time that had passed, that I was bewildered, and gave up all attempts to arrive at any conclusion on the point.

A gray mist continually gathered behind me. When I looked back towards the past, this mist was the medium through which my eyes had to strain for a vision of what had gone by; and the form of the white lady had receded into an unknown region. At length the country of rock began to close again around me, gradually and slowly narrowing, till I found myself walking in a gallery of rock once more, both sides of which I could touch with my outstretched hands. It narrowed yet, until I was forced to move carefully, in order to avoid striking against the projecting pieces of rock. The roof sank lower and lower, until I was compelled, first to stoop, and then to creep on my hands and knees. It recalled terrible dreams of childhood; but I was not much afraid, because I felt sure that this was my path, and my only hope of leaving Fairy Land, of which I was now almost weary.

At length, on getting past an abrupt turn in the passage, through which I had to force myself, I saw, a few yards ahead of me, the long-forgotten daylight shining through a small opening, to which the path, if path it could now be called, led me. With great difficulty I accomplished these last few yards, and came forth to the day. I stood on the shore of a wintry sea, with a wintry sun just a few feet above its horizon-edge. It was bare, and waste, and gray. Hundreds of hopeless waves rushed constantly shorewards, falling exhausted upon a beach of great loose stones, that seemed to stretch miles and miles in both directions. There was nothing for the eye but mingling shades of gray; nothing for the ear but the rush of the coming, the roar of the breaking, and the moan of the retreating wave. No rock lifted up a sheltering severity above the dreariness around; even that from which I had myself emerged rose scarcely a foot above the opening by which I had reached the dismal day, more dismal even than the tomb I had left. A cold, death-like wind swept across the shore, seeming to issue from a pale mouth of cloud upon the horizon. Sign of life was nowhere visible. I wandered over the stones, up and down the beach, a human imbodiment of the nature around me. The wind increased; its keen waves flowed through my soul; the foam rushed higher up the stones; a few dead stars began to gleam in the east; the sound of the waves grew louder and yet more despairing. A dark curtain of cloud was lifted up, and a pale blue rent shone between its foot and the edge of the sea, out from which rushed an icy storm of frozen wind, that tore the waters into spray as it passed, and flung the billows in raving heaps upon the desolate shore. I could bear it no longer.

"I will not be tortured to death," I cried; "I will meet it half-way. The life within me is yet enough to bear me up to the face of Death, and then I die unconquered."

Before it had grown so dark, I had observed, though without any particular interest, that on one part of the shore a low platform of rock seemed to run out far into the midst of the breaking waters.

Towards this I now went, scrambling over smooth stones, to which scarce even a particle of sea-weed clung; and having found it, I got on it, and followed its direction, as near as I could guess, out into the tumbling chaos. I could hardly keep my feet against the wind and sea. The waves repeatedly all but swept me off my path; but I kept on my way, till I reached the end of the low promontory, which, in the fall of the waves, rose a good many feet above the surface, and, in their rise, was covered with their waters. I stood one moment and gazed into the heaving abyss beneath me; then plunged headlong into the mounting wave below. A blessing, like the kiss of a mother, seemed to alight on my soul; a calm, deeper than that which accompanies a hope deferred, bathed my spirit. I sank far into the waters, and sought not to return. I felt as if once more the great arms of the beech-tree were around me, soothing me after the miseries I had passed through, and telling me, like a little sick child, that I should be better to-morrow. The waters of themselves lifted me, as with loving arms, to the surface. I breathed again, but did not unclose my eyes. I would not look on the wintry sea, and the pitiless gray sky. Thus I floated, till something gently touched me. It was a little boat floating beside me. How it came there I could not tell; but it rose and sank on the waters, and kept touching me in its fall, as if with a human will to let me know that help was by me. It was a little gay-coloured boat, seemingly covered with glistering scales like those of a fish, all of brilliant rainbow hues. I scrambled into it, and lay down in the bottom, with a sense of exquisite repose.

Then I drew over me a rich, heavy, purple cloth that was beside me; and, lying still, knew, by the sound of the waters, that my little bark was fleeting rapidly onwards. Finding, however, none of that stormy motion which the sea had manifested when I beheld it from the shore, I opened my eyes; and, looking first up, saw above me the deep violet sky of a warm southern night; and then, lifting my head, saw that I was sailing fast upon a summer sea, in the last border of a southern twilight. The aureole of the sun yet shot the extreme faint tips of its longest rays above the horizon-waves, and withdrew them not. It was a perpetual twilight. The stars, great and earnest, like children's eyes, bent down lovingly towards the waters; and the reflected stars within seemed to float up, as if longing to meet their embraces. But when I looked down, a new wonder met my view. For, vaguely revealed beneath the wave, I floated above my whole Past. The fields of my childhood flitted by; the halls of my youthful labours; the streets of great cities where I had dwelt; and the assemblies of men and women wherein I had wearied myself seeking for rest. But so indistinct were the visions, that sometimes I thought I was sailing on a shallow sea, and that strange rocks and forests of sea-plants beguiled my eye, sufficiently to be transformed, by the magic of the phantasy, into well-known objects and regions. Yet, at times, a beloved form seemed to lie close beneath me in sleep; and the eyelids would tremble as if about to forsake the conscious eye; and the arms would heave upwards, as if in dreams they sought for a satisfying presence. But these motions might come only from the heaving of the waters between those forms and me. Soon I fell asleep, overcome with fatigue and delight. In dreams of unspeakable joy—of restored friendships; of revived embraces; of love which said it had never died; of faces that had vanished long ago, yet said with smiling lips that they knew nothing of the grave; of pardons implored, and granted with such bursting floods of love, that I was almost glad I had sinned—thus I passed through this wondrous twilight. I awoke with the feeling that I had been kissed and loved to my heart's content; and found that my boat was floating motionless by the grassy shore of a little island.

CHAPTER 19

"In still rest, in changeless simplicity, I bear,
uninterrupted, the consciousness of the whole of Humanity
within me." —SCHLEIERMACHERS, Monologen.

"... such a sweetness, such a grace,
In all thy speech appear,
That what to th'eye a beauteous face,
That thy tongue is to the ear."
—COWLEY.

The water was deep to the very edge; and I sprang from the little boat upon a soft grassy turf. The island seemed rich with a profusion of all grasses and low flowers. All delicate lowly things were most plentiful; but no trees rose skywards, not even a bush overtopped the tall grasses, except in one place near the cottage I am about to describe, where a few plants of the gum-cistus, which drops every night all the blossoms that the day brings forth, formed a kind of natural arbour. The whole island lay open to the sky and sea. It rose nowhere more than a few feet above the level of the waters, which flowed deep all around its border. Here there seemed to be neither tide nor storm. A sense of persistent calm and fulness arose in the mind at the sight of the slow, pulse-like rise and fall of the deep, clear, unrippled waters against the bank of the island, for shore it could hardly be called, being so much more like the edge of a full, solemn river. As I walked over the grass towards the cottage, which stood at a little distance from the bank, all the flowers of childhood looked at me with perfect child-eyes out of the grass. My heart, softened by the dreams through which it had passed, overflowed in a sad, tender love towards them. They looked to me like children impregnably fortified in a helpless confidence. The sun stood half-way down the western sky, shining very soft and golden; and there grew a second world of shadows amidst the world of grasses and wild flowers.

The cottage was square, with low walls, and a high pyramidal roof thatched with long reeds, of which the withered blossoms hung over all the eaves. It is noticeable that most of the buildings I saw in Fairy Land were cottages. There was no path to a door, nor, indeed, was there any track worn by footsteps in the island.

The cottage rose right out of the smooth turf. It had no windows that I could see; but there was a door in the centre of the side facing me, up to which I went. I knocked, and the sweetest voice I had ever heard said, "Come in." I entered. A bright fire was burning on a hearth in the centre of the earthern floor, and the smoke found its way out at an opening in the centre of the pyramidal roof. Over the fire hung a little pot, and over the pot bent a woman-face, the most wonderful, I thought, that I had ever beheld. For it was older than any countenance I had ever looked upon. There was not a spot in which a wrinkle could lie, where a wrinkle lay not. And the skin was ancient and brown, like old parchment. The woman's form was tall and spare: and when she stood up to welcome me, I saw that she was straight as an arrow. Could that voice of sweetness have issued from those lips of age? Mild as they were, could they be the portals whence flowed such melody? But the moment I saw her eyes, I no longer wondered at her voice: they were absolutely young—those of a woman of five-and-twenty, large, and of a clear gray. Wrinkles had beset them all about; the eyelids themselves were old, and heavy, and worn; but the eyes were very incarnations of soft light. She held out her hand to me, and the voice of sweetness again greeted me, with the single word, "Welcome." She set an old wooden chair for me, near the fire, and went on with her cooking. A wondrous sense of refuge and repose came upon me. I felt like a boy who has got home from school, miles across the hills, through a heavy storm of wind and snow. Almost, as I gazed on her, I sprang from my seat to kiss those old lips. And when, having finished her cooking, she brought some of the dish she had prepared, and set it on a little table by me, covered with a snow-white cloth, I could not help laying my head on her bosom, and bursting into happy tears. She put her arms round me, saying, "Poor child; poor child!"

As I continued to weep, she gently disengaged herself, and, taking a spoon, put some of the food (I did not know what it was) to my lips, entreating me most endearingly to swallow it. To please her, I made an effort, and succeeded. She went on feeding me like a baby, with one arm round me, till I looked up in her face and smiled: then she gave me the spoon and told me to eat, for it would do me good. I obeyed her, and found myself wonderfully refreshed. Then she drew near the fire an old-fashioned couch that was in the cottage, and making me lie down upon it, sat at my feet, and began to sing. Amazing store of old ballads rippled from her lips, over the pebbles of ancient tunes; and the voice that sang was sweet as the voice of a tuneful maiden that singeth ever from very fulness of song. The songs were almost all sad, but with a sound of comfort. One I can faintly recall. It was something like this:

Sir Aglovaile through the churchyard rode;
   Sing, All alone I lie:
   Little recked he where'er he yode,
   All alone, up in the sky.

Swerved his courser, and plunged with fear
   All alone I lie:
   His cry might have wakened the dead men near,
   All alone, up in the sky.

The very dead that lay at his feet,
   Lapt in the mouldy winding-sheet.

But he curbed him and spurred him, until he stood
   Still in his place, like a horse of wood,

With nostrils uplift, and eyes wide and wan;
   But the sweat in streams from his fetlocks ran.

A ghost grew out of the shadowy air,
   And sat in the midst of her moony hair.

In her gleamy hair she sat and wept;
   In the dreamful moon they lay and slept;

The shadows above, and the bodies below,
   Lay and slept in the moonbeams slow.

And she sang, like the moan of an autumn wind
   Over the stubble left behind:

Alas, how easily things go wrong!
   A sigh too much, or a kiss too long,
   And there follows a mist and a weeping rain,
   And life is never the same again.

Alas, how hardly things go right!
   'Tis hard to watch on a summer night,

For the sigh will come and the kiss will stay,
And the summer night is a winter day.

"Oh, lovely ghosts my heart is woes
  To see thee weeping and wailing so.

Oh, lovely ghost," said the fearless knight,
  "Can the sword of a warrior set it right?

Or prayer of bedesman, praying mild,
  As a cup of water a feverish child,

Sooth thee at last, in dreamless mood
  To sleep the sleep a dead lady should?

Thine eyes they fill me with longing sore,
  As if I had known thee for evermore.

Oh, lovely ghost, I could leave the day
  To sit with thee in the moon away

If thou wouldst trust me, and lay thy head
  To rest on a bosom that is not dead."
  The lady sprang up with a strange ghost-cry,
  And she flung her white ghost-arms on high:

And she laughed a laugh that was not gay,
  And it lengthened out till it died away;

And the dead beneath turned and moaned,
  And the yew-trees above they shuddered and groaned.

"Will he love me twice with a love that is vain?
  Will he kill the poor ghost yet again?

I thought thou wert good; but I said, and wept:
  'Can I have dreamed who have not slept?'

And I knew, alas! or ever I would,
Whether I dreamed, or thou wert good.

When my baby died, my brain grew wild.
I awoke, and found I was with my child."

"If thou art the ghost of my Adelaide,
How is it? Thou wert but a village maid,

And thou seemest an angel lady white,
Though thin, and wan, and past delight."

The lady smiled a flickering smile,
And she pressed her temples hard the while.

"Thou seest that Death for a woman can
Do more than knighthood for a man."

"But show me the child thou callest mine,
Is she out to-night in the ghost's sunshine?"

"In St. Peter's Church she is playing on,
At hide-and-seek, with Apostle John.

When the moonbeams right through the window go,
Where the twelve are standing in glorious show,

She says the rest of them do not stir,
But one comes down to play with her.

Then I can go where I list, and weep,
For good St. John my child will keep."

"Thy beauty filleth the very air,
Never saw I a woman so fair."

GEORGE MACDONALD

"Come, if thou darest, and sit by my side;
    But do not touch me, or woe will betide.

Alas, I am weak: I might well know
    This gladness betokens some further woe.

Yet come. It will come. I will bear it. I can.
    For thou lovest me yet—though but as a man."

The knight dismounted in earnest speed;
    Away through the tombstones thundered the steed,

And fell by the outer wall, and died.
    But the knight he kneeled by the lady's side;

Kneeled beside her in wondrous bliss,
    Rapt in an everlasting kiss:

Though never his lips come the lady nigh,
    And his eyes alone on her beauty lie.

All the night long, till the cock crew loud,
    He kneeled by the lady, lapt in her shroud.

And what they said, I may not say:
    Dead night was sweeter than living day.

How she made him so blissful glad
    Who made her and found her so ghostly sad,

I may not tell; but it needs no touch
    To make them blessed who love so much.

"Come every night, my ghost, to me;
    And one night I will come to thee.

'Tis good to have a ghostly wife:
　　She will not tremble at clang of strife;

She will only hearken, amid the din,
　　Behind the door, if he cometh in."

And this is how Sir Aglovaile
　　Often walked in the moonlight pale.

And oft when the crescent but thinned the gloom,
　　Full orbed moonlight filled his room;

And through beneath his chamber door,
　　Fell a ghostly gleam on the outer floor;

And they that passed, in fear averred
　　That murmured words they often heard.

'Twas then that the eastern crescent shone
　　Through the chancel window, and good St. John

Played with the ghost-child all the night,
　　And the mother was free till the morning light,

And sped through the dawning night, to stay
　　With Aglovaile till the break of day.

And their love was a rapture, lone and high,
　　And dumb as the moon in the topmost sky.

One night Sir Aglovaile, weary, slept
　　And dreamed a dream wherein he wept.

A warrior he was, not often wept he,
　　But this night he wept full bitterly.

He woke—beside him the ghost-girl shone
  Out of the dark: 'twas the eve of St. John.

He had dreamed a dream of a still, dark wood,
  Where the maiden of old beside him stood;

But a mist came down, and caught her away,
  And he sought her in vain through the pathless day,

Till he wept with the grief that can do no more,
  And thought he had dreamt the dream before.

From bursting heart the weeping flowed on;
  And lo! beside him the ghost-girl shone;

Shone like the light on a harbour's breast,
  Over the sea of his dream's unrest;

Shone like the wondrous, nameless boon,
  That the heart seeks ever, night or noon:

Warnings forgotten, when needed most,
  He clasped to his bosom the radiant ghost.

She wailed aloud, and faded, and sank.
  With upturn'd white face, cold and blank,

In his arms lay the corpse of the maiden pale,
  And she came no more to Sir Aglovaile.

Only a voice, when winds were wild,
  Sobbed and wailed like a chidden child.

Alas, how easily things go wrong!
  A sigh too much, or a kiss too long,

And there follows a mist and a weeping rain,
And life is never the same again.

This was one of the simplest of her songs, which, perhaps, is the cause of my being able to remember it better than most of the others. While she sung, I was in Elysium, with the sense of a rich soul upholding, embracing, and overhanging mine, full of all plenty and bounty. I felt as if she could give me everything I wanted; as if I should never wish to leave her, but would be content to be sung to and fed by her, day after day, as years rolled by. At last I fell asleep while she sang.

When I awoke, I knew not whether it was night or day. The fire had sunk to a few red embers, which just gave light enough to show me the woman standing a few feet from me, with her back towards me, facing the door by which I had entered. She was weeping, but very gently and plentifully. The tears seemed to come freely from her heart. Thus she stood for a few minutes; then, slowly turning at right angles to her former position, she faced another of the four sides of the cottage. I now observed, for the first time, that here was a door likewise; and that, indeed, there was one in the centre of every side of the cottage.

When she looked towards the second door, her tears ceased to flow, but sighs took their place. She often closed her eyes as she stood; and every time she closed her eyes, a gentle sigh seemed to be born in her heart, and to escape at her lips. But when her eyes were open, her sighs were deep and very sad, and shook her whole frame. Then she turned towards the third door, and a cry as of fear or suppressed pain broke from her; but she seemed to hearten herself against the dismay, and to front it steadily; for, although I often heard a slight cry, and sometimes a moan, yet she never moved or bent her head, and I felt sure that her eyes never closed. Then she turned to the fourth door, and I saw her shudder, and then stand still as a statue; till at last she turned towards me and approached the fire. I saw that her face was white as death. But she gave one look upwards, and smiled the sweetest, most child-innocent smile; then heaped fresh wood on the fire, and, sitting down by the blaze, drew her wheel near her, and began to spin. While she spun, she murmured a low strange song, to which the hum of the wheel made a kind of infinite symphony. At length she paused in her spinning and singing, and glanced towards me, like a mother who looks whether or not her child gives signs of waking. She smiled when she saw that my eyes were open. I asked her whether it was day yet. She answered, "It is always day here, so long as I keep my fire burning."

I felt wonderfully refreshed; and a great desire to see more of the island awoke within me. I rose, and saying that I wished to look about me, went towards the door by which I had entered.

"Stay a moment," said my hostess, with some trepidation in her voice. "Listen to me. You will not see what you expect when you go out of that door. Only remember this: whenever you wish to come back to me, enter wherever you see this mark."

She held up her left hand between me and the fire. Upon the palm, which appeared almost transparent, I saw, in dark red, a mark like this —> which I took care to fix in my mind.

She then kissed me, and bade me good-bye with a solemnity that awed me; and bewildered me too, seeing I was only going out for a little ramble in an island, which I did not believe larger than could easily be compassed in a few hours' walk at most. As I went she resumed her spinning.

I opened the door, and stepped out. The moment my foot touched the smooth sward, I seemed to issue from the door of an old barn on my father's estate, where, in the hot afternoons, I used to go and lie amongst the straw, and read. It seemed to me now that I had been asleep there. At a little distance in the field, I saw two of my brothers at play. The moment they caught sight of me, they called out to me to come and join them, which I did; and we played together as we had done years ago, till the red sun went down in the west, and the gray fog began to rise from the river. Then we went home together with a strange happiness. As we went, we heard the continually renewed larum of a landrail in the long grass. One of my brothers and I separated to a little distance, and each commenced running towards the part whence the sound appeared to come, in the hope of approaching the spot where the bird was, and so getting at least a sight of it, if we should not be able to capture the little creature. My father's voice recalled us from trampling down the rich long grass, soon to be cut down and laid aside for the winter. I had quite forgotten all about Fairy Land, and the wonderful old woman, and the curious red mark.

My favourite brother and I shared the same bed. Some childish dispute arose between us; and our last words, ere we fell asleep, were not of kindness, notwithstanding the pleasures of the day. When I woke in the morning, I missed him. He had risen early, and had gone to bathe in the river. In another hour, he was brought home drowned. Alas! Alas! If we had only gone to sleep as usual, the one with his arm about the other! Amidst the horror of the moment, a strange conviction flashed across my mind, that I had gone through the very same once before.

I rushed out of the house, I knew not why, sobbing and crying bitterly. I ran through the fields in aimless distress, till, passing the old barn, I caught sight of a red mark on the door. The merest trifles sometimes rivet the attention in the deepest misery; the intellect has so little to do with grief. I went up to look at this mark, which I did not remember ever to have seen before. As I looked at it, I thought I would go in and lie down amongst the straw, for I was very weary with running about and weeping. I opened the door; and there in the cottage sat the old woman as I had left her, at her spinning-wheel.

"I did not expect you quite so soon," she said, as I shut the door behind me. I went up to the couch, and threw myself on it with that fatigue wherewith one awakes from a feverish dream of hopeless grief.

The old woman sang:

The great sun, benighted,
  May faint from the sky;
  But love, once uplighted,
  Will never more die.

Form, with its brightness,
  From eyes will depart:
  It walketh, in whiteness,

The halls of the heart.

Ere she had ceased singing, my courage had returned. I started from the couch, and, without taking leave of the old woman, opened the door of Sighs, and sprang into what should appear.

I stood in a lordly hall, where, by a blazing fire on the hearth, sat a lady, waiting, I knew, for some one long desired. A mirror was near me, but I saw that my form had no place within its depths, so I feared not that I should be seen. The lady wonderfully resembled my marble lady, but was altogether of the daughters of men, and I could not tell whether or not it was she.

It was not for me she waited. The tramp of a great horse rang through the court without. It ceased, and the clang of armour told that his rider alighted, and the sound of his ringing heels approached the hall. The door opened; but the lady waited, for she would meet her lord alone. He strode in: she flew like a home-bound dove into his arms, and nestled on the hard steel. It was the knight of the soiled armour. But now the armour shone like polished glass; and strange to tell, though the mirror reflected not my form, I saw a dim shadow of myself in the shining steel.

"O my beloved, thou art come, and I am blessed."

Her soft fingers speedily overcame the hard clasp of his helmet; one by one she undid the buckles of his armour; and she toiled under the weight of the mail, as she *would* carry it aside. Then she unclasped his greaves, and unbuckled his spurs; and once more she sprang into his arms, and laid her head where she could now feel the beating of his heart. Then she disengaged herself from his embrace, and, moving back a step or two, gazed at him. He stood there a mighty form, crowned with a noble head, where all sadness had disappeared, or had been absorbed in solemn purpose. Yet I suppose that he looked more thoughtful than the lady had expected to see him, for she did not renew her caresses, although his face glowed with love, and the few words he spoke were as mighty deeds for strength; but she led him towards the hearth, and seated him in an ancient chair, and set wine before him, and sat at his feet.

"I am sad," he said, "when I think of the youth whom I met twice in the forests of Fairy Land; and who, you say, twice, with his songs, roused you from the death-sleep of an evil enchantment. There was something noble in him, but it was a noble-ness of thought, and not of deed. He may yet perish of vile fear."

"Ah!" returned the lady, "you saved him once, and for that I thank you; for may I not say that I somewhat loved him? But tell me how you fared, when you struck your battle-axe into the ash-tree, and he came and found you; for so much of the story you had told me, when the beggar-child came and took you away."

"As soon as I saw him," rejoined the knight, "I knew that earthly arms availed not against such as he; and that my soul must meet him in its naked strength. So I unclasped my helm, and flung it on the ground; and, holding my good axe yet in my hand, gazed at him with steady eyes. On he came, a horror indeed, but I did not flinch. Endurance must conquer, where force could not reach. He came nearer and nearer, till the ghastly face was close to mine. A shudder as of death ran through me; but I think I did not move, for he seemed to quail, and retreated. As soon as he gave back, I struck one more sturdy blow on the stem of his tree, that the forest

GEORGE MACDONALD

rang; and then looked at him again. He writhed and grinned with rage and apparent pain, and again approached me, but retreated sooner than before. I heeded him no more, but hewed with a will at the tree, till the trunk creaked, and the head bowed, and with a crash it fell to the earth. Then I looked up from my labour, and lo! the spectre had vanished, and I saw him no more; nor ever in my wanderings have I heard of him again."

"Well struck! Well withstood! My hero," said the lady.

"But," said the knight, somewhat troubled, "dost thou love the youth still?"

"Ah!" she replied, "how can I help it? He woke me from worse than death; he loved me. I had never been for thee, if he had not sought me first. But I love him not as I love thee. He was but the moon of my night; thou art the sun of my day, O beloved."

"Thou art right," returned the noble man. "It were hard, indeed, not to have some love in return for such a gift as he hath given thee. I, too, owe him more than words can speak."

Humbled before them, with an aching and desolate heart, I yet could not restrain my words:

"Let me, then, be the moon of thy night still, O woman! And when thy day is beclouded, as the fairest days will be, let some song of mine comfort thee, as an old, withered, half-forgotten thing, that belongs to an ancient mournful hour of uncompleted birth, which yet was beautiful in its time."

They sat silent, and I almost thought they were listening. The colour of the lady's eyes grew deeper and deeper; the slow tears grew, and filled them, and overflowed. They rose, and passed, hand in hand, close to where I stood; and each looked towards me in passing. Then they disappeared through a door which closed behind them; but, ere it closed, I saw that the room into which it opened was a rich chamber, hung with gorgeous arras. I stood with an ocean of sighs frozen in my bosom. I could remain no longer. She was near me, and I could not see her; near me in the arms of one loved better than I, and I would not see her, and I would not be by her. But how to escape from the nearness of the best beloved? I had not this time forgotten the mark; for the fact that I could not enter the sphere of these living beings kept me aware that, for me, I moved in a vision, while they moved in life. I looked all about for the mark, but could see it nowhere; for I avoided looking just where it was. There the dull red cipher glowed, on the very door of their secret chamber. Struck with agony, I dashed it open, and fell at the feet of the ancient woman, who still spun on, the whole dissolved ocean of my sighs bursting from me in a storm of tearless sobs. Whether I fainted or slept, I do not know; but, as I returned to consciousness, before I seemed to have power to move, I heard the woman singing, and could distinguish the words:

O light of dead and of dying days!
    O Love! in thy glory go,
    In a rosy mist and a moony maze,
    O'er the pathless peaks of snow.

But what is left for the cold gray soul,

112

That moans like a wounded dove?
One wine is left in the broken bowl! —
'Tis — To love, and love and love.
Now I could weep. When she saw me weeping, she sang:
Better to sit at the waters' birth,
Than a sea of waves to win;
To live in the love that floweth forth,
Than the love that cometh in.

Be thy heart a well of love, my child,
Flowing, and free, and sure;
For a cistern of love, though undefiled,
Keeps not the spirit pure.

I rose from the earth, loving the white lady as I had never loved her before.

Then I walked up to the door of Dismay, and opened it, and went out. And lo! I came forth upon a crowded street, where men and women went to and fro in multitudes. I knew it well; and, turning to one hand, walked sadly along the pavement. Suddenly I saw approaching me, a little way off, a form well known to me (*well-known!*—alas, how weak the word!) in the years when I thought my boyhood was left behind, and shortly before I entered the realm of Fairy Land. Wrong and Sorrow had gone together, hand-in-hand as it is well they do.

Unchangeably dear was that face. It lay in my heart as a child lies in its own white bed; but I could not meet her.

"Anything but that," I said, and, turning aside, sprang up the steps to a door, on which I fancied I saw the mystic sign. I entered—not the mysterious cottage, but her home. I rushed wildly on, and stood by the door of her room.

"She is out," I said, "I will see the old room once more."

I opened the door gently, and stood in a great solemn church. A deep-toned bell, whose sounds throbbed and echoed and swam through the empty building, struck the hour of midnight. The moon shone through the windows of the clerestory, and enough of the ghostly radiance was diffused through the church to let me see, walking with a stately, yet somewhat trailing and stumbling step, down the opposite aisle, for I stood in one of the transepts, a figure dressed in a white robe, whether for the night, or for that longer night which lies too deep for the day, I could not tell. Was it she? And was this her chamber? I crossed the church, and followed. The figure stopped, seemed to ascend as it were a high bed, and lay down. I reached the place where it lay, glimmering white. The bed was a tomb. The light was too ghostly to see clearly, but I passed my hand over the face and the hands and the feet, which were all bare. They were cold—they were marble, but I knew them. It grew dark. I turned to retrace my steps, but found, ere long, that I had wandered into what seemed a little chapel. I groped about, seeking the door. Everything I touched belonged to the dead. My hands fell on the cold effigy of a knight who lay with his legs crossed and his sword broken beside him. He lay in his noble rest, and I lived on in ignoble strife. I felt for the left hand and a certain finger; I found there the ring I knew: he was one of my own ancestors. I was in the chapel over the burial-vault of my race. I called aloud: "If any of the dead are moving here, let them take pity upon me, for I, alas! am still alive; and let some dead woman comfort me, for I am a stranger in the land of the dead, and see no light." A warm kiss alighted on my lips through the dark. And I said, "The dead kiss well; I will not be afraid." And a great hand was reached out of the dark, and grasped mine for a moment, mightily and tenderly. I said to myself: "The veil between, though very dark, is very thin."

Groping my way further, I stumbled over the heavy stone that covered the entrance of the vault: and, in stumbling, descried upon the stone the mark, glowing in red fire. I caught the great ring. All my effort could not have moved the huge slab; but it opened the door of the cottage, and I threw myself once more, pale and speechless, on the couch beside the ancient dame. She sang once more:

Thou dreamest: on a rock thou art,
    High o'er the broken wave;
    Thou fallest with a fearful start
    But not into thy grave;
    For, waking in the morning's light,
    Thou smilest at the vanished night

So wilt thou sink, all pale and dumb,
    Into the fainting gloom;
    But ere the coming terrors come,
    Thou wak'st—where is the tomb?
    Thou wak'st—the dead ones smile above,
    With hovering arms of sleepless love.

She paused; then sang again:

We weep for gladness, weep for grief;
    The tears they are the same;
    We sigh for longing, and relief;
    The sighs have but one name,

And mingled in the dying strife,
    Are moans that are not sad
    The pangs of death are throbs of life,
    Its sighs are sometimes glad.

The face is very strange and white:
    It is Earth's only spot
    That feebly flickers back the light

The living seeth not.

I fell asleep, and slept a dreamless sleep, for I know not how long. When I awoke, I found that my hostess had moved from where she had been sitting, and now sat between me and the fourth door.

I guessed that her design was to prevent my entering there. I sprang from the couch, and darted past her to the door. I opened it at once and went out. All I remember is a cry of distress from the woman: "Don't go there, my child! Don't go there!" But I was gone.

I knew nothing more; or, if I did, I had forgot it all when I awoke to consciousness, lying on the floor of the cottage, with my head in the lap of the woman, who was weeping over me, and stroking my hair with both hands, talking to me as a mother might talk to a sick and sleeping, or a dead child. As soon as I looked up and saw her, she smiled through her tears; smiled with withered face and young eyes, till her countenance was irradiated with the light of the smile. Then she bathed my head and face and hands in an icy cold, colourless liquid, which smelt a little of damp earth. Immediately I was able to sit up. She rose and put some food before me. When I had eaten, she said: "Listen to me, my child. You must leave me directly!"

"Leave you!" I said. "I am so happy with you. I never was so happy in my life."

"But you must go," she rejoined sadly. "Listen! What do you hear?"

"I hear the sound as of a great throbbing of water."

"Ah! you do hear it? Well, I had to go through that door—the door of the Timeless" (and she shuddered as she pointed to the fourth door)—"to find you; for if I had not gone, you would never have entered again; and because I went, the waters around my cottage will rise and rise, and flow and come, till they build a great firmament of waters over my dwelling. But as long as I keep my fire burning, they cannot enter. I have fuel enough for years; and after one year they will sink away again, and be just as they were before you came. I have not been buried for a hundred years now." And she smiled and wept.

"Alas! Alas!" I cried. "I have brought this evil on the best and kindest of friends, who has filled my heart with great gifts."

"Do not think of that," she rejoined. "I can bear it very well. You will come back to me some day, I know. But I beg you, for my sake, my dear child, to do one thing. In whatever sorrow you may be, however inconsolable and irremediable it may appear, believe me that the old woman in the cottage, with the young eyes" (and she smiled), "knows something, though she must not always tell it, that would quite satisfy you about it, even in the worst moments of your distress. Now you must go."

"But how can I go, if the waters are all about, and if the doors all lead into other regions and other worlds?"

"This is not an island," she replied; "but is joined to the land by a narrow neck; and for the door, I will lead you myself through the right one."

She took my hand, and led me through the third door; whereupon I found myself standing in the deep grassy turf on which I had landed from the little boat, but upon the opposite side of the cottage. She pointed out the direction I must take, to find the isthmus and escape the rising waters.

Then putting her arms around me, she held me to her bosom; and as I kissed her, I felt as if I were leaving my mother for the first time, and could not help weeping bitterly. At length she gently pushed me away, and with the words, "Go, my son, and do something worth doing," turned back, and, entering the cottage, closed the door behind her. I felt very desolate as I went.

CHAPTER 20

"Thou hadst no fame; that which thou didst like good
Was but thy appetite that swayed thy blood
For that time to the best; for as a blast
That through a house comes, usually doth cast
Things out of order, yet by chance may come
And blow some one thing to his proper room,
So did thy appetite, and not thy zeal,
Sway thee by chance to do some one thing well."
FLETCHER'S *Faithful Shepherdess.*

"The noble hart that harbours vertuous thought
And is with childe of glorious great intent,
Can never rest, until it forth have brought
Th' eternall brood of glorie excellent."
SPENSER, *The Faerie Queene.*

I had not gone very far before I felt that the turf beneath my feet was soaked with the rising waters. But I reached the isthmus in safety. It was rocky, and so much higher than the level of the peninsula, that I had plenty of time to cross. I saw on each side of me the water rising rapidly, altogether without wind, or violent motion, or broken waves, but as if a slow strong fire were glowing beneath it. Ascending a steep acclivity, I found myself at last in an open, rocky country. After travelling for some hours, as nearly in a straight line as I could, I arrived at a lonely tower, built on the top of a little hill, which overlooked the whole neighbouring country. As I approached, I heard the clang of an anvil; and so rapid were the blows, that I despaired of making myself heard till a pause in the work should ensue. It was some minutes before a cessation took place; but when it did, I knocked loudly, and had not long to wait; for, a moment after, the door was partly opened by a noble-looking youth, half-undressed, glowing with heat, and begrimed with the blackness of the forge. In one hand he held a sword, so lately from the furnace that it yet shone with a dull fire. As soon as he saw me, he threw the door wide open, and standing aside, invited me very cordially to enter. I did so; when he shut and bolted the door most carefully, and then led the way inwards. He brought me into a rude hall, which seemed to occupy almost the whole of the ground floor of the little tower, and which I saw was now being used as a workshop. A huge fire roared on the hearth, beside which was an anvil. By the anvil stood, in similar undress, and in a waiting attitude, hammer in hand, a second youth, tall as the former, but far more slightly built. Reversing the usual course of perception in such meetings, I thought them, at first sight, very unlike; and at the second glance, knew that they were brothers. The former, and apparently the elder, was muscular and dark, with curling hair, and large hazel eyes, which sometimes grew wondrously soft. The second was slender and fair, yet with a countenance like an eagle, and an eye which, though pale blue, shone with an almost fierce expression. He stood erect, as if looking from a lofty mountain crag, over a vast plain outstretched below. As soon as we entered the hall, the elder turned to me, and I saw that a glow of satisfaction shone on both their faces. To my surprise and great pleasure, he addressed me thus:

"Brother, will you sit by the fire and rest, till we finish this part of our work?"

I signified my assent; and, resolved to await any disclosure they might be inclined to make, seated myself in silence near the hearth.

The elder brother then laid the sword in the fire, covered it well over, and when it had attained a sufficient degree of heat, drew it out and laid it on the anvil, moving it carefully about, while the younger, with a succession of quick smart blows, appeared either to be welding it, or hammering one part of it to a consenting shape with the rest. Having finished, they laid it carefully in the fire; and, when it was very hot indeed, plunged it into a vessel full of some liquid, whence a blue flame sprang upwards, as the glowing steel entered.

There they left it; and drawing two stools to the fire, sat down, one on each side of me.

"We are very glad to see you, brother. We have been expecting you for some days," said the dark-haired youth.

"I am proud to be called your brother," I rejoined; "and you will not think I refuse the name, if I desire to know why you honour me with it?"

"Ah! then he does not know about it," said the younger. "We thought you had known of the bond betwixt us, and the work we have to do together. You must tell him, brother, from the first."

So the elder began:

"Our father is king of this country. Before we were born, three giant brothers had appeared in the land. No one knew exactly when, and no one had the least idea whence they came. They took possession of a ruined castle that had stood unchanged and unoccupied within the memory of any of the country people. The vaults of this castle had remained uninjured by time, and these, I presume, they made use of at first. They were rarely seen, and never offered the least injury to any one; so that they were regarded in the neighbourhood as at least perfectly harmless, if not rather benevolent beings. But it began to be observed, that the old castle had assumed somehow or other, no one knew when or how, a somewhat different look from what it used to have. Not only were several breaches in the lower part of the walls built up, but actually some of the battlements which yet stood, had been repaired, apparently to prevent them from falling into worse decay, while the more important parts were being restored. Of course, every one supposed the giants must have a hand in the work, but no one ever saw them engaged in it. The peasants became yet more uneasy, after one, who had concealed himself, and watched all night, in the neighbourhood of the castle, reported that he had seen, in full moonlight, the three huge giants working with might and main, all night long, restoring to their former position some massive stones, formerly steps of a grand turnpike stair, a great portion of which had long since fallen, along with part of the wall of the round tower in which it had been built. This wall they were completing, foot by foot, along with the stair. But the people said they had no just pretext for interfering: although the real reason for letting the giants alone was, that everybody was far too much afraid of them to interrupt them.

"At length, with the help of a neighbouring quarry, the whole of the external wall of the castle was finished. And now the country folks were in greater fear than before. But for several years the giants remained very peaceful. The reason of this was afterwards supposed to be the fact, that they were distantly related to several good people in the country; for, as long as these lived, they remained quiet; but as soon as they were all dead the real nature of the giants broke out. Having completed the outside of their castle, they proceeded, by spoiling the country houses around them, to make a quiet luxurious provision for their comfort within. Affairs reached such a pass, that the news of their robberies came to my father's ears; but he, alas! was so crippled in his resources, by a war he was carrying on with a neighbouring prince, that he could only spare a very few men, to attempt the capture of their stronghold. Upon these the giants issued in the night, and slew every man of them. And now, grown bolder by success and impunity, they no longer confined their depredations to property, but began to seize the persons of their distinguished neighbours, knights and ladies, and hold them in durance, the misery of which was heightened by all manner of indignity, until they were redeemed by their friends, at an exorbitant ransom. Many knights have adventured their overthrow, but to their own instead; for they have all been slain, or captured, or forced to make a hasty retreat. To crown their enormities, if any man now attempts their destruction, they, immediately upon his defeat, put one or more of their captives to a shameful death, on a turret in sight of all passers-by; so that they have been much less molested of late; and we, although we have burned, for years, to attack these demons and destroy them, dared not, for the sake of their captives, risk the adventure, before we should have reached at least our earliest manhood. Now, however, we are preparing for the attempt; and the grounds of this preparation are these. Having only the resolution, and not the experience necessary for the undertaking, we went and consulted a lonely woman of wisdom, who lives not very far from here, in the direction of the quarter from which you have come. She received us most kindly, and gave us what seems to us the best of advice. She first inquired what experience we had had in arms. We told her we had been well exercised from our boyhood, and for some years had kept ourselves in constant practice, with a view to this necessity.

"'But you have not actually fought for life and death?' said she.

"We were forced to confess we had not.

"'So much the better in some respects,' she replied. 'Now listen to me. Go first and work with an armourer, for as long time as you find needful to obtain a knowledge of his craft; which will not be long, seeing your hearts will be all in the work. Then go to some lonely tower, you two alone. Receive no visits from man or woman. There forge for yourselves every piece of armour that you wish to wear, or to use, in your coming encounter. And keep up your exercises. As, however, two of you can be no match for the three giants, I will find you, if I can, a third brother, who will take on himself the third share of the fight, and the preparation. Indeed, I have already seen one who will, I think, be the very man for your fellowship, but it will be some time before he comes to me. He is wandering now without an aim. I will show him to you in a glass, and, when he comes, you will know him at once. If he will share your endeavours, you must teach him all you know, and he will repay you well, in present song, and in future deeds.'

"She opened the door of a curious old cabinet that stood in the room. On the inside of this door was an oval convex mirror. Looking in it for some time, we at length saw reflected the place where we stood, and the old dame seated in her chair. Our forms were not reflected. But at the feet of the dame lay a young man, yourself, weeping.

"'Surely this youth will not serve our ends,' said I, 'for he weeps.'

"The old woman smiled. 'Past tears are present strength,' said she.

"'Oh!' said my brother, 'I saw you weep once over an eagle you shot.'

"'That was because it was so like you, brother,' I replied; 'but indeed, this youth may have better cause for tears than that—I was wrong.'

"'Wait a while,' said the woman; 'if I mistake not, he will make you weep till your tears are dry for ever. Tears are the only cure for weeping. And you may have need of the cure, before you go forth to fight the giants. You must wait for him, in your tower, till he comes.'

"Now if you will join us, we will soon teach you to make your armour; and we will fight together, and work together, and love each other as never three loved before. And you will sing to us, will you not?"

"That I will, when I can," I answered; "but it is only at times that the power of song comes upon me. For that I must wait; but I have a feeling that if I work well, song will not be far off to enliven the labour."

This was all the compact made: the brothers required nothing more, and I did not think of giving anything more. I rose, and threw off my upper garments.

"I know the uses of the sword," I said. "I am ashamed of my white hands beside yours so nobly soiled and hard; but that shame will soon be wiped away."

"No, no; we will not work to-day. Rest is as needful as toil. Bring the wine, brother; it is your turn to serve to-day."

The younger brother soon covered a table with rough viands, but good wine; and we ate and drank heartily, beside our work. Before the meal was over, I had learned all their story. Each had something in his heart which made the conviction, that he would victoriously perish in the coming conflict, a real sorrow to him.

Otherwise they thought they would have lived enough. The causes of their trouble were respectively these:

While they wrought with an armourer, in a city famed for workmanship in steel and silver, the elder had fallen in love with a lady as far beneath him in real rank, as she was above the station he had as apprentice to an armourer. Nor did he seek to further his suit by discovering himself; but there was simply so much manhood about him, that no one ever thought of rank when in his company. This is what his brother said about it. The lady could not help loving him in return. He told her when he left her, that he had a perilous adventure before him, and that when it was achieved, she would either see him return to claim her, or hear that he had died with honour. The younger brother's grief arose from the fact, that, if they were both slain, his old father, the king, would be childless. His love for his father was so exceeding, that to one unable to sympathise with it, it would have appeared extravagant. Both loved him equally at heart; but the love of the younger had been more developed, because his thoughts and anxieties had not been otherwise occupied. When at home, he had been his constant companion; and, of late, had ministered to the infirmities of his growing age. The youth was never weary of listening to the tales of his sire's youthful adventures; and had not yet in the smallest degree lost the conviction, that his father was the greatest man in the world. The grandest triumph possible to his conception was, to return to his father, laden with the spoils of one of the hated giants. But they both were in some dread, lest the thought of the loneliness of these two might occur to them, in the moment when decision was most necessary, and disturb, in some degree, the self-possession requisite for the success of their attempt. For, as I have said, they were yet untried in actual conflict. "Now," thought I, "I see to what the powers of my gift must minister." For my own part, I did not dread death, for I had nothing to care to live for; but I dreaded the encounter because of the responsibility connected with it. I resolved however to work hard, and thus grow cool, and quick, and forceful.

The time passed away in work and song, in talk and ramble, in friendly fight and brotherly aid. I would not forge for myself armour of heavy mail like theirs, for I was not so powerful as they, and depended more for any success I might secure, upon nimbleness of motion, certainty of eye, and ready response of hand. Therefore I began to make for myself a shirt of steel plates and rings; which work, while more troublesome, was better suited to me than the heavier labour. Much assistance did the brothers give me, even after, by their instructions, I was able to make some progress alone. Their work was in a moment abandoned, to render any required aid to mine. As the old woman had promised, I tried to repay them with song; and many were the tears they both shed over my ballads and dirges. The songs they liked best to hear were two which I made for them. They were not half so good as many others I knew, especially some I had learned from the wise woman in the cottage; but what comes nearest to our needs we like the best.

I The king sat on his throne
  Glowing in gold and red;
  The crown in his right hand shone,
  And the gray hairs crowned his head.

His only son walks in,
    And in walls of steel he stands:
    Make me, O father, strong to win,
    With the blessing of holy hands."

He knelt before his sire,
    Who blessed him with feeble smile
    His eyes shone out with a kingly fire,
    But his old lips quivered the while.

"Go to the fight, my son,
    Bring back the giant's head;
    And the crown with which my brows have done,
    Shall glitter on thine instead."

"My father, I seek no crowns,
    But unspoken praise from thee;
    For thy people's good, and thy renown,
    I will die to set them free."

The king sat down and waited there,
    And rose not, night nor day;
    Till a sound of shouting filled the air,
    And cries of a sore dismay.

Then like a king he sat once more,
    With the crown upon his head;
    And up to the throne the people bore
    A mighty giant dead.

And up to the throne the people bore
    A pale and lifeless boy.
    The king rose up like a prophet of yore,
    In a lofty, deathlike joy.

He put the crown on the chilly brow:
    "Thou should'st have reigned with me
    But Death is the king of both, and now
    I go to obey with thee.

"Surely some good in me there lay,
  To beget the noble one."
The old man smiled like a winter day,
And fell beside his son.
II "O lady, thy lover is dead," they cried;
  "He is dead, but hath slain the foe;
He hath left his name to be magnified
In a song of wonder and woe."

"Alas! I am well repaid," said she,
  "With a pain that stings like joy:
For I feared, from his tenderness to me,
That he was but a feeble boy.

"Now I shall hold my head on high,
  The queen among my kind;
If ye hear a sound, 'tis only a sigh
For a glory left behind."

The first three times I sang these songs they both wept passionately. But after the third time, they wept no more. Their eyes shone, and their faces grew pale, but they never wept at any of my songs again.

CHAPTER 21

"I put my life in my hands." — *The Book of Judges.*

At length, with much toil and equal delight, our armour was finished. We armed each other, and tested the strength of the defence, with many blows of loving force. I was inferior in strength to both my brothers, but a little more agile than either; and upon this agility, joined to precision in hitting with the point of my weapon, I grounded my hopes of success in the ensuing combat. I likewise laboured to develop yet more the keenness of sight with which I was naturally gifted; and, from the remarks of my companions, I soon learned that my endeavours were not in vain.

The morning arrived on which we had determined to make the attempt, and succeed or perish—perhaps both. We had resolved to fight on foot; knowing that the mishap of many of the knights who had made the attempt, had resulted from the fright of their horses at the appearance of the giants; and believing with Sir Gawain, that, though mare's sons might be false to us, the earth would never prove a traitor. But most of our preparations were, in their immediate aim at least, frustrated.

We rose, that fatal morning, by daybreak. We had rested from all labour the day before, and now were fresh as the lark. We bathed in cold spring water, and dressed ourselves in clean garments, with a sense of preparation, as for a solemn festivity. When we had broken our fast, I took an old lyre, which I had found in the tower and had myself repaired, and sung for the last time the two ballads of which I have said so much already. I followed them with this, for a closing song:

Oh, well for him who breaks his dream

With the blow that ends the strife
And, waking, knows the peace that flows
Around the pain of life!

We are dead, my brothers! Our bodies clasp,
As an armour, our souls about;
This hand is the battle-axe I grasp,
And this my hammer stout.

Fear not, my brothers, for we are dead;
No noise can break our rest;
The calm of the grave is about the head,
And the heart heaves not the breast.

And our life we throw to our people back,
To live with, a further store;
We leave it them, that there be no lack
In the land where we live no more.

Oh, well for him who breaks his dream
With the blow that ends the strife
And, waking, knows the peace that flows
Around the noise of life!

As the last few tones of the instrument were following, like a dirge, the death of the song, we all sprang to our feet. For, through one of the little windows of the tower, towards which I had looked as I sang, I saw, suddenly rising over the edge of the slope on which our tower stood, three enormous heads. The brothers knew at once, by my looks, what caused my sudden movement. We were utterly unarmed, and there was no time to arm.

But we seemed to adopt the same resolution simultaneously; for each caught up his favourite weapon, and, leaving his defence behind, sprang to the door. I snatched up a long rapier, abruptly, but very finely pointed, in my sword-hand, and in the other a sabre; the elder brother seized his heavy battle-axe; and the younger, a great, two-handed sword, which he wielded in one hand like a feather. We had just time to get clear of the tower, embrace and say good-bye, and part to some little distance, that we might not encumber each other's motions, ere the triple giant-brotherhood drew near to attack us. They were about twice our height, and armed to the teeth. Through the visors of their helmets their monstrous eyes shone with a horrible ferocity. I was in the middle position, and the middle giant approached me. My eyes were busy with his armour, and I was not a moment in settling my mode of attack. I saw that his body-armour was somewhat clumsily made, and that the overlappings in the lower part had more play than necessary; and I hoped that, in a fortunate moment, some joint would open a little, in a visible and accessible part. I stood till he came near enough to aim a blow at me with the mace, which has been, in all ages, the favourite weapon of giants, when, of course, I leaped aside, and let the blow fall upon the spot where I had been standing. I expected this would strain the joints of his armour yet more. Full of fury, he made at me again; but I kept him busy, constantly eluding his blows, and hoping thus to fatigue him. He did not seem to fear any assault from me, and I attempted none as yet; but while I watched his motions in order to avoid his blows, I, at the same time, kept equal watch upon those joints of his armour, through some one of which I hoped to reach his life. At length, as if somewhat fatigued, he paused a moment, and drew himself slightly up; I bounded forward, foot and hand, ran my rapier right through to the armour of his back, let go the hilt, and passing under his right arm, turned as he fell, and flew at him with my sabre. At one happy blow I divided the band of his helmet, which fell off, and allowed me, with a second cut across the eyes, to blind him quite; after which I clove his head, and turned, uninjured, to see how my brothers had fared. Both the giants were down, but so were my brothers. I flew first to the one and then to the other couple. Both pairs of combatants were dead, and yet locked together, as in the death-struggle. The elder had buried his battle-axe in the body of his foe, and had fallen beneath him as he fell. The giant had strangled him in his own death-agonies. The younger had nearly hewn off the left leg of his enemy; and, grappled with in the act, had, while they rolled together on the earth, found for his dagger a passage betwixt the gorget and cuirass of the giant, and stabbed him mortally in the throat. The blood from the giant's throat was yet pouring over the hand of his foe, which still grasped the hilt of the dagger sheathed in the wound. They lay silent. I, the least worthy, remained the sole survivor in the lists.

As I stood exhausted amidst the dead, after the first worthy deed of my life, I suddenly looked behind me, and there lay the Shadow, black in the sunshine. I went into the lonely tower, and there lay the useless armour of the noble youths— supine as they.

Ah, how sad it looked! It was a glorious death, but it was death. My songs could not comfort me now. I was almost ashamed that I was alive, when they, the true-hearted, were no more. And yet I breathed freer to think that I had gone through the trial, and had not failed. And perhaps I may be forgiven, if some feelings of pride arose in my bosom, when I looked down on the mighty form that lay dead by my hand.

"After all, however," I said to myself, and my heart sank, "it was only skill. Your giant was but a blunderer."

I left the bodies of friends and foes, peaceful enough when the death-fight was over, and, hastening to the country below, roused the peasants. They came with shouting and gladness, bringing waggons to carry the bodies. I resolved to take the princes home to their father, each as he lay, in the arms of his country's foe. But first I searched the giants, and found the keys of their castle, to which I repaired, followed by a great company of the people. It was a place of wonderful strength. I released the prisoners, knights and ladies, all in a sad condition, from the cruelties and neglects of the giants. It humbled me to see them crowding round me with thanks, when in truth the glorious brothers, lying dead by their lonely tower, were those to whom the thanks belonged. I had but aided in carrying out the thought born in their brain, and uttered in visible form before ever I laid hold thereupon. Yet I did count myself happy to have been chosen for their brother in this great deed.

After a few hours spent in refreshing and clothing the prisoners, we all commenced our journey towards the capital. This was slow at first; but, as the strength and spirits of the prisoners returned, it became more rapid; and in three days we reached the palace of the king. As we entered the city gates, with the huge bulks lying each on a waggon drawn by horses, and two of them inextricably inter-twined with the dead bodies of their princes, the people raised a shout and then a cry, and followed in multitudes the solemn procession.

I will not attempt to describe the behaviour of the grand old king. Joy and pride in his sons overcame his sorrow at their loss. On me he heaped every kindness that heart could devise or hand execute. He used to sit and question me, night after night, about everything that was in any way connected with them and their prepa-rations. Our mode of life, and relation to each other, during the time we spent together, was a constant theme. He entered into the minutest details of the construc-tion of the armour, even to a peculiar mode of riveting some of the plates, with unwearying interest. This armour I had intended to beg of the king, as my sole memorials of the contest; but, when I saw the delight he took in contemplating it, and the consolation it appeared to afford him in his sorrow, I could not ask for it; but, at his request, left my own, weapons and all, to be joined with theirs in a trophy, erected in the grand square of the palace. The king, with gorgeous cere-mony, dubbed me knight with his own old hand, in which trembled the sword of his youth.

During the short time I remained, my company was, naturally, much courted by the young nobles. I was in a constant round of gaiety and diversion, notwithstanding that the court was in mourning. For the country was so rejoiced at the death of the giants, and so many of their lost friends had been restored to the nobility and men of wealth, that the gladness surpassed the grief. "Ye have indeed left your lives to your people, my great brothers!" I said.

But I was ever and ever haunted by the old shadow, which I had not seen all the time that I was at work in the tower. Even in the society of the ladies of the court, who seemed to think it only their duty to make my stay there as pleasant to me as possible, I could not help being conscious of its presence, although it might not be annoying me at the time. At length, somewhat weary of uninterrupted pleasure, and nowise strengthened thereby, either in body or mind, I put on a splendid suit of armour of steel inlaid with silver, which the old king had given me, and, mounting the horse on which it had been brought to me, took my leave of the palace, to visit the distant city in which the lady dwelt, whom the elder prince had loved. I antici-pated a sore task, in conveying to her the news of his glorious fate: but this trial was spared me, in a manner as strange as anything that had happened to me in Fairy Land.

CHAPTER 22

"No one has my form but the I."
   Schoppe, in JEAN PAUL'S Titan.

"Joy's a subtil elf.
   I think man's happiest when he forgets himself."
   CYRIL TOURNEUR, The Revenger's Tragedy.

On the third day of my journey, I was riding gently along a road, apparently little frequented, to judge from the grass that grew upon it. I was approaching a forest. Everywhere in Fairy Land forests are the places where one may most certainly expect adventures. As I drew near, a youth, unarmed, gentle, and beautiful, who had just cut a branch from a yew growing on the skirts of the wood, evidently to make himself a bow, met me, and thus accosted me:

"Sir knight, be careful as thou ridest through this forest; for it is said to be strangely enchanted, in a sort which even those who have been witnesses of its enchantment can hardly describe."

I thanked him for his advice, which I promised to follow, and rode on. But the moment I entered the wood, it seemed to me that, if enchantment there was, it must be of a good kind; for the Shadow, which had been more than usually dark and distressing, since I had set out on this journey, suddenly disappeared. I felt a wonderful elevation of spirits, and began to reflect on my past life, and especially on my combat with the giants, with such satisfaction, that I had actually to remind myself, that I had only killed one of them; and that, but for the brothers, I should never have had the idea of attacking them, not to mention the smallest power of standing to it. Still I rejoiced, and counted myself amongst the glorious knights of old; having even the unspeakable presumption—my shame and self-condemnation at the memory of it are such, that I write it as the only and sorest penance I can perform—to think of myself (will the world believe it?) as side by side with Sir Galahad! Scarcely had the thought been born in my mind, when, approaching me from the left, through the trees, I espied a resplendent knight, of mighty size, whose armour seemed to shine of itself, without the sun. When he drew near, I was astonished to see that this armour was like my own; nay, I could trace, line for line, the correspondence of the inlaid silver to the device on my own. His horse, too, was like mine in colour, form, and motion; save that, like his rider, he was greater and fiercer than his counterpart. The knight rode with beaver up. As he halted right opposite to me in the narrow path, barring my way, I saw the reflection of my countenance in the centre plate of shining steel on his breastplate. Above it rose the same face—his face—only, as I have said, larger and fiercer. I was bewildered. I could not help feeling some admiration of him, but it was mingled with a dim conviction that he was evil, and that I ought to fight with him.

"Let me pass," I said.

"When I will," he replied.

Something within me said: "Spear in rest, and ride at him! else thou art for ever a slave."

I tried, but my arm trembled so much, that I could not couch my lance. To tell the truth, I, who had overcome the giant, shook like a coward before this knight. He gave a scornful laugh, that echoed through the wood, turned his horse, and said, without looking round, "Follow me."

I obeyed, abashed and stupefied. How long he led, and how long I followed, I cannot tell. "I never knew misery before," I said to myself. "Would that I had at least struck him, and had had my death-blow in return! Why, then, do I not call to him to wheel and defend himself? Alas! I know not why, but I cannot. One look from him would cow me like a beaten hound." I followed, and was silent.

At length we came to a dreary square tower, in the middle of a dense forest. It looked as if scarce a tree had been cut down to make room for it. Across the very door, diagonally, grew the stem of a tree, so large that there was just room to squeeze past it in order to enter. One miserable square hole in the roof was the only visible suggestion of a window. Turret or battlement, or projecting masonry of any kind, it had none. Clear and smooth and massy, it rose from its base, and ended with a line straight and unbroken. The roof, carried to a centre from each of the four walls, rose slightly to the point where the rafters met. Round the base lay several little heaps of either bits of broken branches, withered and peeled, or half-whitened bones; I could not distinguish which. As I approached, the ground sounded hollow beneath my horse's hoofs. The knight took a great key from his pocket, and reaching past the stem of the tree, with some difficulty opened the door. "Dismount," he commanded. I obeyed. He turned my horse's head away from the tower, gave him a terrible blow with the flat side of his sword, and sent him madly tearing through the forest.

"Now," said he, "enter, and take your companion with you."

I looked round: knight and horse had vanished, and behind me lay the horrible shadow. I entered, for I could not help myself; and the shadow followed me. I had a terrible conviction that the knight and he were one. The door closed behind me.

Now I was indeed in pitiful plight. There was literally nothing in the tower but my shadow and me. The walls rose right up to the roof; in which, as I had seen from without, there was one little square opening. This I now knew to be the only window the tower possessed. I sat down on the floor, in listless wretchedness. I think I must have fallen asleep, and have slept for hours; for I suddenly became aware of existence, in observing that the moon was shining through the hole in the roof. As she rose higher and higher, her light crept down the wall over me, till at last it shone right upon my head. Instantaneously the walls of the tower seemed to vanish away like a mist. I sat beneath a beech, on the edge of a forest, and the open country lay, in the moonlight, for miles and miles around me, spotted with glimmering houses and spires and towers. I thought with myself, "Oh, joy! It was only a dream; the horrible narrow waste is gone, and I wake beneath a beech-tree, perhaps one that loves me, and I can go where I will." I rose, as I thought, and walked about, and did what I would, but ever kept near the tree; for always, and, of course, since my meeting with the woman of the beech-tree far more than ever, I loved that tree. So the night wore on. I waited for the sun to rise, before I could venture to renew my journey. But as soon as the first faint light of the dawn appeared, instead of shining upon me from the eye of the morning, it stole like a fainting ghost through the little square hole above my head; and the walls came out as the light grew, and the glorious night was swallowed up of the hateful day. The long dreary day passed. My shadow lay black on the floor. I felt no hunger, no need of food. The night came. The moon shone. I watched her light slowly descending the wall, as I might have watched, adown the sky, the long, swift approach of a helping angel. Her rays touched me, and I was free. Thus night after night passed away. I should have died but for this. Every night the conviction returned, that I was free. Every morning I sat wretchedly disconsolate. At length, when the course of the moon no longer permitted her beams to touch me, the night was dreary as the day.

When I slept, I was somewhat consoled by my dreams; but all the time I dreamed, I knew that I was only dreaming. But one night, at length, the moon, a mere shred of pallor, scattered a few thin ghostly rays upon me; and I think I fell asleep and dreamed. I sat in an autumn night before the vintage, on a hill overlooking my own castle. My heart sprang with joy. Oh, to be a child again, innocent, fearless, without shame or desire! I walked down to the castle. All were in consternation at my absence. My sisters were weeping for my loss. They sprang up and clung to me, with incoherent cries, as I entered. My old friends came flocking round me. A gray light shone on the roof of the hall. It was the light of the dawn shining through the square window of my tower. More earnestly than ever, I longed for freedom after this dream; more drearily than ever, crept on the next wretched day. I measured by the sunbeams, caught through the little window in the trap of my tower, how it went by, waiting only for the dreams of the night.

About noon, I started as if something foreign to all my senses and all my experience, had suddenly invaded me; yet it was only the voice of a woman singing. My whole frame quivered with joy, surprise, and the sensation of the unforeseen. Like a living soul, like an incarnation of Nature, the song entered my prison-house. Each tone folded its wings, and laid itself, like a caressing bird, upon my heart. It bathed me like a sea; inwrapt me like an odorous vapour; entered my soul like a long draught of clear spring-water; shone upon me like essential sunlight; soothed me like a mother's voice and hand. Yet, as the clearest forest-well tastes sometimes of the bitterness of decayed leaves, so to my weary, prisoned heart, its cheerfulness had a sting of cold, and its tenderness unmanned me with the faintness of long-departed joys. I wept half-bitterly, half-luxuriously; but not long. I dashed away the tears, ashamed of a weakness which I thought I had abandoned. Ere I knew, I had walked to the door, and seated myself with my ears against it, in order to catch every syllable of the revelation from the unseen outer world. And now I heard each word distinctly. The singer seemed to be standing or sitting near the tower, for the sounds indicated no change of place. The song was something like this:

The sun, like a golden knot on high,
  Gathers the glories of the sky,
  And binds them into a shining tent,
  Roofing the world with the firmament.
  And through the pavilion the rich winds blow,
  And through the pavilion the waters go.
  And the birds for joy, and the trees for prayer,
  Bowing their heads in the sunny air,
  And for thoughts, the gently talking springs,
  That come from the centre with secret things —
  All make a music, gentle and strong,
  Bound by the heart into one sweet song.
  And amidst them all, the mother Earth
  Sits with the children of her birth;
  She tendeth them all, as a mother hen
  Her little ones round her, twelve or ten:
  Oft she sitteth, with hands on knee,
  Idle with love for her family.
  Go forth to her from the dark and the dust,
  And weep beside her, if weep thou must;
  If she may not hold thee to her breast,
  Like a weary infant, that cries for rest
  At least she will press thee to her knee,
  And tell a low, sweet tale to thee,
  Till the hue to thy cheeky and the light to thine eye,
  Strength to thy limbs, and courage high
  To thy fainting heart, return amain,
  And away to work thou goest again.
  From the narrow desert, O man of pride,
  Come into the house, so high and wide.

Hardly knowing what I did, I opened the door. Why had I not done so before? I do not know.

At first I could see no one; but when I had forced myself past the tree which grew across the entrance, I saw, seated on the ground, and leaning against the tree, with her back to my prison, a beautiful woman. Her countenance seemed known to me, and yet unknown. She looked at me and smiled, when I made my appearance.

"Ah! were you the prisoner there? I am very glad I have wiled you out."

"Do you know me then?" "Do you not know me? But you hurt me, and that, I suppose, makes it easy for a man to forget. You broke my globe. Yet I thank you. Perhaps I owe you many thanks for breaking it. I took the pieces, all black, and wet with crying over them, to the Fairy Queen. There was no music and no light in them now. But she took them from me, and laid them aside; and made me go to sleep in a great hall of white, with black pillars, and many red curtains. When I woke in the morning, I went to her, hoping to have my globe again, whole and sound; but she sent me away without it, and I have not seen it since. Nor do I care for it now. I have something so much better. I do not need the globe to play to me; for I can sing. I could not sing at all before. Now I go about everywhere through Fairy Land, singing till my heart is like to break, just like my globe, for very joy at my own songs. And wherever I go, my songs do good, and deliver people. And now I have delivered you, and I am so happy."

She ceased, and the tears came into her eyes.

All this time, I had been gazing at her; and now fully recognised the face of the child, glorified in the countenance of the woman.

I was ashamed and humbled before her; but a great weight was lifted from my thoughts. I knelt before her, and thanked her, and begged her to forgive me.

"Rise, rise," she said; "I have nothing to forgive; I thank you. But now I must be gone, for I do not know how many may be waiting for me, here and there, through the dark forests; and they cannot come out till I come."

She rose, and with a smile and a farewell, turned and left me. I dared not ask her to stay; in fact, I could hardly speak to her. Between her and me, there was a great gulf. She was uplifted, by sorrow and well-doing, into a region I could hardly hope ever to enter. I watched her departure, as one watches a sunset. She went like a radiance through the dark wood, which was henceforth bright to me, from simply knowing that such a creature was in it.

She was bearing the sun to the unsunned spots. The light and the music of her broken globe were now in her heart and her brain. As she went, she sang; and I caught these few words of her song; and the tones seemed to linger and wind about the trees after she had disappeared:

Thou goest thine, and I go mine —
  Many ways we wend;
  Many days, and many ways,
  Ending in one end.

Many a wrong, and its curing song;
  Many a road, and many an inn;
  Room to roam, but only one home
  For all the world to win.

And so she vanished. With a sad heart, soothed by humility, and the knowledge of her peace and gladness, I bethought me what now I should do. First, I must leave the tower far behind me, lest, in some evil moment, I might be once more caged within its horrible walls. But it was ill walking in my heavy armour; and besides I had now no right to the golden spurs and the resplendent mail, fitly dulled with long neglect. I might do for a squire; but I honoured knighthood too highly, to call myself any longer one of the noble brotherhood. I stripped off all my armour, piled it under the tree, just where the lady had been seated, and took my unknown way, eastward through the woods. Of all my weapons, I carried only a short axe in my hand.

Then first I knew the delight of being lowly; of saying to myself, "I am what I am, nothing more." "I have failed," I said, "I have lost myself—would it had been my shadow." I looked round: the shadow was nowhere to be seen. Ere long, I learned that it was not myself, but only my shadow, that I had lost. I learned that it is better, a thousand-fold, for a proud man to fall and be humbled, than to hold up his head in his pride and fancied innocence. I learned that he that will be a hero, will barely be a man; that he that will be nothing but a doer of his work, is sure of his manhood. In nothing was my ideal lowered, or dimmed, or grown less precious; I only saw it too plainly, to set myself for a moment beside it. Indeed, my ideal soon became my life; whereas, formerly, my life had consisted in a vain attempt to behold, if not my ideal in myself, at least myself in my ideal. Now, however, I took, at first, what perhaps was a mistaken pleasure, in despising and degrading myself. Another self seemed to arise, like a white spirit from a dead man, from the dumb and trampled self of the past. Doubtless, this self must again die and be buried, and again, from its tomb, spring a winged child; but of this my history as yet bears not the record.

Self will come to life even in the slaying of self; but there is ever something deeper and stronger than it, which will emerge at last from the unknown abysses of the soul: will it be as a solemn gloom, burning with eyes? Or a clear morning after the rain? Or a smiling child, that finds itself nowhere, and everywhere?

CHAPTER 23

"High erected thought, seated in a heart of courtesy."
SIR PHILIP SIDNEY.

"A sweet attractive kinde of grace,
  A full assurance given by lookes,
  Continuall comfort in a face,
  The lineaments of Gospel bookes."
MATTHEW ROYDON, on Sir Philip Sidney.

I had not gone far, for I had but just lost sight of the hated tower, when a voice of another sort, sounding near or far, as the trees permitted or intercepted its passage, reached me. It was a full, deep, manly voice, but withal clear and melodious. Now it burst on the ear with a sudden swell, and anon, dying away as suddenly, seemed to come to me across a great space. Nevertheless, it drew nearer; till, at last, I could distinguish the words of the song, and get transient glimpses of the singer, between the columns of the trees. He came nearer, dawning upon me like a growing thought. He was a knight, armed from head to heel, mounted upon a strange-looking beast, whose form I could not understand. The words which I heard him sing were like these:

Heart be stout,
  And eye be true;
  Good blade out!
  And ill shall rue.

Courage, horse!
    Thou lackst no skill;
    Well thy force
    Hath matched my will.

For the foe
    With fiery breath,
    At a blow,
    Is still in death.

Gently, horse!
    Tread fearlessly;
    'Tis his corse
    That burdens thee.

The sun's eye
    Is fierce at noon;
    Thou and I
    Will rest full soon.

And new strength
    New work will meet;
    Till, at length,
    Long rest is sweet.

And now horse and rider had arrived near enough for me to see, fastened by the long neck to the hinder part of the saddle, and trailing its hideous length on the ground behind, the body of a great dragon. It was no wonder that, with such a drag at his heels, the horse could make but slow progress, notwithstanding his evident dismay. The horrid, serpent-like head, with its black tongue, forked with red, hanging out of its jaws, dangled against the horse's side. Its neck was covered with long blue hair, its sides with scales of green and gold. Its back was of corrugated skin, of a purple hue. Its belly was similar in nature, but its colour was leaden, dashed with blotches of livid blue. Its skinny, bat-like wings and its tail were of a dull gray. It was strange to see how so many gorgeous colours, so many curving lines, and such beautiful things as wings and hair and scales, combined to form the horrible creature, intense in ugliness.

The knight was passing me with a salutation; but, as I walked towards him, he reined up, and I stood by his stirrup. When I came near him, I saw to my surprise and pleasure likewise, although a sudden pain, like a birth of fire, sprang up in my heart, that it was the knight of the soiled armour, whom I knew before, and whom I had seen in the vision, with the lady of the marble. But I could have thrown my arms around him, because she loved him. This discovery only strengthened the resolution I had formed, before I recognised him, of offering myself to the knight, to wait upon him as a squire, for he seemed to be unattended. I made my request in as few words as possible. He hesitated for a moment, and looked at me thoughtfully. I saw that he suspected who I was, but that he continued uncertain of his suspicion. No doubt he was soon convinced of its truth; but all the time I was with him, not a word crossed his lips with reference to what he evidently concluded I wished to leave unnoticed, if not to keep concealed.

"Squire and knight should be friends," said he: "can you take me by the hand?" And he held out the great gauntleted right hand. I grasped it willingly and strongly. Not a word more was said. The knight gave the sign to his horse, which again began his slow march, and I walked beside and a little behind.

We had not gone very far before we arrived at a little cottage; from which, as we drew near, a woman rushed out with the cry:

"My child! My child! Have you found my child?"

"I have found her," replied the knight, "but she is sorely hurt. I was forced to leave her with the hermit, as I returned. You will find her there, and I think she will get better. You see I have brought you a present. This wretch will not hurt you again." And he undid the creature's neck, and flung the frightful burden down by the cottage door.

The woman was now almost out of sight in the wood; but the husband stood at the door, with speechless thanks in his face.

"You must bury the monster," said the knight. "If I had arrived a moment later, I should have been too late. But now you need not fear, for such a creature as this very rarely appears, in the same part, twice during a lifetime."

"Will you not dismount and rest you, Sir Knight?" said the peasant, who had, by this time, recovered himself a little.

"That I will, thankfully," said he; and, dismounting, he gave the reins to me, and told me to unbridle the horse, and lead him into the shade. "You need not tie him up," he added; "he will not run away."

When I returned, after obeying his orders, and entered the cottage, I saw the knight seated, without his helmet, and talking most familiarly with the simple host. I stood at the open door for a moment, and, gazing at him, inwardly justified the white lady in preferring him to me. A nobler countenance I never saw. Loving-kindness beamed from every line of his face. It seemed as if he would repay himself for the late arduous combat, by indulging in all the gentleness of a womanly heart. But when the talk ceased for a moment, he seemed to fall into a reverie. Then the exquisite curves of the upper lip vanished. The lip was lengthened and compressed at the same moment. You could have told that, within the lips, the teeth were firmly closed. The whole face grew stern and determined, all but fierce; only the eyes burned on like a holy sacrifice, uplift on a granite rock.

The woman entered, with her mangled child in her arms. She was pale as her little burden. She gazed, with a wild love and despairing tenderness, on the still, all but dead face, white and clear from loss of blood and terror.

The knight rose. The light that had been confined to his eyes, now shone from his whole countenance. He took the little thing in his arms, and, with the mother's help, undressed her, and looked to her wounds. The tears flowed down his face as he did so. With tender hands he bound them up, kissed the pale cheek, and gave her back to her mother. When he went home, all his tale would be of the grief and joy of the parents; while to me, who had looked on, the gracious countenance of the armed man, beaming from the panoply of steel, over the seemingly dead child, while the powerful hands turned it and shifted it, and bound it, if possible even more gently than the mother's, formed the centre of the story.

After we had partaken of the best they could give us, the knight took his leave, with a few parting instructions to the mother as to how she should treat the child.

I brought the knight his steed, held the stirrup while he mounted, and then followed him through the wood. The horse, delighted to be free of his hideous load, bounded beneath the weight of man and armour, and could hardly be restrained from galloping on. But the knight made him time his powers to mine, and so we went on for an hour or two. Then the knight dismounted, and compelled me to get into the saddle, saying: "Knight and squire must share the labour."

Holding by the stirrup, he walked along by my side, heavily clad as he was, with apparent ease. As we went, he led a conversation, in which I took what humble part my sense of my condition would permit me.

"Somehow or other," said he, "notwithstanding the beauty of this country of Faerie, in which we are, there is much that is wrong in it. If there are great splendours, there are corresponding horrors; heights and depths; beautiful women and awful fiends; noble men and weaklings. All a man has to do, is to better what he can. And if he will settle it with himself, that even renown and success are in themselves of no great value, and be content to be defeated, if so be that the fault is not his; and so go to his work with a cool brain and a strong will, he will get it done; and fare none the worse in the end, that he was not burdened with provision and precaution."

"But he will not always come off well," I ventured to say.

"Perhaps not," rejoined the knight, "in the individual act; but the result of his lifetime will content him."

"So it will fare with you, doubtless," thought I; "but for me—"

Venturing to resume the conversation after a pause, I said, hesitatingly:

"May I ask for what the little beggar-girl wanted your aid, when she came to your castle to find you?"

He looked at me for a moment in silence, and then said—

"I cannot help wondering how you know of that; but there is something about you quite strange enough to entitle you to the privilege of the country; namely, to go unquestioned. I, however, being only a man, such as you see me, am ready to tell you anything you like to ask me, as far as I can. The little beggar-girl came into the hall where I was sitting, and told me a very curious story, which I can only recollect very vaguely, it was so peculiar. What I can recall is, that she was sent to gather wings. As soon as she had gathered a pair of wings for herself, she was to fly away, she said, to the country she came from; but where that was, she could give no information.

"She said she had to beg her wings from the butterflies and moths; and wherever she begged, no one refused her. But she needed a great many of the wings of butterflies and moths to make a pair for her; and so she had to wander about day after day, looking for butterflies, and night after night, looking for moths; and then she begged for their wings. But the day before, she had come into a part of the forest, she said, where there were multitudes of splendid butterflies flitting about, with wings which were just fit to make the eyes in the shoulders of hers; and she knew she could have as many of them as she liked for the asking; but as soon as she began to beg, there came a great creature right up to her, and threw her down, and walked over her. When she got up, she saw the wood was full of these beings stalking about, and seeming to have nothing to do with each other. As soon as ever she began to beg, one of them walked over her; till at last in dismay, and in growing horror of the senseless creatures, she had run away to look for somebody to help her. I asked her what they were like. She said, like great men, made of wood, without knee-or elbow-joints, and without any noses or mouths or eyes in their faces. I laughed at the little maiden, thinking she was making child's game of me; but, although she burst out laughing too, she persisted in asserting the truth of her story."

"'Only come, knight, come and see; I will lead you.'

"So I armed myself, to be ready for anything that might happen, and followed the child; for, though I could make nothing of her story, I could see she was a little human being in need of some help or other. As she walked before me, I looked attentively at her. Whether or not it was from being so often knocked down and walked over, I could not tell, but her clothes were very much torn, and in several places her white skin was peeping through. I thought she was hump-backed; but on looking more closely, I saw, through the tatters of her frock—do not laugh at me —a bunch on each shoulder, of the most gorgeous colours. Looking yet more closely, I saw that they were of the shape of folded wings, and were made of all kinds of butterfly wings and moth wings, crowded together like the feathers on the individual butterfly pinion; but, like them, most beautifully arranged, and producing a perfect harmony of colour and shade. I could now more easily believe the rest of her story; especially as I saw, every now and then, a certain heaving motion in the wings, as if they longed to be uplifted and outspread. But beneath her scanty garments complete wings could not be concealed, and indeed, from her own story, they were yet unfinished.

"After walking for two or three hours (how the little girl found her way, I could not imagine), we came to a part of the forest, the very air of which was quivering with the motions of multitudes of resplendent butterflies; as gorgeous in colour, as if the eyes of peacocks' feathers had taken to flight, but of infinite variety of hue and form, only that the appearance of some kind of eye on each wing predomi- nated. 'There they are, there they are!' cried the child, in a tone of victory mingled with terror. Except for this tone, I should have thought she referred to the butter- flies, for I could see nothing else. But at that moment an enormous butterfly, whose wings had great eyes of blue surrounded by confused cloudy heaps of more dingy colouring, just like a break in the clouds on a stormy day towards evening, settled near us. The child instantly began murmuring: 'Butterfly, butterfly, give me your wings'; when, the moment after, she fell to the ground, and began crying as if hurt. I drew my sword and heaved a great blow in the direction in which the child had fallen. It struck something, and instantly the most grotesque imitation of a man became visible. You see this Fairy Land is full of oddities and all sorts of incredibly ridiculous things, which a man is compelled to meet and treat as real existences, although all the time he feels foolish for doing so. This being, if being it could be called, was like a block of wood roughly hewn into the mere outlines of a man; and hardly so, for it had but head, body, legs, and arms—the head without a face, and the limbs utterly formless. I had hewn off one of its legs, but the two portions moved on as best they could, quite independent of each other; so that I had done no good. I ran after it, and clove it in twain from the head downwards; but it could not be convinced that its vocation was not to walk over people; for, as soon as the little girl began her begging again, all three parts came bustling up; and if I had not interposed my weight between her and them, she would have been trampled again under them. I saw that something else must be done. If the wood was full of the creatures, it would be an endless work to chop them so small that they could do no injury; and then, besides, the parts would be so numerous, that the butterflies would be in danger from the drift of flying chips. I served this one so, however; and then told the girl to beg again, and point out the direction in which one was coming. I was glad to find, however, that I could now see him myself, and wondered how they could have been invisible before. I would not allow him to walk over the child; but while I kept him off, and she began begging again, another appeared; and it was all I could do, from the weight of my armour, to protect her from the stupid, persevering efforts of the two. But suddenly the right plan occurred to me. I tripped one of them up, and, taking him by the legs, set him up on his head, with his heels against a tree. I was delighted to find he could not move. Meantime the poor child was walked over by the other, but it was for the last time. Whenever one appeared, I followed the same plan—tripped him up and set him on his head; and so the little beggar was able to gather her wings without any trouble, which occupation she continued for several hours in my company."

"What became of her?" I asked.

"I took her home with me to my castle, and she told me all her story; but it seemed to me, all the time, as if I were hearing a child talk in its sleep. I could not arrange her story in my mind at all, although it seemed to leave hers in some certain order of its own. My wife—"

Here the knight checked himself, and said no more. Neither did I urge the conversation farther.

Thus we journeyed for several days, resting at night in such shelter as we could get; and when no better was to be had, lying in the forest under some tree, on a couch of old leaves.

I loved the knight more and more. I believe never squire served his master with more care and joyfulness than I. I tended his horse; I cleaned his armour; my skill in the craft enabled me to repair it when necessary; I watched his needs; and was well repaid for all by the love itself which I bore him.

"This," I said to myself, "is a true man. I will serve him, and give him all worship, seeing in him the imbodiment of what I would fain become. If I cannot be noble myself, I will yet be servant to his nobleness." He, in return, soon showed me such signs of friendship and respect, as made my heart glad; and I felt that, after all, mine would be no lost life, if I might wait on him to the world's end, although no smile but his should greet me, and no one but him should say, "Well done! He was a good servant!" at last. But I burned to do something more for him than the ordinary routine of a squire's duty permitted.

One afternoon, we began to observe an appearance of roads in the wood. Branches had been cut down, and openings made, where footsteps had worn no path below. These indications increased as we passed on, till, at length, we came into a long, narrow avenue, formed by felling the trees in its line, as the remaining roots evidenced. At some little distance, on both hands, we observed signs of similar avenues, which appeared to converge with ours, towards one spot. Along these we indistinctly saw several forms moving, which seemed, with ourselves, to approach the common centre. Our path brought us, at last, up to a wall of yew-trees, growing close together, and intertwining their branches so, that nothing could be seen beyond it. An opening was cut in it like a door, and all the wall was trimmed smooth and perpendicular. The knight dismounted, and waited till I had provided for his horse's comfort; upon which we entered the place together.

It was a great space, bare of trees, and enclosed by four walls of yew, similar to that through which we had entered. These trees grew to a very great height, and did not divide from each other till close to the top, where their summits formed a row of conical battlements all around the walls. The space contained was a parallelogram of great length. Along each of the two longer sides of the interior, were ranged three ranks of men, in white robes, standing silent and solemn, each with a sword by his side, although the rest of his costume and bearing was more priestly than soldierly. For some distance inwards, the space between these opposite rows was filled with a company of men and women and children, in holiday attire. The looks of all were directed inwards, towards the further end. Far beyond the crowd, in a long avenue, seeming to narrow in the distance, went the long rows of the white-robed men. On what the attention of the multitude was fixed, we could not tell, for the sun had set before we arrived, and it was growing dark within. It grew darker and darker. The multitude waited in silence. The stars began to shine down into the enclosure, and they grew brighter and larger every moment. A wind arose, and swayed the pinnacles of the tree-tops; and made a strange sound, half like music, half like moaning, through the close branches and leaves of the tree-walls. A young girl who stood beside me, clothed in the same dress as the priests, bowed her head, and grew pale with awe.

The knight whispered to me, "How solemn it is! Surely they wait to hear the voice of a prophet. There is something good near!"

But I, though somewhat shaken by the feeling expressed by my master, yet had an unaccountable conviction that here was something bad. So I resolved to be keenly on the watch for what should follow.

Suddenly a great star, like a sun, appeared high in the air over the temple, illuminating it throughout; and a great song arose from the men in white, which went rolling round and round the building, now receding to the end, and now approaching, down the other side, the place where we stood. For some of the singers were regularly ceasing, and the next to them as regularly taking up the song, so that it crept onwards with gradations produced by changes which could not themselves be detected, for only a few of those who were singing ceased at the same moment. The song paused; and I saw a company of six of the white-robed men walk up the centre of the human avenue, surrounding a youth gorgeously attired beneath his robe of white, and wearing a chaplet of flowers on his head. I followed them closely, with my keenest observation; and, by accompanying their slow progress with my eyes, I was able to perceive more clearly what took place when they arrived at the other end. I knew that my sight was so much more keen than that of most people, that I had good reason to suppose I should see more than the rest could, at such a distance. At the farther end a throne stood upon a platform, high above the heads of the surrounding priests. To this platform I saw the company begin to ascend, apparently by an inclined plane or gentle slope. The throne itself was elevated again, on a kind of square pedestal, to the top of which led a flight of steps. On the throne sat a majestic-looking figure, whose posture seemed to indicate a mixture of pride and benignity, as he looked down on the multitude below. The company ascended to the foot of the throne, where they all kneeled for some minutes; then they rose and passed round to the side of the pedestal upon which the throne stood. Here they crowded close behind the youth, putting him in the foremost place, and one of them opened a door in the pedestal, for the youth to enter. I was sure I saw him shrink back, and those crowding behind pushed him in. Then, again, arose a burst of song from the multitude in white, which lasted some time. When it ceased, a new company of seven commenced its march up the centre. As they advanced, I looked up at my master: his noble countenance was full of reverence and awe. Incapable of evil himself, he could scarcely suspect it in another, much less in a multitude such as this, and surrounded with such appearances of solemnity. I was certain it was the really grand accompaniments that overcame him; that the stars overhead, the dark towering tops of the yew-trees, and the wind that, like an unseen spirit, sighed through their branches, bowed his spirit to the belief, that in all these ceremonies lay some great mystical meaning which, his humility told him, his ignorance prevented him from understanding.

More convinced than before, that there was evil here, I could not endure that my master should be deceived; that one like him, so pure and noble, should respect what, if my suspicions were true, was worse than the ordinary deceptions of priest-craft. I could not tell how far he might be led to countenance, and otherwise support their doings, before he should find cause to repent bitterly of his error. I watched the new procession yet more keenly, if possible, than the former. This time, the central figure was a girl; and, at the close, I observed, yet more indubitably, the shrinking back, and the crowding push. What happened to the victims, I never learned; but I had learned enough, and I could bear it no longer. I stooped, and whispered to the young girl who stood by me, to lend me her white garment. I wanted it, that I might not be entirely out of keeping with the solemnity, but might have at least this help to passing unquestioned. She looked up, half-amused and half-bewildered, as if doubting whether I was in earnest or not. But in her perplexity, she permitted me to unfasten it, and slip it down from her shoulders.

I easily got possession of it; and, sinking down on my knees in the crowd, I rose apparently in the habit of one of the worshippers.

Giving my battle-axe to the girl, to hold in pledge for the return of her stole, for I wished to test the matter unarmed, and, if it was a man that sat upon the throne, to attack him with hands bare, as I supposed his must be, I made my way through the crowd to the front, while the singing yet continued, desirous of reaching the platform while it was unoccupied by any of the priests. I was permitted to walk up the long avenue of white robes unmolested, though I saw questioning looks in many of the faces as I passed. I presume my coolness aided my passage; for I felt quite indifferent as to my own fate; not feeling, after the late events of my history, that I was at all worth taking care of; and enjoying, perhaps, something of an evil satisfaction, in the revenge I was thus taking upon the self which had fooled me so long. When I arrived on the platform, the song had just ceased, and I felt as if all were looking towards me. But instead of kneeling at its foot, I walked right up the stairs to the throne, laid hold of a great wooden image that seemed to sit upon it, and tried to hurl it from its seat. In this I failed at first, for I found it firmly fixed. But in dread lest, the first shock of amazement passing away, the guards would rush upon me before I had effected my purpose, I strained with all my might; and, with a noise as of the cracking, and breaking, and tearing of rotten wood, something gave way, and I hurled the image down the steps. Its displacement revealed a great hole in the throne, like the hollow of a decayed tree, going down apparently a great way. But I had no time to examine it, for, as I looked into it, up out of it rushed a great brute, like a wolf, but twice the size, and tumbled me headlong with itself, down the steps of the throne. As we fell, however, I caught it by the throat, and the moment we reached the platform, a struggle commenced, in which I soon got uppermost, with my hand upon its throat, and knee upon its heart. But now arose a wild cry of wrath and revenge and rescue. A universal hiss of steel, as every sword was swept from its scabbard, seemed to tear the very air in shreds. I heard the rush of hundreds towards the platform on which I knelt. I only tightened my grasp of the brute's throat. His eyes were already starting from his head, and his tongue was hanging out. My anxious hope was, that, even after they had killed me, they would be unable to undo my gripe of his throat, before the monster was past breathing. I therefore threw all my will, and force, and purpose, into the grasping hand. I remember no blow. A faintness came over me, and my consciousness departed.

CHAPTER 24

"We are ne'er like angels till our passions die."
  DEKKER.

"This wretched Inn, where we scarce stay to bait,
  We call our Dwelling-Place:
  We call one Step a Race:
  But angels in their full enlightened state,
  Angels, who Live, and know what 'tis to Be,
  Who all the nonsense of our language see,
  Who speak things, and our words, their ill-drawn
  pictures, scorn,
  When we, by a foolish figure, say,
  Behold an old man dead! then they
  Speak properly, and cry, Behold a man-child born!"
  COWLEY.

I was dead, and right content. I lay in my coffin, with my hands folded in peace. The knight, and the lady I loved, wept over me.

Her tears fell on my face.

"Ah!" said the knight, "I rushed amongst them like a madman. I hewed them down like brushwood. Their swords battered on me like hail, but hurt me not. I cut a lane through to my friend. He was dead. But he had throttled the monster, and I had to cut the handful out of its throat, before I could disengage and carry off his body. They dared not molest me as I brought him back."

"He has died well," said the lady.

My spirit rejoiced. They left me to my repose. I felt as if a cool hand had been laid upon my heart, and had stilled it. My soul was like a summer evening, after a heavy fall of rain, when the drops are yet glistening on the trees in the last rays of the down-going sun, and the wind of the twilight has begun to blow. The hot fever of life had gone by, and I breathed the clear mountain-air of the land of Death. I had never dreamed of such blessedness. It was not that I had in any way ceased to be what I had been. The very fact that anything can die, implies the existence of some-thing that cannot die; which must either take to itself another form, as when the seed that is sown dies, and arises again; or, in conscious existence, may, perhaps, continue to lead a purely spiritual life. If my passions were dead, the souls of the passions, those essential mysteries of the spirit which had imbodied themselves in the passions, and had given to them all their glory and wonderment, yet lived, yet glowed, with a pure, undying fire. They rose above their vanishing earthly garments, and disclosed themselves angels of light. But oh, how beautiful beyond the old form! I lay thus for a time, and lived as it were an unradiating existence; my soul a motionless lake, that received all things and gave nothing back; satisfied in still contemplation, and spiritual consciousness.

Ere long, they bore me to my grave. Never tired child lay down in his white bed, and heard the sound of his playthings being laid aside for the night, with a more luxurious satisfaction of repose than I knew, when I felt the coffin settle on the firm earth, and heard the sound of the falling mould upon its lid. It has not the same hollow rattle within the coffin, that it sends up to the edge of the grave. They buried me in no graveyard. They loved me too much for that, I thank them; but they laid me in the grounds of their own castle, amid many trees; where, as it was spring-time, were growing primroses, and blue-bells, and all the families of the woods

Now that I lay in her bosom, the whole earth, and each of her many births, was as a body to me, at my will. I seemed to feel the great heart of the mother beating into mine, and feeding me with her own life, her own essential being and nature. I heard the footsteps of my friends above, and they sent a thrill through my heart. I knew that the helpers had gone, and that the knight and the lady remained, and spoke low, gentle, tearful words of him who lay beneath the yet wounded sod. I rose into a single large primrose that grew by the edge of the grave, and from the window of its humble, trusting face, looked full in the countenance of the lady. I felt that I could manifest myself in the primrose; that it said a part of what I wanted to say; just as in the old time, I had used to betake myself to a song for the same end. The flower caught her eye. She stooped and plucked it, saying, "Oh, you beautiful creature!" and, lightly kissing it, put it in her bosom. It was the first kiss she had ever given me. But the flower soon began to wither, and I forsook it.

It was evening. The sun was below the horizon; but his rosy beams yet illumi-nated a feathery cloud, that floated high above the world. I arose, I reached the cloud; and, throwing myself upon it, floated with it in sight of the sinking sun. He sank, and the cloud grew gray; but the grayness touched not my heart. It carried its rose-hue within; for now I could love without needing to be loved again. The moon came gliding up with all the past in her wan face. She changed my couch into a ghostly pallor, and threw all the earth below as to the bottom of a pale sea of dreams. But she could not make me sad. I knew now, that it is by loving, and not by being loved, that one can come nearest the soul of another; yea, that, where two love, it is the loving of each other, and not the being loved by each other, that originates and perfects and assures their blessedness. I knew that love gives to him that loveth, power over any soul beloved, even if that soul know him not, bringing him inwardly close to that spirit; a power that cannot be but for good; for in proportion as selfishness intrudes, the love ceases, and the power which springs therefrom dies. Yet all love will, one day, meet with its return. All true love will, one day, behold its own image in the eyes of the beloved, and be humbly glad. This is possible in the realms of lofty Death. "Ah! my friends," thought I, "how I will tend you, and wait upon you, and haunt you with my love."

"My floating chariot bore me over a great city. Its faint dull sound steamed up into the air—a sound—how composed?" How many hopeless cries," thought I, "and how many mad shouts go to make up the tumult, here so faint where I float in eternal peace, knowing that they will one day be stilled in the surrounding calm, and that despair dies into infinite hope, and the seeming impossible there, is the law here!

"But, O pale-faced women, and gloomy-browed men, and forgotten children, how I will wait on you, and minister to you, and, putting my arms about you in the dark, think hope into your hearts, when you fancy no one is near! Soon as my senses have all come back, and have grown accustomed to this new blessed life, I will be among you with the love that healeth."

With this, a pang and a terrible shudder went through me; a writhing as of death convulsed me; and I became once again conscious of a more limited, even a bodily and earthly life.

CHAPTER 25

"Our life is no dream; but it ought to become one,
and perhaps will." —NOVALIS.

"And on the ground, which is my modres gate,
I knocke with my staf; erlich and late,
And say to hire, Leve mother, let me in."
CHAUCER, The Pardoneres Tale.

Sinking from such a state of ideal bliss, into the world of shadows which again closed around and infolded me, my first dread was, not unnaturally, that my own shadow had found me again, and that my torture had commenced anew. It was a sad revulsion of feeling. This, indeed, seemed to correspond to what we think death is, before we die. Yet I felt within me a power of calm endurance to which I had hitherto been a stranger. For, in truth, that I should be able if only to think such things as I had been thinking, was an unspeakable delight. An hour of such peace made the turmoil of a lifetime worth striving through.

I found myself lying in the open air, in the early morning, before sunrise. Over me rose the summer heaven, expectant of the sun. The clouds already saw him, coming from afar; and soon every dewdrop would rejoice in his individual presence within it.

I lay motionless for a few minutes; and then slowly rose and looked about me. I was on the summit of a little hill; a valley lay beneath, and a range of mountains closed up the view upon that side. But, to my horror, across the valley, and up the height of the opposing mountains, stretched, from my very feet, a hugely expanding shade. There it lay, long and large, dark and mighty. I turned away with a sick despair; when lo! I beheld the sun just lifting his head above the eastern hill, and the shadow that fell from me, lay only where his beams fell not. I danced for joy. It was only the natural shadow, that goes with every man who walks in the sun. As he arose, higher and higher, the shadow-head sank down the side of the opposite hill, and crept in across the valley towards my feet.

Now that I was so joyously delivered from this fear, I saw and recognised the country around me. In the valley below, lay my own castle, and the haunts of my childhood were all about me hastened home. My sisters received me with unspeakable joy; but I suppose they observed some change in me, for a kind of respect, with a slight touch of awe in it, mingled with their joy, and made me ashamed. They had been in great distress about me. On the morning of my disappearance, they had found the floor of my room flooded; and, all that day, a wondrous and nearly impervious mist had hung about the castle and grounds. I had been gone, they told me, twenty-one days. To me it seemed twenty-one years. Nor could I yet feel quite secure in my new experiences. When, at night, I lay down once more in my own bed, I did not feel at all sure that when I awoke, I should not find myself in some mysterious region of Fairy Land. My dreams were incessant and perturbed; but when I did awake, I saw clearly that I was in my own home.

My mind soon grew calm; and I began the duties of my new position, somewhat instructed, I hoped, by the adventures that had befallen me in Fairy Land. Could I translate the experience of my travels there, into common life? This was the question. Or must I live it all over again, and learn it all over again, in the other forms that belong to the world of men, whose experience yet runs parallel to that of Fairy Land? These questions I cannot answer yet. But I fear.

Even yet, I find myself looking round sometimes with anxiety, to see whether my shadow falls right away from the sun or no. I have never yet discovered any inclination to either side. And if I am not unfrequently sad, I yet cast no more of a shade on the earth, than most men who have lived in it as long as I. I have a strange feeling sometimes, that I am a ghost, sent into the world to minister to my fellow men, or, rather, to repair the wrongs I have already done.

May the world be brighter for me, at least in those portions of it, where my darkness falls not.

Thus I, who set out to find my Ideal, came back rejoicing that I had lost my Shadow.

When the thought of the blessedness I experienced, after my death in Fairy Land, is too high for me to lay hold upon it and hope in it, I often think of the wise woman in the cottage, and of her solemn assurance that she knew something too good to be told. When I am oppressed by any sorrow or real perplexity, I often feel as if I had only left her cottage for a time, and would soon return out of the vision, into it again. Sometimes, on such occasions, I find myself, unconsciously almost, looking about for the mystic mark of red, with the vague hope of entering her door, and being comforted by her wise tenderness. I then console myself by saying: "I have come through the door of Dismay; and the way back from the world into which that has led me, is through my tomb. Upon that the red sign lies, and I shall find it one day, and be glad."

I will end my story with the relation of an incident which befell me a few days ago. I had been with my reapers, and, when they ceased their work at noon, I had lain down under the shadow of a great, ancient beech-tree, that stood on the edge of the field. As I lay, with my eyes closed, I began to listen to the sound of the leaves overhead. At first, they made sweet inarticulate music alone; but, by-and-by, the sound seemed to begin to take shape, and to be gradually moulding itself into words; till, at last, I seemed able to distinguish these, half-dissolved in a little ocean of circumfluent tones: "A great good is coming—is coming—is coming to thee, Anodos;" and so over and over again. I fancied that the sound reminded me of the voice of the ancient woman, in the cottage that was four-square. I opened my eyes, and, for a moment, almost believed that I saw her face, with its many wrinkles and its young eyes, looking at me from between two hoary branches of the beech overhead. But when I looked more keenly, I saw only twigs and leaves, and the infinite sky, in tiny spots, gazing through between. Yet I know that good is coming to me— that good is always coming; though few have at all times the simplicity and the courage to believe it. What we call evil, is the only and best shape, which, for the person and his condition at the time, could be assumed by the best good. And so, *Farewell.*

CROSS PURPOSES AND THE SHADOWS

BY
GEORGE MACDONALD

PART I
CROSS PURPOSES

CHAPTER 1

Once upon a time, the Queen of Fairyland, finding her own subjects far too well-behaved to be amusing, took a sudden longing to have a mortal or two at her Court. So, after looking about her for some time, she fixed upon two to bring to Fairyland.

But how were they to be brought?

"Please your majesty," said at last the daughter of the prime-minister,

"I will bring the girl."

The speaker, whose name was Peaseblossom, after her great-great-grandmother, looked so graceful, and hung her head so apologetically, that the Queen said at once,—

"How will you manage it, Peaseblossom?"

"I will open the road before her, and close it behind her."

"I have heard that you have pretty ways of doing things; so you may try."

The court happened to be held in an open forest-glade of smooth turf, upon which there was just one mole-heap. As soon as the Queen had given her permission to Peaseblossom, up through the mole-heap came the head of a goblin, which cried out,—

"Please your majesty, I will bring the boy."

"You!" exclaimed the Queen. "How will you do it?"

The goblin began to wriggle himself out of the earth, as if he had been a snake, and the whole world his skin, till the court was convulsed with laughter. As soon as he got free, he began to roll over and over, in every possible manner, rotatory and cylindrical, all at once, until he reached the wood. The courtiers followed, holding their sides, so that the Queen was left sitting upon her throne in solitary state.

When they reached the wood, the goblin, whose name was Toadstool, was nowhere to be seen. While they were looking for him, out popped his head from the mole-heap again, with the words,—

"So, your majesty."

"You have taken your own time to answer," said the Queen, laughing.

"And my own way too, eh! your majesty?" rejoined Toadstool, grinning.

"No doubt. Well, you may try."

And the goblin, making as much of a bow as he could with only half his neck above ground, disappeared under it.

CHAPTER 2

No mortal, or fairy either, can tell where Fairyland begins and where it ends. But somewhere on the borders of Fairyland there was a nice country village, in which lived some nice country people.

Alice was the daughter of the squire, a pretty, good-natured girl, whom her friends called fairy-like, and others called silly.

One rosy summer evening, when the wall opposite her window was flaked all over with rosiness, she threw herself down on her bed, and lay gazing at the wall. The rose-colour sank through her eyes and dyed her brain, and she began to feel as if she were reading a story-book. She thought she was looking at a western sea, with the waves all red with sunset. But when the colour died out, Alice gave a sigh to see how commonplace the wall grew. "I wish it was always sunset!" she said, half aloud. "I don't like gray things."

"I will take you where the sun is always setting, if you like, Alice," said a sweet, tiny voice near her. She looked down on the coverlet of the bed, and there, looking up at her, stood a lovely little creature. It seemed quite natural that the little lady should be there; for many things we never could believe, have only to happen, and then there is nothing strange about them. She was dressed in white, with a cloak of sunset-red—the colours of the sweetest of sweet-peas. On her head was a crown of twisted tendrils, with a little gold beetle in front.

"Are you a fairy?" said Alice.

"Yes. Will you go with me to the sunset?"

"Yes, I will."

When Alice proceeded to rise, she found that she was no bigger than the fairy; and when she stood up on the counterpane, the bed looked like a great hall with a painted ceiling. As she walked towards Peaseblossom, she stumbled several times over the tufts that made the pattern. But the fairy took her by the hand and led her towards the foot of the bed. Long before they reached it, however, Alice saw that the fairy was a tall, slender lady, and that she herself was quite her own size. What she had taken for tufts on the counterpane were really bushes of furze, and broom, and heather, on the side of a slope.

"Where are we?" asked Alice.

"Going on," answered the fairy.

Alice, not liking the reply, said,—

"I want to go home."

"Good-bye, then!" answered the fairy.

Alice looked round. A wide, hilly country lay all about them. She could not even tell from what quarter they had come.

"I must go with you, I see," she said.

Before they reached the bottom, they were walking over the loveliest meadow-grass. A little stream went cantering down beside them, without channel or bank, sometimes running between the blades, sometimes sweeping the grass all one way under it. And it made a great babbling for such a little stream and such a smooth course.

Gradually the slope grew gentler, and the stream flowed more softly and spread out wider. At length they came to a wood of long, straight poplars, growing out of the water, for the stream ran into the wood, and there stretched out into a lake. Alice thought they could go no farther; but Peaseblossom led her straight on, and they walked through.

It was now dark; but everything under the water gave out a pale, quiet light. There were deep pools here and there, but there was no mud, or frogs, or water-lizards, or eels. All the bottom was pure, lovely grass, brilliantly green. Down the banks of the pools she saw, all under water, primroses and violets and pimpernels. Any flower she wished to see she had only to look for, and she was sure to find it. When a pool came in their way, the fairy swam, and Alice swam by her; and when they got out they were quite dry, though the water was as delightfully wet as water should be. Besides the trees, tall, splendid lilies grew out of it, and hollyhocks and irises and sword-plants, and many other long-stemmed flowers. From every leaf and petal of these, from every branch-tip and tendril, dropped bright water. It gathered slowly at each point, but the points were so many that there was a constant musical plashing of diamond rain upon the still surface of the lake. As they went on, the moon rose and threw a pale mist of light over the whole, and the diamond drops turned to half-liquid pearls, and round every tree-top was a halo of moonlight, and the water went to sleep, and the flowers began to dream.

"Look," said the fairy; "those lilies are just dreaming themselves into a child's sleep. I can see them smiling. This is the place out of which go the things that appear to children every night."

"Is this dreamland, then?" asked Alice.

"If you like," answered the fairy.

"How far am I from home?"

"The farther you go, the nearer home you are."

Then the fairy lady gathered a bundle of poppies and gave it to Alice. The next deep pool that they came to, she told her to throw it in. Alice did so, and following it, laid her head upon it. That moment she began to sink. Down and down she went, till at last she felt herself lying on the long, thick grass at the bottom of the pool, with the poppies under her head and the clear water high over it. Up through it she saw the moon, whose bright face looked sleepy too, disturbed only by the little ripples of the rain from the tall flowers on the edges of the pool.

She fell fast asleep, and all night dreamed about home.

CHAPTER 3

Richard—which is name enough for a fairy story—was the son of a widow in Alice's village. He was so poor that he did not find himself generally welcome; so he hardly went anywhere, but read books at home, and waited upon his mother. His manners, therefore, were shy, and sufficiently awkward to give an unfavourable impression to those who looked at outsides. Alice would have despised him; but he never came near enough for that.

Now Richard had been saving up his few pence in order to buy an umbrella for his mother; for the winter would come, and the one she had was almost torn to ribands. One bright summer evening, when he thought umbrellas must be cheap, he was walking across the market-place to buy one: there, in the middle of it, stood an odd-looking little man, actually selling umbrellas. Here was a chance for him! When he drew nearer, he found that the little man, while vaunting his umbrellas to the skies, was asking such absurdly small prices for them, that no one would venture to buy one. He had opened and laid them all out at full stretch on the market-place—about five-and-twenty of them, stick downwards, like little tents— and he stood beside, haranguing the people. But he would not allow one of the crowd to touch his umbrellas. As soon as his eye fell upon Richard, he changed his tone, and said, "Well, as nobody seems inclined to buy, I think, my dear umbrellas, we had better be going home." Whereupon the umbrellas got up, with some diffi- culty, and began hobbling away. The people stared at each other with open mouths, for they saw that what they had taken for a lot of umbrellas, was in reality a flock of black geese. A great turkey-cock went gobbling behind them, driving them all down a lane towards the forest. Richard thought with himself, "There is more in this than I can account for. But an umbrella that could lay eggs would be a very jolly umbrella." So by the time the people were beginning to laugh at each other, Richard was half-way down the lane at the heels of the geese. There he stooped and caught one of them, but instead of a goose he had a huge hedgehog in his hands, which he dropped in dismay; whereupon it waddled away a goose as before, and the whole of them began cackling and hissing in a way that he could not mistake. For the turkey-cock, he gobbled and gabbled and choked himself and got right again in the most ridiculous manner. In fact, he seemed sometimes to forget that he was a turkey, and laughed like a fool. All at once, with a simultaneous long-necked hiss, they flew into the wood, and the turkey after them. But Richard soon got up with them again, and found them all hanging by their feet from the trees, in two rows, one on each side of the path, while the turkey was walking on. Him Richard followed; but the moment he reached the middle of the suspended geese, from every side arose the most frightful hisses, and their necks grew longer and longer, till there were nearly thirty broad bills close to his head, blowing in his face, in his ears, and at the back of his neck. But the turkey, looking round and seeing what was going on, turned and walked back. When he reached the place, he looked up at the first and gobbled at him in the wildest manner. That goose grew silent and dropped from the tree. Then he went to the next, and the next, and so on, till he had gobbled them all off the trees, one after another. But when Richard expected to see them go after the turkey, there was nothing there but a flock of huge mushrooms and puff-balls.

"I have had enough of this," thought Richard. "I will go home again."

"Go home, Richard," said a voice close to him.

Looking down, he saw, instead of the turkey, the most comical-looking little man he had ever seen.

"Go home, Master Richard," repeated he, grinning.

"Not for your bidding," answered Richard.

"Come on, then, Master Richard."

"Nor that either, without a good reason."

"I will give you such an umbrella for your mother."

"I don't take presents from strangers."

"Bless you, I'm no stranger here! Oh, no! not at all." And he set off in the manner usual with him, rolling every way at once.

Richard could not help laughing and following. At length Toadstool plumped into a great hole full of water. "Served him right!" thought Richard. "Served him right!" bawled the goblin, crawling out again, and shaking the water from him like a spaniel. "This is the very place I wanted, only I rolled too fast." However, he went on rolling again faster than before, though it was now uphill, till he came to the top of a considerable height, on which grew a number of palm-trees.

"Have you a knife, Richard?" said the goblin, stopping all at once, as if he had been walking quietly along, just like other people.

Richard pulled out a pocket-knife and gave it to the creature, who instantly cut a deep gash in one of the trees. Then he bounded to another and did the same, and so on till he had gashed them all. Richard, following him, saw that a little stream, clearer than the clearest water, began to flow from each, increasing in size the longer it flowed. Before he had reached the last there was quite a tinkling and rustling of the little rills that ran down the stems of the palms. This grew and grew, till Richard saw that a full rivulet was flowing down the side of the hill.

"Here is your knife, Richard," said the goblin; but by the time he had put it in his pocket, the rivulet had grown to a small torrent.

"Now, Richard, come along," said Toadstool, and threw himself into the torrent.

"I would rather have a boat," returned Richard.

"Oh, you stupid!" cried Toadstool crawling up the side of the hill, down which the stream had already carried him some distance.

With every contortion that labour and difficulty could suggest, yet with incredible rapidity, he crawled to the very top of one of the trees, and tore down a huge leaf, which he threw on the ground, and himself after it, rebounding like a ball. He then laid the leaf on the water, held it by the stem, and told Richard to get upon it. He did so. It went down deep in the middle with his weight. Toadstool let it go, and it shot down the stream like an arrow. This began the strangest and most delightful voyage. The stream rushed careering and curveting down the hill-side, bright as a diamond, and soon reached a meadow plain. The goblin rolled alongside of the boat like a bundle of weeds; but Richard rode in triumph through the low grassy country upon the back of his watery steed. It went straight as an arrow, and, strange to tell, was heaped up on the ground, like a ridge of water or a wave, only rushing on endways. It needed no channel, and turned aside for no opposition. It flowed over everything that crossed its path, like a great serpent of water, with folds fitting into all the ups and downs of the way. If a wall came in its course it flowed against it, heaping itself up on itself till it reached the top, whence it plunged to the foot on the other side, and flowed on. Soon he found that it was running gently up a grassy hill. The waves kept curling back as if the wind blew them, or as if they could hardly keep from running down again. But still the stream mounted and flowed, and the waves with it. It found it difficult, but it could do it. When they reached the top, it bore them across a heathy country, rolling over purple heather, and blue harebells, and delicate ferns, and tall foxgloves crowded with bells purple and white. All the time the palm-leaf curled its edges away from the water, and made a delightful boat for Richard, while Toadstool tumbled along in the stream like a porpoise. At length the water began to run very fast, and went faster and faster, till suddenly it plunged them into a deep lake, with a great splash, and stopped there. Toadstool went out of sight, and came up gasping and grinning, while Richard's boat tossed and heaved like a vessel in a storm at sea; but not a drop of water came in. Then the goblin began to swim, and pushed and tugged the boat along. But the lake was so still, and the motion so pleasant, that Richard fell fast asleep.

CHAPTER 4

When he woke he found himself still afloat upon the broad palm-leaf. He was alone in the middle of a lake, with flowers and trees growing in and out of it everywhere. The sun was just over the tree-tops. A drip of water from the flowers greeted him with music; the mists were dissolving away, and where the sunlight fell on the lake the water was clear as glass. Casting his eyes downward, he saw, just beneath him, far down at the bottom, Alice drowned, as he thought. He was in the act of plunging in, when he saw her open her eyes, and at the same moment begin to float up. He held out his hand, but she repelled it with disdain, and swimming to a tree, sat down on a low branch, wondering how ever the poor widow's son could have found his way into Fairyland. She did not like it. It was an invasion of privilege.

"How did you come here, young Richard?" she asked, from six yards off.

"A goblin brought me."

"Ah! I thought so. A fairy brought me."

"Where is your fairy?"

"Here I am," said Peaseblossom, rising slowly to the surface just by the tree on which Alice was seated.

"Where is your goblin?" retorted Alice.

"Here I am," bawled Toadstool, rushing out of the water like a salmon, and casting a summersault in the air before he fell in again with a tremendous splash. His head rose again close beside Peaseblossom, who being used to such creatures only laughed.

"Isn't he handsome?" he grinned.

"Yes, very. He wants polishing, though."

"You could do that for yourself, you know. Shall we change?"

"I don't mind. You'll find her rather silly."

"That's nothing. The boy's too sensible for me."

He dived, and rose at Alice's feet. She shrieked with terror. The fairy floated away like a water-lily towards Richard. "What a lovely creature!" thought he; but hearing Alice shriek again, he said,

"Don't leave Alice; she's frightened at that queer creature.—I don't think there's any harm in him, though, Alice."

"Oh, no! He won't hurt her," said Peaseblossom. "I'm tired of her. He's going to take her to the court, and I will take you."

"I don't want to go."

"But you must. You can't go home again. You don't know the way."

"Richard! Richard!" cried Alice, in an agony.

Richard sprang from his boat, and was by her side in a moment.

"He pinched me," cried Alice.

Richard hit the goblin a terrible blow on the head; but it took no more effect upon him than if his head had been a round ball of india-rubber. He gave Richard a furious look, however, and bawling out, "You'll repent that, Dick!" vanished under the water.

"Come along, Richard; make haste; he will murder you," cried the fairy.

"It is all your fault," said Richard. "I won't leave Alice."

Then the fairy saw it was all over with her and Toadstool; for they can do nothing with mortals against their will. So she floated away across the water in Richard's boat, holding her robe for a sail, and vanished, leaving the two alone in the lake.

"You have driven away my fairy!" cried Alice. "I shall never get home now. It is all your fault, you naughty young man."

"I drove away the goblin," remonstrated Richard.

"Will you please to sit on the other side of the tree? I wonder what my papa would say if he saw me talking to you!"

"Will you come to the next tree, Alice?" said Richard, after a pause.

Alice, who had been crying all the time that Richard was thinking, said "I won't." Richard, therefore, plunged into the water without her, and swam for the tree. Before he had got half-way, however, he heard Alice crying "Richard! Richard!" This was just what he wanted. So he turned back, and Alice threw herself into the water. With Richard's help she swam pretty well, and they reached the tree. "Now for the next!" said Richard; and they swam to the next, and then to the third. Every tree they reached was larger than the last, and every tree before them was larger still. So they swam from tree to tree, till they came to one that was so large that they could not see round it. What was to be done? Clearly to climb this tree. It was a dreadful prospect for Alice, but Richard proceeded to climb; and by putting her feet where he put his, and now and then getting hold of his ankle, she managed to make her way up. There were a great many stumps where branches had withered off, and the bark was nearly as rough as a hill-side, so there was plenty of foothold for them. When they had climbed a long time, and were getting very tired indeed, Alice cried out, "Richard, I shall drop—I shall. Why did you come this way?" And she began once more to cry. But at that moment Richard caught hold of a branch above his head, and reaching down his other hand got hold of Alice, and held her till she had recovered a little. In a few moments more they reached the fork of the tree, and there they sat and rested. "This is capital!" said Richard, cheerily.

"What is?" asked Alice, sulkily.

"Why, we have room to rest, and there's no hurry for a minute or two.

I'm tired."

"You selfish creature!" said Alice. "If you are tired, what must I be!"

"Tired too," answered Richard. "But we've got on bravely. And look! what's that?"

By this time the day was gone, and the night so near, that in the shadows of the tree all was dusky and dim. But there was still light enough to discover that in a niche of the tree sat a huge horned owl, with green spectacles on his beak, and a book in one foot. He took no heed of the intruders, but kept muttering to himself. And what do you think the owl was saying? I will tell you. He was talking about the book that he held upside down in his foot.

"Stupid book this-s-s-s! Nothing in it at all! Everything upside down!

Stupid ass-s-s-s! Says owls can't read! I can read backwards!"

"I think that is the goblin again," said Richard, in a whisper. "However, if you ask a plain question, he must give you a plain answer, for they are not allowed to tell downright lies in Fairyland."

"Don't ask him, Richard; you know you gave him a dreadful blow."

"I gave him what he deserved, and he owes me the same.—Hallo! which is the way out?"

He wouldn't say if you please, because then it would not have been a plain question.

"Down-stairs," hissed the owl, without ever lifting his eyes from the book, which all the time he read upside down, so learned was he.

"On your honour, as a respectable old owl?" asked Richard.

"No," hissed the owl; and Richard was almost sure that he was not really an owl. So he stood staring at him for a few moments, when all at once, without lifting his eyes from the book, the owl said, "I will sing a song," and began:—

"Nobody knows the world but me.
    When they're all in bed, I sit up to see
    I'm a better student than students all,
    For I never read till the darkness fall;
    And I never read without my glasses,
    And that is how my wisdom passes.
      Howlowlwhoolhoolwoolool.

"I can see the wind. Now who can do that?
    I see the dreams that he has in his hat;
    I see him snorting them out as he goes—
    Out at his stupid old trumpet-nose.
    Ten thousand things that you couldn't think
    I write them down with pen and ink.
      Howlowlwhoolootwhitit that's wit.

163

"You may call it learning—'tis mother-wit.
   No one else sees the lady-moon sit
   On the sea, her nest, all night, but the owl,
   Hatching the boats and the long-legged fowl.
   When the oysters gape to sing by rote,
   She crams a pearl down each stupid throat.
   Howlowlwhitit that's wit, there's a fowl!"

And so singing, he threw the book in Richard's face, spread out his great, silent, soft wings, and sped away into the depths of the tree. When the book struck Richard, he found that it was only a lump of wet moss.

While talking to the owl he had spied a hollow behind one of the branches. Judging this to be the way the owl meant, he went to see, and found a rude, ill-defined staircase going down into the very heart of the trunk. But so large was the tree that this could not have hurt it in the least. Down this stair, then, Richard scrambled as best he could, followed by Alice—not of her own will, she gave him clearly to understand, but because she could do no better. Down, down they went, slipping and falling sometimes, but never very far, because the stair went round and round. It caught Richard when he slipped, and he caught Alice when she did. They had begun to fear that there was no end to the stair, it went round and round so steadily, when, creeping through a crack, they found themselves in a great hall, supported by thousands of pillars of gray stone. Where the little light came from they could not tell. This hall they began to cross in a straight line, hoping to reach one side, and intending to walk along it till they came to some opening. They kept straight by going from pillar to pillar, as they had done before by the trees. Any honest plan will do in Fairyland, if you only stick to it. And no plan will do if you do not stick to it.

It was very silent, and Alice disliked the silence more than the dimness,—so much, indeed, that she longed to hear Richard's voice. But she had always been so cross to him when he had spoken, that he thought it better to let her speak first; and she was too proud to do that. She would not even let him walk alongside of her, but always went slower when he wanted to wait for her; so that at last he strode on alone. And Alice followed. But by degrees the horror of silence grew upon her, and she felt at last as if there was no one in the universe but herself. The hall went on widening around her; their footsteps made no noise; the silence grew so intense that it seemed on the point of taking shape. At last she could bear it no longer. She ran after Richard, got up with him, and laid hold of his arm.

He had been thinking for some time what an obstinate, disagreeable girl Alice was, and wishing he had her safe home to be rid of her, when, feeling a hand, and looking round, he saw that it was the disagreeable girl. She soon began to be companionable after a fashion, for she began to think, putting everything together, that Richard must have been several times in Fairyland before now. "It is very strange," she said to herself; "for he is quite a poor boy, I am sure of that. His arms stick out beyond his jacket like the ribs of his mother's umbrella. And to think of me wandering about Fairyland with him!"

The moment she touched his arm, they saw an arch of blackness before them. They had walked straight to a door—not a very inviting one, for it opened upon an utterly dark passage. Where there was only one door, however, there was no difficulty about choosing. Richard walked straight through it; and from the greater fear of being left behind, Alice faced the lesser fear of going on. In a moment they were in total darkness. Alice clung to Richard's arm, and murmured, almost against her will, "Dear Richard!" It was strange that fear should speak like love; but it was in Fairyland. It was strange, too, that as soon as she spoke thus, Richard should fall in love with her all at once. But what was more curious still was, that, at the same moment, Richard saw her face. In spite of her fear, which had made her pale, she looked very lovely.

"Dear Alice!" said Richard, "how pale you look!"

"How can you tell that, Richard, when all is as black as pitch?"

"I can see your face. It gives out light. Now I see your hands. Now I can see your feet. Yes, I can see every spot where you are going to—No, don't put your foot there. There is an ugly toad just there."

The fact was, that the moment he began to love Alice, his eyes began to send forth light. What he thought came from Alice's face, really came from his eyes. All about her and her path he could see, and every minute saw better; but to his own path he was blind. He could not see his hand when he held it straight before his face, so dark was it. But he could see Alice, and that was better than seeing the way —ever so much.

At length Alice too began to see a face dawning through the darkness. It was Richard's face; but it was far handsomer than when she saw it last. Her eyes had begun to give light too. And she said to herself—"Can it be that I love the poor widow's son?—I suppose that must be it," she answered herself, with a smile; for she was not disgusted with herself at all. Richard saw the smile, and was glad. Her paleness had gone, and a sweet rosiness had taken its place. And now she saw Richard's path as he saw hers, and between the two sights they got on well.

They were now walking on a path betwixt two deep waters, which never moved, shining as black as ebony where the eyelight fell. But they saw ere long that this path kept growing narrower and narrower. At last, to Alice's dismay, the black waters met in front of them.

"What is to be done now, Richard?" she said.

When they fixed their eyes on the water before them, they saw that it was swarming with lizards, and frogs, and black snakes, and all kinds of strange and ugly creatures, especially some that had neither heads, nor tails, nor legs, nor fins, nor feelers, being, in fact, only living lumps. These kept jumping out and in, and sprawling upon the path. Richard thought for a few moments before replying to Alice's question, as, indeed, well he might. But he came to the conclusion that the path could not have gone on for the sake of stopping there; and that it must be a kind of finger that pointed on where it was not allowed to go itself. So he caught up Alice in his strong arms, and jumped into the middle of the horrid swarm. And just as minnows vanish if you throw anything amongst them, just so these wretched creatures vanished, right and left and every way.

He found the water broader than he had expected; and before he got over, he found Alice heavier than he could have believed; but upon a firm, rocky bottom, Richard waded through in safety. When he reached the other side, he found that the bank was a lofty, smooth, perpendicular rock, with some rough steps cut in it. By and by the steps led them right into the rock, and they were in a narrow passage once more, but, this time, leading up. It wound round and round, like the thread of a great screw. At last, Richard knocked his head against something, and could go no farther. The place was close and hot. He put up his hands, and pushed what felt like a warm stone: it moved a little.

"Go down, you brutes!" growled a voice above, quivering with anger. "You'll upset my pot and my cat, and my temper too, if you push that way. Go down!"

Richard knocked very gently, and said: "Please let us out."

"Oh, yes, I dare say! Very fine and soft-spoken! Go down, you goblin brutes! I've had enough of you. I'll scald the hair off your ugly heads if you do that again. Go down, I say!"

Seeing fair speech was of no avail, Richard told Alice to go down a little, out of the way; and, setting his shoulders to one end of the stone, heaved it up; whereupon down came the other end, with a pot, and a fire, and a cat which had been asleep beside it. She frightened Alice dreadfully as she rushed past her, showing nothing but her green lamping eyes.

Richard, peeping up, found that he had turned a hearth-stone upside down. On the edge of the hole stood a little crooked old man, brandishing a mop-stick in a tremendous rage, and hesitating only where to strike him. But Richard put him out of his difficulty by springing up and taking the stick from him. Then, having lifted Alice out, he returned it with a bow, and, heedless of the maledictions of the old man, proceeded to get the stone and the pot up again. For puss, she got out of herself.

Then the old man became a little more friendly, and said: "I beg your pardon, I thought you were goblins. They never will let me alone. But you must allow, it was rather an unusual way of paying a morning call." And the creature bowed conciliatingly.

"It was, indeed," answered Richard. "I wish you had turned the door to us instead of the hearth-stone." For he did not trust the old man. "But," he added, "I hope you will forgive us."

"Oh, certainly, certainly, my dear young people! Use your freedom. But such young people have no business to be out alone. It is against the rules."

"But what is one to do—I mean two to do—when they can't help it?"

"Yes, yes, of course; but now, you know, I must take charge of you. So you sit there, young gentleman; and you sit there, young lady."

He put a chair for one at one side of the hearth, and for the other at the other side, and then drew his chair between them. The cat got upon his hump, and then set up her own. So here was a wall that would let through no moonshine. But although both Richard and Alice were very much amused, they did not like to be parted in this peremptory manner. Still they thought it better not to anger the old man any more—in his own house, too.

But he had been once angered, and that was once too often, for he had made it a rule never to forgive without taking it out in humiliation.

It was so disagreeable to have him sitting there between them, that they felt as if they were far asunder. In order to get the better of the fancy, they wanted to hold each other's hand behind the dwarf's back. But the moment their hands began to approach, the back of the cat began to grow long, and its hump to grow high; and, in a moment more, Richard found himself crawling wearily up a steep hill, whose ridge rose against the stars, while a cold wind blew drearily over it. Not a habitation was in sight; and Alice had vanished from his eyes. He felt, however, that she must be somewhere on the other side, and so climbed and climbed to get over the brow of the hill, and down to where he thought she must be. But the longer he climbed, the farther off the top of the hill seemed; till at last he sank quite exhausted, and—must I confess it?—very nearly began to cry. To think of being separated from Alice all at once, and in such a disagreeable way! But he fell a-thinking instead, and soon said to himself: "This must be some trick of that wretched old man. Either this mountain is a cat or it is not. If it is a mountain, this won't hurt it; if it is a cat, I hope it will." With that, he pulled out his pocket-knife, and feeling for a soft place, drove it at one blow up to the handle in the side of the mountain.

A terrific shriek was the first result; and the second, that Alice and he sat looking at each other across the old man's hump, from which the cat-a-mountain had vanished. Their host sat staring at the blank fireplace, without ever turning round, pretending to know nothing of what had taken place.

"Come along, Alice," said Richard, rising. "This won't do. We won't stop here."

Alice rose at once, and put her hand in his. They walked towards the door. The old man took no notice of them. The moon was shining brightly through the window; but instead of stepping out into the moonlight when they opened the door, they stepped into a great beautiful hall, through the high gothic windows of which the same moon was shining. Out of this hall they could find no way, except by a staircase of stone which led upwards. They ascended it together. At the top Alice let go Richard's hand to peep into a little room, which looked all the colours of the rainbow, just like the inside of a diamond. Richard went a step or two along a corridor, but finding she had left him, turned and looked into the chamber. He could see her nowhere. The room was full of doors; and she must have mistaken the door. He heard her voice calling him, and hurried in the direction of the sound. But he could see nothing of her. "More tricks," he said to himself. "It is of no use to stab this one. I must wait till I see what can be done." Still he heard Alice calling him, and still he followed, as well as he could. At length he came to a doorway, open to the air, through which the moonlight fell. But when he reached it, he found that it was high up in the side of a tower, the wall of which went straight down from his feet, without stair or descent of any kind. Again he heard Alice call him, and lifting his eyes, saw her, across a wide castle-court, standing at another door just like the one he was at, with the moon shining full upon her.

"All right, Alice!" he cried. "Can you hear me?"

"Yes," answered she.

"Then listen. This is all a trick. It is all a lie of that old wretch in the kitchen. Just reach out your hand, Alice dear."

Alice did as Richard asked her; and, although they saw each other many yards off across the court, their hands met.

"There! I thought so!" exclaimed Richard triumphantly. "Now, Alice, I don't believe it is more than a foot or two down to the court below, though it looks like a hundred feet. Keep fast hold of my hand, and jump when I count three." But Alice drew her hand from him in sudden dismay; whereupon Richard said, "Well, I will try first," and jumped. The same moment his cheery laugh came to Alice's ears, and she saw him standing safe on the ground, far below.

"Jump, dear Alice, and I will catch you," said he.

"I can't; I am afraid," answered she.

"The old man is somewhere near you. You had better jump," said Richard.

Alice sprang from the wall in terror, and only fell a foot or two into Richard's arms. The moment she touched the ground, they found themselves outside the door of a little cottage which they knew very well, for it was only just within the wood that bordered on their village. Hand in hand they ran home as fast as they could. When they reached a little gate that led into her father's grounds, Richard bade Alice good-bye. The tears came in her eyes. Richard and she seemed to have grown quite man and woman in Fairyland, and they did not want to part now. But they felt that they must. So Alice ran in the back way, and reached her own room before anyone had missed her. Indeed, the last of the red had not quite faded from the west.

As Richard crossed the market-place on his way home, he saw an umbrella-man just selling the last of his umbrellas. He thought the man gave him a queer look as he passed, and felt very much inclined to punch his head. But remembering how useless it had been to punch the goblin's head, he thought it better not.

In reward of their courage, the Fairy Queen sent them permission to visit Fairyland as often as they pleased; and no goblin or fairy was allowed to interfere with them.

For Peaseblossom and Toadstool, they were both banished from court, and compelled to live together, for seven years, in an old tree that had just one green leaf upon it.

Toadstool did not mind it much, but Peaseblossom did.

THE SHADOWS

Old Ralph Rinkelmann made his living by comic sketches, and all but lost it again by tragic poems. So he was just the man to be chosen king of the fairies, for in Fairyland the sovereignty is elective.

It is no doubt very strange that fairies should desire to have a mortal king; but the fact is, that with all their knowledge and power, they cannot get rid of the feeling that some men are greater than they are, though they can neither fly nor play tricks. So at such times as there happens to be twice the usual number of sensible electors, such a man as Ralph Rinkelmann gets to be chosen.

They did not mean to insist on his residence; for they needed his presence only on special occasions. But they must get hold of him somehow, first of all, in order to make him king. Once he was crowned, they could get him as often as they pleased; but before this ceremony there was a difficulty. For it is only between life and death that the fairies have power over grown-up mortals, and can carry them off to their country. So they had to watch for an opportunity.

Nor had they to wait long. For old Ralph was taken dreadfully ill; and while hovering between life and death, they carried him off, and crowned him king of Fairyland. But after he was crowned, it was no wonder, considering the state of his health, that he should not be able to sit quite upright on the throne of Fairyland; or that, in consequence, all the gnomes and goblins, and ugly, cruel things that live in the holes and corners of the kingdom, should take advantage of his condition, and run quite wild, playing him, king as he was, all sorts of tricks; crowding about his throne, climbing up the steps, and actually scrambling and quarrelling like mice about his ears and eyes, so that he could see and think of nothing else. But I am not going to tell anything more about this part of his adventures just at present. By strong and sustained efforts, he succeeded, after much trouble and suffering, in reducing his rebellious subjects to order. They all vanished to their respective holes and corners; and King Ralph, coming to himself, found himself in his bed, half propped up with pillows.

But the room was full of dark creatures, which gambolled about in the firelight in such a strange, huge, though noiseless fashion, that he thought at first that some of his rebellious goblins had not been subdued with the rest, but had followed him beyond the bounds of Fairyland into his own private house in London. How else could these mad, grotesque hippopotamus-calves make their ugly appearance in Ralph Rinkelmann's bed-room? But he soon found out that although they were like the underground goblins, they were very different as well, and would require quite different treatment. He felt convinced that they were his subjects too, but that he must have overlooked them somehow at his late coronation—if indeed they had been present; for he could not recollect that he had seen anything just like them before. He resolved, therefore, to pay particular attention to their habits, ways, and characters; else he saw plainly that they would soon be too much for him; as indeed this intrusion into his chamber, where Mrs. Rinkelmann, who must be queen if he was king, sat taking some tea by the fireside, evidently foreshadowed. But she, perceiving that he was looking about him with a more composed expression than his face had worn for many days, started up, and came quickly and quietly to his side, and her face was bright with gladness. Whereupon the fire burned up more cheerily; and the figures became more composed and respectful in their behaviour, retreating towards the wall like well-trained attendants. Then the king of Fairyland had some tea and dry toast, and leaning back on his pillows, nearly fell asleep; but not quite, for he still watched the intruders.

Presently the queen left the room to give some of the young princes and princesses their tea; and the fire burned lower, and behold, the figures grew as black and as mad in their gambols as ever! Their favourite games seemed to be Hide and Seek; Touch and Go; Grin and Vanish; and many other such; and all in the king's bed-chamber, too; so that it was quite alarming. It was almost as bad as if the house had been haunted by certain creatures which shall be nameless in a fairy story, because with them Fairyland will not willingly have much to do.

"But it is a mercy that they have their slippers on!" said the king to himself; for his head ached.

As he lay back, with his eyes half shut and half open, too tired to pay longer attention to their games, but, on the whole, considerably more amused than offended with the liberties they took, for they seemed good-natured creatures, and more frolicsome than positively ill-mannered, he became suddenly aware that two of them had stepped forward from the walls, upon which, after the manner of great spiders, most of them preferred sprawling, and now stood in the middle of the floor at the foot of his majesty's bed, becking and bowing and ducking in the most grotesquely obsequious manner; while every now and then they turned solemnly round upon one heel, evidently considering that motion the highest token of homage they could show.

"What do you want?" said the king.

"That it may please your majesty to be better acquainted with us," answered they. "We are your majesty's subjects."

"I know you are. I shall be most happy," answered the king.

"We are not what your majesty takes us for, though. We are not so foolish as your majesty thinks us."

"It is impossible to take you for anything that I know of," rejoined the king, who wished to make them talk, and said whatever came uppermost;—"for soldiers, sailors, or anything: you will not stand still long enough. I suppose you really belong to the fire brigade; at least, you keep putting its light out."

"Don't jest, please your majesty." And as they said the words—for they both spoke at once throughout the interview—they performed a grave somerset towards the king.

"Not jest!" retorted he; "and with you? Why, you do nothing but jest. What are you?"

"The Shadows, sire. And when we do jest, sire, we always jest in earnest. But perhaps your majesty does not see us distinctly."

"I see you perfectly well," returned the king.

"Permit me, however," rejoined one of the Shadows; and as he spoke he approached the king; and lifting a dark forefinger, he drew it lightly but carefully across the ridge of his forehead, from temple to temple. The king felt the soft gliding touch go, like water, into every hollow, and over the top of every height of that mountain-chain of thought. He had involuntarily closed his eyes during the operation, and when he unclosed them again, as soon as the finger was withdrawn, he found that they were opened in more senses than one. The room appeared to have extended itself on all sides, till he could not exactly see where the walls were; and all about it stood the Shadows motionless. They were tall and solemn; rather awful, indeed, in their appearance, notwithstanding many remarkable traits of grotesqueness, for they looked just like the pictures of Puritans drawn by Cavaliers, with long arms, and very long, thin legs, from which hung large loose feet, while in their countenances length of chin and nose predominated. The solemnity of their mien, however, overcame all the oddity of their form, so that they were very eerie indeed to look at, dressed as they all were in funereal black. But a single glance was all that the king was allowed to have; for the former operator waved his dusky palm across his vision, and once more the king saw only the fire-lighted walls, and dark shapes flickering about upon them. The two who had spoken for the rest seemed likewise to have vanished. But at last the king discovered them, standing one on each side of the fireplace. They kept close to the chimney-wall, and talked to each other across the length of the chimney-piece; thus avoiding the direct rays of the fire, which, though light is necessary to their appearing to human eyes, do not agree with them at all—much less give birth to them, as the king was soon to learn. After a few minutes they again approached the bed, and spoke thus:—

"It is now getting dark, please your majesty. We mean, out of doors in the snow. Your majesty may see, from where he is lying, the cold light of its great winding-sheet—a famous carpet for the Shadows to dance upon, your majesty. All our brothers and sisters will be at church now, before going to their night's work."

"Do they always go to church before they go to work?"

"They always go to church first."

"Where is the church?"

"In Iceland. Would your majesty like to see it?"

"How can I go and see it, when, as you know very well, I am ill in bed? Besides,

I should be sure to take cold in a frosty night like this, even if I put on the blankets, and took the feather-bed for a muff."

A sort of quivering passed over their faces, which seemed to be their mode of laughing. The whole shape of the face shook and fluctuated as if it had been some dark fluid; till by slow degrees of gathering calm, it settled into its former rest. Then one of them drew aside the curtains of the bed, and the window-curtains not having been yet drawn, the king beheld the white glimmering night outside, struggling with the heaps of darkness that tried to quench it; and the heavens full of stars, flashing and sparkling like live jewels. The other Shadow went towards the fire and vanished in it.

Scores of Shadows immediately began an insane dance all about the room; disappearing, one after the other, through the uncovered window, and gliding darkly away over the face of the white snow; for the window looked at once on a field of snow. In a few moments, the room was quite cleared of them; but instead of being relieved by their absence, the king felt immediately as if he were in a dead-house, and could hardly breathe for the sense of emptiness and desolation that fell upon him. But as he lay looking out on the snow, which stretched blank and wide before him, he spied in the distance a long dark line which drew nearer and nearer, and showed itself at last to be all the Shadows, walking in a double row, and carrying in the midst of them something like a bier. They vanished under the window, but soon reappeared, having somehow climbed up the wall of the house; for they entered in perfect order by the window, as if melting through the transparency of the glass.

They still carried the bier or litter. It was covered with richest furs, and skins of gorgeous wild beasts, whose eyes were replaced by sapphires and emeralds, that glittered and gleamed in the fire and snow light. The outermost skin sparkled with frost, but the inside ones were soft and warm and dry as the down under a swan's wing. The Shadows approached the bed, and set the litter upon it. Then a number of them brought a huge fur robe, and wrapping it round the king, laid him on the litter in the midst of the furs. Nothing could be more gentle and respectful than the way in which they moved him; and he never thought of refusing to go. Then they put something on his head, and, lifting the litter, carried him once round the room, to fall into order. As he passed the mirror he saw that he was covered with royal ermine, and that his head wore a wonderful crown of gold, set with none but red stones: rubies and carbuncles and garnets, and others whose names he could not tell, glowed gloriously around his head, like the salamandrine essence of all the Christmas fires over the world. A sceptre lay beside him—a rod of ebony, surmounted by a cone-shaped diamond, which, cut in a hundred facets, flashed all the hues of the rainbow, and threw coloured gleams on every side, that looked like Shadows too, but more ethereal than those that bore him. Then the Shadows rose gently to the window, passed through it, and sinking slowing upon the field of outstretched snow, commenced an orderly gliding rather than march along the frozen surface. They took it by turns to bear the king, as they sped with the swiftness of thought, in a straight line towards the north. The pole-star rose above their heads with visible rapidity; for indeed they moved quite as fast as sad thoughts, though not with all the speed of happy desires. England and Scotland slid past the litter of the king of the Shadows. Over rivers and lakes they skimmed and glided. They climbed the high mountains, and crossed the valleys with a fearless bound;

till they came to John-o'-Groat's house and the Northern Sea. The sea was not frozen; for all the stars shone as clear out of the deeps below as they shone out of the deeps above; and as the bearers slid along the blue-gray surface, with never a furrow in their track, so pure was the water beneath that the king saw neither surface, bottom, nor substance to it, and seemed to be gliding only through the blue sphere of heaven, with the stars above him, and the stars below him, and between the stars and him nothing but an emptiness, where, for the first time in his life, his soul felt that it had room enough.

At length they reached the rocky shores of Iceland. There they landed, still pursuing their journey. All this time the king felt no cold; for the red stones in his crown kept him warm, and the emerald and sapphire eyes of the wild beasts kept the frosts from settling upon his litter.

Oftentimes upon their way they had to pass through forests, caverns, and rock-shadowed paths, where it was so dark that at first the king feared he should lose his Shadows altogether. But as soon as they entered such places, the diamond in his sceptre began to shine and glow, and flash, sending out streams of light of all the colours that painter's soul could dream of; in which light the Shadows grew livelier and stronger than ever, speeding through the dark ways with an all but blinding swiftness. In the light of the diamond, too, some of their forms became more simple and human, while others seemed only to break out into a yet more untamable absurdity. Once, as they passed through a cave, the king actually saw some of their eyes—strange shadow-eyes; he had never seen any of their eyes before. But at the same moment when he saw their eyes, he knew their faces too, for they turned them full upon him for an instant; and the other Shadows, catching sight of these, shrank and shivered, and nearly vanished. Lovely faces they were; but the king was very thoughtful after he saw them, and continued rather troubled all the rest of the journey. He could not account for those faces being there, and the faces of Shadows, too, with living eyes.

But he soon found that amongst the Shgadows a man must learn never to be surprised at anything; for if he does not, he will soon grow quite stupid, in consequence of the endless recurrence of surprises.

At last they climbed up the bed of a little stream, and then, passing through a narrow rocky defile, came out suddenly upon the side of a mountain, overlooking a blue frozen lake in the very heart of mighty hills. Overhead, the aurora borealis was shivering and flashing like a battle of ten thousand spears. Underneath, its beams passed faintly over the blue ice and the sides of the snow-clad mountains, whose tops shot up like huge icicles all about, with here and there a star sparkling on the very tip of one. But as the northern lights in the sky above, so wavered and quivered, and shot hither and thither, the Shadows on the surface of the lake below; now gathering in groups, and now shivering asunder; now covering the whole surface of the lake, and anon condensed into one dark knot in the centre. Every here and there on the white mountains might be seen two or three shooting away towards the tops, to vanish beyond them, so that their number was gradually, though not visibly, diminishing.

"Please your majesty," said the Shadows, "this is our church—the Church of the Shadows."

And so saying, the king's body-guard set down the litter upon a rock, and plunged into the multitudes below. They soon returned, however, and bore the king down into the middle of the lake. All the Shadows came crowding round him, respectfully but fearlessly; and sure never such a grotesque assembly revealed itself before to mortal eyes. The king had seen all kind of gnomes, goblins, and kobolds at his coronation; but they were quite rectilinear figures compared with the insane lawlessness of form in which the Shadows rejoiced; and the wildest gambols of the former were orderly dances of ceremony beside the apparently aimless and wilful contortions of figure, and metamorphoses of shape, in which the latter indulged. They retained, however, all the time, to the surprise of the king, an identity, each of his own type, inexplicably perceptible through every change. Indeed this preservation of the primary idea of each form was more wonderful than the bewildering and ridiculous alterations to which the form itself was every moment subjected.

"What are you?" said the king, leaning on his elbow, and looking around him.

"The Shadows, your majesty," answered several voices at once.

"What Shadows?"

"The human Shadows. The Shadows of men, and women, and their children."

"Are you not the shadows of chairs and tables, and pokers and tongs, just as well?"

At this question a strange jarring commotion went through the assembly with a shock. Several of the figures shot up as high as the aurora, but instantly settled down again to human size, as if overmastering their feelings, out of respect to him who had roused them. One who had bounded to the highest visible icy peak, and as suddenly returned, now elbowed his way through the rest, and made himself spokesman for them during the remaining part of the dialogue.

"Excuse our agitation, your majesty," said he. "I see your majesty has not yet thought proper to make himself acquainted with our nature and habits."

"I wish to do so now," replied the king.

"We are the Shadows," repeated the Shadow solemnly.

"Well?" said the king.

"We do not often appear to men."

"Ha!" said the king.

"We do not belong to the sunshine at all. We go through it unseen, and only by a passing chill do men recognize an unknown presence."

"Ha!" said the king again.

"It is only in the twilight of the fire, or when one man or woman is alone with a single candle, or when any number of people are all feeling the same thing at once, making them one, that we show ourselves, and the truth of things."

"Can that be true that loves the night?" said the king.

"The darkness is the nurse of light," answered the Shadow.

"Can that be true which mocks at forms?" said the king.

"Truth rides abroad in shapeless storms," answered the Shadow.

"Ha! ha!" thought Ralph Rinkelmann, "it rhymes. The Shadow caps my questions with his answers. Very strange!" And he grew thoughtful again.

The Shadow was the first to resume.

"Please your majesty, may we present our petition?"

"By all means," replied the king. "I am not well enough to receive it in proper state."

"Never mind, your majesty. We do not care for much ceremony; and indeed none of us are quite well at present. The subject of our petition weighs upon us."

"Go on," said the king.

"Sire," began the Shadow, "our very existence is in danger. The various sorts of artificial light, both in houses and in men, women, and children, threaten to end our being. The use and the disposition of gaslights, especially high in the centres, blind the eyes by which alone we can be perceived. We are all but banished from towns. We are driven into villages and lonely houses, chiefly old farm-houses, out of which, even, our friends the fairies are fast disappearing. We therefore petition our king, by the power of his art, to restore us to our rights in the house itself, and in the hearts of its inhabitants."

"But," said the king, "you frighten the children."

"Very seldom, your majesty; and then only for their good. We seldom seek to frighten anybody. We mostly want to make people silent and thoughtful; to awe them a little, your majesty."

"You are much more likely to make them laugh," said the king.

"Are we?" said the Shadow.

And approaching the king one step, he stood quite still for a moment. The diamond of the king's sceptre shot out a vivid flame of violet light, and the king stared at the Shadow in silence, and his lip quivered. He never told what he saw then; but he would say:

"Just fancy what it might be if some flitting thoughts were to persist in staying to be looked at."

"It is only," resumed the Shadow, "when our thoughts are not fixed upon any particular object, that our bodies are subject to all the vagaries of elemental influences. Generally, amongst worldly men and frivolous women, we only attach ourselves to some article of furniture or of dress; and they never doubt that we are mere foolish and vague results of the dashing of the waves of the light against the solid forms of which their houses are full. We do not care to tell them the truth, for they would never see it. But let the worldly man—or the frivolous woman —and then—"

At each of the pauses indicated, the mass of Shadows throbbed and heaved with emotion; but they soon settled again into comparative stillness. Once more the Shadow addressed himself to speak. But suddenly they all looked up, and the king, following their gaze, saw that the aurora had begun to pale.

"The moon is rising," said the Shadow. "As soon as she looks over the mountains into the valley, we must be gone, for we have plenty to do by the moon; we are powerful in her light. But if your majesty will come here to-morrow night, your majesty may learn a great deal more about us, and judge for himself whether it be fit to accord our petition; for then will be our grand annual assembly, in which we report to our chiefs the things we have attempted, and the good or bad success we have had."

"If you send for me," returned the king, "I will come."

Ere the Shadow could reply, the tip of the moon's crescent horn peeped up from behind an icy pinnacle, and one slender ray fell on the lake. It shone upon no Shadows. Ere the eye of the king could again seek the earth after beholding the first brightness of the moon's resurrection, they had vanished; and the surface of the lake glittered gold and blue in the pale moonlight.

There the king lay, alone in the midst of the frozen lake, with the moon staring at him. But at length he heard from somewhere a voice that he knew.

"Will you take another cup of tea, dear?" said Mrs. Rinkelmann.

And Ralph, coming slowly to himself, found that he was lying in his own bed.

"Yes, I will," he answered; "and rather a large piece of toast, if you please; for I have been a long journey since I saw you last."

"He has not come to himself quite," said Mrs. Rinkelmann, between her and herself.

"You would be rather surprised," continued Ralph, "if I told you where I had been."

"I dare say I should," responded his wife.

"Then I will tell you," rejoined Ralph.

But at that moment, a great Shadow bounced out of the fire with a single huge leap, and covered the whole room. Then it settled in one corner, and Ralph saw it shaking its fist at him from the end of a preposterous arm. So he took the hint, and held his peace. And it was as well for him. For I happen to know something about the Shadows too; and I know that if he had told his wife all about it just then, they would not have sent for him the following evening.

But as the king, after finishing his tea and toast, lay and looked about him, the Shadows dancing in his room seemed to him odder and more inexplicable than ever. The whole chamber was full of mystery. So it generally was, but now it was more mysterious than ever. After all that he had seen in the Shadow-church, his own room and its Shadows were yet more wonderful and unintelligible than those.

This made it the more likely that he had seen a true vision; for instead of making common things look commonplace, as a false vision would have done, it had made common things disclose the wonderful that was in them.

"The same applies to all arts as well," thought Ralph Rinkelmann.

The next afternoon, as the twilight was growing dusky, the king lay wondering whether or not the Shadows would fetch him again. He wanted very much to go, for he had enjoyed the journey exceedingly, and he longed, besides, to hear some of the Shadows tell their stories. But the darkness grew deeper and deeper, and the shadows did not come. The cause was, that Mrs. Rinkelmann sat by the fire in the gloaming; and they could not carry off the king while she was there. Some of them tried to frighten her away by playing the oddest pranks on the walls, and floor, and ceiling; but altogether without effect; the queen only smiled, for she had a good conscience. Suddenly, however, a dreadful scream was heard from the nursery, and Mrs. Rinkelmann rushed upstairs to see what was the matter. No sooner had she gone than the two warders of the chimney-corners stepped out into the middle of the room, and said, in a low voice,—

"Is your majesty ready?"

"Have you no hearts?" said the king; "or are they as black as your faces? Did you not hear the child scream? I must know what is the matter with her before I go."

"Your majesty may keep his mind easy on that point," replied the warders. "We had tried everything we could think of to get rid of her majesty the queen, but without effect. So a young madcap Shadow, half against the will of the older ones of us, slipped upstairs into the nursery; and has, no doubt, succeeded in appalling the baby, for he is very lithe and long-legged.—Now, your majesty."

"I will have no such tricks played in my nursery," said the king, rather angrily. "You might put the child beside itself."

"Then there would be twins, your majesty. And we rather like twins."

"None of your miserable jesting! You might put the child out of her wits."

"Impossible, sire; for she has not got into them yet."

"Go away," said the king.

"Forgive us, your majesty. Really, it will do the child good; for that Shadow will, all her life, be to her a symbol of what is ugly and bad. When she feels in danger of hating or envying anyone, that Shadow will come back to her mind and make her shudder."

"Very well," said the king. "I like that. Let us go."

The Shadows went through the same ceremonies and preparations as before; during which, the young Shadow before-mentioned contrived to make such grimaces as kept the baby in terror, and the queen in the nursery, till all was ready. Then with a bound that doubled him up against the ceiling, and a kick of his legs six feet out behind him, he vanished through the nursery door, and reached the king's bed-chamber just in time to take his place with the last who were melting through the window in the rear of the litter, and settling down upon the snow beneath. Away they went as before, a gliding blackness over the white carpet. And it was Christmas-eve.

When they came in sight of the mountain-lake, the king saw that it was crowded over its whole surface with a changeful intermingling of Shadows. They were all talking and listening alternately, in pairs, trios, and groups of every size. Here and there large companies were absorbed in attention to one elevated above the rest, not in a pulpit, or on a platform, but on the stilts of his own legs, elongated for the nonce. The aurora, right overhead, lighted up the lake and the sides of the mountains, by sending down from the zenith, nearly to the surface of the lake, great folded vapours, luminous with all the colours of a faint rainbow.

Many, however, as the words were that passed on all sides, not a shadow of a sound reached the ears of the king: the shadow-speech could not enter his corporeal organs. One of his guides, however, seeing that the king wanted to hear and could not, went through a strange manipulation of his head and ears; after which he could hear perfectly, though still only the voice to which, for the time, he directed his attention. This, however, was a great advantage, and one which the king longed to carry back with him to the world of men.

The king now discovered that this was not merely the church of the Shadows, but their news exchange at the same time. For, as the shadows have no writing or printing, the only way in which they can make each other acquainted with their doings and thinkings, is to meet and talk at this word-mart and parliament of shades. And as, in the world, people read their favourite authors, and listen to their favourite speakers, so here the Shadows seek their favourite Shadows, listen to their adventures, and hear generally what they have to say.

Feeling quite strong, the king rose and walked about amongst them, wrapped in his ermine robe, with his red crown on his head, and his diamond sceptre in his hand. Every group of Shadows to which he drew near, ceased talking as soon as they saw him approach; but at a nod they went on again directly, conversing and relating and commenting, as if no one was there of other kind or of higher rank than themselves. So the king heard a good many stories. At some of them he laughed, and at some of them he cried. But if the stories that the Shadows told were printed, they would make a book that no publisher could produce fast enough to satisfy the buyers. I will record some of the things that the king heard, for he told them to me soon after. In fact, I was for some time his private secretary.

"I made him confess before a week was over," said a gloomy old Shadow.

"But what was the good of that?" rejoined a pert young one. "That could not undo what was done."

"Yes, it could."

"What! bring the dead to life?"

"No; but comfort the murderer. I could not bear to see the pitiable misery he was in. He was far happier with the rope round his neck, than he was with the purse in his pocket. I saved him from killing himself too."

"How did you make him confess?"

"Only by wallowing on the wall a little."

"How could that make him tell?"

"He knows."

The Shadow was silent; and the king turned to another, who was preparing to speak.

"I made a fashionable mother repent."

"How?" broke from several voices, in whose sound was mingled a touch of incredulity.

"Only by making a little coffin on the wall," was the reply.

"Did the fashionable mother confess too?"

"She had nothing more to confess than everybody knew."

"What did everybody know then?"

"That she might have been kissing a living child, when she followed a dead one to the grave.—The next will fare better."

"I put a stop to a wedding," said another.

"Horrid shade!" remarked a poetic imp.

"How?" said others. "Tell us how."

"Only by throwing a darkness, as if from the branch of a sconce, over the forehead of a fair girl.—They are not married yet, and I do not think they will be. But I loved the youth who loved her. How he started! It was a revelation to him."

"But did it not deceive him?"

"Quite the contrary."

"But it was only a shadow from the outside, not a shadow coming through from the soul of the girl."

"Yes. You may say so. But it was all that was wanted to make the meaning of her forehead manifest—yes, of her whole face, which had now and then, in the pauses of his passion, perplexed the youth. All of it, curled nostrils, pouting lips, projecting chin, instantly fell into harmony with that darkness between her eyebrows. The youth understood it in a moment, and went home miserable. And they're not married yet."

"I caught a toper alone, over his magnum of port," said a very dark Shadow;

"and didn't I give it him! I made delirium tremens first; and then I settled into a funeral, passing slowly along the length of the opposite wall. I gave him plenty of plumes and mourning coaches. And then I gave him a funeral service, but I could not manage to make the surplice white, which was all the better for such a sinner. The wretch stared till his face passed from purple to grey, and actually left his fifth glass only, unfinished, and took refuge with his wife and children in the drawing-room, much to their surprise. I believe he actually drank a cup of tea; and although I have often looked in since, I have never caught him again, drinking alone at least."

"But does he drink less? Have you done him any good?"

"I hope so; but I am sorry to say I can't feel sure about it."

"Humph! Humph! Humph!" grunted various shadow throats.

"I had such fun once!" cried another. "I made such game of a young clergyman!"

"You have no right to make game of anyone."

"Oh yes, I have—when it is for his good. He used to study his sermons—where do you think?"

"In his study, of course. Where else should it be?"

"Yes and no. Guess again."

"Out amongst the faces in the streets."

"Guess again."

"In still green places in the country?"

"Guess again."

"In old books?"

"Guess again."

"No, no. Tell us."

"In the looking glass. Ha! ha! ha!"

"He was fair game; fair shadow game."

"I thought so. And I made such fun of him one night on the wall! He had sense enough to see that it was himself, and very like an ape. So he got ashamed, turned the mirror with its face to the wall, and thought a little more about his people, and a little less about himself. I was very glad; for, please your majesty,"—and here the speaker turned towards the king—"we don't like the creatures that live in the mirrors. You call them ghosts, don't you?"

Before the king could reply, another had commenced. But the story about the clergyman had made the king wish to hear one of the shadow-sermons. So he turned him towards a long Shadow, who was preaching to a very quiet and listening crowd. He was just concluding his sermon.

"Therefore, dear Shadows, it is the more needful that we love one another as much as we can, because that is not much. We have no such excuse for not loving as mortals have, for we do not die like them. I suppose it is the thought of that death that makes them hate so much. Then again, we go to sleep all day, most of us, and not in the night, as men do. And you know that we forget everything that happened the night before; therefore, we ought to love well, for the love is short. Ah! dear Shadow, whom I love now with all my shadowy soul, I shall not love thee to-morrow eve, I shall not know thee; I shall pass thee in the crowd and never dream that the Shadow whom I now love is near me then. Happy Shades! for we only remember our tales until we have told them here, and then they vanish in the shadow-churchyard, where we bury only our dead selves. Ah! brethren, who would be a man and remember? Who would be a man and weep? We ought indeed to love one another, for we alone inherit oblivion; we alone are renewed with eternal birth; we alone have no gathered weight of years. I will tell you the awful fate of one Shadow who rebelled against his nature, and sought to remember the past. He said, 'I will remember this eve.' He fought with the genial influences of kindly sleep when the sun rose on the awful dead day of light; and although he could not keep quite awake, he dreamed of the foregone eve, and he never forgot his dream. Then he tried again the next night, and the next, and the next; and he tempted another Shadow to try it with him. But at last their awful fate overtook them; for, instead of continuing to be Shadows, they began to cast shadows, as foolish men say; and so they thickened and thickened till they vanished out of our world. They are now condemned to walk the earth, a man and a woman, with death behind them, and memories within them. Ah, brother Shades! let us love one another, for we shall soon forget. We are not men, but Shadows."

The king turned away, and pitied the poor Shadows far more than they pitied men.

"Oh! how we played with a musician one night!" exclaimed a Shadow in another group, to which the king had first directed a passing thought, and then had stopped to listen.—"Up and down we went, like the hammers and dampers on his piano. But he took his revenge on us. For after he had watched us for half an hour in the twilight, he rose and went to his instrument, and played a shadow-dance that fixed us all in sound for ever. Each could tell the very notes meant for him; and as long as he played, we could not stop, but went on dancing and dancing after the music, just as the magician—I mean the musician—pleased. And he punished us well; for he nearly danced us all off our legs and out of shape into tired heaps of collapsed and palpitating darkness. We won't go near him for some time again, if we can only remember it. He had been very miserable all day, he was so poor; and we could not think of any way of comforting him except making him laugh. We did not succeed, with our wildest efforts; but it turned out better than we had expected, after all; for his shadow-dance got him into notice, and he is quite popular now, and making money fast.—If he does not take care, we shall have other work to do with him by and by, poor fellow!"

"I and some others did the same for a poor play-writer once. He had a Christmas piece to write, and [not] being an original genius, it was not so easy for him to find a subject as it is for most of his class. I saw the trouble he was in, and collecting a few stray Shadows, we acted, in dumb-show of course, the funniest bit of nonsense we could think of; and it was quite successful. The poor fellow watched every motion, roaring with laughter at us, and delight at the ideas we put into his head. He turned it all into words, and scenes, and actions; and the piece came off with a splendid success."

"But how long we have to look for a chance of doing anything worth doing," said a long, thin, especially lugubrious Shadow. "I have only done one thing worth telling ever since we met last. But I am proud of that."

"What was it? What was it?" rose from twenty voices.

"I crept into a dining-room, one twilight, soon after Christmas-day. I had been drawn thither by the glow of a bright fire shining through red window-curtains. At first I thought there was no one there, and was on the point of leaving the room, and going out again into the snowy street, when I suddenly caught the sparkle of eyes. I found that they belonged to a little boy who lay very still on a sofa. I crept into a dark corner by the sideboard, and watched him. He seemed very sad, and did nothing but stare into the fire. At last he sighed out,—'I wish mamma would come home.' 'Poor boy!' thought I, 'there is no help for that but mamma.' Yet I would try to while away the time for him. So out of my corner I stretched a long shadow arm, reaching all across the ceiling, and pretended to make a grab at him. He was rather frightened at first; but he was a brave boy, and soon saw that it was all a joke. So when I did it again, he made a clutch at me; and then we had such fun! For though he often sighed and wished mamma would come home, he always began again with me; and on we went with the wildest games. At last his mother's knock came to the door, and starting up in delight, he rushed into the hall to meet her, and forgot all about poor black me. But I did not mind that in the least; for when I glided out after him into the hall, I was well repaid for my trouble by hearing his mother say to him,—'Why, Charlie, my dear, you look ever so much better since I left you!' At that moment I slipped through the closing door, and as I ran across the snow, I heard the mother say,—'What shadow can that be, passing so quickly?' And Charlie answered with a merry laugh,—'Oh! mamma, I suppose it must be the funny shadow that has been playing such games with me all the time you were out.' As soon as the door was shut, I crept along the wall and looked in at the dining-room window. And I heard his mamma say, as she led him into the room, 'What an imagination the boy has!' Ha! ha! ha! Then she looked at him, and the tears came in her eyes; and she stooped down over him, and I heard the sounds of a mingling kiss and sob."

"I always look for nurseries full of children," said another; "and this winter I have been very fortunate. I am sure children belong especially to us. One evening, looking about in a great city, I saw through the window into a large nursery, where the odious gas had not yet been lighted. Round the fire sat a company of the most delightful children I had ever seen. They were waiting patiently for their tea. It was too good an opportunity to be lost. I hurried away, and gathering together twenty of the best Shadows I could find, returned in a few moments; and entering the nursery, we danced on the walls one of our best dances. To be sure it was mostly extemporized; but I managed to keep it in harmony by singing this song, which I made as we went on. Of course the children could not hear it; they only saw the motions that answered to it; but with them they seemed to be very much delighted indeed, as I shall presently prove to you. This was the song:—

'Swing, swang, swingle, swuff,
    Flicker, flacker, fling, fluff!
    Thus we go,
    To and fro;
    Here and there,
    Everywhere,
    Born and bred;
    Never dead,
    Only gone.

'On! Come on.

181

Looming, glooming,
Spreading, fuming,
Shattering, scattering,
Parting, darting,
Settling, starting,
All our life
Is a strife,
And a wearying for rest
On the darkness' friendly breast.

'Joining, splitting,
Rising, sitting,
Laughing, shaking,
Sides all aching,
Grumbling, grim, and gruff.
Swingle, swangle, swuff!

'Now a knot of darkness;
Now dissolved gloom;
Now a pall of blackness
Hiding all the room.
Flicker, flacker, fluff!
Black, and black enough!

'Dancing now like demons;
Lying like the dead;
Gladly would we stop it,
And go down to bed!
But our work we still must do,
Shadow men, as well as you.

'Rooting, rising, shooting,
Heaving, sinking, creeping;
Hid in corners crooning;
Splitting, poking, leaping,
Gathering, towering, swooning.
When we're lurking,
Yet we're working,
For our labour we must do,
Shadow men, as well as you.
Flicker, flacker, fling, fluff!
Swing, swang, swingle, swuff!'

"'How thick the Shadows are!' said one of the children—a thoughtful little girl.

"'I wonder where they come from,' said a dreamy little boy.

"'I think they grow out of the wall,' answered the little girl; 'for I have been watching them come; first one and then another, and then a whole lot of them. I am sure they grow out of the walls.'

"'Perhaps they have papas and mammas,' said an older boy, with a smile.

"'Yes, yes; and the doctor brings them in his pocket,' said another, a consequential little maiden.

"'No; I'll tell you,' said the older boy: 'they're ghosts.'

"'But ghosts are white.'

"'Oh! but these have got black coming down the chimney.'

"'No,' said a curious-looking, white-faced boy of fourteen, who had been reading by the firelight, and had stopped to hear the little ones talk; 'they're body ghosts; they're not soul ghosts.'

"'A silence followed, broken by the first, the dreamy-eyed boy, who said,—

"'I hope they didn't make me;' at which they all burst out laughing. Just then the nurse brought in their tea, and when she proceeded to light the gas, we vanished."

"I stopped a murder," cried another.

"How? How? How?"

"I will tell you. I had been lurking about a sick-room for some time, where a miser lay, apparently dying. I did not like the place at all, but I felt as if I should be wanted there. There were plenty of lurking-places about, for the room was full of all sorts of old furniture, especially cabinets, chests, and presses. I believe he had in that room every bit of the property he had spent a long life in gathering. I found that he had gold and gold in those places; for one night, when his nurse was away, he crept out of bed, mumbling and shaking, and managed to open one of his chests, though he nearly fell down with the effort. I was peeping over his shoulder, and such a gleam of gold fell upon me, that it nearly killed me. But hearing his nurse coming, he slammed the lid down, and I recovered.

"I tried very hard, but I could not do him any good. For although I made all sorts of shapes on the walls and ceiling, representing evil deeds that he had done, of which there were plenty to choose from, I could make no shapes on his brain or conscience. He had no eyes for anything but gold. And it so happened that his nurse had neither eyes nor heart for anything else either.

"'One day, as she was seated beside his bed, but where he could not see her, stirring some gruel in a basin, to cool it from him, I saw her take a little phial from her bosom, and I knew by the expression of her face both what it was and what she was going to do with it. Fortunately the cork was a little hard to get out, and this gave me one moment to think.

"The room was so crowded with all sorts of things, that although there were no curtains on the four-post bed to hide from the miser the sight of his precious treasures, there was yet but one small part of the ceiling suitable for casting myself upon in the shape I wished to assume. And this spot was hard to reach. But having discovered that upon this very place lay a dull gleam of firelight thrown from a strange old dusty mirror that stood away in some corner, I got in front of the fire, spied where the mirror was, threw myself upon it, and bounded from its face upon the oval pool of dim light on the ceiling, assuming, as I passed, the shape of an old stooping hag, who poured something from a phial into a basin. I made the handle of the spoon with my own nose, ha! ha!" And the shadow-hand caressed the shadow-tip of the shadow-nose, before the shadow-tongue resumed.

"The old miser saw me: he would not taste the gruel that night, although his nurse coaxed and scolded till they were both weary. She pretended to taste it herself, and to think it very good; but at last retired into a corner, and after making as if she were eating it, took good care to pour it all out into the ashes."

"But she must either succeed, or starve him, at last," interposed a Shadow.

"I will tell you."

"And," interposed a third, "he was not worth saving."

"He might repent," suggested another who was more benevolent.

"No chance of that," returned the former. "Misers never do. The love of money has less in it to cure itself than any other wickedness into which wretched men can fall. What a mercy it is to be born a Shadow! Wickedness does not stick to us. What do we care for gold!—Rubbish!"

"Amen! Amen! Amen!" came from a hundred shadow-voices.

"You should have let her murder him, and so you would have been quit of him."

"And besides, how was he to escape at last? He could never get rid of her, you know."

"I was going to tell you," resumed the narrator, "only you had so many shadow-remarks to make, that you would not let me."

"Go on; go on."

"There was a little grandchild who used to come and see him sometimes—the only creature the miser cared for. Her mother was his daughter; but the old man would never see her, because she had married against his will. Her husband was now dead, but he had not forgiven her yet. After the shadow he had seen, however, he said to himself, as he lay awake that night—I saw the words on his face—'How shall I get rid of that old devil? If I don't eat I shall die; and if I do eat I shall be poisoned. I wish little Mary would come. Ah! her mother would never have served me so.' He lay awake, thinking such things over and over again, all night long, and I stood watching him from a dark corner, till the dayspring came and shook me out. When I came back next night, the room was tidy and clean. His own daughter, a sad-faced but beautiful woman, sat by his bedside; and little Mary was curled up on the floor by the fire, imitating us, by making queer shadows on the ceiling with her twisted hands. But she could not think how ever they got there. And no wonder, for I helped her to some very unaccountable ones."

"I have a story about a granddaughter, too," said another, the moment that speaker ceased.

"Tell it. Tell it."

"Last Christmas-day," he began, "I and a troop of us set out in the twilight to find some house where we could all have something to do; for we had made up our minds to act together. We tried several, but found objections to them all. At last we espied a large lonely country-house, and hastening to it, we found great preparations making for the Christmas dinner. We rushed into it, scampered all over it, and made up our minds in a moment that it would do. We amused ourselves in the nursery first, where there were several children being dressed for dinner. We generally do go to the nursery first, your majesty. This time we were especially charmed with a little girl about five years old, who clapped her hands and danced about with delight at the antics we performed; and we said we would do something for her if we had a chance. The company began to arrive; and at every arrival we rushed to the hall, and cut wonderful capers of welcome. Between times we scudded away to see how the dressing went on. One girl about eighteen was delightful. She dressed herself as if she did not care much about it, but could not help doing it prettily. When she took her last look at the phantom in the glass, she half smiled to it.—But we do not like those creatures that come into the mirrors at all, your majesty. We don't understand them. They are dreadful to us.—She looked rather sad and pale, but very sweet and hopeful. So we wanted to know all about her, and soon found out that she was a distant relation and a great favourite of the gentleman of the house, an old man, in whose face benevolence was mingled with obstinacy and a deep shade of the tyrannical. We could not admire him much; but we would not make up our minds all at once: Shadows never do.

"The dinner-bell rang, and down we hurried. The children all looked happy, and we were merry. But there was one cross fellow among the servants, and didn't we plague him! and didn't we get fun out of him! When he was bringing up dishes, we lay in wait for him at every corner, and sprang upon him from the floor, and from over the banisters, and down from the cornices. He started and stumbled and blundered so in consequence, that his fellow-servants thought he was tipsy. Once he dropped a plate, and had to pick up the pieces, and hurry away with them; and didn't we pursue him as he went! It was lucky for him his master did not see how he went on; but we took care not to let him get into any real scrape, though he was quite dazed with the dodging of the unaccountable shadows. Sometimes he thought the walls were coming down upon him; sometimes that the floor was gaping to swallow him; sometimes that he would be knocked to pieces by the hurrying to and fro, or be smothered in the black crowd.

"When the blazing plum-pudding was carried in we made a perfect shadow-carnival about it, dancing and mumming in the blue flames, like mad demons. And how the children screamed with delight!

"The old gentleman, who was very fond of children, was laughing his heartiest laugh, when a loud knock came to the hall-door. The fair maiden started, turned paler, and then red as the Christmas fire. I saw it, and flung my hands across her face. She was very glad, and I know she said in her heart, 'You kind Shadow!' which paid me well. Then I followed the rest into the hall, and found there a jolly, handsome, brown-faced sailor, evidently a son of the house. The old man received him with tears in his eyes, and the children with shouts of joy. The maiden escaped in the confusion, just in time to save herself from fainting. We crowded about the lamp to hide her retreat, and nearly put it out; and the butler could not get it to burn up before she had glided into her place again, relieved to find the room so dark. The sailor only had seen her go, and now he sat down beside her, and, without a word, got hold of her hand in the gloom. When we all scattered to the walls and the corners, and the lamp blazed up again, he let her hand go.

"During the rest of the dinner the old man watched the two, and saw that there was something between them, and was very angry. For he was an important man in his own estimation, and they had never consulted him. The fact was, they had never known their own minds till the sailor had gone upon his last voyage, and

185

had learned each other's only this moment.—We found out all this by watching them, and then talking together about it afterwards.—The old gentleman saw, too, that his favourite, who was under such obligation to him for loving her so much, loved his son better than him; and he grew by degrees so jealous that he overshadowed the whole table with his morose looks and short answers. That kind of shadowing is very different from ours; and the Christmas dessert grew so gloomy that we Shadows could not bear it, and were delighted when the ladies rose to go to the drawing-room. The gentlemen would not stay behind the ladies, even for the sake of the well-known wine. So the moody host, notwithstanding his hospitality, was left alone at the table in the great silent room. We followed the company upstairs to the drawing-room, and thence to the nursery for snap-dragon; but while they were busy with this most shadowy of games, nearly all the Shadows crept downstairs again to the dining-room, where the old man still sat, gnawing the bone of his own selfishness. They crowded into the room, and by using every kind of expansion— blowing themselves out like soap-bubbles—they succeeded in heaping up the whole room with shade upon shade. They clustered thickest about the fire and the lamp, till at last they almost drowned them in hills of darkness.

"Before they had accomplished so much, the children, tired with fun and frolic, had been put to bed. But the little girl of five years old, with whom we had been so pleased when first we arrived, could not go to sleep. She had a little room of her own; and I had watched her to bed, and now kept her awake by gambolling in the rays of the night-light. When her eyes were once fixed upon me, I took the shape of her grandfather, representing him on the wall as he sat in his chair, with his head bent down and his arms hanging listlessly by his sides. And the child remembered that that was just as she had seen him last; for she had happened to peep in at the dining-room door after all the rest had gone upstairs. 'What if he should be sitting there still,' thought she, 'all alone in the dark!' She scrambled out of bed and crept down.

"Meantime the others had made the room below so dark, that only the face and white hair of the old man could be dimly discerned in the shadowy crowd. For he had filled his own mind with shadows, which we Shadows wanted to draw out of him. Those shadows are very different from us, your majesty knows. He was thinking of all the disappointments he had had in life, and of all the ingratitude he had met with. And he thought far more of the good he had done, than the good others had got. 'After all I have done for them,' said he, with a sigh of bitterness, 'not one of them cares a straw for me. My own children will be glad when I am gone!'—At that instant he lifted up his eyes and saw, standing close by the door, a tiny figure in a long night-gown. The door behind her was shut. It was my little friend, who had crept in noiselessly. A pang of icy fear shot to the old man's heart, but it melted away as fast, for we made a lane through us for a single ray from the fire to fall on the face of the little sprite; and he thought it was a child of his own that had died when just the age of her child-niece, who now stood looking for her grandfather among the Shadows. He thought she had come out of her grave in the cold darkness to ask why her father was sitting alone on Christmas-day. And he felt he had no answer to give his little ghost, but one he would be ashamed for her to hear. But his grandchild saw him now, and walked up to him with a childish stateliness, stumbling once or twice on what seemed her long shroud. Pushing through the crowded shadows, she reached him, climbed upon his knee, laid her little long-

186

haired head on his shoulders, and said,—'Ganpa! you goomy? Isn't it your Kissy-Day too, ganpa?'

"A new fount of love seemed to burst from the clay of the old man's heart. He clasped the child to his bosom, and wept. Then, without a word, he rose with her in his arms, carried her up to her room, and laying her down in her bed, covered her up, kissed her sweet little mouth unconscious of reproof, and then went to the drawing-room.

"As soon as he entered, he saw the culprits in a quiet corner alone. He went up to them, took a hand of each, and joining them in both his, said, 'God bless you!' Then he turned to the rest of the company, and 'Now,' said he, 'let's have a Christmas carol.'—And well he might; for though I have paid many visits to the house, I have never seen him cross since; and I am sure that must cost him a good deal of trouble."

"We have just come from a great palace," said another, "where we knew there were many children, and where we thought to hear glad voices, and see royally merry looks. But as soon as we entered, we became aware that one mighty Shadow shrouded the whole; and that Shadow deepened and deepened, till it gathered in darkness about the reposing form of a wise prince. When we saw him, we could move no more, but clung heavily to the walls, and by our stillness added to the sorrow of the hour. And when we saw the mother of her people weeping with bowed head for the loss of him in whom she had trusted, we were seized with such a longing to be Shadows no more, but winged angels, which are the white shadows cast in heaven from the Light of Light, so as to gather around her, and hover over her with comforting, that we vanished from the walls, and found ourselves floating high above the towers of the palace, where we met the angels on their way, and knew that our service was not needed."

By this time there was a glimmer of approaching moonlight, and the king began to see several of those stranger Shadows, with human faces and eyes, moving about amongst the crowd. He knew at once that they did not belong to his dominion. They looked at him, and came near him, and passed slowly, but they never made any obeisance, or gave sign of homage. And what their eyes said to him, the king only could tell. And he did not tell.

"What are those other Shadows that move through the crowd?" said he to one of his subjects near him.

The Shadow started, looked round, shivered slightly, and laid his finger on his lips. Then leading the king a little aside, and looking carefully about him once more,—

"I do not know," said he in a low tone, "what they are. I have heard of them often, but only once did I ever see any of them before. That was when some of us one night paid a visit to a man who sat much alone, and was said to think a great deal. We saw two of those sitting in the room with him, and he was as pale as they were. We could not cross the threshold, but shivered and shook, and felt ready to melt away. Is not your majesty afraid of them too?"

But the king made no answer; and before he could speak again, the moon had climbed above the mighty pillars of the church of the Shadows, and looked in at the great window of the sky.

The shapes had all vanished; and the king, again lifting up his eyes, saw but the wall of his own chamber, on which flickered the Shadow of a Little Child. He looked down, and there, sitting on a stool by the fire, he saw one of his own little ones, waiting to say good-night to his father, and go to bed early, that he might rise early too, and be very good and happy all Christmas-day.

And Ralph Rinkelmann rejoiced that he was a man, and not a Shadow.

But as the Shadows vanished they left the sense of song in the king's brain. And the words of their song must have been something like these:—

"Shadows, Shadows, Shadows all!
    Shadow birth and funeral!
    Shadow moons gleam overhead;
    Over shadow-graves we tread.
    Shadow-hope lives, grows, and dies.
    Shadow-love from shadow-eyes
    Shadow-ward entices on
    To shadow-words on shadow-stone,
    Closing up the shadow-tale
    With a shadow-shadow-wail.

"Shadow-man, thou art a gloom
    Cast upon a shadow-tomb
    Through the endless shadow air,
    From the shadow sitting there,
    On a moveless shadow-throne,
    Glooming through the ages gone;
    North and south, and in and out,
    East and west, and all about,
    Flinging Shadows everywhere
    On the shadow-painted air
    Shadow-man, thou hast no story;
    Nothing but a shadow-glory."

But Ralph Rinkelmann said to himself,—

    "They are but Shadows that sing thus; for a Shadow can see but Shadows. A man sees a man where a Shadow sees only a Shadow."

    And he was comforted in himself.

THE LIGHT PRINCESS

BY
GEORGE MACDONALD

1. WHAT! NO CHILDREN?

Once upon a time, so long ago that I have quite forgotten the date, there lived a king and queen who had no children.

And the king said to himself, "All the queens of my acquaintance have children, some three, some seven, and some as many as twelve; and my queen has not one. I feel ill-used." So he made up his mind to be cross with his wife about it. But she bore it all like a good patient queen as she was. Then the king grew very cross indeed. But the queen pretended to take it all as a joke, and a very good one too.

"Why don't you have any daughters, at least?" said he. "I don't say sons; that might be too much to expect."

"I am sure, dear king, I am very sorry," said the queen.

"So you ought to be," retorted the king; "you are not going to make a virtue of that, surely."

But he was not an ill-tempered king, and in any matter of less moment would have let the queen have her own way with all his heart. This, however, was an affair of state.

The queen smiled.

"You must have patience with a lady, you know, dear king," said she.

She was, indeed, a very nice queen, and heartily sorry that she could not oblige the king immediately.

2. WON'T I, JUST?

The king tried to have patience, but he succeeded very badly. It was more than he deserved, therefore, when, at last, the queen gave him a daughter—as lovely a little princess as ever cried.

The day drew near when the infant must be christened. The king wrote all the invitations with his own hand. Of course somebody was forgotten. Now it does not generally matter if somebody is forgotten, only you must mind who. Unfortunately, the king forgot without intending to forget; and so the chance fell upon the Princess Makemnoit, which was awkward. For the princess was the king's own sister; and he ought not to have forgotten her. But she had made herself so disagreeable to the old king, their father, that he had forgotten her in making his will; and so it was no wonder that her brother forgot her in writing his invitations. But poor relations don't do anything to keep you in mind of them. Why don't they? The king could not see into the garret she lived in, could he?

She was a sour, spiteful creature. The wrinkles of contempt crossed the wrinkles of peevishness, and made her face as full of wrinkles as a pat of butter. If ever a king could be justified in forgetting anybody, this king was justified in forgetting his sister, even at a christening. She looked very odd, too. Her forehead was as large as all the rest of her face, and projected over it like a precipice. When she was angry, her little eyes flashed blue. When she hated anybody, they shone yellow and green. What they looked like when she loved anybody, I do not know; for I never heard of her loving anybody but herself, and I do not think she could have managed that if she had not somehow got used to herself. But what made it highly imprudent in the king to forget her was that she was awfully clever. In fact, she was a witch; and when she bewitched anybody, he very soon had enough of it; for she beat all the wicked fairies in wickedness, and all the clever ones in cleverness. She despised all the modes we read of in history, in which offended fairies and witches have taken their revenges; and therefore, after waiting and waiting in vain for an invitation, she made up her mind at last to go without one, and make the whole family miserable, like a princess as she was.

So she put on her best gown, went to the palace, was kindly received by the happy monarch, who forgot that he had forgotten her, and took her place in the procession to the royal chapel. When they were all gathered about the font, she contrived to get next to it, and throw something into the water; after which she maintained a very respectful demeanour till the water was applied to the child's face. But at that moment she turned round in her place three times, and muttered the following words, loud enough for those beside her to hear:—

"Light of spirit, by my charms,
   Light of body, every part,
   Never weary human arms—
   Only crush thy parents' heart!"

They all thought she had lost her wits, and was repeating some foolish nursery rhyme; but a shudder went through the whole of them notwithstanding. The baby, on the contrary, began to laugh and crow; while the nurse gave a start and a smothered cry, for she thought she was struck with paralysis: she could not feel the baby in her arms. But she clasped it tight and said nothing. The mischief was done.

3. SHE CAN'T BE OURS.

Her atrocious aunt had deprived the child of all her gravity. If you ask me how this was effected, I answer, "In the easiest way in the world. She had only to destroy gravitation." For the princess was a philosopher, and knew all the ins and outs of the laws of gravitation as well as the ins and outs of her boot-lace. And being a witch as well, she could abrogate those laws in a moment; or at least so clog their wheels and rust their bearings, that they would not work at all. But we have more to do with what followed than with how it was done.

The first awkwardness that resulted from this unhappy privation was, that the moment the nurse began to float the baby up and down, she flew from her arms towards the ceiling. Happily, the resistance of the air brought her ascending career to a close within a foot of it. There she remained, horizontal as when she left her nurse's arms, kicking and laughing amazingly. The nurse in terror flew to the bell, and begged the footman, who answered it, to bring up the house-steps directly. Trembling in every limb, she climbed upon the steps, and had to stand upon the very top, and reach up, before she could catch the floating tail of the baby's long clothes.

When the strange fact came to be known, there was a terrible commotion in the palace. The occasion of its discovery by the king was naturally a repetition of the nurse's experience. Astonished that he felt no weight when the child was laid in his arms, he began to wave her up and not down, for she slowly ascended to the ceiling as before, and there remained floating in perfect comfort and satisfaction, as was testified by her peals of tiny laughter. The king stood staring up in speechless amazement, and trembled so that his beard shook like grass in the wind. At last, turning to the queen, who was just as horror-struck as himself, he said, gasping, staring, and stammering,—

"She can't be ours, queen!"

Now the queen was much cleverer than the king, and had begun already to suspect that "this effect defective came by cause."

"I am sure she is ours," answered she. "But we ought to have taken better care of her at the christening. People who were never invited ought not to have been present."

"Oh, ho!" said the king, tapping his forehead with his forefinger, "I have it all. I've found her out. Don't you see it, queen? Princess Makemnoit has bewitched her." "That's just what I say," answered the queen.

"I beg your pardon, my love; I did not hear you.—John! bring the steps I get on my throne with."

For he was a little king with a great throne, like many other kings.

The throne-steps were brought, and set upon the dining-table, and John got upon the top of them. But he could not reach the little princess, who lay like a baby-laughter-cloud in the air, exploding continuously. "Take the tongs, John," said his Majesty; and getting up on the table, he handed them to him.

John could reach the baby now, and the little princess was handed down by the tongs.

4. WHERE IS SHE?

One fine summer day, a month after these her first adventures, during which time she had been very carefully watched, the princess was lying on the bed in the queen's own chamber, fast asleep. One of the windows was open, for it was noon, and the day was so sultry that the little girl was wrapped in nothing less ethereal than slumber itself. The queen came into the room, and not observing that the baby was on the bed, opened another window. A frolicsome fairy wind, which had been watching for a chance of mischief, rushed in at the one window, and taking its way over the bed where the child was lying, caught her up, and rolling and floating her along like a piece of flue, or a dandelion seed, carried her with it through the opposite window, and away. The queen went down-stairs, quite ignorant of the loss she had herself occasioned.

When the nurse returned, she supposed that her Majesty had carried her off, and, dreading a scolding, delayed making inquiry about her. But hearing nothing, she grew uneasy, and went at length to the queen's boudoir, where she found her Majesty.

"Please, your Majesty, shall I take the baby?" said she.

"Where is she?" asked the queen.

"Please forgive me. I know it was wrong."

"What do you mean?" said the queen, looking grave.

"Oh! don't frighten me, your Majesty!" exclaimed the nurse, clasping her hands.

The queen saw that something was amiss, and fell down in a faint. The nurse rushed about the palace, screaming, "My baby! my baby!"

Every one ran to the queen's room. But the queen could give no orders. They soon found out, however, that the princess was missing, and in a moment the palace was like a beehive in a garden; and in one minute more the queen was brought to herself by a great shout and a clapping of hands. They had found the princess fast asleep under a rose-bush, to which the elvish little wind-puff had carried her, finishing its mischief by shaking a shower of red rose-leaves all over the little white sleeper. Startled by the noise the servants made, she woke, and, furious with glee, scattered the rose-leaves in all directions, like a shower of spray in the sunset.

She was watched more carefully after this, no doubt; yet it would be endless to relate all the odd incidents resulting from this peculiarity of the young princess. But there never was a baby in a house, not to say a palace, that kept the household in such constant good humour, at least below-stairs. If it was not easy for her nurses to hold her, at least she made neither their arms nor their hearts ache. And she was so nice to play at ball with! There was positively no danger of letting her fall. They might throw her down, or knock her down, or push her down, but couldn't let her down. It is true, they might let her fly into the fire or the coal-hole, or through the window; but none of these accidents had happened as yet. If you heard peals of laughter resounding from some unknown region, you might be sure enough of the cause. Going down into the kitchen, or the room, you would find Jane and Thomas, and Robert and Susan, all and sum, playing at ball with the little princess. She was the ball herself, and did not enjoy it the less for that. Away she went, flying from one to another, screeching with laughter. And the servants loved the ball itself better even than the game. But they had to take some care how they threw her, for if she received an upward direction, she would never come down again without being fetched.

5. WHAT IS TO BE DONE?

But above-stairs it was different. One day, for instance, after breakfast, the king went into his counting-house, and counted out his money. The operation gave him no pleasure.

"To think," said he to himself, "that every one of these gold sovereigns weighs a quarter of an ounce, and my real, live, flesh-and-blood princess weighs nothing at all!"

And he hated his gold sovereigns, as they lay with a broad smile of self-satisfaction all over their yellow faces.

The queen was in the parlour, eating bread and honey. But at the second mouthful she burst out crying, and could not swallow it.

The king heard her sobbing. Glad of anybody, but especially of his queen, to quarrel with, he clashed his gold sovereigns into his money-box, clapped his crown on his head, and rushed into the parlour.

"What is all this about?" exclaimed he. "What are you crying for, queen?"

"I can't eat it," said the queen, looking ruefully at the honey-pot.

"No wonder!" retorted the king. "You've just eaten your breakfast—two turkey eggs, and three anchovies."

"Oh, that's not it!" sobbed her Majesty. "It's my child, my child!"

"Well, what's the matter with your child? She's neither up the chimney nor down the draw-well. Just hear her laughing."

Yet the king could not help a sigh, which he tried to turn into a cough, saying—

"It is a good thing to be light-hearted, I am sure, whether she be ours or not."

"It is a bad thing to be light-headed," answered the queen, looking with prophetic soul far into the future.

"'Tis a good thing to be light-handed," said the king.

"'Tis a bad thing to be light-fingered," answered the queen.

"'Tis a good thing to be light-footed," said the king.

"'Tis a bad thing—" began the queen; but the king interrupted her.

"In fact," said he, with the tone of one who concludes an argument in which he has had only imaginary opponents, and in which, therefore, he has come off triumphant—"in fact, it is a good thing altogether to be light-bodied."

"But it is a bad thing altogether to be light-minded," retorted the queen, who was beginning to lose her temper.

This last answer quite discomfited his Majesty, who turned on his heel, and betook himself to his counting-house again. But he was not half-way towards it, when the voice of his queen overtook him.

"And it's a bad thing to be light-haired," screamed she, determined to have more last words, now that her spirit was roused.

The queen's hair was black as night; and the king's had been, and his daughter's was, golden as morning. But it was not this reflection on his hair that arrested him; it was the double use of the word light. For the king hated all witticisms, and punning especially. And besides, he could not tell whether the queen meant light-haired or light-heired; for why might she not aspirate her vowels when she was exasperated herself?

He turned upon his other heel, and rejoined her. She looked angry still, because she knew that she was guilty, or, what was much the same, knew that HE thought so.

"My dear queen," said he, "duplicity of any sort is exceedingly objectionable between married people of any rank, not to say kings and queens; and the most objectionable form duplicity can assume is that of punning."

"There!" said the queen, "I never made a jest, but I broke it in the making. I am the most unfortunate woman in the world!"

She looked so rueful, that the king took her in his arms; and they sat down to consult.

"Can you bear this?" said the king.

"No, I can't," said the queen.

"Well, what's to be done?" said the king.

"I'm sure I don't know," said the queen. "But might you not try an apology?"

"To my old sister, I suppose you mean?" said the king.

"Yes," said the queen.

"Well, I don't mind," said the king.

So he went the next morning to the house of the princess, and, making a very humble apology, begged her to undo the spell. But the princess declared, with a grave face, that she knew nothing at all about it. Her eyes, however, shone pink, which was a sign that she was happy. She advised the king and queen to have patience, and to mend their ways. The king returned disconsolate. The queen tried to comfort him.

"We will wait till she is older. She may then be able to suggest something herself. She will know at least how she feels, and explain things to us."

"But what if she should marry?" exclaimed the king, in sudden consternation at the idea.

"Well, what of that?" rejoined the queen. "Just think! If she were to have children! In the course of a hundred years the air might be as full of floating children as of gossamers in autumn."

"That is no business of ours," replied the queen. "Besides, by that time they will have learned to take care of themselves."

A sigh was the king's only answer.

He would have consulted the court physicians; but he was afraid they would try experiments upon her.

6. SHE LAUGHS TOO MUCH.

Meantime, notwithstanding awkward occurrences, and griefs that she brought upon her parents, the little princess laughed and grew—not fat, but plump and tall. She reached the age of seventeen, without having fallen into any worse scrape than a chimney; by rescuing her from which, a little bird-nesting urchin got fame and a black face. Nor, thoughtless as she was, had she committed anything worse than laughter at everybody and everything that came in her way. When she was told, for the sake of experiment, that General Clanrunfort was cut to pieces with all his troops, she laughed; when she heard that the enemy was on his way to besiege her papa's capital, she laughed hugely; but when she was told that the city would certainly be abandoned to the mercy of the enemy's soldiery—why, then she laughed immoderately. She never could be brought to see the serious side of anything. When her mother cried, she said,—

"What queer faces mamma makes! And she squeezes water out of her cheeks? Funny mamma!"

And when her papa stormed at her, she laughed, and danced round and round him, clapping her hands, and crying—

"Do it again, papa. Do it again! It's SUCH fun! Dear, funny papa!"

And if he tried to catch her, she glided from him in an instant, not in the least afraid of him, but thinking it part of the game not to be caught. With one push of her foot, she would be floating in the air above his head; or she would go dancing backwards and forwards and sideways, like a great butterfly. It happened several times, when her father and mother were holding a consultation about her in private, that they were interrupted by vainly repressed outbursts of laughter over their heads; and looking up with indignation, saw her floating at full length in the air above them, whence she regarded them with the most comical appreciation of the position.

One day an awkward accident happened. The princess had come out upon the lawn with one of her attendants, who held her by the hand. Spying her father at the other side of the lawn, she snatched her hand from the maid's, and sped across to him. Now when she wanted to run alone, her custom was to catch up a stone in each hand, so that she might come down again after a bound. Whatever she wore as part of her attire had no effect in this way: even gold, when it thus became as it were a part of herself, lost all its weight for the time. But whatever she only held in her hands retained its downward tendency. On this occasion she could see nothing to catch up but a huge toad, that was walking across the lawn as if he had a hundred years to do it in. Not knowing what disgust meant, for this was one of her peculiarities, she snatched up the toad and bounded away. She had almost reached her father, and he was holding out his arms to receive her, and take from her lips the kiss which hovered on them like a butterfly on a rosebud, when a puff of wind blew her aside into the arms of a young page, who had just been receiving a message from his Majesty. Now it was no great peculiarity in the princess that, once she was set agoing, it always cost her time and trouble to check herself. On this occasion there was no time. She must kiss-and she kissed the page. She did not mind it much; for she had no shyness in her composition; and she knew, besides, that she could not help it. So she only laughed, like a musical box. The poor page fared the worst. For the princess, trying to correct the unfortunate tendency of the kiss, put out her hands to keep her off the page; so that, along with the kiss, he received, on the other cheek, a slap with the huge black toad, which she poked right into his eye. He tried to laugh, too, but the attempt resulted in such an odd contortion of countenance, as showed that there was no danger of his pluming himself on the kiss. As for the king, his dignity was greatly hurt, and he did not speak to the page for a whole month.

I may here remark that it was very amusing to see her run, if her mode of progression could properly be called running. For first she would make a bound; then, having alighted, she would run a few steps, and make another bound. Sometimes she would fancy she had reached the ground before she actually had, and her feet would go backwards and forwards, running upon nothing at all, like those of a chicken on its back. Then she would laugh like the very spirit of fun; only in her laugh there was something missing. What it was, I find myself unable to describe. I think it was a certain tone, depending upon the possibility of sorrow— MORBIDEZZA, perhaps. She never smiled.

7. TRY METAPHYSICS.

After a long avoidance of the painful subject, the king and queen resolved to hold a council of three upon it; and so they sent for the princess. In she came, sliding and flitting and gliding from one piece of furniture to another, and put herself at last in an armchair, in a sitting posture. Whether she could be said to sit, seeing she received no support from the seat of the chair, I do not pretend to determine.

"My dear child," said the king, "you must be aware by this time that you are not exactly like other people."

"Oh, you dear funny papa! I have got a nose, and two eyes, and all the rest. So have you. So has mamma."

"Now be serious, my dear, for once," said the queen.

"No, thank you, mamma; I had rather not."

"Would you not like to be able to walk like other people?" said the king.

"No indeed, I should think not. You only crawl. You are such slow coaches!"

"How do you feel, my child?" he resumed, after a pause of discomfiture.

"Quite well, thank you."

"I mean, what do you feel like?"

"Like nothing at all, that I know of."

"You must feel like something."

"I feel like a princess with such a funny papa, and such a dear pet of a queen-mamma!"

"Now really!" began the queen; but the princess interrupted her.

"Oh Yes," she added, "I remember. I have a curious feeling sometimes, as if I were the only person that had any sense in the whole world."

She had been trying to behave herself with dignity; but now she burst into a violent fit of laughter, threw herself backwards over the chair, and went rolling about the floor in an ecstasy of enjoyment. The king picked her up easier than one does a down quilt, and replaced her in her former relation to the chair. The exact preposition expressing this relation I do not happen to know.

"Is there nothing you wish for?" resumed the king, who had learned by this time that it was useless to be angry with her.

"Oh, you dear papa!—yes," answered she.

"What is it, my darling?"

"I have been longing for it—oh, such a time!—ever since last night." "Tell me what it is."

"Will you promise to let me have it?"

The king was on the point of saying Yes, but the wiser queen checked him with a single motion of her head. "Tell me what it is first," said he.

"No no. Promise first."

"I dare not. What is it?"

"Mind, I hold you to your promise.—It is—to be tied to the end of a string—a very long string indeed, and be flown like a kite. Oh, such fun! I would rain rose-water, and hail sugar-plums, and snow whipped-cream, and—and—and—"

A fit of laughing checked her; and she would have been off again over the floor, had not the king started up and caught her just in time. Seeing nothing but talk could be got out of her, he rang the bell, and sent her away with two of her ladies-in-waiting.

"Now, queen," he said, turning to her Majesty, "what IS to be done?"

"There is but one thing left," answered she. "Let us consult the college of Meta-physicians."

"Bravo!" cried the king; "we will."

Now at the head of this college were two very wise Chinese philosophers-by name Hum-Drum, and Kopy-Keck. For them the king sent; and straightway they came. In a long speech he communicated to them what they knew very well already—as who did not?—namely, the peculiar condition of his daughter in rela-tion to the globe on which she dwelt; and requested them to consult together as to what might be the cause and probable cure of her INFIRMITY. The king laid stress upon the word, but failed to discover his own pun. The queen laughed; but Hum-Drum and Kopy-Keck heard with humility and retired in silence.

The consultation consisted chiefly in propounding and supporting, for the thou-sandth time, each his favourite theories. For the condition of the princess afforded delightful scope for the discussion of every question arising from the division of thought-in fact, of all the Metaphysics of the Chinese Empire. But it is only justice to say that they did not altogether neglect the discussion of the practical question, what was to be done.

Hum-Drum was a Materialist, and Kopy-Keck was a Spiritualist. The former was slow and sententious; the latter was quick and flighty: the latter had generally the first word; the former the last.

"I reassert my former assertion," began Kopy-Keck, with a plunge. "There is not a fault in the princess, body or soul; only they are wrong put together. Listen to me now, Hum-Drum, and I will tell you in brief what I think. Don't speak. Don't answer me. I won't hear you till I have done.— At that decisive moment, when souls seek their appointed habitations, two eager souls met, struck, rebounded, lost their way, and arrived each at the wrong place. The soul of the princess was one of those, and she went far astray. She does not belong by rights to this world at all, but to some other planet, probably Mercury. Her proclivity to her true sphere destroys all the natural influence which this orb would otherwise possess over her corporeal frame. She cares for nothing here. There is no relation between her and this world.

"She must therefore be taught, by the sternest compulsion, to take an interest in the earth as the earth. She must study every department of its history—its animal history; its vegetable history; its mineral history; its social history; its moral history; its political history, its scientific history; its literary history; its musical history; its artistical history; above all, its metaphysical history. She must begin with the Chinese dynasty and end with Japan. But first of all she must study geology, and especially the history of the extinct races of animals-their natures, their habits, their loves, their hates, their revenges. She must—"

"Hold, h-o-o-old!" roared Hum-Drum. "It is certainly my turn now. My rooted and insubvertible conviction is, that the causes of the anomalies evident in the princess's condition are strictly and solely physical. But that is only tantamount to acknowledging that they exist. Hear my opinion.— From some cause or other, of no importance to our inquiry, the motion of her heart has been reversed. That remarkable combination of the suction and the force-pump works the wrong way-I mean in the case of the unfortunate princess: it draws in where it should force out, and forces out where it should draw in. The offices of the auricles and the ventricles are subverted. The blood is sent forth by the veins, and returns by the arteries. Consequently it is running the wrong way through all her corporeal organism—lungs and all. Is it then at all mysterious, seeing that such is the case, that on the other particular of gravitation as well, she should differ from normal humanity? My proposal for the cure is this:—

"Phlebotomize until she is reduced to the last point of safety. Let it be effected, if necessary, in a warm bath. When she is reduced to a state of perfect asphyxy, apply a ligature to the left ankle, drawing it as tight as the bone will bear. Apply, at the same moment, another of equal tension around the right wrist. By means of plates constructed for the purpose, place the other foot and hand under the receivers of two air-pumps. Exhaust the receivers. Exhibit a pint of French brandy, and await the result."

"Which would presently arrive in the form of grim Death," said Kopy-Keck.

"If it should, she would yet die in doing our duty," retorted Hum-Drum.

But their Majesties had too much tenderness for their volatile offspring to subject her to either of the schemes of the equally unscrupulous philosophers. Indeed, the most complete knowledge of the laws of nature would have been unserviceable in her case; for it was impossible to classify her. She was a fifth imponderable body, sharing all the other properties of the ponderable.

8. TRY A DROP OF WATER.

Perhaps the best thing for the princess would have been to fall in love. But how a princess who had no gravity could fall into anything is a difficulty—perhaps THE difficulty.

As for her own feelings on the subject, she did not even know that there was such a beehive of honey and stings to be fallen into. But now I come to mention another curious fact about her.

The palace was built on the shores of the loveliest lake in the world; and the princess loved this lake more than father or mother. The root of this preference no doubt, although the princess did not recognise it as such, was, that the moment she got into it, she recovered the natural right of which she had been so wickedly deprived—namely, gravity. Whether this was owing to the fact that water had been employed as the means of conveying the injury, I do not know. But it is certain that she could swim and dive like the duck that her old nurse said she was. The manner in which this alleviation of her misfortune was discovered was as follows.

One summer evening, during the carnival of the country, she had been taken upon the lake by the king and queen, in the royal barge. They were accompanied by many of the courtiers in a fleet of little boats. In the middle of the lake she wanted to get into the lord chancellor's barge, for his daughter, who was a great favourite with her, was in it with her father. Now though the old king rarely condescended to make light of his misfortune, yet, Happening on this occasion to be in a particularly good humour, as the barges approached each other, he caught up the princess to throw her into the chancellor's barge. He lost his balance, however, and, dropping into the bottom of the barge, lost his hold of his daughter; not, however, before imparting to her the downward tendency of his own person, though in a somewhat different direction; for, as the king fell into the boat, she fell into the water. With a burst of delighted laughter she disappeared in the lake. A cry of horror ascended from the boats. They had never seen the princess go down before.

Half the men were under water in a moment; but they had all, one after another, come up to the surface again for breath, when—tinkle, tinkle, babble, and gush! came the princess's laugh over the water from far away. There she was, swimming like a swan. Nor would she come out for king or queen, chancellor or daughter. She was perfectly obstinate.

But at the same time she seemed more sedate than usual. Perhaps that was because a great pleasure spoils laughing. At all events, after this, the passion of her life was to get into the water, and she was always the better behaved and the more beautiful the more she had of it. Summer and winter it was quite the same; only she could not stay so long in the water when they had to break the ice to let her in. Any day, from morning till evening in summer, she might be descried—a streak of white in the blue water—lying as still as the shadow of a cloud, or shooting along like a dolphin; disappearing, and coming up again far off, just where one did not expect her. She would have been in the lake of a night, too, if she could have had her way; for the balcony of her window overhung a deep pool in it; and through a shallow reedy passage she could have swum out into the wide wet water, and no one would have been any the wiser. Indeed, when she happened to wake in the moonlight she could hardly resist the temptation. But there was the sad difficulty of getting into it. She had as great a dread of the air as some children have of the water. For the slightest gust of wind would blow her away; and a gust might arise in the stillest moment. And if she gave herself a push towards the water and just failed of reaching it, her situation would be dreadfully awkward, irrespective of the wind; for at best there she would have to remain, suspended in her nightgown, till she was seen and angled for by someone from the window.

"Oh! if I had my gravity," thought she, contemplating the water, "I would flash off this balcony like a long white sea-bird, headlong into the darling wetness. Heigh-ho!"

This was the only consideration that made her wish to be like other people.

Another reason for her being fond of the water was that in it alone she enjoyed any freedom. For she could not walk out without a cortege, consisting in part of a troop of light horse, for fear of the liberties which the wind might take with her. And the king grew more apprehensive with increasing years, till at last he would not allow her to walk abroad at all without some twenty silken cords fastened to as many parts of her dress, and held by twenty noblemen. Of course horseback was out of the question. But she bade good-by to all this ceremony when she got into the water.

And so remarkable were its effects upon her, especially in restoring her for the time to the ordinary human gravity, that Hum-Drum and Kopy-Keck agreed in recommending the king to bury her alive for three years; in the hope that, as the water did her so much good, the earth would do her yet more. But the king had some vulgar prejudices against the experiment, and would not give his consent. Foiled in this, they yet agreed in another recommendation; which, seeing that one imported his opinions from China and the other from Thibet, was very remarkable indeed. They argued that, if water of external origin and application could be so efficacious, water from a deeper source might work a perfect cure; in short, that if the poor afflicted princess could by any means be made to cry, she might recover her lost gravity.

But how was this to be brought about? Therein lay all the difficulty—to meet

207

which the philosophers were not wise enough. To make the princess cry was as impossible as to make her weigh. They sent for a professional beggar; commanded him to prepare his most touching oracle of woe; helped him out of the court charade box, to whatever he wanted for dressing up, and promised great rewards in the event of his success. But it was all in vain. She listened to the mendicant artist's story, and gazed at his marvellous make up, till she could contain herself no longer, and went into the most undignified contortions for relief, shrieking, positively screeching with laughter.

When she had a little recovered herself, she ordered her attendants to drive him away, and not give him a single copper; whereupon his look of mortified discomfiture wrought her punishment and his revenge, for it sent her into violent hysterics, from which she was with difficulty recovered.

But so anxious was the king that the suggestion should have a fair trial, that he put himself in a rage one day, and, rushing up to her room, gave her an awful whipping. Yet not a tear would flow. She looked grave, and her laughing sounded uncommonly like screaming—that was all. The good old tyrant, though he put on his best gold spectacles to look, could not discover the smallest cloud in the serene blue of her eyes.

9. PUT ME IN AGAIN.

It must have been about this time that the son of a king, who lived a thousand miles from Lagobel set out to look for the daughter of a queen. He travelled far and wide, but as sure as he found a princess, he found some fault in her. Of course he could not marry a mere woman, however beautiful; and there was no princess to be found worthy of him. Whether the prince was so near perfection that he had a right to demand perfection itself, I cannot pretend to say. All I know is, that he was a fine, handsome, brave, generous, well-bred, and well-behaved youth, as all princes are.

In his wanderings he had come across some reports about our princess; but as everybody said she was bewitched, he never dreamed that she could bewitch him. For what indeed could a prince do with a princess that had lost her gravity? Who could tell what she might not lose next? She might lose her visibility, or her tangibility; or, in short, the power of making impressions upon the radical sensorium; so that he should never be able to tell whether she was dead or alive. Of course he made no further inquiries about her. One day he lost sight of his retinue in a great forest. These forests are very useful in delivering princes from their courtiers, like a sieve that keeps back the bran. Then the princes get away to follow their fortunes. In this way they have the advantage of the princesses, who are forced to marry before they have had a bit of fun. I wish our princesses got lost in a forest sometimes.

One lovely evening, after wandering about for many days, he found that he was approaching the outskirts of this forest; for the trees had got so thin that he could see the sunset through them; and he soon came upon a kind of heath. Next he came upon signs of human neighbourhood; but by this time it was getting late, and there was nobody in the fields to direct him.

After travelling for another hour, his horse, quite worn out with long labour and lack of food, fell, and was unable to rise again. So he continued his journey on foot.

GEORGE MACDONALD

At length he entered another wood—not a wild forest, but a civilized wood, through which a footpath led him to the side of a lake. Along this path the prince pursued his way through the gathering darkness. Suddenly he paused, and listened. Strange sounds came across the water. It was, in fact, the princess laughing. Now there was something odd in her laugh, as I have already hinted; for the hatching of a real hearty laugh requires the incubation of gravity; and perhaps this was how the prince mistook the laughter for screaming. Looking over the lake, he saw something white in the water; and, in an instant, he had torn off his tunic, kicked off his sandals, and plunged in. He soon reached the white object, and found that it was a woman. There was not light enough to show that she was a princess, but quite enough to show that she was a lady, for it does not want much light to see that.

Now I cannot tell how it came about,—whether she pretended to be drowning, or whether he frightened her, or caught her so as to embarrass her,—but certainly he brought her to shore in a fashion ignominious to a swimmer, and more nearly drowned than she had ever expected to be; for the water had got into her throat as often as she had tried to speak.

At the place to which he bore her, the bank was only a foot or two above the water; so he gave her a strong lift out of the water, to lay her on the bank. But, her gravitation ceasing the moment she left the water, away she went up into the air, scolding and screaming.

"You naughty, naughty, NAUGHTY, NAUGHTY man!" she cried.

No one had ever succeeded in putting her into a passion before.—When the prince saw her ascend, he thought he must have been bewitched, and have mistaken a great swan for a lady. But the princess caught hold of the topmost cone upon a lofty fir. This came off; but she caught at another; and, in fact, stopped herself by gathering cones, dropping them as the stalks gave way. The prince, meantime, stood in the water, staring, and forgetting to get out. But the princess disappearing, he scrambled on shore, and went in the direction of the tree. There he found her climbing down one of the branches towards the stem. But in the darkness of the wood, the prince continued in some bewilderment as to what the phenomenon could be; until, reaching the ground, and seeing him standing there, she caught hold of him, and said,—

"I'll tell papa."

"Oh no, you won't!" returned the prince.

"Yes, I will," she persisted. "What business had you to pull me down out of the water, and throw me to the bottom of the air? I never did you any harm."

"Pardon me. I did not mean to hurt you."

"I don't believe you have any brains; and that is a worse loss than your wretched gravity. I pity you."

The prince now saw that he had come upon the bewitched princess, and had already offended her. But before he could think what to say next, she burst out angrily, giving a stamp with her foot that would have sent her aloft again but for the hold she had of his arm,—

"Put me up directly."

"Put you up where, you beauty?" asked the prince.

He had fallen in love with her almost, already; for her anger made her more charming than any one else had ever beheld her; and, as far as he could see, which

210

certainly was not far, she had not a single fault about her, except, of course, that she had not any gravity. No prince, however, would judge of a princess by weight. The loveliness of her foot he would hardly estimate by the depth of the impression it could make in mud.

"Put you up where, you beauty?" asked the prince.

"In the water, you stupid!" answered the princess.

"Come, then," said the prince.

The condition of her dress, increasing her usual difficulty in walking, compelled her to cling to him; and he could hardly persuade himself that he was not in a delightful dream, notwithstanding the torrent of musical abuse with which she overwhelmed him. The prince being therefore in no hurry, they came upon the lake at quite another part, where the bank was twenty-five feet high at least; and when they had reached the edge, he turned towards the princess, and said,—

"How am I to put you in?" "That is your business," she answered, quite snappishly. "You took me out—put me in again."

"Very well," said the prince; and, catching her up in his arms, he sprang with her from the rock. The princess had just time to give one delighted shriek of laughter before the water closed over them. When they came to the surface, she found that, for a moment or two, she could not even laugh, for she had gone down with such a rush, that it was with difficulty she recovered her breath. The instant they reached the surface—

"How do you like falling in?" said the prince.

After some effort the princess panted out,—

"Is that what you call FALLING IN?"

"Yes," answered the prince, "I should think it a very tolerable specimen."

"It seemed to me like going up," rejoined she.

"My feeling was certainly one of elevation too," the prince conceded.

The princess did not appear to understand him, for she retorted his question:—

"How do YOU like falling in?" said the princess.

"Beyond everything," answered he; "for I have fallen in with the only perfect creature I ever saw."

"No more of that: I am tired of it," said the princess.

Perhaps she shared her father's aversion to punning.

"Don't you like falling in then?" said the prince.

"It is the most delightful fun I ever had in my life," answered she. "I never fell before. I wish I could learn. To think I am the only person in my father's kingdom that can't fall!"

Here the poor princess looked almost sad.

"I shall be most happy to fall in with you any time you like," said the prince, devotedly.

"Thank you. I don't know. Perhaps it would not be proper. But I don't care. At all events, as we have fallen in, let us have a swim together."

"With all my heart," responded the prince.

And away they went, swimming, and diving, and floating, until at last they heard cries along the shore, and saw lights glancing in all directions. It was now quite late, and there was no moon.

"I must go home," said the princess. "I am very sorry, for this is delightful."

"So am I," returned the prince. "But I am glad I haven't a home to go to—at least, I don't exactly know where it is."

"I wish I hadn't one either," rejoined the princess; "it is so stupid! I have a great mind," she continued, "to play them all a trick. Why couldn't they leave me alone? They won't trust me in the lake for a single night!—You see where that green light is burning? That is the window of my room. Now if you would just swim there with me very quietly, and when we are all but under the balcony, give me such a push—up you call it-as you did a little while ago, I should be able to catch hold of the balcony, and get in at the window; and then they may look for me till to-morrow morning!"

"With more obedience than pleasure," said the prince, gallantly; and away they swam, very gently.

"Will you be in the lake to-morrow night?" the prince ventured to ask.

"To be sure I will. I don't think so. Perhaps," was the princess's somewhat strange answer.

But the prince was intelligent enough not to press her further; and merely whispered, as he gave her the parting lift, "Don't tell."

The only answer the princess returned was a roguish look. She was already a yard above his head. The look seemed to say, "Never fear. It is too good fun to spoil that way."

So perfectly like other people had she been in the water, that even yet the prince could scarcely believe his eyes when he saw her ascend slowly, grasp the balcony, and disappear through the window. He turned, almost expecting to see her still by his side. But he was alone in the water. So he swam away quietly, and watched the lights roving about the shore for hours after the princess was safe in her chamber. As soon as they disappeared, he landed in search of his tunic and sword, and, after some trouble, found them again. Then he made the best of his way round the lake to the other side. There the wood was wilder, and the shore steeper-rising more immediately towards the mountains which surrounded the lake on all sides, and kept sending it messages of silvery streams from morning to night, and all night long. He soon found a spot whence he could see the green light in the princess's room, and where, even in the broad daylight, he would be in no danger of being discovered from the opposite shore. It was a sort of cave in the rock, where he provided himself a bed of withered leaves, and lay down too tired for hunger to keep him awake. All night long he dreamed that he was swimming with the princess.

10. LOOK AT THE MOON.

Early the next morning the prince set out to look for something to eat, which he soon found at a forester's hut, where for many following days he was supplied with all that a brave prince could consider necessary. And having plenty to keep him alive for the present, he would not think of wants not yet in existence. Whenever Care intruded, this prince always bowed him out in the most princely manner. When he returned from his breakfast to his watch-cave, he saw the princess already floating about in the lake, attended by the king and queen whom he knew by their crowns—and a great company in lovely little boats, with canopies of all the colours of the rainbow, and flags and streamers of a great many more. It was a very bright day, and soon the prince, burned up with the heat, began to long for the cold water and the cool princess. But he had to endure till twilight; for the boats had provisions on board, and it was not till the sun went down that the gay party began to vanish. Boat after boat drew away to the shore, following that of the king and queen, till only one, apparently the princess's own boat, remained. But she did not want to go home even yet, and the prince thought he saw her order the boat to the shore without her. At all events, it rowed away; and now, of all the radiant company, only one white speck remained. Then the prince began to sing. And this is what he sung:—

"Lady fair,
   Swan-white,
   Lift thine eyes,
   Banish night
   By the might
   Of thine eyes.
   Snowy arms,

Oars of snow,
Oar her hither,
Plashing low.
Soft and slow,
Oar her hither.
Stream behind her
O'er the lake,
Radiant whiteness!
In her wake
Following, following for her sake.
Radiant whiteness!
Cling about her,
Waters blue;
Part not from her,
But renew
Cold and true
Kisses round her.
Lap me round,
Waters sad,
That have left her.
Make me glad,
For ye had
Kissed her ere ye left her."

Before he had finished his song, the princess was just under the place where he sat, and looking up to find him. Her ears had led her truly.

"Would you like a fall, princess?" said the prince, looking down.

"Ah! there you are! Yes, if you please, prince," said the princess, looking up.

"How do you know I am a prince, princess?" said the prince.

"Because you are a very nice young man, prince," said the princess.

"Come up then, princess."

"Fetch me, prince."

The prince took off his scarf, then his sword-belt, then his tunic, and tied them all together, and let them down. But the line was far too short. He unwound his turban, and added it to the rest, when it was all but long enough; and his purse completed it. The princess just managed to lay hold of the knot of money, and was beside him in a moment. This rock was much higher than the other, and the splash and the dive were tremendous. The princess was in ecstasies of delight, and their swim was delicious.

Night after night they met, and swam about in the dark clear lake; where such was the prince's gladness, that (whether the princess's way of looking at things infected him, or he was actually getting light-headed) he often fancied that he was swimming in the sky instead of the lake. But when he talked about being in heaven, the princess laughed at him dreadfully.

When the moon came, she brought them fresh pleasure. Everything looked strange and new in her light, with an old, withered, yet unfading newness. When the moon was nearly full, one of their great delights was, to dive deep in the water,

214

and then, turning round, look up through it at the great blot of light close above them, shimmering and trembling and wavering, spreading and contracting, seeming to melt away, and again grow solid. Then they would shoot up through the blot; and lo! there was the moon, far off, clear and steady and cold, and very lovely, at the bottom of a deeper and bluer lake than theirs, as the princess said.

The prince soon found out that while in the water the princess was very like other people. And besides this, she was not so forward in her questions or pert in her replies at sea as on shore. Neither did she laugh so much; and when she did laugh, it was more gently. She seemed altogether more modest and maidenly in the water than out of it.

But when the prince, who had really fallen in love when he fell in the lake, began to talk to her about love, she always turned her head towards him and laughed. After a while she began to look puzzled, as if she were trying to understand what he meant, but could not—revealing a notion that he meant something. But as soon as ever she left the lake, she was so altered, that the prince said to himself, "If I marry her, I see no help for it: we must turn merman and mermaid, and go out to sea at once."

11. HISS!

The princess's pleasure in the lake had grown to a passion, and she could scarcely bear to be out of it for an hour. Imagine then her consternation, when, diving with the prince one night, a sudden suspicion seized her that the lake was not so deep as it used to be. The prince could not imagine what had happened. She shot to the surface, and, without a word, swam at full speed towards the higher side of the lake. He followed, begging to know if she was ill, or what was the matter. She never turned her head, or took the smallest notice of his question. Arrived at the shore, she coasted the rocks with minute inspection. But she was not able to come to a conclusion, for the moon was very small, and so she could not see well. She turned therefore and swam home, without saying a word to explain her conduct to the prince, of whose presence she seemed no longer conscious. He withdrew to his cave, in great perplexity and distress.

Next day she made many observations, which, alas! strengthened her fears. She saw that the banks were too dry; and that the grass on the shore, and the trailing plants on the rocks, were withering away. She caused marks to be made along the borders, and examined them, day after day, in all directions of the wind; till at last the horrible idea became a certain fact—that the surface of the lake was slowly sinking.

The poor princess nearly went out of the little mind she had. It was awful to her to see the lake, which she loved more than any living thing, lie dying before her eyes. It sank away, slowly vanishing. The tops of rocks that had never been seen till now, began to appear far down in the clear water. Before long they were dry in the sun. It was fearful to think of the mud that would soon lie there baking and festering, full of lovely creatures dying, and ugly creatures coming to life, like the unmaking of a world. And how hot the sun would be without any lake! She could not bear to swim in it any more, and began to pine away. Her life seemed bound up

216

with it; and ever as the lake sank, she pined. People said she would not live an hour after the lake was gone.

But she never cried.

A Proclamation was made to all the kingdom, that whosoever should discover the cause of the lake's decrease, would be rewarded after a princely fashion. Hum-Drum and Kopy-Keck applied themselves to their physics and metaphysics; but in vain. Not even they could suggest a cause.

Now the fact was that the old princess was at the root of the mischief. When she heard that her niece found more pleasure in the water than any one else out of it, she went into a rage, and cursed herself for her want of foresight.

"But," said she, "I will soon set all right. The king and the people shall die of thirst; their brains shall boil and frizzle in their skulls before I will lose my revenge."

And she laughed a ferocious laugh, that made the hairs on the back of her black cat stand erect with terror.

Then she went to an old chest in the room, and opening it, took out what looked like a piece of dried seaweed. This she threw into a tub of water. Then she threw some powder into the water, and stirred it with her bare arm, muttering over it words of hideous sound, and yet more hideous import. Then she set the tub aside, and took from the chest a huge bunch of a hundred rusty keys, that clattered in her shaking hands. Then she sat down and proceeded to oil them all. Before she had finished, out from the tub, the water of which had kept on a slow motion ever since she had ceased stirring it, came the head and half the body of a huge gray snake. But the witch did not look round. It grew out of the tub, waving itself backwards and forwards with a slow horizontal motion, till it reached the princess, when it laid its head upon her shoulder, and gave a low hiss in her ear. She started—but with joy; and seeing the head resting on her shoulder, drew it towards her and kissed it. Then she drew it all out of the tub, and wound it round her body. It was one of those dreadful creatures which few have ever beheld—the White Snakes of Darkness.

Then she took the keys and went down to her cellar; and as she unlocked the door she said to herself,—

"This is worth living for!"

Locking the door behind her, she descended a few steps into the cellar, and crossing it, unlocked another door into a dark, narrow passage. She locked this also behind her, and descended a few more steps. If any one had followed the witch-princess, he would have heard her unlock exactly one hundred doors, and descend a few steps after unlocking each. When she had unlocked the last, she entered a vast cave, the roof of which was supported by huge natural pillars of rock. Now this roof was the under side of the bottom of the lake.

She then untwined the snake from her body, and held it by the tail high above her. The hideous creature stretched up its head towards the roof of the cavern, which it was just able to reach. It then began to move its head backwards and forwards, with a slow oscillating motion, as if looking for something. At the same moment the witch began to walk round and round the cavern, coming nearer to the centre every circuit; while the head of the snake described the same path over the roof that she did over the floor, for she kept holding it up. And still it kept slowly oscillating. Round and round the cavern they went, ever lessening the circuit, till at last the snake made a sudden dart, and clung to the roof with its mouth.

"That's right, my beauty!" cried the princess; "drain it dry."

She let it go, left it hanging, and sat down on a great stone, with her black cat, which had followed her all round the cave, by her side. Then she began to knit and mutter awful words. The snake hung like a huge leech, sucking at the stone; the cat stood with his back arched, and his tail like a piece of cable, looking up at the snake; and the old woman sat and knitted and muttered. Seven days and seven nights they remained thus; when suddenly the serpent dropped from the roof as if exhausted, and shrivelled up till it was again like a piece of dried seaweed. The witch started to her feet, picked it up, put it in her pocket, and looked up at the roof. One drop of water was trembling on the spot where the snake had been sucking. As soon as she saw that, she turned and fled, followed by her cat. Shutting the door in a terrible hurry, she locked it, and having muttered some frightful words, sped to the next, which also she locked and muttered over; and so with all the hundred doors, till she arrived in her own cellar. Then she sat down on the floor ready to faint, but listening with malicious delight to the rushing of the water, which she could hear distinctly through all the hundred doors.

But this was not enough. Now that she had tasted revenge, she lost her patience. Without further measures, the lake would be too long in disappearing. So the next night, with the last shred of the dying old moon rising, she took some of the water in which she had revived the snake, put it in a bottle, and set out, accompanied by her cat. Before morning she had made the entire circuit of the lake, muttering fearful words as she crossed every stream, and casting into it some of the water out of her bottle. When she had finished the circuit she muttered yet again, and flung a handful of water towards the moon. Thereupon every spring in the country ceased to throb and bubble, dying away like the pulse of a dying man. The next day there was no sound of falling water to be heard along the borders of the lake. The very courses were dry; and the mountains showed no silvery streaks down their dark sides. And not alone had the fountains of mother Earth ceased to flow; for all the babies throughout the country were crying dreadfully—only without tears.

12. WHERE IS THE PRINCE?

Never since the night when the princess left him so abruptly had the prince had a single interview with her. He had seen her once or twice in the lake; but as far as he could discover, she had not been in it any more at night. He had sat and sung, and looked in vain for his Nereid; while she, like a true Nereid, was wasting away with her lake, sinking as it sank, withering as it dried. When at length he discovered the change that was taking place in the level of the water, he was in great alarm and perplexity. He could not tell whether the lake was dying because the lady had forsaken it; or whether the lady would not come because the lake had begun to sink. But he resolved to know so much at least.

He disguised himself, and, going to the palace, requested to see the lord chamberlain. His appearance at once gained his request; and the lord chamberlain, being a man of some insight, perceived that there was more in the prince's solicitation than met the ear. He felt likewise that no one could tell whence a solution of the present difficulties might arise. So he granted the prince's prayer to be made shoe-black to the princess. It was rather cunning in the prince to request such an easy post, for the princess could not possibly soil as many shoes as other princesses.

He soon learned all that could be told about the princess. He went nearly distracted; but after roaming about the lake for days, and diving in every depth that remained, all that he could do was to put an extra polish on the dainty pair of boots that was never called for.

For the princess kept her room, with the curtains drawn to shut out the dying lake, But she could not shut it out of her mind for a moment. It haunted her imagination so that she felt as if the lake were her soul, drying up within her, first to mud, then to madness and death. She thus brooded over the change, with all its dreadful accompaniments, till she was nearly distracted. As for the prince, she had forgotten him. However much she had enjoyed his company in the water, she did not care for him without it. But she seemed to have forgotten her father and mother too. The lake went on sinking. Small slimy spots began to appear, which glittered steadily amidst the changeful shine of the water. These grew to broad patches of mud, which widened and spread, with rocks here and there, and floundering fishes and crawling eels swarming. The people went everywhere catching these, and looking for anything that might have dropped from the royal boats.

At length the lake was all but gone, only a few of the deepest pools remaining unexhausted.

It happened one day that a party of youngsters found themselves on the brink of one of these pools in the very centre of the lake. It was a rocky basin of considerable depth. Looking in, they saw at the bottom something that shone yellow in the sun. A little boy jumped in and dived for it. It was a plate of gold covered with writing. They carried it to the king. On one side of it stood these words:—

"Death alone from death can save.
　　Love is death, and so is brave—
　　Love can fill the deepest grave.
　　Love loves on beneath the wave."

Now this was enigmatical enough to the king and courtiers. But the reverse of the plate explained it a little. Its writing amounted to this:—

"If the lake should disappear, they must find the hole through which the water ran. But it would be useless to try to stop it by any ordinary means. There was but one effectual mode.—The body of a living man could alone stanch the flow. The man must give himself of his own will; and the lake must take his life as it filled. Otherwise the offering would be of no avail. If the nation could not provide one hero, it was time it should perish."

13. HERE I AM.

This was a very disheartening revelation to the king—not that he was unwilling to sacrifice a subject, but that he was hopeless of finding a man willing to sacrifice himself. No time was to be lost, however, for the princess was lying motionless on her bed, and taking no nourishment but lake-water, which was now none of the best. Therefore the king caused the contents of the wonderful plate of gold to be published throughout the country.

No one, however, came forward.

The prince, having gone several days' journey into the forest, to consult a hermit whom he had met there on his way to Lagobel, knew nothing of the oracle till his return.

When he had acquainted himself with all the particulars, he sat down and thought,—

"She will die if I don't do it, and life would be nothing to me without her; so I shall lose nothing by doing it. And life will be as pleasant to her as ever, for she will soon forget me. And there will be so much more beauty and happiness in the world!—To be sure, I shall not see it." (Here the poor prince gave a sigh.) "How lovely the lake will be in the moonlight, with that glorious creature sporting in it like a wild goddess!—It is rather hard to be drowned by inches, though. Let me see —that will be seventy inches of me to drown." (Here he tried to laugh, but could not.) "The longer the better, however," he resumed: "for can I not bargain that the princess shall be beside me all the time? So I shall see her once more, kiss her perhaps,—who knows?—and die looking in her eyes. It will be no death. At least, I shall not feel it. And to see the lake filling for the beauty again!—All right! I am ready."

He kissed the princess's boot, laid it down, and hurried to the king's apartment. But feeling, as he went, that anything sentimental would be disagreeable, he

GEORGE MACDONALD

resolved to carry off the whole affair with nonchalance. So he knocked at the door of the king's counting-house, where it was all but a capital crime to disturb him.

When the king heard the knock he started up, and opened the door in a rage. Seeing only the shoeblack, he drew his sword. This, I am sorry to say, was his usual mode of asserting his regality when he thought his dignity was in danger. But the prince was not in the least alarmed.

"Please your Majesty, I'm your butler," said he.

"My butler! you lying rascal! What do you mean?"

"I mean, I will cork your big bottle."

"Is the fellow mad?" bawled the king, raising the point of his sword.

"I will put a stopper—plug—what you call it, in your leaky lake, grand monarch," said the prince.

The king was in such a rage that before he could speak he had time to cool, and to reflect that it would be great waste to kill the only man who was willing to be useful in the present emergency, seeing that in the end the insolent fellow would be as dead as if he had died by his Majesty's own hand. "Oh!" said he at last, putting up his sword with difficulty, it was so long; "I am obliged to you, you young fool! Take a glass of wine?"

"No, thank you," replied the prince.

"Very well," said the king. "Would you like to run and see your parents before you make your experiment?"

"No, thank you," said the prince.

"Then we will go and look for the hole at once," said his Majesty, and proceeded to call some attendants.

"Stop, please your Majesty; I have a condition to make," interposed the prince.

"What!" exclaimed the king, "a condition! and with me! How dare you?"

"As you please," returned the prince, coolly. "I wish your Majesty a good morning."

"You wretch! I will have you put in a sack, and stuck in the hole."

"Very well, your Majesty," replied the prince, becoming a little more respectful, lest the wrath of the king should deprive him of the pleasure of dying for the princess. "But what good will that do your Majesty? Please to remember that the oracle says the victim must offer himself."

"Well, you have offered yourself," retorted the king.

"Yes, upon one condition."

"Condition again!" roared the king, once more drawing his sword. "Begone! Somebody else will be glad enough to take the honour off your shoulders."

"Your Majesty knows it will not be easy to get another to take my place."

"Well, what is your condition?" growled the king, feeling that the prince was right.

"Only this," replied the prince: "that, as I must on no account die before I am fairly drowned, and the waiting will be rather wearisome, the princess, your daughter, shall go with me, feed me with her own hands, and look at me now and then to comfort me; for you must confess it IS rather hard. As soon as the water is up to my eyes, she may go and be happy, and forget her poor shoeblack."

Here the prince's voice faltered, and he very nearly grew sentimental, in spite of his resolution.

"Why didn't you tell me before what your condition was? Such a fuss about nothing!" exclaimed the king.

"Do you grant it?" persisted the prince. "Of course I do," replied the king.

"Very well. I am ready."

"Go and have some dinner, then, while I set my people to find the place."

The king ordered out his guards, and gave directions to the officers to find the hole in the lake at once. So the bed of the lake was marked out in divisions and thoroughly examined, and in an hour or so the hole was discovered. It was in the middle of a stone, near the centre of the lake, in the very pool where the golden plate had been found. It was a three-cornered hole of no great size. There was water all round the stone, but very little was flowing through the hole.

14. THIS IS VERY KIND OF YOU.

The prince went to dress for the occasion, for he was resolved to die like a prince.

When the princess heard that a man had offered to die for her, she was so transported that she jumped off the bed, feeble as she was, and danced about the room for joy. She did not care who the man was; that was nothing to her. The hole wanted stopping; and if only a man would do, why, take one. In an hour or two more everything was ready. Her maid dressed her in haste, and they carried her to the side of the lake. When she saw it she shrieked, and covered her face with her hands. They bore her across to the stone where they had already placed a little boat for her.

The water was not deep enough to float it, but they hoped it would be, before long. They laid her on cushions, placed in the boat wines and fruits and other nice things, and stretched a canopy over all.

In a few minutes the prince appeared. The princess recognized him at once, but did not think it worth while to acknowledge him.

"Here I am," said the prince. "Put me in."

"They told me it was a shoeblack," said the princess.

"So I am," said the prince. "I blacked your little boots three times a day, because they were all I could get of you. Put me in."

The courtiers did not resent his bluntness, except by saying to each other that he was taking it out in impudence.

But how was he to be put in? The golden plate contained no instructions on this point. The prince looked at the hole, and saw but one way. He put both his legs into it, sitting on the stone, and, stooping forward, covered the corner that remained open with his two hands. In this uncomfortable position he resolved to abide his fate, and turning to the people, said,—

"Now you can go."

The king had already gone home to dinner.

"Now you can go," repeated the princess after him, like a parrot.

The people obeyed her and went.

Presently a little wave flowed over the stone, and wetted one of the prince's knees. But he did not mind it much. He began to sing, and the song he sang was this:—

"As a world that has no well,
   Darting bright in forest dell;
   As a world without the gleam
   Of the downward-going stream;
   As a world without the glance
   Of the ocean's fair expanse;
   As a world where never rain
   Glittered on the sunny plain;—
   Such, my heart, thy world would be,
   If no love did flow in thee.
   As a world without the sound
   Of the rivulets underground;
   Or the bubbling of the spring
   Out of darkness wandering;
   Or the mighty rush and flowing
   Of the river's downward going;
   Or the music-showers that drop
   On the outspread beech's top;
   Or the ocean's mighty voice,
   When his lifted waves rejoice;—
   Such, my soul, thy world would be,
   If no love did sing in thee.
   Lady, keep thy world's delight;
   Keep the waters in thy sight.
   Love hath made me strong to go,
   For thy sake, to realms below,
   Where the water's shine and hum
   Through the darkness never come;
   Let, I pray, one thought of me
   Spring, a little well, in thee;
   Lest thy loveless soul be found
   Like a dry and thirsty ground."

"Sing again, prince. It makes it less tedious," said the princess.

But the prince was too much overcome to sing any more, and a long pause followed.

"This is very kind of you, prince," said the princess at last, quite coolly, as she lay in the boat with her eyes shut.

"I am sorry I can't return the compliment," thought the prince; "but you are worth dying for, after all."

Again a wavelet, and another, and another flowed over the stone, and wetted both the prince's knees; but he did not speak or move. Two—three—four hours passed in this way, the princess apparently asleep, and the prince very patient. But he was much disappointed in his position, for he had none of the consolation he had hoped for.

At last he could bear it no longer.

"Princess!" said he.

But at the moment up started the princess, crying,—

"I'm afloat! I'm afloat!"

And the little boat bumped against the stone.

"Princess!" repeated the prince, encouraged by seeing her wide awake and looking eagerly at the water.

"Well?" said she, without looking round.

"Your papa promised that you should look at me, and you haven't looked at me once."

"Did he? Then I suppose I must. But I am so sleepy!"

"Sleep then, darling, and don't mind me," said the poor prince.

"Really, you are very good," replied the princess. "I think I will go to sleep again."

"Just give me a glass of wine and a biscuit first," said the prince, very humbly.

"With all my heart," said the princess, and gaped as she said it.

She got the wine and the biscuit, however, and leaning over the side of the boat towards him, was compelled to look at him.

"Why, prince," she said, "you don't look well! Are you sure you don't mind it?"

"Not a bit," answered he, feeling very faint indeed. "Only I shall die before it is of any use to you, unless I have something to eat."

"There, then," said she, holding out the wine to him.

"Ah! you must feed me. I dare not move my hands. The water would run away directly."

"Good gracious!" said the princess; and she began at once to feed him with bits of biscuit and sips of wine.

As she fed him, he contrived to kiss the tips of her fingers now and then. She did not seem to mind it, one way or the other. But the prince felt better.

"Now for your own sake, princess," said he, "I cannot let you go to sleep. You must sit and look at me, else I shall not be able to keep up."

"Well, I will do anything I can to oblige you," answered she, with condescension; and, sitting down, she did look at him, and kept looking at him with wonderful steadiness, considering all things.

The sun went down, and the moon rose, and, gush after gush, the waters were rising up the prince's body. They were up to his waist now.

"Why can't we go and have a swim?" said the princess. "There seems to be water enough just about here."

"I shall never swim more," said the prince.

"Oh, I forgot," said the princess, and was silent.

So the water grew and grew, and rose up and up on the prince. And the princess sat and looked at him. She fed him now and then. The night wore on. The waters rose and rose. The moon rose likewise higher and higher, and shone full on the face of the dying prince. The water was up to his neck.

"Will you kiss me, princess?" said he, feebly.

The nonchalance was all gone now.

"Yes, I will," answered the princess, and kissed him with a long, sweet, cold kiss.

"Now," said he, with a sigh of content, "I die happy."

He did not speak again. The princess gave him some wine for the last time: he was past eating. Then she sat down again, and looked at him. The water rose and rose. It touched his chin. It touched his lower lip. It touched between his lips. He shut them hard to keep it out. The princess began to feel strange. It touched his upper lip. He breathed through his nostrils. The princess looked wild. It covered his nostrils. Her eyes looked scared, and shone strange in the moonlight. His head fell back; the water closed over it, and the bubbles of his last breath bubbled up through the water. The princess gave a shriek, and sprang into the lake.

She laid hold first of one leg, and then of the other, and pulled and tugged, but she could not move either. She stopped to take breath, and that made her think that HE could not get any breath. She was frantic. She got hold of him, and held his head above the water, which was possible now his hands were no longer on the hole. But it was of no use, for he was past breathing.

Love and water brought back all her strength. She got under the water, and pulled and pulled with her whole might, till at last she got one leg out. The other easily followed. How she got him into the boat she never could tell; but when she did, she fainted away. Coming to herself, she seized the oars, kept herself steady as best she could, and rowed and rowed, though she had never rowed before. Round rocks, and over shallows, and through mud she rowed, till she got to the landing-stairs of the palace. By this time her people were on the shore, for they had heard her shriek. She made them carry the prince to her own room, and lay him in her bed, and light a fire, and send for the doctors.

"But the lake, your Highness!" said the chamberlain, who, roused by the noise, came in, in his nightcap.

"Go and drown yourself in it!" she said.

This was the last rudeness of which the princess was ever guilty; and one must allow that she had good cause to feel provoked with the lord chamberlain.

Had it been the king himself, he would have fared no better. But both he and the queen were fast asleep. And the chamberlain went back to his bed. Somehow, the doctors never came. So the princess and her old nurse were left with the prince. But the old nurse was a wise woman, and knew what to do.

They tried everything for a long time without success. The princess was nearly distracted between hope and fear, but she tried on and on, one thing after another, and everything over and over again.

At last, when they had all but given it up, just as the sun rose, the prince opened his eyes.

15. LOOK AT THE RAIN!

The princess burst into a passion of tears, and fell on the floor. There she lay for an hour, and her tears never ceased. All the pent-up crying of her life was spent now. And a rain came on, such as had never been seen in that country. The sun shone all the time, and the great drops, which fell straight to the earth, shone likewise. The palace was in the heart of a rainbow. It was a rain of rubies, and sapphires, and emeralds, and topazes. The torrents poured from the mountains like molten gold; and if it had not been for its subterraneous outlet, the lake would have overflowed and inundated the country. It was full from shore to shore.

But the princess did not heed the lake. She lay on the floor and wept, and this rain within doors was far more wonderful than the rain out of doors.

For when it abated a little, and she proceeded to rise, she found, to her astonishment, that she could not. At length, after many efforts, she succeeded in getting upon her feet. But she tumbled down again directly. Hearing her fall, her old nurse uttered a yell of delight, and ran to her, screaming,—

"My darling child! she's found her gravity!"

"Oh, that's it! is it?" said the princess, rubbing her shoulder and her knee alternately. "I consider it very unpleasant. I feel as if I should be crushed to pieces."

"Hurrah!" cried the prince from the bed. "If you've come round, princess, so have I. How's the lake?"

"Brimful," answered the nurse.

"Then we're all happy."

"That we are indeed!" answered the princess, sobbing.

And there was rejoicing all over the country that rainy day. Even the babies forgot their past troubles, and danced and crowed amazingly. And the king told stories, and the queen listened to them. And he divided the money in his box, and she the honey in her pot, among all the children. And there was such jubilation as was never heard of before.

Of course the prince and princess were betrothed at once. But the princess had to learn to walk, before they could be married with any propriety. And this was not so easy at her time of life, for she could walk no more than a baby. She was always falling down and hurting herself.

"Is this the gravity you used to make so much of?" said she one day to the prince, as he raised her from the floor. "For my part, I was a great deal more comfortable without it."

"No, no, that's not it. This is it," replied the prince, as he took her up, and carried her about like a baby, kissing her all the time. "This is gravity."

"That's better," said she. "I don't mind that so much."

And she smiled the sweetest, loveliest smile in the prince's face. And she gave him one little kiss in return for all his; and he thought them overpaid, for he was beside himself with delight. I fear she complained of her gravity more than once after this, notwithstanding.

It was a long time before she got reconciled to walking. But the pain of learning it was quite counterbalanced by two things, either of which would have been sufficient consolation. The first was, that the prince himself was her teacher; and the second, that she could tumble into the lake as often as she pleased. Still, she preferred to have the prince jump in with her; and the splash they made before was nothing to the splash they made now.

The lake never sank again. In process of time, it wore the roof of the cavern quite through, and was twice as deep as before.

The only revenge the princess took upon her aunt was to tread pretty hard on her gouty toe the next time she saw her. But she was sorry for it the very next day, when she heard that the water had undermined her house, and that it had fallen in the night, burying her in its ruins; whence no one ever ventured to dig up her body. There she lies to this day.

So the prince and princess lived and were happy; and had crowns of gold, and clothes of cloth, and shoes of leather, and children of boys and girls, not one of whom was ever known, on the most critical occasion, to lose the smallest atom of his or her due proportion of gravity.

THE GIANT'S HEART

BY
GEORGE MACDONALD

THE GIANT'S HEART

There was once a giant who lived on the borders of Giantland where it touched on the country of common people.

Everything in Giantland was so big that the common people saw only a mass of awful mountains and clouds; and no living man had ever come from it, as far as anybody knew, to tell what he had seen in it.

Somewhere near these borders, on the other side, by the edge of a great forest, lived a labourer with his wife and a great many children. One day Tricksey-Wee, as they called her, teased her brother Buffy-Bob, till he could not bear it any longer, and gave her a box on the ear. Tricksey-Wee cried; and Buffy-Bob was so sorry and so ashamed of himself that he cried too, and ran off into the wood. He was so long gone that Tricksey-Wee began to be frightened, for she was very fond of her brother; and she was so distressed that she had first teased him and then cried, that at last she ran into the wood to look for him, though there was more chance of losing herself than of finding him. And, indeed, so it seemed likely to turn out; for, running on without looking, she at length found herself in a valley she knew nothing about. And no wonder; for what she thought was a valley with round, rocky sides, was no other than the space between two of the roots of a great tree that grew on the borders of Giantland. She climbed over the side of it, and went towards what she took for a black, round-topped mountain, far away; but which she soon discovered to be close to her, and to be a hollow place so great that she could not tell what it was hollowed out of. Staring at it, she found that it was a doorway; and going nearer and staring harder, she saw the door, far in, with a knocker of iron upon it, a great many yards above her head, and as large as the anchor of a big ship. Now, nobody had ever been unkind to Tricksey-Wee, and therefore she was not afraid of anybody. For Buffy-Bob's box on the ear she did not think worth considering. So spying a little hole at the bottom of the door which had been nibbled by some giant mouse, she crept through it, and found herself in an enormous hall. She could not have seen the other end of it at all, except for the great fire that was burning there, diminished to a spark in the distance. Towards this fire she ran as fast as she could, and was not far from it when something fell before her with a great clatter, over which she tumbled, and went rolling on the floor. She was not much hurt however, and got up in a moment. Then she saw that what she had fallen over was not unlike a great iron bucket. When she examined it more closely, she discovered that it was a thimble; and looking up to see who had dropped it, beheld a huge face, with spectacles as big as the round windows in a church, bending over her, and looking everywhere for the thimble. Tricksey-Wee immediately laid hold of it in both her arms, and lifted it about an inch nearer to the nose of the peering giantess. This movement made the old lady see where it was, and, her finger popping into it, it vanished from the eyes of Tricksey-Wee, buried in the folds of a white stocking like a cloud in the sky, which Mrs. Giant was busy darning. For it was Saturday night, and her husband would wear nothing but white stockings on Sunday. To be sure he did eat little children, but only *very* little ones; and if ever it crossed his mind that it was wrong to do so, he always said to himself that he wore whiter stockings on Sunday than any other giant in all Giantland.

At the same instant Tricksey-Wee heard a sound like the wind in a tree full of leaves, and could not think what it could be; till, looking up, she found that it was the giantess whispering to her; and when she tried very hard she could hear what she said well enough.

"Run away, dear little girl," she said, "as fast as you can; for my husband will be home in a few minutes."

"But I've never been naughty to your husband," said Tricksey-Wee, looking up in the giantess's face.

"That doesn't matter. You had better go. He is fond of little children, particularly little girls."

"Oh, then he won't hurt me."

"I am not sure of that. He is so fond of them that he eats them up; and I am afraid he couldn't help hurting you a little. He's a very good man though."

"Oh! then—" began Tricksey-Wee, feeling rather frightened; but before she could finish her sentence she heard the sound of footsteps very far apart and very heavy. The next moment, who should come running towards her, full speed, and as pale as death, but Buffy-Bob. She held out her arms, and he ran into them. But when she tried to kiss him, she only kissed the back of his head; for his white face and round eyes were turned to the door.

"Run, children; run and hide!" said the giantess.

"Come, Buffy," said Tricksey; "yonder's a great brake; we'll hide in it."

The brake was a big broom; and they had just got into the bristles of it when they heard the door open with a sound of thunder, and in stalked the giant. You would have thought you saw the whole earth through the door when he opened it, so wide was it; and when he closed it, it was like nightfall.

"Where is that little boy?" he cried, with a voice like the bellowing of a cannon. "He looked a very nice boy indeed. I am almost sure he crept through the mouse-hole at the bottom of the door. Where is he, my dear?"

"I don't know," answered the giantess.

"But you know it is wicked to tell lies; don't you, my dear?" retorted the giant.

"Now, you ridiculous old Thunderthump!" said his wife, with a smile as broad as the sea in the sun, "how can I mend your white stockings and look after little boys? You have got plenty to last you over Sunday, I am sure. Just look what good little boys they are!"

Tricksey-Wee and Buffy-Bob peered through the bristles, and discovered a row of little boys, about a dozen, with very fat faces and goggle eyes, sitting before the fire, and looking stupidly into it. Thunderthump intended the most of these for pickling, and was feeding them well before salting them. Now and then, however, he could not keep his teeth off them, and would eat one by the bye, without salt.

He strode up to the wretched children. Now, what made them very wretched indeed was, that they knew if they could only keep from eating, and grow thin, the giant would dislike them, and turn them out to find their way home; but notwithstanding this, so greedy were they, that they ate as much as ever they could hold. The giantess, who fed them, comforted herself with thinking that they were not real boys and girls, but only little pigs pretending to be boys and girls.

"Now tell me the truth," cried the giant, bending his face down over them. They shook with terror, and every one hoped it was somebody else the giant liked best. "Where is the little boy that ran into the hall just now? Whoever tells me a lie shall be instantly boiled."

"He's in the broom," cried one dough-faced boy. "He's in there, and a little girl with him."

"The naughty children," cried the giant, "to hide from *me!*" And he made a stride towards the broom.

"Catch hold of the bristles, Bobby. Get right into a tuft, and hold on," cried Tricksey-Wee, just in time.

The giant caught up the broom, and seeing nothing under it, set it down again with a force that threw them both on the floor. He then made two strides to the boys, caught the dough-faced one by the neck, took the lid off a great pot that was boiling on the fire, popped him in as if he had been a trussed chicken, put the lid on again, and saying, "There, boys! See what comes of lying!" asked no more questions; for, as he always kept his word, he was afraid he might have to do the same to them all; and he did not like boiled boys. He like to eat them crisp, as radishes, whether forked or not, ought to be eaten. He then sat down, and asked his wife if his supper was ready. She looked into the pot, and throwing the boy out with the ladle, as if he had been a black beetle that had tumbled in and had had the worst of it, answered that she thought it was. Whereupon he rose to help her; and taking the pot from the fire, poured the whole contents, bubbling and splashing, into a dish like a vat. Then they sat down to supper. The children in the broom could not see what they had; but it seemed to agree with them, for the giant talked like thunder, and the giantess answered like the sea, and they grew chattier and chattier. At length the giant said,—

"I don't feel quite comfortable about that heart of mine." And as he spoke, instead of laying his hand on his bosom, he waved it away towards the corner where the children were peeping from the broom-bristles, like frightened little mice.

"Well, you know, my darling Thunderthump," answered his wife, "I always thought it ought to be nearer home. But you know best, of course."

"Ha! ha! You don't know where it is, wife. I moved it a month ago."

"What a man you are, Thunderthump! You trust any creature alive rather than your wife."

Here the giantess gave a sob which sounded exactly like a wave going flop into the mouth of a cave up to the roof.

"Where have you got it now?" she resumed, checking her emotion.

"Well, Doodlem, I don't mind telling *you*," answered the giant, soothingly. "The great she-eagle has got it for a nest egg. She sits on it night and day, and thinks she will bring the greatest eagle out of it that ever sharpened his beak on the rocks of Mount Skycrack. I can warrant no one else will touch it while she has got it. But she is rather capricious, and I confess I am not easy about it; for the least scratch of one of her claws would do for me at once. And she *has* claws."

I refer anyone who doubts this part of my story to certain chronicles of Giant-land preserved among the Celtic nations. It was quite a common thing for a giant to put his heart out to nurse, because he did not like the trouble and responsibility of doing it himself; although I must confess it was a dangerous sort of plan to take, especially with such a delicate viscus as the heart.

All this time Buffy-Bob and Tricksey-Wee were listening with long ears.

"Oh!" thought Tricksey-Wee, "if I could but find the giant's cruel heart, wouldn't I give it a squeeze!"

The giant and giantess went on talking for a long time. The giantess kept advising the giant to hide his heart somewhere in the house; but he seemed afraid of the advantage it would give her over him.

"You could hide it at the bottom of the flour-barrel," said she.

"That would make me feel chokey," answered he.

"Well, in the coal-cellar. Or in the dust-hole—that's the place! No one would think of looking for your heart in the dust-hole."

"Worse and worse!" cried the giant.

"Well, the water-butt," suggested she.

"No, no; it would grow spongy there," said he.

"Well, what *will* you do with it?"

"I will leave it a month longer where it is, and then I will give it to the Queen of the Kangaroos, and she will carry it in her pouch for me. It is best to change its place, you know, lest my enemies should scent it out. But, dear Doodlem, it's a fretting care to have a heart of one's own to look after. The responsibility is too much for me. If it were not for a bite of a radish now and then, I never could bear it."

Here the giant looked lovingly towards the row of little boys by the fire, all of whom were nodding, or asleep on the floor.

"Why don't you trust it to me, dear Thunderthump?" said his wife. "I would take the best possible care of it."

"I don't doubt it, my love. But the responsibility would be too much for *you*. You would no longer be my darling, light-hearted, airy, laughing Doodlem. It would transform you into a heavy, oppressed woman, weary of life—as I am."

The giant closed his eyes and pretended to go to sleep. His wife got his stockings, and went on with her darning. Soon the giant's pretence became reality, and the giantess began to nod over her work.

"Now, Buffy," whispered Tricksey-Wee, "now's our time. I think it's moonlight, and we had better be off. There's a door with a hole for the cat just behind us."

"All right," said Bob; "I'm ready."

So they got out of the broom-brake and crept to the door. But to their great disappointment, when they got through it, they found themselves in a sort of shed. It was full of tubs and things, and, though it was built of wood only, they could not find a crack.

"Let us try this hole," said Tricksey; for the giant and giantess were sleeping behind them, and they dared not go back.

"All right," said Bob.

He seldom said anything else than *All right*.

Now this hole was in a mound that came in through the wall of the shed, and went along the floor for some distance. They crawled into it, and found it very dark. But groping their way along, they soon came to a small crack, through which they saw grass, pale in the moonshine. As they crept on, they found the hole began to get wider and lead upwards.

"What is that noise of rushing?" said Buffy-Bob.

"I can't tell," replied Tricksey; "for, you see, I don't know what we are in."

The fact was, they were creeping along a channel in the heart of a giant tree; and the noise they heard was the noise of the sap rushing along in its wooden pipes. When they laid their ears to the wall, they heard it gurgling along with a pleasant noise.

"It sounds kind and good," said Tricksey. "It is water running. Now it must be running from somewhere to somewhere. I think we had better go on, and we shall come somewhere."

It was now rather difficult to go on, for they had to climb as if they were climbing a hill; and now the passage was wide. Nearly worn out, they saw light overhead at last, and creeping through a crack into the open air, found themselves on the fork of a huge tree. A great, broad, uneven space lay around them, out of which spread boughs in every direction, the smallest of them as big as the biggest tree in the country of common people. Overhead were leaves enough to supply all the trees they had ever seen. Not much moonlight could come through, but the leaves would glimmer white in the wind at times. The tree was full of giant birds. Every now and then, one would sweep through, with a great noise. But, except an occasional chirp, sounding like a shrill pipe in a great organ, they made no noise. All at once an owl began to hoot. He thought he was singing. As soon as he began, other birds replied, making rare game of him. To their astonishment, the children found they could understand every word they sang. And what they sang was something like this:—

"I will sing a song.
  I'm the Owl."
   "Sing a song, you Sing-song
   Ugly fowl!
   What will you sing about,
   Night in and Day out?"
   "Sing about the night;
   I'm the Owl."

"You could not see for the light,
   Stupid fowl."
"Oh! the Moon! and the Dew!
   And the Shadows!—tu-whoo!"

The owl spread out his silent, soft, sly wings, and lighting between Tricksey-Wee and Buffy-Bob, nearly smothered them, closing up one under each wing. It was like being buried in a down bed. But the owl did not like anything between his sides and his wings, so he opened his wings again, and the children made haste to get out. Tricksey-Wee immediately went in front of the bird, and looking up into his huge face, which was as round as the eyes of the giantess's spectacles, and much bigger, dropped a pretty courtesy, and said,—"Please, Mr. Owl, I want to whisper to you."

"Very well, small child," answered the owl, looking important, and stooping his ear towards her. "What is it?"

"Please tell me where the eagle lives that sits on the giant's heart."

"Oh, you naughty child! That's a secret. For shame!"

And with a great hiss that terrified them, the owl flew into the tree. All birds are fond of secrets; but not many of them can keep them so well as the owl.

So the children went on because they did not know what else to do. They found the way very rough and difficult, the tree was so full of humps and hollows. Now and then they plashed into a pool of rain; now and then they came upon twigs growing out of the trunk where they had no business, and they were as large as full-grown poplars. Sometimes they came upon great cushions of soft moss, and on one of them they lay down and rested. But they had not lain long before they spied a large nightingale sitting on a branch, with its bright eyes looking up at the moon. In a moment more he began to sing, and the birds about him began to reply, but in a different tone from that in which they had replied to the owl. Oh, the birds did call the nightingale such pretty names! The nightingale sang, and the birds replied like this:—

"I will sing a song.
   I'm the nightingale."
"Sing a song, long, long,
   Little Neverfail!
 What will you sing about,
   Light in or light out?"
"Sing about the light
   Gone away;
 Down, away, and out of sight—
   Poor lost Day!
 Mourning for the Day dead,
   O'er his dim bed."

The nightingale sang so sweetly, that the children would have fallen asleep but for fear of losing any of the song. When the nightingale stopped they got up and wandered on. They did not know where they were going, but they thought it best to keep going on, because then they might come upon something or other. They were very sorry they had forgotten to ask the nightingale about the eagle's nest, but his music had put everything else out of their heads. They resolved, however, not to forget the next time they had a chance. So they went on and on, till they were both tired, and Tricksey-Wee said at last, trying to laugh,—

"I declare my legs feel just like a Dutch doll's."

"Then here's the place to go to bed in," said Buffy-Bob.

They stood at the edge of a last year's nest, and looked down with delight into the round, mossy cave. Then they crept gently in, and, lying down in each other's arms, found it so deep, and warm, and comfortable, and soft, that they were soon fast asleep.

Now, close beside them, in a hollow, was another nest, in which lay a lark and his wife; and the children were awakened, very early in the morning, by a dispute between Mr. and Mrs. Lark.

"Let me up," said the lark.

"It is not time," said the lark's wife.

"It is," said the lark, rather rudely. "The darkness is quite thin. I can almost see my own beak."

"Nonsense!" said the lark's wife. "You know you came home yesterday morning quite worn out—you had to fly so very high before you saw him. I am sure he would not mind if you took it a little easier. Do be quiet and go to sleep again."

"That's not it at all," said the lark. "He doesn't want me. I want him.

Let me up, I say."

He began to sing; and Tricksey-Wee and Buffy-Bob, having now learned the way, answered him:—

"I will sing a song.
    I'm the Lark."
  "Sing, sing, Throat-strong,
    Little Kill-the-dark.
  What will you sing about,
  Now the night is out?"
"I can only call;
    I can't think.
  Let me up—that's all.
    Let me drink!
  Thirsting all the long night
  For a drink of light."

By this time the lark was standing on the edge of his nest and looking at the children.

"Poor little things! You can't fly," said the lark.

"No; but we can look up," said Tricksey.

"Ah, you don't know what it is to see the very first of the sun."

"But we know what it is to wait till he comes. He's no worse for your seeing him first, is he?"

"Oh no, certainly not," answered the lark, with condescension, and then, bursting into his *Jubilate*, he sprang aloft, clapping his wings like a clock running down.

"Tell us where—" began Buffy-Bob.

But the lark was out of sight. His song was all that was left of him.

That was everywhere, and he was nowhere.

"Selfish bird!" said Buffy. "It's all very well for larks to go hunting the sun, but they have no business to despise their neighbours, for all that."

"Can I be of any use to you?" said a sweet bird-voice out of the nest.

This was the lark's wife, who stayed at home with the young larks while her husband went to church.

"Oh! thank you. If you please," answered Tricksey-Wee.

And up popped a pretty brown head; and then up came a brown feathery body; and last of all came the slender legs on to the edge of the nest. There she turned, and, looking down into the nest, from which came a whole litany of chirpings for breakfast, said, "Lie still, little ones." Then she turned to the children.

"My husband is King of the Larks," she said.

Buffy-Bob took off his cap, and Tricksey-Wee courtesied very low.

"Oh, it's not me," said the bird, looking very shy. "I am only his wife. It's my husband." And she looked up after him into the sky, whence his song was still falling like a shower of musical hailstones. Perhaps *she* could see him.

"He's a splendid bird," said Buffy-Bob; "only you know he *will* get up a little too early."

"Oh, no! he doesn't. It's only his way, you know. But tell me what I can do for you."

"Tell us, please, Lady Lark, where the she-eagle lives that sits on Giant Thunderthump's heart."

"Oh! that is a secret."

"Did you promise not to tell?"

"No; but larks ought to be discreet. They see more than other birds."

"But you don't fly up high like your husband, do you?"

"Not often. But it's no matter. I come to know things for all that."

"Do tell me, and I will sing you a song," said Tricksey-Wee.

"Can you sing too?—You have got no wings!"

"Yes. And I will sing you a song I learned the other day about a lark and his wife."

"Please do," said the lark's wife. "Be quiet, children, and listen."

Tricksey-Wee was very glad she happened to know a song which would please the lark's wife, at least, whatever the lark himself might have thought of it, if he had heard it. So she sang,—

"'Good morrow, my lord!' in the sky alone,
   Sang the lark, as the sun ascended his throne.
   'Shine on me, my lord; I only am come,
   Of all your servants, to welcome you home.

I have flown a whole hour, right up, I swear,
To catch the first shine of your golden hair!'
"'Must I thank you, then,' said the king, 'Sir Lark,
For flying so high, and hating the dark?
You ask a full cup for half a thirst:
Half is love of me, and half love to be first.
There's many a bird that makes no haste,
But waits till I come. That's as much to my taste.
"And the king hid his head in a turban of cloud;
And the lark stopped singing, quite vexed and cowed.
But he flew up higher, and thought, 'Anon,
The wrath of the king will be over and gone,
And his crown, shining out of its cloudy fold,
Will change my brown feathers to a glory of gold.'
"So he flew, with the strength of a lark he flew.
But as he rose, the cloud rose too;
And not a gleam of the golden hair
Came through the depth of the misty air;
Till, weary with flying, with sighing sore,
The strong sun-seeker could do no more.
"His wings had had no chrism of gold,
And his feathers felt withered and worn and old;
So he quivered and sank, and dropped like a stone.
And there on his nest, where he left her, alone,
Sat his little wife on her little eggs,
Keeping them warm with wings and legs.
"Did I say alone? Ah, no such thing!
Full in her face was shining the king.
'Welcome, Sir Lark! You look tired,' said he.
'*Up* is not always the best way to me.
While you have been singing so high and away,
I've been shining to your little wife all day.'
"He had set his crown all about the nest,
And out of the midst shone her little brown breast;
And so glorious was she in russet gold,
That for wonder and awe Sir Lark grew cold.
He popped his head under her wing, and lay
As still as a stone, till the king was away."

As soon as Tricksey-Wee had finished her song, the lark's wife began a low, sweet, modest little song of her own; and after she had piped away for two or three minutes, she said,—

"You dear children, what can I do for you?"

"Tell us where the she-eagle lives, please," said Tricksey-Wee.

"Well, I don't think there can be much harm in telling such wise, good children," said Lady Lark; "I am sure you don't want to do any mischief."

"Oh, no; quite the contrary," said Buffy-Bob.

"Then I'll tell you. She lives on the very topmost peak of Mount Skycrack; and the only way to get up is to climb on the spiders' webs that cover it from top to bottom."

"That's rather serious," said Tricksey-Wee.

"But you don't want to go up, you foolish little thing! You can't go. And what do you want to go up for?"

"That is a secret," said Tricksey-Wee.

"Well, it's no business of mine," rejoined Lady Lark, a little offended, and quite vexed that she had told them. So she flew away to find some breakfast for her little ones, who by this time were chirping very impatiently. The children looked at each other, joined hands, and walked off.

In a minute more the sun was up, and they soon reached the outside of the tree. The bark was so knobby and rough, and full of twigs, that they managed to get down, though not without great difficulty. Then, far away to the north, they saw a huge peak, like the spire of a church, going right up into the sky. They thought this must be Mount Skycrack, and turned their faces towards it. As they went on, they saw a giant or two, now and then, striding about the fields or through the woods, but they kept out of their way. Nor were they in much danger; for it was only one or two of the border giants that were so very fond of children.

At last they came to the foot of Mount Skycrack. It stood in a plain alone, and shot right up, I don't know how many thousand feet, into the air, a long, narrow, spearlike mountain. The whole face of it, from top to bottom, was covered with a network of spiders' webs, with threads of various sizes, from that of silk to that of whipcord. The webs shook and quivered, and waved in the sun, glittering like silver. All about ran huge greedy spiders, catching huge silly flies, and devouring them.

Here they sat down to consider what could be done. The spiders did not heed them, but ate away at the flies.—Now, at the foot of the mountain, and all round it, was a ring of water, not very broad, but very deep. As they sat watching them, one of the spiders, whose web was woven across this water, somehow or other lost his hold, and fell in on his back. Tricksey-Wee and Buffy-Bob ran to his assistance, and laying hold each of one of his legs, succeeded, with the help of the other legs, which struggled spiderfully, in getting him out upon dry land. As soon as he had shaken himself, and dried himself a little, the spider turned to the children, saying,—

"And now, what can I do for you?"

"Tell us, please," said they, "how we can get up the mountain to the she-eagle's nest."

"Nothing is easier," answered the spider. "Just run up there, and tell them all I sent you, and nobody will mind you."

"But we haven't got claws like you, Mr. Spider," said Buffy.

"Ah! no more you have, poor unprovided creatures! Still, I think we can manage it. Come home with me."

"You won't eat us, will you?" said Buffy.

"My dear child," answered the spider, in a tone of injured dignity, "I eat nothing but what is mischievous or useless. You have helped me, and now I will help you."

The children rose at once, and climbing as well as they could, reached the spider's nest in the centre of the web. Nor did they find it very difficult; for whenever too great a gap came, the spider spinning a strong cord stretched it just where they would have chosen to put their feet next. He left them in his nest, after bringing them two enormous honey-bags, taken from bees that he had caught; but presently about six of the wisest of the spiders came back with him. It was rather horrible to look up and see them all round the mouth of the nest, looking down on them in contemplation, as if wondering whether they would be nice eating. At length one of them said,—"Tell us truly what you want with the eagle, and we will try to help you."

Then Tricksey-Wee told them that there was a giant on the borders who treated little children no better than radishes, and that they had narrowly escaped being eaten by him; that they had found out that the great she-eagle of Mount Skycrack was at present sitting on his heart; and that, if they could only get hold of the heart, they would soon teach the giant better behaviour.

"But," said their host, "if you get at the heart of the giant, you will find it as large as one of your elephants. What can you do with it?"

"The least scratch will kill it," replied Buffy-Bob.

"Ah! but you might do better than that," said the spider.—"Now we have resolved to help you. Here is a little bag of spider-juice. The giants cannot bear spiders, and this juice is dreadful poison to them. We are all ready to go up with you, and drive the eagle away. Then you must put the heart into this other bag, and bring it down with you; for then the giant will be in your power."

"But how can we do that?" said Buffy. "The bag is not much bigger than a pudding-bag."

"But it is as large as you will be able to carry."

"Yes; but what are we to do with the heart?"

"Put it in the bag, to be sure. Only, first, you must squeeze a drop out of the other bag upon it. You will see what will happen."

"Very well; we will do as you tell us," said Tricksey-Wee. "And now, if you please, how shall we go?"

"Oh, that's our business," said the first spider. "You come with me, and my grandfather will take your brother. Get up."

So Tricksey-Wee mounted on the narrow part of the spider's back, and held fast. And Buffy-Bob got on the grandfather's back. And up they scrambled, over one web after another, up and up—so fast! And every spider followed; so that, when Tricksey-Wee looked back, she saw a whole army of spiders scrambling after them.

"What can we want with so many?" she thought; but she said nothing.

The moon was now up, and it was a splendid sight below and around them. All Giantland was spread out under them, with its great hills, lakes, trees, and animals. And all above them was the clear heaven, and Mount Skycrack rising into it, with its endless ladders of spider-webs, glittering like cords made of moonbeams. And up the moonbeams went, crawling, and scrambling, and racing, a huge army of huge spiders.

At length they reached all but the very summit, where they stopped. Tricksey-Wee and Buffy-Bob could see above them a great globe of feathers, that finished off the mountain like an ornamental knob.

"But how shall we drive her off?" said Buffy.

"We'll soon manage that," answered the grandfather-spider. "Come on you, down there."

Up rushed the whole army, past the children, over the edge of the nest, on to the she-eagle, and buried themselves in her feathers. In a moment she became very restless, and went pecking about with her beak. All at once she spread out her wings, with a sound like a whirlwind, and flew off to bathe in the sea; and then the spiders began to drop from her in all directions on their gossamer wings. The children had to hold fast to keep the wind of the eagle's flight from blowing them off. As soon as it was over, they looked into the nest, and there lay the giant's heart—an awful and ugly thing.

"Make haste, child!" said Tricksey's spider.

So Tricksey took her bag, and squeezed a drop out of it upon the heart. She thought she heard the giant give a far-off roar of pain, and she nearly fell from her seat with terror. The heart instantly began to shrink. It shrunk and shrivelled till it was nearly gone; and Buffy-Bob caught it up and put it into his bag. Then the two spiders turned and went down again as fast as they could. Before they got to the bottom, they heard the shrieks of the she-eagle over the loss of her egg; but the spiders told them not to be alarmed, for her eyes were too big to see them.—By the time they reached the foot of the mountain, all the spiders had got home, and were busy again catching flies, as if nothing had happened.

After renewed thanks to their friends, the children set off, carrying the giant's heart with them.

"If you should find it at all troublesome, just give it a little more spider-juice directly," said the grandfather, as they took their leave.

Now, the giant had given an awful roar of pain the moment they anointed his heart, and had fallen down in a fit, in which he lay so long that all the boys might have escaped if they had not been so fat. One did, and got home in safety. For days the giant was unable to speak. The first words he uttered were,—

"Oh, my heart! my heart!"

"Your heart is safe enough, dear Thunderstump," said his wife. "Really, a man of your size ought not to be so nervous and apprehensive. I am ashamed of you."

"You have no heart, Doodlem," answered he. "I assure you that at this moment mine is in the greatest danger. It has fallen into the hands of foes, though who they are I cannot tell."

Here he fainted again; for Tricksey-Wee, finding the heart begin to swell a little, had given it the least touch of spider-juice.

Again he recovered, and said,—

"Dear Doodlem, my heart is coming back to me. It is coming nearer and nearer."

After lying silent for hours, he exclaimed,—

"It is in the house, I know!"

And he jumped up and walked about, looking in every corner.

As he rose, Tricksey-Wee and Buffy-Bob came out of the hole in the tree-root, and through the cat-hole in the door, and walked boldly towards the giant. Both kept their eyes busy watching him. Led by the love of his own heart, the giant soon spied them, and staggered furiously towards them.

"I will eat you, you vermin!" he cried. "Here with my heart!"

Tricksey gave the heart a sharp pinch. Down fell the giant on his knees, blubbering, and crying, and begging for his heart.

"You shall have it, if you behave yourself properly," said Tricksey.

"How shall I behave myself properly?" asked he, whimpering.

"Take all those boys and girls, and carry them home at once."

"I'm not able; I'm too ill. I should fall down."

"Take them up directly."

"I can't, till you give me my heart."

"Very well!" said Tricksey; and she gave the heart another pinch.

The giant jumped to his feet, and catching up all the children, thrust some into his waistcoat pockets, some into his breast pocket, put two or three into his hat, and took a bundle of them under each arm. Then he staggered to the door.

All this time poor Doodlem was sitting in her arm-chair, crying, and mending a white stocking.

The giant led the way to the borders. He could not go so fast but that Buffy and Tricksey managed to keep up with him. When they reached the borders, they thought it would be safer to let the children find their own way home. So they told him to set them down. He obeyed.

"Have you put them all down, Mr. Thunderthump?" asked Tricksey-Wee.

"Yes," said the giant.

"That's a lie!" squeaked a little voice; and out came a head from his waistcoat pocket.

Tricksey-Wee pinched the heart till the giant roared with pain.

"You're not a gentleman. You tell stories," she said.

"He was the thinnest of the lot," said Thunderthump, crying.

"Are you all there now, children?" asked Tricksey.

"Yes, ma'am," returned they, after counting themselves very carefully, and with some difficulty; for they were all stupid children.

"Now," said Tricksey-Wee to the giant, "will you promise to carry off no more children, and never to eat a child again all you life?"

"Yes, yes! I promise," answered Thunderthump, sobbing.

"And you will never cross the borders of Giantland?"

"Never."

"And you shall never again wear white stockings on a Sunday, all your life long. —Do you promise?"

The giant hesitated at this, and began to expostulate; but Tricksey-Wee, believing it would be good for his morals, insisted; and the giant promised.

Then she required of him, that, when she gave him back his heart, he should give it to his wife to take care of for him for ever after.

The poor giant fell on his knees, and began again to beg. But

Tricksey-Wee giving the heart a slight pinch, he bawled out,—

"Yes, yes! Doodlem shall have it, I swear. Only she must not put it in the flour-barrel, or in the dust-hole."

"Certainly not. Make your own bargain with her.—And you promise not to interfere with my brother and me, or to take any revenge for what we have done?"

"Yes, yes, my dear children; I promise everything. Do, pray, make haste and give me back my poor heart."

"Wait there, then, till I bring it to you."

"Yes, yes. Only make haste, for I feel very faint."

Tricksey-Wee began to undo the mouth of the bag. But Buffy-Bob, who had got very knowing on his travels, took out his knife with the pretence of cutting the string; but, in reality, to be prepared for any emergency.

No sooner was the heart out of the bag, than it expanded to the size of a bullock;

and the giant, with a yell of rage and vengeance, rushed on the two children, who had stepped sideways from the terrible heart. But Buffy-Bob was too quick for Thunderthump. He sprang to the heart, and buried his knife in it, up to the hilt. A fountain of blood spouted from it; and with a dreadful groan the giant fell dead at the feet of little Tricksey-Wee, who could not help being sorry for him after all.

THE GOLDEN KEY

BY
GEORGE MACDONALD

THE GOLDEN KEY

There was a boy who used to sit in the twilight and listen to his great-aunt's stories.

She told him that if he could reach the place where the end of the rainbow stands he would find there a golden key.

"And what is the key for?" the boy would ask. "What is it the key of? What will it open?"

"That nobody knows," his aunt would reply. "He has to find that out."

"I suppose, being gold," the boy once said, thoughtfully, "that I could get a good deal of money for it if I sold it."

"Better never find it than sell it," returned his aunt. And then the boy went to bed and dreamed about the golden key.

Now, all that his great-aunt told the boy about the golden key would have been nonsense, had it not been that their little house stood on the borders of Fairyland. For it is perfectly well known that out of Fairyland nobody ever can find where the rainbow stands. The creature takes such good care of its golden key, always flitting from place to place, lest anyone should find it! But in Fairyland it is quite different. Things that look real in this country look very thin indeed in Fairyland, while some of the things that here cannot stand still for a moment, will not move there. So it was not in the least absurd of the old lady to tell her nephew such things about the golden key.

"Did you ever know anybody find it?" he asked one evening.

"Yes. Your father, I believe, found it."

"And what did he do with it, can you tell me?"

"He never told me."

"What was it like?"

"He never showed it to me."

"How does a new key come there always?"

"I don't know. There it is."

"Perhaps it is the rainbow's egg."

"Perhaps it is. You will be a happy boy if you find the nest."

"Perhaps it comes tumbling down the rainbow from the sky."

"Perhaps it does."

One evening, in summer, he went into his own room, and stood at the lattice-window, and gazed into the forest which fringed the outskirts of Fairyland. It came close up to his great-aunt's garden, and, indeed, sent some straggling trees into it. The forest lay to the east, and the sun, which was setting behind the cottage, looked straight into the dark wood with his level red eye. The trees were all old, and had few branches below, so that the sun could see a great way into the forest; and the boy, being keen-sighted, could see almost as far as the sun. The trunks stood like rows of red columns in the shine of the red sun, and he could see down aisle after aisle in the vanishing distance. And as he gazed into the forest he began to feel as if the trees were all waiting for him, and had something they could not go on with till he came to them. But he was hungry, and wanted his supper. So he lingered.

Suddenly, far among the trees, as far as the sun could shine, he saw a glorious thing. It was the end of a rainbow, large and brilliant. He could count all the seven colours, and could see shade after shade beyond the violet; while before the red stood a colour more gorgeous and mysterious still. It was a colour he had never seen before. Only the spring of the rainbow-arch was visible. He could see nothing of it above the trees.

"The golden key!" he said to himself, and darted out of the house, and into the wood.

He had not gone far before the sun set. But the rainbow only glowed the brighter: for the rainbow of Fairyland is not dependent upon the sun as ours is. The trees welcomed him. The bushes made way for him. The rainbow grew larger and brighter; and at length he found himself within two trees of it.

It was a grand sight, burning away there in silence, with its gorgeous, its lovely, its delicate colours, each distinct, all combining. He could now see a great deal more of it. It rose high into the blue heavens, but bent so little that he could not tell how high the crown of the arch must reach. It was still only a small portion of a huge bow.

He stood gazing at it till he forgot himself with delight—even forgot the key which he had come to seek. And as he stood it grew more wonderful still. For in each of the colours, which was as large as the column of a church, he could faintly see beautiful forms slowly ascending as if by the steps of a winding stair. The forms appeared irregularly—now one, now many, now several, now none—men and women and children—all different, all beautiful.

He drew nearer to the rainbow. It vanished. He started back a step in dismay. It was there again, as beautiful as ever. So he contented himself with standing as near it as he might, and watching the forms that ascended the glorious colours towards the unknown height of the arch, which did not end abruptly, but faded away in the blue air, so gradually that he could not say where it ceased.

When the thought of the golden key returned, the boy very wisely proceeded to mark out in his mind the space covered by the foundation of the rainbow, in order that he might know where to search, should the rainbow disappear. It was based chiefly upon a bed of moss.

Meantime it had grown quite dark in the wood. The rainbow alone was visible by its own light. But the moment the moon rose the rainbow vanished. Nor could any change of place restore the vision to the boy's eyes. So he threw himself down upon the mossy bed, to wait till the sunlight would give him a chance of finding the key. There he fell fast asleep.

When he woke in the morning the sun was looking straight into his eyes. He turned away from it, and the same moment saw a brilliant little thing lying on the moss within a foot of his face. It was the golden key. The pipe of it was of plain gold, as bright as gold could be. The handle was curiously wrought and set with sapphires. In a terror of delight he put out his hand and took it, and had it.

He lay for a while, turning it over and over, and feeding his eyes upon its beauty. Then he jumped to his feet, remembering that the pretty thing was of no use to him yet. Where was the lock to which the key belonged? It must be somewhere, for how could anybody be so silly as make a key for which there was no lock? Where should he go to look for it? He gazed about him, up into the air, down to the earth, but saw no keyhole in the clouds, in the grass, or in the trees.

Just as he began to grow disconsolate, however, he saw something glimmering in the wood. It was a mere glimmer that he saw, but he took it for a glimmer of rainbow, and went towards it.—And now I will go back to the borders of the forest.

Not far from the house where the boy had lived there was another house, the owner of which was a merchant, who was much away from home. He had lost his wife some years before, and had only one child, a little girl, whom he left to the charge of two servants, who were very idle and careless. So she was neglected and left untidy, and was sometimes ill-used besides.

Now, it is well known that the little creatures commonly called fairies, though there are many different kinds of fairies in Fairyland, have an exceeding dislike to untidiness. Indeed, they are quite spiteful to slovenly people. Being used to all the lovely ways of the trees and flowers, and to the neatness of the birds and all wood-land creatures, it makes them feel miserable, even in their deep woods and on their grassy carpets, to think that within the same moonlight lies a dirty, uncomfortable, slovenly house. And this makes them angry with the people that live in it, and they would gladly drive them out of the world if they could. They want the whole earth nice and clean. So they pinch the maids black and blue, and play them all manner of uncomfortable tricks.

But this house was quite a shame, and the fairies in the forest could not endure it. They tried everything on the maids without effect, and at last resolved upon making a clean riddance, beginning with the child. They ought to have known that it was not her fault, but they have little principle and much mischief in them, and they thought that if they got rid of her the maids would be sure to be turned away.

So one evening, the poor little girl having been put to bed early, before the sun was down, the servants went off to the village, locking the door behind them. The child did not know she was alone, and lay contentedly looking out of her window towards the forest, of which, however, she could not see much, because of the ivy and other creeping plants which had straggled across her window. All at once she saw an ape making faces at her out of the mirror, and the heads carved upon a great old wardrobe grinning fearfully. Then two old spider-legged chairs came forward into the middle of the room, and began to dance a queer, old-fashioned dance. This set her laughing, and she forgot the ape and the grinning heads. So the fairies saw they had made a mistake, and sent the chairs back to their places. But they knew that she had been reading the story of Silverhair all day. So the next moment she heard the voices of the three bears upon the stair, big voice, middle voice, and little voice, and she heard their soft, heavy tread, as if they had had stockings over their boots, coming nearer and nearer to the door of her room, till she could bear it no longer. She did just as Silverhair did, and as the fairies wanted her to do: she darted to the window, pulled it open, got upon the ivy, and so scrambled to the ground. She then fled to the forest as fast as she could run.

Now, although she did not know it, this was the very best way she could have gone; for nothing is ever so mischievous in its own place as it is out of it; and, besides, these mischievous creatures were only the children of Fairyland, as it were, and there are many other beings there as well; and if a wanderer gets in among them, the good ones will always help him more than the evil ones will be able to hurt him.

The sun was now set, and the darkness coming on, but the child thought of no danger but the bears behind her. If she had looked round, however, she would have seen that she was followed by a very different creature from a bear. It was a curious creature, made like a fish, but covered, instead of scales, with feathers of all colours, sparkling like those of a humming-bird. It had fins, not wings, and swam through the air as a fish does through the water. Its head was like the head of a small owl.

After running a long way, and as the last of the light was disappearing, she passed under a tree with drooping branches. It dropped its branches to the ground all about her, and caught her as in a trap. She struggled to get out, but the branches pressed her closer and closer to the trunk. She was in great terror and distress, when the air-fish, swimming into the thicket of branches, began tearing them with its beak. They loosened their hold at once, and the creature went on attacking them, till at length they let the child go. Then the air-fish came from behind her, and swam on in front, glittering and sparkling all lovely colours; and she followed.

It led her gently along till all at once it swam in at a cottage-door. The child followed still. There was a bright fire in the middle of the floor, upon which stood a pot without a lid, full of water that boiled and bubbled furiously. The air-fish swam straight to the pot and into the boiling water, where it lay quiet. A beautiful woman rose from the opposite side of the fire and came to meet the girl. She took her up in her arms, and said,—

"Ah, you are come at last! I have been looking for you a long time."

She sat down with her on her lap, and there the girl sat staring at her. She had never seen anything so beautiful. She was tall and strong, with white arms and neck, and a delicate flush on her face. The child could not tell what was the colour of her hair, but could not help thinking it had a tinge of dark green. She had not one ornament upon her, but she looked as if she had just put off quantities of diamonds and emeralds. Yet here she was in the simplest, poorest little cottage, where she was evidently at home. She was dressed in shining green.

The girl looked at the lady, and the lady looked at the girl.

"What is your name?" asked the lady.

"The servants always call me Tangle."

"Ah, that was because your hair was so untidy. But that was their fault, the naughty women! Still it is a pretty name, and I will call you Tangle too. You must not mind my asking you questions, for you may ask me the same questions, every one of them, and any others that you like. How old are you?"

"Ten," answered Tangle.

"You don't look like it," said the lady.

"How old are you, please?" returned Tangle.

"Thousands of years old," answered the lady.

"You don't look like it," said Tangle.

"Don't I? I think I do. Don't you see how beautiful I am?"

And her great blue eyes looked down on the little Tangle, as if all the stars in the sky were melted in them to make their brightness.

"Ah! but," said Tangle, "when people live long they grow old. At least I always thought so."

"I have no time to grow old," said the lady. "I am too busy for that. It is very idle to grow old.—But I cannot have my little girl so untidy. Do you know I can't find a clean spot on your face to kiss?"

"Perhaps," suggested Tangle, feeling ashamed, but not too much so to say a word for herself—"perhaps that is because the tree made me cry so."

"My poor darling!" said the lady, looking now as if the moon were melted in her eyes, and kissing her little face, dirty as it was, "the naughty tree must suffer for making a girl cry."

"And what is your name, please?" asked Tangle.

"Grandmother," answered the lady.

"Is it really?"

"Yes, indeed. I never tell stories, even in fun."

"How good of you!"

"I couldn't if I tried. It would come true if I said it, and then I should be punished enough." And she smiled like the sun through a summer-shower.

"But now," she went on, "I must get you washed and dressed, and then we shall have some supper."

"Oh! I had supper long ago," said Tangle.

"Yes, indeed you had," answered the lady—"three years ago. You don't know that it is three years since you ran away from the bears. You are thirteen and more now."

Tangle could only stare. She felt quite sure it was true.

"You will not be afraid of anything I do with you—will you?" said the lady.

"I will try very hard not to be; but I can't be certain, you know," replied Tangle.

"I like your saying so, and I shall be quite satisfied," answered the lady.

She took off the girl's night-gown, rose with her in her arms, and going to the wall of the cottage, opened a door. Then Tangle saw a deep tank, the sides of which were filled with green plants, which had flowers of all colours. There was a roof over it like the roof of the cottage. It was filled with beautiful clear water, in which swam a multitude of such fishes as the one that had led her to the cottage. It was the light their colours gave that showed the place in which they were.

The lady spoke some words Tangle could not understand, and threw her into the tank.

The fishes came crowding about her. Two or three of them got under her head and kept it up. The rest of them rubbed themselves all over her, and with their wet feathers washed her quite clean. Then the lady, who had been looking on all the time, spoke again; whereupon some thirty or forty of the fishes rose out of the water underneath Tangle, and so bore her up to the arms the lady held out to take her. She carried her back to the fire, and, having dried her well, opened a chest, and taking out the finest linen garments, smelling of grass and lavender, put them upon her, and over all a green dress, just like her own, shining like hers, and soft like hers, and going into just such lovely folds from the waist, where it was tied with a brown cord, to her bare feet.

"Won't you give me a pair of shoes too, Grandmother?" said Tangle.

"No, my dear; no shoes. Look here. I wear no shoes."

So saying she lifted her dress a little, and there were the loveliest white feet, but no shoes. Then Tangle was content to go without shoes too. And the lady sat down with her again, and combed her hair, and brushed it, and then left it to dry while she got the supper.

First she got bread out of one hole in the wall; then milk out of another; then several kinds of fruit out of a third; and then she went to the pot on the fire, and took out the fish, now nicely cooked, and, as soon as she had pulled off its feathered skin, ready to be eaten.

"But," exclaimed Tangle. And she stared at the fish, and could say no more.

"I know what you mean," returned the lady. "You do not like to eat the messenger that brought you home. But it is the kindest return you can make. The creature was afraid to go until it saw me put the pot on, and heard me promise it should be boiled the moment it returned with you. Then it darted out of the door at once. You saw it go into the pot of itself the moment it entered, did you not?"

"I did," answered Tangle, "and I thought it very strange; but then I saw you, and forgot all about the fish."

"In Fairyland," resumed the lady, as they sat down to the table, "the ambition of the animals is to be eaten by the people; for that is their highest end in that condition. But they are not therefore destroyed. Out of that pot comes something more than the dead fish, you will see."

Tangle now remarked that the lid was on the pot. But the lady took no further notice of it till they had eaten the fish, which Tangle found nicer than any fish she had ever tasted before. It was as white as snow, and as delicate as cream. And the moment she had swallowed a mouthful of it, a change she could not describe began to take place in her. She heard a murmuring all about her, which became more and more articulate, and at length, as she went on eating, grew intelligible. By the time she had finished her share, the sounds of all the animals in the forest came crowding through the door to her ears; for the door still stood wide open, though it was pitch dark outside; and they were no longer sounds only; they were speech, and speech that she could understand. She could tell what the insects in the cottage were saying to each other too. She had even a suspicion that the trees and flowers all about the cottage were holding midnight communications with each other; but what they said she could not hear.

As soon as the fish was eaten, the lady went to the fire and took the lid off the pot. A lovely little creature in human shape, with large white wings, rose out of it, and flew round and round the roof of the cottage; then dropped, fluttering, and nestled in the lap of the lady. She spoke to it some strange words, carried it to the door, and threw it out into the darkness. Tangle heard the flapping of its wings die away in the distance.

"Now have we done the fish any harm?" she said, returning.

"No," answered Tangle, "I do not think we have. I should not mind eating one every day."

"They must wait their time, like you and me too, my little Tangle."

And she smiled a smile which the sadness in it made more lovely.

"But," she continued, "I think we may have one for supper to-morrow."

So saying she went to the door of the tank, and spoke; and now Tangle understood her perfectly.

"I want one of you," she said,—"the wisest."

Thereupon the fishes got together in the middle of the tank, with their heads forming a circle above the water, and their tails a larger circle beneath it. They were holding a council, in which their relative wisdom should be determined. At length one of them flew up into the lady's hand, looking lively and ready.

"You know where the rainbow stands?" she asked.

"Yes, Mother, quite well," answered the fish.

"Bring home a young man you will find there, who does not know where to go."

The fish was out of the door in a moment. Then the lady told Tangle it was time to go to bed; and, opening another door in the side of the cottage, showed her a little arbour, cool and green, with a bed of purple heath growing in it, upon which she threw a large wrapper made of the feathered skins of the wise fishes, shining gorgeous in the firelight.

Tangle was soon lost in the strangest, loveliest dreams. And the beautiful lady was in every one of her dreams.

In the morning she woke to the rustling of leaves over her head, and the sound of running water. But, to her surprise, she could find no door—nothing but the moss-grown wall of the cottage. So she crept through an opening in the arbour, and stood in the forest. Then she bathed in a stream that ran merrily through the trees, and felt happier; for having once been in her grandmother's pond, she must be clean and tidy ever after; and, having put on her green dress, felt like a lady.

She spent that day in the wood, listening to the birds and beasts and creeping things. She understood all that they said, though she could not repeat a word of it; and every kind had a different language, while there was a common though more limited understanding between all the inhabitants of the forest. She saw nothing of the beautiful lady, but she felt that she was near her all the time; and she took care not to go out of sight of the cottage. It was round, like a snow-hut or a wigwam; and she could see neither door nor window in it. The fact was, it had no windows; and though it was full of doors, they all opened from the inside, and could not even be seen from the outside.

She was standing at the foot of a tree in the twilight, listening to a quarrel between a mole and a squirrel, in which the mole told the squirrel that the tail was the best of him, and the squirrel called the mole Spade-fists, when, the darkness having deepened around her, she became aware of something shining in her face, and looking round, saw that the door of the cottage was open, and the red light of the fire flowing from it like a river through the darkness. She left Mole and Squirrel to settle matters as they might, and darted off to the cottage. Entering, she found the pot boiling on the fire, and the grand, lovely lady sitting on the other side of it.

"I've been watching you all day," said the lady. "You shall have something to eat by and by, but we must wait till our supper comes home."

She took Tangle on her knee, and began to sing to her—such songs as made her

255

wish she could listen to them for ever. But at length in rushed the shining fish, and snuggled down in the pot. It was followed by a youth who had outgrown his worn garments. His face was ruddy with health, and in his hand he carried a little jewel, which sparkled in the firelight.

The first words the lady said were,—

"What is that in your hand, Mossy?"

Now Mossy was the name his companions had given him, because he had a favourite stone covered with moss, on which he used to sit whole days reading; and they said the moss had begun to grow upon him too.

Mossy held out his hand. The moment the lady saw that it was the golden key, she rose from her chair, kissed Mossy on the forehead, made him sit down on her seat, and stood before him like a servant. Mossy could not bear this, and rose at once. But the lady begged him, with tears in her beautiful eyes, to sit, and let her wait on him.

"But you are a great, splendid, beautiful lady," said Mossy.

"Yes, I am. But I work all day long—that is my pleasure; and you will have to leave me so soon!"

"How do you know that, if you please, madam?" asked Mossy.

"Because you have got the golden key."

"But I don't know what it is for. I can't find the key-hole. Will you tell me what to do?"

"You must look for the key-hole. That is your work. I cannot help you. I can only tell you that if you look for it you will find it."

"What kind of box will it open? What is there inside?"

"I do not know. I dream about it, but I know nothing."

"Must I go at once?"

"You may stop here to-night, and have some of my supper. But you must go in the morning. All I can do for you is to give you clothes. Here is a girl called Tangle, whom you must take with you."

"That *will* be nice," said Mossy.

"No, no!" said Tangle. "I don't want to leave you, please, Grandmother."

"You must go with him, Tangle. I am sorry to lose you, but it will be the best thing for you. Even the fishes, you see, have to go into the pot, and then out into the dark. If you fall in with the Old Man of the Sea, mind you ask him whether he has not got some more fishes ready for me. My tank is getting thin."

So saying, she took the fish from the pot, and put the lid on as before. They sat down and ate the fish, and then the winged creature rose from the pot, circled the roof, and settled on the lady's lap. She talked to it, carried it to the door, and threw it out into the dark. They heard the flap of its wings die away in the distance.

The lady then showed Mossy into just such another chamber as that of Tangle; and in the morning he found a suit of clothes laid beside him. He looked very handsome in them. But the wearer of Grandmother's clothes never thinks about how he or she looks, but thinks always how handsome other people are.

Tangle was very unwilling to go.

"Why should I leave you? I don't know the young man," she said to the lady.

"I am never allowed to keep my children long. You need not go with him except you please, but you must go some day; and I should like you to go with him, for he has the golden key. No girl need be afraid to go with a youth that has the golden key. You will take care of her, Mossy, will you not?"

"That I will," said Mossy.

And Tangle cast a glance at him, and thought she should like to go with him.

"And," said the lady, "if you should lose each other as you go through the—the —I never can remember the name of that country,—do not be afraid, but go on and on."

She kissed Tangle on the mouth and Mossy on the forehead, led them to the door, and waved her hand eastward. Mossy and Tangle took each other's hand and walked away into the depth of the forest. In his right hand Mossy held the golden key.

They wandered thus a long way, with endless amusement from the talk of the animals. They soon learned enough of their language to ask them necessary questions. The squirrels were always friendly, and gave them nuts out of their own hoards; but the bees were selfish and rude, justifying themselves on the ground that Tangle and Mossy were not subjects of their queen, and charity must begin at home, though indeed they had not one drone in their poorhouse at the time. Even the blinking moles would fetch them an earth-nut or a truffle now and then, talking as if their mouths, as well as their eyes and ears, were full of cotton wool, or their own velvety fur. By the time they got out of the forest they were very fond of each other, and Tangle was not in the least sorry that her grandmother had sent her away with Mossy.

At length the trees grew smaller, and stood farther apart, and the ground began to rise, and it got more and more steep, till the trees were all left behind, and the two were climbing a narrow path with rocks on each side. Suddenly they came upon a rude doorway, by which they entered a narrow gallery cut in the rock. It grew darker and darker, till it was pitch-dark, and they had to feel their way. At length the light began to return, and at last they came out upon a narrow path on the face of a lofty precipice. This path went winding down the rock to a wide plain, circular in shape, and surrounded on all sides by mountains. Those opposite to them were a great way off, and towered to an awful height, shooting up sharp, blue, ice-enamelled pinnacles. An utter silence reigned where they stood. Not even the sound of water reached them.

Looking down, they could not tell whether the valley below was a grassy plain or a great still lake. They had never seen any space look like it. The way to it was difficult and dangerous, but down the narrow path they went, and reached the bottom in safety. They found it composed of smooth, light-coloured sandstone, undulating in parts, but mostly level. It was no wonder to them now that they had not been able to tell what it was, for this surface was everywhere crowded with shadows. The mass was chiefly made up of the shadows of leaves innumerable, of all lovely and imaginative forms, waving to and fro, floating and quivering in the breath of a breeze whose motion was unfelt, whose sound was unheard. No forests clothed the mountain-sides, no trees were anywhere to be seen, and yet the shadows of the leaves, branches, and stems of all various trees covered the valley as far as their eyes could reach. They soon spied the shadows of flowers mingled with those of the leaves, and now and then the shadow of a bird with open beak, and throat distended with song. At times would appear the forms of strange, graceful creatures, running up and down the shadow-boles and along the branches, to disappear in the wind-tossed foliage. As they walked they waded knee-deep in the lovely lake. For the shadows were not merely lying on the surface of the ground, but heaped up above it like substantial forms of darkness, as if they had been cast upon a thousand different planes of the air. Tangle and Mossy often lifted their heads and gazed upwards to discry whence the shadows came; but they could see nothing more than a bright mist spread above them, higher than the tops of the mountains, which stood clear against it. No forests, no leaves, no birds were visible.

After a while, they reached more open spaces, where the shadows were thinner; and came even to portions over which shadows only flitted, leaving them clear for such as might follow. Now a wonderful form, half bird-like half human, would float across on outspread sailing pinions. Anon an exquisite shadow group of gambolling children would be followed by the loveliest female form, and that again by the grand stride of a Titanic shape, each disappearing in the surrounding press of shadowy foliage. Sometimes a profile of unspeakable beauty or grandeur would appear for a moment and vanish. Sometimes they seemed lovers that passed linked arm in arm, sometimes father and son, sometimes brothers in loving contest, sometimes sisters entwined in gracefullest community of complex form. Sometimes wild horses would tear across, free, or bestrode by noble shadows of ruling men. But some of the things which pleased them most they never knew how to describe.

About the middle of the plain they sat down to rest in the heart of a heap of shadows. After sitting for a while, each, looking up, saw the other in tears: they were each longing after the country whence the shadows fell.

"We *must* find the country from which the shadows come," said Mossy.

"We must, dear Mossy," responded Tangle. "What if your golden key should be the key to *it*?"

"Ah! that would be grand," returned Mossy.—"But we must rest here for a little, and then we shall be able to cross the plain before night."

So he lay down on the ground, and about him on every side, and over his head, was the constant play of the wonderful shadows. He could look through them, and see the one behind the other, till they mixed in a mass of darkness. Tangle, too, lay admiring, and wondering, and longing after the country whence the shadows came. When they were rested they rose and pursued their journey.

How long they were in crossing this plain I cannot tell; but before night Mossy's hair was streaked with gray, and Tangle had got wrinkles on her forehead.

As evening grew on, the shadows fell deeper and rose higher. At length they reached a place where they rose above their heads, and made all dark around them. Then they took hold of each other's hand, and walked on in silence and in some dismay. They felt the gathering darkness, and something strangely solemn besides, and the beauty of the shadows ceased to delight them. All at once Tangle found that she had not a hold of Mossy's hand, though when she lost it she could not tell.

"Mossy, Mossy!" she cried aloud in terror.

But no Mossy replied.

A moment after, the shadows sank to her feet, and down under her feet, and the mountains rose before her. She turned towards the gloomy region she had left, and called once more upon Mossy. There the gloom lay tossing and heaving, a dark, stormy, foamless sea of shadows, but no Mossy rose out of it, or came climbing up the hill on which she stood. She threw herself down and wept in despair.

Suddenly she remembered that the beautiful lady had told them, if they lost each other in a country of which she could not remember the name, they were not to be afraid, but to go straight on.

"And besides," she said to herself, "Mossy has the golden key, and so no harm will come to him, I do believe."

She rose from the ground, and went on.

Before long she arrived at a precipice, in the face of which a stair was cut. When she had ascended half-way, the stair ceased, and the path led straight into the mountain. She was afraid to enter, and turning again towards the stair, grew giddy at sight of the depth beneath her, and was forced to throw herself down in the mouth of the cave.

When she opened her eyes, she saw a beautiful little figure with wings standing beside her, waiting.

"I know you," said Tangle. "You are my fish."

"Yes. But I am a fish no longer. I am an aeranth now."

"What is that?" asked Tangle.

"What you see I am," answered the shape. "And I am come to lead you through the mountain."

"Oh! thank you, dear fish—aeranth, I mean," returned Tangle, rising.

Thereupon the aeranth took to his wings, and flew on through the long, narrow passage, reminding Tangle very much of the way he had swum on before her when he was a fish. And the moment his white wings moved, they began to throw off a continuous shower of sparks of all colours, which lighted up the passage before them.—All at once he vanished, and Tangle heard a low, sweet sound, quite different from the rush and crackle of his wings. Before her was an open arch, and through it came light, mixed with the sound of sea-waves.

She hurried out, and fell, tired and happy, upon the yellow sand of the shore. There she lay, half asleep with weariness and rest, listening to the low plash and retreat of the tiny waves, which seemed ever enticing the land to leave off being land, and become sea. And as she lay, her eyes were fixed upon the foot of a great rainbow standing far away against the sky on the other side of the sea. At length she fell fast asleep.

When she awoke, she saw an old man with long white hair down to his shoulders, leaning upon a stick covered with green buds, and so bending over her.

"What do you want here, beautiful woman?" he said.

"Am I beautiful? I am so glad!" said Tangle, rising. "My grandmother is beautiful."

"Yes. But what do you want?" he repeated, kindly.

"I think I want you. Are not you the Old Man of the Sea?"

"I am."

"Then Grandmother says, have you any more fishes ready for her?"

"We will go and see, my dear," answered the old man, speaking yet more kindly than before. "And I can do something for you, can I not?"

"Yes—show me the way up to the country from which the shadows fall," said Tangle.

For there she hoped to find Mossy again.

"Ah! indeed, that would be worth doing," said the old man. "But I cannot, for I do not know the way myself. But I will send you to the Old Man of the Earth. Perhaps he can tell you. He is much older than I am."

Leaning on his staff, he conducted her along the shore to a steep rock, that looked like a petrified ship turned upside down. The door of it was the rudder of a great vessel, ages ago at the bottom of the sea. Immediately within the door was a stair in the rock, down which the old man went, and Tangle followed. At the bottom the old man had his house, and there he lived.

As soon as she entered it, Tangle heard a strange noise, unlike anything she had ever heard before. She soon found that it was the fishes talking. She tried to understand what they said; but their speech was so old-fashioned, and rude, and undefined, that she could not make much of it.

"I will go and see about those fishes for my daughter," said the Old
Man of the Sea.

And moving a slide in the wall of his house, he first looked out, and then tapped upon a thick piece of crystal that filled the round opening. Tangle came up behind him, and peeping through the window into the heart of the great deep green ocean, saw the most curious creatures, some very ugly, all very odd, and with especially queer mouths, swimming about everywhere, above and below, but all coming towards the window in answer to the tap of the Old Man of the Sea. Only a few could get their mouths against the glass; but those who were floating miles away yet turned their heads towards it. The old man looked through the whole flock carefully for some minutes, and then turning to Tangle, said,—

"I am sorry I have not got one ready yet. I want more time than she does. But I will send some as soon as I can."

He then shut the slide.

Presently a great noise arose in the sea. The old man opened the slide again, and tapped on the glass, whereupon the fishes were all as still as sleep.

"They were only talking about you," he said. "And they do speak such nonsense! —To-morrow," he continued, "I must show you the way to the Old Man of the Earth. He lives a long way from here."

"Do let me go at once," said Tangle.

"No. That is not possible. You must come this way first."

He led her to a hole in the wall, which she had not observed before. It was covered with the green leaves and white blossoms of a creeping plant.

"Only white-blossoming plants can grow under the sea," said the old man. "In there you will find a bath, in which you must lie till I call you."

Tangle went in, and found a smaller room or cave, in the further corner of which was a great basin hollowed out of a rock, and half-full of the clearest sea-water. Little streams were constantly running into it from cracks in the wall of the cavern. It was polished quite smooth inside, and had a carpet of yellow sand in the bottom of it. Large green leaves and white flowers of various plants crowded up and over it, draping and covering it almost entirely.

No sooner was she undressed and lying in the bath, than she began to feel as if the water were sinking into her, and she were receiving all the good of sleep without undergoing its forgetfulness. She felt the good coming all the time. And she grew happier and more hopeful than she had been since she lost Mossy. But she could not help thinking how very sad it was for a poor old man to live there all alone, and have to take care of a whole seaful of stupid and riotous fishes.

After about an hour, as she thought, she heard his voice calling her, and rose out of the bath. All the fatigue and aching of her long journey had vanished. She was as whole, and strong, and well as if she had slept for seven days.

Returning to the opening that led into the other part of the house, she started back with amazement, for through it she saw the form of a grand man, with a majestic and beautiful face, waiting for her.

"Come," he said; "I see you are ready."

She entered with reverence.

"Where is the Old Man of the Sea?" she asked, humbly.

"There is no one here but me," he answered, smiling. "Some people call me the Old Man of the Sea. Others have another name for me, and are terribly frightened when they meet me taking a walk by the shore. Therefore I avoid being seen by them, for they are so afraid, that they never see what I really am. You see me now.— But I must show you the way to the Old Man of the Earth."

He led her into the cave where the bath was, and there she saw, in the opposite corner, a second opening in the rock.

"Go down that stair, and it will bring you to him," said the Old Man of the Sea.

With humble thanks Tangle took her leave. She went down the winding stair, till she began to fear there was no end to it. Still down and down it went, rough and broken, with springs of water bursting out of the rocks and running down the steps beside her. It was quite dark about her, and yet she could see. For after being in that bath, people's eyes always give out a light they can see by. There were no creeping things in the way. All was safe and pleasant though so dark and damp and deep.

At last there was not one step more, and she found herself in a glimmering cave. On a stone in the middle of it sat a figure with its back towards her—the figure of an old man bent double with age. From behind she could see his white beard spread out on the rocky floor in front of him. He did not move as she entered, so she passed round that she might stand before him and speak to him.

The moment she looked in his face, she saw that he was a youth of marvellous beauty. He sat entranced with the delight of what he beheld in a mirror of something like silver, which lay on the floor at his feet, and which from behind she had taken for his white beard. He sat on, heedless of her presence, pale with the joy of his vision. She stood and watched him. At length, all trembling, she spoke. But her voice made no sound. Yet the youth lifted up his head. He showed no surprise, however, at seeing her—only smiled a welcome.

"Are you the Old Man of the Earth?" Tangle had said.

And the youth answered, and Tangle heard him, though not with her ears:—

"I am. What can I do for you?"

"Tell me the way to the country whence the shadows fall."

"Ah! that I do not know. I only dream about it myself. I see its shadows sometimes in my mirror: the way to it I do not know. But I think the Old Man of the Fire must know. He is much older than I am. He is the oldest man of all."

"Where does he live?"

"I will show you the way to his place. I never saw him myself."

So saying, the young man rose, and then stood for a while gazing at Tangle.

"I wish I could see that country too," he said. "But I must mind my work."

He led her to the side of the cave, and told her to lay her ear against the wall.

"What do you hear?" he asked.

"I hear," answered Tangle, "the sound of a great water running inside the rock."

"That river runs down to the dwelling of the oldest man of all—the Old Man of the Fire. I wish I could go to see him. But I must mind my work. That river is the only way to him."

Then the Old Man of the Earth stooped over the floor of the cave, raised a huge stone from it, and left it leaning. It disclosed a great hole that went plumb-down.

"That is the way," he said.

"But there are no stairs."

"You must throw yourself in. There is no other way."

She turned and looked him full in the face—stood so for a whole minute, as she thought: it was a whole year—then threw herself headlong into the hole.

When she came to herself, she found herself gliding down fast and deep. Her head was under water, but that did not signify, for, when she thought about it, she could not remember that she had breathed once since her bath in the cave of the Old Man of the Sea. When she lifted up her head a sudden and fierce heat struck her, and she sank it again instantly, and went sweeping on.

Gradually the stream grew shallower. At length she could hardly keep her head under. Then the water could carry her no farther. She rose from the channel, and went step for step down the burning descent. The water ceased altogether. The heat was terrible. She felt scorched to the bone, but it did not touch her strength. It grew hotter and hotter. She said, "I can bear it no longer." Yet she went on.

At the long last, the stair ended at a rude archway in an all but glowing rock. Through this archway Tangle fell exhausted into a cool mossy cave. The floor and walls were covered with moss—green, soft, and damp. A little stream spouted from a rent in the rock and fell into a basin of moss. She plunged her face into it and drank. Then she lifted her head and looked around. Then she rose and looked again. She saw no one in the cave. But the moment she stood upright she had a marvellous sense that she was in the secret of the earth and all its ways. Everything she had seen, or learned from books; all that her grandmother had said or sung to her; all the talk of the beasts, birds, and fishes; all that had happened to her on her journey with Mossy, and since then in the heart of the earth with the Old man and the Older man—all was plain: she understood it all, and saw that everything meant the same thing, though she could not have put it into words again.

The next moment she descried, in a corner of the cave, a little naked child sitting on the moss. He was playing with balls of various colours and sizes, which he disposed in strange figures upon the floor beside him. And now Tangle felt that there was something in her knowledge which was not in her understanding. For she knew there must be an infinite meaning in the change and sequence and individual forms of the figures into which the child arranged the balls, as well as in the varied harmonies of their colours, but what it all meant she could not tell.* He went on busily, tirelessly, playing his solitary game, without looking up, or seeming to know that there was a stranger in his deep-withdrawn cell. Diligently as a lacemaker shifts her bobbins, he shifted and arranged his balls. Flashes of meaning would now pass from them to Tangle, and now again all would be not merely obscure, but utterly dark. She stood looking for a long time, for there was fascination in the sight; and the longer she looked the more an indescribable vague intelligence went on rousing itself in her mind. For seven years she had stood there watching the naked child with his coloured balls, and it seemed to her like seven hours, when all at once the shape the balls took, she knew not why, reminded her of the Valley of Shadows, and she spoke:—

"Where is the Old Man of the Fire?" she said.

* I think I must be indebted to Novalis for these geometrical figures.

"Here I am," answered the child, rising and leaving his balls on the moss. "What can I do for you?"

There was such an awfulness of absolute repose on the face of the child that Tangle stood dumb before him. He had no smile, but the love in his large gray eyes was deep as the centre. And with the repose there lay on his face a shimmer as of moonlight, which seemed as if any moment it might break into such a ravishing smile as would cause the beholder to weep himself to death. But the smile never came, and the moonlight lay there unbroken. For the heart of the child was too deep for any smile to reach from it to his face.

"Are you the oldest man of all?" Tangle at length, although filled with awe, ventured to ask.

"Yes, I am. I am very, very old. I am able to help you, I know. I can help everybody." And the child drew near and looked up in her face so that she burst into tears.

"Can you tell me the way to the country the shadows fall from?" she sobbed.

"Yes. I know the way quite well. I go there myself sometimes. But you could not go my way; you are not old enough. I will show you how you can go."

"Do not send me out into the great heat again," prayed Tangle.

"I will not," answered the child.

And he reached up, and put his little cool hand on her heart.

"Now," he said, "you can go. The fire will not burn you. Come."

He led her from the cave, and following him through another archway, she found herself in a vast desert of sand and rock. The sky of it was of rock, lowering over them like solid thunderclouds; and the whole place was so hot that she saw, in bright rivulets, the yellow gold and white silver and red copper trickling molten from the rocks. But the heat never came near her.

When they had gone some distance, the child turned up a great stone, and took something like an egg from under it. He next drew a long curved line in the sand with his finger, and laid the egg in it. He then spoke something Tangle could not understand. The egg broke, a small snake came out, and, lying in the line in the sand, grew and grew till he filled it. The moment he was thus full-grown, he began to glide away, undulating like a sea-wave.

"Follow that serpent," said the child. "He will lead you the right way."

Tangle followed the serpent. But she could not go far without looking back at the marvellous child. He stood alone in the midst of the glowing desert, beside a fountain of red flame that had burst forth at his feet, his naked whiteness glimmering a pale rosy red in the torrid fire. There he stood, looking after her, till, from the lengthening distance, she could see him no more. The serpent went straight on, turning neither to the right nor left.

Meantime Mossy had got out of the Lake of Shadows, and, following his mournful, lonely way, had reached the sea-shore. It was a dark, stormy evening. The sun had set. The wind was blowing from the sea. The waves had surrounded the rock within which lay the old man's house. A deep water rolled between it and the shore, upon which a majestic figure was walking alone.

Mossy went up to him and said,—

"Will you tell me where to find the Old Man of the Sea?"

"I am the Old Man of the Sea," the figure answered.

"I see a strong kingly man of middle age," returned Mossy.

Then the old man looked at him more intently, and said,—

"Your sight, young man, is better than that of most who take this way. The night is stormy: come to my house and tell me what I can do for you."

Mossy followed him. The waves flew from before the footsteps of the Old Man of the Sea, and Mossy followed upon dry sand.

When they had reached the cave, they sat down and gazed at each other.

Now Mossy was an old man by this time. He looked much older than the Old Man of the Sea, and his feet were very weary.

After looking at him for a moment, the old man took him by the hand and led him into his inner cave. There he helped him to undress, and laid him in the bath. And he saw that one of his hands Mossy did not open.

"What have you in that hand?" he asked.

Mossy opened his hand, and there lay the golden key.

"Ah!" said the old man, "that accounts for your knowing me. And I know the way you have to go."

"I want to find the country whence the shadows fall," said Mossy.

"I dare say you do. So do I. But meantime, one thing is certain.—What is that key for, do you think?"

"For a key-hole somewhere. But I don't know why I keep it. I never could find the key-hole. And I have lived a good while, I believe," said Mossy, sadly. "I'm not sure that I'm not old. I know my feet ache."

"Do they?" said the old man, as if he really meant to ask the question; and Mossy, who was still lying in the bath, watched his feet for a moment before he replied,—"No, they do not. Perhaps I am not old either."

"Get up and look at yourself in the water."

He rose and looked at himself in the water, and there was not a gray hair on his head or a wrinkle on his skin.

"You have tasted of death now," said the old man. "Is it good?"

"It is good," said Mossy. "It is better than life."

"No, said the old man: it is only more life.—Your feet will make no holes in the water now."

"What do you mean?"

"I will show you that presently."

They returned to the outer cave, and sat and talked together for a long time. At length the Old Man of the Sea rose, and said to Mossy,—

"Follow me."

He led him up the stair again, and opened another door. They stood on the level of the raging sea, looking towards the east. Across the waste of waters, against the bosom of a fierce black cloud, stood the foot of a rainbow, glowing in the dark.

"This indeed is my way," said Mossy, as soon as he saw the rainbow, and stepped out upon the sea. His feet made no holes in the water. He fought the wind, and clomb the waves, and went on towards the rainbow.

The storm died away. A lovely day and a lovelier night followed. A cool wind blew over the wide plain of the quiet ocean. And still Mossy journeyed eastward. But the rainbow had vanished with the storm.

Day after day he held on, and he thought he had no guide. He did not see how a shining fish under the water directed his steps. He crossed the sea, and came to a great precipice of rock, up which he could discover but one path. Nor did this lead him farther than half-way up the rock, where it ended on a platform. Here he stood and pondered.—It could not be that the way stopped here, else what was the path for? It was a rough path, not very plain, yet certainly a path.—He examined the face of the rock. It was smooth as glass. But as his eyes kept roving hopelessly over it, something glittered, and he caught sight of a row of small sapphires. They bordered a little hole in the rock.

"The key-hole!" he cried.

He tried the key. It fitted. It turned. A great clang and clash, as of iron bolts on huge brazen caldrons, echoed thunderously within. He drew out the key. The rock in front of him began to fall. He retreated from it as far as the breadth of the platform would allow. A great slab fell at his feet. In front was still the solid rock, with this one slab fallen forward out of it. But the moment he stepped upon it, a second fell, just short of the edge of the first, making the next step of a stair, which thus kept dropping itself before him as he ascended into the heart of the precipice. It led him into a hall fit for such an approach—irregular and rude in formation, but floor, sides, pillars, and vaulted roof, all one mass of shining stones of every colour that light can show. In the centre stood seven columns, ranged from red to violet. And on the pedestal of one of them sat a woman, motionless, with her face bowed upon her knees. Seven years had she sat there waiting. She lifted her head as Mossy drew near. It was Tangle. Her hair had grown to her feet, and was rippled like the windless sea on broad sands. Her face was beautiful, like her grandmother's, and as still and peaceful as that of the Old Man of the Fire. Her form was tall and noble. Yet Mossy knew her at once.

"How beautiful you are, Tangle!" he said, in delight and astonishment.

"Am I?" she returned. "Oh, I have waited for you so long! But you, you are like the Old Man of the Sea. No. You are like the Old Man of the Earth. No, no. You are like the oldest man of all. You are like them all. And yet you are my own old Mossy! How did you come here? What did you do after I lost you? Did you find the key-hole? Have you got the key still?"

She had a hundred questions to ask him, and he a hundred more to ask her. They told each other all their adventures, and were as happy as man and woman could be. For they were younger and better, and stronger and wiser, than they had ever been before.

It began to grow dark. And they wanted more than ever to reach the country whence the shadows fall. So they looked about them for a way out of the cave. The door by which Mossy entered had closed again, and there was half a mile of rock between them and the sea. Neither could Tangle find the opening in the floor by which the serpent had led her thither. They searched till it grew so dark that they could see nothing, and gave it up.

After a while, however, the cave began to glimmer again. The light came from the moon, but it did not look like moonlight, for it gleamed through those seven pillars in the middle, and filled the place with all colours. And now Mossy saw that there was a pillar beside the red one, which he had not observed before. And it was of the same new colour that he had seen in the rainbow when he saw it first in the fairy forest. And on it he saw a sparkle of blue. It was the sapphires round the key-hole.

He took his key. It turned in the lock to the sound of Aeolian music. A door opened upon slow hinges, and disclosed a winding stair within. The key vanished from his fingers. Tangle went up. Mossy followed. The door closed behind them. They climbed out of the earth; and, still climbing, rose above it. They were in the rainbow. Far abroad, over ocean and land, they could see through its transparent walls the earth beneath their feet. Stairs beside stairs wound up together, and beautiful beings of all ages climbed along with them.

They knew that they were going up to the country whence the shadows fall.

And by this time I think they must have got there.

AT THE BACK OF THE
NORTH WIND

BY
ELIZABETH LEWIS
AND
GEORGE MACDONALD

DIAMOND MAKES THE ACQUAINTANCE OF NORTH WIND

There was once a little boy named Diamond and he slept in a low room over a coach house. In fact, his room was just a loft where they kept hay and straw and oats for the horses. Little Diamond's father was a coachman and he had named his boy after a favorite horse.

Diamond's father had built him a bed in the loft with boards all around it, because there was so little room in their own end of the coach house. So when little Diamond lay there in bed, he could hear the horses under him munching away in the dark or moving sleepily in their dreams. His father put old Diamond, the horse after whom he was named, in the stall under the bed because he was quiet and did not go to sleep standing, but lay down like a reasonable creature.

Little Diamond sometimes woke in the middle of the night and felt his bed shaking in the blasts of the north wind. Then he could not help wondering if the wind should blow the house down and he should fall down into the manger, whether old Diamond might not eat him up before he knew him in his night gown. And though old Diamond was quiet all night long, yet when he woke up he got up like an earthquake. Then little Diamond knew what o'clock it was, or at least what was to be done next, which was—to go to sleep again as fast as he could!

Often there was hay at little Diamond's feet as he lay in bed, and hay at his head, piled up in great heaps to the very roof. Sometimes there was none at all. That was when they had used it all and had not yet bought more. Soon they bought more, and then it was only through a little lane with two or three turnings in it that he could reach his bed at all.

Sometimes when his mother undressed him in her room and told him to trot away to bed by himself, he would creep into the heart of the hay first. There he would lie, thinking how cold it was outside in the wind and how warm it would be inside his bed; and how he would go to his bed when he pleased; only he wouldn't just yet; he would get a little colder first. As he grew colder lying in the hay, his bed seemed to him to grow warmer. Then at last, he would scramble out of the hay, shoot like an arrow into his bed, cover himself up, snuggle down, and think what a happy boy he was!

He had not the least idea that the wind got in at a chink in the wall and blew about him all night. But the back of his bed was of boards only an inch thick, and on the other side of them was the north wind. Now these boards were soft and crumbly, and it happened that a soft part in them had worn away.

One night after he lay down, little Diamond found that a knot had come out of one of them and the wind was blowing in upon him. He jumped out of bed again, got a little wisp of hay, twisted it up and folded it in the middle. In this way, he made it into a cork and stuck it into the knot-hole to keep the wind out. But the wind began to blow loudly and angrily. Just as Diamond was falling asleep, out blew his hay cork and hit him on the nose!

It was just hard enough to wake him up and let him hear the wind whistling through the hole. He searched about for his hay cork, found it, and stuck it in harder. He was just dropping off to sleep once more, when pop! with an angry whistle behind it, the cork struck him again, this time on the cheek. Up he rose once more, got some more hay to make a new cork, and stuck it into the hole as hard as ever he could. But he was scarcely laid down again, before pop! it came on his fore-head. So he gave it up, drew the bed-clothes over his head, and was soon fast asleep.

Next day, little Diamond forgot all about the hole. But his mother found it when she was making up his bed and pasted a piece of thick brown paper over it. So when Diamond snuggled down into his bed that night, he did not think of it at all. But before he dropped asleep, he heard a queer sound and lifted his head to listen. Was somebody talking to him? The wind was rising again and beginning to blow and whistle. Was it the wind? He moved about to find out who or what it was, and at last, happened to put his hand upon the knot-hole with the paper pasted over it. Against this he laid his ear and then he heard the voice quite distinctly.

"What do you mean, little boy, by closing up my window?"

"What window?" asked Diamond.

"You stuffed hay into it three times last night! I had to blow it out again three times!"

"You can't mean this little hole? It isn't a window. It is a hole in my bed."

"I did not say a window. I said it was my window!"

"But it can't be a window!" said Diamond. "Windows are holes to see out of."

"Well, that is just what I made this window for."

"But you are outside," answered Diamond. "You can't want a window."

"You are quite mistaken. Windows are to see out of, you say. Well, I am in my house, and I want windows to see out of."

"But you have made a window into my bed."

"Well, your mother has three windows into my dancing hall, and you have three into my garret."

"Dear me!" said Diamond. "Still you can hardly expect me to keep a window in my bed for you. Now, can you?"

"Come!" said the voice. "You just open that window!"

"Well," said Diamond, "mother says I should be obliging. Still it is rather hard. You see, the north wind will blow right in my face if I do!"

"I am the North Wind!" said the voice.

"O-o-oh!" said Diamond. "Then will you promise not to blow in my face if I open your window?"

"I cannot promise that," said the North Wind.

"But you will give me the tooth-ache. Mother has it already."

"But what is to become of me without a window!" cried the voice.

"I am sure I don't know. All I say is that it will be worse for me than for you."

"No, it will not," replied the voice. "You shall not be the worse for it—I promise you that. You will be much the better for it. Just believe what I say, and do as I tell you."

"Well, I can pull the clothes over my head," said Diamond. So he felt around with his little sharp nails, got hold of one edge of the paper and tore it off. In came a long whistling stream of cold that struck his little naked chest. He scrambled and tumbled in under the bed-clothes and covered himself up. There was no paper between him and the voice now, and he felt—not frightened exactly—but a little queer.

"What a strange person this North Wind must be," thought Diamond, "to live in what they call 'Out-of-Doors,' I suppose, and make windows into people's beds."

Now the voice began again. He could hear it quite plainly, even with his head under the bed-clothes. It was still more gentle now, though it was six times as large and loud as before. And he thought it sounded a little like his mother's.

"What is your name, little boy?" it asked.

"Diamond," answered Diamond under the bed-clothes.

"What a funny name!"

"It is a very nice name," replied the boy.

"I am not so sure of that," said the voice.

"Well, I am!" returned Diamond. "I think it is a very pretty name."

"Diamond is a useless thing, rather," said the voice.

"That is not true. Diamond is very useful—and as big as two—and so quiet all night! But doesn't he make a jolly row in the morning, getting up on his four great legs! It is like thunder!"

"You do not seem to know what a diamond is!" cried the voice.

"Oh, don't I, just! Diamond is a great and good horse, and he sleeps right under me. He is old Diamond and I am young Diamond. Or, if you like it better, Mr. North Wind, if you are so particular, he is big Diamond and I am little Diamond. And I do not know which of us my father likes best!"

A beautiful laugh, soft and musical, sounded somewhere near him. But the boy kept his head under the clothes.

"I am not Mr. North Wind," said the voice.

"You told me you were the North Wind," cried Diamond.

"I did not say Mr. North Wind," said the voice.

"Well, I do say Mr. for my mother tells me always to be polite."

"Then let me tell you that I do not think it at all polite for you to say Mr. to me," answered the voice.

"Isn't it? Well, I am sorry then."

"But you ought to know better," said the voice. "You can't think it is polite to lie there with your head under the bed-clothes and never look to see what kind of a person you are talking to! I want you to come out with me."

"I want to go to sleep!" said Diamond.

"Will you take your head out of the bed-clothes?" said the voice a little angrily.

"No!" said Diamond crossly.

The moment he said the word a fierce blast of wind crashed in the wall and swept the clothes off him. He started up in a fright. Leaning over him was the large, beautiful, pale face of a woman. Her dark eyes had begun to flash a little but the rest of her face was very sweet and beautiful. What was very strange, though, was that away from her head streamed out her black hair in every direction like dark clouds. Soon it fell down about her again and then her face came out of it like the moon out of the clouds.

"Will you go with me now, little Diamond?" asked the North Wind bending over him and speaking very gently.

"Yes, yes!" cried Diamond, stretching out his arms toward her. "Yes, I will go with you, dear North Wind. I am not a bit afraid. I will go! But," he added, "how shall I get my clothes? They are in mother's room and the door is locked."

"Oh never mind your clothes. You will not be cold. Nobody is cold with the North Wind."

"I thought everybody was," said Diamond.

"That is a great mistake. People are not cold when they are with the North Wind —only when they are against it. Now will you come?"

"Yes, dear North Wind. You are so beautiful I am quite ready to go with you."

"Ah, but I may not always look beautiful. If you see me with my face all black, don't be frightened. If you see me flapping wings like bat's wings, as big as the whole sky, don't be afraid. If you hear me raging, you must believe that I am just doing my work. Nay, Diamond, if I change into a serpent or a tiger, you must not let go your hold of me, for it will be I just the same. And now, come!"

She turned away and went so swiftly that she was gone before Diamond was more than started. When he finally got down the stairs and out into the yard, no one did he see. And there he stood with his bare feet on the hard stones of the paved yard.

"I dare say she is hiding somewhere to see what I will do," said Diamond. So around the end of the stable he went to see if he could find her. But at once, sharp as a knife, the wind came against his little chest and bare legs. And stronger and stronger the wind seemed to blow. It was so cold! All at once, he remembered that she had said that people were not cold if they went with the North Wind. So he turned his back and trotted again toward the yard and sure enough, he began to feel almost warm once more!

On and on, North Wind blew him and, presently, she seemed to shove him right against a small door in a wall. It opened and she blew him through it and out into the very middle of the lawn of the house next door. It was here that Mr. Coleman lived who was his father's master and who owned big Diamond. So little Diamond did not feel entirely strange, and then, too, there was a light in one window that looked friendly. As long as he could see that, Diamond could not feel quite alone or lonely. But all at once, the light went almost out. Then indeed, he felt that it was dreadful to be out in the night alone, when every body else was gone to bed! That was more than he could bear and it was not strange that he burst out crying.

Some one in the house heard the sound of his sobbing and came out and found him there. He was taken into the house and into a room which had a bright light and a warm fire in it. Beside this, he found Miss Coleman, the young lady daughter of the house, who was having her long dark hair brushed out before going to bed. Somehow in that state, she looked just like the beautiful North Wind that he had been searching for. Without stopping to think, he ran right into her arms for comfort.

After he was warmed and comforted, they took him back home and knocked on the door to arouse his mother, to come and get him. She was much surprised to see him, you may be sure. She carried him up to his bed again and tucked him snugly in. And there he fell fast asleep.

DIAMOND'S FIRST TRIP WITH THE NORTH WIND

Diamond awoke very early the next morning and thought what a curious dream he had had. But the memory of it grew brighter and brighter until it did not look altogether like a dream. In fact he began to doubt whether he had not really been abroad in the wind at night.

All that week it was hard weather. The grass showed white in the morning with the hoar frost which clung to every blade. As Diamond's shoes were not good and his mother had not saved up quite enough money to get him the new pair she so much wanted for him, she would not let him run out. But at length, she brought home his new shoes. No sooner did she find that they fitted him, than she told him he might run out into the yard and amuse himself.

The sun was going down when he flew from the door like a bird from its cage. A great fire of sunset burned over the top of the gate that led to the stables. Above the fire in the sky, lay a large lake of green light, above that a golden cloud, and over that the blue of the wintry heavens. Diamond thought that next to his own home, he had never seen any place he would like so much to live in as that sky.

As he wandered about, he came to stand by the little door which opened upon the lawn of the house next door. That made him remember how the wind had driven him to this same spot on the night of his dream. So he thought he would just go in and see if things looked at all as they did then. But not a flower was to be seen in the beds on the lawn! Even the brave old chrysanthemums and Christmas roses had passed away before the frost. What? Yes! There was one. He ran and knelt down to look at it.

It was a primrose—a tiny, tiny thing, but perfect in shape—a baby wonder. As he stooped his face to see it close, a little wind began to blow. Two or three long leaves that stood up behind the flower shook and wavered and quivered. But the primrose lay still in the green hollow, looking up at the sky and not seeming to

274

know at all that the wind was blowing. It looked like a golden eye that the black wintry earth had opened to look at the sky with.

That very same night, after Diamond had been asleep for a little, he awoke all at once in the dark.

"Open the window, Diamond," said a voice.

Now Diamond's mother had once more pasted up North Wind's window.

"Are you North Wind?" said Diamond. "I do not hear you blowing."

"No, but you hear me talking. Open the window for I haven't over much time."

"Yes," said Diamond. "But please, North Wind, where's the use? You left me all alone last time."

"That was your fault," returned North Wind. "I had work to do and you kept me waiting."

Diamond was already scratching at the paper like ten mice and, getting hold of the edge of it, tore it off. The next instant a young girl glided across the bed and stood on the floor.

"Oh, dear!" said Diamond quite dismayed. "I didn't know—who are you, please?"

"I am North Wind."

"But you are no bigger than I am!"

"Do you think I care how big or how little I am? And of course, I am little this evening! Didn't you see me behind the leaves of the primrose? Didn't you see them blowing? Make haste, now, if you want to go with me! Dress as fast as you can and I will go and shake the leaves of the primrose till you come!"

"Don't hurt it!" said Diamond.

North Wind broke out into a little laugh like the breaking of silver bubbles and was gone in a moment. Diamond saw the gleam of something vanishing down the stair. He dressed himself as fast as ever he could and crept out into the yard, through the door in the wall, and away to the primrose. Behind it stood North Wind leaning over it.

"Come along!" she said jumping up and holding out her hand. She led him across the garden and with one bound was on top of the wall. Then she reached down her hand to Diamond. He gave a great spring and stood beside her.

Another bound, and they stood in the road by the river. It was full tide and the stars were shining clear in its depths. But they had not walked beside it far before its surface was covered with ripples and the stars had vanished. North Wind was now as tall as a full-grown girl. Her hair was flying about her head and the wind was blowing a breeze down the river. But she turned aside and went up a narrow lane.

"I have some rather disagreeable work to do to-night," she said. "And disagreeable work must be looked after first."

So saying, she laid hold of Diamond and began to run, gliding along faster and faster. She made many turnings and windings. Once they ran through a hall where they found both the front and back doors open. At the foot of the stair, North Wind stood still and Diamond, hearing a great growl, started in terror. There, instead of North Wind, was a huge wolf by his side! He let go his hold and the wolf bounded

275

up the stair. The windows of the house rattled and shook and there came the sound of a fall.

"Surely," thought Diamond, "North Wind can't be eating one of the children!"

He started to rush up after her, but she met him on the stair, took him by the hand and hurried him out of the house.

"I hope you haven't eaten a baby, North Wind!" he said very solemnly.

North Wind laughed merrily and went tripping on faster. Her grassy robe swept and swirled about her steps. Wherever it passed over withered leaves, they went fleeing and whirling away and running on their edges all about her feet. "No, I did not eat a baby," she said, "as you would know if you had not let go of me. I merely scared an ugly nurse who was calling a child bad names. I flew at her throat and she tumbled over with a crash. I had to put on a bad shape before she could see me. I put on a wolf's shape for that is what she is growing to be inside."

They were now climbing the slope of a grassy ascent. At the top, North Wind stood and turned her face toward London. The stars were still shining clear and cold overhead. There was not a cloud to be seen.

"Now," said North Wind, "do not let go of me again. I might have lost you the last time, only I was not in a hurry then. Now I am in a hurry."

As she spoke, she was growing larger and larger. Her head went up and up toward the stars. As she grew, her hair, longer and longer, lifted itself from her head and went out in black waves. She put her hands behind her head and began weaving and knotting her hair together. Then she took up Diamond in her hands and threw him over her shoulder saying, "I have made a place for you in my hair. Get in, Diamond."

Diamond soon found the woven nest and crept into it. The next moment he was rising in the air. North Wind grew towering up to the place of the clouds. Her hair went streaming out from her till it spread like a mist over the stars. She flung herself abroad in space. Diamond made a little place through the woven meshes of her hair and peeped through that, for he did not dare look over the top of his nest.

The earth was rushing past like a river or a sea below him. Trees and water and green grass hurried away beneath. Now there was nothing but the roofs of houses sweeping along like a great torrent of stones and rocks. Chimneys fell and tiles flew from the roofs. There was a great roaring for the wind was dashing against London like a stormy sea. Diamond, of course, at the back of North Wind, was in a calm but he could hear it. Around and around and around, swept North Wind, her dark hair rolling and flowing, sweeping the people all into their homes and the bad smells out of the streets.

Suddenly, Diamond saw a little girl coming along a street. She was dreadfully blown by the wind, and a broom she was trailing behind her was very troublesome. It seemed as if the wind had a spite at her! It kept worrying her and tearing at her rags. She was so lonely there!

"Oh, please, North Wind," cried Diamond, "won't you help that little girl?"

"I cannot leave my work, Diamond. But you can help her if you like. Only, I can't wait for you. And mind, the wind will get hold of you too!"

"But how shall I get home again," cried Diamond, "if you don't wait for me?"

"Well, you must think of that!" said North Wind.

"Oh," cried Diamond. "I am sure the wind will blow her over! I must help her anyway! Let me go!"

Without a word, North Wind dropped into the street and set him down. The same moment, he was caught in the coils of the blast and all but swept away. North Wind vanished. The wind was roaring along the street. The little girl was scudding before it, her hair flying, while behind her she dragged her broom with which she swept her crossing. Her little legs were going as fast as they could, to keep her from falling.

"Stop! stop! little girl!" shouted Diamond, starting in pursuit.

"I can't!" wailed the girl. "The wind won't let me!"

Diamond ran after her and caught hold of her frock but it tore in his hand. Then he ran fast enough to get in front of her and turning around, caught her in his arms. Just then, he thought he got a glimpse of North Wind turning the corner in front of them. They must go with her of course, and sure enough, when they turned the corner after her, they found it quite quiet there.

"Now, you must lead me," said Diamond. "You show me the way you must go to get home and I will take care of you."

So the little girl put her free hand in his and began to lead him. They went around turning after turning, till they stopped at a cellar-door in a very dirty lane. There the little girl knocked.

"What an awful place!" said Diamond. "I should not like to live here."

"Oh yes, you would, if you had no where else to go!" answered the girl. "I only hope they'll let me in."

"Don't they always let you in?" said Diamond.

"No, they don't. And then I have to stay in the street all night and scud back to my crossing the first thing in the morning. You see they don't answer, now!"

"Well," said Diamond, "I don't want to get in. I want to go back to my mother. Come with me and I will take you to my own home."

The little girl thought this would be much better than sitting in the streets all night. So they started off. The trouble was that Diamond was not at all sure that he could find the way without North Wind. But the only thing to do was to try. So they wandered on and on, turning in this direction and that, without any reason for one way more than another. At last, they got out of the thick of the houses into a kind of waste place. By this time, they were both very tired, and Diamond was inclined to cry. For he said to himself that he had not done the little girl any good and he had lost his own way home. But in this, he was wrong for she was far happier in having him with her, and making people happier is one of the best ways of doing them good.

They sat down and rested themselves a little and then went on. After a time, they found themselves on a rising ground that sloped rather steeply on the other side. The moment they reached the top, a gust of wind seized them and blew them down hill as fast as they could run. Nor could Diamond stop before he went bang! against one of the doors in a wall. To his dismay, it burst open. When they came to themselves, they peeped in. It was the back door of a garden.

"Oh! oh!" cried Diamond after staring for a few moments. "I know this place— know it well! It is Mr. Coleman's garden and here I am at home again. Oh, I am so glad! Come in, little girl! Come in with me and my mother will give you some breakfast."

"No, no! I can't!" said the little girl. "We have been so long coming. Look up! Don't you see that it is morning now? I must hurry back to my crossing and sweep it and get money to take home or they will beat me! I cannot stay. Good-bye, little boy, good-bye!"

She started back at once, ran up the hill and disappeared behind it. Diamond called after her and called, but she did not even turn round. He was sorry to see her go but there was no help for it. So when she was gone quite out of sight, he shut the door of the garden as best he could, and ran through the kitchen garden to the stables. And wasn't he glad to get into his own blessed bed again!

NORTH WIND SINKS A SHIP

It was some time before he saw North Wind again. He saw the little girl before that but it was only for a moment. It happened in this way. His father was taking the horse, Diamond, to have new shoes put on him, and knowing that little Diamond, like all small boys, liked a ride, he set him on the horse and taking the bridle led the two Diamonds away.

The blacksmith's shop was some distance away, deeper in London. As they crossed the angle of a square, Diamond, who was looking about to see if any one noticed him riding upon the big horse like a man, saw a little girl sweeping a crossing before a lady and holding out her hand for a penny. The lady had no penny and the little girl was disappointed.

Diamond could not stand that. He knew the little girl and he knew that he had a penny in his pocket. He slid off the horse in a sort of tumble and ran to her, holding out the penny. She did not know him at first, but when he smiled at her, she did. He stuffed the penny into her hand and ran back, for he knew his father would not care to wait. After that, he did not see little Nanny for a long time.

He played often now on the lawn of the house next door—Mr. Coleman's lawn—as the summer drew near, warm and splendid. One evening, he was sitting in a little summer-house at the foot of the lawn, before which was a bed of tulips. They were closed for the night but the wind was waving them slightly. All at once, out of one of them, there flew a big buzzing bumblebee.

"There! That's something done!" said a voice—a gentle, merry, childish voice but so tiny! "I was afraid he would have to stay there all night."

Diamond looked all about and then he saw the tiniest creature, sliding down the stem of the tulip.

"Are you the fairy that herds the bees?" he asked kneeling down beside the tulip bed.

"I am not a fairy," answered the little creature. "You stupid Diamond, have you never seen me before?"

As she spoke, a moan of wind bent the tulips almost to the ground and then he recognized North Wind.

"But there!" added the little creature, "I must not stay to chatter. I have to go and sink a ship to-night."

"Sink a ship!" cried Diamond. "And drown the men and women in it? How dreadful! Still I cannot believe you are cruel, North Wind!"

"No, I could not be cruel, and yet I must often do what looks cruel to those who do not know. But the people they say I drown, I only carry away to the back of the north wind—only I never saw the place."

"But how can you carry them there if you never saw the place? And how is it that you never saw it?"

"Because it is behind me. You cannot see your own back, you know. But run along now if you want to go with me to-night. I cannot take you till you have been to bed and gone to sleep. I'll look about and do something till you are ready. Do you see that man over there on the river in the boat who is just floating about? Now watch!"

She flashed like a dragon-fly across the water whose surface rippled and puckered as she passed. The next moment, the man in the boat glanced about him and bent to his oars. The boat flew over the rippling water. The same instant almost, North Wind perched again upon the river wall.

"How did you do that?" asked Diamond.

"I just blew in his face and blew the mist out of him."

"But what for? I don't understand!" said Diamond. Hearing no answer, he looked down at the wall. North Wind was gone. Away across the river went a long ripple—what sailors call a cat's paw. The man in the boat at once put up his sail. The moon was coming to herself on the edge of a great cloud and the sail began to shine white. Diamond rubbed his eyes and wondered what it was all about. But he felt that he could not know more till he had gone to bed, so he turned away and started for home. He stopped to look out of a window before going to bed. Above the moon, the clouds were streaming different ways, and the wind was rising as he fell asleep.

He woke in the middle of the night and the darkness. A terrible noise was rumbling overhead like the rolling beat of great drums. For a while, he could not come quite awake. But a second peal of thunder broke over his head and a great blast of wind followed which tore some tiles off the roof and, through the hole this made, sent a spout of wind down into his face. At the same moment, he heard a mighty, yet musical voice say, "Come up, Diamond! It's all ready. I am waiting for you." Then a gigantic arm was reached down which drew him up and clasped him against North Wind's breast.

"Oh, North Wind!" he murmured. But the words vanished from his lips as he had seen the soap bubbles, that burst too soon, vanish from the mouth of his pipe. The wind caught them and they were no-where.

At the same moment, a peal of thunder which shook Diamond's heart against his side boomed out of the heavens; I cannot say, out of the sky, for there was no sky. Diamond had not seen the lightning for he had been busy trying to find the face of North Wind. Every moment, the folds of her garment would sweep across his eyes and blind him. But between them, he could just catch glimpses of the great glories of her eyes looking down at him through the rifts of the huge clouds over his head.

"Oh dear North Wind!" cried the boy. "Why do you do like this? Must you go and sink the ship? It is not like you! Here you are, taking care of a poor little boy like me, with one arm, and there you are, sinking the ship with the other! No, no! It can't be like you!"

"Then you must believe that I am cruel," answered the strong voice of North Wind, sounding about him out of the clouds.

"No, dear North Wind, I can't believe that. I don't believe it. I will not believe it. How could you know how to put on such a beautiful face if you did not love me and love all the rest too? No! You may sink as many ships as you like—though I shall not like to see it!"

"That is quite another thing!" said North Wind.

As she spoke, she gave one spring from the roof and rushed up into the clouds. As if the clouds knew she had come, they burst into fresh thunderous light. Diamond seemed to be borne through an ocean of dazzling flame. The winds were writhing around him like a storm of serpents. For they were in the midst of the clouds and mists which of course took the shapes of the wind, eddying, and wreathing, and whirling, and shooting, and dashing about like gray and black water.

Now it blinded him by smiting him upon the eyes. Now it deafened him by bellowing in his ears. But he did not mind it. He only gasped at first, and then laughed, for the arm of North Wind was about him and he felt quite safe, though he knew that they were sweeping with the speed of the wind itself toward the sea! But before they reached it, Diamond felt North Wind's hair beginning to fall down about him.

"Is the storm over, North Wind?" he called out.

"No, Diamond. I am only waiting for a moment to set you down. You will not like to see the ship sunk and I am going to give you a place to stop in till I come back. Look!"

With one sweep of her great white arm, she flung yards deep of darkness, like a great curtain, from before the face of the boy. And lo! it was a blue night lit up with stars. Where it did not shine with stars, it shimmered with a milky whiteness of stars except where, just before them, the gray towers of a cathedral blotted out the sky.

"A good place for you to wait in," said North Wind and swept down upon the cathedral roof. They went in through an open door in one of the towers. Diamond found himself at the top of a stone stair which went twisting away down into the darkness. North Wind held his hand, and after a little, led him out upon a narrow gallery which ran all around the central part of the church. Below him, lay the inside of the church like a great silent gulf hollowed in stone. On and on, they walked along this narrow gallery till at last they reached a much broader stairway leading on down and down until at length, it led them down into the church itself.

There he felt himself clasped in the arms of North Wind who held him close and kissed him on the forehead. The next moment, she was gone, and Diamond heard a moaning about the church which grew and grew to a roaring. The storm was up again and he knew that North Wind's hair was flying.

The church was dark. Only a little light came through the windows which were almost all of that precious old stained glass so much lovelier than the new. There was not enough light in the stars to show the colors in them. Diamond began to feel his way about the place, and for a little while went wandering up and down. His pattering foot-steps waked soft answering echoes in the stone house. It was as if the great cathedral somehow knew that his little self was there and went on giving back an answer to every step he took.

At last, he gave a great sigh and said, "I am so tired!" He did not hear the gentle echo which answered from far away over his head. For at that moment, he came against the lowest of a few steps that stretched across the church, and fell down and hurt his arm. He cried a little at first, and then crawled up the steps on his hands and knees. At the top, he came to a little bit of carpet on which he lay down. And there he lay staring at the dull windows that rose nearly a hundred feet above his head.

The moon was at that moment just on the edge of the horizon. And lo! with the moon, lovely figures began to dawn in the windows. He lay and looked at them backward over his head, wondering if they would come down. He heard a low, soft murmuring as if they were talking to themselves about him. But his eyes grew tired, and more and more tired. His eyelids grew so heavy that they would keep tumbling down over his eyes. He kept lifting them and lifting them. But every time, they were heavier than the last. It was no use! They were too much for him. Sometimes before he got them half way up, down they went again. At length, he gave it up quite, and the moment he gave it up, he was fast asleep!

When his eyes came wide open again, there were no lovely figures—or even windows—but a dark heap of hay all about him. The small panes in the roof of his loft were glimmering blue in the light of the morning. Old Diamond was coming awake down below in the stable. In a moment more he was on his feet and shaking himself so that young Diamond's bed trembled under him.

"He is grand at shaking himself!" said Diamond. "I wish I could shake myself like that. But then I can wash myself and he can't. What fun it would be to see old Diamond washing his face with his hoofs and iron shoes! Wouldn't it be a picture!"

He dressed himself quickly and ran out. Down the stairs he went and through the little door out upon the lawn of Mr. Coleman's house next door. He wanted to see how things looked since last night. There was the little summer-house with the tulip bed before it where he had been sitting the evening before, crushed to the ground! Over it lay the great elm tree which the wind had broken across! As he stood looking at it, a gentleman who was staying at the Coleman house came out upon the lawn.

"Dear me!" said the gentleman. "There has been terrible work here! This is the North Wind's doing! What a pity! I wish we lived at the back of it, I am sure!"

"Where is that, sir?" asked Diamond.

"Away in the Hyperborean regions," answered the gentleman. He smiled for he knew well enough that Diamond would not understand that big word which means the country away in the far, far north.

"I never heard of that place," returned Diamond.

"No," said the gentleman. "I suppose not. But if this tree had been there, it would not have been blown down. There is no wind in that country."

"That must be the place," said Diamond to himself, "where North Wind said she would take the people whom she sunk with the ship. Next time I see her, I am going to ask her to take me to see that land, too."

THE LAND AT THE BACK OF THE
NORTH WIND

One morning, Diamond's mother did not think he was feeling very well and when he told her that he had a little headache, she was sure of it. Now there was an aunt of his living at Sandwich and his mother decided to send him there for a change. So giving him two pence for spending money, she packed him off to Sandwich for a visit.

He soon made great friends with an old woman who kept a toy-shop there, where he spent his two pence. One hot day when he had been walking about more than he ought and was tired, he went into the toy-shop to rest. The old woman had gone out but he thought it would be all right for him to sit down on a box and rest.

All at once, he heard a gentle whirring somewhere amongst the toys. Among them was a whistle that had a wind-mill at the end which turned when you blew the whistle. No one was blowing the whistle now and yet the wind-mill was turning and turning and turning.

"What can it mean?" said Diamond out loud after watching for a few moments.

"It means me," answered the tiniest voice he had ever heard.

"Who are you, please?" asked Diamond.

"Well, really, I begin to be ashamed of you!" cried the voice. "You are as bad as a baby that doesn't know its mother in a new bonnet!"

"Not quite so bad as that, dear North Wind," said Diamond. "And I am so glad to see you. Did you sink the ship?"

"Yes."

"And drown everybody?"

"Not quite. One boat got away with six or seven men in it."

"And you took the others to that queer place the gentleman spoke of," said

Diamond to himself. Aloud he said, "Please, North Wind, I want you to take me to the country at the back of the north wind."

"That is not so easy," said North Wind and was silent so long that he thought she must have gone away. But presently she spoke again.

"It is not so easy," she said thoughtfully. "But we shall see. We shall see. You must go home, now, my dear, for you do not seem very well."

So Diamond went home. That afternoon, his head began to ache very much and he had to go to bed. In the middle of the night, his aunt came in to feel his forehead and to give him a drink of lemonade. Then he went off to sleep, but was awake again soon, for a burst of wind blew open his lattice window. The same moment, he found himself in a cloud of North Wind's hair, with her beautiful face, set in it like a moon, bending over him.

"Quick! Diamond!" she said. "I have found such a chance!"

"But I am not well," said Diamond.

"I know. But you will be better for it."

"Very well," said Diamond; and getting out of bed, he jumped into North Wind's arms. Sure enough, the moment he felt her arms fold about him, he began to feel better. It was a moonless night and very dark, with glimpses of stars when the clouds parted.

"We shall soon get to where the waves are dashing about," said North Wind. And soon, Diamond looking down saw the white glimmer of breaking water far below him.

"You see, Diamond," said North Wind, "it is very difficult to get you to the back of the north wind for that country lies in the very north itself. Now, of course, I cannot blow northwards, for then I should have to be South Wind. The north is where I come from—it is my home though I never get nearer to it than the outer door. I can only sit on the door-step and hear the voices in there, behind me. Since I cannot blow in that direction to get there, I have just to draw into myself and grow weaker and fainter as I go. That makes it hard for me to carry anything—even you —with me when I go that way. So I must get some help. Let me get rid of a few of these clouds. There! What do you see now?"

"A boat," said Diamond.

"A ship," said North Wind, "whose captain I know well. I have often helped him to sail his eighty miles a day northward."

"He must have tacked often to do that," said Diamond who had been watching the ships at Sandwich.

"Yes, that gave him a share in the business. It is not good at all—mind that, Diamond—to do everything for those you love and not give them a share in the doing. It is not being really kind to them. If South Wind had blown that ship straight north, the captain would just have smoked his pipe all day and got stupider and stupider. But now I am going to put you aboard his ship. Do you see that round thing on the deck like the top of a drum? Below that is where they keep their spare sails. I am going to blow it off and drop you through upon the sails. You will find it nice and warm and dry. Just coil yourself up there and go to sleep."

A moment more, and he felt himself tumbled in on the heap of sails. Hour after hour, he lay comfortably there. He could hear the straining of the masts, the creaking of the boom, and the singing of the ropes with the roaring of the wind;

also the surge of the waves past the ship's sides and the thud with which every now and then one would strike her.

All at once arose a terrible uproar. The cover was blown off again, a fierce wind rushed in, snatched him up and bore him aloft into the clouds. Down below, he saw the little vessel, he had been in, tossing on the waves like a sea-bird with folded wing. Near it was a bigger ship which was on its way to the north pole.

"That big ship will give us a lift now," said North Wind. Swooping down she tucked him snugly in amongst some flags. And now on and on, they sped toward the north. How long it was, Diamond did not know, but one night she whispered in his ear, "Come up on deck, Diamond."

Everything looked very strange. Here and there on all sides, were huge masses of floating ice looking like cathedrals and castles and crags, and beyond them a blue sea. Some of the icebergs were drifting northward, one passing very near the ship. North Wind seized Diamond and with a single bound, lighted on it. The same instant, South Wind began to blow and North Wind hurried Diamond down the north side of the berg and into a cave. There she sat down as if weary on a ledge of ice.

Diamond was enraptured with the color of the air in the cave, a deep, dazzling, lovely blue that was always in motion, boiling and sparkling. But when he looked at North Wind he was frightened.

He saw that her form and face were growing, not small, but transparent like something dissolving away. He could see the side of the blue cave through her very heart. She melted slowly away till all that was left was a pale face with two great lucid eyes in it.

"She is dying away!" he said. "Of course, as we go northward, she is dying away more and more."

After a little, he went out and sat on the edge of his floating island and looked down into the green ocean. When he got tired of that, he went back into the blue cave. He felt as if in a dream. He was not hungry, but he sucked little bits of the berg at times.

At length, far off on the horizon, there rose into the sky a shining peak, and his berg floated right toward it. Other peaks came into view as he went on, and at last his berg floated up to a projecting rock. Diamond stepped ashore and a little way before him saw a lofty ridge of ice with a gap in it like the opening of a valley. As he got nearer, he saw it was not a gap but the form of a woman, her hands in her lap and her hair hanging to the ground.

"It is North Wind on her door-step!" said Diamond joyfully and hurried on.

She sat motionless with drooping head and did not move nor speak. He was sure it was North Wind but he thought she must be dead at last. Her face was white as the snow, her eyes blue as the ice cave, and she had on a greenish robe like the color in the hollows of a glacier.

He walked toward her instantly and put out his hand to lay it on her. There was nothing there but intense cold. All grew white about him. He groped on further. The white thickened about him and he felt himself stumbling and falling. But as he fell, he rolled over the threshold. It was thus that Diamond got to the back of the north wind.

And what did he find? There was no North Wind in sight nor snow nor ice. It was a country where even the ground smelled sweetly, though Diamond thought the odour must come out of the flowers. A gentle air breathed in his face but he was not quite sure he did not miss the wind. A river as clear as crystal ran not only through the grass but over it too. It murmured a low, sweet song as it ran. There was no sun nor moon but a pure cloudless light always, and the blue arch of the sky seemed like a harp playing the soft airs of Heaven. There were many people there and all the people seemed happy and yet as if they were going to be happier some day.

Nothing ever went wrong at the back of the north wind and the only thing one ever missed was some one he loved who had not yet got there. But if one at the back of the north wind wanted to know how things were going with any one he loved, he had only to go to a certain tree, and climb up and sit down in the branches.

One day, when Diamond was sitting in this tree, he began to long very much to get home again. And no wonder! For he saw his mother crying. Now if you wished anything at the back of the north wind, you could follow your wish if you could find the way. So Diamond knew that he must now find North Wind. He could not go home without her and therefore he must find her. He went all about searching and searching. One day as he was looking and looking, he thought he caught a glimpse of the ice ridge and the misty form of North Wind seated as he had left her. He ran as hard as he could. Yes, he was sure it was she. He pushed on through the whiteness, which began to thicken around him. It was harder and harder to go but he struggled on and at last reached her and sank wearily down at her knees. At that same moment, the country at her back vanished from Diamond's view.

North Wind was as still as Diamond had left her. But as he touched her, her face began to change like that of one waking from sleep. He clambered up upon her breast. She gave a great sigh, slowly lifted her arms, and slowly folded them about him, until she clasped him close.

"Have you been sitting here ever since I went through you, dear North Wind? It has been like a hundred years!" said Diamond.

"It has been just seven days," said North Wind smiling. "Come now, we will go."

The next moment, Diamond sat alone on the rock. North Wind had vanished. But something like a cockchafer flew past his face. Around and around him in circles it went.

"Come along, Diamond," it said in his ear. "It is time we were setting out for Sandwich."

It seemed to drop to the ground but when he looked Diamond could see nothing but a little spider with long legs which made its way over the ice toward the south. It grew and grew till Diamond discovered that it was not a spider but a weasel. Away glided the weasel and away went Diamond after it. The weasel grew and grew and grew till he saw it was not a weasel but a cat. Away went the cat and away went Diamond after it. When he came up with it, it was not a cat but a leopard. The leopard grew to a jaguar and the jaguar to a Bengal tiger.

Of none of them was Diamond afraid for he had been at North Wind's back and he could be afraid of her no longer whatever she did or grew to be. The tiger flew over the snow in a straight line for the south, growing less and less to Diamond's eyes till it was only a black speck upon the whiteness. Then it vanished altogether.

And now Diamond felt that he would rather not run any further and that the ice had got very rough. Besides he was near the precipices that bounded the sea. So he slowed up his pace to a walk and said to himself, "North Wind will come back for me, I know. She is just teasing me a little. Then, too, she must get started some way to grow bigger and bigger all the time!"

"Here I am, dear boy," said North Wind's voice behind him.

Diamond turned and saw her as he liked best to see her, standing beside him a tall, beautiful woman.

"Where is the tiger?" he said. "But of course, you were the tiger. It puzzles me a little. I saw it such a long way off before me, and there you are behind me. It is odd, you know."

"None of these things is odder to me than to see you eat bread and butter," said North Wind.

"I should just like to see a slice of bread and butter!" cried Diamond. "I am afraid to say how long it is since I had anything to eat!"

"You shall have some soon. I am glad to find you want some!"

She swept him up in her arms and bounded into the air. Her tresses began to lift and rise and spread and stream and flow and flutter. And North Wind and Diamond went flying southward. The sea slid away from under them like a great web of shot silk, blue shot with gray, and green shot with purple. The stars appeared to sail away past them, like golden boats on a blue sea turned upside down. Diamond himself went fast, fast, fast—he went fast asleep in North Wind's arms.

DIAMOND'S FATHER LOSES HIS EMPLOYMENT

When he woke once more, a face was bending over him. It was not North Wind's, however; it was his mother's. He put out his arms to her and she clasped him to her heart and burst out crying.

"What is the matter, mother?" cried Diamond.

"Oh, Diamond dear! You have been so ill!" she said.

"Why no, mother dear. I have only been at the back of the North Wind," returned Diamond.

"I thought you were dead," said his mother.

At that moment, the doctor came in. He drew his mother aside and told her not to talk to Diamond. He must be kept as quiet as possible. And indeed, Diamond felt very strange and weak. But he soon got better with chicken broth and other nice things.

And it was a good thing that he could get well and strong again. For since he had come to Sandwich, a sad thing had happened to his father. Mr. Coleman, his father's employer, had failed in business. It had come about in this way. Miss Coleman, who had looked so like North Wind that night on which he had seen her having her long black hair combed beside the fire, had a lover, a Mr. Evans. Now Mr. Evans was poor and felt ashamed to marry Miss Coleman until he had made more money and could live finely. This was a sort of false pride and it brought about great trouble for them all.

For Mr. Coleman took Mr. Evans into partnership to help him along. As soon as that happened, Mr. Evans began to urge Mr. Coleman to go into business ventures which were not honest but in which they could make a great deal of money. It was not so bad at first, but as they went on, it became more and more dishonest.

They could not seem to get out of it, however, and get back to carrying on their business in the right way. So North Wind had to take a hand and teach them better. It was Mr. Coleman's ship she sank that night when she carried Diamond into the cathedral to wait for her. In the one boat-load of people which North Wind drove off to a desert island, was Mr. Evans. He had gone along on the ship to manage the business. Now he found that it would have been better to have been poor and stayed at home to marry Miss Coleman than to be ship-wrecked and have to live on a desert island because he longed so to be rich.

The loss of the ship ruined Mr. Coleman. He had to sell off his house and his horses, old Diamond among them, and go and live in a poor little house in a much less pleasant place. He had to begin again to work and learn how much better it is to be honest and contented than to try to get rich quickly. And poor Miss Coleman thought her lover was drowned and was very, very unhappy.

Nobody suffers alone. When old Diamond was sold, young Diamond's father was thrown out of work. Then he had no way to earn money to keep Diamond and his mother and the new little baby brother who had come to them. How Diamond did wish he was big enough to do something! But of course, he could think of nothing he could do. Besides he had to get well and strong first, anyway. His father sent word that he and his mother were to stay down at Sandwich until he found something to do and a place where he could make a home for them. It was a very fortunate thing that Diamond's aunt was glad to keep them with her as long as ever they were willing to stay.

One day when Diamond was getting strong enough to go out, his mother got his aunt's husband, who had a little pony cart, to carry them down to the sea-shore. A whiff of sea air, she said, would do them both good. They sat down on the edge of the rough grass which bordered the sand. Away before them stretched the sparkling waters of the ocean, every wave of which flashed out its delight in the face of the great sun. On each hand, the shore rounded outward, forming a little bay. Dry sand was about their feet, and under them thin wiry grass.

After a time, his mother stretched out her hand for the basket which she had brought with her and she and Diamond had their dinner. Diamond did enjoy it, the drive and the fresh air had made him so hungry! But he was sorry that his mother looked so sad and depressed. He knew she was thinking about his father and how they now had no home. But there was nothing for him to do. So he lay down on the sand again, feeling sleepy, and gazed sleepily out over the sand. "What is that, mother!" he said.

"Only a bit of paper," she answered looking where he pointed.

"It flutters more than a bit of paper would, I think," said Diamond.

"I'll go and see if you like," said his mother.

She rose and went and found that it was a little book partly buried in the sand. Several of its leaves were clear of the sand and these the wind kept blowing about in a very fluttering manner. She took it up and brought it to Diamond.

"What is it, mother?" he asked.

"Rhymes, I think," said she.

"I am so sleepy," he said. "Do read some of them to me."

"Well, I will," she said and began one. "But this is such nonsense," she said again. "I will try to find a better one."

She turned the leaves, searching, but three times with sudden puffs the wind blew the leaves rustling back to the same verses.

"I wonder if that is North Wind," said Diamond to himself. To his mother he said, "Do read that one. It sounded very nice. I am sure it is a good one."

His mother thought it might amuse him although she could not find any sense in it. So she read on like this:

I know a river
whose waters run asleep,
run, run ever,
singing in the shallows,
dumb in the hollows
sleeping so deep;
and all the swallows
that dip their feathers
in the hollows
or in the shallows
are the merriest swallows of all!

"Why!" whispered Diamond to himself sleepily, "that is what the river sang when I was at the back of the north wind."

And so with the daisies
the little white daisies
they grow and they blow
and they spread out their crown
and they praise the sun;
and when he goes down
their praising is done
and they fold up their crown
till over the plain
he is rising amain
and they're at it again!
praising and praising
such low songs raising
that no one hears them
but the sun who rears them!
and the sheep that bite them
awake or asleep
are the quietest sheep
with the merriest bleat!
and the little lambs
are the merriest lambs!
they forget to eat
for the frolic in their feet!

"Merriest, merriest, merriest," murmured Diamond as he sank deeper and deeper in sleep. "That is what the song of the river is telling me. Even I can be merry and

cheerful—and that will help some. And so I will—when—I—wake—up—again."
And he went off sound asleep.

It was not very long after this that Diamond and his mother could go home again. His father had now found something to do and this is how it came about. He one day met a cabman who was a friend of his and this friend said to him, "Why don't you set up as a cabman yourself—and buy a cab?"

"I haven't enough money to buy a horse with—and a cab," said Diamond's father.

"Look here," answered his friend. "I just bought an old horse the other day, cheap. He is no good for the hansom I drive, for when folks take a hansom, they want to drive like the wind. But for a four-wheeler that takes families and their luggage, he's the very horse. I bought him cheap and I'll sell him cheap."

"Oh, I don't want him," said Diamond's father.

"Well, come and see him anyway," said his friend. So he went.

What was his delight on going into the stable to find that the horse was no other than his own old Diamond! Diamond, grown very thin and bony and long-legged. The horse hearing his master's voice, turned his long neck. And when his old friend went up to him and laid his hand on his side, he whinnied for joy and laid his big head on his master's breast. This settled the matter. Diamond's father put his arms around old Diamond's neck and fairly cried.

The end of it was that Diamond's father bought old Diamond again, together with a four-wheeled cab. As there were some rooms to be had over the stable, he took them, wrote to his wife to come home, and set up as a cabman.

It was late in the afternoon when Diamond and his mother and the baby reached London. His father was waiting for them with his own cab but they had not told Diamond who the horse was. For his father wanted to enjoy the pleasure of his surprise when he found it out. He got in with his mother without looking at the horse and was quite proud of riding home in his father's cab.

When he got to the stables where their rooms were he could not help being a little dismayed at first. But he thought of the song of the river at the back of the north wind and just looked about for things that were pleasant. He said to himself that it was a fine thing that all their old furniture was there. Then he began to search out the advantages of the place.

A thick, dull rain was falling and that was depressing. But the weather would change and there was a good fire burning in the room, which a neighbor had made for them. The tea things were put out and the kettle was boiling on the fire. And with a good fire and tea and bread and butter, things cannot be so very bad.

But Diamond's father and mother were rather miserable and Diamond began to feel a kind of darkness spreading over him. At the same moment, he said, "This will never do! I can't give in to this. I've been at the back of the north wind. Things go right there and they must be made to go right here!"

So he said out loud, "What nice bread and butter this is!" And when he had eaten it, he began to amuse the baby who was soon shrieking with laughter. His father and mother had to laugh too and things began to look better.

It was indeed a change for them all, not only from Sandwich but from their old place. Instead of the great river where the huge barges with their brown and yellow sails went up and down, their windows now looked out upon a dirty paved yard.

There was no garden more for Diamond to run into when he pleased, with gay flowers about his feet, and lofty trees over his head.

Neither was there a wooden wall at the back of his bed with a hole in it for North Wind to come in at when she liked. Indeed, there was such a high wall that North Wind seldom got into the place. And the wall at the head of Diamond's new bed only divided it from the room where a cabman lived who drank too much beer and came home to quarrel with and abuse his wife. It was dreadful for Diamond to hear the scolding and the crying. But he was determined it should not make him miserable for he had been at the back of the north wind.

DIAMOND LEARNS TO DRIVE A HORSE

The wind blew loudly all night long, the first night Diamond slept in his new home, but he did not hear it. My own belief is that when Diamond slept too soundly to remember anything about it in the morning, he had been all night at the back of the north wind. Sometimes something did seem to remain in his mind like the low far-off murmur of the river singing its song. He sometimes tried to hold on to the words it sung. But ever as he came awaker—as he would say—one line faded away and then another. At last there was nothing left but the sense that everything went right there and could—and must—be made to go right here.

That was how he awoke that first morning and he jumped up at once saying, "I've been ill a long time and given a great deal of trouble. Now let's see how I can help my mother."

When he went into her room, he found her lighting the fire and his father just getting up. So he took up the baby who was awake too and cared for him till his mother had the breakfast ready. She was looking gloomy and his father too was silent. Diamond felt that in a few minutes, he would be just as miserable. But he tried with all his might to be jolly with the baby and presently his mother just had to smile.

"Why, Diamond, child!" she said at last. "You are as good to your mother as if you were a girl—nursing the baby and toasting the bread, and sweeping up the hearth. I declare a body would think you had been among the fairies."

"I've been at the back of the north wind," said Diamond to himself happily.

And now his father was more cheerful too. "Won't you come out and see the cab, Diamond?" he asked.

"Yes, father, in just a minute after I put the baby down."

So his father went on ahead. When Diamond got out into the yard, the horse was between the shafts. Diamond went around to look at him. The sight of him made him feel very queer. He could not make it out. What horse was it that looked

294

so familiar? When he came around in front and the old horse put out his long neck and began rubbing against him, Diamond saw it could be no other than old Diamond and he just put his arms around his neck and cried.

"Isn't it jolly, father!" he said. "Was there ever anybody so lucky as we! Dear old Diamond!" He hugged the horse again and kissed both his big, hairy cheeks. He could only manage one at a time, however—the other cheek was so far off on the other side of old Diamond's big head. And now his father took up the reins to drive off.

"Oh, father, do let me drive a bit!" cried Diamond jumping up on the box beside him. His father put the reins into his hands and began to show him how to drive. He let Diamond drive quite a little way and then the boy jumped down and ran gaily back to his mother.

Now it happened that the man who sold old Diamond back to his father, saw how delighted little Diamond was to learn to drive. And that evening, shortly before Diamond's father came home, the man asked Diamond's mother if the boy might not go a little way with him.

"He cannot go far," said his mother, "for he is not very strong yet."

"I will take him only as far as the square," said the man.

Diamond's mother said he might go as far as that. Dancing with delight, Diamond ran to get his cap and in a few minutes was jumping into the cab. The man gave him the reins and showed him how to drive safely through the gate and Diamond got along famously. Just as they were turning into the square, they had an adventure. It was getting quite dusky. A cab was coming rapidly from the other direction, and Diamond pulling aside and the other driver pulling up, they just escaped a collision. And there was his father!

"Why, Diamond, it is a bad beginning to run into your own father," he said.

"But, father, wouldn't it have been a bad ending for you to run into your own son!" answered the boy. And both men laughed heartily.

"He is a good little driver, though," said the man. "He would be fit to drive on his own hook in a week or two. But he had better go back with you now."

"Come along then, Diamond," said his father. Diamond jumped across into the other cab and they drove away home.

It was not long before Diamond was a great favorite with all the men about the stables—he was so jolly! It was not the best place in the world for him to be brought up in and at first he did hear a good many rough and bad words. But as he did not like them, he never learned to say them and they did him little harm. Before long, the men grew rather ashamed to use them. One would nudge the other to remind him that the boy was within hearing and the words choked themselves before they got any further.

One day, they gave him a curry comb and brush to try his hand on old Diamond's coat. He used them deftly and thoroughly as far as he could reach.

"You must make haste and grow," the men told him. "It won't do to clean a horse half way up and leave his back dirty, you know."

"Put me up," said Diamond. In a moment he was on the old horse's back with the comb and brush. There he combed and brushed and combed and brushed. Every now and then, old Diamond would whisk his tail and once he sent the comb flying out of the stable door to the great amusement of the men. But they brought it back to him and Diamond finished his task.

"Oh, dear!" said Diamond, when he had done. "I'm so tired!" And he laid himself down at full length on old Diamond's back. The men were much amused and from that time were always ready to teach him to drive.

So in one way and another, he did learn to drive all sorts of horses, and through the most crowded streets in London city. One day his father took him on his own cab and as they were standing waiting for a passenger, his father left him alone for a few minutes. Hearing a noise, Diamond looked around to see what it was. There was a crossing near the cab-stand where a girl was sweeping. Some young roughs had picked a quarrel with her and were now trying to pull her broom away from her. Diamond was off his box in a moment and running to the help of the girl. The roughs began to act worse than ever. Just then Diamond's father came back and sent them flying. The girl thanked Diamond and began sweeping again as if nothing had happened.

She did not forget her friends, however. A moment after, she came running up with her broom over her shoulder, calling "Cab, there! Cab!" And when Diamond's father reached the curbstone, who should it be but Mrs. Coleman and Miss Coleman! Diamond and his father were very happy to see them again and gladly drove them home. When they wanted to pay for it, Diamond's father would not hear of it, but jumped on his box and drove away.

It was a long time since Diamond had seen North Wind or even thought much about her. Now, as his father drove along, he was thinking not about her but about the crossing sweeper. He was wondering what made him feel as if he knew her quite well when he could not remember anything of her. But a picture arose in his mind of a little girl running before the wind, and dragging her broom after her. From that, he recalled the whole adventure of the night when he had gone out with North Wind and made her put him down in a London street.

A few nights after this, Diamond woke up suddenly, believing he heard the north wind thundering along. But it was something quite different. South Wind was moaning around the chimneys, to be sure, for she was not very happy that night. But it was not her voice that had wakened Diamond. It was a loud angry voice, now growling like that of a beast, now raving like that of a madman. It was the voice of the drunken cabman whose room was just through the wall at the back of Diamond's bed.

At length, there came a cry from the woman and a scream from the baby. Diamond thought it was time somebody did something. He jumped up and went to see. The voice of the crying baby guided him to the right door and he peeped in. The drunken cabman had dropped into a chair, his wife lay sobbing on the bed, and the baby was wailing in its cradle.

Diamond's first thought was to run away from the misery of it. But he remembered at once that he had been at the back of the north wind. People who had been there must always try to destroy misery wherever they saw it. But what could he do? Well, there was the baby. He stole in and lifted it into his arms and soon had it on his knee, smiling at the light that came in from the street lamp. He began to sing to it in a low voice—the song of the river as it ran over the soft grass and among the flowers in the country at the back of the north wind. He sang on till the baby went sound asleep. He himself got sleepier and sleepier, though the cabman and his wife only got wider awake all the time. At length, Diamond found himself nodding. He got up and laid the baby gently in its cradle and stole quietly out and home again to his own bed.

"Wife," said the cabman, "did you see that angel?"

"Yes," answered his wife, "it is little Diamond who lives in the next yard."

She knew him well enough. She was the neighbor who had the fire lighted and the tea ready for them when Diamond and his mother came home from Sandwich on that rainy, gloomy night. Her husband was somehow very sorry now and ashamed of the misery he had caused—was it the song of the river which Diamond had sung that caused it? He tried hard to forget where the drink shop stood and for a good many weeks managed to keep away from it.

One day when their cab was waiting for a fare, Diamond jumped down to run a little and stretch his legs. He strolled up to the crossing where Nanny and her broom were to be found in all weathers. Just as he was going to speak to her a tall gentleman stepped upon the crossing. He was glad to find it clean and he gave the girl a penny. When she made him a courtesy, he looked at her again and said, "Where do you live, my child?"

"Paradise Row," she answered. "Next door to the Adam and Eve—down the area."

"Whom do you live with?" he asked.

"My wicked old granny," she replied.

"You should not call your granny wicked," said the gentleman.

"But she is!" said Nanny. "If you don't believe me, you can come and take a look at her."

The gentleman looked very grave at hearing her. It was not a nice way for a little girl to talk. He was turning away, when he saw the face of Diamond looking up into his own.

"Please," said Diamond, "her granny is very cruel to her sometimes—and shuts her out in the streets at night if she happens to be late."

"So, my little man. And what can you do?" asked the gentleman turning towards him.

"Drive a cab," said Diamond proudly.

"Anything else?" asked the gentleman smiling.

"Take care of the baby," said Diamond; "clean father's boots and make him a bit of toast for his tea."

"You are a useful little man," said the gentleman. "Can you read?"

"No, but father and mother can and they are going to teach me soon."

"Well, here is a penny for you, and when you learn to read, come to me and I will give you six-pence and a book with fine pictures in it."

He gave Diamond a card with his address on it. "Thank you," said Diamond and put the card into his pocket. The gentleman walked away but he saw Diamond give the penny to Nanny and say, "I have a father and mother and little brother and you have nothing but a wicked old granny. You may have my penny."

The girl put the penny in her pocket and Diamond asked, "Is she as cruel as ever?"

"Just the same. But I get more coppers, so I can buy myself some food. She is so blind that she doesn't see that I do not eat her old scraps. I hide them in my pocket."

"What do you want them for?"

"To give to cripple Jim. His leg was broken when he was young, so he isn't good for much. But I love Jim. I always keep something for him."

"Diamond! Diamond!" called his father, just then.

So Diamond ran back and told him about the gentleman and showed him the card he had given him.

"Why, it is not many doors from our stables!" cried his father looking at the address. "Take care of it, Diamond. One needs all the friends he can get in this world."

"We've got many friends," said Diamond. "Haven't we? There's mother and the baby and old Diamond—and the man next door who drinks—and his wife and baby—and Mrs. Coleman and Miss Coleman—and—and a many!"

His father just laughed and drove off.

DIAMOND DRIVES THE CAB

The question of the tall gentleman as to whether Diamond could read or not, set his father to thinking it was high time he could. As soon as old Diamond was fed and bedded, he began the task of teaching him that very night. It was not much of a task to Diamond for his father took for the lesson book the same one which North Wind had waved the leaves of on the sands at Sandwich. Within a month, he was able to spell out most of the verses for himself. But he never found in it the river song which he thought his mother had read from it. Could it have been North Wind doing the reading in his mother's voice?

It was not long before Diamond managed with many blunders to read all the rhymes in his book to his mother. Then he said, "In a week or so, I shall be able to go to the tall gentleman and tell him I can read." But before the week was out he had another reason for going to the gentleman, whose name he found out was Mr. Raymond. For three days, Nanny had not been at her crossing. Diamond was quite anxious about her, fearing she must be ill. On the fourth day not seeing her yet, he said to his father, "I want to go and look after Nanny. She can't be well."

"All right," said his father. "Only take care of yourself, Diamond."

So Diamond set off to find his way to Nanny's home. It was a long distance and he had to ask his way over and over again. But he kept on without getting discouraged and at last he came to it.

Happily for Diamond, the ugly old granny had gone out. He laid his ear to the door and thought he heard a moaning within. He tried the door and found it was not locked. It was a dreary place indeed—and very dark, for the window was below the level of the street and was covered with mud. And the smell in the room was dreadful!

He could see next to nothing at first but he heard the moaning plainly enough now. Soon he found his friend lying with closed eyes and a white suffering face on a heap of rags in a corner. He went up to her and spoke but she made him no answer. She did not even hear him. Taking out a lump of barley sugar candy he had brought for her he laid it down beside her and hurried away. He was going to find Mr. Raymond and see if he could not do something for Nanny.

It was a long walk to Mr. Raymond's door but he got there at last. Yet after all, the servant was not going to let him in, only Mr. Raymond came out into the hall just then and saw him and recognized him at once.

"Come in, my little man," he said. "I suppose you have come to claim your six-pence."

"No, sir, not that."

"What! Can't you read yet?"

"Yes," said Diamond. "I can now a little. But I've come to tell you about Nanny— the little girl at the crossing."

"Oh, yes, I remember her," said Mr. Raymond. "What is it about Nanny?"

Diamond told him all about her—how she was sick, and how dark it was where she lived and with bad smells. Now, Mr. Raymond was one of the kindest men in London and was well known at the children's hospital. He hurried there now, and some one went from there at once to find Nanny. Before night, they sent a litter for her and soon the little girl was lying in a nice clean bed, though she was too sick to know anything about it.

Diamond overheard a doctor say to Mr. Raymond, "How do you suppose the little chap knew what to do about Nanny?"

"He doesn't know that I have been at the back of the north wind," he said to himself. "If you have once been there, it just comes to you how to do a little to help."

After Nanny had been well seen to, Mr. Raymond took the boy home with him and they soon settled the matter of the six-pence between them.

"And now, what will you do with it?" the gentleman asked him.

"Take it home to my mother," answered Diamond. "She has a tea-pot with a broken spout and she keeps all her money in it. It isn't much but she saves it up to buy shoes for me. And there's the baby—he'll want shoes soon. And every six-pence is something, isn't it?"

"To be sure, my little man. And here is the book for you, full of pictures and stories."

There were poems in it too, and Diamond at once began to puzzle out one of them which ran like this:

I have only one foot, but thousands of toes;
  My one foot stands but never goes.
I have many arms and they are mighty, all;
And hundreds of fingers large and small.
From the ends of my fingers my beauty grows,
I breathe with my hair and I drink with my toes.
In the summer, with song I shake and quiver,
But in winter, I fast and groan and shiver.

When Diamond ran home with his new book in his hand, he found his father at home already. He was sitting by the fire and looking rather miserable for his head ached and he looked sick. The next day, he had to stay in bed while his wife nursed him, and Diamond took care of the baby. By the next day, he was very ill indeed. And it was not long before their money was all gone.

Diamond's mother could not help crying over it but she came into Diamond's room so that the poor sick father should not hear it. Diamond was frightened when he heard her sobbing and said, "Is father worse?"

"No, no," said his mother, "he is better. But the money is all gone and what are we to do?"

"Don't cry," said Diamond. "We'll get along some how. Let me read to you out of North Wind's book."

So he read a little story about the early bird that caught the nice fat worm.

"I wish you were like that little bird, dear," said his mother, "and could catch something to eat!"

After she was gone away, Diamond lay thinking and somehow he seemed to hear the murmur of North Wind's river blowing through his thoughts and telling him about something he could do. The next morning he got up as soon as he heard the men moving in the yard. When he went down, the stable was just opened. "I'm the early bird, I think," he said to himself, "and I hope I'll catch the worm."

He would not ask any one to help him because he was afraid he would be kept from doing what he wanted. With the aid of an old chair, he got the harness on old Diamond. The dear old horse opened his mouth for the bit just as if Diamond was giving him an apple. He fastened the cheek-strap very carefully, and got all the pieces of harness on and buckled. By this time some of the men were watching him to see if he would get it all done by himself. And when he put old Diamond between the shafts, got his whip, and jumped up on the box, the men broke into a cheer.

The cheer brought his mother to the window and when she saw her little boy setting out all alone in the cab, she called "Diamond! Diamond!" But Diamond did not hear her for the rattle of the cab and so he drove away. He was very much afraid no one would hire him because he was such a little driver. But before he got to his regular stand, he was hailed by a man who wanted to catch a train and was in too great a hurry to think about the driver. He got a good fare for that and reached the cab-stand the first one after all. As the other cabmen came, he told them about his father and said that he was going to drive the cab in his place.

"Well, you are a plucky one!" they all said. "And you shall have a fair chance with the rest."

And he did, for another gentleman came up very soon for him. When he saw the boy, he was much astonished. "Are you the driver of this cab?" he asked. "Yes, sir," answered Diamond, showing his father's badge of which he was proud.

"You are the youngest cabman I ever saw!" said the gentleman greatly amused. "But I believe I'll risk you!"

He jumped in and soon found that Diamond got him over the ground very well. The trip was one of several miles and the gentleman paid him three shillings for the drive. When Diamond got back, he stopped at a stand where he had never been before and got down to put on old Diamond's nose-bag of oats. The men there did not treat him very nicely and a group of rough boys came up and began to torment him. But who do you think came to his rescue? Why, the drunken cabman whose room was next to Diamond's and whose baby Diamond had once rocked and put to sleep.

"What is up here?" the cabman asked.

"Do you see this young snip?" the boys cried, "He pretends to drive a cab!"

"Yes, I do see him," said the cabman. "I see you, too. You'd better take yourselves away from here or you won't find me very agreeable!"

And they went in a hurry!

When Diamond went home that night, he carried one pound, one shilling and six-pence. His mother had grown very anxious and was almost afraid to look when she heard his cab coming at last. But there was the old horse, and there was the cab, all right! And there was Diamond on the box his face as triumphant as a full moon! One of the men took the horse to put him up and Diamond ran into the house and into the arms of his mother!

"See! See!" he cried. "Here is the worm I caught!" He poured out the six-pences and shillings into her lap. His mother burst out crying again, but with joy this time and ran to show his father. Then how pleased he was! And Diamond snatched up the baby and began to sing and dance, he was so happy!

The next morning, Diamond was up almost as early as before. But the men would not let him do the harnessing any more. They got the cab all ready for him and sent him in to eat all the breakfast he could and get well bundled up. His first passenger was a young woman to be taken to the docks. When he started back some roughs came along and tried to steal his fare. But a pale-faced man came up and beat them off with his stick, and told Diamond to drive away. Diamond begged him to get into the cab and ride. The man said he could not spare the money to ride—he was too poor.

"Oh, do come!" said Diamond. "I don't want the money. You helped me. Let me help you."

"Well," said the man, "if you will take me to Chiswick, I can pay for that. Drive to the Wilderness—Mr. Coleman's place. I'll show you when we get there."

Now Diamond had been thinking he had seen the gentleman before and when he said this, it flashed upon him that it was Mr. Evans who had been going to marry Miss Coleman. North Wind had sunk his and Mr. Coleman's ship because their business was not honest and was making bad men of them. She had carried Mr. Evans away to a desert island. He had just got back again and was poor now and humble and willing to begin to work again in an honest way.

It was plain he did not know that Mr. Coleman had been ruined too and had been forced to sell the Wilderness and move into a poor house in the city. But Diamond knew, and as he drove along he was thinking what he ought to do. The gentleman would not find Miss Coleman at the Wilderness. And if he told him where she lived now, perhaps he would not go to see her because he would be so ashamed of having brought all this trouble on her by trying so hard to be rich.

Still he must want to see her very much and she must want to see him. So

Diamond made up his mind to drive straight to where Miss Coleman lived now, and then they could explain to each other. So on he went.

Now the wind was blowing furiously and when old Diamond finally got to Miss Coleman's house and held back to stop, one of the straps of the harness broke. Diamond jumped down and opened the cab door and asked the gentleman if he would not step into this house where friends of his lived and wait while he mended the strap. Then he ran and rang the bell and whispered to the maid who came to call Miss Coleman. A few minutes later, he was not at all sure he had done the right thing. For suddenly there came the sound of a great cry and then a running to and fro in the house. But after a little while, they came and called him in and Miss Coleman put her arms around him and hugged him tight!

The rest of the day, he did very well. And what a story he had to tell his father and mother that night about Mr. Evans and the Colemans. They were sure he had done right and he was so glad!

DIAMOND VISITS NANNY

For a fortnight, Diamond went on driving his cab and helping his family. Some people began to know him and to look for him to drive them where they wanted to go. One old gentleman who lived near the stables hired him to carry him into the city every morning at a certain hour. And Diamond was as regular as clock work. After that fortnight, his father was able to go out again. Then Diamond began to think about little Nanny and went off to inquire about her.

The first day his father took up his work again, Diamond went with him as usual. In the afternoon, however, his father went home and left Diamond to drive the cab for the rest of the day. It was hard for old Diamond to do all the work but they could not afford to have another horse. They saved him as much as they could and fed him well and he did bravely.

The next morning, his father was so much stronger that Diamond thought he might go and ask Mr. Raymond to take him to see Nanny. Mr. Raymond was quite willing to go and so they walked over to the hospital which was close at hand.

When Diamond followed Mr. Raymond into the room where those children lay who had got over the worst of their illness, and were growing better, he saw a number of little iron beds. Each one of them stood with its head to the wall and in each one was a child whose face showed just how far it had left the pain behind and was getting well. Diamond looked all around but he could see no Nanny. He turned to Mr. Raymond with a question in his eyes.

"Well?" said Mr. Raymond.

"Nanny's not here," said Diamond.

"Oh, yes, she is."

"I don't see her!"

"I do, though. There she is."

He pointed to a bed right in front of where Diamond was standing.

"That's not Nanny!" cried Diamond.

"Yes, it is Nanny. I have seen her a great many times since you have, and that is she."

So Diamond looked again and looked hard. "If that is Nanny," said Diamond to himself, "then she must have been at the back of the north wind. That is why she looks so different." He said nothing aloud, only stared. And as he stared, something of the face of the old Nanny began to come out in the face of the new Nanny. The old Nanny had been somewhat rough in her speech, her face rather hard, and she had not kept herself clean—how could she! Now, in her fresh white bed, she looked sweet and gentle and refined.

"Surely North Wind has had something to do with it," thought Diamond. In her weeks of sickness, had North Wind carried Nanny to the country at her back—as she once had carried him—and changed her from a rough girl to a gentle maiden? As he gazed, the best of the old face, the good and true part of the old Nanny, dawned upon him like the moon coming out of a cloud. He saw that it was Nanny, indeed—but very worn and grown almost beautiful.

He went up to her and she smiled. He had heard her laugh, but he had never seen her smile before. "Nanny, do you know me?" asked Diamond. She only smiled again. She was not likely to forget him. To be sure, she did not know that it was he who had got her there. But he was the only boy except cripple Jim who had ever been kind to her.

Mr. Raymond walked about talking to the other children, while Diamond visited with Nanny. Then after a time, he stood in the middle of the room and told them a nice fairy story. He often did that and the children watched for his visits. After he finished the story, he had to go. Diamond took leave of Nanny and promised to go and see her again soon and went away with Mr. Raymond.

Now Mr. Raymond had been turning over in his mind what he could do for Diamond and for Nanny. He knew Diamond's father somewhat. But he wanted to find out better what sort of a man he was and whether he was worth doing anything for. He decided to see if he would do anything for any body else. For that would be the very best way to find out if it were worth while to do anything for him. So as they walked away together, he said to little Diamond, "Nanny must leave the hospital soon, Diamond. They cannot keep her as long as they would like. They cannot keep her till she is quite strong. There are always so many sick children they want to take in and make better. The question is what will she do when they send her out again?"

"That is just what I can't tell," said Diamond, "though I've been thinking it over and over. Her crossing was taken long ago. I couldn't bear to see Nanny fighting for it, especially with the poor lame boy who has taken it. Besides she has no better right to it than he has. Nobody gave it to her. She just took it and now he has taken it."

"She would get sick again, anyway," said Mr. Raymond, "if she went to sweeping again right away in the wet. If somebody could only teach her something to do it would be better. Perhaps if she could be taught to be nice and clean and to speak only gentle words——"

"Mother could teach her that!" interrupted Diamond.

"And to dress babies and feed them and take care of them," Mr. Raymond went on, "she might get a place as nurse maid somewhere. People would give her money for that."

"Why, I'll ask mother!" cried Diamond. "She could learn to dress our baby, you know, with me to show her how!"

"But you will have to give her food then. And your father, not being strong, has enough to do already without that."

"Still there am I!" said Diamond. "I'll help him out with it. When he gets tired of driving, up I get. And I could drive more if Nanny was at home to help mother."

"Now I wonder," said Mr. Raymond, "if you couldn't do better with two horses. I am going away for a few months and I am willing to let your father have my horse while I am gone. He is nearly as old as your Diamond. I don't want to part with him and yet I don't want him to be idle. Nobody ought to be idle, not even a horse. Still I do not want him to be worked hard. Will you tell your father what I say and see if he wants to take charge of him?"

"Yes, I will," said Diamond. "And he will come and see you about it."

So when Diamond went home, he told his father all about it. But when his father went to see about it, he found that he must agree to work the horse only six hours a day. Then too he must take Nanny from the hospital and feed her, and teach her to be useful and keep her as long as he had Mr. Raymond's horse. Diamond's father could not help thinking that it was a pretty close bargain and so it was. Mr. Raymond wanted to find out if Diamond's father was the kind of man who was willing to help some one else without getting any advantage out of it for himself. Then it would be worth while to help him. Diamond's father was that kind of a man. So when he heard all about Nanny, he decided to accept Mr. Raymond's offer and do the best he could.

Nanny was not fit to be moved for some time yet and Diamond went to see her as often as he could. But he went out to drive old Diamond every day now for a few hours at least. Then he had to help mind his baby brother for part of the time. So he did not go to the hospital as often as he would have liked. When he did go, he sat by Nanny's bed and told her all that had happened to him since he had been there before. In her turn Nanny would tell him of what went on in the hospital—what visitors they had and things like that.

"Day before yesterday," said Nanny one day, "a lady came to see us. She was a very beautiful lady. She sat down beside my bed and let me stroke her hand. She had on a most beautiful ring with a rich red stone in it. When she saw me looking at it, she slipped it off her finger and put it on mine. She said I might wear her lovely ruby for a little while if it would make me happy."

"Her ruby!" cried Diamond. "How funny that is! Our new horse's name is Ruby. And we took him so that we could take you to live with us, while you are getting strong again. I do believe a ruby is for good luck!"

"It did me good right then," said Nanny. "For that night I had such a lovely dream. It began with a red sunset like my darling ruby ring. Then somehow a wind came out of it and blew me along out of the dirty streets into a yard with a lovely lawn of soft grass."

"That was North Wind, I know!" cried Diamond. "That is what she does to me."

"I do not know what you mean," said Nanny. "I do not know anything about

North Wind. But all at once there was no more ruby sunset but a great golden moon hanging very low and seeming to be shining just to be good to me. It was easy, I suppose, for me to dream about the moon. I've always been used to watching her. She was the only thing worth looking at in our street, at night."

"Don't call it your street," said Diamond. "You are not going back to it. You are coming to us, you know."

"That is too good to be true!" said Nanny.

"No, no!" cried Diamond. "How could anything be too good to be true? To be true is to be the very best thing of all. It sounds like your wicked old granny to say that!"

"Do you know, Diamond," said Nanny, "I do not think my old granny is my real old granny at all. I don't think she was ever any one's granny or mother. That was why she was not good to me. Perhaps she never had any mother when she was little to be good to her. And somebody must first be good to you, don't you think, before you can learn how to be good to any body else? Isn't that so? But where was I in my dream? Oh yes, the big yellow moon came down closer and closer to the grass in front of me. Then somehow, it seemed to be my ruby lady. She reached out soft warm arms of golden light and took me up. I sank against her breast into very downy, golden clouds and went to sleep and left off having pain. And yet I didn't sleep but knew it all the time, and just swung softly there all night long."

"Wasn't it really North Wind?" said Diamond to himself. "Perhaps it was North Wind though she doesn't know it. Maybe the moon does just the same. What if it should some day carry her to that same country—at the back of my North Wind! Who knows?"

The nurse now came and told him it was time to go. Nanny had closed her eyes as if she were tired or asleep. So Diamond arose quietly and tip-toed away.

THINGS GO HARD WITH DIAMOND'S FAMILY

It was a great delight to Diamond, when at length Nanny was well enough to leave the hospital and go to their house. She was not strong yet but Diamond's mother was very careful of her. She took care she should have nothing to do that she was not fit for. If Nanny had been taken straight from the street, it is pretty sure she would not have been so pleasant in a nice house nor so easy to teach. But the kindness they had shown her in the hospital while she was ill so long had changed her quite a little.

As she got better, the colour came back to her cheeks, her step grew lighter and quicker, her smile shone out more readily, and it was clear she would soon be a treasure of help. It was great fun to see Diamond teaching her how to hold the baby and wash and dress him. Nanny had never had a little brother or sister to care for and she and Diamond often had to laugh over her awkwardness. But she was soon able to do it all as well as Diamond himself.

Things, however, did not go very well with Diamond's father from the first coming of the horse, Ruby. It almost seemed as if the red beast brought bad luck with him. The fares were fewer and the pay less. Ruby's work did indeed make the week's income at first a little more than it used to be. But then there were two more to feed. After the first month, however, he fell lame, and for the whole of the next month, Diamond's father did not dare work him at all. It cost just as much to feed him and all he did was to stand in the stable and grow fat.

And after he got well again, it was not much better. Times had then become hard and fewer and fewer people felt that they could afford to ride in cabs. The cabmen got fewer and fewer shillings to live on. Diamond's household had less and less to buy food and clothing with. Then too, Diamond's mother was poorly for a new baby was coming.

Diamond's father began to feel gloomier and gloomier and if Diamond had not made himself remember that he had been at the back of the north wind, he would

308

have been gloomy himself. But when his father came home, Diamond would get out his book and show him how well he could read. Besides he taught Nanny how to read and as she was a very clever little girl, she picked it up very fast. Nanny was such a comfort about the house that Diamond's father just had to cheer up a little when he came home at night and the dull day's work was over.

After the new baby came, Diamond sang to her and of course he had to make up new songs to sing to her because she was a little sister baby. It would never do, he said, to sing the little brother songs to her. While he sang, his father and mother could not help listening and forgetting for the time how bad things were getting to be.

The three months Mr. Raymond had spoken of were now gone and Diamond's father was very anxious for him to come back and take Ruby off his hands, for he did not seem to work enough to pay for his keep. Then he was so lazy and fat, while poor old Diamond had got so thin he was just skin and bones! For Diamond's father was an honest man and felt that he must stick to his promise to feed Ruby while he kept him, whether old Diamond got enough to eat or not. But he did wish Mr. Raymond would come, though when he looked at Nanny he felt that he would be sorry to lose her. For it was understood that a place as a nurse girl would be found for her when Ruby was taken away.

Mr. Raymond did not come, however, and things got worse and worse. Diamond could do little but drive old Diamond in the cab whenever he could be of help that way, and sing to the two babies at home. At last, one week was worse than anything they had yet had. They were almost without bread before it was over.

It was Friday night, and Diamond like the rest of the household had had very little to eat that day. His mother would always pay the week's rent before she spent anything even for food. His father had been very gloomy—so gloomy that he was very cross. It had been a stormy winter and even now that spring had come, the north wind often blew. When Diamond went to his bed, which was in a tiny room in the roof, he heard it like the sea, moaning. As he fell asleep, he still heard the moaning, and presently, he heard the voice of North Wind calling him. His heart beat very fast, it was such a long time since he had heard that voice! He jumped out of bed, but did not see her. Yet she kept on calling.

"Diamond, come here! Diamond, come here!" the voice repeated again and again.

"Dear North Wind," said Diamond, "I want so much to come to you but I can't tell where to find you."

"Come here, Diamond!" was all her answer.

So he opened his door and trotted down the long stair and out into the yard. A great puff of wind at once came against him. He turned and went with it, and it blew him up to the stable door and kept on blowing.

"She wants me to go into the stable," said Diamond. "But the door is locked."

Just then, a great blast of wind brought down the key upon the stones at his feet from where it was kept hanging high above his head. He picked it up, opened the door, and went in without much noise. And what did he hear? He heard the two horses, Diamond and Ruby, talking to each other. They talked in a strange language, yet somehow he could understand it.

"You ought to be ashamed of yourself," old Diamond was saying, "sleek and fat as you are, and so lazy you get along no faster than a big dray-horse that is pulling tons!"

"Oh, I like to be fat and lazy!" said Ruby.

"And you like to hear master abused on account of you, too, I dare say," replied old Diamond angrily. "Why don't you get up a little speed, while you are drawing a fare, at least! The abuse master gets for your sake is quite shameful! No wonder he doesn't get many fares when he has you!"

"Well, if I worked as hard as I could, I'd be a bag of bones like you!"

"I'm proud to work!" said old Diamond. "I wouldn't be as fat as you, not for all you're worth. You are a disgrace! Look at the horse next you. He is something like a horse—all skin and bones. He knows he has got his master's wife and children to support and he works like a horse!"

"I might get lamed again, if I didn't go slowly and carefully," said Ruby.

"Lame again!" snorted old Diamond. "It's my belief you lamed yourself on purpose so you could stay in the stable and stuff yourself and grow fat! You selfish beast!"

"I might get angry at you," said Ruby, "if I didn't know a little better than you do how things are coming out. What do you think my master would say if he were to come back—and he may come any day now—and find me all worn down to a rack of bones and lamed into the bargain? Do you think anything would make him believe that your master had used me right and as he promised he would? And isn't it better he should live a little hard himself and prove himself to be an honest man who does what he says he'll do? You don't know everything, old Diamond. You would not probably believe me if I told you that enduring bad things is often just a way for bringing good things about. But you'll see!"

Old Diamond just snorted sleepily in reply and gave all his attention to doubling up his knees and getting down upon the floor to go to sleep. The racket he made gave young Diamond a start. With a shiver, he seemed to come awake and see the stable door standing open. He trotted out of it, back up the long stairs, and tumbled into bed. But Ruby's words kept sounding in his head.

"Is it like what's in my book?" he said to himself sleepily,—"that about a blessing in disguise, when things look bad but are working out all right—like things at the back of the north wind?" He got sleepier, however, as he tried to think and was fast asleep before he knew it. The next morning, he sang to the baby more cheerily than ever and here is part of the song he sung:

Where did you come from, Baby dear?
    Out of everywhere into here.

Where did you get your eyes so blue?
    Out of the sky as I came through.

Where did you get this pearly ear?
God spoke and it came out to hear.

But how did you come to us, you dear?
God thought of you and so I am here.

"You never made that song, Diamond," said his mother.

"No, mother. But it's mine just the same, for I love it."

"Does loving a thing make it yours?"

"I think so, mother. Baby's mine because I love her, and so are you. Love makes the only my-ness, doesn't it, mother?"

"Perhaps so, Diamond. Yes, I think it does," said his mother.

When his father came home for his dinner he looked very sad. He had not got a single fare the whole morning.

"We shall just have to go to the work-house," he said and dropped into a chair in despair. Just then, came a knock at the door and in walked Mr. Raymond! Of course, he wanted to see the horses at once. And when he saw how fat Ruby was and how poor was faithful old Diamond—and when, moreover, he remembered how poor and starved the family looked though Nanny was still there and kindly treated—he knew that Diamond's father had been stanch and true to his bargain, though it had turned out to be a hard one. He was a man worth helping—that was clear! And Mr. Raymond was now ready to help him as much as he needed.

He first pointed out that old Diamond needed only to be fattened up and Ruby thinned down to make of them a fine pair of horses for his country home to which he was now going. And Diamond's father should go along as coachman. There would be regular wages again and a much more comfortable home in the country.

"And now, will you sell me old Diamond?" asked Mr. Raymond. "If you will, here are twenty pounds for him, if you think that is enough."

"I will sell him to you, sir," answered Diamond's father, "if you promise to let me buy him back if I can, if you ever wish to sell him. I could not part with him without that. Though as to who calls him his, that is nothing. For I believe it's true what my little Diamond says—that it's loving a thing that makes it yours."

"You shall have that chance," said Mr. Raymond. So the bargain was made. How Diamond capered about at the thought of going to the beautiful country to live and having a yard and grass to play on! It would be like the old home at Mr. Coleman's —perhaps even nicer than that. How he danced the baby and sang to it!

"And North Wind told me, Baby dear! She sang in my ears how bad things are just a chance to make good things come!"

DIAMOND IN HIS NEW HOME

Before the end of the month, Ruby had got a great deal thinner and old Diamond a good deal fatter. They really began to look fit to go in double harness. Diamond's father and mother got their things all packed up and were ready to go into the country at the shortest notice. They were now so peaceful, and so happy over the prospect that they believed it worth all the trouble and worry they had gone through.

Nanny had been so happy since she left the hospital and had been living with Diamond's family that she did not think the country would make her any happier. Besides she would have to leave cripple Jim behind and maybe never see him again. She had known cripple Jim much longer than she had known Diamond and he had no one else to care about him.

Diamond had taken a great deal of time and trouble to find Jim. For Jim had moved his home and had not heard of Nanny's illness till long after she was taken to the hospital. He was much too shy to go and inquire about her there. But when at length she went to live with Diamond's family, Jim was willing enough to go and see her. It was after one of his visits during which he and Nanny had talked things over that Diamond found out that Nanny thought it would not be so very pleasant to go to the country. The sun and the moon and the trees and the flowers did not seem much to Nanny without Jim.

Diamond thought it over and that same night he went to see Mr. Raymond. He wanted to tell him about Jim and Nanny and ask him what they could do about it. "Jim can shine shoes very well indeed, sir," said Diamond. "If you could take Jim into the country too, to clean your shoes and do other odd jobs, then Nanny would like it better. She is so fond of Jim."

Mr. Raymond thought it all over and finally decided that there would be something for Jim to do.

So on a certain day, Diamond's father took his mother and Diamond himself and his little brother and sister and Nanny and Jim down by train to a place called "The Mound," where Mr. Raymond was to live. He went back to London that same night. The next day, he drove Ruby and Diamond down with the carriage behind them, and Mr. Raymond and a lady in the carriage. For Mr. Raymond was now married. And the moment Nanny saw Mrs. Raymond, she recognized her as the lady who had let her wear the beautiful ruby ring when she was ill in the hospital.

The weather was very hot at first, and the woods very shadowy, and the wild flowers mainly gone. But there were plenty of the loveliest grass and daisies about the house. Diamond's chief pleasure seemed to be to lie among them and breathe the pure air. As he lay there, he dreamed often of the country at the back of the north wind and tried to remember the songs the river used to sing. For this was more like being at the back of the north wind than anything he had known since he left it. But though he did lie happily in the grass and dream of her, of North Wind herself, he neither saw nor heard anything for some months.

Mr. Raymond's house was called "The Mound" because it stood upon a steep little knoll that had been made on purpose. It was built for Queen Elizabeth as a hunting tower—a place, that is, from the top of which you could see the country for miles on all sides. From a window the Queen was able to follow with her eyes the flying deer, and the hunters in the chase. The mound had been cast up so as to give the house an outlook over the neighboring heights and woods.

Diamond's father and mother lived in a little cottage a short distance from the house. It was a real cottage with a roof of thick thatch which, in June and July, the wind sprinkled with the red and white petals of the rose tree climbing up the walls. But Mr. and Mrs. Raymond wanted Diamond to be a page in their own house. So he was dressed in the little blue suit of a page and lived at "The Mound" itself.

"Would you be afraid to sleep alone, Diamond?" asked his mistress. "There is a little room at the top of the house—all alone. Perhaps you would not mind sleeping there."

"I can sleep anywhere," said Diamond. "And I like best to be high up. Should I be able to see out?"

"I will show you the place," she answered, and taking him by the hand, she led him up and up the oval winding stair into one of the two towers that were on the house. Near the top, they entered a tiny room with two windows from which you could see all over the country. Diamond clapped his hands with delight!

"You would like this room, then, Diamond?" asked his mistress.

"It is the grandest room in the house!" he answered. "I shall be near the stars and yet not far from the tops of the trees. That is just what I like!"

I daresay he thought also that it would be a nice place for North Wind to call at, in passing. Below him spread a lake of green leaves with glimpses of grass here and there at the bottom. As he looked down, he saw a squirrel appear suddenly and as suddenly vanish among the top-most branches.

"Aha! Mr. Squirrel!" he cried. "My nest is built higher than yours!"

"I will have a bell hung at your door which I can ring when I want you," said his mistress. And so Diamond became a little page in the house.

But after all, his master and mistress seemed to want to keep him out of doors as much as possible. And his father and mother sometimes looked at him very anxiously. Diamond thought that no one seemed to ask him to do much. Often they gave him a story book and sent him out to sit in the sweet air and sunshine at the foot of a big beech tree.

He did not see much of Nanny and Jim. Somehow they liked to slip off together when their work was over. They did not understand the many fancies that Diamond talked about, but they could understand each other very well. They were never unkind to him but they liked better to go off by themselves. Diamond did not mind much. He was never lonely. And then he had a beautiful place where he went and where he saw lovely things that no one else saw.

He called this place his nest. He went to it by going up a little rope ladder that hung from a branch of the big beech tree. When he reached the limb the rope hung from, he went on climbing higher and higher. Up among the leafy branches and away at the top, out of sight, he found a safe and comfortable seat which he called his nest.

"What do you see up there, Diamond," some one asked him once.

"I can see the first star peeping out of the sky. I don't see anything more except a few leaves and the big sky over me. It goes swinging about. The earth is all behind my back. There comes another star! The wind with its kisses makes me feel as if I were in North Wind's arms."

He thought he would be quite happy if only he could remember some of the songs the river sang to him when he was in the country at the back of the north wind. They seemed to be murmuring in his ear most of the time. Yet somehow they were just far enough off so that he could not catch the words.

His little brother and baby sister often played about on the grass with him and often he made up songs to sing to the baby. But these never seemed to be just like the river's songs after all. One of them was about his nest up in the beech tree and it ran like this:

What would you see if I took you up
    To my little nest in the air?
    You would see the sky like a clean blue cup
    Turned upside downwards there.

What would you do if I took you there,
    To my little nest in the tree?
    My child with cries would trouble the air
    To get what she could but see.

What would you get in the top of the tree,
    For all your crying and grief?
    Not a star would you clutch of all you see—
    You could only gather a leaf.

But when you had lost your greedy grief

Content to see from afar,
You would find in your hand a withering leaf,
In your heart a shining star!

ANOTHER VISIT FROM NORTH WIND

One night when he reached his own room, he opened both his windows, one of which looked to the north and the other to the east, to find how the wind blew. It blew right in at the north window. Diamond was glad for he thought perhaps North Wind herself would come now. But as she always came of herself and never when he was looking for her, and, indeed, almost never when he was thinking of her, he shut the east window and went to bed.

He awoke in the dim blue night. The moon had vanished from that side of the house. He thought he heard a knocking at his door.

"Somebody wants me!" he said, and jumping out of bed ran to open the door.

But there was no one there. He closed it again, and the noise still going on, found that another door in the room was rattling. It belonged to a closet he thought, but he had never been able to open it. The wind blowing in at the window must be shaking it. He would go and see if that was it.

The door now opened quite easily. To his surprise, instead of a closet he found a long narrow room. The moon, which was sinking in the west, shone in at an open window at the other end. This room had a low ceiling and spread the whole length of the house close under the roof. It was quite empty. The yellow light of the half moon streamed over the dark floor.

He was so delighted to find this strange moonlit place close to his own snug little room that he began to dance and skip about the floor. The wind came in through the door he had left open. It blew about him as he danced and he kept turning toward it that it might blow in his face.

He kept picturing to himself the many places, lovely and desolate, the hill sides and farm yards and tree-tops and meadows, over which it had blown on its way to "The Mound." As he danced he grew more and more delighted with the motion and the wind. His feet grew stronger and his body lighter. At length, it seemed as if he were borne up on the air and could almost fly.

So strong did this feeling become that at last he began to doubt whether he was not in one of those precious dreams he so often had, in which he floated about on the wind at will. Then something made him look up. To his unspeakable delight, he found his uplifted hands lying in those of North Wind! Yes, North Wind was dancing with him round and round the long bare room, her hair now falling to the floor, now floating to the ceiling. The sweetest of smiles was playing about her beautiful mouth. She did not stoop in order to dance with him but held his hands high in hers.

When he saw her, he gave one spring and his arms were about her neck and her arms holding him to her breast. The same moment, she swept with him out of the open window through which the moon was shining. Making a wide and sweeping circuit, she settled with him in his own little nest at the top of the big beech tree. Diamond was so entirely happy that he did not care to speak a word. But presently, he felt as if he were going to sleep and that would be to lose so much that he was not willing to do it.

"Please, dear North Wind," said he, "I am so happy that I am afraid it is a dream. How am I to know that it is not a dream?"

"What does it matter?" returned North Wind. "The dream—if it is a dream—is a pleasant one, is it not?"

"That is just why I want it to be true! It is not for the dream itself—I mean it is not for the pleasure of it," answered Diamond, "for I have that whether it is a dream or not. It is for you, North Wind! I cannot bear to find it a dream because then I should lose you! You would be nobody then and I could not bear that. You are not just a dream, dear North Wind, are you? Do say no, for I shall not dare dream of you again if you are nobody at all."

"Either I am not a dream, or there is something better which is not a dream, Diamond," said North Wind in a rather sorrowful tone.

"But it is not something better, it is you I want, North Wind," he persisted.

She made no answer but rose with him in her arms and sailed away over the tree-tops till they came to a meadow where a flock of sheep was feeding.

"Do you remember the song you made up here in this meadow to sing to the baby?" asked North Wind, "about Bo-peep's sheep that ran away from her to follow after the sun? And when she went after them, she could not find the old sheep at all —only some lambs—twice as many new lambs?"

"Oh, yes," said Diamond. "But I do not like that song. It seems to say that one is just as good as another—or that two new ones are better than the one old one you had before. But somehow when once you have looked into anybody's eyes—deep down into them, I mean—no one else will do for you any more. Nobody ever so beautiful or so good will make up to you for that one going out of sight. So you see, North Wind, I cannot help being frightened to think that perhaps I am only dreaming and that you are nowhere at all! Do tell me that you are my own real beautiful North Wind!"

Again she rose and shot high up into the air. Diamond lay quiet in her arms waiting for her to speak. He tried to see up into her face, for he was dreadfully afraid she did not answer him because she could not tell him she was not a dream. But her hair fell all over her face so that he could not see it. This frightened him still more.

"Do speak, North Wind!" he said at last.

317

"I am thinking what I can say," said North Wind slowly. "And say it so that a little boy like you can understand."

As she spoke, she was settling quietly down on a grassy hill side in the midst of a wild, furzy common. There was a rabbit warren underneath. Some of the rabbits came out of their holes in the moonlight. They looked very sober and wise, like patriarchs standing in their tent doors and looking about them before going to bed. When they saw North Wind, instead of turning around and vanishing again with a thump of their heels, they cantered slowly up to her. They snuffed all about her with their long upper lips which moved every way at once. That was their way of kissing her. Every now and then, she stroked down their long furry backs or lifted and played with their long ears.

"I think," she said to Diamond after they had been sitting silent for a long time, "that if I were only a dream, you would not have been able to love me so. You love me when you are not with me, don't you?"

"Indeed I do!" answered Diamond stroking her hand. "I see! I see! How could I be able to love you as I do if you were not there at all, you know? Besides I would not be able to dream anything half so beautiful all out of my own head. Or if I did, I could not love a fancy of my own like that, could I?"

"I think not. Besides, would you not have forgotten me wholly when you woke again? People almost always forget their dreams. But you have seen me in many shapes, Diamond. You remember I was a wolf once—don't you?"

"Yes, a good wolf that frightened a bad, wicked nurse!"

"Well, if I were to turn to an ugly shape again, would you still wish I were not a dream?"

"Yes, for I should know you were still beautiful inside, and that you loved me still. I should not like you to look ugly, you know. And I shouldn't believe it was really you a bit!"

"That's my own Diamond! Then I will try to tell you all I know about it. I don't think I am just what you fancy me to be. I have to shape myself in various ways to various people. But the heart of me is true. People call me by dreadful names and think they know all about me. But they don't. Sometimes they call me Bad Fortune or Evil Chance or Ruin—as Mr. Evans did when I sank his ship. Then people have another name for me which they think the most dreadful of all."

"What is that?" asked Diamond smiling up in her face. "And does it only mean another way in which you do them good though they think you are doing them ill?"

"Yes," answered North Wind, "it is just like that. But I will not tell you that name —not just now. Only will you always remember, if you should hear it, not to be the least afraid of it—or of me? Will you promise, Diamond?"

"Yes, North Wind, I promise," said Diamond. "I will never be afraid of you."

"Do you remember having to go through me to get into the country at my back?" asked North Wind, "after the long, long, long ride in the ship and the journey on the iceberg?"

"Yes, yes, I do! How tired you were, North Wind, when we got at last on to the iceberg and South Wind began to blow! And how thin and weak you grew in the beautiful blue cave in the side of the ice. Afterward when I landed and found you in the cleft in the ice ridge, sitting on your own door-step, how cold you were, North Wind! And so white, all but your lovely eyes! When I went up close to you, my own heart grew like a lump of ice. And when I tried to clasp you, the white grew so thick all about me, and then I forgot for a while."

"You were very near then, Diamond, to knowing what my other name is. But did I hurt you at all, dear boy? Would you be afraid of me if you had to go through me again?"

"No. Why should I? It was delicious to forget like that! It was like going into the softest and sweetest sleep! I should be glad enough to do it again, if it was only to get another peep at the country at your back."

"But you did not then see the real country at the back of the north wind, Diamond," said North Wind.

"Didn't I, North Wind? Oh, I'm so sorry! I thought I did. What did I see?"

"Only a picture of it—a sort of vision of it—and only while you seemed to be asleep. The real country at my real back is ever so much more beautiful than that. You shall see it one day—perhaps before very long."

"Do they sing songs there?" asked Diamond.

"Yes," replied North Wind. "You have not forgotten the lovely river as clear as glass that ran over and through the grass and flowers, have you? Nor the soft sweet songs it was always singing?"

"No," said Diamond. "I remember that best of all. But I could not keep the words of any one of its songs in mind, do what I would. And I did try."

"That was my fault," said North Wind.

"How was that?" asked the little boy.

"Because I could not hear it plainly enough myself to teach it to you. But you will hear the very song itself when you get to the back of——"

"My own dear North Wind," said Diamond, finishing the sentence for her, and stroking the arm that held him leaning against her.

"And now, I will take you home again," said North Wind. "It won't do to tire you too much."

"Oh, no, no!" pleaded Diamond. "I am not in the least tired."

"It is better, though," said North Wind.

"Very well; if you wish it," yielded Diamond, but with a sigh.

"You are a dear boy," said North Wind. "I will come for you again to-morrow night and take you out for a longer time. We shall make a little journey together, in fact. We shall start earlier, and as the moon will be somewhat later, we shall have clear moonlight all the way."

She rose in air and swept over the meadow and the trees. In a few minutes, "The Mound" appeared below them. She sank down to the house and floated in at the window of Diamond's room. There she laid him on his bed and covered him over. In a moment, he had sunk into a dreamless sleep.

NORTH WIND CARRIES
DIAMOND AWAY

The next night, Diamond was tired, but was waiting eagerly for the promised visit of North Wind. He was seated by his open window, with his head on his hand and rather afraid he could not sleep. Suddenly, he started and found he had already been asleep. He looked out of the window and saw something white against his beech tree. It was North Wind. Her hair and her garments went floating away behind her over the tree whose top was swaying about while the other trees were quite still.

"Are you ready, Diamond?" she asked.

"Yes," answered Diamond, "quite ready."

In a moment, she was at the window and her arms came in and took him. She sailed away so swiftly that he could at first mark nothing but the speed with which the clouds above and the dim earth below went rushing past. Soon he began to see that the sky was very lovely with mottled clouds all about the moon on which she threw faint colours like those of an opal.

The night was warm and in North Wind's arms he did not feel the wind which down below was making waves in the ripe grain and ripples on the rivers and lakes. At length, they came down just where a little spring bubbled out of a hill side.

"I am going to take you along this little brook," said North Wind. "I am not needed for anything else to-night and we will just have a lovely little time."

She stooped over the stream and holding Diamond down close to the surface of it glided along, level with its flow, as it ran down the hill. The song of the brook came up into Diamond's ears and grew and grew and changed with every turn. It seemed to Diamond to be singing the story of its life to him. And so it was. It began with a musical tinkle which changed to a babble and then to a gentle rushing.

Sometimes its song would almost cease. Then it broke out again, tinkle, babble, and rush, all at once. At the bottom of the hill, they came to a small river into which the brook flowed with a muffled but merry sound. Along the surface of the river, darkly clear in the moonlight below them, they floated. Now, where it widened out into a little lake, they would hover for a moment over a bed of water-lilies. They watched them swing about, folded in sleep, as the water on which they leaned swayed in the presence of North Wind. Now they would watch the fishes asleep among their roots below.

Sometimes, North Wind held Diamond over a deep hollow curving into the bank and let him look far into its cool stillness. Sometimes she would leave the river and sweep across a clover field. The bees were all at home and the clover was asleep. Then she would return and follow the river. Now the armies of wheat and of oats would hang over its rush from the opposite bank. Now the willows would dip low branches into its still waters. Now it would lead them through stately trees and grassy banks into a lovely garden where the roses and lilies were asleep and the flowers folded up, or only a few awake sending out strong, sweet odours.

Wider and wider grew the stream until they came upon boats lying along its banks which rocked a little in the flutter of North Wind's garments. Then came houses on the banks, each standing in a lovely lawn with grand trees. In parts, the river was so high that some of the grass and some of the roots of the trees were under water. As they glided through the stems, Diamond could see the grass at the bottom of the water. How like it was to the river which ran through the country at the back of the north wind! And now he seemed to hear more and more clearly its murmured song till at last the words came out plainly.

The sun is gone down,
    And the moon's in the sky.
    But the sun will come up
    And the moon be laid by.

The flower is asleep
    But it is not dead.
    When the morning shines
    It will lift its head.

When winter comes
    Will it die? Oh, no!
    It will only hide
    From the frost and snow.

Sure is the summer,
    Sure is the sun.
    The night and the winter
    Are shadows that run!

They left the river and began to float about and over the houses one after another—beautiful rich houses which like fine trees had taken hundreds of years to grow. Scarcely a light was to be seen, and not a movement to be heard. All the people lay fast asleep in dreams.

But a little later they came floating past a window in which a light was burning. Diamond heard a moan coming from it and looked up anxiously into North Wind's face. By a shaded lamp, a lady in a soft white wrapper sat trying to read and forget the pain which made her moan softly while she read. North Wind seemed to read Diamond's thought and floated silently in at the window. Diamond began singing softly the song of the river with its soothing murmuring strain. When he finished, out of the window they slipped away and floated on.

"Did she hear, North Wind?" said Diamond. "Did she know we were trying to help her—and will it help her?"

"She heard you," answered North Wind. "She heard with her heart, though, and not with her ears. She will not forget, but she will never understand till——"

"Till she gets to the back of the north wind," said Diamond.

North Wind smiled. Then she turned so that he could look down at the place over which they were passing.

"Oh!" he cried out suddenly. "I know where we are now. This is my old home before we moved into the city. Do let me get down and go into the old garden, North Wind, and run into mother's room, and into old Diamond's stall. I wonder if the hole is at the back of my bed still—your window, you know. Oh, I should like to stay here all the rest of the night! It won't take you long to get home from here, will it, North Wind?"

"No," she answered; "you shall stay as long as you like."

"Oh, how jolly!" cried Diamond.

North Wind sailed over the house with him and set him down on the lawn at the back. Diamond ran about the lawn for a little while in the moonlight. He found part of it cut up into flower beds and the small summer house and great elm tree were gone. It was so changed! He didn't like it and ran into the stable. There were no horses there at all. He ran upstairs but the rooms were all empty. The only thing left that he cared about was the hole in the wall where his little bed had stood. All besides was desolate. He turned and ran down the stairs again and out upon the lawn. There he threw himself down and began to cry. It was all so dreary and lost!

"I liked the place so much!" he thought to himself. "But now—there is nothing left to like. I suppose it is only the people in a place that make you like it and when they are gone there is nothing left to like. It's as if it were dead! North Wind told me I might stop as long as I wanted to, but I have stopped too long already! Oh, North Wind!" he cried aloud turning his face up toward the sky.

The moon was under a cloud and all was looking dull and dismal. A star shot from the sky. It fell in the grass beside him. The moment it lighted, there stood North Wind!

"Oh!" cried Diamond joyfully. "Were you the shooting star?"

"Yes," said North Wind.

"And did you hear me call?"

"Yes."

"As high up as that?"

"Yes, I heard you quite well."

"Take me home, North Wind. Take me home!"

"Have you had enough of your old home already?"

"Yes. It is not home here any more."

"Why is that, do you think?" asked North Wind.

"Is it because its soul is gone? Yes, that must be it, is it not, North Wind?"

"Yes, Diamond, that is it. Its soul is gone," said North Wind.

She lifted him into her arms to bear him away. How long they floated about he did not know. But presently all was changed. He was in his own room again. And there was North Wind in the doorway of the long narrow room that opened out of his room, and in which the night before he was dancing when he looked up to find his lifted hands clasped in hers and saw her lovely face smiling down upon him.

Now she was a different North Wind. She was just as he had seen her sitting on her own door-step in the far, far north. She was as white as snow and her eyes as blue as the heart of an iceberg.

"That's how she would look when she thought I might be afraid of her," he said to himself. Then he spoke aloud. "I am not afraid of you, dear North Wind," he cried. "See! I am not a bit afraid of you!" Stretching out both his hands to clasp her he pressed up close against her and laid his head upon her breast. And then he fell asleep.

In the morning, they found little Diamond lying on the floor of the big attic room—fast asleep, as they thought, and with such a happy smile on his face. But when they took him up, they found he was not asleep. He had gone to that lovely country at the back of the north wind—to stay.

THE PRINCESS AND THE GOBLIN

BY
GEORGE MACDONALD

ILLUSTRATED
BY
JESSIE WILLCOX SMITH

WHY THE PRINCESS HAS A STORY
ABOUT HER

There was once a little princess who—

"But, Mr. Author, why do you always write about princesses?"

"Because every little girl is a princess."

"You will make them vain if you tell them that."

"Not if they understand what I mean."

"Then what do you mean?"

"What do you mean by a princess?"

"The daughter of a king."

"Very well, then every little girl is a princess, and there would be no need to say anything about it, except that she is always in danger of forgetting her rank, and behaving as if she had grown out of the mud. I have seen little princesses behave like the children of thieves and lying beggars, and that is why they need, to be told they are princesses. And that is why, when I tell a story of this kind, I like to tell it about a princess. Then I can say better what I mean, because I can then give her every beautiful thing I want her to have."

"Please go on."

There was once a little princess whose father was king over a great country full of mountains and valleys. His palace was built upon one of the mountains, and was very grand and beautiful. The princess, whose name was Irene, was born there, but she was sent soon after her birth, because her mother was not very strong, to be brought up by country people in a large house, half castle, half farm-house, on the side of another mountain, about halfway between its base and its peak.

The princess was a sweet little creature, and at the time my story begins was about eight years old. I think, but she got older very fast. Her face was fair and pretty, with eyes like two bits of night-sky, each with a star dissolved in the blue. Those eyes you would have thought must have known they came from there, so often were they turned up in that direction. The ceiling of her nursery was blue, with stars in it, as like the sky as they could make it. But I doubt if ever she saw the real sky with the stars in it, for a reason which I had better mention at once.

These mountains were full of hollow places underneath; huge caverns, and winding ways, some with water running through them, and some shining with all colors of the rainbow when a light was taken in. There would not have been much known about them, had there not been mines there, great deep pits, with long galleries and passages running off from them, which had been dug to get at the ore of which the mountains were full. In the course of digging, the miners came upon many of these natural caverns. A few of them had far-off openings out on the side of a mountain, or into a ravine.

Now in these subterranean caverns lived a strange race of beings, called by some gnomes, by some kobolds, by some goblins. There was a legend current in the country that at one time they lived above ground, and were very like other people. But for some reason or other, concerning which there were different legendary theories, the king had laid what they thought too severe taxes upon them, or had required observances of them they did not like, or had begun to treat them with more severity in some way or other, and impose stricter laws; and the consequence was that they had all disappeared from the face of the country. According to the legend, however, instead of going to some other country, they had all taken refuge in the subterranean caverns, whence they never came out but at night, and then seldom showed themselves in any numbers, and never to many people at once. It was only in the least frequented and most difficult parts of the mountains that they were said to gather even at night in the open air. Those who had caught sight of any of them said that they had greatly altered in the course of generations; and no wonder, seeing they lived away from the sun, in cold and wet and dark places. They were now, not ordinarily ugly, but either absolutely hideous, or ludicrously grotesque both in face and form. There was no invention, they said, of the most lawless imagination expressed by pen or pencil, that could surpass the extravagance of their appearance. And as they grew mis-shapen in body, they had grown in knowledge and cleverness, and now were able to do things no mortal could see the possibility of. But as they grew in cunning, they grew in mischief, and their great delight was in every way they could think of to annoy the people who lived in the open-air-story above them. They had enough of affection left for each other, to preserve them from being absolutely cruel for cruelty's sake to those that came in their way; but still they so heartily cherished the ancestral grudge against those who occupied their former possession, and especially against the descendants of the king who had caused their expulsion, that they sought every opportunity of tormenting them in ways that were as odd as their inventors; and although dwarfed and mis-shapen, they had strength equal to their cunning. In the process of time they had got a king, and a government of their own, whose chief business, beyond their own simple affairs, was to devise trouble for their neighbors. It will now be pretty evident why the little princess had never seen the sky at night. They were much too afraid of the goblins to let her out of the house then, even in company with ever so many attendants; and they had good reason, as we shall see by-and-by.

THE PRINCESS LOSES HERSELF

I have said the Princess Irene was about eight years old when my story begins. And this is how it begins.

One very wet day, when the mountain was covered with mist which was constantly gathering itself together into rain-drops, and pouring down on the roofs of the great old house, whence it fell in a fringe of water from the eaves all round about it, the princess could not of course go out. She got very tired, so tired that even her toys could no longer amuse her. You would wonder at that if I had time to describe to you one half of the toys she had. But then you wouldn't have the toys themselves, and that makes all the difference: you can't get tired of a thing before you have it. It was a picture, though, worth seeing—the princess sitting in the nursery with the sky-ceiling over her head, at a great table covered with her toys. If the artist would like to draw this, I should advise him not to meddle with the toys. I am afraid of attempting to describe them, and I think he had better not try to draw them. He had better not. He can do a thousand things I can't, but I don't think he could draw those toys. No man could better make the princess herself than he could, though—leaning with her back bowed into the back of the chair, her head hanging down, and her hands in her lap, very miserable as she would say herself, not even knowing what she would like, except to go out and get very wet, catch a particularly nice cold, and have to go to bed and take gruel. The next moment after you see her sitting there, her nurse goes out of the room.

She ran for some distance, turned several times, and then began to be afraid.

Even that is a change, and the princess wakes up a little, and looks about her. Then she tumbles off her chair, and runs out of the door, not the same door the nurse went out of, but one which opened at the foot of a curious old stair of worm-eaten oak, which looked as if never any one had set foot upon it. She had once before been up six steps, and that was sufficient reason, in such a day, for trying to find out what was at the top of it.

Up and up she ran—such a long way it seemed to her! until she came to the top of the third flight. There she found the landing was the end of a long passage. Into this she ran. It was full of doors on each side. There were so many that she did not care to open any, but ran on to the end, where she turned into another passage, also full of doors. When she had turned twice more, and still saw doors and only doors about her, she began to get frightened. It was so silent! And all those doors must hide rooms with nobody in them! That was dreadful. Also the rain made a great trampling noise on the roof. She turned and started at full speed, her little footsteps echoing through the sounds of the rain—back for the stairs and her safe nursery. So she thought, but she had lost herself long ago. It doesn't follow that she was lost, because she had lost herself though.

She ran for some distance, turned several times, and then began to be afraid. Very soon she was sure that she had lost the way back. Rooms everywhere, and no stair! Her little heart beat as fast as her little feet ran, and a lump of tears was growing in her throat. But she was too eager and perhaps too frightened to cry for some time. At last her hope failed her. Nothing but passages and doors every-where! She threw herself on the floor, and began to wail and cry.

She did not cry long, however, for she was as brave as could be expected of a princess of her age. After a good cry, she got up, and brushed the dust from her frock. Oh what old dust it was! Then she wiped her eyes with her hands, for princesses don't always have their handkerchiefs in their pockets any more than some other little girls I know of. Next, like a true princess, she resolved on going wisely to work to find her way back: she would walk through the passages, and look in every direction for the stair. This she did, but without success. She went over the same ground again and again without knowing it, for the passages and doors were all alike. At last, in a corner, through a half-open door, she did see a stair. But alas! it went the wrong way: instead of going down, it went up. Frightened as she was, however, she could not help wishing to see where yet further the stair could lead. It was very narrow, and so steep that she went up like a four-legged creature on her hands and feet.

THE PRINCESS AND—WE SHALL
SEE WHO

WHEN she came to the top, she found herself in a little square place, with three doors, two opposite each other, and one opposite the top of the stair. She stood for a moment, without an idea in her little head what to do next. But as she stood, she began to hear a curious humming sound. Could it be the rain? No. It was much more gentle, and even monotonous than the sound of the rain, which now she scarcely heard. The low sweet humming sound went on, sometimes stopping for a little while and then beginning again. It was more like the hum of a very happy bee that had found a rich well of honey in some globular flower, than anything else I can think of at this moment. Where could it come from? She laid her ear first to one of the doors to hearken if it was there—then to another. When she laid her ear against the third door, there could be no doubt where it came from: it must be from something in that room. What could it be? She was rather afraid, but her curiosity was stronger than her fear, and she opened the door very gently and peeped in. What do you think she saw? A very old lady who sat spinning.

"Oh, Mr. Editor! I know the story you are going to tell: it's The Sleeping Beauty; only you're spinning too, and making it longer."

"No, indeed, it is not that story. Why should I tell one that every properly educated child knows already? More old ladies than one have sat spinning in a garret. Besides, the old lady in that story was only spinning with a spindle, and this one was spinning with a spinning wheel, else how could the princess have heard the sweet noise through the door? Do you know the difference? Did you ever see a spindle or a spinning wheel? I daresay you never did. Well, ask your mamma to explain to you the difference. Between ourselves, however, I shouldn't wonder if she didn't know much better than you. Another thing is, that this is not a fairy story; but a goblin story. And one thing more, this old lady spinning was not an old nurse—but—you shall see who. I think I have now made it quite plain that this is

332

not that lovely story of The Sleeping Beauty. It is quite a new one, I assure you, and I will try to tell it as prettily as I can."

Perhaps you will wonder how the princess could tell that the old lady was an old lady, when I inform you that not only was she beautiful, but her skin was smooth and white. I will tell you more. Her hair was combed back from her forehead and face, and hung loose far down and all over her back. That is not much like an old lady—is it? Ah! but it was white almost as snow. And although her face was so smooth, her eyes looked so wise that you could not have helped seeing she must be old. The princess, though she could not have told you why, did think her very old indeed—quite fifty—she said to herself. But she was rather older than that, as you shall hear.

While the princess stared bewildered, with her head just inside the door, the old lady lifted hers, and said in a sweet, but old and rather shaky voice, which mingled very pleasantly with the continued hum of her wheel:

"Come in, my dear; come in. I am glad to see you."

That the princess was a real princess, you might see now quite plainly; for she didn't hang on to the handle of the door, and stare without moving, as I have known some do who ought to have been princesses, but were only rather vulgar little girls. She did as she was told, stepped inside the door at once, and shut it gently behind her.

"Come to me, my dear," said the old lady.

And again the princess did as she was told. She approached the old lady— rather slowly, I confess, but did not stop until she stood by her side, and looked up in her face with her blue eyes and the two melted stars in them.

"Why, what have you been doing with your eyes, child?" asked the old lady.

"Crying," answered the princess.

"Why, child?"

"Because I couldn't find my way down again."

"But you could find your way up."

"Not at first—not for a long time."

"But your face is streaked like the back of a zebra. Hadn't you a handkerchief to wipe your eyes with?"

"No."

"Then why didn't you come to me to wipe them for you?"

"Please I didn't know you were here. I will next time."

"There's a good child!" said the old lady.

Then she stopped her wheel, and rose, and, going out of the room, returned with a little silver basin and a soft white towel, with which she washed and wiped the bright little face. And the princess thought her hands were so smooth and nice!

When she carried away the basin and towel, the little princess wondered to see how straight and tall she was, for, although she was so old, she didn't stoop a bit. She was dressed in black velvet with thick white heavy-looking lace about it; and on the black dress her hair shone like silver. There was hardly any more furniture in the room than there might have been in that of the poorest old woman who made her bread by her spinning. There was no carpet on the floor—no table anywhere— nothing but the spinning-wheel and the chair beside it. When she came back, she sat down again, and without a word began her spinning once more, while Irene, who had never seen a spinning-wheel, stood by her side and looked on. When the old lady had succeeded in getting her thread fairly in operation again, she said to the princess, but without looking at her:

"Do you know my name, child?"

"No, I don't know it," answered the princess.

"My name is Irene."

"That's my name!" cried the princess.

"I know that. I let you have mine. I haven't got your name. You've got mine."

"How can that be?" asked the princess, bewildered. "I've always had my name."

"Your papa, the king, asked me if I had any objection to your having it; and of course I hadn't. I let you have it with pleasure."

"It was very kind of you to give me your name—and such a pretty one," said the princess.

"Oh, not so very kind!" said the old lady. "A name is one of those things one can give away and keep all the same. I have a good many such things. Wouldn't you like to know who I am, child?"

"Yes, that I should—very much."

"I'm your great-great-grandmother," said the lady.

"What's that?" asked the princess.

"I'm your father's mother's father's mother."

"Oh, dear! I can't understand that," said the princess.

"I daresay not. I didn't expect you would. But that's no reason why I shouldn't say it."

"Oh no!" answered the princess.

"I will explain it all to you when you are older," the lady went on. "But you will be able to understand this much now: I came here to take care of you."

"Is it long since you came? Was it yesterday? Or was it to-day, because it was so wet that I couldn't get out?"

"I've been here ever since you came yourself."

"What a long time!" said the princess. "I don't remember it at all."

"No. I suppose not."

"But I never saw you before."

"No. But you shall see me again."

"Do you live in this room always?"

"I don't sleep in it. I sleep on the opposite side of the landing. I sit here most of the day."

"I shouldn't like it. My nursery is much prettier. You must be a queen too, if you are my great big grandmother."

"Yes, I am a queen."

"Where is your crown then?"

"In my bedroom."

"I should like to see it."

"You shall some day—not to-day."

"I wonder why nursie never told me."

"Nursie doesn't know. She never saw me."

"But somebody knows that you are in the house?"

"No; nobody."

"How do you get your dinner then?"

"I keep poultry—of a sort."

"Where do you keep them?"

"I will show you."

"And who makes the chicken broth for you?"

"I never kill any of my chickens."

"Then I can't understand."

"What did you have for breakfast this morning?"

"Oh! I had bread and milk, and an egg.—I daresay you eat their eggs."

"Yes, that's it. I eat their eggs."

"Is that what makes your hair so white?"

"No, my dear. It's old age. I am very old."

"I thought so. Are you fifty?"

"Yes—more than that."

"Are you a hundred?"

"Yes—more than that. I am too old for you to guess. Come and see my chickens."

Again she stopped her spinning. She rose, took the princess by the hand, led her out of the room, and opened the door opposite the stair. The princess expected to see a lot of hens and chickens, but instead of that, she saw the blue sky first, and then the roofs of the house, with a multitude of the loveliest pigeons, mostly white, but of all colors, walking about, making bows to each other, and talking a language she could not understand. She clapped her hands with delight, and up rose such a flapping of wings, that she in her turn was startled.

She clapped her hands with delight, and up rose such a flapping of wings.

"You've frightened my poultry," said the old lady, smiling.

"And they've frightened me," said the princess, smiling too. "But what very nice poultry! Are the eggs nice?"

"Yes, very nice."

"What a small egg-spoon you must have! Wouldn't it be better to keep hens, and get bigger eggs?"

"How should I feed them, though?"

"I see," said the princess. "The pigeons feed themselves. They've got wings."

"Just so. If they couldn't fly, I couldn't eat their eggs."

"But how do you get at the eggs? Where are their nests?"

The lady took hold of a little loop of string in the wall at the side of the door, and lifting a shutter showed a great many pigeon-holes with nests, some with young ones and some with eggs in them. The birds came in at the other side, and she took out the eggs on this side. She closed it again quickly, lest the young ones should be frightened.

"Oh what a nice way!" cried the princess. "Will you give me an egg to eat? I'm rather hungry."

"I will some day, but now you must go back, or nursie will be miserable about you. I daresay she's looking for you everywhere."

"Except here," answered the princess. "Oh how surprised she will be when I tell her about my great big grand-grandmother!"

"Yes, that she will!" said the old lady with a curious smile. "Mind you tell her all about it exactly."

"That I will. Please will you take me back to her?"

"I can't go all the way, but I will take you to the top of the stair, and then you must run down quite fast into your own room."

The little princess put her hand in the old lady's, who, looking this way and that, brought her to the top of the first stair, and thence to the bottom of the second, and did not leave her till she saw her half way down the third. When she heard the cry of her nurse's pleasure at finding her, she turned and walked up the stairs again, very fast indeed for such a very great grandmother, and sat down to her spinning with another strange smile on her sweet old face.

About this spinning of hers I will tell you more next time.

Guess what she was spinning.

WHAT THE NURSE THOUGHT OF IT

"Why, where can you have been, princess?" asked the nurse, taking her in her arms. "It's very unkind of you to hide away so long. I began to be afraid—"

Here she checked herself.

"What were you afraid of, nursie?" asked the princess.

"Never mind," she answered. "Perhaps I will tell you another day. Now tell me where you have been?"

"I've been up a long way to see my very great, huge, old grandmother," said the princess.

"What do you mean by that?" asked the nurse, who thought she was making fun.

"I mean that I've been a long way up and up to see my great grandmother. Ah, nursie, you don't know what a beautiful mother of grandmothers I've got upstairs. She is such an old lady! with such lovely white hair!—as white as my silver cup. Now, when I think of it, I think her hair must be silver."

"What nonsense you are talking, princess!" said the nurse.

"I'm not talking nonsense," returned Irene, rather offended. "I will tell you all about her. She's much taller than you, and much prettier."

"Oh, I daresay!" remarked the nurse.

"And she lives upon pigeon's eggs."

"Most likely," said the nurse.

"And she sits in an empty room, spin-spinning all day long."

"Not a doubt of it," said the nurse.

"And she keeps her crown in her bedroom."

"Of course—quite the proper place to keep her crown in. She wears it in bed, I'll be bound."

"She didn't say that. And I don't think she does. That wouldn't be comfortable—would it? I don't think my papa wears his crown for a night-cap. Does he, nursie?"

"I never asked him. I daresay he does."

"And she's been there ever since I came here—ever so many years."

"Anybody could have told you that," said the nurse, who did not believe a word Irene was saying.

"Why didn't you tell me then?"

"There was no necessity. You could make it all up for yourself."

"You don't believe me then!" exclaimed the princess, astonished and angry, as well she might be.

"Did you expect me to believe you, princess?" asked the nurse coldly. "I know princesses are in the habit of telling make-believes, but you are the first I ever heard of who expected to have them believed," she added, seeing that the child was strangely in earnest.

The princess burst into tears.

"Well, I must say," remarked the nurse, now thoroughly vexed with her for crying, "it is not at all becoming in a princess to tell stories and expect to be believed just because she is a princess."

"But it's quite true, I tell you, nursie."

"You've dreamt it, then, child."

"No, I didn't dream it. I went up-stairs, and I lost myself, and if I hadn't found the beautiful lady, I should never have found myself."

"Oh, I daresay!"

"Well, you just come up with me, and see if I'm not telling the truth."

"Indeed I have other work to do. It's your dinner-time, and I won't have any more such nonsense."

The princess wiped her eyes, and her face grew so hot that they were soon quite dry. She sat down to her dinner, but ate next to nothing. Not to be believed does not at all agree with princesses; for a real princess cannot tell a lie. So all the afternoon she did not speak a word. Only when the nurse spoke to her, she answered her, for a real princess is never rude—even when she does well to be offended.

Of course the nurse was not comfortable in her mind—not that she suspected the least truth in Irene's story, but that she loved her dearly, and was vexed with herself for having been cross to her. She thought her crossness was the cause of the princess' unhappiness, and had no idea that she was really and deeply hurt at not being believed. But, as it became more and more plain during the evening in every motion and look, that, although she tried to amuse herself with her toys, her heart was too vexed and troubled to enjoy them, her nurse's discomfort grew and grew. When bedtime came, she undressed and laid her down, but the child, instead of holding up her little mouth to be kissed, turned away from her and lay still. Then nursie's heart gave way altogether, and she began to cry. At the sound of her first sob, the princess turned again, and held her face to kiss her as usual. But the nurse had her handkerchief to her eyes, and did not see the movement.

"Nursie," said the princess, "why won't you believe me?"

"Because I can't believe you," said the nurse, getting angry again.

"Ah! then you can't help it," said Irene, "and I will not be vexed with you any more. I will give you a kiss and go to sleep."

"You little angel!" cried the nurse, and caught her out of bed, and walked about the room with her in her arms, kissing and hugging her.

"You will let me take you to see my dear old great big grandmother, won't you?" said the princess, as she laid her down again.

"And you won't say I'm ugly, any more—will you, princess?"

"Nursie! I never said you were ugly. What can you mean?"

"Well, if you didn't say it, you meant it."

"Indeed, I never did."

"You said I wasn't so pretty as that—"

"As my beautiful grandmother—yes, I did say that; and I say it again, for it's quite true."

"Then I do think you are unkind!" said the nurse, and put her handkerchief to her eyes again.

"Nursie, dear, everybody can't be as beautiful as every other body, you know. You are very nice-looking, but if you had been as beautiful as my grandmother—"

"Bother your grandmother!" said the nurse.

"Nurse, that's very rude. You are not fit to be spoken to—till you can behave better."

The princess turned away once more, and again the nurse was ashamed of herself.

"I'm sure I beg your pardon, princess," she said, though still in an offended tone. But the princess let the tone pass, and heeded only the words.

"You won't say it again, I am sure," she answered, once more turning toward her nurse. "I was only going to say that if you had been twice as nice-looking as you are, some king or other would have married you, and then what would have become of me?"

"You are an angel!" repeated the nurse, again embracing her.

"Now," insisted Irene, "you will come and see my grandmother—won't you?"

"I will go with you anywhere you like, my cherub," she answered; and in two minutes the weary little princess was fast asleep.

THE PRINCES LETS WELL ALONE

When she woke the next morning, the first thing she heard was the rain still falling. Indeed, this day was so like the last, that it would have been difficult to tell where was the use of it. The first thing she thought of, however, was not the rain, but the lady in the tower; and the first question that occupied her thoughts was whether she should not ask the nurse to fulfill her promise this very morning, and go with her to find her grandmother as soon as she had had her breakfast. But she came to the conclusion that perhaps the lady would not be pleased if she took anyone to see her without first asking leave; especially as it was pretty evident, seeing she lived on pigeons' eggs, and cooked them herself, that she did not want the household to know she was there. So the princess resolved to take the first opportunity of running up alone and asking whether she might bring her nurse. She believed the fact that she could not otherwise convince her she was telling the truth, would have much weight with her grandmother.

The princess and her nurse were the best of friends all dressing time, and the princess in consequence ate an enormous little breakfast.

"I wonder, Lootie"—that was her pet-name for her nurse—"what pigeons' eggs taste like?" she said, as she was eating her egg—not quite a common one, for they always picked out the pinky ones for her.

"We'll get you a pigeon's egg, and you shall judge for yourself," said the nurse.

"Oh, no, no!" returned Irene, suddenly reflecting they might disturb the old lady in getting it, and that even if they did not, she would have one less in consequence.

"What a strange creature you are," said the nurse—"first to want a thing and then to refuse it!"

But she did not say it crossly, and the princess never minded any remarks that were not unfriendly.

"Well, you see, Lootie, there are reasons," she returned, and said no more, for she did not want to bring up the subject of their former strife, lest her nurse should

340

offer to go before she had had her grandmother's permission to bring her. Of course she could refuse to take her, but then she would believe her less than ever.

Now the nurse, as she said herself afterward, could not be every moment in the room, and as never before yesterday had the princess given her the smallest reason for anxiety, it had not yet come into her head to watch her more closely. So she soon gave her a chance, and the very first that offered, Irene was off and up the stairs again.

This day's adventure, however, did not turn out like yesterday's, although it began like it; and indeed to-day is very seldom like yesterday, if people would note the differences—even when it rains. The princess ran through passage after passage, and could not find the stair of the tower. My own suspicion is that she had not gone up high enough, and was searching on the second instead of the third floor. When she turned to go back, she failed equally in her search after the stair. She was lost once more.

Something made it even worse to bear this time, and it was no wonder that she cried again. Suddenly it occurred to her that it was after having cried before that she had found her grandmother's stair. She got up at once, wiped her eyes, and started upon a fresh quest. This time, although she did not find what she hoped, she found what was next best: she did not come on a stair that went up, but she came upon one that went down. It was evidently not the stair she had come up, yet it was a good deal better than none; so down she went, and was singing merrily before she reached the bottom. There, to her surprise, she found herself in the kitchen. Although she was not allowed to go there alone, her nurse had often taken her, and she was a great favorite with the servants. So there was a general rush at her the moment she appeared, for every one wanted to have her; and the report of where she was soon reached the nurse's ears. She came at once to fetch her; but she never suspected how she had got there, and the princess kept her own counsel.

Her failure to find the old lady not only disappointed her, but made her very thoughtful. Sometimes she came almost to the nurse's opinion that she had dreamed all about her; but that fancy never lasted very long. She wondered much whether she should ever see her again, and thought it very sad not to have been able to find her when she particularly wanted her. She resolved to say nothing more to her nurse on the subject, seeing it was so little in her power to prove her words.

THE LITTLE MINER

The next day the great cloud still hung over the mountain, and the rain poured like water from a full sponge. The princess was very fond of being out of doors, and she nearly cried when she saw that the weather was no better. But the mist was not of such a dark dingy gray; there was light in it; and as the hours went on, it grew brighter and brighter, until it was almost too brilliant to look at; and late in the afternoon, the sun broke out so gloriously that Irene clapped her hands, crying,

"See, see, Lootie! The sun has had his face washed. Look how bright he is! Do get my hat, and let us go out for a walk. Oh dear! oh dear! how happy I am!"

Lootie was very glad to please the princess. She got her hat and cloak, and they set out together for a walk up the mountain; for the road was so hard and steep that the water could not rest upon it, and it was always dry enough for walking a few minutes after the rain ceased. The clouds were rolling away in broken pieces, like great, overwoolly sheep, whose wool the sun had bleached till it was almost too white for the eyes to bear. Between them the sky shone with a deeper and purer blue, because of the rain. The trees on the road-side were hung all over with drops, which sparkled in the sun like jewels. The only things that were no brighter for the rain, were the brooks that ran down the mountain; they had changed from the clearness of crystal to a muddy brown; but what they lost in color they gained in sound—or at least in noise, for a brook when it is swollen is not so musical as before. But Irene was in raptures with the great brown streams tumbling down everywhere; and Lootie shared in her delight, for she too had been confined to the house for three days. At length she observed that the sun was getting low, and said it was time to be going back. She made the remark again and again, but, every time, the princess begged her to go on just a little farther and a little farther; reminding her that it was much easier to go down hill, and saying that when they did turn, they would be at home in a moment. So on and on they did go, now to look at a group of ferns over whose tops a stream was pouring in a watery arch, now to pick

342

a shining stone from a rock by the wayside, now to watch the flight of some bird. Suddenly the shadow of a great mountain peak came up from behind, and shot in front of them. When the nurse saw it, she started and shook, and tremulously grasping the hand of the princess turned and began to run down the hill.

"What's all the haste, nursie?" asked Irene, running alongside of her.

"We must not be out a moment longer."

"But we can't help being out a good many moments longer."

It was too true. The nurse almost cried. They were much too far from home. It was against express orders to be out with the princess one moment after the sun was down; and they were nearly a mile up the mountain! If his Majesty, Irene's papa, were to hear of it, Lootie would certainly be dismissed; and to leave the princess would break her heart. It was no wonder she ran. But Irene was not in the least frightened, not knowing anything to be frightened at. She kept on chattering as well as she could, but it was not easy.

"Lootie! Lootie! why do you run so fast? It shakes my teeth when I talk."

"Then don't talk," said Lootie.

But the princess went on talking. She was always saying, "Look, look, Lootie," but Lootie paid no more heed to anything she said, only ran on.

"Look, look, Lootie! Don't you see that funny man peeping over the rock?"

Lootie only ran the faster. They had to pass the rock and when they came nearer, the princess clearly saw that it was only a large fragment of the rock itself that she had mistaken for a man.

"Look, look, Lootie! There's such a curious creature at the foot of that old tree. Look at it, Lootie! It's making faces at us, I do think."

Lootie gave a stifled cry, and ran faster still—so fast, that Irene's little legs could not keep up with her, and she fell with a clash. It was a hard down-hill road, and she had been running very fast—so it was no wonder she began to cry. This put the nurse nearly beside herself; but all she could do was to run on, the moment she got the princess on her feet again.

"Who's that laughing at me?" said the princess, trying to keep in her sobs, and running too fast for her grazed knees.

"Nobody, child," said the nurse, almost angrily.

But that instant there came a burst of coarse tittering from somewhere near, and a hoarse indistinct voice that seemed to say, "Lies! lies! lies!"

"Oh!" cried the nurse with a sigh that was almost a scream, and ran on faster than ever.

"Nursie! Lootie! I can't run any more. Do let us walk a bit."

"What am I to do?" said the nurse. "Here, I will carry you."

She caught her up; but found her much too heavy to run with, and had to set her down again. Then she looked wildly about her, gave a great cry, and said—

"We've taken the wrong turning somewhere, and I don't know where we are. We are lost, lost!"

The terror she was in had quite bewildered her. It was true enough they had lost the way. They had been running down into a little valley in which there was no house to be seen.

Now Irene did not know what good reason there was for her nurse's terror, for the servants had all strict orders never to mention the goblins to her, but it was very discomposing to see her nurse in such a fright. Before, however, she had time to

343

grow thoroughly alarmed like her, she heard the sound of whistling, and that revived her. Presently she saw a boy coming up the road from the valley to meet them. He was the whistler; but before they met, his whistling changed to singing. And this is something like what he sang:

"Ring! dod! bang!
    Go the hammers' clang!
    Hit and turn and bore!
    Whizz and puff and roar!
    Thus we rive the rocks.
    Force the goblin locks.
    See the shining ore!
    One, two, three—
    Bright as gold can be!
    Four, five, six—
    Shovels, mattocks, picks!
    Seven, eight, nine—
    Light your lamp at mine.
    Ten, eleven, twelve—
    Loosely hold the helve.
    We're the merry miner-boys,
    Make the goblins hold their noise."

"I wish you would hold your noise," said the nurse rudely, for the very word goblin at such a time and in such a place made her tremble. It would bring the goblins upon them to a certainty, she thought, to defy them in that way. But whether the boy heard her or not, he did not stop his singing.

"Thirteen, fourteen, fifteen—
    This is worth the siftin';
    Sixteen, seventeen, eighteen—
    There's the match, and lay't in.
    Nineteen, twenty—
    Goblins in a plenty."

"Do be quiet," cried the nurse, in a whispered shriek. But the boy, who was now close at hand, still went on.

"Hush! scush! scurry!
    There you go in a hurry!
    Gobble! gobble! gobblin'!
    There you go a wobblin';
    Hobble, hobble, hobblin'!

Cobble! cobble! cobblin'!
Hob-bob-goblin—Huuuuuh!"

"There!" said the boy, as he stood still opposite them. "There! that'll do for them. They can't bear singing, and they can't stand that song. They can't sing themselves, for they have no more voice than a crow; and they don't like other people to sing."

The boy was dressed in a miner's dress, with a curious cap on his head. He was a very nice-looking boy, with eyes as dark as the mines in which he worked, and as sparkling as the crystals in their rocks. He was about twelve years old. His face was almost too pale for beauty, which came of his being so little in the open air and the sunlight—for even vegetables grown in the dark are white; but he looked happy, merry indeed—perhaps at the thought of having routed the goblins; and his bearing as he stood before them had nothing clownish or rude about it.

"I saw them," he went on, "as I came up; and I'm very glad I did. I knew they were after somebody, but I couldn't see who it was. They won't touch you so long as I'm with you."

"Why, who are you?" asked the nurse, offended at the freedom with which he spoke to them.

"I'm Peter's son."

"Who's Peter?"

"Peter the miner."

"I don't know him."

"I'm his son, though."

"And why should the goblins mind you, pray?"

"Because I don't mind them. I'm used to them."

"What difference does that make?"

"If you're not afraid of them, they're afraid of you. I'm not afraid of them. That's all. But it's all that's wanted—up here, that is. It's a different thing down there. They won't always mind that song even, down there. And if anyone sings it, they stand grinning at him awfully; and if he gets frightened, and misses a word, or says a wrong one, they—oh! don't they give it him!"

"What do they do to him?" asked Irene, with a trembling voice.

"Don't go frightening the princess," said the nurse.

"The princess!" repeated the little miner, taking off his curious cap. "I beg your pardon; but you oughtn't to be out so late. Everybody knows that's against the law."

"Yes, indeed it is!" said the nurse, beginning to cry again. "And I shall have to suffer for it."

"What does that matter?" said the boy. "It must be your fault. It is the princess who will suffer for it. I hope they didn't hear you call her the princess. If they did, they're sure to know her again: they're awfully sharp."

"Lootie! Lootie!" cried the princess. "Take me home."

"Don't go on like that," said the nurse to the boy, almost fiercely. "How could I help it? I lost my way."

"You shouldn't have been out so late. You wouldn't have lost your way if you hadn't been frightened," said the boy. "Come along. I'll soon set you right again. Shall I carry your little Highness?"

"Impertinence!" murmured the nurse, but she did not say it aloud, for she thought if she made him angry, he might take his revenge by telling some one belonging to the house, and then it would be sure to come to the king's ears.

"No, thank you," said Irene. "I can walk very well, though I can't run so fast as nursie. If you will give me one hand, Lootie will give me another, and then I shall get on famously."

They soon had her between them, holding a hand of each.

"Now let's run," said the nurse.

"No, no," said the little miner. "That's the worst thing you can do. If you hadn't run before, you would not have lost your way. And if you run now, they will be after you in a moment."

"I don't want to run," said Irene.

"You don't think of me," said the nurse.

"Yes, I do, Lootie. The boy says they won't touch us if we don't run."

"Yes; but if they know at the house that I've kept you out so late, I shall be turned away, and that would break my heart."

"Turned away, Lootie. Who would turn you away?"

"Your papa, child."

"But I'll tell him it was all my fault. And you know it was, Lootie."

"He won't mind that. I'm sure he won't."

"Then I'll cry, and go down on my knees to him, and beg him not to take away my own dear Lootie."

The nurse was comforted at hearing this, and said no more. They went on, walking pretty fast, but taking care not to run a step.

"I want to talk to you," said Irene to the little miner; "but it's so awkward! I don't know your name."

"My name's Curdie, little princess."

"What a funny name! Curdie! What more?"

"Curdie Peterson. What's your name, please?"

"Irene."

"What more?"

"I don't know what more.—What more is my name, Lootie?"

"Princesses haven't got more than one name. They don't want it."

"Oh then, Curdie, you must call me just Irene, and no more."

"No, indeed," said the nurse indignantly. "He shall do no such thing."

"What shall he call me, then, Lootie?"

"Your royal Highness."

"My royal Highness! What's that? No, no, Lootie, I will not be called names. I don't like them. You said to me once yourself that it's only rude children that call names; and I'm sure Curdie wouldn't be rude.—Curdie, my name's Irene."

"Well, Irene," said Curdie, with a glance at the nurse which showed he enjoyed teasing her, "it's very kind of you to let me call you anything. I like your name very much."

He expected the nurse to interfere again; but he soon saw that she was too frightened to speak. She was staring at something a few yards before them, in the middle of the path, where it narrowed between rocks so that only one could pass at a time.

"It's very much kinder of you to go out of your way to take us home," said Irene.

"I'm not going out of my way yet," said Curdie. "It's on the other side those rocks the path turns off to my father's."

"You wouldn't think of leaving us till we're safe home, I'm sure," gasped the nurse.

"Of course not," said Curdie.

"You dear, good, kind Curdie! I'll give you a kiss when we get home," said the princess.

The nurse gave her a great pull by the hand she held. But at that instant the something in the middle of the way, which had looked like a great lump of earth brought down by the rain, began to move. One after another it shot out four long things, like two arms and two legs, but it was now too dark to tell what they were. The nurse began to tremble from head to foot. Irene clasped Curdie's hand yet faster, and Curdie began to sing again.

"One, two—
  Hit and hew!
  Three, four—
  Blast and bore!
  Five, six—
  There's a fix!
  Seven, eight—
  Hold it straight.
  Nine, ten—
  Hit again!
  Hurry! scurry!
  Bother! smother!
  There's a toad
  In the road!
  Smash it!
  Squash it!
  Fry it!
  Dry it!
  You're another!
  Up and off!
  There's enough!—Huuuuuh!"

As he uttered the last words, Curdie let go his hold of his companion, and rushed at the thing in the road, as if he would trample it under his feet. It gave a great spring, and ran straight up one of the rocks like a huge spider. Curdie turned back laughing, and took Irene's hand again. She grasped his very tight, but said nothing till they had passed the rocks. A few yards more and she found herself on a part of the road she knew, and was able to speak again.

"Do you know, Curdie, I don't quite like your song; it sounds to me rather rude," she said.

"Well, perhaps it is," answered Curdie. "I never thought of that; it's a way we have. We do it because they don't like it."

"Who don't like it?"

"The cobs, as we call them."

"Don't!" said the nurse.

"Why not?" said Curdie.

"I beg you won't. Please don't."

"Oh, if you ask me that way, of course I won't; though I don't a bit know why. Look! there are the lights of your great house down below. You'll be at home in five minutes now."

Nothing more happened. They reached home in safety. Nobody had missed them, or even known they had gone out; and they arrived at the door belonging to their part of the house without anyone seeing them. The nurse was rushing in with a hurried and not over-gracious good-night to Curdie; but the princess pulled her hand from hers, and was just throwing her arms around Curdie's neck, when she caught her again and dragged her away.

"Never mind, Princess Irene," he said. "You mustn't kiss me to-night. But you sha'n't break your word. I will come another time."

"Lootie, Lootie, I promised Curdie a kiss," cried Irene.

"A princess mustn't give kisses. It's not at all proper," said Lootie.

"But I promised," said the princess.

"There's no occasion; he's only a miner-boy."

"He is a good boy, and a brave boy, and he has been very kind to us. Lootie! Lootie! I promised."

"Then you shouldn't have promised."

"Lootie, I promised him a kiss."

"Your royal Highness," said Lootie, suddenly growing very respectful, "must come in directly."

"Nurse, a princess must not break her word," said Irene, drawing herself up and standing stockstill.

Lootie did not know which the king might count the worst—to let the princess be out after sunset, or to let her kiss a miner-boy. She did not know that, being a gentleman, as many kings have been, he would have counted neither of them the worse. However much he might have disliked his daughter to kiss the miner-boy, he would not have had her break her word for all the goblins in creation. But, as I say, the nurse was not lady enough to understand this, and so she was in a great difficulty, for, if she insisted, some one might hear the princess cry and run to see, and then all would come out. But here Curdie came again to the rescue.

"Never mind, Princess Irene," he said. "You mustn't kiss me to-night. But you sha'n't break your word. I will come another time. You may be sure I will."

"Oh, thank you, Curdie!" said the princess, and stopped crying.

"Good night, Irene; good night, Lootie," said Curdie, and turned and was out of sight in a moment.

"I should like to see him!" muttered the nurse, as she carried the princess to the nursery.

"You will see him," said Irene. "You may be sure Curdie will keep his word. He's sure to come again."

"I should like to see him!" repeated the nurse, and said no more. She did not want to open a new cause of strife with the princess by saying more plainly what she meant. Glad enough that she had succeeded both in getting home unseen, and in keeping the princess from kissing the miner's boy, she resolved to watch her far better in future. Her carelessness had already doubled the danger she was in. Formerly the goblins were her only fear; now she had to protect her charge from Curdie as well.

THE MINES

Curdie went home whistling. He resolved to say nothing about the princess for fear of getting the nurse into trouble, for while he enjoyed teasing her because of her absurdity, he was careful not to do her any harm. He saw no more of the goblins, and was soon fast asleep in his bed.

He woke in the middle of the night, and thought he heard curious noises outside. He sat up and listened; then got up, and, opening the door very quietly, went out. When he peeped round the corner, he saw, under his own window, a group of stumpy creatures, whom he at once recognized by their shape. Hardly, however, had he begun his "One, two, three!" when they broke asunder, scurried away, and were out of sight. He returned laughing, got into bed again, and was fast asleep in a moment.

Reflecting a little over the matter in the morning, he came to the conclusion that, as nothing of the kind had ever happened before, they must be annoyed with him for interfering to protect the princess. By the time he was dressed, however, he was thinking of something quite different, for he did not value the enmity of the goblins in the least.

As soon as they had had breakfast, he set off with his father for the mine.

They entered the hill by a natural opening under a huge rock, where a little stream rushed out. They followed its course for a few yards, when the passage took a turn, and sloped steeply into the heart of the hill. With many angles and windings and branchings off, and sometimes with steps where it came upon a natural gulf, it led them deep into the hill before they arrived at the place where they were at present digging out the precious ore. This was of various kinds, for the mountain was very rich with the better sorts of metals. With flint and steel, and tinder box, they lighted their lamps, then fixed them on their heads, and were soon hard at work with their pickaxes and shovels and hammers. Father and son were at work near each other, but not in the same gang—the passages out of which the ore was dug, they called gangs—for when the lode, or vein of ore, was small, one miner would have to dig away alone in a passage no bigger than gave him just room to work—sometimes in uncomfortable cramped positions. If they stopped for a moment they could hear everywhere around them, some nearer, some farther off, the sounds of their companions burrowing away in all directions in the inside of the great mountain—some boring holes in the rock in order to blow it up with gunpowder, others shoveling the broken ore into baskets to be carried to the mouth of the mine, others hitting away with their pickaxes. Sometimes, if the miner was in a very lonely part, he would hear only a tap-tapping, no louder than that of a woodpecker, for the sound would come from a great distance off through the solid mountain rock.

The work was hard at best, for it is very warm underground; but it was not particularly unpleasant, and some of the miners, when they wanted to earn a little more money for a particular purpose, would stop behind the rest, and work all night. But you could not tell night from day down there, except from feeling tired and sleepy; for no light of the sun ever came into those gloomy regions. Some who had thus remained behind during the night, although certain there were none of their companions at work, would declare the next morning that they heard, every time they halted for a moment to take breath, a tap-tapping all about them, as if the mountain were then more full of miners than ever it was during the day; and some in consequence would never stay over night, for all knew those were the sounds of the goblins. They worked only at night, for the miners' night was the goblins' day. Indeed, the greater number of the miners were afraid of the goblins: for there were strange stories well known amongst them of the treatment some had received whom the goblins had surprised at their work during the night. The more coura-geous of them, however, amongst them Peter Peterson and Curdie, who in this took after his father, had stayed in the mine all night again and again, and although they had several times encountered a few stray goblins, had never yet failed in driving them away. As I have indicated already, the chief defence against them was verse, for they hated verse of every kind, and some kinds they could not endure at all. I suspect they could not make any themselves, and that was why they disliked it so much. At all events, those who were most afraid of them were those who could neither make verses themselves, nor remember the verses that other people made for them; while those who were never afraid were those who could make verses for themselves; for although there were certain old rhymes which were very effectual, yet it was well known that a new rhyme, if of the right sort, was even more distasteful to them, and therefore more effectual in putting them to flight.

Perhaps my readers may be wondering what the goblins could be about, working all night long, seeing they never carried up the ore and sold it; but when I have informed them concerning what Curdie learned the very next night, they will be able to understand.

For Curdie had determined, if his father would permit him, to remain there alone this night—and that for two reasons: first, he wanted to get extra wages in order that he might buy a very warm red petticoat for his mother, who had begun to complain of the cold of the mountain air sooner than usual this autumn; and second, he had just a faint glimmering of hope of finding out what the goblins were about under his window the night before.

When he told his father, he made no objection, for he had great confidence in his boy's courage and resources.

"I'm sorry I can't stay with you," said Peter; "but I want to go and pay the parson a visit this evening, and besides I've had a bit of a headache all day."

"I'm sorry for that, father," said Curdie.

"Oh! it's not much. You'll be sure to take care of yourself, won't you?"

"Yes, father; I will. I'll keep a sharp lookout, I promise you."

Curdie was the only one who remained in the mine. About six o'clock the rest went away, every one bidding him good night, and telling him to take care of himself; for he was a great favorite with them all.

"Don't forget your rhymes," said one.

"No, no," answered Curdie.

"It's no matter if he does," said another, "for he'll only have to make a new one."

"Yes, but he mightn't be able to make it fast enough," said another; "and while it was cooking in his head, they might take a mean advantage and set upon him."

"I'll do my best," said Curdie. "I'm not afraid."

"We all know that," they returned, and left him.

THE GOBLINS

For some time Curdie worked away briskly, throwing all the ore he had disengaged on one side behind him, to be ready for carrying out in the morning. He heard a good deal of goblin-tapping, but it all sounded far away in the hill, and he paid it little heed. Toward midnight he began to feel rather hungry; so he dropped his pickaxe, got a lump of bread which in the morning he had laid in a damp hole in the rock, sat down on a heap of ore and ate his supper. Then he leaned back for five minutes' rest before beginning his work again, and laid his head against the rock. He had not kept the position for one minute before he heard something which made him sharpen his ears. It sounded like a voice inside the rock. After a while he heard it again. It was a goblin-voice—there could be no doubt about that—and this time he could make out the words.

"Hadn't we better be moving?" it said.

A rougher and deeper voice replied:

"There's no hurry. That wretched little mole won't be through to-night, if he work ever so hard. He's by no means at the thinnest place."

"But you still think the lode does come through into our house?" said the first voice.

"Yes, but a good bit farther on than he has got to yet. If he had struck a stroke more to the side just here," said the goblin, tapping the very stone, as it seemed to Curdie, against which his head lay, "he would have been through; but he's a couple of yards past it now, and if he follow the lode it will be a week before it leads him in. You see it back there—a long way. Still, perhaps, in case of accident, it would be as well to be getting out of this. Helfer, you'll take the great chest. That's your business, you know."

"Yes, dad," said a third voice. "But you must help me to get it on my back. It's awfully heavy, you know."

"Well, it isn't just a bag of smoke, I admit. But you're as strong as a mountain, Helfer."

"You say so, dad. I think myself I'm all right. But I could carry ten times as much if it wasn't for my feet."

"That is your weak point, I confess, my boy."

"Ain't it yours, too, father?"

"Well, to be honest, it is a goblin-weakness. Why they come so soft, I declare I haven't an idea."

"Specially when your head's so hard, you know, father."

"Yes, my boy. The goblin's glory is his head. To think how the fellows up above there have to put on helmets and things when they go fighting. Ha! ha!"

"But why don't we wear shoes like them, father? I should like it—specially when I've got a chest like that on my head."

"Well, you see, it's not the fashion. The king never wears shoes."

"The queen does."

"Yes; but that's for distinction. The first queen, you see—I mean the king's first wife—wore shoes of course, because she came from upstairs; and so, when she died, the next queen would not be inferior to her as she called it, and would wear shoes too. It was all pride. She is the hardest in forbidding them to the rest of the women."

"I'm sure I wouldn't wear them—no, not for—that I wouldn't!" said the first voice, which was evidently that of the mother of the family. "I can't think why either of them should."

"Didn't I tell you the first was from upstairs?" said the other. "That was the only silly thing I ever knew his Majesty guilty of. Why should he marry an outlandish woman like that—one of our natural enemies too?"

"I suppose he fell in love with her."

"Pooh! pooh! He's just as happy now with one of his own people."

"Did she die very soon? They didn't tease her to death, did they?"

"Oh dear no! The king worshipped her very footmarks."

"What made her die, then? Didn't the air agree with her?"

"She died when the young prince was born."

"How silly of her! We never do that. It must have been because she wore shoes."

"I don't know that."

"Why do they wear shoes up there?"

"Ah! now that's a sensible question, and I will answer it. But in order to do so, I must first tell you a secret. I once saw the queen's feet."

"Without her shoes?"

"Yes—without her shoes."

"No! Did you? How was it?"

"Never you mind how it was. She didn't know I saw them. And what do you think!—they had toes!"

"Toes! What's that?"

"You may well ask! I should never have known if I had not seen the queen's feet. Just imagine! the ends of her feet were split up into five or six thin pieces!"

"Oh, horrid! How could the king have fallen in love with her?"

"You forget that she wore shoes. That is just why she wore them. That is why all the men, and women too, upstairs wear shoes. They can't bear the sight of their own feet without them."

"Ah! now I understand. If ever you wish for shoes again, Helfer, I'll hit your feet —I will."

"No, no, mother; pray don't."

"Then don't you."

"But with such a big box on my head—"

A horrid scream followed, which Curdie interpreted as in reply to a blow from his mother upon the feet of her eldest goblin.

"Well, I never knew so much before!" remarked a fourth voice.

"Your knowledge is not universal quite yet," said the father. "You were only fifty last month. Mind you see to the bed and bedding. As soon as we've finished our supper, we'll be up and going. Ha! ha! ha!"

"What are you laughing at, husband?"

"I'm laughing to think what a mess the miners will find themselves in—somewhere before this day ten years."

"Why, what do you mean?"

"Oh, nothing."

"Oh yes, you do mean something. You always do mean something."

"It's more than you do, then, wife."

"That may be; but it's not more than I find out, you know."

"Ha! ha! You're a sharp one. What a mother you've got, Helfer!"

"Yes, father."

"Well, I suppose I must tell you. They're all at the palace consulting about it to-night; and as soon as we've got away from this thin place, I'm going there to hear what night they fix upon. I should like to see that young ruffian there on the other side, struggling in the agonies of—"

He dropped his voice so low that Curdie could hear only a growl. The growl went on in a low bass for a good while, as inarticulate as if the goblin's tongue had been a sausage; and it was not until his wife spoke again that it rose to its former pitch.

"But what shall we do when you are at the palace?" she asked.

"I will see you safe in the new house I've been digging for you for the last two months. Podge, you mind the table and chairs. I commit them to your care. The table has seven legs—each chair three. I shall require them all at your hands."

After this arose a confused conversation about the various household goods and their transport; and Curdie heard nothing more that was of any importance.

He now knew at least one of the reasons for the constant sound of the goblin hammers and pickaxes at night. They were making new houses for themselves, to which they might retreat when the miners should threaten to break into their dwellings. But he had learned two things of far greater importance. The first was, that some grievous calamity was preparing, and almost ready to fall upon the heads of the miners; the second was—the one weak point of a goblin's body: he had not known that their feet were so tender as he had now reason to suspect. He had heard it said that they had no toes: he had never had opportunity of inspecting them closely enough in the dusk in which they always appeared, to satisfy himself whether it was a correct report. Indeed, he had not been able even to satisfy himself as to whether they had no fingers, although that also was commonly said to be the fact. One of the miners, indeed, who had had more schooling than the rest, was wont to argue that such must have been the primordial condition of humanity, and that education and handicraft had developed both toes and fingers—with which proposition Curdie had once heard his father sarcastically agree, alleging in support of it the probability that babies' gloves were a traditional remnant of the old state of things; while the stockings of all ages, no regard being paid in them to the toes, pointed in the same direction. But what was of importance was the fact concerning the softness of the goblin-feet, which he foresaw might be useful to all miners. What he had to do in the mean time, however, was to discover, if possible, the special evil design the goblins had now in their heads.

Although he knew all the gangs and all the natural galleries with which they communicated in the mined part of the mountain, he had not the least idea where the palace of the king of the gnomes was; otherwise he would have set out at once on the enterprise of discovering what the said design was. He judged, and rightly, that it must lie in a farther part of the mountain, between which and the mine there was as yet no communication. There must be one nearly completed, however; for it could be but a thin partition which now separated them. If only he could get through in time to follow the goblins as they retreated! A few blows would doubtless be sufficient—just where his ear now lay; but if he attempted to strike there with his pickaxe, he would only hasten the departure of the family, put them on their guard, and perhaps lose their involuntary guidance. He therefore began to feel the wall with his hands, and soon found that some of the stones were loose enough to be drawn out with little noise.

Laying hold of a large one with both his hands, he drew it gently out, and let it down softly.

"What was that noise?" said the goblin father.

Curdie blew out his light, lest it should shine through.

"It must be that one miner that stayed behind the rest," said the mother.

"No; he's been gone a good while. I haven't heard a blow for an hour. Besides, it wasn't like that."

"Then I suppose it must have been a stone carried down the brook inside."

"Perhaps. It will have more room by and by."

Curdie kept quite still. After a little while, hearing nothing but the sounds of their preparations for departure, mingled with an occasional word of direction, and anxious to know whether the removal of the stone had made an opening into the goblins' house, he put in his hand to feel. It went in a good way, and then came in contact with something soft. He had but a moment to feel it over, it was so quickly withdrawn: it was one of the toeless goblin-feet. The owner of it gave a cry of fright.

"What's the matter, Helfer?" asked his mother.

"A beast came out of the wall, and licked my foot."

"Nonsense! There are no wild beasts in our country," said his father.

"But it was, father. I felt it."

"Nonsense, I say. Will you malign your native realms and reduce them to a level with the country up-stairs? That is swarming with wild beasts of every description."

"But I did feel it, father."

"I tell you to hold your tongue. You are no patriot."

Curdie suppressed his laughter, and lay still as a mouse—but no stiller, for every moment he kept nibbling away with his fingers at the edges of the hole. He was slowly making it bigger, for here the rock had been very much shattered with the blasting.

There seemed to be a good many in the family, to judge from the mass of confused talk which now and then came through the hole; but when all were speaking together, and just as if they had bottle-brushes—each at least one—in their throats, it was not easy to make out much that was said. At length he heard once more what the father-goblin was saying.

"Now then," he said, "get your bundles on your backs. Here, Helfer, I'll help you up with your chest."

"I wish it was my chest, father."

"Your turn will come in good time enough! Make haste. I must go to the meeting at the palace to-night. When that's over, we can come back and clear out the last of the things before our enemies return in the morning. Now light your torches, and come along. What a distinction it is to provide our own light, instead of being dependent on a thing hung up in the air—a most disagreeable contrivance—intended no doubt to blind us when we venture out under its baleful influence! Quite glaring and vulgar, I call it, though no doubt useful to poor creatures who haven't the wit to make light for themselves!"

Curdie could hardly keep himself from calling through to know whether they made the fire to light their torches by. But a moment's reflection showed him that they would have said they did, inasmuch as they struck two stones together, and the fire came.

THE HALL OF THE GOBLIN PALACE

A sound of many soft feet followed, but soon ceased. Then Curdie flew at the hole like a tiger, and tore and pulled. The sides gave way, and it was soon large enough for him to crawl through. He would not betray himself by rekindling his lamp, but the torches of the retreating company, departing in a straight line up a long avenue from the door of their cave, threw back light enough to afford him a glance round the deserted home of the goblins. To his surprise, he could discover nothing to distinguish it from an ordinary cave in the rock, upon many of which he had come with the rest of the miners in the progress of their excavations. The goblins had talked of coming back for the rest of their household gear: he saw nothing that would have made him suspect a family had taken shelter there for a single night. The floor was rough and stony; the walls full of projecting corners; the roof in one place twenty feet high, in another endangering his forehead; while on one side a stream, no thicker than a needle, it is true, but still sufficient to spread a wide dampness over the wall, flowed down the face of the rock. But the troop in front of him was toiling under heavy burdens. He could distinguish Helfer now and then, in the flickering light and shade, with his heavy chest on his bending shoulders; while the second brother was almost buried in what looked like a great feather-bed. "Where do they get the feathers?" thought Curdie; but in a moment the troop disappeared at a turn of the way, and it was now both safe and necessary for Curdie to follow them, lest they should be round the next turning before he saw them again, for so he might lose them altogether. He darted after them like a grayhound. When he reached the corner and looked cautiously round, he saw them again at some distance down another long passage. None of the galleries he saw that night bore signs of the work of man—or of goblin either. Stalactites far older than the mines hung from their roofs; and their floors were rough with boulders and large round stones, showing that there water must have once run. He waited again at this corner till they had disappeared round the next, and so followed them a long way through one passage after another. The passages grew more and more lofty, and were more and more covered in the roof with shining stalactites.

It was a strange enough procession which he followed. But the strangest part of it was the household animals which crowded amongst the feet of the goblins. It was true they had no wild animals down there—at least they did not know of any; but they had a wonderful number of tame ones. I must, however, reserve any contributions toward the natural history of these for a later position in my story.

At length, turning a corner too abruptly, he had almost rushed into the middle of the goblin family; for there they had already set down all their burdens on the floor of a cave considerably larger than that which they had left. They were as yet too breathless to speak, else he would have had warning of their arrest. He started back, however, before any one saw him, and retreating a good way, stood watching till the father should come out to go to the palace. Before very long, both he and his son Helfer appeared and kept on in the same direction as before, while Curdie followed them again with renewed precaution. For a long time he heard no sound except something like the rush of a river inside the rock; but at length what seemed the far-off noise of a great shouting reached his ears, which however presently ceased. After advancing a good way farther, he thought he heard a single voice. It sounded clearer and clearer as he went on, until at last he could almost distinguish the words. In a moment or two, keeping after the goblins round another corner, he once more started back—this time in amazement.

He was at the entrance of a magnificent cavern, of an oval shape, once probably a huge natural reservoir of water, now the great palace hall of the goblins. It rose to a tremendous height, but the roof was composed of such shining materials, and the multitude of torches carried by the goblins who crowded the floor lighted up the place so brilliantly, that Curdie could see to the top quite well. But he had no idea how immense the place was, until his eyes had got accustomed to it, which was not for a good many minutes. The rough projections on the walls, and the shadows thrown upward from them by the torches, made the sides of the chamber look as if they were crowded with statues upon brackets and pedestals, reaching in irregular tiers from floor to roof. The walls themselves were, in many parts, of gloriously shining substances, some of them gorgeously colored besides, which powerfully contrasted with the shadows. Curdie could not help wondering whether his rhymes would be of any use against such a multitude of goblins as filled the floor of the hall, and indeed felt considerably tempted to begin his shout of One, two, three! but as there was no reason for routing them, and much for endeavoring to discover their designs, he kept himself perfectly quiet, and peeping round the edge of the doorway, listened with both his sharp ears.

At the other end of the hall, high above the heads of the multitude, was a terrace-like ledge of considerable height, caused by the receding of the upper part of the cavern wall. Upon this sat the king and his court, the king on a throne hollowed out of a huge block of green copper ore, and his court upon lower seats around it. The king had been making them a speech, and the applause which followed it was what Curdie had heard. One of the court was now addressing the multitude. What he heard him say was to the following effect:

"Hence it appears that two plans have been for some time together working in the strong head of his Majesty for the deliverance of his people. Regardless of the fact that we were the first possessors of the regions they now inhabit, regardless equally of the fact that we abandoned that region from the loftiest motives; regardless also of the self-evident fact that we excel them as far in mental ability as they excel us in stature, they look upon us as a degraded race, and make a mockery of all our finer feelings. But the time has almost arrived when—thanks to his Majesty's inventive genius—it will be in our power to take a thorough revenge upon them once for all, in respect of their unfriendly behavior."

"May it please your Majesty—" cried a voice close by the door, which Curdie recognized as that of the goblin he had followed.

"Who is he that interrupts the Chancellor?" cried another from near the throne.

"Glump," answered several voices.

"He is our trusty subject," said the king himself, in a slow and stately voice: "let him come forward and speak."

A lane was parted through the crowd, and Glump having ascended the platform and bowed to the king, spoke as follows:

"Sire, I would have held my peace, had I not known that I only knew how near was the moment to which the Chancellor had just referred. In all probability, before another day is past, the enemy will have broken through into my house—the partition between being even now not more than a foot in thickness."

"Not quite so much," thought Curdie to himself.

"This very evening I have had to remove my household effects; therefore the sooner we are ready to carry out the plan, for the execution of which his Majesty has been making such magnificent preparations, the better. I may just add, that within the last few days I have perceived a small outbreak in my dining-room, which combined with observations upon the course of the river escaping where the evil men enter, has convinced me that close to the spot must lie a deep gulf in its channel. This discovery will, I trust, add considerably to the otherwise immense forces at his Majesty's disposal."

He ceased, and the king graciously acknowledged his speech with a bend of his head; whereupon Glump, after a bow to his Majesty, slid down amongst the rest of the undistinguished multitude. Then the Chancellor rose and resumed.

"The information which the worthy Glump has given us," he said, "might have been of considerable import at the present moment, but for that other design already referred to, which naturally takes precedence. His Majesty, unwilling to proceed to extremities, and well aware that such measures sooner or later result in violent reactions, has excogitated a more fundamental and comprehensive measure, of which I need say no more. Should his Majesty be successful—as who dares to doubt?—then a peace, all to the advantage of the goblin kingdom, will be established for a generation at least, rendered absolutely secure by the pledge which his royal Highness the prince will have and hold for the good behavior of his relatives. Should his Majesty fail—which who shall dare even to imagine in his most secret thoughts?—then will be the time for carrying out with rigor the design to which Glump referred, and for which our preparations are even now all but completed. The failure of the former will render the latter imperative."

Curdie perceiving that the assembly was drawing to a close, and that there was little chance of either plan being more fully discovered, now thought it prudent to make his escape before the goblins began to disperse, and slipped quietly away.

There was not much danger of meeting any goblins, for all the men at least were left behind him in the palace; but there was considerable danger of his taking a wrong turning, for he had now no light, and had therefore to depend upon his memory and his hands. After he had left behind him the glow that issued from the door of Glump's new abode, he was utterly without guide, so far as his eyes were concerned.

He was most anxious to get back through the hole before the goblins should return to fetch the remains of their furniture. It was not that he was in the least afraid of them, but, as it was of the utmost importance that he should thoroughly discover what the plans they were cherishing were, he must not occasion the slightest suspicion that they were watched by a miner.

He hurried on, feeling his way along the walls of rock. Had he not been very courageous, he must have been very anxious, for he could not but know that if he lost his way it would be the most difficult thing in the world to find it again. Morning would bring no light into these regions; and toward him least of all, who was known as a special rhymster and persecutor, could goblins be expected to exercise courtesy? Well might he wish that he had brought his lamp and tinder-box with him, of which he had not thought when he crept so eagerly after the goblins! He wished it all the more when, after a while, he found his way blocked up, and could get no farther. It was of no use to turn back, for he had not the least idea where he had begun to go wrong. Mechanically, however, he kept feeling about the walls that hemmed him in. His hand came upon a place where a tiny stream of water was running down the face of the rock. "What a stupid I am!" he said to himself. "I am actually at the end of my journey!—and there are the goblins coming back to fetch their things!" he added, as the red glimmer of their torches appeared at the end of the long avenue that led up to the cave. In a moment he had thrown himself on the floor, and wriggled backward through the hole. The floor on the other side was several feet lower, which made it easier to get back. It was all he could do to lift the largest stone he had taken out of the hole, but he did manage to shove it in again. He sat down on the ore-heap and thought.

He was pretty sure that the latter plan of the goblins was to inundate the mine by breaking outlets for the water accumulated in the natural reservoirs of the mountain, as well as running through portions of it. While the part hollowed by the miners remained shut off from that inhabited by the goblins, they had had no opportunity of injuring them thus; but now that a passage was broken through, and the goblins' part proved the higher in the mountain, it was clear to Curdie that the mine could be destroyed in an hour. Water was always the chief danger to which the miners were exposed. They met with a little choke-damp sometimes, but never with the explosive fire-damp so common in coal mines. Hence they were careful as soon as they saw any appearance of water.

As the result of his reflections while the goblins were busy in their old home, it seemed to Curdie that it would be best to build up the whole of this gang, filling it with stone, and clay or lime, so that there should be no smallest channel for the water to get into. There was not, however, any immediate danger, for the execution of the goblins' plan was contingent upon the failure of that unknown design which was to take precedence of it; and he was most anxious to keep the door of communication open, that he might if possible discover what that former plan was. At the same time they could not then resume their intermitted labors for the inundation without his finding it out; when by putting all hands to the work, the one existing outlet might in a single night be rendered impenetrable to any weight of water; for by filling the gang entirely up, their embankment would be buttressed by the sides of the mountain itself.

As soon as he found that the goblins had again retired, he lighted his lamp, and proceeded to fill the hole he had made with such stones as he could withdraw when he pleased. He then thought it better, as he might have occasion to be up a good many nights after this, to go home and have some sleep.

How pleasant the night-air felt upon the outside of the mountain after what he had gone through in the inside of it! He hurried up the hill, without meeting a single goblin on the way, and called and tapped at the window until he woke his father, who soon rose and let him in. He told him the whole story, and, just as he had expected, his father thought it best to work that lode no farther, but at the same time to pretend occasionally to be at work there still, in order that the goblins might have no suspicions. Both father and son then went to bed, and slept soundly until the morning.

THE PRINCESS'S KING-PAPA

The weather continued fine for weeks, and the little princess went out every day. So long a period of fine weather had indeed never been known upon that mountain. The only uncomfortable thing was that her nurse was so nervous and particular about being in before the sun was down, that often she would take to her heels when nothing worse than a fleecy cloud crossing the sun threw a shadow on the hillside; and many an evening they were home a full hour before the sunlight had left the weathercock on the stables. If it had not been for such behavior, Irene would by this time have almost forgotten the goblins. She never forgot Curdie, but him she remembered for his own sake, and indeed would have remembered him if only because a princess never forgets her debts until they are paid.

One splendid sunshiny day, about an hour after noon, Irene, who was playing on a lawn in the garden, heard the distant blast of a bugle. She jumped up with a cry of joy, for she knew by that particular blast that her father was on his way to see her. This part of the garden lay on the slope of the hill, and allowed a full view of the country below. So she shaded her eyes with her hand, and looked far away to catch the first glimpse of shining armor. In a few moments a little troop came glittering round the shoulder of a hill. Spears and helmets were sparkling and gleaming, banners were flying, horses prancing, and again came the bugle-blast, which was to her like the voice of her father calling across the distance, "Irene, I'm coming." On and on they came, until she could clearly distinguish the king. He rode a white horse, and was taller than any of the men with him. He wore a narrow circle of gold set with jewels around his helmet, and as he came still nearer, Irene could discern the flashing of the stones in the sun. It was a long time since he had been to see her, and her little heart beat faster and faster as the shining troop approached, for she loved her king-papa very dearly, and was nowhere so happy as in his arms. When they reached a certain point, after which she could see them no more from the garden, she ran to the gate, and there stood till up they came clanging and stamping, with one more bright bugle-blast which said, "Irene, I am come."

By this time the people of the house were all gathered at the gate, but Irene stood alone in front of them. When the horseman pulled up, she ran to the side of the white horse, and held up her arms. The king stooped, and took her hands. In an instant she was on the saddle, and clasped in his great strong arms. I wish I could describe the king, so that you could see him in your mind. He had gentle blue eyes, but a nose that made him look like an eagle. A long dark beard, streaked with silvery lines, flowed from his mouth almost to his waist, and as Irene sat on the saddle and hid her glad face upon his bosom, it mingled with the golden hair which her mother had given her, and the two together were like a cloud with streaks of the sun woven through it. After he had held her to his heart for a minute, he spoke to his white horse, and the great beautiful creature, which had been prancing so proudly a little while before, walked as gently as a lady—for he knew he had a little lady on his back—through the gate and up to the door of the house. Then the king set her on the ground, and, dismounting, took her hand and walked with her into the great hall, which was hardly ever entered except when he came to see his little princess. There he sat down with two of his councillors who had accompanied him, to have some refreshment, and Irene bestowed herself on his right hand, and drank her milk out of a wooden bowl curiously carved.

In an instant she was on the saddle, and clasped in his great strong arms.

After the king had eaten and drunk, he turned to the princess and said, stroking her hair—

"Now, my child, what shall we do next?"

THE PRINCESS AND THE GOBLIN

This was the question he almost always put to her first after their meal together; and Irene had been waiting for it with some impatience, for now, she thought, she should be able to settle a question which constantly perplexed her.

"I should like you to take me to see my great old grandmother."

The king looked grave, and said—

"What does my little daughter mean?"

"I mean the Queen Irene that lives up in the tower—the very old lady, you know, with the long hair of silver."

The king only gazed at his little princess with a look which she could not understand.

"She's got her crown in her bedroom," she went on; "but I've not been in there yet. You know she's here, don't you?"

"No," said the king very quietly.

"Then it must be all a dream," said Irene. "I half thought it was; but I couldn't be sure. Now I am sure of it. Besides, I couldn't find her the next time I went up."

At that moment a snow-white pigeon flew in at an open window and, with a flutter, settled upon Irene's head. She broke into a merry laugh, cowered a little and put up her hands to her head, saying—

"Dear dovey, don't peck me. You'll pull out my hair with your long claws, if you don't have a care."

The king stretched out his hand to take the pigeon, but it spread its wings and flew again through the open window, when its whiteness made one flash in the sun and vanished. The king laid his hand on the princess's head, held it back a little, gazed in her face, smiled half a smile and sighed half a sigh.

"Come, my child; we'll have a walk in the garden together," he said.

"You won't come up and see my huge, great, beautiful grandmother, then, king-papa?" said the princess.

"Not this time," said the king very gently. "She has not invited me, you know, and great old ladies like her do not choose to be visited without leave asked and given."

The garden was a very lovely place. Being upon a mountain side, there were parts in it where the rocks came through in great masses, and all immediately about them remained quite wild. Tufts of heather grew upon them, and other hardy mountain plants and flowers, while near them would be lovely roses and lilies, and all pleasant garden flowers. This mingling of the wild mountain with the civilized garden was very quaint, and it was impossible for any number of gardeners to make such a garden look formal and stiff.

Against one of these rocks was a garden-seat, shadowed, from the afternoon sun by the overhanging of the rock itself. There was a little winding path up to the top of the rock, and on the top another seat; but they sat on the seat at its foot, because the sun was hot; and there they talked together of many things. At length the king said:

"You were out late one evening, Irene."

"Yes, papa. It was my fault; and Lootie was very sorry."

"I must talk to Lootie about it," said the king.

"Don't speak loud to her, please, papa," said Irene. "She's been so afraid of being late ever since! Indeed she has not been naughty. It was only a mistake for once."

"Once might be too often," murmured the king to himself, as he stroked his child's head.

I cannot tell you how he had come to know. I am sure Curdie had not told him. Some one about the palace must have seen them, after all. He sat for a good while thinking. There was no sound to be heard except that of a little stream which ran merrily out of an opening in the rock by where they sat, and sped away down the hill through the garden. Then he rose, and leaving Irene where she was, went into the house and sent for Lootie, with whom he had a talk that made her cry.

When in the evening he rode away upon his great white horse, he left six of his attendants behind him, with orders that three of them should watch outside the house every night, walking round and round it from sunset to sunrise. It was clear he was not quite comfortable about the princess.

THE OLD LADY'S BEDROOM

Nothing more happened worth telling for some time. The autumn came and went by. There were no more flowers in the garden. The winds blew strong, and howled among the rocks. The rain fell, and drenched the few yellow and red leaves that could not get off the bare branches. Again and again there would be a glorious morning followed by a pouring afternoon, and sometimes, for a week together, there would be rain, nothing but rain, all day, and then the most lovely cloudless night, with the sky all out in full-blown stars—not one missing. But the princess could not see much of them, for she went to bed early. The winter drew on, and she found things growing dreary. When it was too stormy to go out, and she had got tired of her toys, Lootie would take her about the house, sometimes to the house-keeper's room, where the housekeeper, who was a good, kind old woman, made much of her—sometimes to the servants' hall or the kitchen, where she was not princess merely, but absolute queen, and ran a great risk of being spoiled. Sometimes she would run of herself to the room where the men-at-arms whom the king had left, sat, and they showed her their arms and accoutrements, and did what they could to amuse her. Still at times she found it very dreary, and often and often wished that her huge great grandmother had not been a dream.

One morning the nurse left her with the housekeeper for a while. To amuse her, she turned out the contents of an old cabinet upon the table. The little princess found her treasures, queer ancient ornaments and many things the uses of which she could not imagine, far more interesting than her own toys, and sat playing with them for two hours or more. But at length, in handling a curious old-fashioned brooch, she ran the pin of it into her thumb, and gave a little scream with the sharp-ness of the pain, but would have thought little more of it, had not the pain increased and her thumb begun to swell. This alarmed the housekeeper greatly. The nurse was fetched; the doctor was sent for; her hand was poulticed, and long before her usual time she was put to bed. The pain still continued, and although she fell asleep and dreamed a good many dreams, there was the pain always in every dream. At last it woke her up.

The moon was shining brightly into the room. The poultice had fallen off her hand, and it was burning hot. She fancied if she could hold it into the moonlight, that would cool it. So she got out of bed, without waking the nurse who lay at the other end of the room, and went to the window. When she looked out, she saw one of the men-at-arms walking in the garden, with the moonlight glancing on his armor. She was just going to tap on the window and call him, for she wanted to tell him all about it, when she bethought herself that that might wake Lootie, and she would put her into bed again. So she resolved to go to the window of another room, and call him from there. It was so much nicer to have somebody to talk to than to lie awake in bed with the burning pain in her hand. She opened the door very gently and went through the nursery, which did not look into the garden, to go to the other window. But when she came to the foot of the old staircase, there was the moon shining down from some window high up, and making the worm-eaten oak look very strange and delicate and lovely. In a moment she was putting her little feet one after the other in the silvery path up the stair, looking behind as she went, to see the shadow they made in the middle of the silver. Some little girls would have been afraid to find themselves thus alone in the middle of the night, but Irene was a princess.

As she went slowly up the stairs, not quite sure that she was not dreaming, suddenly a great longing woke up in her heart to try once more whether she could not find the old, old lady with the silvery hair.

"If she is a dream," she said to herself, "then I am the likelier to find her, if I am dreaming."

So up and up she went, stair after stair, until she came to the many rooms—all just as she had seen them before. Through passage after passage she softly sped, comforting herself that if she should lose her way it would not matter much, because when she woke she would find herself in her own bed, with Lootie not far off. But as if she had known every step of the way, she walked straight to the door at the foot of the narrow stair that led to the tower.

"What if I should realliality-really find my beautiful old grandmother up there!" she said to herself, as she crept up the steep steps.

When she reached the top, she stood a moment listening in the dark, for there was no moon there. Yes! it was! it was the hum of the spinning-wheel! What a diligent grandmother to work both day and night!

She tapped gently at the door.

"Come in, Irene," said the sweet voice.

The princess opened the door, and entered. There was the moonlight streaming in at the window, and in the middle of the moonlight sat the old lady in her black dress with the white lace, and her silvery hair mingling with the moonlight, so that you could not have distinguished one from the other.

"Come in, Irene," she said again. "Can you tell me what I am spinning?"

"She speaks," thought Irene, "just as if she had seen me five minutes ago, or yesterday at the farthest.—No," she answered; "I don't know what you are spinning. Please, I thought you were a dream. Why couldn't I find you before, great-great-grandmother?"

"That you are hardly old enough to understand. But you would have found me sooner if you hadn't come to think I was a dream. I will give you one reason, though, why you couldn't find me. I didn't want you to find me."

"Why, please?"

"Because I did not want Lootie to know I was here."

"But you told me to tell Lootie."

"Yes. But I knew Lootie would not believe you. If she were to see me sitting spinning here, she wouldn't believe me either."

"Why."

"Because she couldn't. She would rub her eyes, and go away and say she felt queer, and forget half of it and more, and then say it had been all a dream."

"Just like me," said Irene, feeling very much ashamed of herself.

"Yes, a good deal like you, but not just like you; for you've come again; and Lootie wouldn't have come again. She would have said, No, no—she had had enough of such nonsense."

"Is it naughty of Lootie then?"

"It would be naughty of you. I've never done anything for Lootie."

"And you did wash my face and hands for me," said Irene, beginning to cry.

The old lady smiled a sweet smile and said—

"I'm not vexed with you, my child—nor with Lootie either. But I don't want you to say anything more to Lootie about me. If she should ask you, you must just be silent. But I do not think she will ask you."

All the time they talked, the old lady kept on spinning.

"You haven't told me yet what I am spinning," she said.

"Because I don't know. It's very pretty stuff."

It was indeed very pretty stuff. There was a good bunch of it on the distaff attached to the spinning-wheel, and in the moonlight it shone like—what shall I say it was like? It was not white enough for silver—yes, it was like silver, but shone gray rather than white, and glittered only a little. And the thread the old lady drew out from it was so fine that Irene could hardly see it.

"I am spinning this for you, my child."

"For me! What am I to do with it, please?"

"I will tell you by and by. But first I will tell you what it is. It is spider-webs—of a particular kind. My pigeons bring it me from over the great sea. There is only one forest where the spiders live who make this particular kind—the finest and strongest of any. I have nearly finished my present job. What is on the rock now will be quite sufficient. I have a week's work there yet, though," she added, looking at the bunch.

"Do you work all day and night too, great-great-great-great grandmother?" said the princess, thinking to be very polite with so many greats.

"I am not quite so great as all that," she answered, smiling almost merrily. "If you call me grandmother, that will do.—No. I don't work every night—only moonlit nights, and then no longer than the moon shines upon my wheel. I sha'n't work much longer to-night."

"And what will you do next, grandmother?"

"Go to bed. Would you like to see my bedroom?"

"Yes, that I should."

"Then I think I won't work any longer to-night. I shall be in good time."

The old lady rose, and left her wheel standing just as it was. You see there was no good in putting it away, for where there was not any furniture, there was no danger of being untidy.

Then she took Irene by the hand, but it was her bad hand, and Irene gave a little cry of pain.

"My child!" said, her grandmother, "what is the matter?"

Irene held her hand into the moonlight, that the old lady might see it, and told her all about it, at which she looked grave. But she only said—"Give me your other hand"; and, having led her out upon the little dark landing, opened the door on the opposite side of it. What was Irene's surprise to see the loveliest room she had ever seen in her life! It was large and lofty, and dome-shaped. From the centre hung a lamp as round as a ball, shining as if with the brightest moonlight, which made everything visible in the room, though not so clearly that the princess could tell what many of the things were. A large oval bed stood in the middle, with a coverlid of rose-color, and velvet curtains all round it of a lovely pale blue. The walls were also blue—spangled all over with what looked like stars of silver.

The old lady left her, and going to a strange-looking cabinet, opened it and took out a curious silver casket. Then she sat down on a low chair, and calling Irene, made her kneel before her, while she looked at her hand. Having examined it, she opened the casket, and took from it a little ointment. The sweetest odor filled the room—like that of roses and lilies—as she rubbed the ointment gently all over the hot swollen hand. Her touch was so pleasant and cool, that it seemed to drive away the pain and heat wherever it came.

"Oh, grandmother! it is so nice!" said Irene. "Thank you; thank you."

Then the old lady went to a chest of drawers, and took out a large handkerchief of gossamer-like cambric, which she tied around her hand.

"I don't think that I can let you go away to-night," she said. "Do you think you would like to sleep with me?"

"Oh, yes, yes, dear grandmother!" said Irene, and would have clapped her hands, forgetting that she could not.

"You won't be afraid then to go to bed with such an old woman?"

"No. You are so beautiful, grandmother."

"But I am very old."

"And I suppose I am very young. You won't mind sleeping with such a very young woman, grandmother?"

"You sweet little pertness!" said the old lady, and drew her toward her, and kissed her on the forehead and the cheek and the mouth.

Then she got a large silver basin, and having poured some water into it, made Irene sit on the chair, and washed her feet. This done, she was ready for bed. And oh, what a delicious bed it was into which her grandmother laid her! She hardly could have told she was lying upon anything: she felt nothing but the softness. The old lady having undressed herself, lay down beside her.

"Why don't you put out your moon?" asked the princess.

"That never goes out, night or day," she answered. "In the darkest night, if any of my pigeons are out on a message, they always see my moon, and know where to fly to."

"But if somebody besides the pigeons were to see it—somebody about the house, I mean—they would come to look what it was, and find you."

"The better for them then," said the old lady. "But it does not happen above five times in a hundred years that any one does see it. The greater part of those who do, take it for a meteor, wink their eyes, and forget it again. Besides, nobody could find the room except I pleased. Besides again—I will tell you a secret—if that light were to go out, you would fancy yourself lying in a bare garret, on a heap of old straw, and would not see one of the pleasant things round about you all the time."

"I hope it will never go out," said the princess.

"I hope not. But it is time we both went to sleep. Shall I take you in my arms?"

The little princess nestled close up to the old lady, who took her in both her arms, and held her close to her bosom.

"Oh dear! this is so nice!" said the princess. "I didn't know anything in the whole world could be so comfortable. I should like to lie here for ever."

"You may if you will," said the old lady. "But I must put you to one trial—not a very hard one, I hope.—This night week you must come back to me. If you don't, I do not know when you may find me again, and you will soon want me very much."

"Oh! please, don't let me forget."

"You shall not forget. The only question is whether you will believe I am anywhere—whether you will believe I am anything but a dream. You may be sure I will do all I can to help you to come. But it will rest with yourself after all. On the night of next Friday, you must come to me. Mind now."

"I will try," said the princess.

"Then good night," said the old lady, and kissed the forehead which lay in her bosom.

In a moment more the little princess was dreaming in the midst of the loveliest dreams—of summer seas and moonlight and mossy springs and great murmuring trees, and beds of wild flowers with such odors as she had never smelled before. But after all, no dream could be more lovely than what she had left behind when she fell asleep.

In the morning she found herself in her own bed. There was no handkerchief or anything else on her hand, only a sweet odor lingering about it. The swelling had all gone down; the prick of the brooch had vanished:—in fact her hand was perfectly well.

A SHORT CHAPTER ABOUT CURDIE

Curdie spent many nights in the mine. His father and he had taken Mrs. Peterson into the secret, for they knew mother could hold her tongue, which was more than could be said of all the miners' wives. But Curdie did not tell her that every night he spent in the mine, part of it went in earning a new red petticoat for her.

Mrs. Peterson was such a nice good mother! All mothers are more or less, but Mrs. Peterson was nice and good all more and no less. She made a little heaven in that poor cottage on the hillside—for her husband and son to go home to out of the dreary earth in which they worked. I doubt if the princess was very much happier even in the arms of her huge great-grandmother than Peter and Curdie were in the arms of Mrs. Peterson. True, her hands were hard, and chapped, and large, but it was with work for them; and therefore in the sight of the angels, her hands were so much the more beautiful. And if Curdie worked hard to get her a petticoat, she worked hard every day to get him comforts which he would have missed much more than she would a new petticoat even in winter. Not that she and Curdie ever thought of how much they worked for each other: that would have spoiled everything.

When left alone in the mine, Curdie always worked on for an hour or two first, following the lode which, according to Glump, would lead at last into the deserted habitation. After that, he would set out on a reconnoitering expedition. In order to manage this, or rather the return from it, better than the first time, he had bought a huge ball of fine string, having learned the trick from Hop-o'-my-Thumb, whose history his mother had often told him. Not that Hop-o'-my-Thumb had ever used a ball of string—I should be sorry to be supposed so far out in my classics—but the principle was the same as that of the pebbles. The end of this string he fastened to his pickaxe, which figured no bad anchor, and then, with the ball in his hand, unrolling as he went, set out in the dark through the natural gangs of the goblins' territory. The first night or two he came upon nothing worth remembering; saw only a little of the home-life of the cobs in the various caves they called houses; failed in coming upon anything to cast light upon the foregoing design which kept the inundation for the present in the background. But at length, I think on the third or fourth night, he found, partly guided by the noise of their implements, a company of evidently the best sappers and miners amongst them, hard at work. What were they about? It could not well be the inundation, seeing that had in the meantime been postponed to something else. Then what was it? He lurked and watched, every now and then in the greatest risk of being detected, but without success. He had again and again to retreat in haste, a proceeding rendered the more difficult that he had to gather up his string as he returned upon its course. It was not that he was afraid of the goblins, but that he was afraid of their finding out that they were watched, which might have prevented the discovery at which he aimed. Sometimes his haste had to be such that, when he reached home toward morning, his string for lack of time to wind it up as he "dodged the cobs," would be in what seemed the most hopeless entanglement; but after a good sleep though a short one, he always found his mother had got it right again. There it was, wound in a most respectable ball, ready for use the moment he should want it!

"I can't think how you do it, mother," he would say.

"I follow the thread," she would answer—"just as you do in the mine."

She never had more to say about it; but the less clever she was with her words, the more clever she was with her hands; and the less his mother said, the more, Curdie believed, she had to say.

But still he had made no discovery as to what the goblin miners were about.

THE COBS' CREATURES

About this time, the gentlemen whom the king had left behind him to watch over the princess, had each occasion to doubt the testimony of his own eyes, for more than strange were the objects to which they would bear witness. They were of one sort—creatures—but so grotesque and misshapen as to be more like a child's drawings upon his slate than anything natural. They saw them only at night, while on guard about the house. The testimony of the man who first reported having seen one of them was that, as he was walking slowly round the house, while yet in the shadow, he caught sight of a creature standing on its hind legs in the moonlight, with its fore feet upon a window-ledge, staring in at the window. Its body might have been that of a dog or wolf—he thought, but he declared on his honor that its head was twice the size it ought to have been for the size of its body, and as round as a ball, while the face, which it turned upon him as it fled, was more like one carved by a boy upon the turnip inside which he is going to put a candle, than anything else he could think of. It rushed into the garden. He sent an arrow after it, and thought he must have struck it; for it gave an unearthly howl, and he could not find his arrow any more than the beast, although he searched all about the place where it vanished. They laughed at him until he was driven to hold his tongue; and said he must have taken too long a pull at the ale-jug. But before two nights were over, he had one to side with him; for he too had seen something strange, only quite different from that reported by the other. The description the second man gave of the creature he had seen was yet more grotesque and unlikely. They were both laughed at by the rest; but night after night another came over to their side, until at last there was only one left to laugh at all his companions. Two nights more passed, and he saw nothing; but on the third, he came rushing from the garden to the other two before the house, in such an agitation that they declared—for it was their turn now—that the band of his helmet was cracking under his chin with the rising of his hair inside it. Running with him into that part of the garden which I

374

have already described, they saw a score of creatures, to not one of which they could give a name, and not one of which was like another, hideous and ludicrous at once, gamboling on the lawn in the moonlight. The supernatural or rather subnatural ugliness of their faces, the length of legs and necks in some, and the apparent absence of both or either in others, made the spectators, although in one consent as to what they saw, yet doubtful, as I have said, of the evidence of their own eyes— and ears as well; for the noises they made, although not loud, were as uncouth and varied as their forms, and could be described neither as grunts nor squeaks nor roars nor howls nor barks nor yells nor screams nor croaks nor hisses nor mews nor shrieks, but only as something like all of them mingled in one horrible dissonance. Keeping in the shade, the watchers had a few moments to recover themselves before the hideous assembly suspected their presence; but all at once, as if by common consent, they scampered off in the direction of a great rock, and vanished before the men had come to sufficiently to think of following them.

My readers will suspect what these were; but I will now give them full information concerning them. They were of course household animals belonging to the goblins, whose ancestors had taken their ancestors many centuries before from the upper regions of light into the lower regions of darkness. The original stocks of these horrible creatures were very much the same as the animals now seen about farms and homes in the country, with the exception of a few of them, which had been wild creatures, such as foxes, and indeed wolves and small bears, which the goblins, from their proclivity toward the animal creation, had caught when cubs and tamed. But in the course of time, all had undergone even greater changes than had passed upon their owners. They had altered—that is, their descendants had altered—into such creatures as I have not attempted to describe except in the vaguest manner—the various parts of their bodies assuming, in an apparently arbitrary and self-willed manner, the most abnormal developments. Indeed, so little did any distinct type predominate in some of the bewildering results, that you could only have guessed at any known animal as the original, and even then, what likeness remained would be more one of general expression than of definable conformation. But what increased the gruesomeness tenfold, was that, from constant domestic, or indeed rather family association with the goblins, their countenances had grown in grotesque resemblance to the human. No one understands animals who does not see that every one of them, even amongst the fishes, it may be with a dimness and vagueness infinitely remote, yet shadows the human: in the case of these the human resemblance had greatly increased: while their owners had sunk toward them, they hod risen toward their owners. But the conditions of subterranean life being equally unnatural for both, while the goblins were worse, the creatures had not improved by the approximation, and its result would have appeared far more ludicrous than consoling to the warmest lover of animal nature. I shall now explain how it was that just then these animals began to show themselves about the king's country house.

The goblins, as Curdie had discovered, were mining on—at work both day and night, in divisions, urging the scheme after which he lay in wait. In the course of their tunneling, they had broken into the channel of a small stream, but the break being in the top of it, no water had escaped to interfere with their work. Some of the creatures, hovering as they often did about their masters, had found the hole, and had, with the curiosity which had grown to a passion from the restraints of their unnatural circumstances, proceeded to explore the channel. The stream was the same which ran out by the seat on which Irene and her king-papa had sat as I have told, and the goblin-creatures found it jolly fun to get out for a romp on a smooth lawn such as they had never seen in all their poor miserable lives. But although they had partaken enough of the nature of their owners to delight in annoying and alarming any of the people whom they met on the mountain, they were of course incapable of designs of their own, or of intentionally furthering those of their masters.

For several nights after the men-at-arms were at length of one mind as to the facts of the visits of some horrible creatures, whether bodily or spectral they could not yet say, they watched with special attention that part of the garden where they had last seen them. Perhaps indeed they gave in consequence too little attention to the house. But the creatures were too cunning to be easily caught; nor were the watchers quick-eyed enough to descry the head, or the keen eyes in it, which, from the opening whence the stream issued, would watch them in turn, ready, the moment they left the lawn to report the place clear.

THAT NIGHT WEEK

During the whole of the week, Irene had been thinking every other moment of her promise to the old lady, although even now she could not feel quite sure that she had not been dreaming. Could it really be that an old lady lived up in the top of the house with pigeons and a spinning-wheel, and a lamp that never went out? She was, however, none the less determined, on the coming Friday, to ascend the three stairs, walk through the passages with the many doors, and try to find the tower in which she had either seen or dreamed her grandmother.

Her nurse could not help wondering what had come to the child—she would sit so thoughtfully silent, and even in the midst of a game with her, would so suddenly fall into a dreamy mood. But Irene took care to betray nothing, whatever efforts Lootie might make to get at her thoughts. And Lootie had to say to herself, "What an odd child she is!" and give it up.

At length the long looked-for Friday arrived, and lest Lootie should be moved to watch her, Irene endeavored to keep herself as quiet as possible. In the afternoon she asked for her doll's house, and went on arranging and rearranging the various rooms and their inhabitants for a whole hour. Then she gave a sigh and threw herself back in her chair. One of the dolls would not sit, and another would not stand, and they were all very tiresome. Indeed there was one that would not even lie down, which was too bad. But it was now getting dark, and the darker it got the more exited Irene became, and the more she felt it necessary to be composed.

"I see you want your tea, princess," said the nurse: "I will go and get it. The room feels close: I will open the window a little. The evening is mild: it won't hurt you."

"There's no fear of that, Lootie," said Irene, wishing she had put off going for the tea till it was darker, when she might have made her attempt with every advantage.

I fancy Lootie was longer in returning than she had intended; for when Irene, who had been lost in thought, looked up, she saw it was nearly dark, and at the same moment caught sight of a pair of eyes, bright with a green light, glowering at her through the open window. The next instant something leaped into the room. It was like a cat, with legs as long as a horse's, Irene said, but its body no bigger and its legs no thicker than those of a cat. She was too frightened to cry out, but not too frightened to jump from her chair and run from the room.

It is plain enough to every one of my readers what she ought to have done—and indeed Irene thought of it herself; but when she came to the foot of the old stair, just outside the nursery door, she imagined the creature running up those long ascents after her, and pursuing her through the dark passages—which, after all, might lead to no tower! That thought was too much. Her heart failed her, and turning from the stair, she rushed along to the hall, whence, finding the front-door open, she darted into the court, pursued—at least she thought so—by the creature. No one happening to see her, on she ran, unable to think for fear, and ready to run anywhere to elude the awful creature with the stilt-legs. Not daring to look behind her, she rushed straight out of the gate, and up the mountain. It was foolish indeed —thus to run farther and farther from all who could help her, as if she had been seeking a fit spot for the goblin-creature to eat her in at his leisure; but that is the way fear serves us: it always takes the side of the thing that we are afraid of.

The princess was soon out of breath with running up hill; but she ran on, for she fancied the horrible creature just behind her, forgetting that, had it been after her, such legs as those must have overtaken her long ago. At last she could run no longer, and fell, unable even to scream, by the roadside, where she lay for some-time, half dead with terror. But finding nothing lay hold of her, and her breath beginning to come back, she ventured at length to get half up, and peer anxiously about her. It was now so dark that she could see nothing. Not a single star was out. She could not even tell in what direction the house lay, and between her and home she fancied the dreadful creature lying ready to pounce upon her. She saw now that she ought to have run up the stairs at once. It was well she did not scream; for, although very few of the goblins had come out for weeks, a stray idler or two might have heard her. She sat down upon a stone, and nobody but one who had done something wrong could have been more miserable. She had quite forgotten her promise to visit her grandmother. A rain-drop fell on her face. She looked up, and for a moment her terror was lost in astonishment. At first she thought the rising moon had left her place, and drawn nigh to see what could be the matter with the little girl, sitting alone, without hat or cloak, on the dark bare mountain; but she soon saw she was mistaken, for there was no light on the ground at her feet, and no shadow anywhere. But a great silvery globe was hanging in the air; and as she gazed at the lovely thing, her courage revived. If she were but indoors again she would fear nothing, not even the terrible creature with the long legs! But how was she to find her way back? What could that light be? Could it be—? No, it couldn't. But what if it should be—yes—it must be—her great-great-grandmother's lamp, which guided her pigeons home through the darkest night! She jumped up: she had but to keep that light in view, and she must find the house.

Her heart grew strong. Speedily, yet softly, she walked down the hill, hoping to pass the watching creature unseen. Dark as it was, there was little danger now of choosing the wrong road. And—which was most strange—the light that filled her eyes from the lamp, instead of blinding them for a moment to the object upon which they next fell, enabled her for a moment to see it, despite the darkness. By looking at the lamp and then dropping her eyes, she could see the road for a yard or two in front of her, and this saved her from several falls, for the road was very rough. But all at once, to her dismay, it vanished, and the terror of the beast, which had left her the moment she began to return, again laid hold of her heart. The same instant, however, she caught the light of the windows, and knew exactly where she was. It was too dark to run, but she made what haste she could, and reached the gate in safety. She found the house door still open, ran through the hall, and, without even looking into the nursery, bounded straight up the stair, and the next, and the next; then turning to the right, ran through the long avenue of silent rooms, and found her way at once to the door at the foot of the tower stair.

When first the nurse missed her, she fancied she was playing her a trick, and for some time took no trouble about her; but at last, getting frightened, she had begun to search; and when the princess entered, the whole household was hither and thither, over the house, hunting for her. A few seconds after she reached the stair of the tower, they had even begun to search the neglected rooms, in which they would never have thought of looking had they not already searched every other place they could think of in vain. But by this time she was knocking at the old lady's door.

WOVEN AND THEN SPUN

"Come in, Irene," said the silvery voice of her grandmother.

The princess opened the door, and peeped in. But the room was quite dark, and there was no sound of the spinning-wheel. She grew frightened once more, thinking that, although the room was there, the old lady might be a dream after all. Every little girl knows how dreadful it is to find a room empty where she thought somebody was; but Irene had to fancy for a moment that the person she came to find was nowhere at all. She remembered however that at night she spun only in the moonlight, and concluded that must be why there was no sweet, bee-like humming: the old lady might be somewhere in the darkness. Before she had time to think another thought, she heard her voice again, saying as before—

"Come in, Irene."

From the sound, she understood at once that she was not in the room beside her. Perhaps she was in her bedroom. She turned across the passage, feeling her way to the other door. When her hand fell on the lock, again the old lady spoke—

"Shut the other door behind you, Irene. I always close the door of my workroom when I go to my chamber."

Irene wondered to hear her voice so plainly through the door; having shut the other, she opened it and went in. Oh, what a lovely haven to reach from the darkness and fear through which she had come! The soft light made her feel as if she were going into the heart of the milkiest pearl; while the blue walls and their silver stars for a moment perplexed her with the fancy that they were in reality the sky which she had left outside a minute ago covered with rainclouds.

"I've lighted a fire for you, Irene: you're cold and wet," said her grandmother.

Then Irene looked again, and saw that what she had taken for a huge bouquet of red roses on a low stand against the wall, was in fact a fire which burned in the shapes of the loveliest and reddest roses, glowing gorgeously between the heads and wings of two cherubs of shining silver. And when she came nearer, she found that the smell of roses with which the room was filled, came from the fire-roses on the hearth. Her grandmother was dressed in the loveliest pale-blue velvet, over which her hair, no longer white, but of a rich gold color, streamed like a cataract, here falling in dull gathered heaps, there rushing away in smooth shining falls. And even as she looked, the hair seemed pouring down from her head, and vanishing in a golden mist ere it reached the floor. It flowed from under the edge of a circle of shining silver, set with alternated pearls and opals. On her dress was no ornament whatever, neither was there a ring on her hand, or a necklace or carcanet about her neck. But her slippers glimmered with the light of the Milky-way, for they were covered with seed-pearls and opals in one mass. Her face was that of a woman of three-and-twenty.

The princess was so bewildered with astonishment and admiration that she could hardly thank her, and drew nigh with timidity, feeling dirty and uncomfortable. The lady was seated on a low chair by the side of the fire, with hands outstretched to take her, but the princess hung back with a troubled smile.

"Come," and she still held out her arms.

"Why, what's the matter?" asked her grandmother. "You haven't been doing anything wrong—I know that by your face, though it is rather miserable. What's the matter, my dear?"

And still she held out her arms.

"Dear grandmother," said Irene, "I'm not so sure that I haven't done something wrong. I ought to have run up to you at once when the long-legged cat came in at the window, instead of running out on the mountain, and making myself such a fright."

"You were taken by surprise, my child, and are not so likely to do it again. It is when people do wrong things willfully that they are the more likely to do them again. Come."

And still she held out her arms.

"But, grandmother, you're so beautiful and grand with your crown on! and I am so dirty with mud and rain!—I should quite spoil your beautiful blue dress."

With a merry little laugh, the lady sprang from her chair, more lightly far than Irene herself could, caught the child to her bosom, and kissing the tear-stained face over and over, sat down with her in her lap.

"Oh, grandmother! you'll make yourself such a mess!" cried Irene, clinging to her.

"You darling! do you think I care more for my dress than for my little girl? Beside—look here!"

As she spoke she set her down, and Irene saw to her dismay that the lovely dress was covered with the mud of her fall on the mountain road. But the lady stooped to the fire, and taking from it, by the stalk in her fingers, one of the burning roses, passed it once and again and a third time over the front of her dress; and when Irene looked, not a single stain was to be discovered.

"There!" said her grandmother, "you won't mind coming to me now?"

But Irene again hung back, eyeing the flaming rose which the lady held in her hand.

"You're not afraid of the rose—are you?" she said, and she was about to throw it on the hearth again.

"Oh! don't, please!" cried Irene. "Won't you hold it to my frock and my hands and my face? And I'm afraid my feet and my knees want it too!"

"No," answered her grandmother, smiling a little sadly, as she threw the rose from her; "it is too hot for you yet. It would set your frock in a flame. Besides, I don't want to make you clean to-night. I want your nurse and the rest of the people to see you as you are, for you will have to tell them how you ran away for fear of the long-legged cat. I should like to wash you, but they would not believe you then. Do you see that bath behind you?"

The princess looked, and saw a large oval tub of silver, shining brilliantly in the light of the wonderful lamp.

"Go and look into it," said the lady.

Irene went, and came back very silently, with her eyes shining.

"What did you see?" asked her grandmother.

"The sky and the moon and the stars," she answered. "It looked as if there was no bottom to it."

The lady smiled a pleased, satisfied smile, and was silent also for a few moments. Then she said—

"Any time you want a bath, come to me. I know you have a bath every morning, but sometimes you want one at night too."

"Thank you, grandmother; I will—I will indeed," answered Irene, and was again silent for some moments thinking. Then she said, "How was it, grandmother, that I saw your beautiful lamp—not the light of it only—but the great round silver lamp itself, hanging alone in the great open air high up? It was your lamp I saw—wasn't it?"

"Yes, my child; it was my lamp."

"Then how was it? I don't see a window all round."

"When I please, I can make the lamp shine through the walls—shine so strong that it melts them away from before the sight, and shows itself as you saw it. But, as I told you, it is not everybody can see it."

"How is it that I can then? I'm sure I don't know."

"It is a gift born with you. And one day I hope everybody will have it."

"But how do you make it shine through the walls?"

"Ah! that you would not understand if I were to try ever so much to make you —not yet—not yet. But," added the lady rising, "you must sit in my chair while I get you the present I have been preparing for you. I told you my spinning was for you. It is finished now, and I am going to fetch it. I have been keeping it warm under one of my brooding pigeons."

Irene sat down in the low chair, and her grandmother left her, shutting the door behind her. The child sat gazing, now at the rose-fire, now at the starry walls, now at the silvery light; and a great quietness came over her heart. If all the long-legged cats in the world had come rushing helter-skelter at her then, she would not have been afraid of them for a single moment. How this was, however, she could not tell; —she only knew there was no fear in her, and everything was so right and safe that it could not get in.

She had been gazing at the lovely lamp for some minutes fixedly: turning her eyes, she found the wall had vanished, for she was looking out on the dark cloudy night. But though she heard the wind blowing, none of it blew upon her. In a moment more, the clouds themselves parted, or rather vanished like the wall, and she looked straight into the starry herds, flashing gloriously in the dark blue. It was but for a moment. The clouds gathered again and shut out the stars; the wall gathered again and shut out the clouds; and there stood the lady beside her with the loveliest smile on her face, and a shimmering ball in her hand, about the size of a pigeon's egg.

"There, Irene; there is my work for you!" she said, holding out the ball to the princess.

She took it in her hand, and looked at it all over. It sparkled a little, and shone here and shone there, but not much. It was of a sort of gray whiteness, something like spun glass.

"Is this all your spinning, grandmother?" she asked.

"All since you came to the house. There is more there than you think."

"How pretty it is! What am I to do with it?"

"That I will now explain to you," answered the lady, turning from her, and going to her cabinet.

She came back with a small ring in her hand. Then she took the ball from Irene's, and did something with the two—Irene could not tell what.

"Give me your hand," she said.

Irene held up her right hand.

"Yes, that is the hand I want," said the lady, and put the ring on the forefinger of it.

"What a beautiful ring!" said Irene. "What is the stone called?"

"It is a fire-opal."

"Please, am I to keep it?"

"Always."

"Oh, thank you, grandmother! It's prettier than anything I ever saw, except those
—of all colors—in your—Please, is that your crown?"

"Yes, it is my crown. The stone in your ring is of the same sort—only not so
good. It has only red, but mine have all colors, you see."

"Yes, grandmother. I will take such care of it!—But—" she added, hesitating.

"But what?" asked her grandmother.

"What am I to say when Lootie asks me where I got it?"

"You will ask her where you got it," answered the lady smiling.

"I don't see how I can do that."

"You will though."

"Of course I will if you say so. But you know I can't pretend not to know."

"Of course not. But don't trouble yourself about it. You will see when the time
comes."

So saying, the lady turned, and threw the little ball into the rose-fire.

"Oh, grandmother!" exclaimed Irene; "I thought you had spun it for me."

"So I did, my child. And you've got it."

"No; it's burnt in the fire."

The lady put her hand in the fire, brought out the ball, glimmering as before,
and held it toward her. Irene stretched out her hand to take it, but the lady turned,
and going to her cabinet, opened a drawer, and laid the ball in it.

"Have I done anything to vex you, grandmother?" said Irene pitifully.

"No, my darling. But you must understand that no one ever gives anything to
another properly and really without keeping it. That ball is yours."

"Oh! I'm not to take it with me! You are going to keep it for me!"

"You are to take it with you. I've fastened the end of it to the ring on your
finger."

Irene looked at the ring.

"I can't see it there, grandmother," she said.

"Feel—a little way from the ring—toward the cabinet," said the lady.

"Oh! I do feel it!" exclaimed the princess. "But I can't see it," she added, looking
close to her outstretched hand.

"No. The thread is too fine for you to see it. You can only feel it. Now you can
fancy how much spinning that took, although it does seem such a little ball."

"But what use can I make of it, if it lies in your cabinet?"

"That is what I will explain to you. It would be of no use to you—it wouldn't be
yours at all if it did not lie in my cabinet. Now listen. If ever you find yourself in
any danger—such, for example, as you were in this evening—you must take off
your ring, and put it under the pillow of your bed. Then you must lay your forefinger, the same that wore the ring, upon the thread, and follow the thread wherever it
leads you."

"Oh, how delightful! It will lead me to you, grandmother, I know!"

"Yes. But, remember, it may seem to you a very roundabout way indeed, and
you must not double the thread. Of one thing you may be sure, that while you hold
it, I hold it too."

"It is very wonderful!" said Irene thoughtfully. Then suddenly becoming aware,
she jumped up, crying—"Oh, grandmother! here I have been sitting all this time in
your chair, and you standing! I beg your pardon."

The lady laid her hand on her shoulder and said:

"Sit down again, Irene. Nothing pleases me better than to see any one sit in my chair. I am only too glad to stand so long as any one will sit in it."

"How kind of you!" said the princess, and sat down again.

"It makes me happy," said the lady.

"But," said Irene, still puzzled, "won't the thread get in somebody's way and be broken, if the one end is fast to my ring and the other laid in your cabinet?"

"You will find all that arranges itself. I am afraid it is time for you to go."

"Mightn't I stay and sleep with you to-night, grandmother?"

"No, not to-night. If I had meant you to stay to-night, I should have given you a bath; but you know everybody in the house is miserable about you, and it would be cruel to keep them so all night. You must go down stairs."

"I'm so glad, grandmother, you didn't say—go home—for this is my home. Mayn't I call this my home?"

"You may, my child. And I trust you will always think it your home. Now come. I must take you back without any one seeing you."

"Please, I want to ask you one question more," said Irene. "Is it because you have your crown on that you look so young?"

"No, child," answered her grandmother; "it is because I felt so young this evening, that I put my crown on. And it occurred to me that you would like to see your old grandmother in her best."

"Why do you call yourself old? You're not old, grandmother."

"I am very old indeed. It is so silly of people—I don't mean you, for you are such a tiny, and couldn't know better—but it is so silly of people to fancy that old age means crookedness and witheredness and feebleness and sticks and spectacles and rheumatism and forgetfulness! It is so silly! Old age has nothing whatever to do with all that. The right old age means strength and beauty and mirth and courage and clear eyes and strong painless limbs. I am older than you are able to think, and—"

"And look at you, grandmother!" cried Irene, jumping up, and flinging her arms about her neck. "I won't be so silly again, I promise you. At least—I'm rather afraid to promise—but if I am, I promise to be sorry for it—I do. I wish I were as old as you, grandmother. I don't think you are ever afraid of anything."

"Not for long, at least, my child. Perhaps by the time I am two thousand years of age, I shall, indeed, never be afraid of anything. But I must confess that I have sometimes been afraid about my children—sometimes about you, Irene."

"Oh, I'm so sorry, grandmother!—To-night, I suppose, you mean."

"Yes—a little to-night; but a good deal when you had all but made up your mind that I was a dream, and no real great-great-grandmother. You must not suppose that I am blaming you for that, I daresay it was out of your power to help it."

"I don't know, grandmother," said the princess, beginning to cry. "I can't always do myself as I should like. And I don't always try. I'm very sorry anyhow."

The lady stooped, lifted her in her arms, and sat down with her in her chair, holding her close to her bosom. In a few minutes the princess had sobbed herself to sleep. How long she slept, I do not know. When she came to herself she was sitting in her own high chair at the nursery table, with her doll's-house before her.

THE RING

The same moment her nurse came into the room, sobbing. When she saw her sitting there, she started back with a loud cry of amazement and joy. Then running to her, she caught her up in her arms and covered her dear little face with kisses.

"My precious darling princess! where have you been? What has happened to you? We've all been crying our eyes out, and searching the house from top to bottom for you."

"Not quite from the top," thought Irene to herself; and she might have added —"not quite to the bottom," perhaps, if she had known all. But the one she would not, and the other she could not say.

"Oh, Lootie! I've had such a dreadful adventure!" she replied, and told her all about the cat with the long legs, and how she ran out upon the mountain, and came back again. But she said nothing of her grandmother or her lamp.

"And there we've been searching for you all over the house for more than an hour and a half!" exclaimed the nurse. "But that's no matter, now we've got you! Only, princess, I must say," she added, her mood changing, "what you ought to have done was to call for your own Lootie to come and help you, instead of running out of the house, and up the mountain, in that wild—I must say, foolish fashion."

"Well, Lootie," said Irene quietly, "perhaps if you had a big cat, all legs, running at you, you mightn't exactly know which was the wisest thing to do at the moment."

"I wouldn't run up the mountain, anyhow," returned Lootie.

"Not if you had time to think about it. But when those creatures came at you that night on the mountain, you were so frightened yourself that you lost your way home."

This put a stop to Lootie's reproaches. She had been on the point of saying that the long-legged cat must have been a twilight fancy of the princess's, but the memory of the horrors of that night, and of the talking-to which the king had given her in consequence, prevented her from saying that which after all she did not half believe—having a strong suspicion that the cat was a goblin; for the fact was that she knew nothing of the difference between the goblins and their creatures: she counted them all just goblins.

Without another word she went and got some fresh tea and bread and butter for the princess. Before she returned, the whole household, headed by the housekeeper, burst into the nursery to exult over their darling. The gentlemen-at-arms followed, and were ready enough to believe all she told them about the long-legged cat. Indeed, though wise enough to say nothing about it, they remembered with no little horror, just such a creature amongst those they had surprised at their gambols upon the princess's lawn. In their own hearts they blamed themselves for not having kept better watch. And their captain gave order that from this night the front door and all the windows on the ground floor should be locked immediately the sun set, and opened after upon no pretence whatever. The men-at-arms redoubled their vigilance, and for some time there was no further cause of alarm.

When the princess woke the next morning, her nurse was bending over her.

"How your ring does glow this morning, princess!—just like a fiery rose!" she said.

"Does it, Lootie?" returned Irene. "Who gave me the ring, Lootie? I know I've had it a long time, but where did I get it? I don't remember."

"I think it must have been your mother gave it you, princess; but really, for as long as you have worn it, I don't remember that ever I heard," answered her nurse.

"I will ask my king-papa the next time he comes," said Irene.

SPRING-TIME

The spring, so dear to all creatures, young and old, came at last, and before the first few days of it had gone, the king rode through its budding valleys to see his little daughter. He had been in a distant part of his dominions all the winter, for he was not in the habit of stopping in one great city, or of visiting only his favorite country houses, but he moved from place to place, that all his people might know him. Wherever he journeyed, he kept a constant lookout for the ablest and best men to put into office, and wherever he found himself mistaken, and those he had appointed incapable or unjust, he removed them at once. Hence you see it was his care of the people that kept him from seeing his princess so often as he would have liked. You may wonder why he did not take her about with him; but there were several reasons against his doing so, and I suspect her great-great-grandmother had had a principal hand in preventing it. Once more Irene heard the bugle-blast, and once more she was at the gate to meet her father as he rode up on his great white horse.

After they had been alone for a little while, she thought of what she had resolved to ask him.

"Please, king-papa," she said, "will you tell me where I got this pretty ring? I can't remember."

The king looked at it. A strange, beautiful smile spread like sunshine over his face, and an answering smile, but at the same time a questioning one, spread like moonlight over Irene's.

"It was your queen-mamma's once," he said.

"And why isn't it hers now?" asked Irene.

"She does not want it now," said the king, looking grave.

"Why doesn't she want it now?"

"Because she's gone where all those rings are made."

"And when shall I see her?" asked the princess.

"Not for some time yet," answered the king, and the tears came in his eyes.

Irene did not remember her mother, and did not know why her father looked so, and why the tears came in his eyes; but she put her arms round his neck and kissed him, and asked no more questions.

The king was much disturbed on hearing the report of the gentlemen-at-arms concerning the creatures they had seen; and I presume would have taken Irene with him that very day, but for what the presence of the ring on her finger assured him of. About an hour before he left, Irene saw him go up the old stair; and he did not come down again till they were just ready to start; and she thought with herself that he had been up to see the old lady. When he went away, he left the other six gentlemen behind him, that there might be six of them always on guard.

And now, in the lovely spring-weather, Irene was out on the mountain the greater part of the day. In the warmer hollows there were lovely primroses, and not so many that she ever got tired of them. As often as she saw a new one opening an eye of light in the blind earth, she would clap her hands with gladness, and, unlike some children I know, instead of pulling it, would touch it as tenderly as if it had been a new baby, and, having made its acquaintance, would leave it as happy as she found it. She treated the plants on which they grew like birds' nests; every fresh flower was like a new little bird to her. She would pay a visit to all the flower-nests she knew, remembering each by itself. She would go down on her hands and knees beside one and say "Good morning! Are you all smelling very sweet this morning? Good-bye!" And then she would go to another nest, and say the same. It was a favorite amusement with her. There were many flowers up and down, and she loved them all, but the primroses were her favorites.

"They're not too shy, and they're not a bit forward," she would say to Lootie.

There were goats too about, over the mountain, and when the little kids came, she was as pleased with them as with the flowers. The goats belonged to the miners mostly—a few of them to Curdie's mother; but there were a good many wild ones that seemed to belong to nobody. These the goblins counted theirs, and it was upon them partly that they lived. They set snares and dug pits for them; and did not scruple to take what tame ones happened to be caught; but they did not try to steal them in any other manner, because they were afraid of the dogs the hill-people kept to watch them, for the knowing dogs always tried to bite their feet. But the goblins had a kind of sheep of their own—very queer creatures, which they drove out to feed at night, and the other goblin-creatures were wise enough to keep good watch over them, for they knew they should have their bones by and by.

CURDIE'S CLUE

Curdie was as watchful as ever, but was almost getting tired of his ill-success. Every other night or so he followed the goblins about, as they went on digging and boring, and getting as near them as he could, watched them from behind stones and rocks; but as yet he seemed no nearer finding out what they had in view. As at first, he always kept hold of the end of his string, while his pickaxe left just outside the hole by which he entered the goblins' country from the mine, continued to serve as an anchor and hold fast the other end. The goblins hearing no more noise in that quarter, had ceased to apprehend an immediate invasion, and kept no watch.

One night, after dodging about and listening till he was nearly falling asleep with weariness, he began to roll up his ball, for he had resolved to go home to bed. It was not long, however, before he began to feel bewildered. One after another he passed goblin-houses, caves that is, occupied by goblin families, and at length was sure they were many more than he had passed as he came. He had to use great caution to pass unseen—they lay so close together. Could his string have led him wrong? He still followed winding it, and still it led him into more thickly populated quarters, until he became quite uneasy, and indeed apprehensive; for although he was not afraid of the cobs, he was afraid of not finding his way out. But what could he do? It was of no use to sit down and wait for the morning—the morning made no difference here. It was all dark, and always dark; and if his string failed him he was helpless. He might even arrive within a yard of the mine, and never know it. Seeing he could do nothing better, he would at least find where the end of the string was, and if possible how it had come to play him such a trick. He knew by the size of the ball that he was getting pretty near the last of it, when he began to feel a tugging and pulling at it. What could it mean? Turning a sharp corner, he thought he heard strange sounds. These grew, as he went on, to a scuffling and growling and squeaking; and the noise increased, until, turning a second sharp corner, he found himself in the midst of it, and the same moment tumbled over a

390

wallowing mass, which he knew must be a knot of the cobs' creatures. Before he could recover his feet, he had caught some great scratches on his face, and several severe bites on his legs and arms. But as he scrambled to get up, his hand fell upon his pickaxe, and before the horrid beasts could do him any serious harm, he was laying about with it right and left in the dark. The hideous cries which followed gave him the satisfaction of knowing that he had punished some of them pretty smartly for their rudeness, and by their scampering and their retreating howls, he perceived that he had routed them. He stood a little, weighing his battle-axe in his hand as if it had been the most precious lump of metal—but indeed no lump of gold itself could have been so precious at that time as that common tool—then untied the end of the string from it, put the ball in his pocket, and still stood thinking. It was clear that the cobs' creatures had found his axe, had between them carried it off, and had so led him he knew not where. But for all his thinking he could not tell what he ought to do, until suddenly he became aware of a glimmer of light in the distance. Without a moment's hesitation he set out for it, as fast as the unknown and rugged way would permit. Yet again turning a corner, led by the dim light, he spied something quite new in his experience of the underground regions— a small irregular shape of something shining. Going up to it, he found it was a piece of mica, or Muscovy glass, called sheep-silver in Scotland, and the light flickering as if from a fire behind it. After trying in vain for some time to discover an entrance to the place where it was burning, he came at length to a small chamber in which an opening high in the wall revealed a glow beyond. To this opening he managed to scramble up, and then he saw a strange sight.

Below sat a little group of goblins around a fire, the smoke of which vanished in the darkness far aloft. The sides of the cave were full of shining minerals like those of the palace-hall; and the company was evidently of a superior order, for every one wore stones about head, or arms, or waist, shining, dull, gorgeous colors in the light of the fire. Nor had Curdie looked long before he recognized the king himself, and found that he had made his way into the inner apartment of the royal family. He had never had such a good chance of hearing something! He crept through the hole as softly as he could, scrambled a good way down the wall toward them without attracting attention, and then sat down and listened. The king, evidently the queen, and probably the crown-prince and the prime minister were talking together. He was sure of the queen by her shoes, for as she warmed her feet at the fire, he saw them quite plainly.

"That will be fun!" said the one he took for the crown-prince.

It was the first whole sentence he heard.

"I don't see why you should think it such a grand affair!" said his stepmother, tossing her head backward.

"You must remember, my spouse," interposed his Majesty, as if making excuse for his son, "he has got the same blood in him. His mother—"

"Don't talk to me of his mother! You positively encourage his unnatural fancies. Whatever belongs to that mother, ought to be cut out of him."

"You forget yourself, my dear!" said the king.

"I don't," said the queen, "nor you either. If you expect me to approve of such coarse tastes, you will find yourself mistaken. I don't wear shoes for nothing."

"You must acknowledge, however," the king said, with a little groan, "that this at least is no whim of Harelip's, but a matter of state-policy. You are well aware that his gratification comes purely from the pleasure of sacrificing himself to the public good. Does it not, Harelip?"

"Yes, father; of course it does. Only it will be nice to make her cry. I'll have the skin taken off between her toes, and tie them up till they grow together. Then her feet will be like other people's, and there will be no occasion for her to wear shoes."

"Do you mean to insinuate I've got toes, you unnatural wretch?" cried the queen; and she moved angrily toward Harelip. The councilor, however, who was betwixt them, leaned forward so as to prevent her touching him, but only as if to address the prince.

"Your royal Highness," he said, "possibly requires to be reminded that you have got three toes yourself—one on one foot, two on the other."

"Ha! ha! ha!" shouted the queen triumphantly.

The councilor, encouraged by this mark of favor, went on.

"It seems to me, your royal Highness, it would greatly endear you to your future people, proving to them that you are not the less one of themselves that you had the misfortune to be born of a sun-mother, if you were to command upon yourself the comparatively slight operation which, in a more extended form, you so wisely meditate with regard to your future princess."

"Ha! ha! ha!" laughed the queen, louder than before, and the king and the minister joined in the laugh. It was anything but a laughing matter to Harelip. He growled, and for a few moments the others continued to express their enjoyment of his discomfiture.

The queen was the only one Curdie could see with any distinctness. She sat sideways to him, and the light of the fire shone full upon her face. He could not consider her handsome. Her nose was certainly broader at the end than its extreme length, and her eyes, instead of being horizontal, were set up like two perpendicular eggs, one on the broad, the other on the small, end. Her mouth was no bigger than a small buttonhole until she laughed, when it stretched from ear to ear—only to be sure her ears were very nearly in the middle of her cheeks.

Anxious to hear everything they might say, Curdie ventured to slide down a smooth part of the rock just under him, to a projection below, upon which he thought to rest. But whether he was not careful enough, or the projection gave way, down he came with a rush on the floor of the cavern, bringing with him a great rumbling shower of stones.

The goblins jumped from their seats in more anger than consternation, for they had never yet seen anything to be afraid of in the palace. But when they saw Curdie with his pick in his hand, their rage was mingled with fear, for they took him for the first of an invasion of miners. The king notwithstanding drew himself up to his full height of four feet, spread himself to his full breadth of three and a half, for he was the handsomest and squarest of all the goblins, and strutting up to Curdie, planted himself with outspread feet before him, and said with dignity—

"Pray what right have you in my palace?"

"The right of necessity, your majesty," answered Curdie. "I lost my way, and did not know where I was wandering to."

"How did you get in?"

"By a hole in the mountain."

"But you are a miner! Look at your pickaxe!"

Curdie did look at it, answering,

"I came upon it, lying on the ground, a little way from here. I tumbled over some wild beasts who were playing with it. Look, your majesty." And Curdie showed him how he was scratched and bitten.

The king was pleased to find him behave more politely than he had expected from what his people had told him concerning the miners, for he attributed it to the power of his own presence; but he did not therefore feel friendly to the intruder.

"You will oblige me by walking out of my dominions at once," he said, well knowing what a mockery lay in the words.

"With pleasure, if your majesty will give me a guide," said Curdie.

"I will give you a thousand," said the king, with a scoffing air of magnificent liberality.

"One will be quite sufficient," said Curdie.

But the king uttered a strange shout, half halloo, half roar, and in rushed goblins till the cave was swarming. He said something to the first of them which Curdie could not hear, and it was passed from one to another till in a moment the farthest in the crowd had evidently heard and understood it. They began to gather about him in a way he did not relish, and he retreated toward the wall. They pressed upon him.

The goblins fell back a little when he began, and made horrible grimaces all through the rhyme.

"Stand back," said Curdie, grasping his pickaxe tighter by his knee.

They only grinned and pressed closer. Curdie bethought himself, and began to rhyme.

"Ten, twenty, thirty—
    You're all so very dirty!
    Twenty, thirty, forty—
    You're all so thick and snorty!

"Thirty, forty, fifty—
    You're all so puff-and-snifty!
    Forty, fifty, sixty—
    Beast and man so mixty!

"Fifty, sixty, seventy—
    Mixty, maxty, leaventy—
    Sixty, seventy, eighty—
    All your cheeks so slaty.

"Seventy, eighty, ninety,
    All your hands so flinty!
    Eighty, ninety, hundred,
    Altogether dundred!"

The goblins fell back a little when he began, and made horrible grimaces all through the rhyme, as if eating something so disagreeable that it set their teeth on edge and gave them the creeps; but whether it was that the rhyming words were most of them no words at all, for a new rhyme being considered more efficacious, Curdie had made it on the spur of the moment, or whether it was that the presence of the king and queen gave them courage, I cannot tell; but the moment the rhyme was over, they crowded on him again, and out shot a hundred long arms, with a multitude of thick nailless fingers at the end of them, to lay hold upon him. Then Curdie heaved up his axe. But being as gentle as courageous and not wishing to kill any of them, he turned the end which was square and blunt like a hammer, and with that came down a great blow on the head of the goblin nearest him. Hard as the heads of all goblins are, he thought he must feel that. And so he did, no doubt; but he only gave a horrible cry, and sprung at Curdie's throat. Curdie however drew back in time, and just at that critical moment, remembered the vulnerable part of the goblin-body. He made a sudden rush at the king, and stamped with all his might on his Majesty's feet. The king gave a most unkingly howl, and almost fell into the fire. Curdie then rushed into the crowd, stamping right and left. The goblins drew back howling on every side as he approached, but they were so crowded that few of those he attacked could escape his tread; and the shrieking and roaring that filled the cave would have appalled Curdie, but for the good hope it gave him. They were tumbling over each other in heaps in their eagerness to rush from the cave, when a new assailant suddenly faced him:—the queen, with flaming eyes and expanded nostrils, her hair standing half up from her head, rushed at him. She trusted in her shoes; they were of granite—hollowed like French sabots. Curdie would have endured much rather than hurt a woman, even if she was a goblin; but here was an affair of life and death: forgetting her shoes, he made a great stamp on one of her feet. But she instantly returned it with very different effect, causing him frightful pain and almost disabling him. His only chance with her would have been to attack the granite shoes with his pickaxe, but before he could think of that, she had caught him up in her arms, and was rushing with him across the cave. She dashed him into a hole in the wall, with a force that almost stunned him. But although he could not move, he was not too far gone to hear her great cry, and the rush of multitudes of soft feet, followed by the sounds of something heaved up against the rock; after which came a multitudinous patter of stones falling near him. The last had not ceased when he grew very faint, for his head had been badly cut, and at last insensible.

When he came to himself, there was perfect silence about him, and utter darkness, but for the merest glimmer in one tiny spot. He crawled to it, and found that they had heaved a slab against the mouth of the hole, past the edge of which a poor little gleam found its way from the fire. He could not move it a hair's breadth, for they had piled a great heap of stones against it. He crawled back to where he had been lying, in the faint hope of finding his pickaxe. But after a vain search, he was at last compelled to acknowledge himself in an evil plight. He sat down and tried to think, but soon fell fast asleep.

GOBLIN COUNSELS

He must have slept a long time, for when he awoke, he felt wonderfully restored—indeed he felt almost well, and he was also very hungry. There were voices in the outer cave.

Once more then, it was night; for the goblins slept during the day, and went about their affairs during the night.

In the universal and constant darkness of their dwelling, they had no reason to prefer the one arrangement to the other; but from aversion to the sun-people, they chose to be busy when there was least chance of their being met either by the miners below, when they were burrowing, or by the people of the mountain above, when they were feeding their sheep or catching their goats. And indeed it was only when the sun was away that the outside of the mountain was sufficiently like their own dismal regions to be endurable to their mole-eyes, so thoroughly had they become disused to any light beyond that of their own fires and torches.

Curdie listened, and soon found that they were talking of himself.

"How long will it take?" asked Harelip.

"Not many days, I should think," answered the king. "They are poor feeble creatures, those sun-people, and want to be always eating. We can go a week at a time without food, and be all the better for it; but I've been told they eat two or three times every day! Can you believe it?—They must be quite hollow inside—not at all like us, nine-tenths of whose bulk is solid flesh and bone. Yes—I judge a week of starvation will do for him."

"If I may be allowed a word," interposed the queen, "—and I think I ought to have some voice in the matter—"

"The wretch is entirely at your disposal, my spouse," interrupted the king. "He is your property. You caught him yourself. We should never have done it."

The queen laughed. She seemed in far better humor than the night before.

396

"I was about to say," she resumed, "that it does seem a pity to waste so much fresh meat."

"What are you thinking of, my love?" said the king. "The very notion of starving him implies that we are not going to give him any meat, either salt or fresh."

"I'm not such a stupid as that comes to," returned her Majesty. "What I mean is, that by the time he is starved, there will hardly be a picking upon his bones."

The king gave a great laugh.

"Well, my spouse, you may have him when you like," he said. "I don't fancy him for my part. I am pretty sure he is tough eating."

"That would be to honor instead of punish his insolence," returned the queen. "But why should our poor creatures be deprived of so much nourishment? Our little dogs and cats and pigs and small bears would enjoy him very much."

"You are the best of housekeepers, my lovely queen!" said her husband. "Let it be so by all means. Let us have our people in, and get him out and kill him at once. He deserves it. The mischief he might have brought upon us, now that he had penetrated so far as our most retired citadel, is incalculable. Or rather let us tie him hand and foot, and have the pleasure of seeing him torn to pieces by full torchlight in the great hall."

"Better and better!" cried the queen and prince together, both of them clapping their hands. And the prince made an ugly noise with his hare-lip, just as if he had intended to be one at the feast.

"But," added the queen, bethinking herself, "he is so troublesome. For as poor creatures as they are, there is something about those sun-people that is very troublesome. I cannot imagine how it is that with such superior strength and skill and understanding as ours, we permit them to exist at all. Why do we not destroy them entirely, and use their cattle and grazing lands at our pleasure? Of course, we don't want to live in their horrid country! It is far too glaring for our quieter and more refined tastes. But we might use it for a sort of outhouse, you know. Even our creatures' eyes might get used to it, and if they did grow blind, that would be of no consequence, provided they grew fat as well. But we might even keep their great cows and other creatures, and then we should have a few more luxuries, such as cream and cheese, which at present we only taste occasionally, when our brave men have succeeded in carrying some off from their farms."

"It is worth thinking of," said the king; "and I don't know why you should be the first to suggest it, except that you have a positive genius for conquest. But still, as you say, there is something very troublesome about them; and it would be better, as I understand you to suggest, that we should starve him for a day or two first, so that he may be a little less frisky when we take him out."

"Once there was a goblin
　Living in a hole;
　Busy he was cobblin'
　A shoe without a sole.

"By came a birdie:
　'Goblin, what do you do?'

'Cobble at a sturdie
Upper leather shoe.'

"'What's the good o' that, sir?'
Said the little bird,
'Why it's very pat, sir—
Plain without a word.

"'Where 'tis all a hill, sir,
Never can be holes:
Why should their shoes have soles, sir,
When they've got no souls?'"

"What's that horrible noise?" cried the queen, shuddering from pot-metal head to granite shoes.

"I declare," said the king with solemn indignation, "it's the sun-creature in the hole!"

"Stop that disgusting noise!" cried the crown-prince valiantly, getting up and standing in front of the heap of stones, with his face toward Curdie's prison.—"Do now, or I'll break your head."

"Break away," shouted Curdie, and began singing again—

"Once there was a goblin
Living in a hole,—"

"I really cannot bear it," said the queen. "If I could only get at his horrid toes with my slippers again!"

"I think we had better go to bed," said the king.

"It's not time to go to bed," said the queen.

"I would if I was you," said Curdie.

"Impertinent wretch!" said the queen, with the utmost scorn in her voice.

"An impossible if," said his Majesty with dignity.

"Quite," returned Curdie, and began singing again—

"Go to bed,
Goblin, do.
Help the queen
Take off her shoe.

"If you do,
It will disclose

A horrid set
Of sprouting toes."

"What a lie!" roared the queen in a rage.

"By the way, that reminds me," said the king, "that, for as long as we have been married, I have never seen your feet, queen. I think you might take off your shoes when you go to bed! They positively hurt me sometimes."

"I will do just as I like," retorted the queen sulkily.

"You ought to do as your hubby wishes you," said the king.

"I will not," said the queen.

"Then I insist upon it," said the king.

Apparently his Majesty approached the queen for the purpose of following the advice given by Curdie, for the latter heard a scuffle, and then a great roar from the king.

"Will you be quiet then?" said the queen wickedly.

"Yes, yes, queen. I only meant to coax you."

"Hands off!" cried the queen triumphantly. "I'm going to bed. You may come when you like. But as long as I am queen, I will sleep in my shoes. It is my royal privilege. Harelip, go to bed."

"I'm going," said Harelip sleepily.

"So am I," said the king.

"Come along then," said the queen; "and mind you are good, or I'll—"

"Oh, no, no, no!" screamed the king, in the most supplicating of tones.

Curdie heard only a muttered reply in the distance; and then the cave was quite still.

They had left the fire burning, and the light came through brighter than before. Curdie thought it was time to try again if anything could be done. But he found he could not get even a finger through the chink between the slab and the rock. He gave a great rush with his shoulder against the slab, but it yielded no more than if it had been part of the rock. All he could do was to sit down and think again.

By and by he came to the resolution to pretend to be dying, in the hope they might take him out before his strength was too much exhausted to let him have a chance. Then, for the creatures, if he could but find his axe again, he would have no fear of them; and if it were not for the queen's horrid shoes, he would have no fear at all.

Meantime, until they should come again at night, there was nothing for him to do but forge new rhymes, now his only weapons. He had no intention of using them at present, of course; but it was well to have a stock, for he might live to want them, and the manufacture of them would help to while away the time.

IRENE'S CLUE

That same morning, early, the princess woke in a terrible fright. There was a hideous noise in her room—of creatures snarling and hissing and racketing about as if they were fighting. The moment she came to herself, she remembered something she had never thought of again—what her grandmother told her to do when she was frightened. She immediately took off her ring and put it under her pillow. As she did so, she fancied she felt a finger and thumb take it gently from under her palm. "It must be my grandmother!" she said to herself, and the thought gave her such courage that she stopped to put on her dainty little slippers before running from the room. While doing this, she caught sight of a long cloak of sky-blue, thrown over the back of a chair by her bedside. She had never seen it before, but it was evidently waiting for her. She put it on, and then, feeling with the forefinger of her right hand, soon found her grandmother's thread, which she proceeded at once to follow, expecting it would lead her straight up the old stair. When she reached the door, she found it went down and ran along the floor, so that she had almost to crawl in order to keep a hold of it. Then, to her surprise, and somewhat to her dismay, she found that instead of leading her toward the stair it turned in quite the opposite direction. It led her through certain narrow passages toward the kitchen, turning aside ere she reached it, and guiding her to a door which communicated with a small back yard. Some of the maids were already up, and this door was standing open. Across the yard the thread still ran along the ground, until it brought her to a door in the wall which opened upon the mountain side. When she had passed through, the thread rose to about half her height, and she could hold it with ease as she walked. It led her straight up the mountain.

The cause of her alarm was less frightful than she supposed. The cook's great black cat, pursued by the housekeeper's terrier, had bounced against her bedroom door, which had not been properly fastened, and the two had burst into her room together and commenced a battle royal. How the nurse came to sleep through it, was a mystery, but I suspect the old lady had something to do with it.

It was a clear warm morning. The wind blew deliciously over the mountain-side. Here and there she saw a late primrose, but she did not stop to call on them. The sky was mottled with small clouds. The sun was not yet up, but some of their fluffy edges had caught his light and hung out orange and gold-colored fringes upon the air. The dew lay in round drops upon the leaves, and hung like tiny diamonds from the blades of grass about her path.

"How lovely that bit of gossamer is!" thought the princess, looking at a long undulating line that shone at some distance from her up the hill. It was not the time for gossamers though; and Irene soon discovered that it was her own thread she saw shining on before her in the light of the morning. It was leading her she knew not whither; but she had never in her life been out before sunrise, and everything was so fresh and cool and lively and full of something coming, that she felt too happy to be afraid of anything.

After leading her up a good distance, the thread turned to the left, and down the path upon which she and Lootie had met Curdie. But she never thought of that, for now in the morning light, with its far outlook over the country, no path could have been more open and airy and cheerful. She could see the road almost to the horizon, along which she had so often watched her king-papa and his troop come shining, with the bugle-blast cleaving the air before them; and it was like a companion to her. Down and down the path went, then up, and then down, and then up again, getting rugged and more rugged as it went; still along the path went the silvery thread, and still along the thread went Irene's little rosy-tipped forefinger. By and by she came to a little stream that jabbered and prattled down the hill, and up the side of the stream went both path and thread. And still the path grew rougher and steeper, and the mountain grew wilder, till Irene began to think she was going a very long way from home; and when she turned to look back, she saw that the level country had vanished and the rough bare mountain had closed in about her. But still on went the thread, and on went the princess. Everything around her was getting brighter and brighter as the sun came nearer; till at length his first rays all at once alighted on the top of a rock before her, like some golden creature fresh from the sky. Then she saw that the little stream ran out of a hole in that rock, that the path did not go past the rock, and that the thread was leading her straight up to it. A shudder ran through her from head to foot when she found that the thread was actually taking her into the hole out of which the stream ran. It ran out babbling joyously, but she had to go in.

She did not hesitate. Right into the hole she went, which was high enough to let her walk without stooping. For a little way there was a brown glimmer, but at the first turn it all but ceased, and before she had gone many paces she was in total darkness. Then she began to be frightened indeed. Every moment she kept feeling the thread backward, and as she went farther and farther into the darkness of the great hollow mountain, she kept thinking more and more about her grandmother, and all that she had said to her, and how kind she had been, and how beautiful she was, and all about her lovely room, and the fire of roses, and the great lamp that sent its light through stone walls. And she became more and more sure that the thread could not have gone there of itself, and that her grandmother must have sent it. But it tried her dreadfully when the path went down very steep, and especially

when she came to places where she had to go down rough stairs, and even sometimes a ladder. Through one narrow passage after another, over lumps of rock and
sand and clay, the thread guided her, until she came to a small hole through which
she had to creep. Finding no change on the other side—"Shall I ever get back?" she
thought, over and over again, wondering at herself that she was not ten times more
frightened, and often feeling as if she were only walking in the story of a dream.
Sometimes she heard the noise of water, a dull gurgling inside the rock. By and by
she heard the sounds of blows, which came nearer and nearer; but again they grew
duller and almost died away. In a hundred directions she turned, obedient to the
guiding thread.

At last she spied a dull red shine, and came up to the mica-window, and thence
away and round about, and right into a cavern, where glowed the red embers of a
fire. Here the thread began to rise. It rose as high as her head, and higher still. What
should she do if she lost her hold? She was pulling it down! She might break it! She
could see it far up, glowing as red as her fire-opal in the light of the embers.

But presently she came to a huge heap of stones, piled in a slope against the
wall of the cavern. On these she climbed, and soon recovered the level of the thread
—only however to find, the next moment, that it vanished through the heap of
stones, and left her standing on it, with her face to the solid rock. For one terrible
moment, she felt as if her grandmother had forsaken her. The thread which the
spiders had spun far over the seas, which her grandmother had sat in the moonlight and spun again for her, which she had tempered in the rose-fire, and tied to
her opal ring, had left her—had gone where she could no longer follow it—had
brought her into a horrible cavern, and there left her! She was forsaken indeed!

"When shall I wake?" she said to herself in an agony, but the same moment
knew that it was no dream. She threw herself upon the heap, and began to cry. It
was well she did not know what creatures, one of them with stone shoes on her
feet, were lying in the next cave. But neither did she know who was on the other
side of the slab.

At length the thought struck her, that at least she could follow the thread backward, and thus get out of the mountain, and home. She rose at once, and found the
thread. But the instant she tried to feel it backward, it vanished from her touch.
Forward, it led her hand up to the heap of stones—backward, it seemed nowhere.
Neither could she see it as before in the light of the fire. She burst into a wailing cry,
and again threw herself down on the stones.

THE ESCAPE

As the princess lay and sobbed, she kept feeling the thread mechanically, following it with her finger many times up the stones in which it disappeared. By and by she began, still mechanically, to poke her finger in after it between the stones as far as she could. All at once it came into her head that she might remove some of the stones and see where the thread went next. Almost laughing at herself for never having thought of this before, she jumped to her feet. Her fear vanished: once more she was certain her grandmother's thread could not have brought her there just to leave her there; and she began to throw away the stones from the top as fast as she could, sometimes two or three at a handful, sometimes taking both hands to lift one. After clearing them away a little, she found that the thread turned and went straight downward. Hence, as the heap sloped a good deal, growing of course wider toward its base, she had to throw away a multitude of stones to follow the thread. But this was not all, for she soon found that the thread, after going straight down for a little way, turned first sideways in one direction, then sideways in another, and then shot, at various angles, hither and thither inside the heap, so that she began to be afraid that to clear the thread, she must remove the whole huge gathering. She was dismayed at the very idea, but, losing no time, set to work with a will; and with aching back, and bleeding fingers and hands, she worked on, sustained by the pleasure of seeing the heap slowly diminish, and begin to show itself on the opposite side of the fire. Another thing which helped to keep up her courage was, that as often as she uncovered a turn of the thread, instead of lying loose upon the stones, it tightened up; this made her sure that her grandmother was at the end of it somewhere.

She had got about half way down when she started, and nearly fell with fright. Close to her ear as it seemed, a voice broke out singing—

"Jabber, bother, smash!
    You'll have it all in a crash.
    Jabber, smash, bother!
    You'll have the worst of the pother.
    Smash, bother, jabber!—"

Here Curdie stopped, either because he could not find a rhyme to jabber, or because he remembered what he had forgotten when he woke up at the sound of Irene's labors, that his plan was to make the goblins think he was getting weak. But he had uttered enough to let Irene know who he was.

"It's Curdie!" she cried joyfully.

"Hush, hush!" came Curdie's voice again from somewhere. "Speak softly."

"Why, you were singing loud!" said Irene.

"Yes. But they know I am here, and they don't know you are. Who are you?"

"I'm Irene," answered the princess. "I know who you are quite well. You're Curdie."

"Why, how ever did you come here, Irene?"

"My great-great-grandmother sent me; and I think I've found out why. You can't get out, I suppose?"

"No, I can't. What are you doing?"

"Clearing away a huge heap of stones."

"There's a princess!" exclaimed Curdie, in a tone of delight, but still speaking in little more than a whisper. "I can't think how you got here, though."

"My grandmother sent me after her thread."

"I don't know what you mean," said Curdie; "but so you're there, it doesn't much matter."

"Oh, yes it does!" returned Irene. "I should never have been here but for her."

"You can tell me all about it when we get out, then. There's no time to lose now," said Curdie.

And Irene went to work, as fresh as when she began.

"There's such a lot of stones!" she said. "It will take me a long time to get them all away."

"How far on have you got?" asked Curdie.

"I've got about the half way, but the other half is ever so much bigger."

"I don't think you will have to move the lower half. Do you see a slab laid up against the wall?"

Irene looked and felt about with her hands, and soon perceived the outlines of the slab.

"Yes," she answered, "I do."

"Then, I think," rejoined Curdie, "when you have cleared the slab about half way down, or a little more, I shall be able to push it over."

"I must follow my thread," returned Irene, "whatever I do."

"What do you mean?" exclaimed Curdie.

"You will see when you get out of here," answered the princess, and then she went on harder than ever.

But she was soon satisfied that what Curdie wanted done, and what the thread wanted done, were one and the same thing. For she not only saw that by following the turns of the thread she had been clearing the face of the slab, but that, a little more than half way down, the thread went through the chink between the slab and the wall into the place where Curdie was confined, so that she could not follow it any farther until the slab was out of her way. As soon as she found this, she said in a right joyous whisper—

"Now, Curdie! I think if you were to give a great push, the slab would tumble over."

"Stand quite clear of it then," said Curdie, "and let me know when you are ready."

Irene got off the heap, and stood on one side of it.

"Now, Curdie!" she cried.

Curdie gave a great rush with his shoulder against it. Out tumbled the slab on the heap, and out crept Curdie over the top of it.

"You've saved my life, Irene!" he whispered.

"Oh, Curdie! I'm so glad! Let's get out of this horrid place as fast as we can."

"That's easier said than done," returned he.

"Oh, no! it's quite easy," said Irene. "We have only to follow my thread. I am sure that it's going to take us out now."

She had already begun to follow it over the fallen slab into the hole, while Curdie was searching the floor of the cavern for his pickaxe.

"Here it is!" he cried. "No, it is not!" he added, in a disappointed tone. "What can it be then?—I declare it's a torch. That is jolly! It's better almost than my pickaxe. Much better if it weren't for those stone shoes!" he went on, as he lighted the torch by blowing the last embers of the expiring fire.

When he looked up, with the lighted torch casting a glare into the great darkness of the huge cavern, he caught sight of Irene disappearing in the hole out of which he had himself just come.

"Where are you going there?" he cried. "That's not the way out. That's where I couldn't get out."

"I know that," whispered Irene. "But this is the way my thread goes, and I must follow it."

"What nonsense the child talks!" said Curdie to himself. "I must follow her, though, and see that she comes to no harm. She will soon find she can't get out that way, and then she will come with me."

So he crept once more over the slab into the hole with his torch in his hand. But when he looked about in it, he could see her nowhere. And now he discovered that although the hole was narrow, it was much larger than he had supposed; for in one direction the roof came down very low, and the hole went off in a narrow passage, of which he could not see the end. The princess must have crept in there. He got on his knees and one hand, holding the torch with the other, and crept after her. The hole twisted about, in some parts so low that he could hardly get through, in others so high that he could not see the roof, but everywhere it was narrow—far too narrow for a goblin to get through, and so I presume they never thought that Curdie might. He was beginning to feel very uncomfortable lest he could not see the end. The princess when he heard her voice almost close to his ear, whispering—

"Aren't you coming, Curdie?"

And when he turned the next corner, there she stood waiting for him.

"I knew you couldn't go wrong in that narrow hole, but now you must keep by me, for here is a great wide place," she said.

"I can't understand it," said Curdie, half to himself, half to Irene.

"Never mind," she returned. "Wait till we get out."

Curdie, utterly astonished that she had already got so far, and by a path he had known nothing of, thought it better to let her do as she pleased.

"At all events," he said again to himself, "I know nothing about the way, miner as I am; and she seems to think she does know something about it, though how she should, passes my comprehension. So she's just as likely to find her way as I am, and as she insists on taking the lead, I must follow. We can't be much worse off than we are, anyhow."

Curdie went on after her, flashing his torch about.

Reasoning thus, he followed her a few steps, and came out in another great cavern, across which Irene walked in a straight line, as confidently as if she knew every step of the way. Curdie went on after her, flashing his torch about, and trying to see something of what lay around them. Suddenly he started back a pace as the light fell upon something close by which Irene was passing. It was a platform of rock raised a few feet from the floor and covered with sheep skins, upon which lay two horrible figures asleep, at once recognized by Curdie as the king and queen of the goblins. He lowered his torch instantly lest the light should awake them. As he did so, it flashed upon his pickaxe, lying by the side of the queen, whose hand lay close by the handle of it.

"Stop one moment," he whispered. "Hold my torch, and don't let the light on their faces."

Irene shuddered when she saw the frightful creatures whom she had passed without observing them, but she did as he requested, and turning her back, held the torch low in front of her. Curdie drew his pickaxe carefully away, and as he did so, spied one of her feet, projecting from under the skins. The great clumsy granite shoe, exposed thus to his hand, was a temptation not to be resisted. He laid hold of it, and with cautious efforts, drew it off. The moment he succeeded, he saw to his astonishment that what he had sung in ignorance, to annoy the queen, was actually true: she had six horrible toes. Overjoyed at his success, and seeing by the huge bump in the sheep skins where the other foot was, he proceeded to lift them gently, for, if he could only succeed in carrying away the other shoe as well, he would be no more afraid of the goblins than of so many flies. But as he pulled at the second shoe, the queen gave a growl and sat up in bed. The same instant the king awoke also, and sat up beside her.

"Run, Irene!" cried Curdie, for though he was not now in the least afraid for himself, he was for the princess.

Irene looked once round, saw the fearful creatures awake, and like the wise princess she was, dashed the torch on the ground and extinguished it, crying out—

"Here, Curdie, take my hand."

He darted to her side, forgetting neither the queen's shoe nor his pickaxe, and caught hold of her hand, as she sped fearlessly where her thread guided her. They heard the queen give a great bellow; but they had a good start, for it would be some time before they could get torches lighted to pursue them. Just as they thought they saw a gleam behind them, the thread brought them to a very narrow opening, through which Irene crept easily, and Curdie with difficulty.

"Now," said Curdie; "I think we shall be safe."

"Of course we shall," returned Irene.

"Why do you think so?" asked Curdie.

"Because my grandmother is taking care of us."

"That's all nonsense," said Curdie. "I don't know what you mean."

"Then if you don't know what I mean, what right have you to call it nonsense?" asked the princess, a little offended.

"I beg your pardon, Irene," said Curdie; "I did not mean to vex you."

"Of course not," returned the princess. "But why do you think we shall be safe?"

"Because the king and queen are far too stout to get through that hole."

"There may be ways round," said the other.

"To be sure there might; we are not out of it yet," acknowledged Curdie.

"But what do you mean by the king and queen?" asked the princess. "I should never call such creatures as those a king and a queen."

"Their own people do, though," answered Curdie.

The princess asked more questions, and Curdie, as they walked leisurely along, gave her a full account, not only of the character and habits of the goblins, so far as he knew them, but of his own adventures with them, beginning from the very night after that in which he had met her and Lootie upon the mountain. When he had finished, he begged Irene to tell him how it was that she had come to his rescue. So Irene too had to tell a long story, which she did in rather a roundabout manner, interrupted by many questions concerning things she had not explained. But her tale, as he did not believe more than half of it, left everything as unaccountable to him as before, and he was nearly as much perplexed as to what he must think of the princess. He could not believe that she was deliberately telling stories, and the only conclusion he could come to was that Lootie had been playing the child tricks, inventing no end of lies to frighten her for her own purposes.

"But how ever did Lootie come to let you go into the mountain alone?" he asked.

"Lootie knows nothing about it. I left her fast asleep—at least I think so. I hope my grandmother won't let her get into trouble, for it wasn't her fault at all, as my grandmother very well knows."

"But how did you find your way to me?" persisted Curdie.

"I told you already," answered Irene;—"by keeping my finger upon my grandmother's thread, as I am doing now."

"You don't mean you've got the thread there?"

"Of course I do. I have told you so ten times already. I have hardly—except when I was removing the stones—taken my finger off it. There!" she added, guiding Curdie's hand to the thread, "you feel it yourself—don't you?"

"I feel nothing at all," replied Curdie.

"Then what can be the matter with your finger? I feel it perfectly. To be sure it is very thin, and in the sunlight looks just like the thread of a spider, though there are many of them twisted together to make it—but for all that I can't think why you shouldn't feel it as well as I do."

Curdie was too polite to say he did not believe there was any thread there at all. What he did say was—

"Well, I can make nothing of it."

"I can though, and you must be glad of that, for it will do for both of us."

"We're not out yet," said Curdie.

"We soon shall be," returned Irene confidently.

And now the thread went downward, and led Irene's hand to a hole in the floor of the cavern, whence came a sound of running water which they had been hearing for some time.

"It goes into the ground now, Curdie," she said, stopping.

He had been listening to another sound, which his practised ear had caught long ago, and which also had been growing louder. It was the noise the goblin miners made at their work, and they seemed to be at no great distance now. Irene heard it the moment she stopped.

"What is that noise?" she asked. "Do you know, Curdie?"

"Yes. It is the goblins digging and burrowing," he answered.

"And don't you know for what purpose they do it?"

"No; I haven't the least idea. Would you like to see them?" he asked, wishing to have another try after their secret.

"If my thread took me there, I shouldn't much mind; but I don't want to see them, and I can't leave my thread. It leads me down into the hole, and we had better go at once."

"Very well. Shall I go in first?" said Curdie.

"No; better not. You can't feel the thread," she answered, stepping down through a narrow break in the floor of the cavern. "Oh!" she cried, "I am in the water. It is running strong—but it is not deep, and there is just room to walk. Make haste, Curdie."

He tried, but the hole was too small for him to get in.

"Go on a little bit," he said, shouldering his pickaxe.

In a few moments he had cleared a large opening and followed her. They went on, down and down with the running water, Curdie getting more and more afraid it was leading them to some terrible gulf in the heart of the mountain. In one or two places he had to break away the rock to make room before even Irene could get through—at least without hurting herself. But at length they spied a glimmer of light, and in a minute more, they were almost blinded by the full sunlight into which they emerged. It was some little time before the princess could see well enough to discover that they stood in her own garden, close by the seat on which she and her king-papa had sat that afternoon. They had come out by the channel of the little stream. She danced and clapped her hands with delight.

"Now, Curdie!" she cried, "won't you believe what I told you about my grand-mother and her thread?"

For she had felt all the time that Curdie was not believing what she had told him.

"There!—don't you see it shining on before us?" she added.

"I don't see anything," persisted Curdie.

"Then you must believe without seeing," said the princess; "for you can't deny it has brought me out of the mountain."

"I can't deny we are out of the mountain, and I should be very ungrateful indeed to deny that you had brought me out of it."

"I couldn't have done it but for the thread," persisted Irene.

"That's the part I don't understand."

"Well, come along, and Lootie will get you something to eat. I am sure you must want it very much."

"Indeed I do. But my father and mother will be so anxious about me, I must make haste—first up the mountain to tell my mother, and then down into the mine again to acquaint my father."

"Very well, Curdie; but you can't get out without coming this way, and I will take you through the house, for that is nearest."

They met no one by the way, for indeed, as before, the people were here and there and everywhere searching for the princess. When they got in, Irene found that the thread, as she had half expected, went up the old staircase, and a new thought struck her. She turned to Curdie and said—

"My grandmother wants me. Do come up with me, and see her. Then you will know that I have been telling you the truth. Do come—to please me, Curdie. I can't bear you should think I say what is not true."

"I never doubted you believed what you said," returned Curdie. "I only thought you had some fancy in your head that was not correct."

"But do come, dear Curdie."

The little miner could not withstand this appeal, and though he felt shy in what seemed to him such a huge grand house, he yielded, and followed her up the stair.

THE OLD LADY AND CURDIE

Up the stair then they went, and the next and the next, and through the long rows of empty rooms, and up the little tower stairs, Irene growing happier and happier as she ascended. There was no answer when she knocked at length at the door of the workroom, nor could she hear any sound of the spinning-wheel, and once more her heart sank within her—but only for one moment, as she turned and knocked at the other door.

"Come in," answered the sweet voice of her grandmother, and Irene opened the door and entered, followed by Curdie.

"You darling!" cried the lady, who was seated by a fire of red roses mingled with white—"I've been waiting for you, and indeed getting a little anxious about you, and beginning to think whether I had not better go and fetch you myself."

As she spoke she took the little princess in her arms and placed her upon her lap. She was dressed in white now, and looking if possible more lovely than ever.

"I've brought Curdie, grandmother. He wouldn't believe what I told him, and so I've brought him."

"Yes—I see him. He is a good boy, Curdie, and a brave boy. Aren't you glad you have got him out?"

"Yes, grandmother. But it wasn't very good of him not to believe me when I was telling him the truth."

"People must believe what they can, and those who believe more must not be hard upon those who believe less. I doubt if you would have believed it all yourself if you hadn't seen some of it."

"Ah! yes, grandmother, I daresay. I'm sure you are right. But he'll believe now."

"I don't know that," replied her grandmother.

"Won't you, Curdie?" said Irene, looking round at him as she asked the question.

He was standing in the middle of the floor, staring, and looking strangely bewildered. This she thought came of his astonishment at the beauty of the lady.

410

"Make a bow to my grandmother, Curdie," she said.

"I don't see any grandmother," answered Curdie, rather gruffly.

"Don't see my grandmother when I'm sitting in her lap!" exclaimed the princess.

"No I don't," said Curdie, almost sulkily.

"Don't you see the lovely fire of roses—white ones amongst them this time?" asked Irene almost as bewildered as he.

"No I don't," answered Curdie, almost sulkily.

"Nor the blue bed? Nor the rose-colored counterpane? Nor the beautiful light, like the moon, hanging from the roof?"

"You're making game of me, your royal Highness; and after what we have come through together this day, I don't think it is kind of you," said Curdie, feeling very much hurt.

"Then what do you see?" asked Irene, who perceived at once that for her not to believe him was at least as bad as for him not to believe her.

"I see a big, bare garret-room—like the one in mother's cottage, only big enough to take the cottage itself in, and leave a good margin all round," answered Curdie.

"And what more do you see?"

"I see a tub, and a heap of musty straw, and a withered apple and a ray of sunlight coming through a hole in the middle of the roof, and shining on your head, and making all the place look a curious dusky brown. I think you had better drop it, princess, and go down to the nursery, like a good girl."

"But don't you hear my grandmother talking to me?" asked Irene, almost crying.

"No. I hear the cooing of a lot of pigeons. If you won't come down, I will go without you. I think that will be better anyhow, for I'm sure nobody who met us would believe a word we said to them. They would think we made it all up. I don't expect anybody but my own father and mother to believe me. They know I wouldn't tell a story."

"And yet you won't believe me, Curdie?" expostulated the princess, now fairly crying with vexation, and sorrow at the gulf between her and Curdie.

"No. I can't, and I can't help it," said Curdie, turning to leave the room.

"What shall I do, grandmother?" sobbed the princess, turning her face round upon the lady's bosom, and shaking with suppressed sobs.

"You must give him time," said her grandmother; "and you must be content not to be believed for a while. It is very hard to bear; but I have had to bear it, and shall have to bear it many a time yet. I will take care of what Curdie thinks of you in the end. You must let him go now."

"You are not coming, are you?" asked Curdie.

"No, Curdie; my grandmother says I must let you go. Turn to the right when you get to the bottom of all the stairs, and in that way you will arrive safely at the hall where the great door is."

"Oh! I don't doubt I can find my way—without you, princess, or your old grannie's thread either," said Curdie, quite rudely.

"Oh, Curdie! Curdie!"

"I wish I had gone home at once. I'm very much obliged to you, Irene, for getting me out of that hole, but I wish you hadn't made a fool of me afterward."

He said this as he opened the door, which he left open, and, without another word, went down the stairs. Irene listened with dismay to his departing footsteps. Then turning again to the lady—

"What does it all mean, grandmother?" she sobbed, and burst into fresh tears.

"It means, my love, that I did not mean to show myself. Curdie is not yet able to believe some things. Seeing is not believing—it is only seeing. You remember I told you that if Lootie were to see me, she would rub her eyes, forget the half she saw, and call the other half nonsense."

"Yes; but I should have thought Curdie—"

"You are right. Curdie is much farther on than Lootie, and you will see what will come of it. But in the meantime, you must be content, I say, to be misunderstood for a while. We are all very anxious to be understood, and it is very hard not to be. But there is one thing much more necessary."

"What is that, grandmother?"

"To understand other people."

"Yes, grandmother. I must be fair—for if I'm not fair to other people, I'm not worth being understood myself I see. So as Curdie can't help it, I will not be vexed with him, but just wait."

"There's my own dear child," said her grandmother, and pressed her close to her bosom.

"Why weren't you in your workroom, when we came up, grandmother?" asked Irene, after a few moments' silence.

"If I had been there, Curdie would have seen me well enough. But why should I be there rather than in this beautiful room?"

"I thought you would be spinning."

"I've nobody to spin for just at present. I never spin without knowing for whom I am spinning."

"That reminds me—there is one thing that puzzles me," said the princess: "how are you to get the thread out of the mountain again? Surely you won't have to make another for me! That would be such a trouble!"

The lady set her down, and rose, and went to the fire. Putting in her hand, she drew it out again, and held up the shining ball between her finger and thumb.

"I've got it now, you see," she said, coming back to the princess, "all ready for you when you want it."

Going to her cabinet, she laid it in the same drawer as before.

"And here is your ring," she added, taking it from the little finger of her left hand, and putting it on the forefinger of Irene's right hand.

"Oh, thank you, grandmother. I feel so safe now!"

"You are very tired, my child," the lady went on. "Your hands are hurt with the stones, and I have counted nine bruises on you. Just look what you are like."

And she held up to her a little mirror which she had brought from the cabinet. The princess burst into a merry laugh at the sight. She was so draggled with the stream, and dirty with creeping through narrow places, that if she had seen the reflection without knowing it was a reflection, she would have taken herself for some gypsy-child whose face was washed and hair combed about once in a month. The lady laughed too, and lifting her again upon her knee, took off her cloak and night-gown. Then she carried her to the side of the room. Irene wondered what she was going to do with her, but asked no questions—only starting a little when she found that she was going to lay her in the large silver bath; for as she looked into it, again she saw no bottom, but the stars shining miles away as it seemed in a great blue gulf. Her hands closed involuntarily on the beautiful arms that held her, and that was all.

The lady pressed her once more to her bosom, saying—

"Do not be afraid, my child."

"No, grandmother," answered the princess, with a little gasp; and the next instant she sank in the clear cool water.

When she opened her eyes, she saw nothing but a strange lovely blue over and beneath and all about her. The lady and the beautiful room had vanished from her sight, and she seemed utterly alone. But instead of being afraid, she felt more than happy—perfectly blissful. And from somewhere came the voice of the lady, singing a strange sweet song, of which she could distinguish every word; but of the sense she had only a feeling—no understanding. Nor could she remember a single line after it was gone. It vanished, like the poetry in a dream, as fast as it came. In after years, however, she would sometimes fancy that snatches of melody suddenly rising in her brain, must be little phrases and fragments of the air of that song; and the very fancy would make her happier, and abler to do her duty.

How long she lay in the water she did not know. It seemed a long time—not from weariness, but from pleasure. But at last she felt the beautiful hands lay hold of her, and through the gurgling waters she was lifted out into the lovely room. The lady carried her to the fire, and sat down with her in her lap, and dried her tenderly with the softest towel. It was so different from Lootie's drying! When the lady had done, she stooped to the fire, and drew from it her night-gown, as white as snow.

"How delicious!" exclaimed the princess. "It smells of all the roses in the world, I think."

When she stood up on the floor, she felt as if she had been made over again. Every bruise and all weariness were gone, and her hands were soft and whole as ever.

"Now I am going to put you to bed for a good sleep," said her grandmother.

"But what will Lootie be thinking? And what am I to say to her when she asks me where I have been?"

"Don't trouble yourself about it. You will find it all come right," said her grandmother, and laid her into the blue bed, under the rosy counterpane.

"There is just one thing more," said Irene. "I am a little anxious about Curdie. As I brought him into the house, I ought to have seen him safe on his way home."

"I took care of all that," answered the lady. "I told you to let him go, and therefore I was bound to look after him. Nobody saw him, and he is now eating a good dinner in his mother's cottage, far up the mountain."

"Then I will go to sleep," said Irene, and in a few minutes, she was fast asleep.

CURDIE AND HIS MOTHER

Curdie went up the mountain neither whistling nor singing, for he was vexed with Irene for taking him in, as he called it; and he was vexed with himself for having spoken to her so angrily. His mother gave a cry of joy when she saw him, and at once set about getting him something to eat, asking him questions all the time, which he did not answer so cheerfully as usual. When his meal was ready, she left him to eat it, and hurried to the mine to let his father know he was safe. When she came back, she found him fast asleep upon her bed; nor did he wake until the arrival home of his father in the evening.

"Now, Curdie," his mother said, as they sat at supper, "tell us the whole story from beginning to end, just as it all happened."

Curdie obeyed, and told everything to the point where they came out upon the lawn in the garden of the king's house.

"And what happened after that?" asked his mother. "You haven't told us all. You ought to be very happy at having got away from those demons, and instead of that, I never saw you so gloomy. There must be something more. Besides, you do not speak of that lovely child as I should like to hear you. She saved your life at the risk of her own, and yet somehow you don't seem to think much of it."

"She talked such nonsense!" answered Curdie, "and told me a pack of things that weren't a bit true; and I can't get over it."

"What were they?" asked his father. "Your mother may be able to throw some light upon them."

Then Curdie made a clean breast of it, and told them everything.

They all sat silent for some time, pondering the strange tale. At last Curdie's mother spoke.

"You confess, my boy," she said, "there is something about the whole affair you do not understand?"

"Yes, of course, mother," he answered, "I cannot understand how a child knowing nothing about the mountain, or even that I was shut up in it, should come all that way alone, straight to where I was; and then, after getting me out of the hole, lead me out of the mountain, too, where I should not have known a step of the way if it had been as light as in the open air."

"Then you have no right to say that what she told you was not true. She did take you out, and she must have had something to guide her: why not a thread as well as a rope, or anything else? There is something you cannot explain, and her explanation may be the right one."

"It's no explanation at all, mother; and I can't believe it."

"That may be only because you do not understand it. If you did, you would probably find it was an explanation, and believe it thoroughly. I don't blame you for not being able to believe it, but I do blame you for fancying such a child would try to deceive you. Why should she? Depend upon it, she told you all she knew. Until you had found a better way of accounting for it all, you might at least have been more sparing of your judgment."

"That is what something inside me has been saying all the time," said Curdie, hanging down his head. "But what do you make of the grandmother? That is what I can't get over. To take me up to an old garret, and try to persuade me against the sight of my own eyes that it was a beautiful room, with blue walls and silver stars, and no end of things in it, when there was nothing there but an old tub and a withered apple and a heap of straw and a sunbeam! It was too bad! She might have had some old woman there at least who could pass for her precious grandmother!"

"Didn't she speak as if she saw those other things herself, Curdie?"

"Yes. That's what bothers me. You would have thought she really meant and believed that she saw every one of the things she talked about. And not one of them there! It was too bad, I say."

"Perhaps some people can see things other people can't see, Curdie," said his mother very gravely. "I think I will tell you something I saw myself once—only perhaps you won't believe me either!"

"Oh, mother, mother!" cried Curdie, bursting into tears; "I don't deserve that, surely!"

"But what I am going to tell you is very strange," persisted his mother; "and if having heard it, you were to say I must have been dreaming, I don't know that I should have any right to be vexed with you, though I know at least that I was not asleep."

"Do tell me, mother. Perhaps it will help me to think better of the princess."

"That's why I am tempted to tell you," replied his mother. "But first, I may as well mention, that according to old whispers, there is something more than common about the king's family; and the queen was of the same blood, for they were cousins of some degree. There were strange stories told concerning them—all good stories—but strange, very strange. What they were I cannot tell, for I only remember the faces of my grandmother and my mother as they talked together about them. There was wonder and awe—not fear, in their eyes, and they whispered, and never spoke aloud. But what I saw myself, was this: Your father was going to work in the mine, one night, and I had been down with his supper. It was soon after we were married, and not very long before you were born. He came with me to the mouth of the mine, and left me to go home alone, for I knew the way almost as well as the floor of our own cottage. It was pretty dark, and in some parts of the road where the rocks overhung, nearly quite dark. But I got along perfectly well, never thinking of being afraid, until I reached a spot you know well enough, Curdie, where the path has to make a sharp turn out of the way of a great rock on the left-hand side. When I got there, I was suddenly surrounded by about half-a-dozen of the cobs, the first I had ever seen, although I had heard tell of them often enough. One of them blocked up the path, and they all began tormenting and teasing me in a way it makes me shudder to think of even now."

"If I had only been with you!" cried father and son in a breath.

The mother gave a funny little smile, and went on.

"They had some of their horrible creatures with them too, and I must confess I was dreadfully frightened. They had torn my clothes very much, and I was afraid they were going to tear myself to pieces, when suddenly a great white soft light shone upon me. I looked up. A broad ray, like a shining road, came down from a large globe of silvery light, not very high up, indeed not quite so high as the horizon—so it could not have been a new star or another moon or anything of that sort. The cobs dropped persecuting me, and looked dazed, and I thought they were going to run away, but presently they began again. The same moment, however, down the path from the globe of light came a bird, shining like silver in the sun. It gave a few rapid flaps first, and then, with its wings straight out, shot sliding down the slope of the light. It looked to me just like a white pigeon. But whatever it was, when the cobs caught sight of it coming straight down upon them, they took to their heels and scampered away across the mountain, leaving me safe, only much frightened. As soon as it had sent them off, the bird went gliding again up the light, and just at the moment it reached the globe, the light disappeared, just the same as if a shutter had been closed over a window, and I saw it no more. But I had no more trouble with the cobs that night, or at any time afterward."

"How strange!" exclaimed Curdie.

"Yes, it is strange; but I can't help believing it, whether you do or not," said his mother.

"It's exactly as your mother told it to me the very next morning," said his father.

"You don't think I'm doubting my own mother!" cried Curdie.

"There are other people in the world quite as well worth believing as your own mother," said his mother. "I don't know that she's so much the fitter to be believed that she happens to be your mother, Mr. Curdie. There are mothers far more likely to tell lies than that little girl I saw talking to the primroses a few weeks ago. If she were to lie I should begin to doubt my own word."

"But princesses have told lies as well as other people," said Curdie.

"Yes, but not princesses like that child. She's a good girl, I am certain, and that's more than being a princess. Depend upon it you will have to be sorry for behaving so to her, Curdie. You ought at least to have held your tongue."

"I am sorry now," answered Curdie.

"You ought to go and tell her so, then."

"I don't see how I could manage that. They wouldn't let a miner boy like me have a word with her alone; and I couldn't tell her before that nurse of hers. She'd be asking ever so many questions, and I don't know how many of them the little princess would like me to answer. She told me that Lootie didn't know anything about her coming to get me out of the mountain. I am certain she would have prevented her somehow if she had known it. But I may have a chance before long, and meantime I must try to do something for her. I think, father, I have got on the track at last."

"Have you, indeed, my boy?" said Peter. "I am sure you deserve some success; you have worked very hard for it. What have you found out?"

"It's difficult you know, father, inside the mountain, especially in the dark, and not knowing what turns you have taken, to tell the lie of things outside."

"Impossible, my boy, without a chart, or at least a compass," returned his father.

"Well, I think I have nearly discovered in what direction the cobs are mining. If I am right, I know something else that I can put to it, and then one and one will make three."

"They very often do, Curdie, as we miners ought to be well aware. Now tell us, my boy, what the two things are, and see whether we guess at the same third as you."

"I don't see what that has to do with the princess," interposed his mother.

"I will soon let you see that, mother. Perhaps you may think me foolish, but until I am sure there is nothing in my present fancy, I am more determined than ever to go on with my observations. Just as we came to the channel by which we got out, I heard the miners at work somewhere near—I think down below us. Now since I began to watch them, they have mined a good half mile, in a straight line; and so far as I am aware, they are working in no other part of the mountain. But I never could tell in what direction they were going. When we came out in the king's garden, however, I thought at once whether it was possible they were working toward the king's house; and what I want to do to-night is to make sure whether they are or not. I will take a light with me—"

"Oh, Curdie," cried his mother, "then they will see you."

"I'm no more afraid of them now than I was before," rejoined Curdie,—"now that I've got this precious shoe. They can't make another such in a hurry, and one bare foot will do for my purpose. Woman as she may be, I won't spare her next time. But I shall be careful with my light, for I don't want them to see me. I won't stick it in my hat."

"Go on, then, and tell us what you mean to do."

"I mean to take a bit of paper with me and a pencil, and go in at the mouth of the stream by which we came out. I shall mark on the paper as near as I can the angle of every turning I take until I find the cobs at work, and so get a good idea in what direction they are going. If it should prove to be nearly parallel with the stream, I shall know it is toward the king's house they are working."

"And what if you should. How much wiser will you be then?"

"Wait a minute, mother, dear. I told you that when I came upon the royal family in the cave, they were talking of their prince—Harelip, they called him—marrying a sun-woman—that means one of us—one with toes to her feet. Now in the speech one of them made that night at their great gathering, of which I heard only a part, he said that peace would be secured for a generation at least by the pledge the prince would hold for the good behavior of her relatives: that's what he said, and he must have meant the sun-woman the prince was to marry. I am quite sure the king is much too proud to wish his son to marry any but a princess, and much too knowing to fancy that his having a peasant woman for a wife would be of any material advantage to them."

"I see what you are driving at now," said his mother.

417

"But," said his father, "the king would dig the mountain to the plain before he would have his princess the wife of a cob, if he were ten times a prince."

"Yes; but they think so much of themselves!" said his mother. "Small creatures always do. The bantam is the proudest cock in my little yard."

"And I fancy," said Curdie, "if they once get her, they would tell the king they would kill her except, he consented to the marriage."

"They might say so," said his father, "but they wouldn't kill her; they would keep her alive for the sake of the hold it gave them over our king. Whatever he did to them, they would threaten to do the same to the princess."

"And they are bad enough to torment her just for their own amusement—I know that," said his mother.

"Anyhow, I will keep a watch on them, and see what they are up to," said Curdie. "It's too horrible to think of. I daren't let myself do it. But they sha'n't have her—at least if I can help it. So, mother dear—my clue is all right—will you get me a bit of paper and a pencil and a lump of pease-pudding, and I will set out at once. I saw a place where I can climb over the wall of the garden quite easily."

"You must mind and keep out of the way of the men on the watch," said his mother.

"That I will. I don't want them to know anything about it. They would spoil it all. The cobs would only try some other plan—they are such obstinate creatures! I shall take good care, mother. They won't kill and eat me either, if they should come upon me. So you needn't mind them."

His mother got him what he asked for, and Curdie set out. Close beside the door by which the princess left the garden for the mountain, stood a great rock, and by climbing it Curdie got over the wall. He tied his clue to a stone just inside the channel of the stream, and took his pickaxe with him. He had not gone far before he encountered a horrid creature coming toward the mouth. The spot was too narrow for two of almost any size or shape, and besides Curdie had no wish to let the creature pass. Not being able to use his pickaxe, however, he had a severe struggle with him, and it was only after receiving many bites, some of them bad, that he succeeded in killing him with his pocket knife. Having dragged him out, he made haste to get in again before another should stop up the way.

I need not follow him farther in this night's adventures. He returned to his breakfast, satisfied that the goblins were mining in the direction of the palace—on so low a level that their intention must, he thought, be to burrow under the walls of the king's house, and rise up inside it—in order, he fully believed, to lay hands on the little princess, and carry her off for a wife to their horrid Harelip.

IRENE BEHAVES LIKE A PRINCESS

When the princess awoke from the sweetest of sleeps, she found her nurse bending above her, the housekeeper looking over the nurse's shoulder, and the laundry-maid looking over the housekeeper's. The room was full of women-servants; and the gentlemen-at-arms, with a long column of men-servants behind them, were peeping, or trying to peep in at the door of the nursery.

"Are those horrid creatures gone?" asked the princess, remembering first what had terrified her in the morning.

"You naughty little princess!" cried Lootie.

Her face was very pale, with red streaks in it, and she looked as if she were going to shake her; but Irene said nothing—only waited to hear what should come next.

"How could you get under the clothes like that, and make us all fancy you were lost! And keep it up all day too! You are the most obstinate child! It's anything but fun to us, I can tell you!"

It was the only way the nurse could account for her disappearance.

"I didn't do that, Lootie," said Irene, very quietly.

"Don't tell stories!" cried her nurse quite rudely.

"I shall tell you nothing at all," said Irene.

"That's just as bad," said the nurse.

"Just as bad to say nothing at all as to tell stories!" exclaimed the princess. "I will ask my papa about that. He won't say so. And I don't think he will like you to say so."

"Tell me directly what you mean by it!" screamed the nurse, half wild with anger at the princess, and fright at the possible consequences to herself.

"When I tell you the truth, Lootie," said the princess, who somehow did not feel at all angry, "you say to me Don't tell stories: it would appear that I must tell stories before you will believe me."

419

"You are very rude, my dear princess," said the nurse.

"You are so rude, Lootie, that I will not speak to you again till you are sorry. Why should I, when I know you will not believe me?" returned the princess.

For she did know perfectly well that if she were to tell Lootie what she had been about, the more she went on to tell her, the less would she believe her.

"You are the most provoking child!" cried her nurse. "You deserve to be well punished for your wicked behavior."

"Please, Mrs. Housekeeper," said the princess, "will you take me to your room and keep me till my king-papa comes? I will ask him to come as soon as he can."

Every one stared at these words. Up to this moment, they had all regarded her as little more than a baby.

But the housekeeper was afraid of the nurse, and sought to patch matters up, saying—

"I am sure, princess, nursey did not mean to be rude to you."

"I do not think my papa would wish me to have a nurse who spoke to me as Lootie does. If she thinks I tell lies, she had better either say so to my papa, or go away. Sir Walter, will you take charge of me?"

"With the greatest of pleasure, princess," answered the captain of the gentlemen-at-arms, walking with his great stride into the room. The crowd of servants made eager way for him, and he bowed low before the little princess's bed. "I shall send my servant at once, on the fastest horse in the stable, to tell your king-papa that your royal Highness desires his presence. When you have chosen one of these under-servants to wait upon you, I shall order the room to be cleared."

"Thank you very much, Sir Walter," said the princess, and her eye glanced toward a rosy-cheeked girl who had lately come to the house as a scullery-maid.

But when Lootie saw the eyes of her dear princess going in search of another instead of her, she fell upon her knees by the bedside, and burst into a great cry of distress.

"I think, Sir Walter," said the princess, "I will keep Lootie. But I put myself under your care; and you need not trouble my king-papa until I speak to you again. Will you all please to go away? I am quite safe and well, and I did not hide myself for the sake either of amusing myself, or of troubling my people. Lootie, will you please to dress me?"

CURDIE COMES TO GRIEF

Everything was for some time quiet above ground. The king was still away in a distant part of his dominions. The men-at-arms kept watching about the house. They had been considerably astonished by finding at the foot of the rock in the garden, the hideous body of the goblin-creature killed by Curdie; but they came to the conclusion that it had been slain in the mines, and had crept out there to die; and except an occasional glimpse of a live one they saw nothing to cause alarm. Curdie kept watching in the mountain, and the goblins kept burrowing deeper into the earth. As long as they went deeper, there was, Curdie judged, no immediate danger.

To Irene, the summer was as full of pleasure as ever, and for a long time, although she often thought of her grandmother during the day, and often dreamed about her at night, she did not see her. The kids and the flowers were as much her delight as ever, and she made as much friendship with the miners' children she met on the mountain as Lootie would permit; but Lootie had very foolish notions concerning the dignity of a princess, not understanding that the truest princess is just the one who loves all her brothers and sisters best, and who is most able to do them good by being humble toward them. At the same time she was considerably altered for the better in her behavior to the princess. She could not help seeing that she was no longer a mere child, but wiser than her age would account for. She kept foolishly whispering to the servants, however—sometimes that the princess was not right in her mind, sometimes that she was too good to live, and other nonsense of the same sort.

All this time, Curdie had to be sorry, without a chance of confessing, that he had behaved so unkindly to the princess. This perhaps made him the more diligent in his endeavors to serve her. His mother and he often talked on the subject, and she comforted him, and told him she was sure he would some day have the opportunity he so much desired.

Here I should like to remark, for the sake of princes and princesses in general, that it is a low and contemptible thing to refuse to confess a fault, or even an error. If a true princess has done wrong, she is always uneasy until she has had an opportunity of throwing the wrongness away from her by saying, "I did it; and I wish I had not; and I am sorry for having done it." So you see there is some ground for supposing that Curdie was not a miner only, but a prince as well. Many such instances have been known in the world's history.

At length, however, he began to see signs of a change in the proceedings of the goblin excavators: they were going no deeper, but had commenced running on a level; and he watched them, therefore, more closely than ever. All at once, one night, coming to a slope of very hard rock, they began to ascend along the inclined plane of its surface. Having reached its top, they went again on a level for a night or two, after which they began to ascend once more, and kept on at a pretty steep angle. At length Curdie judged it time to transfer his observation to another quarter, and the next night, he did not go to the mine at all; but, leaving his pickaxe and clue at home, and taking only his usual lumps of bread and pease-pudding, went down the mountain to the king's house. He climbed over the wall, and remained in the garden the whole night, creeping on hands and knees from one spot to the other, and lying at full length with his ear to the ground, listening. But he heard nothing except the tread of the men-at-arms as they marched about, whose observation, as the night was cloudy and there was no moon, he had little difficulty in avoiding. For several following nights, he continued to haunt the garden and listen, but with no success.

At length, early one evening, whether it was that he had got careless of his own safety, or that the growing moon had become strong enough to expose him, his watching came to a sudden end. He was creeping from behind the rock where the stream ran out, for he had been listening all round it in the hope it might convey to his ear some indication of the whereabouts of the goblin miners, when just as he came into the moonlight on the lawn, a whizz in his ear and a blow upon his leg startled him. He instantly squatted in the hope of eluding further notice. But when he heard the sound of running feet, he jumped up to take the chance of escape by flight. He fell, however, with a keen shoot of pain, for the bolt of a cross-bow had wounded his leg, and the blood was now streaming from it. He was instantly laid hold of by two or three of the men-at-arms. It was useless to struggle, and he submitted in silence.

"It's a boy!" cried several of them together, in a tone of amazement. "I thought it was one of those demons."

"What are you about here?"

"Going to have a little rough usage apparently," said Curdie laughing, as the men shook him.

"Impertinence will do you no good. You have no business here in the king's grounds, and if you don't give a true account of yourself, you shall fare as a thief."

"Why, what else could he be?" said one.

"He might have been after a lost kid, you know," suggested another.

"I see no good in trying to excuse him. He has no business here anyhow."

"Let me go away then, if you please," said Curdie.

"But we don't please—not except you give a good account of yourself."

"I don't feel quite sure whether I can trust you," said Curdie.

"We are the king's own men-at-arms," said the captain, courteously, for he was taken with Curdie's appearance and courage.

"Well, I will tell you all about it—if you will promise to listen to me and not do anything rash."

"I call that cool!" said one of the party laughing. "He will tell us what mischief he was about, if we promise to do as pleases him."

"I was about no mischief," said Curdie.

But ere he could say more he turned faint, and fell senseless on the grass. Then first they discovered that the bolt they had shot, taking him for one of the goblin creatures, had wounded him.

They carried him into the house, and laid him down in the hall. The report spread that they had caught a robber, and the servants crowded in to see the villain. Amongst the rest came the nurse. The moment she saw him she exclaimed with indignation:

"I declare it's the same young rascal of a miner that was rude to me and the princess on the mountain. He actually wanted to kiss the princess. I took good care of that—the wretch! And he was prowling about—was he? Just like his impudence!"

The princess being fast asleep, and Curdie in a faint, she could misrepresent at her pleasure.

When he heard this, the captain, although he had considerable doubt of its truth, resolved to keep Curdie a prisoner until they could search into the affair. So, after they had brought him round a little, and attended to his wound, which was rather a bad one, they laid him, still exhausted from the loss of blood, upon a mattress in a disused room—one of those already so often mentioned—and locked the door, and left him. He passed a troubled night, and in the morning they found him talking wildly. In the evening he came to himself, but felt very weak, and his leg was exceedingly painful. Wondering where he was, and seeing one of the men-at-arms in the room, he began to question him, and soon recalled the events of the preceding night. As he was himself unable to watch any more, he told the soldier all he knew about the goblins, and begged him to tell his companions, and stir them up to watch with tenfold vigilance; but whether it was that he did not talk quite coherently, or that the whole thing appeared incredible, certainly the man concluded that Curdie was only raving still, and tried to coax him into holding his tongue. This, of course, annoyed Curdie dreadfully, who now felt in his turn what it was not to be believed, and the consequence was that his fever returned, and by the time when, at his persistent entreaties, the captain was called, there could be no doubt that he was raving. They did for him what they could, and promised everything he wanted, but with no intention of fulfilment. At last he went to sleep, and when at length his sleep grew profound and peaceful, they left him, locked the door again, and withdrew, intending to revisit him early in the morning.

THE GOBLIN MINERS

That same night several of the servants were having a chat together before going to bed.

"What can that noise be?" said one of the housemaids, who had been listening for a moment or two.

"I've heard it the last two nights," said the cook. "If there were any about the place, I should have taken it for rats, but my Tom keeps them far enough."

"I've heard though," said the scullery-maid, "that rats move about in great companies sometimes. There may be an army of them invading us. I heard the noises yesterday and to-day too."

"It'll be grand fun then for my Tom and Mrs. Housekeeper's Bob," said the cook. "They'll be friends for once in their lives, and fight on the same side. I'll engage Tom and Bob together will put to flight any number of rats."

"It seems to me," said the nurse, "that the noises are much too loud for that. I have heard them all day, and my princess has asked me several times what they could be. Sometimes they sound like distant thunder, and sometimes like the noises you hear in the mountain from those horrid miners underneath."

"I shouldn't wonder," said the cook, "if it was the miners after all. They may have come on some hole in the mountain through which the noises reach to us. They are always boring and blasting and breaking, you know."

As he spoke there came a great rolling rumble beneath them, and the house quivered. They all started up in affright, and rushing to the hall found the gentle-men-at-arms in consternation also. They had sent to wake their captain, who said from their description that it must have been an earthquake, an occurrence which, although very rare in that country, had taken place almost within the century; and then went to bed again, strange to say, and fell fast asleep without once thinking of Curdie, or associating the noises they had heard with what he had told them. He had not believed Curdie. If he had, he would at once have thought of what he had said, and would have taken precautions. As they heard nothing more, they concluded that Sir Walter was right, and that the danger was over for perhaps another hundred years. The fact, as discovered afterward, was that the goblins had, in working up a second sloping face of stone, arrived at a huge block which lay under the cellars of the house, within the line of the foundations. It was so round that when they succeeded, after hard work, in dislodging it without blasting, it rolled thundering down the slope with a bounding, jarring roll, which shook the foundations of the house. The goblins were themselves dismayed at the noise, for they knew, by careful spying and measuring, that they must now be very near, if not under, the king's house, and they feared giving an alarm. They, therefore, remained quiet for awhile, and when they began to work again, they no doubt thought themselves very fortunate in coming upon a vein of sand which filled a winding fissure in the rock on which the house was built. By scooping this away they soon came out in the king's wine-cellar.

No sooner did they and where they were, than they scurried back again, like rats into their holes, and running at full speed to the goblin palace, announced their success to the king and queen with shouts of triumph. In a moment the goblin royal family and the whole goblin people were on their way in hot haste to the king's house, each eager to have a share in the glory of carrying off that same night the Princess Irene.

The queen went stumping along in one shoe of stone and one of skin. This could not have been pleasant, and my readers may wonder that, with such skillful workmen about her, she had not yet replaced the shoe carried off by Curdie. As the king however had more than one ground of objection to her stone shoes, he no doubt took advantage of the discovery of her toes, and threatened to expose her deformity if she had another made. I presume he insisted on her being content with skin-shoes, and allowed her to wear the remaining granite one on the present occasion only because she was going out to war.

They soon arrived in the king's wine-cellar, and regardless of its huge vessels, of which they did not know the use, began as quietly as they could to force the door that led upward.

THE GOBLINS IN THE KING'S HOUSE

When Curdie fell asleep he began at once to dream. He thought he was ascending the mountain-side from the mouth of the mine, whistling and singing "Ring, dod, bang!" when he came upon a woman and child who were lost; and from that point he went on dreaming all that had happened since he met the princess and Lootie; how he had watched the goblins, and been taken by them, how he had been rescued by the princess; everything indeed, until he was wounded, and imprisoned by the men-at-arms. And now he thought he was lying wide awake where they had laid him, when suddenly he heard a great thundering sound.

"The cobs are coming!" he said. "They didn't believe a word I told them! The cobs'll be carrying off the princess from under their stupid noses! But they sha'n't! that they sha'n't!"

He jumped up, as he thought, and began to dress, but, to his dismay, found that he was still lying in bed.

"Now then I will!" he said. "Here goes! I am up now!"

But yet again he found himself snug in bed. Twenty times he tried, and twenty times he failed; for in fact he was not awake, only dreaming that he was. At length in an agony of despair, fancying he heard the goblins all over the house, he gave a great cry. Then there came, as he thought, a hand upon the lock of the door. It opened, and, looking up, he saw a lady with white hair, carrying a silver box in her hand, enter the room. She came to his bed, he thought, stroked his head and face with cool, soft hands, took the dressing from his leg, rubbed it with something that smelled like roses, and then waved her hands over him three times. At the last wave of her hands everything vanished, he felt himself sinking into the profoundest slumber, and remembered nothing more until he awoke in earnest.

The setting moon was throwing a feeble light through the casement, and the house was full of uproar. There was soft heavy multitudinous stamping, a clashing and clanging of weapons, the voices of men and the cries of women, mixed with a

426

hideous bellowing, which sounded victorious. The cobs were in the house! He sprang from his bed, hurried on some of his clothes, not forgetting his shoes, which were armed with nails; then spying an old hunting-knife, or short sword, hanging on the wall, he caught it, and rushed down the stairs, guided by the sounds of strife, which grew louder and louder.

When he reached the ground floor he found the whole place swarming. All the goblins of the mountain seemed gathered there. He rushed amongst them, shouting—

"One, two,
   Hit and hew!
   Three, four,
   Blast and bore!"

and with every rhyme he came down a great stamp upon a foot, cutting at the same time at their faces—executing, indeed, a sword dance of the wildest description. Away scattered the goblins in every direction,—into closets, upstairs, into chimneys, up on rafters, and down to the cellars. Curdie went on stamping and slashing and singing, but saw nothing of the people of the house until he came to the great hall, in which, the moment he entered it, arose a great goblin shout. The last of the men-at-arms, the captain himself, was on the floor, buried beneath a wallowing crowd of goblins. For, while each knight was busy defending himself as well as he could, by stabs in the thick bodies of the goblins, for he had soon found their heads all but invulnerable, the queen had attacked his legs and feet with her horrible granite shoe, and he was soon down; but the captain had got his back to the wall and stood out longer. The goblins would have torn them all to pieces, but the king had given orders to carry them away alive, and over each of them, in twelve groups, was standing a knot of goblins, while as many as could find room were sitting upon their prostrate bodies.

Curdie burst in dancing and gyrating and stamping and singing like a small incarnate whirlwind,

"Where 'tis all a hole, sir,
   Never can be holes:
   Why should their shoes have soles, sir,
   When they've got no souls?

"But she upon her foot, sir,
   Has a granite shoe:
   The strongest leather boot, sir,
   Six would soon be through."

The queen gave a howl of rage and dismay; and before she recovered her presence of mind, Curdie, having begun with the group nearest him, had eleven of the knights on their legs again.

"Stamp on their feet!" he cried, as each man rose, and in a few minutes the hall was nearly empty, the goblins running from it as fast as they could, howling and shrieking and limping, and cowering every now and then as they ran to cuddle their wounded feet in their hard hands, or to protect them from the frightful stamp-stamp of the armed men.

And now Curdie approached the group which, trusting in the queen and her shoe, kept their guard over the prostrate captain. The king sat on the captain's head, but the queen stood in front, like an infuriated cat, with her perpendicular eyes gleaming green, and her hair standing half up from her horrid head. Her heart was quaking, however, and she kept moving about her skin-shod foot with nervous apprehension. When Curdie was within a few paces, she rushed at him, made one tremendous stamp at his opposing foot, which happily he withdrew in time, and caught him round the waist, to dash him on the marble floor. But just as she caught him, he came down with all the weight of his iron-shod shoe upon her skin-shod foot, and with a hideous howl she dropped him, squatted on the floor and took her foot in both her hands. Meanwhile the rest rushed on the king and the bodyguard sent them flying, and lifted the prostrate captain, who was all but pressed to death. It was some moments before he recovered breath and consciousness.

"Where's the princess?" cried Curdie again and again.

No one knew, and off they all rushed in search of her.

Through every room in the house they went, but nowhere was she to be found. Neither was one of the servants to be seen. But Curdie, who had kept to the lower part of the house, which was now quiet enough, began to hear a confused sound as of a distant hubbub, and set out to find where it came from. The noise grew as his sharp ears guided him to a stair and so to the wine cellar. It was full of goblins, whom the butler was supplying with wine as fast as he could draw it.

While the queen and her party had encountered the men-at-arms, Harelip with another company had gone off to search the house. They captured every one they met, and when they could find no more, they hurried away to carry them safe to the caverns below. But when the butler, who was amongst them, found that their path lay through the wine cellar, he bethought himself of persuading them to taste the wine, and, as he had hoped, they no sooner tasted than they wanted more. The routed goblins, on their way below, joined them, and when Curdie entered, they were all, with outstretched hands, in which were vessels of every description, from sauce-pan to silver cup, pressing around the butler, who sat at the tap of a huge cask, filling and filling. Curdie cast one glance around the place before commencing his attack, and saw in the farthest corner a terrified group of the domestics unwatched, but cowering without courage to attempt their escape. Amongst them was the terror-stricken face of Lootie; but nowhere could he see the princess. Seized with the horrible conviction that Harelip had already carried her off, he rushed amongst them, unable for wrath to sing any more, but stamping and cutting with greater fury than ever.

"Stamp on their feet; stamp on their feet!" he shouted, and in a moment the goblins were disappearing through the hole in the floor like rats and mice.

They could not vanish so fast, however, but that many more goblin feet had to go limping back over the underground ways of the mountain that morning.

Presently however they were reinforced from above by the king and his party, with the redoubtable queen at their head. Finding Curdie again busy amongst her unfortunate subjects, she rushed at him once more with the rage of despair, and this time gave him a bad bruise on the foot. Then a regular stamping fight got up between them, Curdie with the point of his hunting knife keeping her from clasping her mighty arms about him, as he watched his opportunity of getting once more a good stamp at her skin-shod foot. But the queen was more wary as well as more agile than hitherto.

The rest meantime, finding their adversary thus matched for the moment, paused in their headlong hurry, and turned to the shivering group of women in the corner. As if determined to emulate his father and have a sun-woman of some sort to share his future throne, Harelip rushed at them, caught up Lootie and sped with her to the hole. She gave a great shriek, and Curdie heard her, and saw the plight she was in. Gathering all his strength, he gave the queen a sudden cut across the face with his weapon, came down, as she started back, with all his weight on the proper foot, and sprang to Lootie's rescue. The prince had two defenceless feet, and on both of them Curdie stamped just as he reached the hole. He dropped his burden and rolled shrieking into the earth. Curdie made one stab at him as he disappeared, caught hold of the senseless Lootie, and having dragged her back to the corner, there mounted guard over her, preparing once more to encounter the queen. Her face streaming with blood, and her eyes flashing green lightning through it, she came on with her mouth open and her teeth grinning like a tiger's, followed by the king and her bodyguard of the thickest goblins. But the same moment in rushed the captain and his men, and ran at them stamping furiously. They dared not encounter such an onset. Away they scurried, the queen foremost. Of course the right thing would have been to take the king and queen prisoners, and hold them hostages for the princess, but they were so anxious to find her that no one thought of detaining them until it was too late.

Having thus rescued the servants, they set about searching the house once more. None of them could give the least information concerning the princess. Lootie was almost silly with terror, and although scarcely able to walk, would not leave Curdie's side for a single moment. Again he allowed the others to search the rest of the house—where, except a dismayed goblin lurking here and there, they found no one—while he requested Lootie to take him to the princess's room. She was as submissive and obedient as if he had been the king. He found the bed-clothes tossed about, and most of them on the floor, while the princess's garments were scattered all over the room, which was in the greatest confusion. It was only too evident that the goblins had been there, and Curdie had no longer any doubt that she had been carried off at the very first of the inroad. With a pang of despair he saw how wrong they had been in not securing the king and queen and prince; but he determined to find and rescue the princess as she had found and rescued him, or meet the worst fate to which the goblins could doom him.

CURDIE'S GUIDE

Just as the consolation of this resolve dawned upon his mind, and he was turning away for the cellar to follow the goblins into their hole, something touched his hand. It was the slightest touch, and when he looked he could see nothing. Feeling and peering about in the gray of the dawn, his fingers came upon a tight thread. He looked again, and narrowly, but still could see nothing. It flashed upon him that this must be the princess's thread. Without saying a word, for he knew no one would believe him any more than he had believed the princess, he followed the thread with his finger, contrived to give Lootie the slip, and was soon out of the house, and on the mountain-side—surprised that, if the thread were indeed her grandmother's messenger, it should have led the princess, as he supposed it must, into the mountain, where she would be certain to meet the goblins rushing back enraged from their defeat. But he hurried on in the hope of overtaking her first. When he arrived however at the place where the path turned off for the mine, he found that the thread did not turn with it, but went straight up the mountain. Could it be that the thread was leading him home to his mother's cottage? Could the princess be there? He bounded up the mountain like one of its own goats, and before the sun was up, the thread had brought him indeed to his mother's door. There it vanished from his fingers, and he could not find it, search as he might.

The door was on the latch, and he entered. There sat his mother by the fire, and in her arms lay the princess fast asleep.

"Hush, Curdie!" said his mother. "Do not wake her. I'm so glad you're come! I thought the cobs must have got you again!"

With a heart full of delight, Curdie sat down at a corner of the hearth, on a stool opposite his mother's chair, and gazed at the princess, who slept as peacefully as if she had been in her own bed. All at once she opened her eyes and fixed them on him.

There sat his mother by the fire, and in her arms lay the princess fast asleep.

"Oh, Curdie! you're come!" she said quietly. "I thought you would!"

Curdie rose and stood before her with downcast eyes.

"Irene," he said, "I am very sorry I did not believe you."

"Oh, never mind, Curdie!" answered the princess. "You couldn't, you know. You do believe me now, don't you?"

"I can't help it now. I ought to have helped it before."

"Why can't you help it now?"

"Because, just as I was going into the mountain to look for you, I got hold of your thread, and it brought me here."

"Then you've come from my house, have you?"

"Yes, I have."

"I didn't know you were there."

"I've been there two or three days, I believe."

"And I never knew it!—Then perhaps you can tell me why my grandmother has brought me here? I can't think. Something woke me—I didn't know what, but I was frightened, and I felt for the thread, and there it was! I was more frightened still when it brought me out on the mountain, for I thought it was going to take me into it again, and I like the outside of it best. I supposed you were in trouble again, and I had to get you out, but it brought me here instead; and, oh, Curdie! your mother has been so kind to me—just like my own grandmother!"

Here Curdie's mother gave the princess a hug, and the princess turned and gave her a sweet smile, and held up her mouth to kiss her.

"Then you didn't see the cobs?" asked Curdie.

"No; I haven't been into the mountain, I told you, Curdie."

"But the cobs have been into your house—all over it—and into your bedroom making such a row!"

431

"What did they want there? It was very rude of them."

"They wanted you—to carry you off into the mountain with them, for a wife to their Prince Harelip."

"Oh, how dreadful!" cried the princess, shuddering.

"But you needn't be afraid, you know. Your grandmother takes care of you."

"Ah! you do believe in my grandmother then? I'm so glad! She made me think you would some day."

All at once Curdie remembered his dream, and was silent, thinking.

"But how did you come to be in my house, and me not know it?" asked the princess.

Then Curdie had to explain everything—how he had watched for her sake, how he had been wounded and shut up by the soldiers, how he heard the noises and could not rise, and how the beautiful old lady had come to him, and all that followed.

"Poor Curdie! to lie there hurt and ill, and me never to know it!" exclaimed the princess, stroking his rough hand. "I would not have hesitated to come and nurse you, if they had told me."

"I didn't see you were lame," said his mother.

"Am I, mother? Oh—yes—I suppose I ought to be. I declare I've never thought of it since I got up to go down amongst the cobs!"

"Let me see the wound," said his mother.

He pulled down his stocking—when behold, except a great scar, his leg was perfectly sound!

Curdie and his mother gazed in each other's eyes, full of wonder, but Irene called out—

"I thought so, Curdie! I was sure it wasn't a dream. I was sure my grandmother had been to see you.—Don't you smell the roses? It was my grandmother healed your leg, and sent you to help me."

"No, Princess Irene," said Curdie; "I wasn't good enough to be allowed to help you: I didn't believe you. Your grandmother took care of you without me."

"She sent you to help my people, anyhow. I wish my king-papa would come. I do want so to tell him how good you have been!"

"But," said the mother, "we are forgetting how frightened your people must be. —You must take the princess home at once, Curdie—or at least go and tell them where she is."

"Yes, mother. Only I'm dreadfully hungry. Do let me have some breakfast first. They ought to have listened to me, and then they wouldn't have been taken by surprise as they were."

"That is true, Curdie; but it is not for you to blame them much. You remember?"

"Yes, mother, I do. Only I must really have something to eat."

"You shall, my boy—as fast as I can get it," said his mother, rising and setting the princess on her chair.

But before his breakfast was ready, Curdie jumped up so suddenly as to startle both his companions.

"Mother, mother!" he cried, "I was forgetting. You must take the princess home yourself. I must go and wake my father."

Without a word of explanation, he rushed to the place where his father was sleeping. Having thoroughly roused him with what he told him, he darted out of the cottage.

MASON-WORK

He had all at once remembered the resolution of the goblins to carry out their second plan upon the failure of the first. No doubt they were already busy, and the mine was therefore in the greatest danger of being flooded and rendered useless—not to speak of the lives of the miners.

When he reached the mouth of the mine, after rousing all the miners within reach, he found his father and a good many more just entering. They all hurried to the gang by which he had found a way into the goblin country. There the foresight of Peter had already collected a great many blocks of stone, with cement, ready for building up the weak place—well enough known to the goblins. Although there was not room for more than two to be actually building at once, they managed, by setting all the rest to work in preparing the cement, and passing the stones, to finish in the course of the day a huge buttress filling the whole gang, and supported everywhere by the live rock. Before the hour when they usually dropped work, they were satisfied that the mine was secure.

They had heard goblin hammers and pickaxes busy all the time, and at length fancied they heard sounds of water they had never heard before. But that was otherwise accounted for when they left the mine; for they stepped out into a tremendous storm which was raging all over the mountain. The thunder was bellowing, and the lightning lancing out of a huge black cloud which lay above it, and hung down its edges of thick mist over its sides. The lightning was breaking out of the mountain, too, and flashing up into the cloud. From the state of the brooks, now swollen into raging torrents, it was evident that the storm had been storming all day.

The wind was blowing as if it would blow him off the mountain, but, anxious about his mother and the princess, Curdie darted up through the thick of the tempest. Even if they had not set out before the storm came on, he did not judge them safe, for, in such a storm even their poor little house was in danger. Indeed he soon found that but for a huge rock against which it was built, and which protected it both from the blasts and the waters, it must have been swept if it was not blown away; for the two torrents into which this rock parted the rush of water behind it united again in front of the cottage—two roaring and dangerous streams, which his mother and the princess could not possibly have passed. It was with great difficulty that he forced his way through one of them, and up to the door.

The moment his hand fell on the latch, through all the uproar of winds and waters came the joyous cry of the princess:—

"There's Curdie! Curdie! Curdie!"

She was sitting wrapped in blankets on the bed, his mother trying for the hundredth time to light the fire which had been drowned by the rain that came down the chimney. The clay floor was one mass of mud, and the whole place looked wretched. But the faces of the mother and the princess shone as if their troubles only made them merrier. Curdie laughed at sight of them.

"I never had such fun!" said the princess, her eyes twinkling and her pretty teeth shining. "How nice it must be to live in a cottage on the mountain!"

"It all depends on what kind your inside house is," said the mother.

"I know what you mean," said Irene. "That's the kind of thing my grandmother says."

By the time Peter returned, the storm was nearly over, but the streams were so fierce and so swollen, that it was not only out of the question for the princess to go down the mountain, but most dangerous for Peter even or Curdie to make the attempt in the gathering darkness.

"They will be dreadfully frightened about you," said Peter to the princess, "but we cannot help it. We must wait till the morning."

With Curdie's help, the fire was lighted at last, and the mother set about making their supper; and after supper they all told the princess stories till she grew sleepy. Then Curdie's mother laid her in Curdie's bed, which was in a tiny little garret-room. As soon as she was in bed, through a little window low down in the roof she caught sight of her grandmother's lamp shining far away beneath, and she gazed at the beautiful silvery globe until she fell fast asleep.

THE KING AND THE KISS

The next morning the sun rose so bright that Irene said the rain had washed his face and let the light out clean. The torrents were still roaring down the side of the mountain, but they were so much smaller as not to be dangerous in the daylight. After an early breakfast, Peter went to his work, and Curdie and his mother set out to take the princess home. They had difficulty in getting her dry across the streams, and Curdie had again and again to carry her, but at last they got safe on the broader part of the road, and walked gently down toward the king's house. And what should they see as they turned the last corner, but the last of the king's troop riding through the gate!

"Oh, Curdie!" cried Irene, clapping her hands right joyfully, "my king-papa is come."

The moment Curdie heard that, he caught her up in his arms, and set off at full speed, crying—

"Come on, mother dear! The king may break his heart before he knows that she is safe."

Irene clung round his neck, and he ran with her like a deer. When he entered the gate into the court, there sat the king on his horse, with all the people of the house about him, weeping and hanging their heads. The king was not weeping, but his face was white as a dead man's, and he looked as if the life had gone out of him. The men-at-arms he had brought with him, sat with horror-stricken faces, but eyes flashing with rage, waiting only for the word of the king to do something—they did not know what, and nobody knew what.

The day before the men-at-arms belonging to the house, as soon as they were satisfied the princess had been carried away, rushed after the goblins into the hole, but found that they had already so skilfully blockaded the narrowest part, not many feet below the cellar, that without miners and their tools they could do nothing. Not one of them knew where the mouth of the mine lay, and some of those

436

who had set out to find it had been overtaken by the storm and had not even yet returned. Poor Sir Walter was especially filled with shame, and almost entertained the hope that the king would order him to be decapitated, for the very thought of that sweet little face down amongst the goblins was unendurable.

When Curdie ran in at the gate with the princess in his arms, they were all so absorbed in their own misery and awed by the king's presence and grief, that no one observed his arrival. He went straight up to the king, where he sat on his horse.

"Papa! papa!" the princess cried, stretching out her arms to him; "here I am!"

The king started. The color rushed to his face. He gave an inarticulate cry. Curdie held up the princess, and the king bent down and took her from his arms. As he clasped her to his bosom, the big tears went dropping down his cheeks and his beard. And such a shout arose from all the bystanders, that the startled horses pranced and capered, and the armor rang and clattered, and the rocks of the mountain echoed back the noises. The princess greeted them all as she nestled in her father's bosom, and the king did not set her down until she had told them all the story. But she had more to tell about Curdie than about herself, and what she did tell about herself none of them could understand except the king and Curdie, who stood by the king's knee stroking the neck of the great white horse. And still as she told what Curdie had done, Sir Walter and others added to what she told, even Lootie joining in the praises of his courage and energy.

Curdie held his peace, looking quietly up in the king's face. And his mother stood on the outskirts of the crowd listening with delight, for her son's deeds were pleasant in her ears, until the princess caught sight of her.

"And there is his mother, king-papa!" she said. "See—there. She is such a nice mother, and has been so kind to me!"

They all parted asunder as the king made a sign to her to come forward. She obeyed, and he gave her his hand, but could not speak.

"And now, king-papa," the princess went on, "I must tell you another thing. One night long ago Curdie drove the goblins away and brought Lootie and me safe from the mountain. And I promised him a kiss when we got home, but Lootie wouldn't let me give it to him. I would not have you scold Lootie, but I want you to impress upon her that a princess must do as she promises."

"Indeed she must, my child—except it be wrong," said the king. "There, give Curdie a kiss."

And as he spoke he held her toward him.

The princess reached down, threw her arms round Curdie's neck, and kissed him on the mouth, saying—

"There, Curdie! There's the kiss I promised you!"

Then they all went into the house, and the cook rushed to the kitchen, and the servants to their work. Lootie dressed Irene in her shiningest clothes, and the king put off his armor, and put on purple and gold; and a messenger was sent for Peter and all the miners, and there was a great and grand feast, which continued long after the princess was put to bed.

THE SUBTERRANEAN WATERS

The king's harper, who always formed a part of his escort, was chanting a ballad which he made as he went on playing on his instrument—about the princess and the goblins, and the prowess of Curdie, when all at once he ceased, with his eyes on one of the doors of the hall. Thereupon the eyes of the king and his guests turned thitherward also. The next moment, through the open doorway came the princess Irene. She went straight up to her father, with her right hand stretched out a little sideways, and her forefinger, as her father and Curdie understood, feeling its way along the invisible thread. The king took her on his knee, and she said in his ear—

"King-papa, do you hear that noise?"

"I hear nothing," said the king.

"Listen," she said, holding up her forefinger.

The king listened, and a great stillness fell upon the company. Each man, seeing that the king listened, listened also, and the harper sat with his harp between his arms, and his fingers silent upon the strings.

"I do hear a noise," said the king at length—"a noise as of distant thunder. It is coming nearer and nearer. What can it be?"

They all heard it now, and each seemed ready to start to his feet as he listened. Yet all sat perfectly still. The noise came rapidly nearer.

"What can it be?" said the king again.

"I think it must be another storm coming over the mountain," said Sir Walter.

Then Curdie, who at the first word of the king had slipped from his seat, and laid his ear to the ground, rose up quickly, and approaching the king said, speaking very fast—

"Please your Majesty, I think I know what it is. I have no time to explain, for that might make it too late for some of us. Will your Majesty order that everybody leave the house as quickly as possible, and get up the mountain?"

The king, who was the wisest man in the kingdom, knew well there was a time

438

when things must be done, and questions left till afterward. He had faith in Curdie, and rose instantly, with Irene in his arms.

"Every man and woman follow me," he said, and strode out into the darkness.

Before he had reached the gate, the noise had grown to a great thundering roar, and the ground trembled beneath their feet, and before the last of them had crossed the court, out after them from the great hall-door came a huge rush of turbid water, and almost swept them away. But they got safe out of the gate and up the mountain, while the torrent went roaring down the road into the valley beneath.

Curdie had left the king and the princess to look after his mother, whom he and his father, one on each side, caught up when the stream overtook them and carried safe and dry.

When the king had got out of the way of the water, a little up the mountain, he stood with the princess in his arms, looking back with amazement on the issuing torrent, which glimmered fierce and foamy through the night. There Curdie rejoined them.

"Now, Curdie," said the king, "what does it mean! Is this what you expected?"

"It is, your Majesty," said Curdie; and proceeded to tell him about the second scheme of the goblins, who, fancying the miners of more importance to the upper world than they were, had resolved, if they should fail in carrying off the king's daughter, to flood the mine and drown the miners. Then he explained what the miners had done to prevent it. The goblins had, in pursuance of their design, let loose all the underground reservoirs and streams, expecting the water to run down into the mine, which was lower than their part of the mountain, for they had, as they supposed, not knowing of the solid wall close behind, broken a passage through into it. But the readiest outlet the water could find had turned out to be the tunnel they had made to the king's house, the possibility of which catastrophe had not occurred to the mind of the young miner until he placed his ear close to the floor of the hall.

What was then to be done? The house appeared in danger of falling, and every moment the torrent was increasing.

"We must set out at once," said the king. "But how to get at the horses!"

"Shall I see if we can manage that?" said Curdie.

"Do," said the king.

Curdie gathered the men-at-arms, and took them over the garden wall, and so to the stables. They found their horses in terror; the water was rising fast around them, and it was quite time they were got out. But there was no way to get them out, except by riding them through the stream, which was now pouring from the lower windows as well as the door. As one horse was quite enough for any man to manage through such a torrent, Curdie got on the king's white charger, and leading the way, brought them all in safety to the rising ground.

"Look, look, Curdie!" cried Irene, the moment that, having dismounted, he led the horse up to the king.

Curdie did look, and saw, high in the air, somewhere about the top of the king's house, a great globe of light, shining like the purest silver.

"Oh!" he cried in some consternation, "that is your grandmother's lamp! We must get her out. I will go and find her. The house may fall, you know."

"My grandmother is in no danger," said Irene, smiling.

"Here, Curdie, take the princess while I get on my horse," said the king.

Curdie took the princess again, and both turned their eyes to the globe of light. The same moment there shot from it a white bird, which, descending with outstretched wings, made one circle round the king and Curdie and the princess, and then glided up again. The light and the pigeon vanished together.

"Now, Curdie," said the princess, as he lifted her to her father's arms, "you see my grandmother knows all about it, and isn't frightened. I believe she could walk through that water and it wouldn't wet her a bit."

"But, my child," said the king, "you will be cold if you haven't something more on. Run, Curdie, my boy, and fetch anything you can lay your hands on, to keep the princess warm. We have a long ride before us."

Curdie was gone in a moment, and soon returned with a great rich fur, and the news that dead goblins were tossing about in the current through the house. They had been caught in their own snare; instead of the mine they had flooded their own country, whence they were now swept up drowned. Irene shuddered, but the king held her close to his bosom. Then he turned to Sir Walter, and said—

"Bring Curdie's father and mother here."

"I wish," said the king, when they stood before him, "to take your son with me. He shall enter my bodyguard at once, and wait further promotion."

Peter and his wife, overcome, only murmured almost inaudible thanks. But Curdie spoke aloud.

"Please your Majesty," he said, "I cannot leave my father and mother."

"That's right, Curdie!" cried the princess. "I wouldn't if I was you."

The king looked at the princess and then at Curdie with a glow of satisfaction on his countenance.

"I too think you are right, Curdie," he said, "and I will not ask you again. But I shall have a chance of doing something for you some time."

"Your Majesty has already allowed me to serve you," said Curdie.

"But, Curdie," said his mother, "why shouldn't you go with the king? We can get on very well without you."

"But I can't get on very well without you," said Curdie. "The king is very kind, but I could not be half the use to him that I am to you. Please your Majesty, if you wouldn't mind giving my mother a red petticoat! I should have got her one long ago, but for the goblins."

"As soon as we get home," said the king, "Irene and I will search out the warmest one to be found, and send it by one of the gentlemen."

"Yes, that we will, Curdie!" said the princess.

"And next summer we'll come back and see you wear it, Curdie's mother," she added. "Sha'n't we, king-papa?"

"Yes, my love; I hope so," said the king.

Then turning to the miners, he said——

"Will you do the best you can for my servants to-night? I hope they will be able to return to the house to-morrow."

The miners with one voice promised their hospitality.

Then the king commanded his servants to mind whatever Curdie should say to them, and after shaking hands with him and his father and mother, the king and the princess and all their company rode away down the side of the new stream which had already devoured half the road, into the starry night.

THE LAST CHAPTER

All the rest went up the mountain, and separated in groups to the homes of the miners. Curdie and his father and mother took Lootie with them. And the whole way, a light, of which all but Lootie understood the origin, shone upon their path. But when they looked round they could see nothing of the silvery globe.

For days and days the water continued to rush from the doors and windows of the king's house, and a few goblin bodies were swept out into the road.

Curdie saw that something must be done. He spoke to his father and the rest of the miners, and they at once proceeded to make another outlet for the waters. By setting all hands to the work, tunneling here and building there, they soon succeeded; and having also made a little tunnel to drain the water away from under the king's house, they were soon able to get into the wine cellar, where they found a multitude of dead goblins—among the rest the queen, with the skin-shoe gone, and the stone one fast to her ankle—for the water had swept away the barricade which prevented the men-at-arms from following the goblins, and had greatly widened the passage. They built it securely up, and then went back to their labors in the mine.

A good many of the goblins with their creatures escaped from the inundation out upon the mountain. But most of them soon left that part of the country, and most of those who remained grew milder in character, and indeed became very much like the Scotch Brownies. Their skulls became softer as well as their hearts, and their feet grew harder, and by degrees they became friendly with the inhabitants of the mountain and even with the miners. But the latter were merciless to any of the cobs' creatures that came their way, until at length they all but disappeared. Still—

"But, Mr. Author, we would rather hear more about the Princess and Curdie. We don't care about the goblins and their nasty creatures. They frighten us—rather."

441

"But you know if you once get rid of the goblins there is no fear of the princess or of Curdie."

"But we want to know more about them."

"Some day, perhaps, I may tell you the further history of both of them; how Curdie came to visit Irene's grandmother, and what she did for him; and how the princess and he met again after they were older—and how—But there! I don't mean to go any farther at present."

"Then you're leaving the story unfinished, Mr. Author!"

"Not more unfinished than a story ought to be, I hope. If you ever knew a story finished, all I can say is, I never did. Somehow, stories won't finish. I think I know why, but I won't say that either, now."

THE END

THE PRINCESS AND CURDIE

BY
GEORGE MACDONALD

ILLUSTRATIONS
BY
JAMES ALLEN

"Come in, Curdie," said the voice.

THE MOUNTAIN

Curdie was the son of Peter the miner. He lived with his father and mother in a cottage built on a mountain, and he worked with his father inside the mountain.

A mountain is a strange and awful thing. In old times, without knowing so much of their strangeness and awfulness as we do, people were yet more afraid of mountains. But then somehow they had not come to see how beautiful they are as well as awful, and they hated them,—and what people hate they must fear. Now that we have learned to look at them with admiration, perhaps we do not always feel quite awe enough of them. To me they are beautiful terrors.

I will try to tell you what they are. They are portions of the heart of the earth that have escaped from the dungeon down below, and rushed up and out. For the heart of the earth is a great wallowing mass, not of blood, as in the hearts of men and animals, but of glowing hot melted metals and stones. And as our hearts keep us alive, so that great lump of heat keeps the earth alive: it is a huge power of buried sunlight—that is what it is. Now think: out of that caldron, where all the bubbles would be as big as the Alps if it could get room for its boiling, certain bubbles have bubbled out and escaped—up and away, and there they stand in the cool, cold sky—mountains. Think of the change, and you will no more wonder that there should be something awful about the very look of a mountain: from the darkness—for where the light has nothing to shine upon, it is much the same as darkness—from the heat, from the endless tumult of boiling unrest—up, with a sudden heavenward shoot, into the wind, and the cold, and the starshine, and a cloak of snow that lies like ermine above the blue-green mail of the glaciers; and the great sun, their grandfather, up there in the sky; and their little old cold aunt, the moon, that comes wandering about the house at night; and everlasting stillness, except for the wind that turns the rocks and caverns into a roaring organ for the young archangels that are studying how to let out the pent-up praises of their hearts, and the molten music of the streams, rushing ever from the bosoms of the glaciers fresh-born. Think too of the change in their own substance—no longer molten and soft, heaving and glowing, but hard and shining and cold. Think of the creatures scampering over and burrowing in it, and the birds building their nests upon it, and the trees growing out of its sides, like hair to clothe it, and the lovely grass in the valleys, and the gracious flowers even at the very edge of its armour of ice, like the rich embroidery of the garment below, and the rivers galloping down the valleys in a tumult of white and green! And along with all these, think of the terrible precipices down which the traveller may fall and be lost, and the frightful gulfs of blue air cracked in the glaciers, and the dark profound lakes, covered like little arctic oceans with floating lumps of ice. All this outside the mountain! But the inside, who shall tell what lies there? Caverns of awfullest solitude, their walls miles thick, sparkling with ores of gold or silver, copper or iron, tin or mercury, studded perhaps with precious stones—perhaps a brook, with eyeless fish in it, running, running ceaseless, cold and babbling, through banks crusted with carbuncles and golden topazes, or over a gravel of which some of the stones are rubies and emeralds, perhaps diamonds and sapphires—who can tell?—and whoever can't tell is free to think—all waiting to flash, waiting for millions of ages—ever since the earth flew off from the sun, a great blot of fire, and began to cool. Then there are caverns full of water, numbing cold, fiercely hot—hotter than any boiling water. From some of these the water cannot get out, and from others it runs in channels as the blood in the body: little veins bring it down from the ice above into the great caverns of the mountain's heart, whence the arteries let it out again, gushing in pipes and clefts and ducts of all shapes and kinds, through and through its bulk, until it springs newborn to the light, and rushes down the mountain side in torrents, and down the valleys in rivers—down, down, rejoicing, to the mighty lungs of the world, that is the sea, where it is tossed in storms and cyclones, heaved up in billows, twisted in waterspouts, dashed to mist upon rocks, beaten by millions of tails, and breathed by millions of gills, whence at last, melted into vapour by the sun, it is lifted up pure into the air, and borne by the servant winds back to the mountain tops and the snow, the solid ice, and the molten stream.

Well, when the heart of the earth has thus come rushing up among her children, bringing with it gifts of all that she possesses, then straightway into it rush her children to see what they can find there. With pickaxe and spade and crowbar, with boring chisel and blasting powder, they force their way back: is it to search for what toys they may have left in their long-forgotten nurseries? Hence the mountains that lift their heads into the clear air, and are dotted over with the dwellings of men, are tunnelled and bored in the darkness of their bosoms by the dwellers in the houses which they hold up to the sun and air.

Curdie and his father were of these: their business was to bring to light hidden things; they sought silver in the rock and found it, and carried it out. Of the many other precious things in their mountain they knew little or nothing. Silver ore was what they were sent to find, and in darkness and danger they found it. But oh, how sweet was the air on the mountain face when they came out at sunset to go home to wife and mother! They did breathe deep then!

The mines belonged to the king of the country, and the miners were his servants, working under his overseers and officers. He was a real king—that is one who ruled for the good of his people, and not to please himself, and he wanted the silver not to buy rich things for himself, but to help him to govern the country, and pay the armies that defended it from certain troublesome neighbours, and the judges whom he set to portion out righteousness amongst the people, that so they might learn it themselves, and come to do without judges at all. Nothing that could be got from the heart of the earth could have been put to better purposes than the silver the king's miners got for him. There were people in the country who, when it came into their hands, degraded it by locking it up in a chest, and then it grew diseased and was called mammon, and bred all sorts of quarrels; but when first it left the king's hands it never made any but friends, and the air of the world kept it clean.

About a year before this story began, a series of very remarkable events had just ended. I will narrate as much of them as will serve to show the tops of the roots of my tree.

Upon the mountain, on one of its many claws, stood a grand old house, half farmhouse, half castle, belonging to the king; and there his only child, the Princess Irene, had been brought up till she was nearly nine years old, and would doubtless have continued much longer, but for the strange events to which I have referred.

At that time the hollow places of the mountain were inhabited by creatures called goblins, who for various reasons and in various ways made themselves troublesome to all, but to the little princess dangerous. Mainly by the watchful devotion and energy of Curdie, however, their designs had been utterly defeated, and made to recoil upon themselves to their own destruction, so that now there were very few of them left alive, and the miners did not believe there was a single goblin remaining in the whole inside of the mountain.

The king had been so pleased with the boy—then approaching thirteen years of age—that when he carried away his daughter he asked him to accompany them; but he was still better pleased with him when he found that he preferred staying with his father and mother. He was a right good king, and knew that the love of a boy who would not leave his father and mother to be made a great man, was worth ten thousand offers to die for his sake, and would prove so when the right time came. For his father and mother, they would have given him up without a grumble, for they were just as good as the king, and he and they perfectly understood each other; but in this matter, not seeing that he could do anything for the king which one of his numerous attendants could not do as well, Curdie felt that it was for him to decide. So the king took a kind farewell of them all and rode away, with his daughter on his horse before him.

A gloom fell upon the mountain and the miners when she was gone, and Curdie did not whistle for a whole week. As for his verses, there was no occasion to make any now. He had made them only to drive away the goblins, and they were all gone —a good riddance—only the princess was gone too! He would rather have had things as they were, except for the princess's sake. But whoever is diligent will soon be cheerful, and though the miners missed the household of the castle, they yet managed to get on without them.

Peter and his wife, however, were troubled with the fancy that they had stood in the way of their boy's good fortune. It would have been such a fine thing for him and them too, they thought, if he had ridden with the good king's train. How beautiful he looked, they said, when he rode the king's own horse through the river that the goblins had sent out of the hill! He might soon have been a captain, they did believe! The good, kind people did not reflect that the road to the next duty is the only straight one, or that, for their fancied good, we should never wish our children or friends to do what we would not do ourselves if we were in their position. We must accept righteous sacrifices as well as make them.

THE WHITE PIGEON

When in the winter they had had their supper and sat about the fire, or when in the summer they lay on the border of the rock-margined stream that ran through their little meadow, close by the door of their cottage, issuing from the far-up whiteness often folded in clouds, Curdie's mother would not seldom lead the conversation to one peculiar personage said and believed to have been much concerned in the late issue of events. That personage was the great-great-grandmother of the princess, of whom the princess had often talked, but whom neither Curdie nor his mother had ever seen. Curdie could indeed remember, although already it looked more like a dream than he could account for if it had really taken place, how the princess had once led him up many stairs to what she called a beautiful room in the top of the tower, where she went through all the—what should he call it?—the behaviour of presenting him to her grandmother, talking now to her and now to him, while all the time he saw nothing but a bare garret, a heap of musty straw, a sunbeam, and a withered apple. Lady, he would have declared before the king himself, young or old, there was none, except the princess herself, who was certainly vexed that he could not see what she at least believed she saw. And for his mother, she had once seen, long before Curdie was born, a certain mysterious light of the same description with one Irene spoke of, calling it her grandmother's moon; and Curdie himself had seen this same light, shining from above the castle, just as the king and princess were taking their leave. Since that time neither had seen or heard anything that could be supposed connected with her. Strangely enough, however, nobody had seen her go away. If she was such an old lady, she could hardly be supposed to have set out alone and on foot when all the house was asleep. Still, away she must have gone, for of course, if she was so powerful, she would always be about the princess to take care of her.

But as Curdie grew older, he doubted more and more whether Irene had not been talking of some dream she had taken for reality: he had heard it said that children could not always distinguish betwixt dreams and actual events. At the same time there was his mother's testimony: what was he to do with that? His mother, through whom he had learned everything, could hardly be imagined by her own dutiful son to have mistaken a dream for a fact of the waking world. So he rather shrunk from thinking about it, and the less he thought about it, the less he was inclined to believe it when he did think about it, and therefore, of course, the less inclined to talk about it to his father and mother; for although his father was one of those men who for one word they say think twenty thoughts, Curdie was well assured that he would rather doubt his own eyes than his wife's testimony. There were no others to whom he could have talked about it. The miners were a mingled company—some good, some not so good, some rather bad—none of them so bad or so good as they might have been; Curdie liked most of them, and was a favourite with all; but they knew very little about the upper world, and what might or might not take place there. They knew silver from copper ore; they understood the underground ways of things, and they could look very wise with their lanterns in their hands searching after this or that sign of ore, or for some mark to guide their way in the hollows of the earth; but as to great-great-grandmothers, they would have mocked him all the rest of his life for the absurdity of not being absolutely certain that the solemn belief of his father and mother was nothing but ridiculous nonsense. Why, to them the very word "great-great-grandmother" would have been a week's laughter! I am not sure that they were able quite to believe there were such persons as great-great-grandmothers; they had never seen one. They were not companions to give the best of help towards progress, and as Curdie grew, he grew at this time faster in body than in mind—with the usual consequence, that he was getting rather stupid—one of the chief signs of which was that he believed less and less of things he had never seen. At the same time I do not think he was ever so stupid as to imagine that this was a sign of superior faculty and strength of mind. Still, he was becoming more and more a miner, and less and less a man of the upper world where the wind blew. On his way to and from the mine he took less and less notice of bees and butterflies, moths and dragon-flies, the flowers and the brooks and the clouds. He was gradually changing into a commonplace man. There is this difference between the growth of some human beings and that of others: in the one case it is a continuous dying, in the other a continuous resurrection. One of the latter sort comes at length to know at once whether a thing is true the moment it comes before him; one of the former class grows more and more afraid of being taken in, so afraid of it that he takes himself in altogether, and comes at length to believe in nothing but his dinner: to be sure of a thing with him is to have it between his teeth. Curdie was not in a very good way then at that time. His father and mother had, it is true, no fault to find with him—and yet—and yet—neither of them was ready to sing when the thought of him came up. There must be something wrong when a mother catches herself sighing over the time when her boy was in petticoats, or the father looks sad when he thinks how he used to carry him on his shoulder. The boy should enclose and keep, as his life, the old child at the heart of him, and never let it go. He must still, to be a right man, be his mother's darling, and more, his father's pride, and more. The child is not meant to die, but to be for ever fresh-born.

Curdie had made himself a bow and some arrows, and was teaching himself to shoot with them. One evening in the early summer, as he was walking home from the mine with them in his hand, a light flashed across his eyes. He looked, and there was a snow-white pigeon settling on a rock in front of him, in the red light of the level sun. There it fell at once to work with one of its wings, in which a feather or two had got some sprays twisted, causing a certain roughness unpleasant to the fastidious creature of the air. It was indeed a lovely being, and Curdie thought how happy it must be flitting through the air with a flash—a live bolt of light. For a moment he became so one with the bird that he seemed to feel both its bill and its feathers, as the one adjusted the other to fly again, and his heart swelled with the pleasure of its involuntary sympathy. Another moment and it would have been aloft in the waves of rosy light—it was just bending its little legs to spring: that moment it fell on the path broken-winged and bleeding from Curdie's cruel arrow. With a gush of pride at his skill, and pleasure at its success, he ran to pick up his prey. I must say for him he picked it up gently—perhaps it was the beginning of his repentance. But when he had the white thing in his hands—its whiteness stained with another red than that of the sunset flood in which it had been revelling—ah God! who knows the joy of a bird, the ecstasy of a creature that has neither store-house nor barn!—when he held it, I say, in his victorious hands, the winged thing looked up in his face—and with such eyes! asking what was the matter, and where the red sun had gone, and the clouds, and the wind of its flight. Then they closed, but to open again presently, with the same questions in them. And so they closed and opened several times, but always when they opened, their look was fixed on his. It did not once flutter or try to get away; it only throbbed and bled and looked at him. Curdie's heart began to grow very large in his bosom. What could it mean? It was nothing but a pigeon, and why should he not kill a pigeon? But the fact was, that not till this very moment had he ever known what a pigeon was. A good many discoveries of a similar kind have to be made by most of us. Once more it opened its eyes—then closed them again, and its throbbing ceased. Curdie gave a sob: its last look reminded him of the princess—he did not know why. He remembered how hard he had laboured to set her beyond danger, and yet what dangers she had had to encounter for his sake: they had been saviours to each other—and what had he done now? He had stopped saving, and had begun killing! What had he been sent into the world for? Surely not to be a death to its joy and loveliness. He had done the thing that was contrary to gladness; he was a destroyer! He was not the Curdie he had been meant to be! Then the underground waters gushed from the boy's heart. And with the tears came the remembrance that a white pigeon, just before the princess went away with her father, came from somewhere—yes, from the grandmother's lamp, and flew round the king and Irene and himself, and then flew away: this might be that very pigeon! Horrible to think! And if it wasn't, yet it was a white pigeon, the same as it. And if she kept a great many pigeons—and white ones, as Irene had told him, then whose pigeon could he have killed but the grand old princess's? Suddenly everything round about him seemed against him. The red sunset stung him: the rocks frowned at him; the sweet wind that had been laving his face as he walked up the hill, dropped—as if he wasn't fit to be kissed any more. Was the whole world going to cast him out? Would he have to stand there for ever, not knowing what to do, with the dead pigeon in his hand? Things looked bad indeed. Was the whole world going to make a work about a pigeon—a white pigeon? The sun went down. Great clouds gathered over the west, and shortened the twilight. The wind gave a howl, and then lay down again. The clouds gathered thicker. Then came a rumbling. He thought it was thunder. It was a rock that fell inside the mountain. A goat ran past him down the hill, followed by a dog sent to fetch him home. He thought they were goblin creatures, and trembled. He used to despise them. And still he held the dead pigeon tenderly in his hand. It grew darker and darker. An evil something began to move in his heart. "What a fool I am!" he said to himself. Then he grew angry, and was just going to throw the bird from him and whistle, when a brightness shone all round him. He lifted his eyes, and saw a great globe of light—like silver at the hottest heat: he had once seen silver run from the furnace. It shone from somewhere above the roofs of the castle: it must be the great old princess's moon! How could she be there? Of course she was not there! He had asked the whole household, and nobody knew anything about her or her globe either. It couldn't be! And yet what did that signify, when there was the white globe shining, and here was the dead white bird in his hand? That moment the pigeon gave a little flutter. "It's not dead!" cried Curdie, almost with a shriek. The same instant he was running full speed towards the castle, never letting his heels down, lest he should shake the poor wounded bird.

"That moment the pigeon fell on the path, broken-winged and bleeding."

THE MISTRESS OF THE
SILVER MOON

When Curdie reached the castle, and ran into the little garden in front of it, there stood the door wide open. This was as he had hoped, for what could he have said if he had had to knock at it? Those whose business it is to open doors, so often mistake and shut them! But the woman now in charge often puzzled herself greatly to account for the strange fact that however often she shut the door, which, like the rest, she took a great deal of unnecessary trouble to do, she was certain, the next time she went to it, to find it open. I speak now of the great front door, of course: the back door she as persistently kept wide: if people could only go in by that, she said, she would then know what sort they were, and what they wanted. But she would neither have known what sort Curdie was, nor what he wanted, and would assuredly have denied him admittance, for she knew nothing of who was in the tower. So the front door was left open for him, and in he walked.

But where to go next he could not tell. It was not quite dark: a dull, shineless twilight filled the place. All he knew was that he must go up, and that proved enough for the present, for there he saw the great staircase rising before him. When he reached the top of it, he knew there must be more stairs yet, for he could not be near the top of the tower. Indeed by the situation of the stair, he must be a good way from the tower itself. But those who work well in the depths more easily understand the heights, for indeed in their true nature they are one and the same: mines are in mountains; and Curdie from knowing the ways of the king's mines, and being able to calculate his whereabouts in them, was now able to find his way about the king's house. He knew its outside perfectly, and now his business was to get his notion of the inside right with the outside. So he shut his eyes and made a picture of the outside of it in his mind. Then he came in at the door of the picture, and yet kept the picture before him all the time—for you can do that kind of thing in your mind,—and took every turn of the stair over again, always watching to remember, every time he turned his face, how the tower lay, and then when he came to himself at the top where he stood, he knew exactly where it was, and walked at once in the right direction. On his way, however, he came to another stair, and up that he went of course, watching still at every turn how the tower must lie. At the top of this stair was yet another—they were the stairs up which the princess ran when first, without knowing it, she was on her way to find her great-great-grandmother. At the top of the second stair he could go no farther, and must therefore set out again to find the tower, which, as it rose far above the rest of the house, must have the last of its stairs inside itself. Having watched every turn to the very last, he still knew quite well in what direction he must go to find it, so he left the stair and went down a passage that led, if not exactly towards it, yet nearer it. This passage was rather dark, for it was very long, with only one window at the end, and although there were doors on both sides of it, they were all shut. At the distant window glimmered the chill east, with a few feeble stars in it, and its light was dreary and old, growing brown, and looking as if it were thinking about the day that was just gone. Presently he turned into another passage, which also had a window at the end of it; and in at that window shone all that was left of the sunset, a few ashes, with here and there a little touch of warmth: it was nearly as sad as the east, only there was one difference—it was very plainly thinking of to-morrow. But at present Curdie had nothing to do with to-day or to-morrow; his business was with the bird, and the tower where dwelt the grand old princess to whom it belonged. So he kept on his way, still eastward, and came to yet another passage, which brought him to a door. He was afraid to open it without first knocking. He knocked, but heard no answer. He was answered nevertheless; for the door gently opened, and there was a narrow stair—and so steep that, big lad as he was, he too, like the Princess Irene before him, found his hands needful for the climbing. And it was a long climb, but he reached the top at last—a little landing, with a door in front and one on each side. Which should he knock at?

As he hesitated, he heard the noise of a spinning-wheel. He knew it at once, because his mother's spinning-wheel had been his governess long ago, and still taught him things. It was the spinning-wheel that first taught him to make verses, and to sing, and to think whether all was right inside him; or at least it had helped him in all these things. Hence it was no wonder he should know a spinning-wheel when he heard it sing—even although as the bird of paradise to other birds was the song of that wheel to the song of his mother's.

He stood listening so entranced that he forgot to knock, and the wheel went on and on, spinning in his brain songs and tales and rhymes, till he was almost asleep as well as dreaming, for sleep does not always come first. But suddenly came the thought of the poor bird, which had been lying motionless in his hand all the time, and that woke him up, and at once he knocked.

"Come in, Curdie," said a voice.

Curdie shook. It was getting rather awful. The heart that had never much heeded an army of goblins, trembled at the soft word of invitation. But then there was the red-spotted white thing in his hand! He dared not hesitate, though. Gently he opened the door through which the sound came, and what did he see? Nothing at first—except indeed a great sloping shaft of moonlight, that came in at a high window, and rested on the floor. He stood and stared at it, forgetting to shut the door.

"Why don't you come in, Curdie?" said the voice. "Did you never see moonlight before?"

"Never without a moon," answered Curdie, in a trembling tone, but gathering courage.

"Certainly not," returned the voice, which was thin and quavering: "I never saw moonlight without a moon."

"But there's no moon outside," said Curdie.

"Ah! but you're inside now," said the voice.

The answer did not satisfy Curdie; but the voice went on.

"There are more moons than you know of, Curdie. Where there is one sun there are many moons—and of many sorts. Come in and look out of my window, and you will soon satisfy yourself that there is a moon looking in at it."

The gentleness of the voice made Curdie remember his manners. He shut the door, and drew a step or two nearer to the moonlight.

All the time the sound of the spinning had been going on and on, and Curdie now caught sight of the wheel. Oh, it was such a thin, delicate thing—reminding him of a spider's web in a hedge! It stood in the middle of the moonlight, and it seemed as if the moonlight had nearly melted it away. A step nearer, he saw, with a start, two little hands at work with it. And then at last, in the shadow on the other side of the moonlight which came like a river between, he saw the form to which the hands belonged: a small, withered creature, so old that no age would have seemed too great to write under her picture, seated on a stool beyond the spinning-wheel, which looked very large beside her, but, as I said, very thin, like a long-legged spider holding up its own web, which was the round wheel itself. She sat crumpled together, a filmy thing that it seemed a puff would blow away, more like the body of a fly the big spider had sucked empty and left hanging in his web, than anything else I can think of.

When Curdie saw her, he stood still again, a good deal in wonder, a very little in reverence, a little in doubt, and, I must add, a little in amusement at the odd look of the old marvel. Her grey hair mixed with the moonlight so that he could not tell where the one began and the other ended. Her crooked back bent forward over her chest, her shoulders nearly swallowed up her head between them, and her two little hands were just like the grey claws of a hen, scratching at the thread, which to Curdie was of course invisible across the moonlight. Indeed Curdie laughed within himself, just a little, at the sight; and when he thought of how the princess used to talk about her huge great old grandmother, he laughed more. But that moment the little lady leaned forward into the moonlight, and Curdie caught a glimpse of her eyes, and all the laugh went out of him.

"What do you come here for, Curdie?" she said, as gently as before.

Then Curdie remembered that he stood there as a culprit, and worst of all, as one who had his confession yet to make. There was no time to hesitate over it.

"Oh, ma'am! see here," he said, and advanced a step or two, holding out the dead pigeon.

"What have you got there?" she asked.

Again Curdie advanced a few steps, and held out his hand with the pigeon, that she might see what it was, into the moonlight. The moment the rays fell upon it the pigeon gave a faint flutter. The old lady put out her old hands and took it, and held it to her bosom, and rocked it, murmuring over it as if it were a sick baby.

When Curdie saw how distressed she was he grew sorrier still, and said,—

"I didn't mean to do any harm, ma'am. I didn't think of its being yours."

"Ah, Curdie! if it weren't mine, what would become of it now?" she returned. "You say you didn't mean any harm: did you mean any good, Curdie?"

"No," answered Curdie.

"Remember, then, that whoever does not mean good is always in danger of harm. But I try to give everybody fair play; and those that are in the wrong are in far more need of it always than those who are in the right: they can afford to do without it. Therefore I say for you that when you shot that arrow you did not know what a pigeon is. Now that you do know, you are sorry. It is very dangerous to do things you don't know about."

"But, please, ma'am—I don't mean to be rude or to contradict you," said Curdie, "but if a body was never to do anything but what he knew to be good, he would have to live half his time doing nothing."

"There you are much mistaken," said the old quavering voice. "How little you must have thought! Why, you don't seem even to know the good of the things you are constantly doing. Now don't mistake me. I don't mean you are good for doing them. It is a good thing to eat your breakfast, but you don't fancy it's very good of you to do it. The thing is good—not you."

Curdie laughed.

"There are a great many more good things than bad things to do. Now tell me what bad thing you have done to-day besides this sore hurt to my little white friend."

While she talked Curdie had sunk into a sort of reverie, in which he hardly knew whether it was the old lady or his own heart that spoke. And when she asked him that question, he was at first much inclined to consider himself a very good fellow on the whole. "I really don't think I did anything else that was very bad all day," he said to himself. But at the same time he could not honestly feel that he was worth standing up for. All at once a light seemed to break in upon his mind, and he woke up, and there was the withered little atomy of the old lady on the other side of the moonlight, and there was the spinning-wheel singing on and on in the middle of it!

"I know now, ma'am; I understand now," he said. "Thank you, ma'am for spinning it into me with your wheel. I see now that I have been doing wrong the whole day, and such a many days besides! Indeed, I don't know when I ever did right, and yet it seems as if I had done right some time and had forgotten how. When I killed your bird I did not know I was doing wrong, just because I was always doing wrong, and the wrong had soaked all through me."

"What wrong were you doing all day, Curdie? It is better to come to the point, you know," said the old lady, and her voice was gentler even than before.

"I was doing the wrong of never wanting or trying to be better. And now I see that I have been letting things go as they would for a long time. Whatever came into my head I did, and whatever didn't come into my head I didn't do. I never sent anything away, and never looked out for anything to come. I haven't been attending to my mother—or my father either. And now I think of it, I know I have often seen them looking troubled, and I have never asked them what was the matter. And now I see too that I did not ask because I suspected it had something to do with me and my behaviour, and didn't want to hear the truth. And I know I have been grumbling at my work, and doing a hundred other things that are wrong."

"You have got it, Curdie," said the old lady, in a voice that sounded almost as if she had been crying. "When people don't care to be better they must be doing everything wrong. I am so glad you shot my bird!"

"Ma'am!" exclaimed Curdie. "How can you be?"

"Because it has brought you to see what sort you were when you did it, and what sort you will grow to be again, only worse, if you don't mind. Now that you are sorry, my poor bird will be better. Look up, my dovey."

The pigeon gave a flutter, and spread out one of its red-spotted wings across the old woman's bosom.

"I will mend the little angel," she said, "and in a week or two it will be flying again. So you may ease your heart about the pigeon."

"Oh, thank you! thank you!" cried Curdie. "I don't know how to thank you."

"Then I will tell you. There is only one way I care for. Do better, and grow better, and be better. And never kill anything without a good reason for it."

"Ma'am, I will go and fetch my bow and arrows, and you shall burn them yourself."

"I have no fire that would burn your bow and arrows, Curdie."

"Then I promise you to burn them all under my mother's porridge-pot to-morrow morning."

"No, no, Curdie. Keep them, and practise with them every day, and grow a good shot. There are plenty of bad things that want killing, and a day will come when they will prove useful. But I must see first whether you will do as I tell you."

"That I will!" said Curdie. "What is it, ma'am?"

"Only something not to do," answered the old lady; "if you should hear any one speak about me, never to laugh or make fun of me."

"Oh, ma'am!" exclaimed Curdie, shocked that she should think such a request needful.

"Stop, stop," she went on. "People hereabout sometimes tell very odd and in fact ridiculous stories of an old woman who watches what is going on, and occasionally interferes. They mean me, though what they say is often great nonsense. Now what I want of you is not to laugh, or side with them in any way; because they will take that to mean that you don't believe there is any such person a bit more than they do. Now that would not be the case—would it, Curdie?"

"No indeed, ma'am. I've seen you."

The old woman smiled very oddly.

"Yes, you've seen me," she said. "But mind," she continued, "I don't want you to say anything—only to hold your tongue, and not seem to side with them."

"That will be easy," said Curdie, "now that I've seen you with my very own eyes, ma'am."

"Not so easy as you think, perhaps," said the old lady, with another curious smile. "I want to be your friend," she added after a little pause, "but I don't quite know yet whether you will let me."

"Indeed I will, ma'am," said Curdie.

"That is for me to find out," she rejoined, with yet another strange smile. "In the meantime all I can say is, come to me again when you find yourself in any trouble, and I will see what I can do for you—only the canning depends on yourself. I am greatly pleased with you for bringing me my pigeon, doing your best to set right what you had set wrong."

As she spoke she held out her hand to him, and when he took it she made use of his to help herself up from her stool, and—when or how it came about, Curdie could not tell—the same instant she stood before him a tall, strong woman—plainly very old, but as grand as she was old, and only rather severe-looking. Every trace of the decrepitude and witheredness she showed as she hovered like a film about her wheel, had vanished. Her hair was very white, but it hung about her head in great plenty, and shone like silver in the moonlight. Straight as a pillar she stood before the astonished boy, and the wounded bird had now spread out both its wings across her bosom, like some great mystical ornament of frosted silver.

"Oh, now I can never forget you!" cried Curdie. "I see now what you really are!"

"The wounded bird now spread out both its wings across her bosom."

"Did I not tell you the truth when I sat at my wheel?" said the old lady.

"Yes, ma'am," answered Curdie.

"I can do no more than tell you the truth now," she rejoined. "It is a bad thing indeed to forget one who has told us the truth. Now go."

Curdie obeyed, and took a few steps towards the door.

"Please, ma'am,"—"what am I to call you?" he was going to say; but when he turned to speak, he saw nobody. Whether she was there or not he could not tell, however, for the moonlight had vanished, and the room was utterly dark. A great fear, such as he had never before known, came upon him, and almost overwhelmed him. He groped his way to the door, and crawled down the stair—in doubt and anxiety as to how he should find his way out of the house in the dark. And the stair seemed ever so much longer than when he came up. Nor was that any wonder, for down and down he went, until at length his foot struck on a door, and when he rose and opened it, he found himself under the starry, moonless sky at the foot of the tower. He soon discovered the way out of the garden, with which he had some acquaintance already, and in a few minutes was climbing the mountain with a solemn and cheerful heart. It was rather dark, but he knew the way well. As he passed the rock from which the poor pigeon fell wounded with his arrow, a great joy filled his heart at the thought that he was delivered from the blood of the little bird, and he ran the next hundred yards at full speed up the hill. Some dark shadows passed him: he did not even care to think what they were, but let them run. When he reached home, he found his father and mother waiting supper for him.

CURDIE'S FATHER AND MOTHER

The eyes of the fathers and mothers are quick to read their children's looks, and when Curdie entered the cottage, his parents saw at once that something unusual had taken place. When he said to his mother, "I beg your pardon for being so late," there was something in the tone beyond the politeness that went to her heart, for it seemed to come from the place where all lovely things were born before they began to grow in this world. When he set his father's chair to the table, an attention he had not shown him for a long time, Peter thanked him with more gratitude than the boy had ever yet felt in all his life. It was a small thing to do for the man who had been serving him since ever he was born, but I suspect there is nothing a man can be so grateful for as that to which he has the most right. There was a change upon Curdie, and father and mother felt there must be something to account for it, and therefore were pretty sure he had something to tell them. For when a child's heart is all right, it is not likely he will want to keep anything from his parents. But the story of the evening was too solemn for Curdie to come out with all at once. He must wait until they had had their porridge, and the affairs of this world were over for the day. But when they were seated on the grassy bank of the brook that went so sweetly blundering over the great stones of its rocky channel, for the whole meadow lay on the top of a huge rock, then he felt that the right hour had come for sharing with them the wonderful things that had come to him. It was perhaps the loveliest of all hours in the year. The summer was young and soft, and this was the warmest evening they had yet had—dusky, dark even below, while above the stars were bright and large and sharp in the blackest blue sky. The night came close around them, clasping them in one universal arm of love, and although it neither spoke nor smiled, seemed all eye and ear, seemed to see and hear and know everything they said and did. It is a way the night has sometimes, and there is a reason for it. The only sound was that of the brook, for there was no wind, and no trees for it to make its music upon if there had been, for the cottage was high up on the mountain, on a great shoulder of stone where trees would not grow. There, to the accompaniment of the water, as it hurried down to the valley and the sea, talking busily of a thousand true things which it could not understand, Curdie told his tale, outside and in, to his father and mother. What a world had slipped in between the mouth of the mine and his mother's cottage! Neither of them said a word until he had ended.

"Now what am I to make of it, mother? It's so strange!" he said, and stopped.

"It's easy enough to see what Curdie has got to make of it—isn't it, Peter?" said the good woman, turning her face towards all she could see of her husband's.

"It seems so to me," answered Peter, with a smile, which only the night saw, but his wife felt in the tone of his words. They were the happiest couple in that country, because they always understood each other, and that was because they always meant the same thing, and that was because they always loved what was fair and true and right better—not than anything else, but than everything else put together.

"Then will you tell Curdie?" said she.

"You can talk best, Joan," said he. "You tell him, and I will listen—and learn how to say what I think," he added, laughing.

"I," said Curdie, "don't know what to think."

"It does not matter so much," said his mother. "If only you know what to make of a thing, you'll know soon enough what to think of it. Now I needn't tell you, surely, Curdie, what you've got to do with this?"

"I suppose you mean, mother," answered Curdie, "that I must do as the old lady told me?"

"That is what I mean: what else could it be? Am I not right, Peter?"

"Quite right, Joan," answered Peter, "so far as my judgment goes. It is a very strange story, but you see the question is not about believing it, for Curdie knows what came to him."

"And you remember, Curdie," said his mother, "that when the princess took you up that tower once before, and there talked to her great-great-grandmother, you came home quite angry with her, and said there was nothing in the place but an old tub, a heap of straw—oh, I remember your inventory quite well!—an old tub, a heap of straw, a withered apple, and a sunbeam. According to your eyes, that was all there was in the great old musty garret. But now you have had a glimpse of the old princess herself!"

"Yes, mother, I did see her—or if I didn't,—" said Curdie very thoughtfully—then began again. "The hardest thing to believe, though I saw it with my own eyes, was when the thin, filmy creature, that seemed almost to float about in the moon-light like a bit of the silver paper they put over pictures, or like a handkerchief made of spider-threads, took my hand, and rose up. She was taller and stronger than you, mother, ever so much!—at least, she looked so."

"And most certainly was so, Curdie, if she looked so," said Mrs. Peterson.

"Well, I confess," returned her son, "that one thing, if there were no other, would make me doubt whether I was not dreaming after all, for as wide awake as I fancied myself to be."

"Of course," answered his mother, "it is not for me to say whether you were dreaming or not if you are doubtful of it yourself; but it doesn't make me think I am dreaming when in the summer I hold in my hand the bunch of sweet-peas that make my heart glad with their colour and scent, and remember the dry, withered-

461

looking little thing I dibbled into the hole in the same spot in the spring. I only think how wonderful and lovely it all is. It seems just as full of reason as it is of wonder. How it is done I can't tell, only there it is! And there is this in it too, Curdie —of which you would not be so ready to think—that when you come home to your father and mother, and they find you behaving more like a dear good son than you have behaved for a long time, they at least are not likely to think you were only dreaming."

"Still," said Curdie, looking a little ashamed, "I might have dreamed my duty."

"Then dream often, my son; for there must then be more truth in your dreams than in your waking thoughts. But however any of these things may be, this one point remains certain: there can be no harm in doing as she told you. And, indeed, until you are sure there is no such person, you are bound to do it, for you promised."

"It seems to me," said his father, "that if a lady comes to you in a dream, Curdie, and tells you not to talk about her when you wake, the least you can do is to hold your tongue."

"True, father!—Yes, mother, I'll do it," said Curdie.

Then they went to bed, and sleep, which is the night of the soul, next took them in its arms and made them well.

THE MINERS

It much increased Curdie's feeling of the strangeness of the whole affair, that, the next morning, when they were at work in the mine, the party of which he and his father were two, just as if they had known what had happened to him the night before, began talking about all manner of wonderful tales that were abroad in the country, chiefly of course those connected with the mines, and the mountains in which they lay. Their wives and mothers and grandmothers were their chief authorities. For when they sat by their firesides they heard their wives telling their children the selfsame tales, with little differences, and here and there one they had not heard before, which they had heard their mothers and grandmothers tell in one or other of the same cottages. At length they came to speak of a certain strange being they called Old Mother Wotherwop. Some said their wives had seen her. It appeared as they talked that not one had seen her more than once. Some of their mothers and grandmothers, however, had seen her also, and they all had told them tales about her when they were children. They said she could take any shape she liked, but that in reality she was a withered old woman, so old and so withered that she was as thin as a sieve with a lamp behind it; that she was never seen except at night, and when something terrible had taken place, or was going to take place— such as the falling in of the roof of a mine, or the breaking out of water in it. She had more than once been seen—it was always at night—beside some well, sitting on the brink of it, and leaning over and stirring it with her forefinger, which was six times as long as any of the rest. And whoever for months after drank of that well was sure to be ill. To this one of them, however, added that he remembered his mother saying that whoever in bad health drank of the well was sure to get better. But the majority agreed that the former was the right version of the story—for was she not a witch, an old hating witch, whose delight was to do mischief? One said he had heard that she took the shape of a young woman sometimes, as beautiful as an angel, and then was most dangerous of all, for she struck every man who looked

463

upon her stone-blind. Peter ventured the question whether she might not as likely be an angel that took the form of an old woman, as an old woman that took the form of an angel. But nobody except Curdie, who was holding his peace with all his might, saw any sense in the question. They said an old woman might be very glad to make herself look like a young one, but who ever heard of a young and beautiful one making herself look old and ugly? Peter asked why they were so much more ready to believe the bad that was said of her than the good. They answered because she was bad. He asked why they believed her to be bad, and they answered, because she did bad things. When he asked how they knew that, they said, because she was a bad creature. Even if they didn't know it, they said, a woman like that was so much more likely to be bad than good. Why did she go about at night? Why did she appear only now and then, and on such occasions? One went on to tell how one night when his grandfather had been having a jolly time of it with his friends in the market town, she had served him so upon his way home that the poor man never drank a drop of anything stronger than water after it to the day of his death. She dragged him into a bog, and tumbled him up and down in it till he was nearly dead.

"I suppose that was her way of teaching him what a good thing water was," said Peter; but the man, who liked strong drink, did not see the joke.

"They do say," said another, "that she has lived in the old house over there ever since the little princess left it. They say too that the housekeeper knows all about it, and is hand and glove with the old witch. I don't doubt they have many a nice airing together on broomsticks. But I don't doubt either it's all nonsense, and there's no such person at all."

"When our cow died," said another, "she was seen going round and round the cowhouse the same night. To be sure she left a fine calf behind her—I mean the cow did, not the witch. I wonder she didn't kill that too, for she'll be a far finer cow than ever her mother was."

"My old woman came upon her one night, not long before the water broke out in the mine, sitting on a stone on the hill-side with a whole congregation of cobs about her. When they saw my wife they all scampered off as fast as they could run, and where the witch was sitting there was nothing to be seen but a withered bracken bush. I make no doubt myself she was putting them up to it."

And so they went on with one foolish tale after another, while Peter put in a word now and then, and Curdie diligently held his peace. But his silence at last drew attention upon it, and one of them said,—

"Come, young Curdie, what are you thinking of?"

"How do you know I'm thinking of anything?" asked Curdie.

"Because you're not saying anything."

"Does it follow then that, as you are saying so much, you're not thinking at all?" said Curdie.

"I know what he's thinking," said one who had not yet spoken; "—he's thinking what a set of fools you are to talk such rubbish; as if ever there was or could be such an old woman as you say! I'm sure Curdie knows better than all that comes to."

"I think," said Curdie, "it would be better that he who says anything about her should be quite sure it is true, lest she should hear him, and not like to be slandered."

"But would she like it any better if it were true?" said the same man. "If she is what they say—I don't know—but I never knew a man that wouldn't go in a rage to be called the very thing he was."

"If bad things were true of her, and I knew it," said Curdie, "I would not hesitate to say them, for I will never give in to being afraid of anything that's bad. I suspect that the things they tell, however, if we knew all about them, would turn out to have nothing but good in them; and I won't say a word more for fear I should say something that mightn't be to her mind."

They all burst into a loud laugh.

"Hear the parson!" they cried. "He believes in the witch! Ha! ha!"

"He's afraid of her!"

"And says all she does is good!"

"He wants to make friends with her, that she may help him to find the gangue."

"Give me my own eyes and a good divining rod before all the witches in the world! and so I'd advise you too, Master Curdie; that is, when your eyes have grown to be worth anything, and you have learned to cut the hazel fork."

Thus they all mocked and jeered at him, but he did his best to keep his temper and go quietly on with his work. He got as close to his father as he could, however, for that helped him to bear it. As soon as they were tired of laughing and mocking, Curdie was friendly with them, and long before their midday meal all between them was as it had been.

But when the evening came, Peter and Curdie felt that they would rather walk home together without other company, and therefore lingered behind when the rest of the men left the mine.

THE EMERALD

Father and son had seated themselves on a projecting piece of the rock at a corner where three galleries met—the one they had come along from their work, one to the right leading out of the mountain, and the other to the left leading far into a portion of it which had been long disused. Since the inundation caused by the goblins, it had indeed been rendered impassable by the settlement of a quantity of the water, forming a small but very deep lake, in a part where was a considerable descent. They had just risen and were turning to the right, when a gleam caught their eyes, and made them look along the whole gangue. Far up they saw a pale green light, whence issuing they could not tell, about halfway between floor and roof of the passage. They saw nothing but the light, which was like a large star, with a point of darker colour yet brighter radiance in the heart of it, whence the rest of the light shot out in rays that faded towards the ends until they vanished. It shed hardly any light around it, although in itself it was so bright as to sting the eyes that beheld it. Wonderful stories had from ages gone been current in the mines about certain magic gems which gave out light of themselves, and this light looked just like what might be supposed to shoot from the heart of such a gem. They went up the old gallery to find out what it could be.

To their surprise they found, however, that, after going some distance, they were no nearer to it, so far as they could judge, than when they started. It did not seem to move, and yet they moving did not approach it. Still they persevered, for it was far too wonderful a thing to lose sight of so long as they could keep it. At length they drew near the hollow where the water lay, and still were no nearer the light. Where they expected to be stopped by the water, however, water was none: something had taken place in some part of the mine that had drained it off, and the gallery lay open as in former times. And now, to their surprise, the light, instead of being in front of them, was shining at the same distance to the right, where they did not know there was any passage at all. Then they discovered, by the light of the lanterns they carried, that there the water had broken through, and made an adit to a part of the mountain of which Peter knew nothing. But they were hardly well into it, still following the light, before Curdie thought he recognised some of the passages he had so often gone through when he was watching the goblins. After they had advanced a long way, with many turnings, now to the right, now to the left, all at once their eyes seemed to come suddenly to themselves, and they became aware that the light which they had taken to be a great way from them was in reality almost within reach of their hands. The same instant it began to grow larger and thinner, the point of light grew dim as it spread, the greenness melted away, and in a moment or two, instead of the star, a dark, dark and yet luminous face was looking at them with living eyes. And Curdie felt a great awe swell up in his heart, for he thought he had seen those eyes before.

"I see you know me, Curdie," said a voice.

"If your eyes are you, ma'am, then I know you," said Curdie. "But I never saw your face before."

"Yes, you have seen it, Curdie," said the voice.

And with that the darkness of its complexion melted away, and down from the face dawned out the form that belonged to it, until at last Curdie and his father beheld a lady, "beautiful exceedingly," dressed in something pale green, like velvet, over which her hair fell in cataracts of a rich golden colour. It looked as if it were pouring down from her head, and, like the water of the Dustbrook, vanishing in a golden vapour ere it reached the floor. It came flowing from under the edge of a coronet of gold, set with alternated pearls and emeralds. In front of the crown was a great emerald, which looked somehow as if out of it had come the light they had followed. There was no ornament else about her, except on her slippers, which were one mass of gleaming emeralds, of various shades of green, all mingling lovely like the waving of grass in the wind and sun. She looked about five-and-twenty years old. And for all the difference, Curdie knew somehow or other, he could not have told how, that the face before him was that of the old princess, Irene's great-great-grandmother.

By this time all around them had grown light, and now first they could see where they were. They stood in a great splendid cavern, which Curdie recognised as that in which the goblins held their state assemblies. But, strange to tell, the light by which they saw came streaming, sparkling, and shooting from stones of many colours in the sides and roof and floor of the cavern—stones of all the colours of the rainbow, and many more. It was a glorious sight—the whole rugged place flashing with colours—in one spot a great light of deep carbuncular red, in another of sapphirine blue, in another of topaz-yellow; while here and there were groups of stones of all hues and sizes, and again nebulous spaces of thousands of tiniest spots of brilliancy of every conceivable shade. Sometimes the colours ran together, and made a little river or lake of lambent interfusing and changing tints, which, by their variegation, seemed to imitate the flowing of water, or waves made by the wind. Curdie would have gazed entranced, but that all the beauty of the cavern, yes, of all he knew of the whole creation, seemed gathered in one centre of harmony and loveliness in the person of the ancient lady who stood before him in the very summer of beauty and strength. Turning from the first glance at the circumfulgent splendour, it dwindled into nothing as he looked again at the lady. Nothing flashed or glowed or shone about her, and yet it was with a prevision of the truth that he said,—

"I was here once before, ma'am."

"I know that, Curdie," she replied.

"The place was full of torches, and the walls gleamed, but nothing as they do now, and there is no light in the place."

"You want to know where the light comes from?" she said, smiling.

"Yes, ma'am."

"Then see: I will go out of the cavern. Do not be afraid, but watch."

She went slowly out. The moment she turned her back to go, the light began to pale and fade; the moment she was out of their sight the place was black as night, save that now the smoky yellow-red of their lamps, which they thought had gone out long ago, cast a dusky glimmer around them.

WHAT IS IN A NAME?

For a time that seemed to them long, the two men stood waiting, while still the Mother of Light did not return. So long was she absent that they began to grow anxious: how were they to find their way from the natural hollows of the mountain crossed by goblin paths, if their lamps should go out? To spend the night there would mean to sit and wait until an earthquake rent the mountain, or the earth herself fell back into the smelting furnace of the sun whence she had issued—for it was all night and no faintest dawn in the bosom of the world. So long did they wait unrevisited, that, had there not been two of them, either would at length have concluded the vision a home-born product of his own seething brain. And their lamps were going out, for they grew redder and smokier! But they did not lose courage, for there is a kind of capillary attraction in the facing of two souls, that lifts faith quite beyond the level to which either could raise it alone: they knew that they had seen the lady of emeralds, and it was to give them their own desire that she had gone from them, and neither would yield for a moment to the half-doubts and half-dreads that awoke in his heart. And still she who with her absence darkened their air did not return. They grew weary, and sat down on the rocky floor, for wait they would—indeed, wait they must. Each set his lamp by his knee, and watched it die. Slowly it sank, dulled, looked lazy and stupid. But ever as it sank and dulled, the image in his mind of the Lady of Light grew stronger and clearer. Together the two lamps panted and shuddered. First one, then the other went out, leaving for a moment a great red, evil-smelling snuff. Then all was the blackness of darkness up to their very hearts and everywhere around them. Was it? No. Far away—it looked miles away—shone one minute faint point of green light—where, who could tell? They only knew that it shone. It grew larger, and seemed to draw nearer, until at last, as they watched with speechless delight and expectation, it seemed once more within reach of an outstretched hand. Then it spread and melted away as before, and there were eyes—and a face—and a lovely form—and lo! the whole cavern blazing with lights innumerable, and gorgeous, yet soft and interfused—so blended, indeed, that the eye had to search and see in order to separate distinct spots of special colour.

The moment they saw the speck in the vast distance they had risen and stood on their feet. When it came nearer they bowed their heads. Yet now they looked with fearless eyes, for the woman that was old and yet young was a joy to see, and filled their hearts with reverent delight. She turned first to Peter.

"I have known you long," she said. "I have met you going to and from the mine, and seen you working in it for the last forty years."

"How should it be, madam, that a grand lady like you should take notice of a poor man like me?" said Peter, humbly, but more foolishly than he could then have understood.

"I am poor as well as rich," said she. "I too work for my bread, and I show myself no favour when I pay myself my own wages. Last night when you sat by the brook, and Curdie told you about my pigeon, and my spinning, and wondered whether he could believe that he had actually seen me, I heard all you said to each other. I am always about, as the miners said the other night when they talked of me as Old Mother Wotherwop."

The lovely lady laughed, and her laugh was a lightning of delight in their souls.

"Yes," she went on, "you have got to thank me that you are so poor, Peter. I have seen to that, and it has done well for both you and me, my friend. Things come to the poor that can't get in at the door of the rich. Their money somehow blocks it up. It is a great privilege to be poor, Peter—one that no man ever coveted, and but a very few have sought to retain, but one that yet many have learned to prize. You must not mistake, however, and imagine it a virtue; it is but a privilege, and one also that, like other privileges, may be terribly misused. Hadst thou been rich, my Peter, thou wouldst not have been so good as some rich men I know. And now I am going to tell you what no one knows but myself: you, Peter, and your wife have both the blood of the royal family in your veins. I have been trying to cultivate your family tree, every branch of which is known to me, and I expect Curdie to turn out a blossom on it. Therefore I have been training him for a work that must soon be done. I was near losing him, and had to send my pigeon. Had he not shot it, that would have been better; but he repented, and that shall be as good in the end."

She turned to Curdie and smiled.

"Ma'am," said Curdie, "may I ask questions?"

"Why not, Curdie?"

"Because I have been told, ma'am, that nobody must ask the king questions."

"The king never made that law," she answered, with some displeasure. "You may ask me as many as you please—that is, so long as they are sensible. Only I may take a few thousand years to answer some of them. But that's nothing. Of all things time is the cheapest."

"Then would you mind telling me now, ma'am, for I feel very confused about it —are you the Lady of the Silver Moon?"

"Yes, Curdie; you may call me that if you like. What it means is true."

"And now I see you dark, and clothed in green, and the mother of all the light that dwells in the stones of the earth! And up there they call you Old Mother Wotherwop! And the Princess Irene told me you were her great-great-grandmother! And you spin the spider-threads, and take care of a whole people of pigeons; and you are worn to a pale shadow with old age; and are as young as anybody can be, not to be too young; and as strong, I do believe, as I am."

The lady stooped towards a large green stone bedded in the rock of the floor, and looking like a well of grassy light in it. She laid hold of it with her fingers, broke it out, and gave it to Peter.

"There!" cried Curdie, "I told you so. Twenty men could not have done that. And your fingers are white and smooth as any lady's in the land. I don't know what to make of it."

"I could give you twenty names more to call me, Curdie, and not one of them would be a false one. What does it matter how many names if the person is one?"

"Ah! but it is not names only, ma'am. Look at what you were like last night, and what I see you now!"

"Shapes are only dresses, Curdie, and dresses are only names. That which is inside is the same all the time."

"But then how can all the shapes speak the truth?"

"It would want thousands more to speak the truth, Curdie; and then they could not. But there is a point I must not let you mistake about. It is one thing the shape I choose to put on, and quite another the shape that foolish talk and nursery tale may please to put upon me. Also, it is one thing what you or your father may think about me, and quite another what a foolish or bad man may see in me. For instance, if a thief were to come in here just now, he would think he saw the demon of the mine, all in green flames, come to protect her treasure, and would run like a hunted wild goat. I should be all the same, but his evil eyes would see me as I was not."

"I think I understand," said Curdie.

"Peter," said the lady, turning then to him, "you will have to give up Curdie for a little while."

"So long as he loves us, ma'am, that will not matter—much."

"Ah! you are right there, my friend," said the beautiful princess.

And as she said it she put out her hand, and took the hard, horny hand of the miner in it, and held it for a moment lovingly.

"I need say no more," she added, "for we understand each other—you and I, Peter."

The tears came into Peter's eyes. He bowed his head in thankfulness, and his heart was much too full to speak.

Then the great old young beautiful princess turned to Curdie.

"Now, Curdie, are you ready?" she said.

"Yes, ma'am," answered Curdie.

"You do not know what for."

"You do, ma'am. That is enough."

"You could not have given me a better answer, or done more to prepare yourself, Curdie," she returned, with one of her radiant smiles. "Do you think you will know me again?"

"I think so. But how can I tell what you may look like next?"

"Ah, that indeed! How can you tell? Or how could I expect you should? But those who know me well, know me whatever new dress or shape or name I may be in; and by-and-by you will have learned to do so too."

"But if you want me to know you again, ma'am, for certain sure," said Curdie, "could you not give me some sign, or tell me something about you that never changes—or some other way to know you, or thing to know you by?"

"No, Curdie; that would be to keep you from knowing me. You must know me in quite another way from that. It would not be the least use to you or me either if I were to make you know me in that way. It would be but to know the sign of me— not to know me myself. It would be no better than if I were to take this emerald out of my crown and give it you to take home with you, and you were to call it me, and talk to it as if it heard and saw and loved you. Much good that would do you, Curdie! No; you must do what you can to know me, and if you do, you will. You shall see me again—in very different circumstances from these, and, I will tell you so much, it may be in a very different shape. But come now, I will lead you out of this cavern; my good Joan will be getting too anxious about you. One word more: you will allow that the men knew little what they were talking about this morning, when they told all those tales of Old Mother Wotherwop; but did it occur to you to think how it was they fell to talking about me at all?—It was because I came to them; I was beside them all the time they were talking about me, though they were far enough from knowing it, and had very little besides foolishness to say."

As she spoke she turned and led the way from the cavern, which, as if a door had been closed, sunk into absolute blackness behind them. And now they saw nothing more of the lady except the green star, which again seemed a good distance in front of them, and to which they came no nearer, although following it at a quick pace through the mountain. Such was their confidence in her guidance, however, and so fearless were they in consequence, that they felt their way neither with hand nor foot, but walked straight on through the pitch dark galleries. When at length the night of the upper world looked in at the mouth of the mine, the green light seemed to lose its way amongst the stars, and they saw it no more.

Out they came into the cool, blessed night. It was very late, and only starlight. To their surprise, three paces away they saw, seated upon a stone, an old country-woman, in a cloak which they took for black. When they came close up to it, they saw it was red.

"Good evening!" said Peter.

"Good evening!" returned the old woman, in a voice as old as herself.

But Curdie took off his cap and said,—

"I am your servant, princess."

The old woman replied,—

"Come to me in the dove-tower to-morrow night, Curdie—alone."

"I will, ma'am," said Curdie.

So they parted, and father and son went home to wife and mother—two persons in one rich, happy woman.

CURDIE'S MISSION

The next night Curdie went home from the mine a little earlier than usual, to make himself tidy before going to the dove-tower. The princess had not appointed an exact time for him to be there; he would go as near the time he had gone first as he could. On his way to the bottom of the hill, he met his father coming up. The sun was then down, and the warm first of the twilight filled the evening. He came rather wearily up the hill: the road, he thought, must have grown steeper in parts since he was Curdie's age. His back was to the light of the sunset, which closed him all round in a beautiful setting, and Curdie thought what a grand-looking man his father was, even when he was tired. It is greed and laziness and selfishness, not hunger or weariness or cold, that take the dignity out of a man, and make him look mean.

"Ah, Curdie! there you are!" he said, seeing his son come bounding along as if it were morning with him and not evening.

"You look tired, father," said Curdie.

"Yes, my boy. I'm not so young as you."

"Nor so old as the princess," said Curdie.

"Tell me this," said Peter: "why do people talk about going down hill when they begin to get old? It seems to me that then first they begin to go up hill."

"You looked to me, father, when I caught sight of you, as if you had been climbing the hill all your life, and were soon to get to the top."

"Nobody can tell when that will be," returned Peter. "We're so ready to think we're just at the top when it lies miles away. But I must not keep you, my boy, for you are wanted; and we shall be anxious to know what the princess says to you— that is, if she will allow you to tell us."

"I think she will, for she knows there is nobody more to be trusted than my father and mother," said Curdie, with pride.

And away he shot, and ran, and jumped, and seemed almost to fly down the long, winding, steep path, until he came to the gate of the king's house.

There he met an unexpected obstruction: in the open door stood the house-keeper, and she seemed to broaden herself out until she almost filled the doorway.

"So!" she said; "it's you, is it, young man? You are the person that comes in and goes out when he pleases, and keeps running up and down my stairs, without ever saying by your leave, or even wiping his shoes, and always leaves the door open! Don't you know that this is my house?"

"No, I do not," returned Curdie, respectfully. "You forget, ma'am, that it is the king's house."

"That is all the same. The king left it to me to take care of, and that you shall know!"

"Is the king dead, ma'am, that he has left it to you?" asked Curdie, half in doubt from the self-assertion of the woman.

"Insolent fellow!" exclaimed the housekeeper. "Don't you see by my dress that I am in the king's service?"

"And am I not one of his miners?"

"Ah! that goes for nothing. I am one of his household. You are an out-of-doors labourer. You are a nobody. You carry a pickaxe. I carry the keys at my girdle. See!"

"But you must not call one a nobody to whom the king has spoken," said Curdie.

"Go along with you!" cried the housekeeper, and would have shut the door in his face, had she not been afraid that when she stepped back he would step in ere she could get it in motion, for it was very heavy, and always seemed unwilling to shut. Curdie came a pace nearer. She lifted the great house key from her side, and threatened to strike him down with it, calling aloud on Mar and Whelk and Plout, the men-servants under her, to come and help her. Ere one of them could answer, however, she gave a great shriek and turned and fled, leaving the door wide open.

Curdie looked behind him, and saw an animal whose gruesome oddity even he, who knew so many of the strange creatures, two of which were never the same, that used to live inside the mountain with their masters the goblins, had never seen equalled. Its eyes were flaming with anger, but it seemed to be at the housekeeper, for it came cowering and creeping up, and laid its head on the ground at Curdie's feet. Curdie hardly waited to look at it, however, but ran into the house, eager to get up the stairs before any of the men should come to annoy—he had no fear of their preventing him. Without halt or hindrance, though the passages were nearly dark, he reached the door of the princess's workroom, and knocked.

"Come in," said the voice of the princess.

Curdie opened the door,—but, to his astonishment, saw no room there. Could he have opened a wrong door? There was the great sky, and the stars, and beneath he could see nothing—only darkness! But what was that in the sky, straight in front of him? A great wheel of fire, turning and turning, and flashing out blue lights!

"Come in, Curdie," said the voice again.

"I would at once, ma'am," said Curdie, "if I were sure I was standing at your door."

"Why should you doubt it, Curdie?"

"Because I see neither walls nor floor, only darkness and the great sky."

"That is all right, Curdie. Come in."

Curdie stepped forward at once. He was indeed, for the very crumb of a moment, tempted to feel before him with his foot; but he saw that would be to distrust the princess, and a greater rudeness he could not offer her. So he stepped straight in—I will not say without a little tremble at the thought of finding no floor beneath his foot. But that which had need of the floor found it, and his foot was satisfied.

No sooner was he in than he saw that the great revolving wheel in the sky was the princess's spinning-wheel, near the other end of the room, turning very fast. He could see no sky or stars any more, but the wheel was flashing out blue—oh such lovely sky-blue light!—and behind it of course sat the princess, but whether an old woman as thin as a skeleton leaf, or a glorious lady as young as perfection, he could not tell for the turning and flashing of the wheel.

"Listen to the wheel," said the voice which had already grown dear to Curdie: its very tone was precious like a jewel, not as a jewel, for no jewel could compare with it in preciousness.

And Curdie listened and listened.

"What is it saying?" asked the voice.

"It is singing," answered Curdie.

"What is it singing?"

Curdie tried to make out, but thought he could not; for no sooner had he got a hold of something than it vanished again. Yet he listened, and listened, entranced with delight.

"Thank you, Curdie," said the voice.

"Ma'am," said Curdie, "I did try hard for a while, but I could not make anything of it."

"Oh, yes, you did, and you have been telling it to me! Shall I tell you again what I told my wheel, and my wheel told you, and you have just told me without knowing it?"

"Please, ma'am."

Then the lady began to sing, and her wheel spun an accompaniment to her song, and the music of the wheel was like the music of an Æolian harp blown upon by the wind that bloweth where it listeth. Oh! the sweet sounds of that spinning-wheel! Now they were gold, now silver, now grass, now palm-trees, now ancient cities, now rubies, now mountain brooks, now peacock's feathers, now clouds, now snowdrops, and now mid-sea islands. But for the voice that sang through it all, about that I have no words to tell. It would make you weep if I were able to tell you what that was like, it was so beautiful and true and lovely. But this is something like the words of its song:—

The stars are spinning their threads,
   And the clouds are the dust that flies,
   And the suns are weaving them up
   For the time when the sleepers shall rise.

The ocean in music rolls,
   And gems are turning to eyes,

And the trees are gathering souls
For the time when the sleepers shall rise.

The weepers are learning to smile,
    And laughter to glean the sighs;
    Burn and bury the care and guile,
    For the day when the sleepers shall rise.

Oh, the dews and the moths and the daisy-red,
    The larks and the glimmers and flows!
    The lilies and sparrows and daily bread,
    And the something that nobody knows!

The princess stopped, her wheel stopped, and she laughed. And her laugh was sweeter than song and wheel; sweeter than running brook and silver bell; sweeter than joy itself, for the heart of the laugh was love.

"Come now, Curdie, to this side of my wheel, and you will find me," she said; and her laugh seemed sounding on still in the words, as if they were made of breath that had laughed.

Curdie obeyed, and passed the wheel, and there she stood to receive him!—fairer than when he saw her last, a little younger still, and dressed not in green and emeralds, but in pale blue, with a coronet of silver set with pearls, and slippers covered with opals, that gleamed every colour of the rainbow. It was some time before Curdie could take his eyes from the marvel of her loveliness. Fearing at last that he was rude, he turned them away; and, behold, he was in a room that was for beauty marvellous! The lofty ceiling was all a golden vine, whose great clusters of carbuncles, rubies, and chrysoberyls, hung down like the bosses of groined arches, and in its centre hung the most glorious lamp that human eyes ever saw—the Silver Moon itself, a globe of silver, as it seemed, with a heart of light so wondrous potent that it rendered the mass translucent, and altogether radiant.

The room was so large that, looking back, he could scarcely see the end at which he entered; but the other was only a few yards from him—and there he saw another wonder: on a huge hearth a great fire was burning, and the fire was a huge heap of roses, and yet it was fire. The smell of the roses filled the air, and the heat of the flames of them glowed upon his face. He turned an inquiring look upon the lady, and saw that she was now seated in an ancient chair, the legs of which were crusted with gems, but the upper part like a nest of daisies and moss and green grass.

"Curdie," she said in answer to his eyes, "you have stood more than one trial already, and have stood them well: now I am going to put you to a harder. Do you think you are prepared for it?"

"How can I tell, ma'am?" he returned, "seeing I do not know what it is, or what preparation it needs? Judge me yourself, ma'am."

"It needs only trust and obedience," answered the lady.

"I dare not say anything, ma'am. If you think me fit, command me."

"It will hurt you terribly, Curdie, but that will be all; no real hurt, but much real good will come to you from it."

Curdie made no answer, but stood gazing with parted lips in the lady's face.

"Go and thrust both your hands into that fire," she said quickly, almost hurriedly.

Curdie dared not stop to think. It was much too terrible to think about. He rushed to the fire, and thrust both his hands right into the middle of the heap of flaming roses, and his arms halfway up to the elbows. And it did hurt! But he did not draw them back. He held the pain as if it were a thing that would kill him if he let it go—as indeed it would have done. He was in terrible fear lest it should conquer him. But when it had risen to the pitch that he thought he could bear it no longer, it began to fall again, and went on growing less and less until by contrast with its former severity it had become rather pleasant. At last it ceased altogether, and Curdie thought his hands must be burnt to cinders if not ashes, for he did not feel them at all. The princess told him to take them out and look at them. He did so, and found that all that was gone of them was the rough hard skin; they were white and smooth like the princess's.

"Come to me," she said.

He obeyed, and saw, to his surprise, that her face looked as if she had been weeping.

"Oh, princess! what is the matter?" he cried. "Did I make a noise and vex you?"

"No, Curdie," she answered; "but it was very bad."

"Did you feel it too then?"

"Of course I did. But now it is over, and all is well.—Would you like to know why I made you put your hands in the fire?"

Curdie looked at them again—then said,—

"To take the marks of the work off them, and make them fit for the king's court, I suppose."

"No, Curdie," answered the princess, shaking her head, for she was not pleased with the answer. "It would be a poor way of making your hands fit for the king's court to take off them all signs of his service. There is a far greater difference on them than that. Do you feel none?"

"No, ma'am."

"You will, though, by and by, when the time comes. But perhaps even then you might not know what had been given you, therefore I will tell you.—Have you ever heard what some philosophers say—that men were all animals once?"

"No, ma'am."

"It is of no consequence. But there is another thing that is of the greatest consequence—this: that all men, if they do not take care, go down the hill to the animals' country; that many men are actually, all their lives, going to be beasts. People knew it once, but it is long since they forgot it."

"I am not surprised to hear it, ma'am, when I think of some of our miners."

"Ah! but you must beware, Curdie, how you say of this man or that man that he is travelling beastward. There are not nearly so many going that way as at first sight you might think. When you met your father on the hill to-night, you stood and spoke together on the same spot; and although one of you was going up and the other coming down, at a little distance no one could have told which was bound in the one direction and which in the other. Just so two people may be at the same spot in manners and behaviour, and yet one may be getting better and the other worse, which is just the greatest of all differences that could possibly exist between them."

"But, ma'am," said Curdie, "where is the good of knowing that there is such a difference, if you can never know where it is?"

"Now, Curdie, you must mind exactly what words I use, because although the right words cannot do exactly what I want them to do, the wrong words will certainly do what I do not want them to do. I did not say you can never know. When there is a necessity for your knowing, when you have to do important business with this or that man, there is always a way of knowing enough to keep you from any great blunder. And as you will have important business to do by and by, and that with people of whom you yet know nothing, it will be necessary that you should have some better means than usual of learning the nature of them. Now listen. Since it is always what they do, whether in their minds or their bodies, that makes men go down to be less than men, that is, beasts, the change always comes first in their hands—and first of all in the inside hands, to which the outside ones are but as the gloves. They do not know it of course; for a beast does not know that he is a beast, and the nearer a man gets to being a beast the less he knows it. Neither can their best friends, or their worst enemies indeed, see any difference in their hands, for they see only the living gloves of them. But there are not a few who feel a vague something repulsive in the hand of a man who is growing a beast. Now here is what the rose-fire has done for you: it has made your hands so knowing and wise, it has brought your real hands so near the outside of your flesh-gloves, that you will henceforth be able to know at once the hand of a man who is growing into a beast; nay, more—you will at once feel the foot of the beast he is growing, just as if there were no glove made like a man's hand between you and it. Hence of course it follows that you will be able often, and with further education in zoology, will be able always to tell, not only when a man is growing a beast, but what beast he is growing to, for you will know the foot—what it is and what beast's it is. According then to your knowledge of that beast, will be your knowledge of the man you have to do with. Only there is one beautiful and awful thing about it, that if any one gifted with this perception once uses it for his own ends, it is taken from him, and then, not knowing that it is gone, he is in a far worse condition than before, for he trusts to what he has not got."

"How dreadful!" said Curdie. "I must mind what I am about."

"Yes, indeed, Curdie."

"But may not one sometimes make a mistake without being able to help it?"

"Yes. But so long as he is not after his own ends, he will never make a serious mistake."

"I suppose you want me, ma'am, to warn every one whose hand tells me that he is growing a beast—because, as you say, he does not know it himself."

The princess smiled.

"Much good that would do, Curdie! I don't say there are no cases in which it would be of use, but they are very rare and peculiar cases, and if such come you will know them. To such a person there is in general no insult like the truth. He cannot endure it, not because he is growing a beast, but because he is ceasing to be a man. It is the dying man in him that it makes uncomfortable, and he trots, or creeps, or swims, or flutters out of its way—calls it a foolish feeling, a whim, an old wives' fable, a bit of priests' humbug, an effete superstition, and so on."

"And is there no hope for him? Can nothing be done? It's so awful to think of going down, down, down like that!"

"Even when it is with his own will?"

"That's what seems to me to make it worst of all," said Curdie.

"You are right," answered the princess, nodding her head; "but there is this amount of excuse to make for all such, remember—that they do not know what or how horrid their coming fate is. Many a lady, so delicate and nice that she can bear nothing coarser than the finest linen to touch her body, if she had a mirror that could show her the animal she is growing to, as it lies waiting within the fair skin and the fine linen and the silk and the jewels, would receive a shock that might possibly wake her up."

"Why then, ma'am, shouldn't she have it?"

The princess held her peace.

"Come here, Lina," she said after a long pause.

From somewhere behind Curdie, crept forward the same hideous animal which had fawned at his feet at the door, and which, without his knowing it, had followed him every step up the dove-tower. She ran to the princess, and lay down at her feet, looking up at her with an expression so pitiful that in Curdie's heart it overcame all the ludicrousness of her horrible mass of incongruities. She had a very short body, and very long legs made like an elephant's, so that in lying down she kneeled with both pairs. Her tail, which dragged on the floor behind her, was twice as long and quite as thick as her body. Her head was something between that of a polar bear and a snake. Her eyes were dark green, with a yellow light in them. Her under teeth came up like a fringe of icicles, only very white, outside of her upper lip. Her throat looked as if the hair had been plucked off. It showed a skin white and smooth.

"Give Curdie a paw, Lina," said the princess.

The creature rose, and, lifting a long fore leg, held up a great dog-like paw to Curdie. He took it gently. But what a shudder, as of terrified delight, ran through him, when, instead of the paw of a dog, such as it seemed to his eyes, he clasped in his great mining fist the soft, neat little hand of a child! He took it in both of his, and held it as if he could not let it go. The green eyes stared at him with their yellow light, and the mouth was turned up towards him with its constant half-grin; but here was the child's hand! If he could but pull the child out of the beast! His eyes sought the princess. She was watching him with evident satisfaction.

"Ma'am, here is a child's hand!" said Curdie.

"Your gift does more for you than it promised. It is yet better to perceive a hidden good than a hidden evil."

"But," began Curdie.

"I am not going to answer any more questions this evening," interrupted the princess. "You have not half got to the bottom of the answers I have already given you. That paw in your hand now might almost teach you the whole science of natural history—the heavenly sort, I mean."

"I will think," said Curdie. "But oh! please! one word more: may I tell my father and mother all about it?"

"Certainly—though perhaps now it may be their turn to find it a little difficult to believe that things went just as you must tell them."

"They shall see that I believe it all this time," said Curdie.

"Tell them that to-morrow morning you must set out for the court—not like a great man, but just as poor as you are. They had better not speak about it. Tell them also that it will be a long time before they hear of you again, but they must not lose heart. And tell your father to lay that stone I gave him last night in a safe place—not because of the greatness of its price, although it is such an emerald as no prince has in his crown, but because it will be a news-bearer between you and him. As often as he gets at all anxious about you, he must take it and lay it in the fire, and leave it there when he goes to bed. In the morning he must find it in the ashes, and if it be as green as ever, then all goes well with you; if it have lost colour, things go ill with you; but if it be very pale indeed, then you are in great danger, and he must come to me."

"Yes, ma'am," said Curdie. "Please, am I to go now?"

"Yes," answered the princess, and held out her hand to him.

Curdie took it, trembling with joy. It was a very beautiful hand—not small, very smooth, but not very soft—and just the same to his fire-taught touch that it was to his eyes. He would have stood there all night holding it if she had not gently withdrawn it.

"I will provide you a servant," she said, "for your journey, and to wait upon you afterwards."

"But where am I to go, ma'am, and what am I to do? You have given me no message to carry, neither have you said what I am wanted for. I go without a notion whether I am to walk this way or that, or what I am to do when I get I don't know where."

"Curdie!" said the princess, and there was a tone of reminder in his own name as she spoke it, "did I not tell you to tell your father and mother that you were to set out for the court? and you know that lies to the north. You must learn to use far less direct directions than that. You must not be like a dull servant that needs to be told again and again before he will understand. You have orders enough to start with, and you will find, as you go on, and as you need to know, what you have to do. But I warn you that perhaps it will not look the least like what you may have been fancying I should require of you. I have one idea of you and your work, and you have another. I do not blame you for that—you cannot help it yet; but you must be ready to let my idea, which sets you working, set your idea right. Be true and honest and fearless, and all shall go well with you and your work, and all with whom your work lies, and so with your parents—and me too, Curdie," she added after a little pause.

The young miner bowed his head low, patted the strange head that lay at the princess's feet, and turned away.

As soon as he passed the spinning-wheel, which looked, in the midst of the glorious room, just like any wheel you might find in a country cottage—old and worn and dingy and dusty—the splendour of the place vanished, and he saw but the big bare room he seemed at first to have entered, with the moon—the princess's moon no doubt—shining in at one of the windows upon the spinning-wheel.

HANDS

Curdie went home, pondering much, and told everything to his father and mother. As the old princess had said, it was now their turn to find what they heard hard to believe. If they had not been able to trust Curdie himself, they would have refused to believe more than the half of what he reported, then they would have refused that half too, and at last would most likely for a time have disbelieved in the very existence of the princess, what evidence their own senses had given them notwithstanding. For he had nothing conclusive to show in proof of what he told them. When he held out his hands to them, his mother said they looked as if he had been washing them with soft soap, only they did smell of something nicer than that, and she must allow it was more like roses than anything else she knew. His father could not see any difference upon his hands, but then it was night, he said, and their poor little lamp was not enough for his old eyes. As to the feel of them, each of his own hands, he said, was hard and horny enough for two, and it must be the fault of the dulness of his own thick skin that he felt no change on Curdie's palms.

"Here, Curdie," said his mother, "try my hand, and see what beast's paw lies inside it."

"No, mother," answered Curdie, half-beseeching, half-indignant, "I will not insult my new gift by making pretence to try it. That would be mockery. There is no hand within yours but the hand of a true woman, my mother."

"I should like you just to take hold of my hand, though," said his mother. "You are my son, and may know all the bad there is in me."

Then at once Curdie took her hand in his. And when he had it, he kept it, stroking it gently with his other hand.

"Mother," he said at length, "your hand feels just like that of the princess."

"What! my horny, cracked, rheumatic old hand, with its big joints, and its short nails all worn down to the quick with hard work—like the hand of the beautiful princess! Why, my child, you will make me fancy your fingers have grown very dull indeed, instead of sharp and delicate, if you talk such nonsense. Mine is such an ugly hand I should be ashamed to show it to any but one that loved me. But love makes all safe—doesn't it, Curdie?"

"Well, mother, all I can say is that I don't feel a roughness, or a crack, or a big joint, or a short nail. Your hand feels just and exactly, as near as I can recollect, and it's not now more than two hours since I had it in mine,—well, I will say, very like indeed to that of the old princess."

"Go away, you flatterer," said his mother, with a smile that showed how she prized the love that lay beneath what she took for its hyperbole. The praise even which one cannot accept is sweet from a true mouth. "If that is all your new gift can do, it won't make a warlock of you," she added.

"Mother, it tells me nothing but the truth," insisted Curdie, "however unlike the truth it may seem. It wants no gift to tell what anybody's outside hands are like. But by it I know your inside hands are like the princess's."

"And I am sure the boy speaks true," said Peter. "He only says about your hand what I have known ever so long about yourself, Joan. Curdie, your mother's foot is as pretty a foot as any lady's in the land, and where her hand is not so pretty it comes of killing its beauty for you and me, my boy. And I can tell you more, Curdie. I don't know much about ladies and gentlemen, but I am sure your inside mother must be a lady, as her hand tells you, and I will try to say how I know it. This is how: when I forget myself looking at her as she goes about her work—and that happens oftener as I grow older—I fancy for a moment or two that I am a gentleman; and when I wake up from my little dream, it is only to feel the more strongly that I must do everything as a gentleman should. I will try to tell you what I mean, Curdie. If a gentleman—I mean a real gentleman, not a pretended one, of which sort they say there are a many above ground—if a real gentleman were to lose all his money and come down to work in the mines to get bread for his family —do you think, Curdie, he would work like the lazy ones? Would he try to do as little as he could for his wages? I know the sort of the true gentleman—pretty near as well as he does himself. And my wife, that's your mother, Curdie, she's a true lady, you may take my word for it, for it's she that makes me want to be a true gentleman. Wife, the boy is in the right about your hand."

"Now, father, let me feel yours," said Curdie, daring a little more.

"No, no, my boy," answered Peter. "I don't want to hear anything about my hand or my head or my heart. I am what I am, and I hope growing better, and that's enough. No, you shan't feel my hand. You must go to bed, for you must start with the sun."

It was not as if Curdie had been leaving them to go to prison, or to make a fortune, and although they were sorry enough to lose him, they were not in the least heart-broken or even troubled at his going.

As the princess had said he was to go like the poor man he was, Curdie came down in the morning from his little loft dressed in his working clothes. His mother, who was busy getting his breakfast for him, while his father sat reading to her out of an old book, would have had him put on his holiday garments, which, she said, would look poor enough amongst the fine ladies and gentlemen he was going to. But Curdie said he did not know that he was going amongst ladies and gentlemen, and that as work was better than play, his work-day clothes must on the whole be better than his play-day clothes; and as his father accepted the argument, his mother gave in.

When he had eaten his breakfast, she took a pouch made of goatskin, with the long hair on it, filled it with bread and cheese, and hung it over his shoulder. Then his father gave him a stick he had cut for him in the wood, and he bade them good-bye rather hurriedly, for he was afraid of breaking down. As he went out, he caught up his mattock and took it with him. It had on the one side a pointed curve of strong steel, for loosening the earth and the ore, and on the other a steel hammer for breaking the stones and rocks. Just as he crossed the threshold the sun showed the first segment of his disc above the horizon.

THE HEATH

He had to go to the bottom of the hill to get into a country he could cross, for the mountains to the north were full of precipices, and it would have been losing time to go that way. Not until he had reached the king's house was it any use to turn northwards. Many a look did he raise, as he passed it, to the dove-tower, and as long as it was in sight, but he saw nothing of the lady of the pigeons.

On and on he fared, and came in a few hours to a country where there were no mountains more—only hills, with great stretches of desolate heath. Here and there was a village, but that brought him little pleasure, for the people were rougher and worse-mannered than those in the mountains, and as he passed through, the children came behind and mocked him.

"There's a monkey running away from the mines!" they cried.

Sometimes their parents came out and encouraged them.

"He don't want to find gold for the king any longer,—the lazybones!" they would say. "He'll be well taxed down here though, and he won't like that either."

But it was little to Curdie that men who did not know what he was about should not approve of his proceedings. He gave them a merry answer now and then, and held diligently on his way. When they got so rude as nearly to make him angry, he would treat them as he used to treat the goblins, and sing his own songs to keep out their foolish noises. Once a child fell as he turned to run away after throwing a stone at him. He picked him up, kissed him, and carried him to his mother. The woman had run out in terror when she saw the strange miner about, as she thought, to take vengeance on her boy. When he put him in her arms, she blessed him, and Curdie went on his way rejoicing.

And so the day went on, and the evening came, and in the middle of a great desolate heath he began to feel tired, and sat down under an ancient hawthorn, through which every now and then a lone wind that seemed to come from nowhere and to go nowhither sighed and hissed. It was very old and distorted. There was not another tree for miles all around. It seemed to have lived so long, and to have been so torn and tossed by the tempests on that moor, that it had at last gathered a wind of its own, which got up now and then, tumbled itself about, and lay down again.

Curdie had been so eager to get on that he had eaten nothing since his breakfast. But he had had plenty of water, for many little streams had crossed his path. He now opened the wallet his mother had given him, and began to eat his supper. The sun was setting. A few clouds had gathered about the west, but there was not a single cloud anywhere else to be seen.

Now Curdie did not know that this was a part of the country very hard to get through. Nobody lived there, though many had tried to build in it. Some died very soon. Some rushed out of it. Those who stayed longest went raving mad, and died a terrible death. Such as walked straight on, and did not spend a night there, got through well, and were nothing the worse. But those who slept even a single night in it were sure to meet with something they could never forget, and which often left a mark everybody could read. And that old hawthorn might have been enough for a warning—it looked so like a human being dried up and distorted with age and suffering, with cares instead of loves, and things instead of thoughts. Both it and the heath around it, which stretched on all sides as far as he could see, were so withered that it was impossible to say whether they were alive or not.

And while Curdie ate there came a change. Clouds had gathered over his head, and seemed drifting about in every direction, as if not "shepherded by the slow, unwilling wind," but hunted in all directions by wolfish flaws across the plains of the sky. The sun was going down in a storm of lurid crimson, and out of the west came a wind that felt red and hot the one moment, and cold and pale the other. And very strangely it sung in the dreary old hawthorn tree, and very cheerily it blew about Curdie, now making him creep close up to the tree for shelter from its shivery cold, now fan himself with his cap, it was so sultry and stifling. It seemed to come from the death-bed of the sun, dying in fever and ague.

And as he gazed at the sun, now on the verge of the horizon, very large and very red and very dull—for though the clouds had broken away a dusty fog was spread all over him—Curdie saw something strange appear against him, moving about like a fly over his burning face. It looked as if it were coming out of his hot furnace-heart, and was a living creature of some kind surely; but its shape was very uncertain, because the dazzle of the light all around it melted its outlines. It was growing larger, it must be approaching! It grew so rapidly that by the time the sun was half down its head reached the top of his arch, and presently nothing but its legs were to be seen, crossing and recrossing the face of the vanishing disc. When the sun was down he could see nothing of it more, but in a moment he heard its feet galloping over the dry crackling heather, and seeming to come straight for him. He stood up, lifted his pickaxe, and threw the hammer end over his shoulder: he was going to have a fight for his life! And now it appeared again, vague, yet very awful, in the dim twilight the sun had left behind him. But just before it reached him, down from its four long legs it dropped flat on the ground, and came crawling towards him, wagging a huge tail as it came.

485

LINA

It was Lina. All at once Curdie recognised her—the frightful creature he had seen at the princess's. He dropped his pickaxe, and held out his hand. She crept nearer and nearer, and laid her chin in his palm, and he patted her ugly head. Then she crept away behind the tree, and lay down, panting hard. Curdie did not much like the idea of her being behind him. Horrible as she was to look at, she seemed to his mind more horrible when he was not looking at her. But he remembered the child's hand, and never thought of driving her away. Now and then he gave a glance behind him, and there she lay flat, with her eyes closed and her terrible teeth gleaming between her two huge fore-paws.

After his supper and his long day's journey it was no wonder Curdie should now be sleepy. Since the sun set the air had been warm and pleasant. He lay down under the tree, closed his eyes, and thought to sleep. He found himself mistaken however. But although he could not sleep, he was yet aware of resting delightfully. Presently he heard a sweet sound of singing somewhere, such as he had never heard before—a singing as of curious birds far off, which drew nearer and nearer. At length he heard their wings, and, opening his eyes, saw a number of very large birds, as it seemed, alighting around him, still singing. It was strange to hear song from the throats of such big birds. And still singing, with large and round but not the less bird-like voices, they began to weave a strange dance about him, moving their wings in time with their legs. But the dance seemed somehow to be troubled and broken, and to return upon itself in an eddy, in place of sweeping smoothly on. And he soon learned, in the low short growls behind him, the cause of the imperfection: they wanted to dance all round the tree, but Lina would not permit them to come on her side.

Now Curdie liked the birds, and did not altogether like Lina. But neither, nor both together, made a reason for driving away the princess's creature. Doubtless she had been a goblins' creature, but the last time he saw her was in the king's

486

house and the dove-tower, and at the old princess's feet. So he left her to do as she would, and the dance of the birds continued only a semicircle, troubled at the edges, and returning upon itself. But their song and their motions, nevertheless, and the waving of their wings, began at length to make him very sleepy. All the time he had kept doubting every now and then whether they could really be birds, and the sleepier he got, the more he imagined them something else, but he suspected no harm. Suddenly, just as he was sinking beneath the waves of slumber, he awoke in fierce pain. The birds were upon him—all over him—and had begun to tear him with beaks and claws. He had but time, however, to feel that he could not move under their weight, when they set up a hideous screaming, and scattered like a cloud. Lina was amongst them, snapping and striking with her paws, while her tail knocked them over and over. But they flew up, gathered, and descended on her in a swarm, perching upon every part of her body, so that he could see only a huge misshapen mass, which seemed to go rolling away into the darkness. He got up and tried to follow, but could see nothing, and after wandering about hither and thither for some time, found himself again beside the hawthorn. He feared greatly that the birds had been too much for Lina, and had torn her to pieces. In a little while, however, she came limping back, and lay down in her old place. Curdie also lay down, but, from the pain of his wounds, there was no sleep for him. When the light came he found his clothes a good deal torn and his skin as well, but gladly wondered why the wicked birds had not at once attacked his eyes. Then he turned looking for Lina. She rose and crept to him. But she was in far worse plight than he —plucked and gashed and torn with the beaks and claws of the birds, especially about the bare part of her neck, so that she was pitiful to see. And those worst wounds she could not reach to lick.

"Poor Lina!" said Curdie; "you got all those helping me."

She wagged her tail, and made it clear she understood him. Then it flashed upon Curdie's mind that perhaps this was the companion the princess had promised him. For the princess did so many things differently from what anybody looked for! Lina was no beauty certainly, but already, the first night, she had saved his life.

"Come along, Lina," he said; "we want water."

She put her nose to the earth, and after snuffing for a moment, darted off in a straight line. Curdie followed. The ground was so uneven, that after losing sight of her many times, at last he seemed to have lost her altogether. In a few minutes, however, he came upon her waiting for him. Instantly she darted off again. After he had lost and found her again many times, he found her the last time lying beside a great stone. As soon as he came up she began scratching at it with her paws. When he had raised it an inch or two, she shoved in first her nose and then her teeth, and lifted with all the might of her strong neck.

When at length between them they got it up, there was a beautiful little well. He filled his cap with the clearest and sweetest water, and drank. Then he gave to Lina, and she drank plentifully. Next he washed her wounds very carefully. And as he did so, he noted how much the bareness of her neck added to the strange repulsiveness of her appearance. Then he bethought him of the goatskin wallet his mother had given him, and taking it from his shoulders, tried whether it would do to make a collar of for the poor animal. He found there was just enough, and the hair so similar in colour to Lina's, that no one could suspect it of having grown somewhere else. He took his knife, ripped up the seams of the wallet, and began trying the skin to her neck. It was plain she understood perfectly what he wished, for she endeavoured to hold her neck conveniently, turning it this way and that while he contrived, with his rather scanty material, to make the collar fit. As his mother had taken care to provide him with needles and thread, he soon had a nice gorget ready for her. He laced it on with one of his boot-laces, which its long hair covered. Poor Lina looked much better in it. Nor could any one have called it a piece of finery. If ever green eyes with a yellow light in them looked grateful, hers did.

As they had no longer any bag to carry them in, Curdie and Lina now ate what was left of the provisions. Then they set out again upon their journey. For seven days it lasted. They met with various adventures, and in all of them Lina proved so helpful, and so ready to risk her life for the sake of her companion, that Curdie grew not merely very fond but very trustful of her, and her ugliness, which at first only moved his pity, now actually increased his affection for her. One day, looking at her stretched on the grass before him, he said,—

"Oh, Lina! if the princess would but burn you in her fire of roses!"

She looked up at him, gave a mournful whine like a dog, and laid her head on his feet. What or how much he could not tell, but clearly she had gathered something from his words.

MORE CREATURES

One day from morning till night they had been passing through a forest. As soon as the sun was down Curdie began to be aware that there were more in it than themselves. First he saw only the swift rush of a figure across the trees at some distance. Then he saw another and then another at shorter intervals. Then he saw others both further off and nearer. At last, missing Lina and looking about after her, he saw an appearance almost as marvellous as herself steal up to her, and begin conversing with her after some beast fashion which evidently she understood.

Presently what seemed a quarrel arose between them, and stranger noises followed, mingled with growling. At length it came to a fight, which had not lasted long, however, before the creature of the wood threw itself upon its back, and held up its paws to Lina. She instantly walked on, and the creature got up and followed her. They had not gone far before another strange animal appeared, approaching Lina, when precisely the same thing was repeated, the vanquished animal rising and following with the former. Again, and yet again and again, a fresh animal came up, seemed to be reasoned and certainly was fought with and overcome by Lina, until at last, before they were out of the wood, she was followed by forty-nine of the most grotesquely ugly, the most extravagantly abnormal animals imagination can conceive. To describe them were a hopeless task. I knew a boy who used to make animals out of heather roots. Wherever he could find four legs, he was pretty sure to find a head and a tail. His beasts were a most comic menagerie, and right fruitful of laughter. But they were not so grotesque and extravagant as Lina and her followers. One of them, for instance, was like a boa constrictor walking on four little stumpy legs near its tail. About the same distance from its head were two little wings, which it was for ever fluttering as if trying to fly with them. Curdie thought it fancied it did fly with them, when it was merely plodding on busily with its four little stumps. How it managed to keep up he could not think, till once when he missed it from the group: the same moment he caught sight of something at a

489

distance plunging at an awful serpentine rate through the trees, and presently, from behind a huge ash, this same creature fell again into the group, quietly waddling along on its four stumps. Watching it after this, he saw that, when it was not able to keep up any longer, and they had all got a little space ahead, it shot into the wood away from the route, and made a great round, serpenting along in huge billows of motion, devouring the ground, undulating awfully, galloping as if it were all legs together, and its four stumps nowhere. In this mad fashion it shot ahead, and, a few minutes after, toddled in again amongst the rest, walking peacefully and somewhat painfully on its few fours.

From the time it takes to describe one of them it will be readily seen that it would hardly do to attempt a description of each of the forty-nine. They were not a goodly company, but well worth contemplating nevertheless; and Curdie had been too long used to the goblins' creatures in the mines and on the mountain, to feel the least uncomfortable at being followed by such a herd. On the contrary the marvellous vagaries of shape they manifested amused him greatly, and shortened the journey much. Before they were all gathered, however, it had got so dark that he could see some of them only a part at a time, and every now and then, as the company wandered on, he would be startled by some extraordinary limb or feature, undreamed of by him before, thrusting itself out of the darkness into the range of his ken. Probably there were some of his old acquaintances among them, although such had been the conditions of semi-darkness in which alone he had ever seen any of them, that it was not likely he would be able to identify any of them.

On they marched solemnly, almost in silence, for either with feet or voice the creatures seldom made any noise. By the time they reached the outside of the wood it was morning twilight. Into the open trooped the strange torrent of deformity, each one following Lina. Suddenly she stopped, turned towards them, and said something which they understood, although to Curdie's ear the sounds she made seemed to have no articulation. Instantly they all turned, and vanished in the forest, and Lina alone came trotting lithely and clumsily after her master.

THE BAKER'S WIFE

They were now passing through a lovely country of hill and dale and rushing stream. The hills were abrupt, with broken chasms for water-courses, and deep little valleys full of trees. But now and then they came to a larger valley, with a fine river, whose level banks and the adjacent meadows were dotted all over with red and white kine, while on the fields above, that sloped a little to the foot of the hills, grew oats and barley and wheat, and on the sides of the hills themselves vines hung and chestnuts rose. They came at last to a broad, beautiful river, up which they must go to arrive at the city of Gwyntystorm, where the king had his court. As they went the valley narrowed, and then the river, but still it was wide enough for large boats. After this, while the river kept its size, the banks narrowed, until there was only room for a road between the river and the great cliffs that overhung it. At last river and road took a sudden turn, and lo! a great rock in the river, which dividing flowed around it, and on the top of the rock the city, with lofty walls and towers and battlements, and above the city the palace of the king, built like a strong castle. But the fortifications had long been neglected, for the whole country was now under one king, and all men said there was no more need for weapons or walls. No man pretended to love his neighbour, but every one said he knew that peace and quiet behaviour was the best thing for himself, and that, he said, was quite as useful, and a great deal more reasonable. The city was prosperous and rich, and if anybody was not comfortable, everybody else said he ought to be.

When Curdie got up opposite the mighty rock, which sparkled all over with crystals, he found a narrow bridge, defended by gates and portcullis and towers with loopholes. But the gates stood wide open, and were dropping from their great hinges; the portcullis was eaten away with rust, and clung to the grooves evidently immovable; while the loopholed towers had neither floor nor roof, and their tops were fast filling up their interiors. Curdie thought it a pity, if only for their old story, that they should be thus neglected. But everybody in the city regarded these signs of decay as the best proof of the prosperity of the place. Commerce and self-interest, they said, had got the better of violence, and the troubles of the past were whelmed in the riches that flowed in at their open gates. Indeed there was one sect of philosophers in it which taught that it would be better to forget all the past history of the city, were it not that its former imperfections taught its present inhabitants how superior they and their times were, and enabled them to glory over their ancestors. There were even certain quacks in the city who advertised pills for enabling people to think well of themselves, and some few bought of them, but most laughed, and said, with evident truth, that they did not require them. Indeed, the general theme of discourse when they met was, how much wiser they were than their fathers.

Curdie crossed the river, and began to ascend the winding road that led up to the city. They met a good many idlers, and all stared at them. It was no wonder they should stare, but there was an unfriendliness in their looks which Curdie did not like. No one, however, offered them any molestation: Lina did not invite liberties. After a long ascent, they reached the principal gate of the city and entered.

The street was very steep, ascending towards the palace, which rose in great strength above all the houses. Just as they entered, a baker, whose shop was a few doors inside the gate, came out in his white apron, and ran to the shop of his friend the barber on the opposite side of the way. But as he ran he stumbled and fell heavily. Curdie hastened to help him up, and found he had bruised his forehead badly. He swore grievously at the stone for tripping him up, declaring it was the third time he had fallen over it within the last month; and saying what was the king about that he allowed such a stone to stick up for ever on the main street of his royal residence of Gwyntystorm! What was a king for if he would not take care of his people's heads! And he stroked his forehead tenderly.

"Was it your head or your feet that ought to bear the blame of your fall?" asked Curdie.

"Why, you booby of a miner! my feet, of course," answered the baker.

"Nay, then," said Curdie, "the king can't be to blame."

"Oh, I see!" said the baker. "You're laying a trap for me. Of course, if you come to that, it was my head that ought to have looked after my feet. But it is the king's part to look after us all, and have his streets smooth."

"Well, I don't see," said Curdie, "why the king should take care of the baker, when the baker's head won't take care of the baker's feet."

"Who are you to make game of the king's baker?" cried the man in a rage.

But, instead of answering, Curdie went up to the bump on the street which had repeated itself on the baker's head, and turning the hammer end of his mattock, struck it such a blow that it flew wide in pieces. Blow after blow he struck, until he had levelled it with the street.

But out flew the barber upon him in a rage.

"What do you break my window for, you rascal, with your pickaxe?"

"I am very sorry," said Curdie. "It must have been a bit of stone that flew from my mattock. I couldn't help it, you know."

"Couldn't help it! A fine story! What do you go breaking the rock for—the very rock upon which the city stands?"

"Look at your friend's forehead," said Curdie. "See what a lump he has got on it with falling over that same stone."

"What's that to my window?" cried the barber. "His forehead can mend itself; my poor window can't."

"But he's the king's baker," said Curdie, more and more surprised at the man's anger.

"What's that to me? This is a free city. Every man here takes care of himself, and the king takes care of us all. I'll have the price of my window out of you, or the exchequer shall pay for it."

Something caught Curdie's eye. He stooped, picked up a piece of the stone he had just broken, and put it in his pocket.

"I suppose you are going to break another of my windows with that stone!" said the barber.

"Oh no," said Curdie. "I didn't mean to break your window, and I certainly won't break another."

"Give me that stone," said the barber.

Curdie gave it to him, and the barber threw it over the city wall.

"I thought you wanted the stone," said Curdie.

"No, you fool!" answered the barber. "What should I want with a stone?"

Curdie stooped and picked up another.

"Give me that stone," said the barber.

"No," answered Curdie. "You have just told me you don't want a stone, and I do."

The barber took Curdie by the collar.

"Come, now! you pay me for that window."

"How much?" asked Curdie.

The barber said, "A crown." But the baker, annoyed at the heartlessness of the barber, in thinking more of his broken window than the bump on his friend's forehead, interfered.

"No, no," he said to Curdie; "don't you pay any such sum. A little pane like that cost only a quarter."

"Well, to be certain," said Curdie, "I'll give him a half." For he doubted the baker as well as the barber. "Perhaps one day, if he finds he has asked too much, he will bring me the difference."

"Ha! ha!" laughed the barber. "A fool and his money are soon parted."

But as he took the coin from Curdie's hand he grasped it in affected reconciliation and real satisfaction. In Curdie's, his was the cold smooth leathery palm of a monkey. He looked up, almost expecting to see him pop the money in his cheek; but he had not yet got so far as that, though he was well on the road to it: then he would have no other pocket.

"I'm glad that stone is gone, anyhow," said the baker. "It was the bane of my life. I had no idea how easy it was to remove it. Give me your pickaxe, young miner, and I will show you how a baker can make the stones fly."

He caught the tool out of Curdie's hand, and flew at one of the foundation stones of the gateway. But he jarred his arm terribly, scarcely chipped the stone, dropped the mattock with a cry of pain, and ran into his own shop. Curdie picked up his implement, and looking after the baker, saw bread in the window, and followed him in. But the baker, ashamed of himself, and thinking he was coming to laugh at him, popped out of the back door, and when Curdie entered, the baker's wife came from the bakehouse to serve him. Curdie requested to know the price of a certain good-sized loaf.

Now the baker's wife had been watching what had passed since first her husband ran out of the shop, and she liked the look of Curdie. Also she was more honest than her husband. Casting a glance to the back door, she replied,—

"That is not the best bread. I will sell you a loaf of what we bake for ourselves." And when she had spoken she laid a finger on her lips. "Take care of yourself in this place, my son," she added. "They do not love strangers. I was once a stranger here, and I know what I say." Then fancying she heard her husband,—"That is a strange animal you have," she said, in a louder voice.

"Yes," answered Curdie. "She is no beauty, but she is very good, and we love each other. Don't we, Lina?"

Lina looked up and whined. Curdie threw her the half of his loaf, which she ate while her master and the baker's wife talked a little. Then the baker's wife gave them some water, and Curdie having paid for his loaf, he and Lina went up the street together.

THE DOGS OF GWYNTYSTORM

The steep street led them straight up to a large market-place, with butchers' shops, about which were many dogs. The moment they caught sight of Lina, one and all they came rushing down upon her, giving her no chance of explaining herself. When Curdie saw the dogs coming he heaved up his mattock over his shoulder, and was ready, if they would have it so. Seeing him thus prepared to defend his follower, a great ugly bull-dog flew at him. With the first blow Curdie struck him through the brain, and the brute fell dead at his feet. But he could not at once recover his weapon, which stuck in the skull of his foe, and a huge mastiff, seeing him thus hampered, flew at him next. Now Lina, who had shown herself so brave upon the road thither, had grown shy upon entering the city, and kept always at Curdie's heel. But it was her turn now. The moment she saw her master in danger she seemed to go mad with rage. As the mastiff jumped at Curdie's throat, Lina flew at his, seized him with her tremendous jaws, gave one roaring grind, and he lay beside the bull-dog with his neck broken. They were the best dogs in the market, after the judgment of the butchers of Gwyntystorm. Down came their masters, knife in hand.

Curdie drew himself up fearlessly, mattock on shoulder, and awaited their coming, while at his heel his awful attendant showed not only her outside fringe of icicle-teeth, but a double row of right serviceable fangs she wore inside her mouth, and her green eyes flashed yellow as gold. The butchers not liking the look either of them or of the dogs at their feet, drew back, and began to remonstrate in the manner of outraged men.

"Stranger," said the first, "that bull-dog is mine."

"Take him, then," said Curdie, indignant.

"You've killed him!"

"Yes—else he would have killed me."

"That's no business of mine."

"No?"

"No."

"That makes it the more mine, then."

"This sort of thing won't do, you know," said the other butcher.

"That's true," said Curdie.

"That's my mastiff," said the butcher.

"And as he ought to be," said Curdie.

"Your brute shall be burnt alive for it," said the butcher.

"Not yet," answered Curdie. "We have done no wrong. We were walking quietly up your street, when your dogs flew at us. If you don't teach your dogs how to treat strangers, you must take the consequences."

"They treat them quite properly," said the butcher. "What right has any one to bring an abomination like that into our city? The horror is enough to make an idiot of every child in the place."

"We are both subjects of the king, and my poor animal can't help her looks. How would you like to be served like that because you were ugly? She's not a bit fonder of her looks than you are—only what can she do to change them?"

"I'll do to change them," said the fellow.

Thereupon the butchers brandished their long knives and advanced, keeping their eyes upon Lina.

"Don't be afraid, Lina," cried Curdie. "I'll kill one—you kill the other."

Lina gave a howl that might have terrified an army, and crouched ready to spring. The butchers turned and ran.

By this time a great crowd had gathered behind the butchers, and in it a number of boys returning from school, who began to stone the strangers. It was a way they had with man or beast they did not expect to make anything by. One of the stones struck Lina; she caught it in her teeth and crunched it that it fell in gravel from her mouth. Some of the foremost of the crowd saw this, and it terrified them. They drew back; the rest took fright from their retreat; the panic spread; and at last the crowd scattered in all directions. They ran, and cried out, and said the devil and his dam were come to Gwyntystorm. So Curdie and Lina were left standing unmolested in the market-place. But the terror of them spread throughout the city, and everybody began to shut and lock his door, so that by the time the setting sun shone down the street, there was not a shop left open, for fear of the devil and his horrible dam. But all the upper windows within sight of them were crowded with heads watching them where they stood lonely in the deserted market-place.

Curdie looked carefully all round, but could not see one open door. He caught sight of the sign of an inn however, and laying down his mattock, and telling Lina to take care of it, walked up to the door of it and knocked. But the people in the house, instead of opening the door, threw things at him from the windows. They would not listen to a word he said, but sent him back to Lina with the blood running down his face. When Lina saw that, she leaped up in a fury and was rushing at the house, into which she would certainly have broken; but Curdie called her, and made her lie down beside him while he bethought him what next he should do.

"Lina," he said, "the people keep their gates open, but their houses and their hearts shut."

As if she knew it was her presence that had brought this trouble upon him, she rose, and went round and round him, purring like a tigress, and rubbing herself against his legs.

Now there was one little thatched house that stood squeezed in between two tall gables, and the sides of the two great houses shot out projecting windows that nearly met across the roof of the little one, so that it lay in the street like a doll's house. In this house lived a poor old woman, with a grandchild. And because she never gossiped or quarrelled, or chaffered in the market, but went without what she could not afford, the people called her a witch, and would have done her many an ill turn if they had not been afraid of her. Now while Curdie was looking in another direction the door opened, and out came a little dark-haired, black-eyed, gipsy-looking child, and toddled across the market-place towards the outcasts. The moment they saw her coming, Lina lay down flat on the road, and with her two huge fore-paws covered her mouth, while Curdie went to meet her, holding out his arms. The little one came straight to him, and held up her mouth to be kissed. Then she took him by the hand, and drew him towards the house, and Curdie yielded to the silent invitation. But when Lina rose to follow, the child shrunk from her, frightened a little. Curdie took her up, and holding her on one arm, patted Lina with the other hand. Then the child wanted also to pat doggy, as she called her by a right bountiful stretch of courtesy, and having once patted her, nothing would serve but Curdie must let her have a ride on doggy. So he set her on Lina's back, holding her hand, and she rode home in merry triumph, all unconscious of the hundreds of eyes staring at her foolhardiness from the windows about the market-place, or the murmur of deep disapproval that rose from as many lips. At the door stood the grandmother to receive them. She caught the child to her bosom with delight at her courage, welcomed Curdie, and showed no dread of Lina. Many were the significant nods exchanged, and many a one said to another that the devil and the witch were old friends. But the woman was only a wise woman, who having seen how Curdie and Lina behaved to each other, judged from that what sort they were, and so made them welcome to her house. She was not like her fellow-townspeople, for that they were strangers recommended them to her.

The moment her door was shut, the other doors began to open, and soon there appeared little groups about here and there a threshold, while a few of the more courageous ventured out upon the square—all ready to make for their houses again, however, upon the least sign of movement in the little thatched one.

The baker and the barber had joined one of these groups, and were busily wagging their tongues against Curdie and his horrible beast.

"He can't be honest," said the barber; "for he paid me double the worth of the pane he broke in my window."

And then he told them how Curdie broke his window by breaking a stone in the street with his hammer. There the baker struck in.

"Now that was the stone," said he, "over which I had fallen three times within the last month: could it be by fair means he broke that to pieces at the first blow? Just to make up my mind on that point I tried his own hammer against a stone in the gate; it nearly broke both my arms, and loosened half the teeth in my head!"

DERBA AND BARBARA

Meantime the wanderers were hospitably entertained by the old woman and her grandchild, and they were all very comfortable and happy together. Little Barbara sat upon Curdie's knee, and he told her stories about the mines and his adventures in them. But he never mentioned the king or the princess, for all that story was hard to believe. And he told her about his mother and his father, and how good they were. And Derba sat and listened. At last little Barbara fell asleep in Curdie's arms, and her grandmother carried her to bed.

It was a poor little house, and Derba gave up her own room to Curdie, because he was honest and talked wisely. Curdie saw how it was, and begged her to allow him to lie on the floor, but she would not hear of it.

In the night he was waked by Lina pulling at him. As soon as he spoke to her she ceased, and Curdie, listening, thought he heard some one trying to get in. He rose, took his mattock, and went about the house, listening and watching; but although he heard noises now at one place, now at another, he could not think what they meant, for no one appeared. Certainly, considering how she had frightened them all in the day, it was not likely any one would attack Lina at night. By-and-by the noises ceased, and Curdie went back to his bed, and slept undisturbed.

In the morning, however, Derba came to him in great agitation, and said they had fastened up the door, so that she could not get out. Curdie rose immediately and went with her: they found that not only the door, but every window in the house was so secured on the outside that it was impossible to open one of them without using great force. Poor Derba looked anxiously in Curdie's face. He broke out laughing.

"They are much mistaken," he said, "if they fancy they could keep Lina and a miner in any house in Gwyntystorm—even if they built up doors and windows."

With that he shouldered his mattock. But Derba begged him not to make a hole in her house just yet. She had plenty for breakfast, she said, and before it was time for dinner they would know what the people meant by it.

And indeed they did. For within an hour appeared one of the chief magistrates of the city, accompanied by a score of soldiers with drawn swords, and followed by a great multitude of the people, requiring the miner and his brute to yield themselves, the one that he might be tried for the disturbance he had occasioned and the injury he had committed, the other that she might be roasted alive for her part in killing two valuable and harmless animals belonging to worthy citizens. The summons was preceded and followed by flourish of trumpet, and was read with every formality by the city marshal himself.

The moment he ended, Lina ran into the little passage, and stood opposite the door.

"I surrender," cried Curdie.

"Then tie up your brute, and give her here."

"No, no," cried Curdie through the door. "I surrender; but I'm not going to do your hangman's work. If you want my dog, you must take her."

"Then we shall set the house on fire, and burn witch and all."

"It will go hard with us but we shall kill a few dozen of you first," cried Curdie. "We're not the least afraid of you."

With that Curdie turned to Derba, and said:—

"Don't be frightened. I have a strong feeling that all will be well. Surely no trouble will come to you for being good to strangers."

"But the poor dog!" said Derba.

Now Curdie and Lina understood each other more than a little by this time, and not only had he seen that she understood the proclamation, but when she looked up at him after it was read, it was with such a grin, and such a yellow flash, that he saw also she was determined to take care of herself.

"The dog will probably give you reason to think a little more of her ere long," he answered. "But now," he went on, "I fear I must hurt your house a little. I have great confidence, however, that I shall be able to make up to you for it one day."

"Never mind the house, if only you can get safe off," she answered. "I don't think they will hurt this precious lamb," she added, clasping little Barbara to her bosom. "For myself, it is all one; I am ready for anything."

"It is but a little hole for Lina I want to make," said Curdie. "She can creep through a much smaller one than you would think."

Again he took his mattock, and went to the back wall.

"They won't burn the house," he said to himself. "There is too good a one on each side of it."

The tumult had kept increasing every moment, and the city marshal had been shouting, but Curdie had not listened to him. When now they heard the blows of his mattock, there went up a great cry, and the people taunted the soldiers that they were afraid of a dog and his miner. The soldiers therefore made a rush at the door, and cut its fastenings.

The moment they opened it, out leaped Lina, with a roar so unnaturally horrible that the sword-arms of the soldiers dropped by their sides, paralysed with the terror of that cry; the crowd fled in every direction, shrieking and yelling with mortal dismay; and without even knocking down with her tail, not to say biting a man of them with her pulverizing jaws, Lina vanished—no one knew whither, for not one of the crowd had had courage to look upon her.

The moment she was gone, Curdie advanced and gave himself up. The soldiers were so filled with fear, shame, and chagrin, that they were ready to kill him on the spot. But he stood quietly facing them, with his mattock on his shoulder; and the magistrate wishing to examine him, and the people to see him made an example of, the soldiers had to content themselves with taking him. Partly for derision, partly to hurt him, they laid his mattock against his back, and tied his arms to it.

They led him up a very steep street, and up another still, all the crowd following. The king's palace-castle rose towering above them; but they stopped before they reached it, at a low-browed door in a great, dull, heavy-looking building.

The city marshal opened it with a key which hung at his girdle, and ordered Curdie to enter. The place within was dark as night, and while he was feeling his way with his feet, the marshal gave him a rough push. He fell, and rolled once or twice over, unable to help himself because his hands were tied behind him.

It was the hour of the magistrate's second and more important breakfast, and until that was over he never found himself capable of attending to a case with concentration sufficient to the distinguishing of the side upon which his own advantage lay; and hence was this respite for Curdie, with time to collect his thoughts. But indeed he had very few to collect, for all he had to do, so far as he could see, was to wait for what would come next. Neither had he much power to collect them, for he was a good deal shaken.

In a few minutes he discovered, to his great relief, that, from the projection of the pick-end of his mattock beyond his body, the fall had loosened the ropes tied round it. He got one hand disengaged, and then the other; and presently stood free, with his good mattock once more in right serviceable relation to his arms and legs.

THE MATTOCK

While the magistrate reinvigorated his selfishness with a greedy breakfast, Curdie found doing nothing in the dark rather wearisome work. It was useless attempting to think what he should do next, seeing the circumstances in which he was presently to find himself were altogether unknown to him. So he began to think about his father and mother in their little cottage home, high in the clear air of the open mountain-side, and the thought, instead of making his dungeon gloomier by the contrast, made a light in his soul that destroyed the power of darkness and captivity. But he was at length startled from his waking dream by a swell in the noise outside. All the time there had been a few of the more idle of the inhabitants about the door, but they had been rather quiet. Now, however, the sounds of feet and voices began to grow, and grew so rapidly that it was plain a multitude was gathering. For the people of Gwyntystorm always gave themselves an hour of pleasure after their second breakfast, and what greater pleasure could they have than to see a stranger abused by the officers of justice? The noise grew till it was like the roaring of the sea, and that roaring went on a long time, for the magistrate, being a great man, liked to know that he was waited for: it added to the enjoyment of his breakfast, and, indeed, enabled him to eat a little more after he had thought his powers exhausted. But at length, in the waves of the human noises rose a bigger wave, and by the running and shouting and outcry, Curdie learned that the magistrate was approaching.

Presently came the sound of the great rusty key in the lock, which yielded with groaning reluctance; the door was thrown back, the light rushed in, and with it came the voice of the city marshal, calling upon Curdie, by many legal epithets opprobrious, to come forth and be tried for his life, inasmuch as he had raised a tumult in his majesty's city of Gwyntystorm, troubled the hearts of the king's baker and barber, and slain the faithful dogs of his majesty's well-beloved butchers.

He was still reading, and Curdie was still seated in the brown twilight of the vault, not listening, but pondering with himself how this king the city marshal talked of could be the same with the majesty he had seen ride away on his grand white horse, with the Princess Irene on a cushion before him, when a scream of agonized terror arose on the farthest skirt of the crowd, and, swifter than flood or flame, the horror spread shrieking. In a moment the air was filled with hideous howling, cries of unspeakable dismay, and the multitudinous noise of running feet. The next moment, in at the door of the vault bounded Lina, her two green eyes flaming yellow as sunflowers, and seeming to light up the dungeon. With one spring she threw herself at Curdie's feet, and laid her head upon them panting. Then came a rush of two or three soldiers darkening the doorway, but it was only to lay hold of the key, pull the door to, and lock it; so that once more Curdie and Lina were prisoners together.

For a few moments Lina lay panting hard: it is breathless work leaping and roaring both at once, and that in a way to scatter thousands of people. Then she jumped up, and began snuffing about all over the place; and Curdie saw what he had never seen before—two faint spots of light cast from her eyes upon the ground, one on each side of her snuffing nose. He got out his tinder-box—a miner is never without one—and lighted a precious bit of candle he carried in a division of it—just for a moment, for he must not waste it.

The light revealed a vault without any window or other opening than the door. It was very old and much neglected. The mortar had vanished from between the stones, and it was half filled with a heap of all sorts of rubbish, beaten down in the middle, but looser at the sides; it sloped from the door to the foot of the opposite wall: evidently for a long time the vault had been left open, and every sort of refuse thrown into it. A single minute served for the survey, so little was there to note.

Meantime, down in the angle between the back wall and the base of the heap Lina was scratching furiously with all the eighteen great strong claws of her mighty feet.

"Ah, ha!" said Curdie to himself, catching sight of her, "if only they will leave us long enough to ourselves!"

With that he ran to the door, to see if there was any fastening on the inside. There was none: in all its long history it never had had one. But a few blows of the right sort, now from the one, now from the other end of his mattock, were as good as any bolt, for they so ruined the lock that no key could ever turn in it again. Those who heard them fancied he was trying to get out, and laughed spitefully. As soon as he had done, he extinguished his candle, and went down to Lina.

She had reached the hard rock which formed the floor of the dungeon, and was now clearing away the earth a little wider. Presently she looked up in his face and whined, as much as to say, "My paws are not hard enough to get any further."

"Then get out of my way, Lina," said Curdie, "and mind you keep your eyes shining, for fear I should hit you."

So saying, he heaved his mattock, and assailed with the hammer end of it the spot she had cleared.

The rock was very hard, but when it did break it broke in good-sized pieces. Now with hammer, now with pick, he worked till he was weary, then rested, and then set to again. He could not tell how the day went, as he had no light but the lamping of Lina's eyes. The darkness hampered him greatly, for he would not let Lina come close enough to give him all the light she could, lest he should strike her. So he had, every now and then, to feel with his hands to know how he was getting on, and to discover in what direction to strike: the exact spot was a mere imagination.

He was getting very tired and hungry, and beginning to lose heart a little, when out of the ground, as if he had struck a spring of it, burst a dull, gleamy, lead-coloured light, and the next moment he heard a hollow splash and echo. A piece of rock had fallen out of the floor, and dropped into water beneath. Already Lina, who had been lying a few yards off all the time he worked, was on her feet and peering through the hole. Curdie got down on his hands and knees, and looked. They were over what seemed a natural cave in the rock, to which apparently the river had access, for, at a great distance below, a faint light was gleaming upon water. If they could but reach it, they might get out; but even if it was deep enough, the height was very dangerous. The first thing, whatever might follow, was to make the hole larger. It was comparatively easy to break away the sides of it, and in the course of another hour he had it large enough to get through.

And now he must reconnoitre. He took the rope they had tied him with—for Curdie's hindrances were always his furtherance—and fastened one end of it by a slip-knot round the handle of his pickaxe, then dropped the other end through, and laid the pickaxe so that, when he was through himself, and hanging on to the edge, he could place it across the hole to support him on the rope. This done, he took the rope in his hands, and, beginning to descend, found himself in a narrow cleft widening into a cave. His rope was not very long, and would not do much to lessen the force of his fall—he thought with himself—if he should have to drop into the water; but he was not more than a couple of yards below the dungeon when he spied an opening on the opposite side of the cleft: it might be but a shallow hole, or it might lead them out. He dropped himself a little below its level, gave the rope a swing by pushing his feet against the side of the cleft, and so pendulled himself into it. Then he laid a stone on the end of the rope that it should not forsake him, called to Lina, whose yellow eyes were gleaming over the mattock-grating above, to watch there till he returned, and went cautiously in.

It proved a passage, level for some distance, then sloping gently up. He advanced carefully, feeling his way as he went. At length he was stopped by a door —a small door, studded with iron. But the wood was in places so much decayed that some of the bolts had dropped out, and he felt sure of being able to open it. He returned, therefore, to fetch Lina and his mattock. Arrived at the cleft, his strong miner arms bore him swiftly up along the rope and through the hole into the dungeon. There he undid the rope from his mattock, and making Lina take the end of it in her teeth, and get through the hole, he lowered her—it was all he could do, she was so heavy. When she came opposite the passage, with a slight push of her tail she shot herself into it, and let go the rope, which Curdie drew up. Then he lighted his candle and searching in the rubbish found a bit of iron to take the place of his pickaxe across the hole. Then he searched again in the rubbish, and found half an old shutter. This he propped up leaning a little over the hole, with a bit of stick, and heaped against the back of it a quantity of the loosened earth. Next he tied his mattock to the end of the rope, dropped it, and let it hang. Last, he got through the hole himself, and pulled away the propping stick, so that the shutter fell over the hole with a quantity of earth on the top of it. A few motions of hand over hand, and he swung himself and his mattock into the passage beside Lina. There he secured the end of the rope, and they went on together to the door.

THE WINE-CELLAR

He lighted his candle and examined it. Decayed and broken as it was, it was strongly secured in its place by hinges on the one side, and either lock or bolt, he could not tell which, on the other. A brief use of his pocket-knife was enough to make room for his hand and arm to get through, and then he found a great iron bolt —but so rusty that he could not move it. Lina whimpered. He took his knife again, made the hole bigger, and stood back. In she shot her small head and long neck, seized the bolt with her teeth, and dragged it grating and complaining back. A push then opened the door. It was at the foot of a short flight of steps. They ascended, and at the top Curdie found himself in a space which, from the echo to his stamp, appeared of some size, though of what sort he could not at first tell, for his hands, feeling about, came upon nothing. Presently, however, they fell on a great thing: it was a wine-cask.

"Curdie was just setting out to explore the place when he heard steps coming down a stair."

He was just setting out to explore the place by a thorough palpation, when he heard steps coming down a stair. He stood still, not knowing whether the door would open an inch from his nose or twenty yards behind his back. It did neither. He heard the key turn in the lock, and a stream of light shot in, ruining the darkness, about fifteen yards away on his right.

A man carrying a candle in one hand and a large silver flagon in the other, entered, and came towards him. The light revealed a row of huge wine-casks, that stretched away into the darkness of the other end of the long vault. Curdie retreated into the recess of the stair, and peeping round the corner of it, watched him, thinking what he could do to prevent him from locking them in. He came on and on, until Curdie feared he would pass the recess and see them. He was just preparing to rush out, and master him before he should give alarm, not in the least knowing what he should do next, when, to his relief, the man stopped at the third cask from where he stood. He set down his light on the top of it, removed what seemed a large vent-peg, and poured into the cask a quantity of something from the flagon. Then he turned to the next cask, drew some wine, rinsed the flagon, threw the wine away, drew and rinsed and threw away again, then drew and drank, draining to the bottom. Last of all, he filled the flagon from the cask he had first visited, replaced then the vent-peg, took up his candle, and turned towards the door.

"There is something wrong here!" thought Curdie.

"Speak to him, Lina," he whispered.

The sudden howl she gave made Curdie himself start and tremble for a moment. As to the man, he answered Lina's with another horrible howl, forced from him by the convulsive shudder of every muscle of his body, then reeled gasping to and fro, and dropped his candle. But just as Curdie expected to see him fall dead he recovered himself, and flew to the door, through which he darted, leaving it open behind him. The moment he ran, Curdie stepped out, picked up the candle still alight, sped after him to the door, drew out the key, and then returned to the stair and waited. In a few minutes he heard the sound of many feet and voices. Instantly he turned the tap of the cask from which the man had been drinking, set the candle beside it on the floor, went down the steps and out of the little door, followed by Lina, and closed it behind them.

Through the hole in it he could see a little, and hear all. He could see how the light of many candles filled the place, and could hear how some two dozen feet ran hither and thither through the echoing cellar; he could hear the clash of iron, probably spits and pokers, now and then; and at last heard how, finding nothing remarkable except the best wine running to waste, they all turned on the butler, and accused him of having fooled them with a drunken dream. He did his best to defend himself, appealing to the evidence of their own senses that he was as sober as they were. They replied that a fright was no less a fright that the cause was imaginary, and a dream no less a dream that the fright had waked him from it. When he discovered, and triumphantly adduced as corroboration, that the key was gone from the door, they said it merely showed how drunk he had been—either that or how frightened, for he had certainly dropped it. In vain he protested that he had never taken it out of the lock—that he never did when he went in, and certainly had not this time stopped to do so when he came out; they asked him why he had to go to the cellar at such a time of the day, and said it was because he had already drunk all the wine that was left from dinner. He said if he had dropped the key, the key was to be found, and they must help him to find it. They told him they wouldn't move a peg for him. He declared, with much language, he would have them all turned out of the king's service. They said they would swear he was drunk. And so positive were they about it, that at last the butler himself began to think whether it was possible they could be in the right. For he knew that sometimes when he had been drunk he fancied things had taken place which he found afterwards could not have happened. Certain of his fellow-servants, however, had all the time a doubt whether the cellar goblin had not appeared to him, or at least roared at him, to protect the wine. In any case nobody wanted to find the key for him; nothing could please them better than that the door of the wine-cellar should never more be locked. By degrees the hubbub died away, and they departed, not even pulling to the door, for there was neither handle nor latch to it.

As soon as they were gone, Curdie returned, knowing now that they were in the wine-cellar of the palace, as, indeed, he had suspected. Finding a pool of wine in a hollow of the floor, Lina lapped it up eagerly: she had had no breakfast, and was now very thirsty as well as hungry. Her master was in a similar plight, for he had but just begun to eat when the magistrate arrived with the soldiers. If only they were all in bed, he thought, that he might find his way to the larder! For he said to himself that, as he was sent there by the young princess's great-great-grandmother to serve her or her father in some way, surely he must have a right to his food in the palace, without which he could do nothing. He would go at once and reconnoitre.

So he crept up the stair that led from the cellar. At the top was a door, opening on a long passage, dimly lighted by a lamp. He told Lina to lie down upon the stair while he went on. At the end of the passage he found a door ajar, and, peeping through, saw right into a great stone hall, where a huge fire was blazing, and through which men in the king's livery were constantly coming and going. Some also in the same livery were lounging about the fire. He noted that their colours were the same with those he himself, as king's miner, wore; but from what he had seen and heard of the habits of the place, he could not hope they would treat him the better for that.

The one interesting thing at the moment, however, was the plentiful supper with which the table was spread. It was something at least to stand in sight of food, and he was unwilling to turn his back on the prospect so long as a share in it was not absolutely hopeless. Peeping thus, he soon made up his mind that if at any moment the hall should be empty, he would at that moment rush in and attempt to carry off a dish. That he might lose no time by indecision, he selected a large pie upon which to pounce instantaneously. But after he had watched for some minutes, it did not seem at all likely the chance would arrive before supper-time, and he was just about to turn away and rejoin Lina, when he saw that there was not a person in the place. Curdie never made up his mind and then hesitated. He darted in, seized the pie, and bore it, swiftly and noiselessly, to the cellar stair.

THE KING'S KITCHEN

Back to the cellar Curdie and Lina sped with their booty, where, seated on the steps, Curdie lighted his bit of candle for a moment. A very little bit it was now, but they did not waste much of it in examination of the pie; that they effected by a more summary process. Curdie thought it the nicest food he had ever tasted, and between them they soon ate it up. Then Curdie would have thrown the dish along with the bones into the water, that there might be no traces of them; but he thought of his mother, and hid it instead; and the very next minute they wanted it to draw some wine into. He was careful it should be from the cask of which he had seen the butler drink. Then they sat down again upon the steps, and waited until the house should be quiet. For he was there to do something, and if it did not come to him in the cellar, he must go to meet it in other places. Therefore, lest he should fall asleep, he set the end of the helve of his mattock on the ground, and seated himself on the cross part, leaning against the wall, so that as long as he kept awake he should rest, but the moment he began to fall asleep he must fall awake instead. He quite expected some of the servants would visit the cellar again that night, but whether it was that they were afraid of each other, or believed more of the butler's story than they had chosen to allow, not one of them appeared.

When at length he thought he might venture, he shouldered his mattock and crept up the stair. The lamp was out in the passage, but he could not miss his way to the servants' hall. Trusting to Lina's quickness in concealing herself, he took her with him.

When they reached the hall they found it quiet and nearly dark. The last of the great fire was glowing red, but giving little light. Curdie stood and warmed himself for a few moments: miner as he was, he had found the cellar cold to sit in doing nothing; and standing thus he thought of looking if there were any bits of candle about. There were many candlesticks on the supper-table, but to his disappointment and indignation their candles seemed to have been all left to burn out, and some of them, indeed, he found still hot in the neck.

Presently, one after another, he came upon seven men fast asleep, most of them upon tables, one in a chair, and one on the floor. They seemed, from their shape and colour, to have eaten and drunk so much that they might be burned alive without waking. He grasped the hand of each in succession, and found two ox-hoofs, three pig-hoofs, one concerning which he could not be sure whether it was the hoof of a donkey or a pony, and one dog's paw. "A nice set of people to be about a king!" thought Curdie to himself, and turned again to his candle hunt. He did at last find two or three little pieces, and stowed them away in his pockets.

They now left the hall by another door, and entered a short passage, which led them to the huge kitchen, vaulted, and black with smoke. There too the fire was still burning, so that he was able to see a little of the state of things in this quarter also. The place was dirty and disorderly. In a recess, on a heap of brushwood, lay a kitchenmaid, with a table-cover around her, and a skillet in her hand: evidently she too had been drinking. In another corner lay a page, and Curdie noted how like his dress was to his own. In the cinders before the hearth were huddled three dogs and five cats, all fast asleep, while the rats were running about the floor. Curdie's heart ached to think of the lovely child-princess living over such a sty. The mine was a paradise to a palace with such servants in it.

Leaving the kitchen, he got into the region of the sculleries. There horrible smells were wandering about, like evil spirits that come forth with the darkness. He lighted a candle—but only to see ugly sights. Everywhere was filth and disorder. Mangy turn-spit dogs were lying about, and gray rats were gnawing at refuse in the sinks. It was like a hideous dream. He felt as if he should never get out of it, and longed for one glimpse of his mother's poor little kitchen, so clean and bright and airy. Turning from it at last in miserable disgust, he almost ran back through the kitchen, re-entered the hall, and crossed it to another door.

It opened upon a wider passage, leading to an arch in a stately corridor, all its length lighted by lamps in niches. At the end of it was a large and beautiful hall, with great pillars. There sat three men in the royal livery, fast asleep, each in a great arm-chair, with his feet on a huge footstool. They looked like fools dreaming themselves kings; and Lina looked as if she longed to throttle them. At one side of the hall was the grand staircase, and they went up.

Everything that now met Curdie's eyes was rich—not glorious like the splendours of the mountain cavern, but rich and soft—except where, now and then, some rough old rib of the ancient fortress came through, hard and discoloured. Now some dark bare arch of stone, now some rugged and blackened pillar, now some huge beam, brown with the smoke and dust of centuries, looked like a thistle in the midst of daisies, or a rock in a smooth lawn.

They wandered about a good while, again and again finding themselves where they had been before. Gradually, however, Curdie was gaining some idea of the place. By-and-by Lina began to look frightened, and as they went on Curdie saw that she looked more and more frightened. Now, by this time he had come to understand that what made her look frightened was always the fear of frightening, and he therefore concluded they must be drawing nigh to somebody. At last, in a gorgeously-painted gallery, he saw a curtain of crimson, and on the curtain a royal crown wrought in silks and stones. He felt sure this must be the king's chamber, and it was here he was wanted; or, if it was not the place he was bound for, something would meet him and turn him aside; for he had come to think that so long as a man wants to do right he may go where he can: when he can go no further, then it is not the way. "Only," said his father, in assenting to the theory, "he must really want to do right, and not merely fancy he does. He must want it with his heart and will, and not with his rag of a tongue."

So he gently lifted the corner of the curtain, and there behind it was a half-open door. He entered, and the moment he was in, Lina stretched herself along the threshold between the curtain and the door.

THE KING'S CHAMBER

He found himself in a large room, dimly lighted by a silver lamp that hung from the ceiling. Far at the other end was a great bed, surrounded with dark heavy curtains. He went softly towards it, his heart beating fast. It was a dreadful thing to be alone in the king's chamber at the dead of night. To gain courage he had to remind himself of the beautiful princess who had sent him. But when he was about halfway to the bed, a figure appeared from the farther side of it, and came towards him, with a hand raised warningly. He stood still. The light was dim, and he could distinguish little more than the outline of a young girl. But though the form he saw was much taller than the princess he remembered, he never doubted it was she. For one thing, he knew that most girls would have been frightened to see him there in the dead of the night, but like a true princess, and the princess he used to know, she walked straight on to meet him. As she came she lowered the hand she had lifted, and laid the forefinger of it upon her lips. Nearer and nearer, quite near, close up to him she came, then stopped, and stood a moment looking at him.

"You are Curdie," she said.

"And you are the Princess Irene," he returned.

"Then we know each other still," she said, with a sad smile of pleasure. "You will help me."

"That I will," answered Curdie. He did not say, "If I can;" for he knew that what he was sent to do, that he could do. "May I kiss your hand, little princess?"

She was only between nine and ten, though indeed she looked several years older, and her eyes almost those of a grown woman, for she had had terrible trouble of late.

She held out her hand.

"I am not the little princess any more. I have grown up since I saw you last, Mr. Miner."

The smile which accompanied the words had in it a strange mixture of playfulness and sadness.

"So I see, Miss Princess," returned Curdie; "and therefore, being more of a princess, you are the more my princess. Here I am, sent by your great-great-grandmother, to be your servant.—May I ask why you are up so late, princess?"

"Because my father wakes so frightened, and I don't know what he would do if he didn't find me by his bedside. There! he's waking now."

She darted off to the side of the bed she had come from. Curdie stood where he was.

A voice altogether unlike what he remembered of the mighty, noble king on his white horse came from the bed, thin, feeble, hollow, and husky, and in tone like that of a petulant child:—

"I will not, I will not. I am a king, and I will be a king. I hate you and despise you, and you shall not torture me!"

"Never mind them, father dear," said the princess. "I am here, and they shan't touch you. They dare not, you know, so long as you defy them."

"They want my crown, darling; and I can't give them my crown, can I? for what is a king without his crown?"

"They shall never have your crown, my king," said Irene. "Here it is—all safe, you see. I am watching it for you."

Curdie drew near the bed on the other side. There lay the grand old king—he looked grand still, and twenty years older. His body was pillowed high; his beard descended long and white over the crimson coverlid; and his crown, its diamonds and emeralds gleaming in the twilight of the curtains, lay in front of him, his long, thin old hands folded round the rigol, and the ends of his beard straying among the lovely stones. His face was like that of a man who had died fighting nobly; but one thing made it dreadful: his eyes, while they moved about as if searching in this direction and in that, looked more dead than his face. He saw neither his daughter nor his crown: it was the voice of the one and the touch of the other that comforted him. He kept murmuring what seemed words, but was unintelligible to Curdie, although, to judge from the look of Irene's face, she learned and concluded from it.

By degrees his voice sank away and the murmuring ceased, although still his lips moved. Thus lay the old king on his bed, slumbering with his crown between his hands; on one side of him stood a lovely little maiden, with blue eyes, and brown hair going a little back from her temples, as if blown by a wind that no one felt but herself; and on the other a stalwart young miner, with his mattock over his shoulder. Stranger sight still was Lina lying along the threshold—only nobody saw her just then.

A moment more and the king's lips ceased to move. His breathing had grown regular and quiet. The princess gave a sigh of relief, and came round to Curdie.

"We can talk a little now," she said, leading him towards the middle of the room. "My father will sleep now till the doctor wakes him to give him his medicine. It is not really medicine, though, but wine. Nothing but that, the doctor says, could have kept him so long alive. He always comes in the middle of the night to give it him with his own hands. But it makes me cry to see him waked up when so nicely asleep."

"What sort of man is your doctor?" asked Curdie.

"Oh, such a dear, good, kind gentleman!" replied the princess. "He speaks so softly, and is so sorry for his dear king! He will be here presently, and you shall see for yourself. You will like him very much."

"Has your king-father been long ill?" asked Curdie.

"A whole year now," she replied. "Did you not know? That's how your mother never got the red petticoat my father promised her. The lord chancellor told me that not only Gwyntystorm but the whole land was mourning over the illness of the good man."

Now Curdie himself had not heard a word of his majesty's illness, and had no ground for believing that a single soul in any place he had visited on his journey had heard of it. Moreover, although mention had been made of his majesty again and again in his hearing since he came to Gwyntystorm, never once had he heard an allusion to the state of his health. And now it dawned upon him also that he had never heard the least expression of love to him. But just for the time he thought it better to say nothing on either point.

"Does the king wander like this every night?" he asked.

"Every night," answered Irene, shaking her head mournfully. "That is why I never go to bed at night. He is better during the day—a little, and then I sleep—in the dressing-room there, to be with him in a moment if he should call me. It is so sad he should have only me and not my mamma! A princess is nothing to a queen!"

"I wish he would like me," said Curdie, "for then I might watch by him at night, and let you go to bed, princess."

"Don't you know then?" returned Irene, in wonder. "How was it you came?— Ah! you said my grandmother sent you. But I thought you knew that he wanted you."

And again she opened wide her blue stars.

"Not I," said Curdie, also bewildered, but very glad.

"He used to be constantly saying—he was not so ill then as he is now—that he wished he had you about him."

"And I never to know it!" said Curdie, with displeasure.

"The master of the horse told papa's own secretary that he had written to the miner-general to find you and send you up; but the miner-general wrote back to the master of the horse, and he told the secretary, and the secretary told my father, that they had searched every mine in the kingdom and could hear nothing of you. My father gave a great sigh, and said he feared the goblins had got you after all, and your father and mother were dead of grief. And he has never mentioned you since, except when wandering. I cried very much. But one of my grandmother's pigeons with its white wing flashed a message to me through the window one day, and then I knew that my Curdie wasn't eaten by the goblins, for my grandmother wouldn't have taken care of him one time to let him be eaten the next. Where were you, Curdie, that they couldn't find you?"

"We will talk about that another time, when we are not expecting the doctor," said Curdie.

As he spoke, his eyes fell upon something shining on the table under the lamp. His heart gave a great throb, and he went nearer.—Yes, there could be no doubt;—it was the same flagon that the butler had filled in the wine-cellar.

"It looks worse and worse!" he said to himself, and went back to Irene, where she stood half dreaming.

"When will the doctor be here?" he asked once more—this time hurriedly.

514

The question was answered—not by the princess, but by something which that instant tumbled heavily into the room. Curdie flew towards it in vague terror about Lina.

On the floor lay a little round man, puffing and blowing, and uttering incoherent language. Curdie thought of his mattock, and ran and laid it aside.

"Oh, dear Dr. Kelman!" cried the princess, running up and taking hold of his arm; "I am so sorry!" She pulled and pulled, but might almost as well have tried to set up a cannon-ball. "I hope you have not hurt yourself?"

"Not at all, not at all," said the doctor, trying to smile and to rise both at once, but finding it impossible to do either.

"If he slept on the floor he would be late for breakfast," said Curdie to himself, and held out his hand to help him.

But when he took hold of it, Curdie very nearly let him fall again, for what he held was not even a foot: it was the belly of a creeping thing. He managed, however, to hold both his peace and his grasp, and pulled the doctor roughly on his legs—such as they were.

"Your royal highness has rather a thick mat at the door," said the doctor, patting his palms together. "I hope my awkwardness may not have startled his majesty."

While he talked Curdie went to the door: Lina was not there.

The doctor approached the bed.

"And how has my beloved king slept to-night?" he asked.

"No better," answered Irene, with a mournful shake of her head.

"Ah, that is very well!" returned the doctor, his fall seeming to have muddled either his words or his meaning. "We must give him his wine, and then he will be better still."

Curdie darted at the flagon, and lifted it high, as if he had expected to find it full, but had found it empty.

"That stupid butler! I heard them say he was drunk!" he cried in a loud whisper, and was gliding from the room.

"Come here with that flagon, you! page!" cried the doctor.

Curdie came a few steps towards him with the flagon dangling from his hand, heedless of the gushes that fell noiseless on the thick carpet.

"Are you aware, young man," said the doctor, "that it is not every wine can do his majesty the benefit I intend he should derive from my prescription?"

"Quite aware, sir," answered Curdie. "The wine for his majesty's use is in the third cask from the corner."

"Fly, then," said the doctor, looking satisfied.

Curdie stopped outside the curtain and blew an audible breath—no more: up came Lina noiseless as a shadow. He showed her the flagon.

"The cellar, Lina: go," he said.

She galloped away on her soft feet, and Curdie had indeed to fly to keep up with her. Not once did she make even a dubious turn. From the king's gorgeous chamber to the cold cellar they shot. Curdie dashed the wine down the back stair, rinsed the flagon out as he had seen the butler do, filled it from the cask of which he had seen the butler drink, and hastened with it up again to the king's room.

The little doctor took it, poured out a full glass, smelt, but did not taste it, and set it down. Then he leaned over the bed, shouted in the king's ear, blew upon his eyes, and pinched his arm: Curdie thought he saw him run something bright into it.

At last the king half woke. The doctor seized the glass, raised his head, poured the wine down his throat, and let his head fall back on the pillow again. Tenderly wiping his beard, and bidding the princess good-night in paternal tones, he then took his leave. Curdie would gladly have driven his pick into his head, but that was not in his commission, and he let him go.

The little round man looked very carefully to his feet as he crossed the threshold.

"That attentive fellow of a page has removed the mat," he said to himself, as he walked along the corridor. "I must remember him."

COUNTER-PLOTTING

Curdie was already sufficiently enlightened as to how things were going, to see that he must have the princess of one mind with him, and they must work together. It was clear that amongst those about the king there was a plot against him: for one thing, they had agreed in a lie concerning himself; and it was plain also that the doctor was working out a design against the health and reason of his majesty, rendering the question of his life a matter of little moment. It was in itself sufficient to justify the worst fears, that the people outside the palace were ignorant of his majesty's condition: he believed those inside it also—the butler excepted—were ignorant of it as well. Doubtless his majesty's councillors desired to alienate the hearts of his subjects from their sovereign. Curdie's idea was that they intended to kill the king, marry the princess to one of themselves, and found a new dynasty; but whatever their purpose, there was treason in the palace of the worst sort: they were making and keeping the king incapable, in order to effect that purpose. The first thing to be seen to therefore was, that his majesty should neither eat morsel nor drink drop of anything prepared for him in the palace. Could this have been managed without the princess, Curdie would have preferred leaving her in ignorance of the horrors from which he sought to deliver her. He feared also the danger of her knowledge betraying itself to the evil eyes about her; but it must be risked— and she had always been a wise child.

Another thing was clear to him—that with such traitors no terms of honour were either binding or possible, and that, short of lying, he might use any means to foil them. And he could not doubt that the old princess had sent him expressly to frustrate their plans.

While he stood thinking thus with himself, the princess was earnestly watching the king, with looks of childish love and womanly tenderness that went to Curdie's heart. Now and then with a great fan of peacock feathers she would fan him very softly; now and then, seeing a cloud begin to gather upon the sky of his sleeping face, she would climb upon the bed, and bending to his ear whisper into it, then draw back and watch again—generally to see the cloud disperse. In his deepest slumber, the soul of the king lay open to the voice of his child, and that voice had power either to change the aspect of his visions, or, which was better still, to breathe hope into his heart, and courage to endure them.

Curdie came near, and softly called her.

"I can't leave papa just yet," she returned, in a low voice.

"I will wait," said Curdie; "but I want very much to say something."

In a few minutes she came to him where he stood under the lamp.

"Well, Curdie, what is it?" she said.

"Princess," he replied, "I want to tell you that I have found why your grandmother sent me."

"Come this way, then," she answered, "where I can see the face of my king."

Curdie placed a chair for her in the spot she chose, where she would be near enough to mark any slightest change on her father's countenance, yet where their low-voiced talk would not disturb him. There he sat down beside her and told her all the story—how her grandmother had sent her good pigeon for him, and how she had instructed him, and sent him there without telling him what he had to do. Then he told her what he had discovered of the state of things generally in Gwyntystorm, and specially what he had heard and seen in the palace that night.

"Things are in a bad state enough," he said in conclusion;—"lying and selfishness and inhospitality and dishonesty everywhere; and to crown all, they speak with disrespect of the good king, and not a man of them knows he is ill."

"You frighten me dreadfully," said Irene, trembling.

"You must be brave for your king's sake," said Curdie.

"Indeed I will," she replied, and turned a long loving look upon the beautiful face of her father. "But what is to be done? And how am I to believe such horrible things of Dr. Kelman?"

"My dear princess," replied Curdie, "you know nothing of him but his face and his tongue, and they are both false. Either you must beware of him, or you must doubt your grandmother and me; for I tell you, by the gift she gave me of testing hands, that this man is a snake. That round body he shows is but the case of a serpent. Perhaps the creature lies there, as in its nest, coiled round and round inside."

"Horrible!" said Irene.

"Horrible indeed; but we must not try to get rid of horrible things by refusing to look at them, and saying they are not there. Is not your beautiful father sleeping better since he had the wine?"

"Yes."

"Does he always sleep better after having it?"

She reflected an instant.

"No; always worse—till to-night," she answered.

"Then remember that was the wine I got him—not what the butler drew. Nothing that passes through any hand in the house except yours or mine must henceforth, till he is well, reach his majesty's lips."

"But how, dear Curdie?" said the princess, almost crying.

"That we must contrive," answered Curdie. "I know how to take care of the wine; but for his food—now we must think."

"He takes hardly any," said the princess, with a pathetic shake of her little head which Curdie had almost learned to look for.

"The more need," he replied, "there should be no poison in it." Irene shuddered. "As soon as he has honest food he will begin to grow better. And you must be just as careful with yourself, princess," Curdie went on, "for you don't know when they may begin to poison you too."

"There's no fear of me; don't talk about me," said Irene. "The good food!—how are we to get it, Curdie? That is the whole question."

"I am thinking hard," answered Curdie. "The good food? Let me see—let me see! —Such servants as I saw below are sure to have the best of everything for them-selves: I will go and see what I can find on their supper-table."

"The chancellor sleeps in the house, and he and the master of the king's horse always have their supper together in a room off the great hall, to the right as you go down the stair," said Irene. "I would go with you, but I dare not leave my father. Alas! he scarcely ever takes more than a mouthful. I can't think how he lives! And the very thing he would like, and often asks for—a bit of bread—I can hardly ever get for him: Dr. Kelman has forbidden it, and says it is nothing less than poison to him."

"Bread at least he shall have," said Curdie; "and that, with the honest wine, will do as well as anything, I do believe. I will go at once and look for some. But I want you to see Lina first, and know her, lest, coming upon her by accident at any time, you should be frightened."

"I should like much to see her," said the princess.

Warning her not to be startled by her ugliness, he went to the door and called her.

She entered, creeping with downcast head, and dragging her tail over the floor behind her. Curdie watched the princess as the frightful creature came nearer and nearer. One shudder went from head to foot of her, and next instant she stepped to meet her. Lina dropped flat on the floor, and covered her face with her two big paws. It went to the heart of the princess: in a moment she was on her knees beside her, stroking her ugly head, and patting her all over.

"Good dog! Dear ugly dog!" she said.

Lina whimpered.

"I believe," said Curdie, "from what your grandmother told me, that Lina is a woman, and that she was naughty, but is now growing good."

Lina had lifted her head while Irene was caressing her; now she dropped it again between her paws; but the princess took it in her hands, and kissed the fore-head betwixt the gold-green eyes.

"Shall I take her with me or leave her?" asked Curdie.

"Leave her, poor dear," said Irene, and Curdie, knowing the way now, went without her.

He took his way first to the room the princess had spoken of, and there also were the remains of supper; but neither there nor in the kitchen could he find a scrap of plain wholesome-looking bread. So he returned and told her that as soon as it was light he would go into the city for some, and asked her for a handkerchief to tie it in. If he could not bring it himself, he would send it by Lina, who could keep out of sight better than he, and as soon as all was quiet at night he would come to her again. He also asked her to tell the king that he was in the house.

His hope lay in the fact that bakers everywhere go to work early. But it was yet much too early. So he persuaded the princess to lie down, promising to call her if the king should stir.

THE LOAF

His majesty slept very quietly. The dawn had grown almost day, and still Curdie lingered, unwilling to disturb the princess.

At last, however, he called her, and she was in the room in a moment. She had slept, she said, and felt quite fresh. Delighted to find her father still asleep, and so peacefully, she pushed her chair close to the bed, and sat down with her hands in her lap.

Curdie got his mattock from where he had hidden it behind a great mirror, and went to the cellar, followed by Lina. They took some breakfast with them as they passed through the hall, and as soon as they had eaten it went out the back way.

At the mouth of the passage Curdie seized the rope, drew himself up, pushed away the shutter, and entered the dungeon. Then he swung the end of the rope to Lina, and she caught it in her teeth. When her master said, "Now, Lina!" she gave a great spring, and he ran away with the end of the rope as fast as ever he could. And such spring had she made, that by the time he had to bear her weight she was within a few feet of the hole. The instant she got a paw through, she was all through.

Apparently their enemies were waiting till hunger should have cowed them, for there was no sign of any attempt having been made to open the door. A blow or two of Curdie's mattock drove the shattered lock clean from it, and telling Lina to wait there till he came back, and let no one in, he walked out into the silent street, and drew the door to behind him. He could hardly believe it was not yet a whole day since he had been thrown in there with his hands tied at his back.

Down the town he went, walking in the middle of the street, that, if any one saw him, he might see he was not afraid, and hesitate to rouse an attack on him. As to the dogs, ever since the death of their two companions, a shadow that looked like a mattock was enough to make them scamper. As soon as he reached the archway of the city gate he turned to reconnoitre the baker's shop, and perceiving no sign of movement, waited there watching for the first.

After about an hour, the door opened, and the baker's man appeared with a pail in his hand. He went to a pump that stood in the street, and having filled his pail returned with it into the shop. Curdie stole after him, found the door on the latch, opened it very gently, peeped in, saw nobody, and entered. Remembering perfectly from what shelf the baker's wife had taken the loaf she said was the best, and seeing just one upon it, he seized it, laid the price of it on the counter, and sped softly out, and up the street. Once more in the dungeon beside Lina, his first thought was to fasten up the door again, which would have been easy, so many iron fragments of all sorts and sizes lay about; but he bethought himself that if he left it as it was, and they came to find him, they would conclude at once that they had made their escape by it, and would look no farther so as to discover the hole. He therefore merely pushed the door close and left it. Then once more carefully arranging the earth behind the shutter, so that it should again fall with it, he returned to the cellar.

And now he had to convey the loaf to the princess. If he could venture to take it himself, well; if not, he would send Lina. He crept to the door of the servants' hall, and found the sleepers beginning to stir. One said it was time to go to bed; another, that he would go to the cellar instead, and have a mug of wine to waken him up; while a third challenged a fourth to give him his revenge at some game or other.

"Oh, hang your losses!" answered his companion; "you'll soon pick up twice as much about the house, if you but keep your eyes open."

Perceiving there would be risk in attempting to pass through, and reflecting that the porters in the great hall would probably be awake also, Curdie went back to the cellar, took Irene's handkerchief with the loaf in it, tied it round Lina's neck, and told her to take it to the princess.

Using every shadow and every shelter, Lina slid through the servants like a shapeless terror through a guilty mind, and so, by corridor and great hall, up the stair to the king's chamber.

Irene trembled a little when she saw her glide soundless in across the silent dusk of the morning, that filtered through the heavy drapery of the windows, but she recovered herself at once when she saw the bundle about her neck, for it both assured her of Curdie's safety, and gave her hope of her father's. She untied it with joy, and Lina stole away, silent as she had come. Her joy was the greater that the king had woke up a little while before, and expressed a desire for food—not that he felt exactly hungry, he said, and yet he wanted something. If only he might have a piece of nice fresh bread! Irene had no knife, but with eager hands she broke a great piece from the loaf, and poured out a full glass of wine. The king ate and drank, enjoyed the bread and the wine much, and instantly fell asleep again.

It was hours before the lazy people brought their breakfast. When it came, Irene crumbled a little about, threw some into the fire-place, and managed to make the tray look just as usual.

In the meantime, down below in the cellar, Curdie was lying in the hollow between the upper sides of two of the great casks, the warmest place he could find. Lina was watching. She lay at his feet, across the two casks, and did her best so to arrange her huge tail that it should be a warm coverlid for her master.

By-and-by Dr. Kelman called to see his patient; and now that Irene's eyes were opened, she saw clearly enough that he was both annoyed and puzzled at finding his majesty rather better. He pretended however to congratulate him, saying he believed he was quite fit to see the lord chamberlain: he wanted his signature to something important; only he must not strain his mind to understand it, whatever it might be: if his majesty did, he would not be answerable for the consequences. The king said he would see the lord chamberlain, and the doctor went. Then Irene gave him more bread and wine, and the king ate and drank, and smiled a feeble smile, the first real one she had seen for many a day. He said he felt much better, and would soon be able to take matters into his own hands again. He had a strange miserable feeling, he said, that things were going terribly wrong, although he could not tell how. Then the princess told him that Curdie was come, and that at night, when all was quiet, for nobody in the palace must know, he would pay his majesty a visit. Her great-great-grandmother had sent him, she said. The king looked strangely upon her, but, the strange look passed into a smile clearer than the first, and Irene's heart throbbed with delight.

THE LORD CHAMBERLAIN

At noon the lord chamberlain appeared. With a long, low bow, and paper in hand, he stepped softly into the room. Greeting his majesty with every appearance of the profoundest respect, and congratulating him on the evident progress he had made, he declared himself sorry to trouble him, but there were certain papers, he said, which required his signature—and therewith drew nearer to the king, who lay looking at him doubtfully. He was a lean, long, yellow man, with a small head, bald over the top, and tufted at the back and about the ears. He had a very thin, prominent, hooked nose, and a quantity of loose skin under his chin and about the throat, which came craning up out of his neckcloth. His eyes were very small, sharp, and glittering, and looked black as jet. He had hardly enough of a mouth to make a smile with. His left hand held the paper, and the long, skinny fingers of his right a pen just dipped in ink.

But the king, who for weeks had scarcely known what he did, was to-day so much himself as to be aware that he was not quite himself; and the moment he saw the paper, he resolved that he would not sign without understanding and approving of it. He requested the lord chamberlain therefore to read it. His lordship commenced at once but the difficulties he seemed to encounter, and the fits of stammering that seized him, roused the king's suspicion tenfold. He called the princess.

"I trouble his lordship too much," he said to her: "you can read print well, my child—let me hear how you can read writing. Take that paper from his lordship's hand, and read it to me from beginning to end, while my lord drinks a glass of my favourite wine, and watches for your blunders."

"Pardon me, your majesty," said the lord chamberlain, with as much of a smile as he was able to extemporize, "but it were a thousand pities to put the attainments of her royal highness to a test altogether too severe. Your majesty can scarcely with justice expect the very organs of her speech to prove capable of compassing words so long, and to her so unintelligible."

"I think much of my little princess and her capabilities," returned the king, more and more aroused. "Pray, my lord, permit her to try."

"Consider, your majesty: the thing would be altogether without precedent. It would be to make sport of statecraft," said the lord chamberlain.

"Perhaps you are right, my lord," answered the king with more meaning than he intended should be manifest while to his growing joy he felt new life and power throbbing in heart and brain. "So this morning we shall read no farther. I am indeed ill able for business of such weight."

"Will your majesty please sign your royal name here?" said the lord chamberlain, preferring the request as a matter of course, and approaching with the feather end of the pen pointed to a spot where was a great red seal.

"Not to-day, my lord," replied the king.

"It is of the greatest importance, your majesty," softly insisted the other.

"I descried no such importance in it," said the king.

"Your majesty heard but a part."

"And I can hear no more to-day."

"I trust your majesty has ground enough, in a case of necessity like the present, to sign upon the representation of his loyal subject and chamberlain?—Or shall I call the lord chancellor?" he added, rising.

"There is no need. I have the very highest opinion of your judgment, my lord," answered the king; "—that is, with respect to means: we might differ as to ends."

The lord chamberlain made yet further attempts at persuasion; but they grew feebler and feebler, and he was at last compelled to retire without having gained his object. And well might his annoyance be keen! For that paper was the king's will, drawn up by the attorney-general; nor until they had the king's signature to it was there much use in venturing farther. But his worst sense of discomfiture arose from finding the king with so much capacity left, for the doctor had pledged himself so to weaken his brain that he should be as a child in their hands, incapable of refusing anything requested of him: his lordship began to doubt the doctor's fidelity to the conspiracy.

The princess was in high delight. She had not for weeks heard so many words, not to say words of such strength and reason, from her father's lips: day by day he had been growing weaker and more lethargic. He was so much exhausted however after this effort, that he asked for another piece of bread and more wine, and fell fast asleep the moment he had taken them.

The lord chamberlain sent in a rage for Dr. Kelman. He came, and while professing himself unable to understand the symptoms described by his lordship, yet pledged himself again that on the morrow the king should do whatever was required of him.

The day went on. When his majesty was awake, the princess read to him—one story-book after another; and whatever she read, the king listened as if he had never heard anything so good before, making out in it the wisest meanings. Every now and then he asked for a piece of bread and a little wine, and every time he ate and drank he slept, and every time he woke he seemed better than the last time. The princess bearing her part, the loaf was eaten up and the flagon emptied before night. The butler took the flagon away, and brought it back filled to the brim, but both were thirsty as well as hungry when Curdie came again.

Meantime he and Lina, watching and waking alternately, had plenty of sleep. In the afternoon, peeping from the recess, they saw several of the servants enter hurriedly, one after the other, draw wine, drink it, and steal out; but their business was to take care of the king, not of his cellar, and they let them drink. Also, when the butler came to fill the flagon, they restrained themselves, for the villain's fate was not yet ready for him. He looked terribly frightened, and had brought with him a large candle and a small terrier—which latter indeed threatened to be troublesome, for he went roving and sniffing about until he came to the recess where they were. But as soon as he showed himself, Lina opened her jaws so wide, and glared at him so horribly, that, without even uttering a whimper, he tucked his tail between his legs and ran to his master. He was drawing the wicked wine at the moment, and did not see him, else he would doubtless have run too.

When supper-time approached, Curdie took his place at the door into the servants' hall; but after a long hour's vain watch, he began to fear he should get nothing: there was so much idling about, as well as coming and going. It was hard to bear—chiefly from the attractions of a splendid loaf, just fresh out of the oven, which he longed to secure for the king and princess. At length his chance did arrive: he pounced upon the loaf and carried it away, and soon after got hold of a pie.

This time, however, both loaf and pie were missed. The cook was called. He declared he had provided both. One of themselves, he said, must have carried them away for some friend outside the palace. Then a housemaid, who had not long been one of them, said she had seen some one like a page running in the direction of the cellar with something in his hands. Instantly all turned upon the pages, accusing them, one after another. All denied, but nobody believed one of them: where there is no truth there can be no faith.

To the cellar they all set out to look for the missing pie and loaf. Lina heard them coming, as well she might, for they were talking and quarrelling loud, and gave her master warning. They snatched up everything, and got all signs of their presence out at the back door before the servants entered. When they found nothing, they all turned on the chambermaid, and accused her, not only of lying against the pages, but of having taken the things herself. Their language and behaviour so disgusted Curdie, who could hear a great part of what passed, and he saw the danger of discovery now so much increased, that he began to devise how best at once to rid the palace of the whole pack of them. That however, would be small gain so long as the treacherous officers of state continued in it. They must be first dealt with. A thought came to him, and the longer he looked at it the better he liked it.

As soon as the servants were gone, quarrelling and accusing all the way, they returned and finished their supper. Then Curdie, who had long been satisfied that Lina understood almost every word he said, communicated his plan to her, and knew by the wagging of her tail and the flashing of her eyes that she comprehended it. Until they had the king safe through the worst part of the night, however, nothing could be done.

They had now merely to go on waiting where they were till the household should be asleep. This waiting and waiting was much the hardest thing Curdie had to do in the whole affair. He took his mattock, and going again into the long passage, lighted a candle-end, and proceeded to examine the rock on all sides. But this was not merely to pass the time: he had a reason for it. When he broke the stone in the street, over which the baker fell, its appearance led him to pocket a fragment for further examination; and since then he had satisfied himself that it was the kind of stone in which gold is found, and that the yellow particles in it were pure metal. If such stone existed here in any plenty, he could soon make the king rich, and independent of his ill-conditioned subjects. He was therefore now bent on an examination of the rock; nor had he been at it long before he was persuaded that there were large quantities of gold in the half-crystalline white stone, with its veins of opaque white and of green, of which the rock, so far as he had been able to inspect it, seemed almost entirely to consist. Every piece he broke was spotted with particles and little lumps of a lovely greenish yellow—and that was gold. Hitherto he had worked only in silver, but he had read, and heard talk, and knew therefore about gold. As soon as he had got the king free of rogues and villains, he would have all the best and most honest miners, with his father at the head of them, to work this rock for the king.

It was a great delight to him to use his mattock once more. The time went quickly, and when he left the passage to go to the king's chamber, he had already a good heap of fragments behind the broken door.

DR. KELMAN

As soon as he had reason to hope the way was clear, Curdie ventured softly into the hall, with Lina behind him. There was no one asleep on the bench or floor, but by the fading fire sat a girl weeping. It was the same who had seen him carrying off the food, and had been so hardly used for saying so. She opened her eyes when he appeared, but did not seem frightened at him.

"I know why you weep," said Curdie; "and I am sorry for you."

"It is hard not to be believed just because one speaks the truth," said the girl, "but that seems reason enough with some people. My mother taught me to speak the truth, and took such pains with me that I should find it hard to tell a lie, though I could invent many a story these servants would believe at once; for the truth is a strange thing here, and they don't know it when they see it. Show it them, and they all stare as if it were a wicked lie, and that with the lie yet warm that has just left their own mouths!—You are a stranger," she said, and burst out weeping afresh, "but the stranger you are to such a place and such people the better!"

"I am the person," said Curdie, "whom you saw carrying the things from the supper-table." He showed her the loaf. "If you can trust, as well as speak the truth, I will trust you.—Can you trust me?"

She looked at him steadily for a moment.

"I can," she answered.

"One thing more," said Curdie: "have you courage as well as faith?"

"I think so."

"Look my dog in the face and don't cry out.—Come here, Lina."

Lina obeyed. The girl looked at her, and laid her hand on her head.

"Now I know you are a true woman," said Curdie. "—I am come to set things right in this house. Not one of the servants knows I am here. Will you tell them to-morrow morning, that, if they do not alter their ways, and give over drinking, and

528

lying, and stealing, and unkindness, they shall every one of them be driven from the palace?"

"They will not believe me."

"Most likely; but will you give them the chance?"

"I will."

"Then I will be your friend. Wait here till I come again."

She looked him once more in the face, and sat down.

When he reached the royal chamber, he found his majesty awake, and very anxiously expecting him. He received him with the utmost kindness, and at once as it were put himself in his hands by telling him all he knew concerning the state he was in. His voice was feeble, but his eye was clear, and although now and then his words and thoughts seemed to wander, Curdie could not be certain that the cause of their not being intelligible to him did not lie in himself. The king told him that for some years, ever since his queen's death, he had been losing heart over the wickedness of his people. He had tried hard to make them good, but they got worse and worse. Evil teachers, unknown to him, had crept into the schools; there was a general decay of truth and right principle at least in the city; and as that set the example to the nation, it must spread. The main cause of his illness was the despondency with which the degeneration of his people affected him. He could not sleep, and had terrible dreams; while, to his unspeakable shame and distress, he doubted almost everybody. He had striven against his suspicion, but in vain, and his heart was sore, for his courtiers and councillors were really kind; only he could not think why none of their ladies came near his princess. The whole country was discontented, he heard, and there were signs of gathering storm outside as well as inside his borders. The master of the horse gave him sad news of the insubordination of the army; and his great white horse was dead, they told him; and his sword had lost its temper: it bent double the last time he tried it!—only perhaps that was in a dream; and they could not find his shield; and one of his spurs had lost the rowel. Thus the poor king went wandering in a maze of sorrows, some of which were purely imaginary, while others were truer than he understood. He told how thieves came at night and tried to take his crown, so that he never dared let it out of his hands even when he slept; and how, every night, an evil demon in the shape of his physician came and poured poison down his throat. He knew it to be poison, he said, somehow, although it tasted like wine.

Here he stopped, faint with the unusual exertion of talking. Curdie seized the flagon, and ran to the wine-cellar.

In the servants' hall the girl still sat by the fire, waiting for him. As he returned he told her to follow him, and left her at the chamber door till he should rejoin her.

Curdie brings wine to the king.

When the king had had a little wine, he informed him that he had already discovered certain of his majesty's enemies, and one of the worst of them was the doctor, for it was no other demon than the doctor himself who had been coming every night, and giving him a slow poison.

"So!" said the king. "Then I have not been suspicious enough, for I thought it was but a dream! Is it possible Kelman can be such a wretch? Who then am I to trust?"

"Not one in the house, except the princess and myself," said Curdie.

"I will not go to sleep," said the king.

"That would be as bad as taking the poison," said Curdie. "No, no, sire; you must show your confidence by leaving all the watching to me, and doing all the sleeping your majesty can."

The king smiled a contented smile, turned on his side, and was presently fast asleep. Then Curdie persuaded the princess also to go to sleep, and telling Lina to watch, went to the housemaid. He asked her if she could inform him which of the council slept in the palace, and show him their rooms. She knew every one of them, she said, and took him the round of all their doors, telling him which slept in each room. He then dismissed her, and returning to the king's chamber, seated himself behind a curtain at the head of the bed, on the side farthest from the king. He told Lina to get under the bed, and make no noise.

About one o'clock the doctor came stealing in. He looked round for the princess, and seeing no one, smiled with satisfaction as he approached the wine where it stood under the lamp. Having partly filled a glass, he took from his pocket a small phial, and filled up the glass from it. The light fell upon his face from above, and Curdie saw the snake in it plainly visible. He had never beheld such an evil countenance: the man hated the king, and delighted in doing him wrong.

With the glass in his hand, he drew near the bed, set it down, and began his usual rude rousing of his majesty. Not at once succeeding, he took a lancet from his pocket, and was parting its cover with an involuntary hiss of hate between his closed teeth, when Curdie stooped and whispered to Lina, "Take him by the leg, Lina." She darted noiselessly upon him. With a face of horrible consternation, he gave his leg one tug to free it; the next instant Curdie heard the one scrunch with which she crushed the bone like a stick of celery. He tumbled on the floor with a yell.

"Drag him out, Lina," said Curdie.

Lina took him by the collar, and dragged him out. Her master followed to direct her, and they left him lying across the lord chamberlain's door, where he gave another horrible yell, and fainted.

Lina darted noiselessly upon him.

The king had waked at his first cry, and by the time Curdie re-entered he had got at his sword where it hung from the centre of the tester, had drawn it, and was trying to get out of bed. But when Curdie told him all was well, he lay down again as quietly as a child comforted by his mother from a troubled dream. Curdie went to the door to watch.

The doctor's yells had roused many, but not one had yet ventured to appear. Bells were rung violently, but none were answered; and in a minute or two Curdie had what he was watching for. The door of the lord chamberlain's room opened, and, pale with hideous terror, his lordship peeped out. Seeing no one, he advanced to step into the corridor, and tumbled over the doctor. Curdie ran up, and held out his hand. He received in it the claw of a bird of prey—vulture or eagle, he could not tell which.

His lordship, as soon as he was on his legs, taking him for one of the pages, abused him heartily for not coming sooner, and threatened him with dismissal from the king's service for cowardice and neglect. He began indeed what bade fair to be a sermon on the duties of a page, but catching sight of the man who lay at his door, and seeing it was the doctor, he fell out upon Curdie afresh for standing there doing nothing, and ordered him to fetch immediate assistance. Curdie left him, but slipped into the king's chamber, closed and locked the door, and left the rascals to look after each other. Ere long he heard hurrying footsteps, and for a few minutes there was a great muffled tumult of scuffling feet, low voices, and deep groanings; then all was still again.

Irene slept through the whole—so confidently did she rest, knowing Curdie was in her father's room watching over him.

THE PROPHECY

Curdie sat and watched every motion of the sleeping king. All the night, to his ear, the palace lay as quiet as a nursery of healthful children. At sunrise he called the princess.

"How has his Majesty slept?" were her first words as she entered the room.

"Quite quietly," answered Curdie; "that is, since the doctor was got rid of."

"How did you manage that?" inquired Irene; and Curdie had to tell all about it.

"How terrible!" she said. "Did it not startle the king dreadfully?"

"It did rather. I found him getting out of bed, sword in hand."

"The brave old man!" cried the princess.

"Not so old!" said Curdie, "—as you will soon see. He went off again in a minute or so; but for a little while he was restless, and once when he lifted his hand it came down on the spikes of his crown, and he half waked."

"But where is the crown?" cried Irene, in sudden terror.

"I stroked his hands," answered Curdie, "and took the crown from them; and ever since he has slept quietly, and again and again smiled in his sleep."

"I have never seen him do that," said the princess. "But what have you done with the crown, Curdie?"

"Look," said Curdie, moving away from the bedside.

Irene followed him—and there, in the middle of the floor, she saw a strange sight. Lina lay at full length, fast asleep, her tail stretched out straight behind her and her fore-legs before her: between the two paws meeting in front of it, her nose just touching it behind, glowed and flashed the crown, like a nest for the humming-birds of heaven.

Irene gazed, and looked up with a smile.

"But what if the thief were to come, and she not to wake?" she said. "Shall I try her?" And as she spoke she stooped towards the crown.

"No, no, no!" cried Curdie, terrified. "She would frighten you out of your wits. I

533

would do it to show you, but she would wake your father. You have no conception with what a roar she would spring at my throat. But you shall see how lightly she wakes the moment I speak to her.—Lina!"

She was on her feet the same instant, with her great tail sticking out straight behind her, just as it had been lying.

"Good dog!" said the princess, and patted her head. Lina wagged her tail solemnly, like the boom of an anchored sloop. Irene took the crown, and laid it where the king would see it when he woke.

"Now, princess," said Curdie, "I must leave you for a few minutes. You must bolt the door, please, and not open it to any one."

Away to the cellar he went with Lina, taking care, as they passed through the servants' hall, to get her a good breakfast. In about one minute she had eaten what he gave her, and looked up in his face: it was not more she wanted, but work. So out of the cellar they went through the passage, and Curdie into the dungeon, where he pulled up Lina, opened the door, let her out, and shut it again behind her. As he reached the door of the king's chamber, Lina was flying out of the gate of Gwyntystorm as fast as her mighty legs could carry her.

"What's come to the wench?" growled the men-servants one to another, when the chambermaid appeared among them the next morning. There was something in her face which they could not understand, and did not like.

"Are we all dirt?" they said. "What are you thinking about? Have you seen yourself in the glass this morning, miss?"

She made no answer.

"Do you want to be treated as you deserve, or will you speak, you hussy?" said the first woman-cook. "I would fain know what right you have to put on a face like that!"

"You won't believe me," said the girl.

"Of course not. What is it?"

"I must tell you, whether you believe me or not," she said.

"Of course you must."

"It is this, then: if you do not repent of your bad ways, you are all going to be punished—all turned out of the palace together."

"A mighty punishment!" said the butler. "A good riddance, say I, of the trouble of keeping minxes like you in order! And why, pray, should we be turned out? What have I to repent of now, your holiness?"

"That you know best yourself," said the girl.

"A pretty piece of insolence! How should I know, forsooth, what a menial like you has got against me! There are people in this house—oh! I'm not blind to their ways! but every one for himself, say I!—Pray, Miss Judgment, who gave you such an impertinent message to his majesty's household?"

"One who is come to set things right in the king's house."

"Right, indeed!" cried the butler; but that moment the thought came back to him of the roar he had heard in the cellar, and he turned pale and was silent.

The steward took it up next.

"And pray, pretty prophetess," he said, attempting to chuck her under the chin, "what have I got to repent of?"

"That you know best yourself," said the girl. "You have but to look into your books or your heart."

"Can you tell me, then, what I have to repent of?" said the groom of the chambers.

"That you know best yourself," said the girl once more. "The person who told me to tell you said the servants of this house had to repent of thieving, and lying, and unkindness, and drinking; and they will be made to repent of them one way, if they don't do it of themselves another."

Then arose a great hubbub; for by this time all the servants in the house were gathered about her, and all talked together, in towering indignation.

"Thieving, indeed!" cried one. "A pretty word in a house where everything is left lying about in a shameless way, tempting poor innocent girls!—a house where nobody cares for anything, or has the least respect to the value of property!"

"I suppose you envy me this brooch of mine," said another. "There was just a half-sheet of note-paper about it, not a scrap more, in a drawer that's always open in the writing-table in the study! What sort of a place is that for a jewel? Can you call it stealing to take a thing from such a place as that? Nobody cared a straw about it. It might as well have been in the dust-hole! If it had been locked up—then, to be sure!"

"Drinking!" said the chief porter, with a husky laugh. "And who wouldn't drink when he had a chance? Or who would repent it, except that the drink was gone? Tell me that, Miss Innocence."

"Lying!" said a great, coarse footman. "I suppose you mean when I told you yesterday you were a pretty girl when you didn't pout? Lying, indeed! Tell us something worth repenting of! Lying is the way of Gwyntystorm. You should have heard Jabez lying to the cook last night! He wanted a sweetbread for his pup, and pretended it was for the princess! Ha! ha! ha!"

"Unkindness! I wonder who's unkind! Going and listening to any stranger against her fellow-servants, and then bringing back his wicked words to trouble them!" said the oldest and worst of the housemaids. "—One of ourselves, too!— Come, you hypocrite! this is all an invention of yours and your young man's, to take your revenge of us because we found you out in a lie last night. Tell true now: —wasn't it the same that stole the loaf and the pie that sent you with the impudent message?"

As she said this, she stepped up to the housemaid and gave her, instead of time to answer, a box on the ear that almost threw her down; and whoever could get at her began to push and hustle and pinch and punch her.

"You invite your fate," she said quietly.

They fell furiously upon her, drove her from the hall with kicks and blows, hustled her along the passage, and threw her down the stair to the wine-cellar, then locked the door at the top of it, and went back to their breakfast.

In the meantime the king and the princess had had their bread and wine, and the princess, with Curdie's help, had made the room as tidy as she could—they were terribly neglected by the servants. And now Curdie set himself to interest and amuse the king, and prevent him from thinking too much, in order that he might the sooner think the better. Presently, at his majesty's request, he began from the beginning, and told everything he could recall of his life, about his father and mother and their cottage on the mountain, of the inside of the mountain and the work there, about the goblins and his adventures with them. When he came to finding the princess and her nurse overtaken by the twilight on the mountain, Irene took up her share of the tale, and told all about herself to that point, and then Curdie took it up again; and so they went on, each fitting in the part that the other did not know, thus keeping the hoop of the story running straight; and the king listened with wondering and delighted ears, astonished to find what he could so ill comprehend, yet fitting so well together from the lips of two narrators. At last, with the mission given him by the wonderful princess and his consequent adventures, Curdie brought up the whole tale to the present moment. Then a silence fell, and Irene and Curdie thought the king was asleep. But he was far from it; he was thinking about many things. After a long pause he said:—

"Now at last, my children, I am compelled to believe many things I could not and do not yet understand—things I used to hear, and sometimes see, as often as I visited my mother's home. Once, for instance, I heard my mother say to her father —speaking of me—'He is a good, honest boy, but he will be an old man before he understands;' and my grandfather answered, 'Keep up your heart, child: my mother will look after him.' I thought often of their words, and the many strange things besides I both heard and saw in that house; but by degrees, because I could not understand them, I gave up thinking of them. And indeed I had almost forgotten them, when you, my child, talking that day about the Queen Irene and her pigeons, and what you had seen in her garret, brought them all back to my mind in a vague mass. But now they keep coming back to me, one by one, every one for itself; and I shall just hold my peace, and lie here quite still, and think about them all till I get well again."

What he meant they could not quite understand, but they saw plainly that already he was better.

"Put away my crown," he said. "I am tired of seeing it, and have no more any fear of its safety."

They put it away together, withdrew from the bedside, and left him in peace.

THE AVENGERS

There was nothing now to be dreaded from Dr. Kelman, but it made Curdie anxious, as the evening drew near, to think that not a soul belonging to the court had been to visit the king, or ask how he did, that day. He feared, in some shape or other, a more determined assault. He had provided himself a place in the room, to which he might retreat upon approach, and whence he could watch; but not once had he had to betake himself to it.

Towards night the king fell asleep. Curdie thought more and more uneasily of the moment when he must again leave them for a little while. Deeper and deeper fell the shadows. No one came to light the lamp. The princess drew her chair close to Curdie: she would rather it were not so dark, she said. She was afraid of something—she could not tell what; nor could she give any reason for her fear but that all was so dreadfully still. When it had been dark about an hour, Curdie thought Lina might be returned; and reflected that the sooner he went the less danger was there of any assault while he was away. There was more risk of his own presence being discovered, no doubt, but things were now drawing to a crisis, and it must be run. So, telling the princess to lock all the doors of the bedchamber, and let no one in, he took his mattock, and with here a run, and there a halt under cover, gained the door at the head of the cellar-stair in safety. To his surprise he found it locked, and the key was gone. There was no time for deliberation. He felt where the lock was, and dealt it a tremendous blow with his mattock. It needed but a second to dash the door open. Some one laid a hand on his arm.

"Who is it?" said Curdie.

"I told you they wouldn't believe me, sir," said the housemaid. "I have been here all day."

He took her hand, and said, "You are a good, brave girl. Now come with me, lest your enemies imprison you again."

He took her to the cellar, locked the door, lighted a bit of candle, gave her a little wine, told her to wait there till he came, and went out the back way.

Swiftly he swung himself up into the dungeon. Lina had done her part. The place was swarming with creatures—animal forms wilder and more grotesque than ever ramped in nightmare dream. Close by the hole, waiting his coming, her green eyes piercing the gulf below, Lina had but just laid herself down when he appeared. All about the vault and up the slope of the rubbish-heap lay and stood and squatted the forty-nine whose friendship Lina had conquered in the wood. They all came crowding about Curdie.

He must get them into the cellar as quickly as ever he could. But when he looked at the size of some of them, he feared it would be a long business to enlarge the hole sufficiently to let them through. At it he rushed, hitting vigorously at its edge with his mattock. At the very first blow came a splash from the water beneath, but ere he could heave a third, a creature like a tapir, only that the grasping point of its proboscis was hard as the steel of Curdie's hammer, pushed him gently aside, making room for another creature, with a head like a great club, which it began banging upon the floor with terrible force and noise. After about a minute of this battery, the tapir came up again, shoved Clubhead aside, and putting its own head into the hole began gnawing at the sides of it with the finger of its nose, in such a fashion that the fragments fell in a continuous gravelly shower into the water. In a few minutes the opening was large enough for the biggest creature amongst them to get through it.

Next came the difficulty of letting them down: some were quite light, but the half of them were too heavy for the rope, not to say for his arms. The creatures themselves seemed to be puzzling where or how they were to go. One after another of them came up, looked down through the hole, and drew back. Curdie thought if he let Lina down, perhaps that would suggest something; possibly they did not see the opening on the other side. He did so, and Lina stood lighting up the entrance of the passage with her gleaming eyes. One by one the creatures looked down again, and one by one they drew back, each standing aside to glance at the next, as if to say, Now you have a look. At last it came to the turn of the serpent with the long body, the four short legs behind, and the little wings before. No sooner had he poked his head through than he poked it farther through—and farther, and farther yet, until there was little more than his legs left in the dungeon. By that time he had got his head and neck well into the passage beside Lina. Then his legs gave a great waddle and spring, and he tumbled himself, far as there was betwixt them, heels over head into the passage.

"That is all very well for you, Mr. Legserpent!" thought Curdie to himself; "but what is to be done with the rest?"

He had hardly time to think it however, before the creature's head appeared again through the floor. He caught hold of the bar of iron to which Curdie's rope was tied, and settling it securely across the narrowest part of the irregular opening, held fast to it with his teeth. It was plain to Curdie, from the universal hardness amongst them, that they must all, at one time or another, have been creatures of the mines.

He saw at once what this one was after. He had planted his feet firmly upon the floor of the passage, and stretched his long body up and across the chasm to serve as a bridge for the rest. He mounted instantly upon his neck, threw his arms round him as far as they would go, and slid down in ease and safety, the bridge just bending a little as his weight glided over it. But he thought some of the creatures would try his teeth.

One by one the oddities followed, and slid down in safety. When they seemed to be all landed, he counted them: there were but forty-eight. Up the rope again he went, and found one which had been afraid to trust himself to the bridge, and no wonder! for he had neither legs nor head nor arms nor tail: he was just a round thing, about a foot in diameter, with a nose and mouth and eyes on one side of the ball. He had made his journey by rolling as swiftly as the fleetest of them could run. The back of the legserpent not being flat, he could not quite trust himself to roll straight and not drop into the gulf. Curdie took him in his arms, and the moment he looked down through the hole, the bridge made itself again, and he slid into the passage in safety, with Ballbody in his bosom.

He ran first to the cellar, to warn the girl not to be frightened at the avengers of wickedness. Then he called to Lina to bring in her friends.

One after another they came trooping in, till the cellar seemed full of them. The housemaid regarded them without fear.

"Sir," she said, "there is one of the pages I don't take to be a bad fellow."

"Then keep him near you," said Curdie. "And now can you show me a way to the king's chamber not through the servants' hall?"

"There is a way through the chamber of the colonel of the guard," she answered, "but he is ill, and in bed."

"Take me that way," said Curdie.

By many ups and downs and windings and turnings she brought him to a dimly-lighted room, where lay an elderly man asleep. His arm was outside the coverlid, and Curdie gave his hand a hurried grasp as he went by. His heart beat for joy, for he had found a good, honest human hand.

"I suppose that is why he is ill," he said to himself.

It was now close upon supper-time, and when the girl stopped at the door of the king's chamber, he told her to go and give the servants one warning more.

"Say the messenger sent you," he said. "I will be with you very soon."

The king was still asleep. Curdie talked to the princess for a few minutes, told her not to be frightened whatever noises she heard, only to keep her door locked till he came, and left her.

THE VENGEANCE

By the time the girl reached the servants' hall they were seated at supper. A loud, confused exclamation arose when she entered. No one made room for her; all stared with unfriendly eyes. A page, who entered the next minute by another door, came to her side.

"Where do you come from, hussy?" shouted the butler, and knocked his fist on the table with a loud clang.

He had gone to fetch wine, had found the stair door broken open and the cellar-door locked, and had turned and fled. Amongst his fellows, however, he had now regained what courage could be called his.

"From the cellar," she replied. "The messenger broke open the door, and sent me to you again."

"The messenger! Pooh! What messenger?"

"The same who sent me before to tell you to repent."

"What! will you go fooling it still? Haven't you had enough of it?" cried the butler in a rage, and starting to his feet, drew near threateningly.

"I must do as I am told," said the girl.

"Then why don't you do as I tell you, and hold your tongue?" said the butler. "Who wants your preachments? If anybody here has anything to repent of, isn't that enough—and more than enough for him—but you must come bothering about, and stirring up, till not a drop of quiet will settle inside him? You come along with me, young woman; we'll see if we can't find a lock somewhere in the house that'll hold you in!"

"Hands off, Mr. Butler!" said the page, and stepped between.

"Oh, ho!" cried the butler, and pointed his fat finger at him. "That's you, is it, my fine fellow? So it's you that's up to her tricks, is it?"

The youth did not answer, only stood with flashing eyes fixed on him, until, growing angrier and angrier, but not daring a step nearer, he burst out with rude but quavering authority,—

"Leave the house, both of you! Be off, or I'll have Mr. Steward to talk to you. Threaten your masters, indeed! Out of the house with you, and show us the way you tell us of!"

Two or three of the footmen got up and ranged themselves behind the butler.

"Don't say I threaten you, Mr. Butler," expostulated the girl from behind the page. "The messenger said I was to tell you again, and give you one chance more."

"Did the messenger mention me in particular?" asked the butler, looking the page unsteadily in the face.

"No, sir," answered the girl.

"I thought not! I should like to hear him!"

"Then hear him now," said Curdie, who that moment entered at the opposite corner of the hall. "I speak of the butler in particular when I say that I know more evil of him than of any of the rest. He will not let either his own conscience or my messenger speak to him: I therefore now speak myself. I proclaim him a villain, and a traitor to his majesty the king.—But what better is any one of you who cares only for himself, eats, drinks, takes good money, and gives vile service in return, stealing and wasting the king's property, and making of the palace, which ought to be an example of order and sobriety, a disgrace to the country?"

For a moment all stood astonished into silence by this bold speech from a stranger. True, they saw by his mattock over his shoulder that he was nothing but a miner boy, yet for a moment the truth told notwithstanding. Then a great roaring laugh burst from the biggest of the footmen as he came shouldering his way through the crowd towards Curdie.

"Yes, I'm right," he cried; "I thought as much! This messenger, forsooth, is nothing but a gallows-bird—a fellow the city marshal was going to hang, but unfortunately put it off till he should be starved enough to save rope and be throttled with a pack-thread. He broke prison, and here he is preaching!"

As he spoke, he stretched out his great hand to lay hold of him. Curdie caught it in his left hand, and heaved his mattock with the other. Finding, however, nothing worse than an ox-hoof, he restrained himself, stepped back a pace or two, shifted his mattock to his left hand, and struck him a little smart blow on the shoulder. His arm dropped by his side, he gave a roar, and drew back.

His fellows came crowding upon Curdie. Some called to the dogs; others swore; the women screamed; the footmen and pages got round him in a half-circle, which he kept from closing by swinging his mattock, and here and there threatening a blow.

"Whoever confesses to having done anything wrong in this house, however small, however great, and means to do better, let him come to this corner of the room," he cried.

None moved but the page, who went towards him skirting the wall. When they caught sight of him, the crowd broke into a hiss of derision.

"There! see! Look at the sinner! He confesses! actually confesses! Come, what is it you stole? The barefaced hypocrite! There's your sort to set up for reproving other people! Where's the other now?"

But the maid had left the room, and they let the page pass, for he looked dangerous to stop. Curdie had just put him betwixt him and the wall, behind the door, when in rushed the butler with the huge kitchen poker, the point of which he had blown red-hot in the fire, followed by the cook with his longest spit. Through the crowd, which scattered right and left before them, they came down upon Curdie. Uttering a shrill whistle, he caught the poker a blow with his mattock, knocking the point to the ground, while the page behind him started forward, and seizing the point of the spit, held on to it with both hands, the cook kicking him furiously.

Ere the butler could raise the poker again, or the cook recover the spit, with a roar to terrify the dead, Lina dashed into the room, her eyes flaming like candles. She went straight at the butler. He was down in a moment, and she on the top of him, wagging her tail over him like a lioness.

"Don't kill him, Lina," said Curdie.

"Oh, Mr. Miner!" cried the butler.

"Put your foot on his mouth, Lina," said Curdie. "The truth Fear tells is not much better than her lies."

The rest of the creatures now came stalking, rolling, leaping, gliding, hobbling into the room, and each as he came took the next place along the wall, until, solemn and grotesque, all stood ranged, awaiting orders.

And now some of the culprits were stealing to the doors nearest them. Curdie whispered the two creatures next him. Off went Ballbody, rolling and bounding through the crowd like a spent cannon shot, and when the foremost reached the door to the corridor, there he lay at the foot of it grinning; to the other door scuttled a scorpion, as big as a huge crab. The rest stood so still that some began to think they were only boys dressed up to look awful; they persuaded themselves they were only another part of the housemaid and page's vengeful contrivance, and their evil spirits began to rise again. Meantime Curdie had, with a second sharp blow from the hammer of his mattock, disabled the cook, so that he yielded the spit with a groan. He now turned to the avengers.

"Go at them," he said.

The whole nine-and-forty obeyed at once, each for himself, and after his own fashion. A scene of confusion and terror followed. The crowd scattered like a dance of flies. The creatures had been instructed not to hurt much, but to hunt incessantly, until every one had rushed from the house. The women shrieked, and ran hither and thither through the hall, pursued each by her own horror, and snapped at by every other in passing. If one threw herself down in hysterical despair, she was instantly poked or clawed or nibbled up again. Though they were quite as frightened at first, the men did not run so fast; and by-and-by some of them, finding they were only glared at, and followed, and pushed, began to summon up courage once more, and with courage came impudence. The tapir had the big footman in charge: the fellow stood stock-still, and let the beast come up to him, then put out his finger and playfully patted his nose. The tapir gave the nose a little twist, and the finger lay on the floor. Then indeed the footman ran, and did more than run, but nobody heeded his cries. Gradually the avengers grew more severe, and the terrors of the imagination were fast yielding to those of sensuous experience, when a page, perceiving one of the doors no longer guarded, sprang at it, and ran out. Another and another followed. Not a beast went after, until, one by one, they were every one gone from the hall, and the whole menie in the kitchen. There they were beginning to congratulate themselves that all was over, when in came the creatures trooping after them, and the second act of their terror and pain began. They were flung about in all directions; their clothes were torn from them; they were pinched and scratched any and everywhere; Ballbody kept rolling up them and over them, confining his attentions to no one in particular; the scorpion kept grabbing at their legs with his huge pincers; a three-foot centipede kept screwing up their bodies, nipping as he went; varied as numerous were their woes. Nor was it long before the last of them had fled from the kitchen to the sculleries. But thither also they were followed, and there again they were hunted about. They were bespattered with the dirt of their own neglect; they were soused in the stinking water that had boiled greens; they were smeared with rancid dripping; their faces were rubbed in maggots: I dare not tell all that was done to them. At last they got the door into a back-yard open, and rushed out. Then first they knew that the wind was howling and the rain falling in sheets. But there was no rest for them even there. Thither also were they followed by the inexorable avengers, and the only door here was a door out of the palace: out every soul of them was driven, and left, some standing, some lying, some crawling, to the farther buffeting of the waterspouts and whirlwinds ranging every street of the city. The door was flung to behind them, and they heard it locked and bolted and barred against them.

A scene of confusion and terror followed: the crowd scattered like a dance of flies.

MORE VENGEANCE

As soon as they were gone, Curdie brought the creatures back to the servants' hall, and told them to eat up everything on the table. It was a sight to see them all standing round it—except such as had to get upon it—eating and drinking, each after its fashion, without a smile, or a word, or a glance of fellowship in the act. A very few moments served to make everything eatable vanish, and then Curdie requested them to clean the house, and the page who stood by to assist them.

Every one set about it except Ballbody: he could do nothing at cleaning, for the more he rolled, the more he spread the dirt. Curdie was curious to know what he had been, and how he had come to be such as he was; but he could only conjecture that he was a gluttonous alderman whom nature had treated homeopathically.

And now there was such a cleaning and clearing out of neglected places, such a burying and burning of refuse, such a rinsing of jugs, such a swilling of sinks, and such a flushing of drains, as would have delighted the eyes of all true housekeepers and lovers of cleanliness generally.

Curdie meantime was with the king, telling him all he had done. They had heard a little noise, but not much, for he had told the avengers to repress outcry as much as possible; and they had seen to it that the more any one cried out the more he had to cry out upon, while the patient ones they scarcely hurt at all.

Having promised his majesty and her royal highness a good breakfast, Curdie now went to finish the business. The courtiers must be dealt with. A few who were the worst, and the leaders of the rest, must be made examples of; the others should be driven from their beds to the street.

He found the chiefs of the conspiracy holding a final consultation in the smaller room off the hall. These were the lord chamberlain, the attorney-general, the master of the horse, and the king's private secretary: the lord chancellor and the rest, as foolish as faithless, were but the tools of these.

The housemaid had shown him a little closet, opening from a passage behind, where he could overhear all that passed in that room; and now Curdie heard enough to understand that they had determined, in the dead of that night, rather in the deepest dark before the morning, to bring a certain company of soldiers into the palace, make away with the king, secure the princess, announce the sudden death of his majesty, read as his the will they had drawn up, and proceed to govern the country at their ease, and with results: they would at once levy severer taxes, and pick a quarrel with the most powerful of their neighbours. Everything settled, they agreed to retire, and have a few hours' quiet sleep first—all but the secretary, who was to sit up and call them at the proper moment. Curdie stole away, allowed them half an hour to get to bed, and then set about completing his purgation of the palace.

First he called Lina, and opened the door of the room where the secretary sat. She crept in, and laid herself down against it. When the secretary, rising to stretch his legs, caught sight of her eyes, he stood frozen with terror. She made neither motion nor sound. Gathering courage, and taking the thing for a spectral illusion, he made a step forward. She showed her other teeth, with a growl neither more than audible nor less than horrible. The secretary sank fainting into a chair. He was not a brave man, and besides, his conscience had gone over to the enemy, and was sitting against the door by Lina.

To the lord chamberlain's door next, Curdie conducted the legserpent, and let him in.

Now his lordship had had a bedstead made for himself, sweetly fashioned of rods of silver gilt: upon it the legserpent found him asleep, and under it he crept. But out he came on the other side, and crept over it next, and again under it, and so over it, under it, over it, five or six times, every time leaving a coil of himself behind him, until he had softly folded all his length about the lord chamberlain and his bed. This done, he set up his head, looking down with curved neck right over his lordship's, and began to hiss in his face. He woke in terror unspeakable, and would have started up; but the moment he moved, the legserpent drew his coils closer, and closer still, and drew and drew until the quaking traitor heard the joints of his bedstead grinding and gnarring. Presently he persuaded himself that it was only a horrid nightmare, and began to struggle with all his strength to throw it off. There-upon the legserpent gave his hooked nose such a bite, that his teeth met through it —but it was hardly thicker than the bowl of a spoon; and then the vulture knew that he was in the grasp of his enemy the snake, and yielded. As soon as he was quiet the legserpent began to untwist and retwist, to uncoil and recoil himself, swinging and swaying, knotting and relaxing himself with strangest curves and convolutions, always, however, leaving at least one coil around his victim. At last he undid himself entirely, and crept from the bed. Then first the lord chamberlain discovered that his tormentor had bent and twisted the bedstead, legs and canopy and all, so about him, that he was shut in a silver cage out of which it was impos-sible for him to find a way. Once more, thinking his enemy was gone, he began to shout for help. But the instant he opened his mouth his keeper darted at him and bit him, and after three or four such essays, with like result, he lay still.

The master of the horse Curdie gave in charge to the tapir. When the soldier saw him enter—for he was not yet asleep—he sprang from his bed, and flew at him with his sword. But the creature's hide was invulnerable to his blows, and he pecked at his legs with his proboscis until he jumped into bed again, groaning, and covered himself up; after which the tapir contented himself with now and then paying a visit to his toes.

For the attorney-general, Curdie led to his door a huge spider, about two feet long in the body, which, having made an excellent supper, was full of webbing. The attorney-general had not gone to bed, but sat in a chair asleep before a great mirror. He had been trying the effect of a diamond star which he had that morning taken from the jewel-room. When he woke he fancied himself paralysed; every limb, every finger even, was motionless: coils and coils of broad spider-ribbon bandaged his members to his body, and all to the chair. In the glass he saw himself wound about, under and over and around, with slavery infinite. On a footstool a yard off sat the spider glaring at him.

Clubhead had mounted guard over the butler, where he lay tied hand and foot under the third cask. From that cask he had seen the wine run into a great bath, and therein he expected to be drowned. The doctor, with his crushed leg, needed no one to guard him.

And now Curdie proceeded to the expulsion of the rest. Great men or underlings, he treated them all alike. From room to room over the house he went, and sleeping or waking took the man by the hand. Such was the state to which a year of wicked rule had reduced the moral condition of the court, that in it all he found but three with human hands. The possessors of these he allowed to dress themselves and depart in peace. When they perceived his mission, and how he was backed, they yielded without dispute.

Then commenced a general hunt, to clear the house of the vermin. Out of their beds in their night-clothing, out of their rooms, gorgeous chambers or garret nooks, the creatures hunted them. Not one was allowed to escape. Tumult and noise there was little, for the fear was too deadly for outcry. Ferreting them out everywhere, following them upstairs and downstairs, yielding no instant of repose except upon the way out, the avengers persecuted the miscreants, until the last of them was shivering outside the palace gates, with hardly sense enough left to know where to turn.

When they set out to look for shelter, they found every inn full of the servants expelled before them, and not one would yield his place to a superior suddenly levelled with himself. Most houses refused to admit them on the ground of the wickedness that must have drawn on them such a punishment; and not a few would have been left in the streets all night, had not Derba, roused by the vain entreaties at the doors on each side of her cottage, opened hers, and given up everything to them. The lord chancellor was only too glad to share a mattress with a stable-boy, and steal his bare feet under his jacket.

In the morning Curdie appeared, and the outcasts were in terror, thinking he had come after them again. But he took no notice of them: his object was to request Derba to go to the palace: the king required her services. She needed take no trouble about her cottage, he said; the palace was henceforward her home: she was the king's chastelaine over men and maidens of his household. And this very morning she must cook his majesty a nice breakfast.

THE PREACHER

Various reports went undulating through the city as to the nature of what had taken place in the palace. The people gathered, and stared at the house, eyeing it as if it had sprung up in the night. But it looked sedate enough, remaining closed and silent, like a house that was dead. They saw no one come out or go in. Smoke rose from a chimney or two; there was hardly another sign of life. It was not for some little time generally understood that the highest officers of the crown as well as the lowest menials of the palace had been dismissed in disgrace: for who was to recognise a lord chancellor in his night-shirt? and what lord chancellor would, so attired in the street, proclaim his rank and office aloud? Before it was day most of the courtiers crept down to the river, hired boats, and betook themselves to their homes or their friends in the country. It was assumed in the city that the domestics had been discharged upon a sudden discovery of general and unpardonable peculation; for, almost everybody being guilty of it himself, petty dishonesty was the crime most easily credited and least easily passed over in Gwyntystorm.

Now that same day was Religion day, and not a few of the clergy, always glad to seize on any passing event to give interest to the dull and monotonic grind of their intellectual machines, made this remarkable one the ground of discourse to their congregations. More especially than the rest, the first priest of the great temple where was the royal pew, judged himself, from his relation to the palace, called upon to "improve the occasion,"—for they talked ever about improvement at Gwyntystorm, all the time they were going downhill with a rush.

The book which had, of late years, come to be considered the most sacred, was called The Book of Nations, and consisted of proverbs, and history traced through custom: from it the first priest chose his text; and his text was, Honesty is the best Policy. He was considered a very eloquent man, but I can offer only a few of the larger bones of his sermon. The main proof of the verity of their religion, he said, was, that things always went well with those who professed it; and its first fundamental principle, grounded in inborn invariable instinct, was, that every One should take care of that One. This was the first duty of Man. If every one would but obey this law, number one, then would every one be perfectly cared for—one being always equal to one. But the faculty of care was in excess of need, and all that overflowed, and would otherwise run to waste, ought to be gently turned in the direction of one's neighbour, seeing that this also wrought for the fulfilling of the law, inasmuch as the reaction of excess so directed was upon the director of the same, to the comfort, that is, and well-being of the original self. To be just and friendly was to build the warmest and safest of all nests, and to be kind and loving was to line it with the softest of all furs and feathers, for the one precious, comfort-loving self there to lie, revelling in downiest bliss. One of the laws therefore most binding upon men because of its relation to the first and greatest of all duties, was embodied in the Proverb he had just read; and what stronger proof of its wisdom and truth could they desire than the sudden and complete vengeance which had fallen upon those worse than ordinary sinners who had offended against the king's majesty by forgetting that Honesty is the best Policy?

At this point of the discourse the head of the legserpent rose from the floor of the temple, towering above the pulpit, above the priest, then curving downwards, with open mouth slowly descended upon him. Horror froze the sermon-pump. He stared upwards aghast. The great teeth of the animal closed upon a mouthful of the sacred vestments, and slowly he lifted the preacher from the pulpit, like a handful of linen from a wash-tub, and, on his four solemn stumps, bore him out of the temple, dangling aloft from his jaws. At the back of it he dropped him into the dust-hole amongst the remnants of a library whose age had destroyed its value in the eyes of the chapter. They found him burrowing in it, a lunatic henceforth—whose madness presented the peculiar feature, that in its paroxysms he jabbered sense.

Bone-freezing horror pervaded Gwyntystorm. If their best and wisest were treated with such contempt, what might not the rest of them look for? Alas for their city! their grandly respectable city! their loftily reasonable city! Where it was all to end, the Convenient alone could tell!

But something must be done. Hastily assembling, the priests chose a new first priest, and in full conclave unanimously declared and accepted, that the king in his retirement had, through the practice of the blackest magic, turned the palace into a nest of demons in the midst of them. A grand exorcism was therefore indispensable.

In the meantime the fact came out that the greater part of the courtiers had been dismissed as well as the servants, and this fact swelled the hope of the Party of Decency, as they called themselves. Upon it they proceeded to act, and strengthened themselves on all sides.

The action of the king's body-guard remained for a time uncertain. But when at length its officers were satisfied that both the master of the horse and their colonel were missing, they placed themselves under the orders of the first priest.

Everyone dated the culmination of the evil from the visit of the miner and his mongrel; and the butchers vowed, if they could but get hold of them again, they would roast both of them alive. At once they formed themselves into a regiment, and put their dogs in training for attack.

Incessant was the talk, innumerable were the suggestions, and great was the deliberation. The general consent, however, was that as soon as the priests should have expelled the demons, they would depose the king, and, attired in all his regal insignia, shut him in a cage for public show; then choose governors, with the lord chancellor at their head, whose first duty should be to remit every possible tax; and the magistrates, by the mouth of the city marshal, required all able-bodied citizens, in order to do their part towards the carrying out of these and a multitude of other reforms, to be ready to take arms at the first summons.

Things needful were prepared as speedily as possible, and a mighty ceremony, in the temple, in the market-place, and in front of the palace, was performed for the expulsion of the demons. This over, the leaders retired to arrange an attack upon the palace.

But that night events occurred which, proving the failure of their first, induced the abandonment of their second intent. Certain of the prowling order of the community, whose numbers had of late been steadily on the increase, reported frightful things. Demons of indescribable ugliness had been espied careering through the midnight streets and courts. A citizen—some said in the very act of house-breaking, but no one cared to look into trifles at such a crisis—had been seized from behind, he could not see by what, and soused in the river. A well-known receiver of stolen goods had had his shop broken open, and when he came down in the morning had found everything in ruin on the pavement. The wooden image of justice over the door of the city marshal had had the arm that held the sword bitten off. The gluttonous magistrate had been pulled from his bed in the dark, by beings of which he could see nothing but the flaming eyes, and treated to a bath of the turtle soup that had been left simmering by the side of the kitchen fire. Having poured it over him, they put him again into his bed, where he soon learned how a mummy must feel in its cerements. Worst of all, in the market-place was fixed up a paper, with the king's own signature, to the effect that whoever henceforth should show inhospitality to strangers, and should be convicted of the same, should be instantly expelled the city; while a second, in the butchers' quarter, ordained that any dog which henceforward should attack a stranger should be immediately destroyed. It was plain, said the butchers, that the clergy were of no use; they could not exorcise demons! That afternoon, catching sight of a poor old fellow in rags and tatters, quietly walking up the street, they hounded their dogs upon him, and had it not been that the door of Derba's cottage was standing open, and was near enough for him to dart in and shut it ere they reached him, he would have been torn in pieces.

And thus things went on for some days.

BARBARA

In the meantime, with Derba to minister to his wants, with Curdie to protect him, and Irene to nurse him, the king was getting rapidly stronger. Good food was what he most wanted, and of that, at least of certain kinds of it, there was plentiful store in the palace. Everywhere since the cleansing of the lower regions of it, the air was clean and sweet, and under the honest hands of the one housemaid the king's chamber became a pleasure to his eyes. With such changes it was no wonder if his heart grew lighter as well as his brain clearer.

But still evil dreams came and troubled him, the lingering result of the wicked medicines the doctor had given him. Every night, sometimes twice or thrice, he would wake up in terror, and it would be minutes ere he could come to himself. The consequence was that he was always worse in the morning, and had loss to make up during the day. This retarded his recovery greatly. While he slept, Irene or Curdie, one or the other, must still be always by his side.

One night, when it was Curdie's turn with the king, he heard a cry somewhere in the house, and as there was no other child, concluded, notwithstanding the distance of her grandmother's room, that it must be Barbara. Fearing something might be wrong, and noting the king's sleep more quiet than usual, he ran to see. He found the child in the middle of the floor, weeping bitterly, and Derba slumbering peacefully in bed. The instant she saw him the night-lost thing ceased her crying, smiled, and stretched out her arms to him. Unwilling to wake the old woman, who had been working hard all day, he took the child, and carried her with him. She clung to him so, pressing her tear-wet radiant face against his, that her little arms threatened to choke him. When he re-entered the chamber, he found the king sitting up in bed, fighting the phantoms of some hideous dream. Generally upon such occasions, although he saw his watcher, he could not dissociate him from the dream, and went raving on. But the moment his eyes fell upon little Barbara, whom he had never seen before, his soul came into them with a rush, and a smile like the dawn of an eternal day overspread his countenance: the dream was nowhere, and the child was in his heart. He stretched out his arms to her, the child stretched out hers to him, and in five minutes they were both asleep, each in the other's embrace. From that night Barbara had a crib in the king's chamber, and as often as he woke, Irene or Curdie, whichever was watching, took the sleeping child and laid her in his arms, upon which, invariably and instantly, the dream would vanish. A great part of the day too she would be playing on or about the king's bed; and it was a delight to the heart of the princess to see her amusing herself with the crown, now sitting upon it, now rolling it hither and thither about the room like a hoop. Her grandmother entering once while she was pretending to make porridge in it, held up her hands in horror-struck amazement; but the king would not allow her to interfere, for the king was now Barbara's playmate, and his crown their plaything.

The colonel of the guard also was growing better. Curdie went often to see him. They were soon friends, for the best people understand each other the easiest, and the grim old warrior loved the miner boy as if he were at once his son and his angel. He was very anxious about his regiment. He said the officers were mostly honest men, he believed, but how they might be doing without him, or what they might resolve, in ignorance of the real state of affairs, and exposed to every misrepresentation, who could tell? Curdie proposed that he should send for the major, offering to be the messenger. The colonel agreed, and Curdie went—not without his mattock, because of the dogs.

But the officers had been told by the master of the horse that their colonel was dead, and although they were amazed he should be buried without the attendance of his regiment, they never doubted the information. The handwriting itself of their colonel was insufficient, counteracted by the fresh reports daily current, to destroy the lie. The major regarded the letter as a trap for the next officer in command, and sent his orderly to arrest the messenger. But Curdie had had the wisdom not to wait for an answer.

The king's enemies said that he had first poisoned the good colonel of the guard, and then murdered the master of the horse, and other faithful councillors; and that his oldest and most attached domestics had but escaped from the palace with their lives—nor all of them, for the butler was missing. Mad or wicked, he was not only unfit to rule any longer, but worse than unfit to have in his power and under his influence the young princess, only hope of Gwyntystorm and the kingdom.

The moment the lord chancellor reached his house in the country and had got himself clothed, he began to devise how yet to destroy his master; and the very next morning set out for the neighbouring kingdom of Borsagrass, to invite invasion, and offer a compact with its monarch.

PETER

At the cottage on the mountain everything for a time went on just as before. It was indeed dull without Curdie, but as often as they looked at the emerald it was gloriously green, and with nothing to fear or regret, and everything to hope, they required little comforting. One morning, however, at last, Peter, who had been consulting the gem, rather now from habit than anxiety, as a farmer his barometer in undoubtful weather, turned suddenly to his wife, the stone in his hand, and held it up with a look of ghastly dismay.

"Why, that's never the emerald!" said Joan.

"It is," answered Peter; "but it were small blame to any one that took it for a bit of bottle glass!"

For, all save one spot right in the centre, of intensest and most brilliant green, it looked as if the colour had been burnt out of it.

"Run, run, Peter!" cried his wife. "Run and tell the old princess. It may not be too late. The boy must be lying at death's door."

Without a word Peter caught up his mattock, darted from the cottage, and was at the bottom of the hill in less time than he usually took to get halfway.

The door of the king's house stood open; he rushed in and up the stair. But after wandering about in vain for an hour, opening door after door, and finding no way farther up, the heart of the old man had well-nigh failed him. Empty rooms, empty rooms!—desertion and desolation everywhere.

At last he did come upon the door to the tower-stair. Up he darted. Arrived at the top, he found three doors, and, one after the other, knocked at them all. But there was neither voice nor hearing. Urged by his faith and his dread, slowly, hesitatingly, he opened one. It revealed a bare garret-room, nothing in it but one chair and one spinning-wheel. He closed it, and opened the next—to start back in terror, for he saw nothing but a great gulf, a moonless night, full of stars, and, for all the stars, dark, dark!—a fathomless abyss. He opened the third door, and a rush like the tide of a living sea invaded his ears. Multitudinous wings flapped and flashed in the sun, and, like the ascending column from a volcano, white birds innumerable shot into the air, darkening the day with the shadow of their cloud, and then, with a sharp sweep, as if bent sideways by a sudden wind, flew northward, swiftly away, and vanished. The place felt like a tomb. There seemed no breath of life left in it. Despair laid hold upon him; he rushed down thundering with heavy feet. Out upon him darted the housekeeper like an ogress-spider, and after her came her men; but Peter rushed past them, heedless and careless—for had not the princess mocked him?—and sped along the road to Gwyntystorm. What help lay in a miner's mattock, a man's arm, a father's heart, he would bear to his boy.

Joan sat up all night waiting his return, hoping and hoping. The mountain was very still, and the sky was clear; but all night long the miner sped northwards, and the heart of his wife was troubled.

THE SACRIFICE

Things in the palace were in a strange condition: the king playing with a child and dreaming wise dreams, waited upon by a little princess with the heart of a queen, and a youth from the mines, who went nowhere, not even into the king's chamber, without his mattock on his shoulder and a horrible animal at his heels; in a room near by the colonel of his guard, also in bed, without a soldier to obey him; in six other rooms, far apart, six miscreants, each watched by a beast-gaoler; ministers to them all, an old woman, a young woman, and a page; and in the wine-cellar, forty-three animals, creatures more grotesque than ever brain of man invented. None dared approach its gates, and seldom one issued from them.

All the dwellers in the city were united in enmity to the palace. It swarmed with evil spirits, they said, whereas the evil spirits were in the city, unsuspected. One consequence of their presence was that, when the rumour came that a great army was on the march against Gwyntystorm, instead of rushing to their defences, to make new gates, free portcullises and drawbridges, and bar the river, each and all flew first to their treasures, burying them in their cellars and gardens, and hiding them behind stones in their chimneys; and, next to rebellion, signing an invitation to his majesty of Borsagrass to enter at their open gates, destroy their king, and annex their country to his own.

The straits of isolation were soon found in the palace: its invalids were requiring stronger food, and what was to be done? for if the butchers sent meat to the palace, was it not likely enough to be poisoned? Curdie said to Derba he would think of some plan before morning.

But that same night, as soon as it was dark, Lina came to her master, and let him understand she wanted to go out. He unlocked a little private postern for her, left it so that she could push it open when she returned, and told the crocodile to stretch himself across it inside. Before midnight she came back with a young deer.

Early the next morning the legserpent crept out of the wine-cellar, through the broken door behind, shot into the river, and soon appeared in the kitchen with a splendid sturgeon. Every night Lina went out hunting, and every morning Legserpent went out fishing, and both invalids and household had plenty to eat. As to news, the page, in plain clothes, would now and then venture out into the market-place, and gather some.

One night he came back with the report that the army of the king of Borsagrass had crossed the border. Two days after, he brought the news that the enemy was now but twenty miles from Gwyntystorm.

The colonel of the guard rose, and began furbishing his armour—but gave it over to the page, and staggered across to the barracks, which were in the next street. The sentry took him for a ghost or worse, ran into the guard-room, bolted the door, and stopped his ears. The poor colonel, who was yet hardly able to stand, crawled back despairing.

For Curdie, he had already, as soon as the first rumour reached him, resolved, if no other instructions came, and the king continued unable to give orders, to call Lina and the creatures, and march to meet the enemy. If he died, he died for the right, and there was a right end of it. He had no preparations to make, except a good sleep.

He asked the king to let the housemaid take his place by his majesty that night, and went and lay down on the floor of the corridor, no farther off than a whisper would reach from the door of the chamber. There, with an old mantle of the king's thrown over him, he was soon fast asleep.

Somewhere about the middle of the night, he woke suddenly, started to his feet, and rubbed his eyes. He could not tell what had waked him. But could he be awake, or was he not dreaming? The curtain of the king's door, a dull red ever before, was glowing a gorgeous, a radiant purple; and the crown wrought upon it in silks and gems was flashing as if it burned! What could it mean? Was the king's chamber on fire? He darted to the door and lifted the curtain. Glorious terrible sight!

A long and broad marble table, that stood at one end of the room, had been drawn into the middle of it, and thereon burned a great fire, of a sort that Curdie knew—a fire of glowing, flaming roses, red and white. In the midst of the roses lay the king, moaning, but motionless. Every rose that fell from the table to the floor, some one, whom Curdie could not plainly see for the brightness, lifted and laid burning upon the king's face, until at length his face too was covered with the live roses, and he lay all within the fire, moaning still, with now and then a shuddering sob. And the shape that Curdie saw and could not see, wept over the king as he lay in the fire, and often she hid her face in handfuls of her shadowy hair, and from her hair the water of her weeping dropped like sunset rain in the light of the roses. At last she lifted a great armful of her hair, and shook it over the fire, and the drops fell from it in showers, and they did not hiss in the flames, but there arose instead as it were the sound of running brooks. And the glow of the red fire died away, and the glow of the white fire grew gray, and the light was gone, and on the table all was black—except the face of the king, which shone from under the burnt roses like a diamond in the ashes of a furnace.

In the midst of the roses lay the king, moaning, but motionless.

Then Curdie, no longer dazzled, saw and knew the old princess. The room was lighted with the splendour of her face, of her blue eyes, of her sapphire crown. Her golden hair went streaming out from her through the air till it went off in mist and light. She was large and strong as a Titaness. She stooped over the table-altar, put her mighty arms under the living sacrifice, lifted the king, as if he were but a little child, to her bosom, walked with him up the floor, and laid him in his bed. Then darkness fell.

The miner-boy turned silent away, and laid himself down again in the corridor. An absolute joy filled his heart, his bosom, his head, his whole body. All was safe; all was well. With the helve of his mattock tight in his grasp, he sank into a dreamless sleep.

THE KING'S ARMY

He woke like a giant refreshed with wine.

When he went into the king's chamber, the housemaid sat where he had left her, and everything in the room was as it had been the night before, save that a heavenly odour of roses filled the air of it. He went up to the bed. The king opened his eyes, and the soul of perfect health shone out of them. Nor was Curdie amazed in his delight.

"Is it not time to rise, Curdie?" said the king.

"It is, your majesty. To-day we must be doing," answered Curdie.

"What must we be doing to-day, Curdie?"

"Fighting, sire."

"Then fetch me my armour—that of plated steel, in the chest there. You will find the underclothing with it."

As he spoke, he reached out his hand for his sword, which hung in the bed before him, drew it, and examined the blade.

"A little rusty!" he said, "but the edge is there. We shall polish it ourselves to-day —not on the wheel. Curdie, my son, I wake from a troubled dream. A glorious torture has ended it, and I live. I know not well how things are, but thou shalt explain them to me as I get on my armour.—No, I need no bath. I am clean.—Call the colonel of the guard."

In complete steel the old man stepped into the chamber. He knew it not, but the old princess had passed through his room in the night.

"Why, Sir Bronzebeard!" said the king, "you are dressed before me! Thou needest no valet, old man, when there is battle in the wind!"

"Battle, sire!" returned the colonel. "—Where then are our soldiers?"

"Why, there, and here," answered the king, pointing to the colonel first, and then to himself. "Where else, man?—The enemy will be upon us ere sunset, if we be not upon him ere noon. What other thing was in thy brave brain when thou didst don thine armour, friend?"

"Your majesty's orders, sire," answered Sir Bronzebeard.

The king smiled and turned to Curdie.

"And what was in thine, Curdie—for thy first word was of battle?"

"See, your majesty," answered Curdie; "I have polished my mattock. If your majesty had not taken the command, I would have met the enemy at the head of my beasts, and died in comfort, or done better."

"Brave boy!" said the king. "He who takes his life in his hand is the only soldier. Thou shalt head thy beasts to-day.—Sir Bronzebeard, wilt thou die with me if need be?"

"Seven times, my king," said the colonel.

"Then shall we win this battle!" said the king. "—Curdie, go and bind securely the six, that we lose not their guards.—Canst thou find us a horse, think'st thou, Sir Bronzebeard? Alas! they told us our white charger was dead."

"I will go and fright the varletry with my presence, and secure, I trust, a horse for your majesty, and one for myself."

"And look you, brother!" said the king; "bring one for my miner boy too, and a sober old charger for the princess, for she too must go to the battle, and conquer with us."

"Pardon me, sire," said Curdie; "a miner can fight best on foot. I might smite my horse dead under me with a missed blow. And besides, I must be near my beasts."

"As you will," said the king. "—Three horses then, Sir Bronzebeard."

The colonel departed, doubting sorely in his heart how to accoutre and lead from the barrack stables three horses, in the teeth of his revolted regiment.

In the hall he met the housemaid.

"Can you lead a horse?" he asked.

"Yes, sir."

"Are you willing to die for the king?"

"Yes, sir."

"Can you do as you are bid?"

"I can keep on trying, sir."

"Come, then. Were I not a man I would be a woman such as thou."

When they entered the barrack-yard, the soldiers scattered like autumn leaves before a blast of winter. They went into the stable unchallenged—and lo! in a stall, before the colonel's eyes, stood the king's white charger, with the royal saddle and bridle hung high beside him!

"Traitorous thieves!" muttered the old man in his beard, and went along the stalls, looking for his own black charger. Having found him, he returned to saddle first the king's. But the maid had already the saddle upon him, and so girt that the colonel could thrust no finger-tip between girth and skin. He left her to finish what she had so well begun, and went and graithed his own. He then chose for the princess a great red horse, twenty years old, which he knew to possess every equine virtue. This and his own he led to the palace, and the maid led the king's.

The king and Curdie stood in the court, the king in full armour of silvered steel, with a circlet of rubies and diamonds round his helmet. He almost leaped for joy when he saw his great white charger come in, gentle as a child to the hand of the housemaid. But when the horse saw his master in his armour, he reared and bounded in jubilation, yet did not break from the hand that held him. Then out came the princess attired and ready, with a hunting-knife her father had given her by her side. They brought her mother's saddle, splendent with gems and gold, set it on the great red horse, and lifted her to it. But the saddle was so big, and the horse so tall, that the child found no comfort in them.

"Please, king papa," she said, "can I not have my white pony?"

"I did not think of him, little one," said the king. "Where is he?"

"In the stable," answered the maid. "I found him half-starved, the only horse within the gates, the day after the servants were driven out. He has been well fed since."

"Go and fetch him," said the king.

As the maid appeared with the pony, from a side door came Lina and the forty-nine, following Curdie.

"I will go with Curdie and the Uglies," cried the princess; and as soon as she was mounted she got into the middle of the pack.

So out they set, the strangest force that ever went against an enemy. The king in silver armour sat stately on his white steed, with the stones flashing on his helmet; beside him the grim old colonel, armed in steel, rode his black charger; behind the king, a little to the right, Curdie walked afoot, his mattock shining in the sun; Lina followed at his heel; behind her came the wonderful company of Uglies; in the midst of them rode the gracious little Irene, dressed in blue, and mounted on the prettiest of white ponies; behind the colonel, a little to the left, walked the page, armed in a breastplate, headpiece, and trooper's sword he had found in the palace, all much too big for him, and carrying a huge brass trumpet which he did his best to blow; and the king smiled and seemed pleased with his music, although it was but the grunt of a brazen unrest. Alongside of the beasts walked Derba carrying Barbara—their refuge the mountains, should the cause of the king be lost; as soon as they were over the river they turned aside to ascend the cliff, and there awaited the forging of the day's history. Then first Curdie saw that the housemaid, whom they had all forgotten, was following, mounted on the great red horse, and seated in the royal saddle.

Many were the eyes unfriendly of women that had stared at them from door and window as they passed through the city; and low laughter and mockery and evil words from the lips of children had rippled about their ears; but the men were all gone to welcome the enemy, the butchers the first, the king's guard the last. And now on the heels of the king's army rushed out the women and children also, to gather flowers and branches, wherewith to welcome their conquerors.

About a mile down the river, Curdie, happening to look behind him, saw the maid, whom he had supposed gone with Derba, still following on the great red horse. The same moment the king, a few paces in front of him, caught sight of the enemy's tents, pitched where, the cliffs receding, the bank of the river widened to a little plain.

THE BATTLE

He commanded the page to blow his trumpet; and, in the strength of the moment, the youth uttered a right war-like defiance.

But the butchers and the guard, who had gone over armed to the enemy, thinking that the king had come to make his peace also, and that it might thereafter go hard with them, rushed at once to make short work with him, and both secure and commend themselves. The butchers came on first—for the guards had slackened their saddle-girths—brandishing their knives, and talking to their dogs. Curdie and the page, with Lina and her pack, bounded to meet them. Curdie struck down the foremost with his mattock. The page, finding his sword too much for him, threw it away and seized the butcher's knife, which as he rose he plunged into the foremost dog. Lina rushed raging and gnashing amongst them. She would not look at a dog so long as there was a butcher on his legs, and she never stopped to kill a butcher, only with one grind of her jaws crushed a leg of him. When they were all down, then indeed she flashed amongst the dogs.

Meantime the king and the colonel had spurred towards the advancing guard. The king clove the major through skull and collar-bone, and the colonel stabbed the captain in the throat. Then a fierce combat commenced—two against many. But the butchers and their dogs quickly disposed of, up came Curdie and his beasts. The horses of the guard, struck with terror, turned in spite of the spur, and fled in confusion.

Thereupon the forces of Borsagrass, which could see little of the affair, but correctly imagined a small determined body in front of them, hastened to the attack. No sooner did their first advancing wave appear through the foam of the retreating one, than the king and the colonel and the page, Curdie and the beasts, went charging upon them. Their attack, especially the rush of the Uglies, threw the first line into great confusion, but the second came up quickly; the beasts could not be everywhere, there were thousands to one against them, and the king and his three companions were in the greatest possible danger.

"The king and the colonel and the page, Curdie and the beasts, went charging upon them."

A dense cloud came over the sun, and sank rapidly towards the earth. The cloud moved "all together," and yet the thousands of white flakes of which it was made up moved each for itself in ceaseless and rapid motion: those flakes were the wings of pigeons. Down swooped the birds upon the invaders; right in the face of man and horse they flew with swift-beating wings, blinding eyes and confounding brain. Horses reared and plunged and wheeled. All was at once in confusion. The men made frantic efforts to seize their tormentors, but not one could they touch; and they outdoubled them in numbers. Between every wild clutch came a peck of beak and a buffet of pinion in the face. Generally the bird would, with sharp-clapping wings, dart its whole body, with the swiftness of an arrow, against its singled mark, yet so as to glance aloft the same instant, and descend skimming; much as the thin stone, shot with horizontal cast of arm, having touched and torn the surface of the lake, ascends to skim, touch, and tear again. So mingled the feathered multitude in the grim game of war. It was a storm in which the wind was birds, and the sea men. And ever as each bird arrived at the rear of the enemy, it turned, ascended, and sped to the front to charge again.

The moment the battle began, the princess's pony took fright, and turned and fled. But the maid wheeled her horse across the road and stopped him; and they waited together the result of the battle.

And as they waited, it seemed to the princess right strange that the pigeons,

561

every one as it came to the rear, and fetched a compass to gather force for the re-attack, should make the head of her attendant on the red horse the goal around which it turned; so that about them was an unintermittent flapping and flashing of wings, and a curving, sweeping torrent of the side-poised wheeling bodies of birds. Strange also it seemed that the maid should be constantly waving her arm towards the battle. And the time of the motion of her arm so fitted with the rushes of birds, that it looked as if the birds obeyed her gesture, and she were casting living javelins by the thousand against the enemy. The moment a pigeon had rounded her head, it went off straight as bolt from bow, and with trebled velocity.

But of these strange things, others besides the princess had taken note. From a rising ground whence they watched the battle in growing dismay, the leaders of the enemy saw the maid and her motions, and, concluding her an enchantress, whose were the airy legions humiliating them, set spurs to their horses, made a circuit, outflanked the king, and came down upon her. But suddenly by her side stood a stalwart old man in the garb of a miner, who, as the general rode at her, sword in hand, heaved his swift mattock, and brought it down with such force on the forehead of his charger, that he fell to the ground like a log. His rider shot over his head and lay stunned. Had not the great red horse reared and wheeled, he would have fallen beneath that of the general.

It looked as if the birds obeyed her gesture, and she were casting living javelins by the thousand against the enemy.

With lifted sabre, one of his attendant officers rode at the miner. But a mass of pigeons darted in the faces of him and his horse, and the next moment he lay beside his commander. The rest of them turned and fled, pursued by the birds.

"Ah, friend Peter!" said the maid; "thou hast come as I told thee! Welcome and thanks!"

By this time the battle was over. The rout was general. The enemy stormed back upon their own camp, with the beasts roaring in the midst of them, and the king and his army, now reinforced by one, pursuing. But presently the king drew rein.

"Call off your hounds, Curdie, and let the pigeons do the rest," he shouted, and turned to see what had become of the princess.

In full panic fled the invaders, sweeping down their tents, stumbling over their baggage, trampling on their dead and wounded, ceaselessly pursued and buffeted by the white-winged army of heaven. Homeward they rushed the road they had come, straight for the borders, many dropping from pure fatigue, and lying where they fell. And still the pigeons were in their necks as they ran. At length to the eyes of the king and his army nothing was visible save a dust-cloud below, and a bird-cloud above.

Before night the bird-cloud came back, flying high over Gwyntystorm. Sinking swiftly, it disappeared among the ancient roofs of the palace.

JUDGMENT

The king and his army returned, bringing with them one prisoner only, the lord chancellor. Curdie had dragged him from under a fallen tent, not by the hand of a man, but by the foot of a mule.

When they entered the city, it was still as the grave. The citizens had fled home. "We must submit," they cried, "or the king and his demons will destroy us." The king rode through the streets in silence, ill-pleased with his people. But he stopped his horse in the midst of the market-place, and called, in a voice loud and clear as the cry of a silver trumpet, "Go and find your own. Bury your dead, and bring home your wounded." Then he turned him gloomily to the palace.

Just as they reached the gates, Peter, who, as they went, had been telling his tale to Curdie, ended it with the words,—

"And so there I was, in the nick of time to save the two princesses!"

"The two princesses, father! The one on the great red horse was the housemaid," said Curdie, and ran to open the gates for the king.

They found Derba returned before them, and already busy preparing them food. The king put up his charger with his own hands, rubbed him down, and fed him.

When they had washed, and eaten and drunk, he called the colonel, and told Curdie and the page to bring out the traitors and the beasts, and attend him to the market-place.

By this time the people were crowding back into the city, bearing their dead and wounded. And there was lamentation in Gwyntystorm, for no one could comfort himself, and no one had any to comfort him. The nation was victorious, but the people were conquered.

The king stood in the centre of the market-place, upon the steps of the ancient cross. He had laid aside his helmet and put on his crown, but he stood all armed beside, with his sword in his hand. He called the people to him, and, for all the terror of the beasts, they dared not disobey him. Those even, who were carrying their wounded laid them down, and drew near trembling.

Then the king said to Curdie and the page,—

"Set the evil men before me."

To the body of the animal they bound the lord chamberlain, speechless with horror.

He looked upon them for a moment in mingled anger and pity, then turned to the people and said,—

"Behold your trust! Ye slaves, behold your leaders! I would have freed you, but ye would not be free. Now shall ye be ruled with a rod of iron, that ye may learn what freedom is, and love it and seek it. These wretches I will send where they shall mislead you no longer."

He made a sign to Curdie, who immediately brought up the leg serpent. To the body of the animal they bound the lord chamberlain, speechless with horror. The butler began to shriek and pray, but they bound him on the back of Clubhead. One after another, upon the largest of the creatures they bound the whole seven, each through the unveiling terror looking the villain he was. Then said the king,—

"I thank you, my good beasts; and I hope to visit you ere long. Take these evil men with you, and go to your place."

Like a whirlwind they were in the crowd, scattering it like dust. Like hounds they rushed from the city, their burdens howling and raving.

What became of them I have never heard.

Then the king turned once more to the people and said, "Go to your houses;" nor vouchsafed them another word. They crept home like chidden hounds.

The king returned to the palace. He made the colonel a duke, and the page a knight, and Peter he appointed general of all his mines. But to Curdie he said,—

"You are my own boy, Curdie. My child cannot choose but love you, and when you are both grown up—if you both will—you shall marry each other, and be king and queen when I am gone. Till then be the king's Curdie."

Irene held out her arms to Curdie. He raised her in his, and she kissed him.

"And my Curdie too!" she said.

Thereafter the people called him Prince Conrad; but the king always called him either just Curdie, or My miner-boy.

They sat down to supper, and Derba and the knight and the housemaid waited, and Barbara sat on the king's left hand. The housemaid poured out the wine; and as she poured out for Curdie red wine that foamed in the cup, as if glad to see the light whence it had been banished so long, she looked him in the eyes. And Curdie started, and sprang from his seat, and dropped on his knees, and burst into tears. And the maid said with a smile, such as none but one could smile,—

"Did I not tell you, Curdie, that it might be you would not know me when next you saw me?"

Then she went from the room, and in a moment returned in royal purple, with a crown of diamonds and rubies, from under which her hair went flowing to the floor, all about her ruby-slippered feet. Her face was radiant with joy, the joy over-shadowed by a faint mist as of unfulfilment. The king rose and kneeled on one knee before her. All kneeled in like homage. Then the king would have yielded her his royal chair. But she made them all sit down, and with her own hands placed at the table seats for Derba and the page. Then in ruby crown and royal purple she served them all.

THE END

The king sent Curdie out into his dominions to search for men and women that had human hands. And many such he found, honest and true, and brought them to his master. So a new and upright government, a new and upright court, was formed, and strength returned to the nation.

But the exchequer was almost empty, for the evil men had squandered everything, and the king hated taxes unwillingly paid. Then came Curdie and said to the king that the city stood upon gold. And the king sent for men wise in the ways of the earth, and they built smelting furnaces, and Peter brought miners, and they mined the gold, and smelted it, and the king coined it into money, and therewith established things well in the land.

The same day on which he found his boy, Peter set out to go home. When he told the good news to Joan his wife, she rose from her chair and said, "Let us go." And they left the cottage, and repaired to Gwyntystorm. And on a mountain above the city they built themselves a warm house for their old age, high in the clear air.

As Peter mined one day by himself, at the back of the king's wine-cellar, he broke into a cavern all crusted with gems, and much wealth flowed therefrom, and the king used it wisely.

Queen Irene—that was the right name of the old princess—was thereafter seldom long absent from the palace. Once or twice when she was missing, Barbara, who seemed to know of her sometimes when nobody else had a notion whither she had gone, said she was with the dear old Uglies in the wood. Curdie thought that perhaps her business might be with others there as well. All the uppermost rooms in the palace were left to her use, and when any one was in need of her help, up thither he must go. But even when she was there, he did not always succeed in finding her. She, however, always knew that such a one had been looking for her.

Curdie went to find her one day. As he ascended the last stair, to meet him came the well-known scent of her roses; and when he opened her door, lo! there was the same gorgeous room in which his touch had been glorified by her fire! And there burned the fire—a huge heap of red and white roses. Before the hearth stood the princess, an old gray-haired woman, with Lina a little behind her, slowly wagging her tail, and looking like a beast of prey that can hardly so long restrain itself from springing as to be sure of its victim. The queen was casting roses, more and more roses, upon the fire. At last she turned and said, "Now, Lina!"—and Lina dashed burrowing into the fire. There went up a black smoke and a dust, and Lina was never more seen in the palace.

Irene and Curdie were married. The old king died, and they were king and queen. As long as they lived Gwyntystorm was a better city, and good people grew in it. But they had no children, and when they died the people chose a king. And the new king went mining and mining in the rock under the city, and grew more and more eager after the gold, and paid less and less heed to his people. Rapidly they sunk towards their old wickedness. But still the king went on mining, and coining gold by the pailful, until the people were worse even than in the old time. And so greedy was the king after gold, that when at last the ore began to fail, he caused the miners to reduce the pillars which Peter and they that followed him had left standing to bear the city. And from the girth of an oak of a thousand years, they chipped them down to that of a fir tree of fifty.

One day at noon, when life was at its highest, the whole city fell with a roaring crash. The cries of men and the shrieks of women went up with its dust, and then there was a great silence.

Where the mighty rock once towered, crowded with homes and crowned with a palace, now rushes and raves a stone-obstructed rapid of the river. All around spreads a wilderness of wild deer, and the very name of Gwyntystorm has ceased from the lips of men.

THE END.

LILITH

BY
GEORGE MACDONALD

PREFACE

I took a walk on Spaulding's Farm the other afternoon. I saw the setting sun lighting up the opposite side of a stately pine wood. Its golden rays straggled into the aisles of the wood as into some noble hall. I was impressed as if some ancient and altogether admirable and shining family had settled there in that part of the land called Concord, unknown to me,—to whom the sun was servant,—who had not gone into society in the village,—who had not been called on. I saw their park, their pleasure-ground, beyond through the wood, in Spaulding's cranberry-meadow. The pines furnished them with gables as they grew. Their house was not obvious to vision; their trees grew through it. I do not know whether I heard the sounds of a suppressed hilarity or not. They seemed to recline on the sunbeams. They have sons and daughters. They are quite well. The farmer's cart-path, which leads directly through their hall, does not in the least put them out,—as the muddy bottom of a pool is sometimes seen through the reflected skies. They never heard of Spaulding, and do not know that he is their neighbor,—notwithstanding I heard him whistle as he drove his team through the house. Nothing can equal the serenity of their lives. Their coat of arms is simply a lichen. I saw it painted on the pines and oaks. Their attics were in the tops of the trees. They are of no politics. There was no noise of labor. I did not perceive that they were weaving or spinning. Yet I did detect, when the wind lulled and hearing was done away, the finest imaginable sweet musical hum,—as of a distant hive in May, which perchance was the sound of their thinking. They had no idle thoughts, and no one without could see their work, for their industry was not as in knots and excrescences embayed.

But I find it difficult to remember them. They fade irrevocably out of my mind even now while I speak and endeavor to recall them, and recollect myself. It is only after a long and serious effort to recollect my best thoughts that I become again aware of their cohabitancy. If it were not for such families as this, I think I should move out of Concord.

PREFACE

Thoreau: "WALKING."

CHAPTER I. THE LIBRARY

I had just finished my studies at Oxford, and was taking a brief holiday from work before assuming definitely the management of the estate. My father died when I was yet a child; my mother followed him within a year; and I was nearly as much alone in the world as a man might find himself.

I had made little acquaintance with the history of my ancestors. Almost the only thing I knew concerning them was, that a notable number of them had been given to study. I had myself so far inherited the tendency as to devote a good deal of my time, though, I confess, after a somewhat desultory fashion, to the physical sciences. It was chiefly the wonder they woke that drew me. I was constantly seeing, and on the outlook to see, strange analogies, not only between the facts of different sciences of the same order, or between physical and metaphysical facts, but between physical hypotheses and suggestions glimmering out of the metaphysical dreams into which I was in the habit of falling. I was at the same time much given to a premature indulgence of the impulse to turn hypothesis into theory. Of my mental peculiarities there is no occasion to say more.

The house as well as the family was of some antiquity, but no description of it is necessary to the understanding of my narrative. It contained a fine library, whose growth began before the invention of printing, and had continued to my own time, greatly influenced, of course, by changes of taste and pursuit. Nothing surely can more impress upon a man the transitory nature of possession than his succeeding to an ancient property! Like a moving panorama mine has passed from before many eyes, and is now slowly flitting from before my own.

The library, although duly considered in many alterations of the house and additions to it, had nevertheless, like an encroaching state, absorbed one room after another until it occupied the greater part of the ground floor. Its chief room was large, and the walls of it were covered with books almost to the ceiling; the rooms into which it overflowed were of various sizes and shapes, and communicated in modes as various—by doors, by open arches, by short passages, by steps up and steps down.

In the great room I mainly spent my time, reading books of science, old as well as new; for the history of the human mind in relation to supposed knowledge was what most of all interested me. Ptolemy, Dante, the two Bacons, and Boyle were even more to me than Darwin or Maxwell, as so much nearer the vanished van breaking into the dark of ignorance.

In the evening of a gloomy day of August I was sitting in my usual place, my back to one of the windows, reading. It had rained the greater part of the morning and afternoon, but just as the sun was setting, the clouds parted in front of him, and he shone into the room. I rose and looked out of the window. In the centre of the great lawn the feathering top of the fountain column was filled with his red glory. I turned to resume my seat, when my eye was caught by the same glory on the one picture in the room—a portrait, in a sort of niche or little shrine sunk for it in the expanse of book-filled shelves. I knew it as the likeness of one of my ancestors, but had never even wondered why it hung there alone, and not in the gallery, or one of the great rooms, among the other family portraits. The direct sunlight brought out the painting wonderfully; for the first time I seemed to see it, and for the first time it seemed to respond to my look. With my eyes full of the light reflected from it, something, I cannot tell what, made me turn and cast a glance to the farther end of the room, when I saw, or seemed to see, a tall figure reaching up a hand to a book-shelf. The next instant, my vision apparently rectified by the comparative dusk, I saw no one, and concluded that my optic nerves had been momentarily affected from within.

I resumed my reading, and would doubtless have forgotten the vague, evanescent impression, had it not been that, having occasion a moment after to consult a certain volume, I found but a gap in the row where it ought to have stood, and the same instant remembered that just there I had seen, or fancied I saw, the old man in search of a book. I looked all about the spot but in vain. The next morning, however, there it was, just where I had thought to find it! I knew of no one in the house likely to be interested in such a book.

Three days after, another and yet odder thing took place.

In one of the walls was the low, narrow door of a closet, containing some of the oldest and rarest of the books. It was a very thick door, with a projecting frame, and it had been the fancy of some ancestor to cross it with shallow shelves, filled with book-backs only. The harmless trick may be excused by the fact that the titles on the sham backs were either humorously original, or those of books lost beyond hope of recovery. I had a great liking for the masked door.

To complete the illusion of it, some inventive workman apparently had shoved in, on the top of one of the rows, a part of a volume thin enough to lie between it and the bottom of the next shelf: he had cut away diagonally a considerable portion, and fixed the remnant with one of its open corners projecting beyond the book-backs. The binding of the mutilated volume was limp vellum, and one could open the corner far enough to see that it was manuscript upon parchment.

Happening, as I sat reading, to raise my eyes from the page, my glance fell upon this door, and at once I saw that the book described, if book it may be called, was gone. Angrier than any worth I knew in it justified, I rang the bell, and the butler appeared. When I asked him if he knew what had befallen it, he turned pale, and assured me he did not. I could less easily doubt his word than my own eyes, for he had been all his life in the family, and a more faithful servant never lived. He left on me the impression, nevertheless, that he could have said something more.

In the afternoon I was again reading in the library, and coming to a point which demanded reflection, I lowered the book and let my eyes go wandering. The same moment I saw the back of a slender old man, in a long, dark coat, shiny as from much wear, in the act of disappearing through the masked door into the closet beyond. I darted across the room, found the door shut, pulled it open, looked into the closet, which had no other issue, and, seeing nobody, concluded, not without uneasiness, that I had had a recurrence of my former illusion, and sat down again to my reading.

Naturally, however, I could not help feeling a little nervous, and presently glancing up to assure myself that I was indeed alone, started again to my feet, and ran to the masked door—for there was the mutilated volume in its place! I laid hold of it and pulled: it was firmly fixed as usual!

I was now utterly bewildered. I rang the bell; the butler came; I told him all I had seen, and he told me all he knew.

He had hoped, he said, that the old gentleman was going to be forgotten; it was well no one but myself had seen him. He had heard a good deal about him when first he served in the house, but by degrees he had ceased to be mentioned, and he had been very careful not to allude to him.

"The place was haunted by an old gentleman, was it?" I said.

He answered that at one time everybody believed it, but the fact that I had never heard of it seemed to imply that the thing had come to an end and was forgotten.

I questioned him as to what he had seen of the old gentleman.

He had never seen him, he said, although he had been in the house from the day my father was eight years old. My grandfather would never hear a word on the matter, declaring that whoever alluded to it should be dismissed without a moment's warning: it was nothing but a pretext of the maids, he said, for running into the arms of the men! but old Sir Ralph believed in nothing he could not see or lay hold of. Not one of the maids ever said she had seen the apparition, but a footman had left the place because of it.

An ancient woman in the village had told him a legend concerning a Mr. Raven, long time librarian to "that Sir Upward whose portrait hangs there among the books." Sir Upward was a great reader, she said—not of such books only as were wholesome for men to read, but of strange, forbidden, and evil books; and in so doing, Mr. Raven, who was probably the devil himself, encouraged him. Suddenly they both disappeared, and Sir Upward was never after seen or heard of, but Mr. Raven continued to show himself at uncertain intervals in the library. There were some who believed he was not dead; but both he and the old woman held it easier to believe that a dead man might revisit the world he had left, than that one who went on living for hundreds of years should be a man at all.

He had never heard that Mr. Raven meddled with anything in the house, but he might perhaps consider himself privileged in regard to the books. How the old woman had learned so much about him he could not tell; but the description she gave of him corresponded exactly with the figure I had just seen.

"I hope it was but a friendly call on the part of the old gentleman!" he concluded, with a troubled smile.

I told him I had no objection to any number of visits from Mr. Raven, but it would be well he should keep to his resolution of saying nothing about him to the servants. Then I asked him if he had ever seen the mutilated volume out of its place; he answered that he never had, and had always thought it a fixture. With that he went to it, and gave it a pull: it seemed immovable.

CHAPTER II. THE MIRROR

Nothing more happened for some days. I think it was about a week after, when what I have now to tell took place.

I had often thought of the manuscript fragment, and repeatedly tried to discover some way of releasing it, but in vain: I could not find out what held it fast.

But I had for some time intended a thorough overhauling of the books in the closet, its atmosphere causing me uneasiness as to their condition. One day the intention suddenly became a resolve, and I was in the act of rising from my chair to make a beginning, when I saw the old librarian moving from the door of the closet toward the farther end of the room. I ought rather to say only that I caught sight of something shadowy from which I received the impression of a slight, stooping man, in a shabby dress-coat reaching almost to his heels, the tails of which, disparting a little as he walked, revealed thin legs in black stockings, and large feet in wide, slipper-like shoes.

At once I followed him: I might be following a shadow, but I never doubted I was following something. He went out of the library into the hall, and across to the foot of the great staircase, then up the stairs to the first floor, where lay the chief rooms. Past these rooms, I following close, he continued his way, through a wide corridor, to the foot of a narrower stair leading to the second floor. Up that he went also, and when I reached the top, strange as it may seem, I found myself in a region almost unknown to me. I never had brother or sister to incite to such romps as make children familiar with nook and cranny; I was a mere child when my guardian took me away; and I had never seen the house again until, about a month before, I returned to take possession.

Through passage after passage we came to a door at the bottom of a winding wooden stair, which we ascended. Every step creaked under my foot, but I heard no sound from that of my guide. Somewhere in the middle of the stair I lost sight of him, and from the top of it the shadowy shape was nowhere visible. I could not even imagine I saw him. The place was full of shadows, but he was not one of them.

I was in the main garret, with huge beams and rafters over my head, great spaces around me, a door here and there in sight, and long vistas whose gloom was thinned by a few lurking cobwebbed windows and small dusky skylights. I gazed with a strange mingling of awe and pleasure: the wide expanse of garret was my own, and unexplored!

In the middle of it stood an unpainted inclosure of rough planks, the door of which was ajar. Thinking Mr. Raven might be there, I pushed the door, and entered.

The small chamber was full of light, but such as dwells in places deserted: it had a dull, disconsolate look, as if it found itself of no use, and regretted having come. A few rather dim sunrays, marking their track through the cloud of motes that had just been stirred up, fell upon a tall mirror with a dusty face, old-fashioned and rather narrow—in appearance an ordinary glass. It had an ebony frame, on the top of which stood a black eagle, with outstretched wings, in his beak a golden chain, from whose end hung a black ball.

I had been looking at rather than into the mirror, when suddenly I became aware that it reflected neither the chamber nor my own person. I have an impression of having seen the wall melt away, but what followed is enough to account for any uncertainty:—could I have mistaken for a mirror the glass that protected a wonderful picture?

I saw before me a wild country, broken and heathy. Desolate hills of no great height, but somehow of strange appearance, occupied the middle distance; along the horizon stretched the tops of a far-off mountain range; nearest me lay a tract of moorland, flat and melancholy.

Being short-sighted, I stepped closer to examine the texture of a stone in the immediate foreground, and in the act espied, hopping toward me with solemnity, a large and ancient raven, whose purply black was here and there softened with gray. He seemed looking for worms as he came. Nowise astonished at the appearance of a live creature in a picture, I took another step forward to see him better, stumbled over something—doubtless the frame of the mirror—and stood nose to beak with the bird: I was in the open air, on a houseless heath!

CHAPTER III. THE RAVEN

I turned and looked behind me: all was vague and uncertain, as when one cannot distinguish between fog and field, between cloud and mountain-side. One fact only was plain—that I saw nothing I knew. Imagining myself involved in a visual illusion, and that touch would correct sight, I stretched my arms and felt about me, walking in this direction and that, if haply, where I could see nothing, I might yet come in contact with something; but my search was vain. Instinctively then, as to the only living thing near me, I turned to the raven, which stood a little way off, regarding me with an expression at once respectful and quizzical. Then the absurdity of seeking counsel from such a one struck me, and I turned again, overwhelmed with bewilderment, not unmingled with fear. Had I wandered into a region where both the material and psychical relations of our world had ceased to hold? Might a man at any moment step beyond the realm of order, and become the sport of the lawless? Yet I saw the raven, felt the ground under my feet, and heard a sound as of wind in the lowly plants around me!

"How DID I get here?" I said—apparently aloud, for the question was immediately answered.

"You came through the door," replied an odd, rather harsh voice.

I looked behind, then all about me, but saw no human shape. The terror that madness might be at hand laid hold upon me: must I henceforth place no confidence either in my senses or my consciousness? The same instant I knew it was the raven that had spoken, for he stood looking up at me with an air of waiting. The sun was not shining, yet the bird seemed to cast a shadow, and the shadow seemed part of himself.

I beg my reader to aid me in the endeavour to make myself intelligible—if here understanding be indeed possible between us. I was in a world, or call it a state of things, an economy of conditions, an idea of existence, so little correspondent with the ways and modes of this world—which we are apt to think the only world, that the best choice I can make of word or phrase is but an adumbration of what I would convey. I begin indeed to fear that I have undertaken an impossibility, undertaken to tell what I cannot tell because no speech at my command will fit the forms in my mind. Already I have set down statements I would gladly change did I know how to substitute a truer utterance; but as often as I try to fit the reality with nearer words, I find myself in danger of losing the things themselves, and feel like one in process of awaking from a dream, with the thing that seemed familiar gradually yet swiftly changing through a succession of forms until its very nature is no longer recognisable.

I bethought me that a bird capable of addressing a man must have the right of a man to a civil answer; perhaps, as a bird, even a greater claim.

A tendency to croak caused a certain roughness in his speech, but his voice was not disagreeable, and what he said, although conveying little enlightenment, did not sound rude.

"I did not come through any door," I rejoined.

"I saw you come through it!—saw you with my own ancient eyes!" asserted the raven, positively but not disrespectfully.

"I never saw any door!" I persisted.

"Of course not!" he returned; "all the doors you had yet seen—and you haven't seen many—were doors in; here you came upon a door out! The strange thing to you," he went on thoughtfully, "will be, that the more doors you go out of, the farther you get in!"

"Oblige me by telling me where I am."

"That is impossible. You know nothing about whereness. The only way to come to know where you are is to begin to make yourself at home."

"How am I to begin that where everything is so strange?"

"By doing something."

"What?"

"Anything; and the sooner you begin the better! for until you are at home, you will find it as difficult to get out as it is to get in."

"I have, unfortunately, found it too easy to get in; once out I shall not try again!"

"You have stumbled in, and may, possibly, stumble out again. Whether you have got in UNFORTUNATELY remains to be seen."

"Do you never go out, sir?"

"When I please I do, but not often, or for long. Your world is such a half-baked sort of place, it is at once so childish and so self-satisfied—in fact, it is not sufficiently developed for an old raven—at your service!"

"Am I wrong, then, in presuming that a man is superior to a bird?"

"That is as it may be. We do not waste our intellects in generalising, but take man or bird as we find him.—I think it is now my turn to ask you a question!"

"You have the best of rights," I replied, "in the fact that you CAN do so!"

"Well answered!" he rejoined. "Tell me, then, who you are—if you happen to know."

"How should I help knowing? I am myself, and must know!"

"If you know you are yourself, you know that you are not somebody else; but do you know that you are yourself? Are you sure you are not your own father?—or, excuse me, your own fool?—Who are you, pray?"

I became at once aware that I could give him no notion of who I was. Indeed,

who was I? It would be no answer to say I was who! Then I understood that I did
not know myself, did not know what I was, had no grounds on which to determine
that I was one and not another. As for the name I went by in my own world, I had
forgotten it, and did not care to recall it, for it meant nothing, and what it might be
was plainly of no consequence here. I had indeed almost forgotten that there it was
a custom for everybody to have a name! So I held my peace, and it was my
wisdom; for what should I say to a creature such as this raven, who saw through
accident into entity?

"Look at me," he said, "and tell me who I am."

As he spoke, he turned his back, and instantly I knew him. He was no longer a
raven, but a man above the middle height with a stoop, very thin, and wearing a
long black tail-coat. Again he turned, and I saw him a raven.

"I have seen you before, sir," I said, feeling foolish rather than surprised.

"How can you say so from seeing me behind?" he rejoined. "Did you ever see
yourself behind? You have never seen yourself at all!—Tell me now, then, who
I am."

"I humbly beg your pardon," I answered: "I believe you were once the librarian
of our house, but more WHO I do not know."

"Why do you beg my pardon?"

"Because I took you for a raven," I said—seeing him before me as plainly a
raven as bird or man could look.

"You did me no wrong," he returned. "Calling me a raven, or thinking me one,
you allowed me existence, which is the sum of what one can demand of his fellow-
beings. Therefore, in return, I will give you a lesson:—No one can say he is himself,
until first he knows that he IS, and then what HIMSELF is. In fact, nobody is
himself, and himself is nobody. There is more in it than you can see now, but not
more than you need to see. You have, I fear, got into this region too soon, but none
the less you must get to be at home in it; for home, as you may or may not know, is
the only place where you can go out and in. There are places you can go into, and
places you can go out of; but the one place, if you do but find it, where you may go
out and in both, is home."

He turned to walk away, and again I saw the librarian. He did not appear to
have changed, only to have taken up his shadow. I know this seems nonsense, but I
cannot help it.

I gazed after him until I saw him no more; but whether distance hid him, or he
disappeared among the heather, I cannot tell.

Could it be that I was dead, I thought, and did not know it? Was I in what we
used to call the world beyond the grave? and must I wander about seeking my
place in it? How was I to find myself at home? The raven said I must do something:
what could I do here?—And would that make me somebody? for now, alas, I was
nobody!

I took the way Mr. Raven had gone, and went slowly after him. Presently I saw
a wood of tall slender pine-trees, and turned toward it. The odour of it met me on
my way, and I made haste to bury myself in it.

Plunged at length in its twilight glooms, I spied before me something with a
shine, standing between two of the stems. It had no colour, but was like the translucent trembling of the hot air that rises, in a radiant summer noon, from the sun-
baked ground, vibrant like the smitten chords of a musical instrument. What it was

grew no plainer as I went nearer, and when I came close up, I ceased to see it, only the form and colour of the trees beyond seemed strangely uncertain. I would have passed between the stems, but received a slight shock, stumbled, and fell. When I rose, I saw before me the wooden wall of the garret chamber. I turned, and there was the mirror, on whose top the black eagle seemed but that moment to have perched.

Terror seized me, and I fled. Outside the chamber the wide garret spaces had an UNCANNY look. They seemed to have long been waiting for something; it had come, and they were waiting again! A shudder went through me on the winding stair: the house had grown strange to me! something was about to leap upon me from behind! I darted down the spiral, struck against the wall and fell, rose and ran. On the next floor I lost my way, and had gone through several passages a second time ere I found the head of the stair. At the top of the great stair I had come to myself a little, and in a few moments I sat recovering my breath in the library.

Nothing should ever again make me go up that last terrible stair! The garret at the top of it pervaded the whole house! It sat upon it, threatening to crush me out of it! The brooding brain of the building, it was full of mysterious dwellers, one or other of whom might any moment appear in the library where I sat! I was nowhere safe! I would let, I would sell the dreadful place, in which an aërial portal stood ever open to creatures whose life was other than human! I would purchase a crag in Switzerland, and thereon build a wooden nest of one story with never a garret above it, guarded by some grand old peak that would send down nothing worse than a few tons of whelming rock!

I knew all the time that my thinking was foolish, and was even aware of a certain undertone of contemptuous humour in it; but suddenly it was checked, and I seemed again to hear the croak of the raven.

"If I know nothing of my own garret," I thought, "what is there to secure me against my own brain? Can I tell what it is even now generating?—what thought it may present me the next moment, the next month, or a year away? What is at the heart of my brain? What is behind my THINK? Am I there at all?—Who, what am I?"

I could no more answer the question now than when the raven put it to me in— at—"Where in?—where at?" I said, and gave myself up as knowing anything of myself or the universe.

I started to my feet, hurried across the room to the masked door, where the mutilated volume, sticking out from the flat of soulless, bodiless, non-existent books, appeared to beckon me, went down on my knees, and opened it as far as its position would permit, but could see nothing. I got up again, lighted a taper, and peeping as into a pair of reluctant jaws, perceived that the manuscript was verse. Further I could not carry discovery. Beginnings of lines were visible on the left-hand page, and ends of lines on the other; but I could not, of course, get at the beginning and end of a single line, and was unable, in what I could read, to make any guess at the sense. The mere words, however, woke in me feelings which to describe was, from their strangeness, impossible. Some dreams, some poems, some musical phrases, some pictures, wake feelings such as one never had before, new in colour and form—spiritual sensations, as it were, hitherto unproved: here, some of the phrases, some of the senseless half-lines, some even of the individual words affected me in similar fashion—as with the aroma of an idea, rousing in me a great longing to know what the poem or poems might, even yet in their mutilation, hold or suggest.

I copied out a few of the larger shreds attainable, and tried hard to complete some of the lines, but without the least success. The only thing I gained in the effort was so much weariness that, when I went to bed, I fell asleep at once and slept soundly.

In the morning all that horror of the empty garret spaces had left me.

CHAPTER IV. SOMEWHERE OR NOWHERE?

The sun was very bright, but I doubted if the day would long be fine, and looked into the milky sapphire I wore, to see whether the star in it was clear. It was even less defined than I had expected. I rose from the breakfast-table, and went to the window to glance at the stone again. There had been heavy rain in the night, and on the lawn was a thrush breaking his way into the shell of a snail.

As I was turning my ring about to catch the response of the star to the sun, I spied a keen black eye gazing at me out of the milky misty blue. The sight startled me so that I dropped the ring, and when I picked it up the eye was gone from it. The same moment the sun was obscured; a dark vapour covered him, and in a minute or two the whole sky was clouded. The air had grown sultry, and a gust of wind came suddenly. A moment more and there was a flash of lightning, with a single sharp thunder-clap. Then the rain fell in torrents.

I had opened the window, and stood there looking out at the precipitous rain, when I descried a raven walking toward me over the grass, with solemn gait, and utter disregard of the falling deluge. Suspecting who he was, I congratulated myself that I was safe on the ground-floor. At the same time I had a conviction that, if I were not careful, something would happen.

He came nearer and nearer, made a profound bow, and with a sudden winged leap stood on the window-sill. Then he stepped over the ledge, jumped down into the room, and walked to the door. I thought he was on his way to the library, and followed him, determined, if he went up the stair, not to take one step after him. He turned, however, neither toward the library nor the stair, but to a little door that gave upon a grass-patch in a nook between two portions of the rambling old house. I made haste to open it for him. He stepped out into its creeper-covered porch, and stood looking at the rain, which fell like a huge thin cataract; I stood in the door behind him. The second flash came, and was followed by a lengthened roll of more distant thunder. He turned his head over his shoulder and looked at me, as much

584

as to say, "You hear that?" then swivelled it round again, and anew contemplated the weather, apparently with approbation. So human were his pose and carriage and the way he kept turning his head, that I remarked almost involuntarily,

"Fine weather for the worms, Mr. Raven!"

"Yes," he answered, in the rather croaky voice I had learned to know, "the ground will be nice for them to get out and in!—It must be a grand time on the steppes of Uranus!" he added, with a glance upward; "I believe it is raining there too; it was, all the last week!"

"Why should that make it a grand time?" I asked.

"Because the animals there are all burrowers," he answered, "—like the field-mice and the moles here.—They will be, for ages to come."

"How do you know that, if I may be so bold?" I rejoined.

"As any one would who had been there to see," he replied. "It is a great sight, until you get used to it, when the earth gives a heave, and out comes a beast. You might think it a hairy elephant or a deinotherium—but none of the animals are the same as we have ever had here. I was almost frightened myself the first time I saw the dry-bog-serpent come wallowing out—such a head and mane! and SUCH eyes! —but the shower is nearly over. It will stop directly after the next thunder-clap. There it is!"

A flash came with the words, and in about half a minute the thunder. Then the rain ceased.

"Now we should be going!" said the raven, and stepped to the front of the porch.

"Going where?" I asked.

"Going where we have to go," he answered. "You did not surely think you had got home? I told you there was no going out and in at pleasure until you were at home!"

"I do not want to go," I said.

"That does not make any difference—at least not much," he answered. "This is the way!"

"I am quite content where I am."

"You think so, but you are not. Come along."

He hopped from the porch onto the grass, and turned, waiting.

"I will not leave the house to-day," I said with obstinacy.

"You will come into the garden!" rejoined the raven.

"I give in so far," I replied, and stepped from the porch.

The sun broke through the clouds, and the raindrops flashed and sparkled on the grass. The raven was walking over it.

"You will wet your feet!" I cried.

"And mire my beak," he answered, immediately plunging it deep in the sod, and drawing out a great wriggling red worm. He threw back his head, and tossed it in the air. It spread great wings, gorgeous in red and black, and soared aloft.

"Tut! tut!" I exclaimed; "you mistake, Mr. Raven: worms are not the larvæ of butterflies!"

"Never mind," he croaked; "it will do for once! I'm not a reading man at present, but sexton at the—at a certain graveyard—cemetery, more properly—in— at—no matter where!"

"I see! you can't keep your spade still: and when you have nothing to bury, you must dig something up! Only you should mind what it is before you make it fly! No creature should be allowed to forget what and where it came from!"

"Why?" said the raven.

"Because it will grow proud, and cease to recognise its superiors."

No man knows it when he is making an idiot of himself.

"Where DO the worms come from?" said the raven, as if suddenly grown curious to know.

"Why, from the earth, as you have just seen!" I answered.

"Yes, last!" he replied. "But they can't have come from it first—for that will never go back to it!" he added, looking up.

I looked up also, but could see nothing save a little dark cloud, the edges of which were red, as if with the light of the sunset.

"Surely the sun is not going down!" I exclaimed, struck with amazement.

"Oh, no!" returned the raven. "That red belongs to the worm."

"You see what comes of making creatures forget their origin!" I cried with some warmth.

"It is well, surely, if it be to rise higher and grow larger!" he returned. "But indeed I only teach them to find it!"

"Would you have the air full of worms?"

"That is the business of a sexton. If only the rest of the clergy understood it as well!"

In went his beak again through the soft turf, and out came the wriggling worm. He tossed it in the air, and away it flew.

I looked behind me, and gave a cry of dismay: I had but that moment declared I would not leave the house, and already I was a stranger in the strange land!

"What right have you to treat me so, Mr. Raven?" I said with deep offence. "Am I, or am I not, a free agent?"

"A man is as free as he chooses to make himself, never an atom freer," answered the raven.

"You have no right to make me do things against my will!"

"When you have a will, you will find that no one can."

"You wrong me in the very essence of my individuality!" I persisted.

"If you were an individual I could not, therefore now I do not. You are but beginning to become an individual."

All about me was a pine-forest, in which my eyes were already searching deep, in the hope of discovering an unaccountable glimmer, and so finding my way home. But, alas! how could I any longer call that house HOME, where every door, every window opened into OUT, and even the garden I could not keep inside!

I suppose I looked discomfited.

"Perhaps it may comfort you," said the raven, "to be told that you have not yet left your house, neither has your house left you. At the same time it cannot contain you, or you inhabit it!"

"I do not understand you," I replied. "Where am I?"

"In the region of the seven dimensions," he answered, with a curious noise in his throat, and a flutter of his tail. "You had better follow me carefully now for a moment, lest you should hurt some one!"

"There is nobody to hurt but yourself, Mr. Raven! I confess I should rather like to hurt you!"

"That you see nobody is where the danger lies. But you see that large tree to your left, about thirty yards away?"

"Of course I do: why should I not?" I answered testily.

"Ten minutes ago you did not see it, and now you do not know where it stands!"

"I do."

"Where do you think it stands?"

"Why THERE, where you know it is!"

"Where is THERE?"

"You bother me with your silly questions!" I cried. "I am growing tired of you!"

"That tree stands on the hearth of your kitchen, and grows nearly straight up its chimney," he said.

"Now I KNOW you are making game of me!" I answered, with a laugh of scorn.

"Was I making game of you when you discovered me looking out of your star-sapphire yesterday?"

"That was this morning—not an hour ago!"

"I have been widening your horizon longer than that, Mr. Vane; but never mind!"

"You mean you have been making a fool of me!" I said, turning from him.

"Excuse me: no one can do that but yourself!"

"And I decline to do it."

"You mistake."

"How?"

"In declining to acknowledge yourself one already. You make yourself such by refusing what is true, and for that you will sorely punish yourself."

"How, again?"

"By believing what is not true."

"Then, if I walk to the other side of that tree, I shall walk through the kitchen fire?"

"Certainly. You would first, however, walk through the lady at the piano in the breakfast-room. That rosebush is close by her. You would give her a terrible start!"

"There is no lady in the house!"

"Indeed! Is not your housekeeper a lady? She is counted such in a certain country where all are servants, and the liveries one and multitudinous!"

"She cannot use the piano, anyhow!"

"Her niece can: she is there—a well-educated girl and a capital musician."

"Excuse me; I cannot help it: you seem to me to be talking sheer nonsense!"

"If you could but hear the music! Those great long heads of wild hyacinth are inside the piano, among the strings of it, and give that peculiar sweetness to her playing!—Pardon me: I forgot your deafness!"

"Two objects," I said, "cannot exist in the same place at the same time!"

"Can they not? I did not know!—I remember now they do teach that with you. It is a great mistake—one of the greatest ever wiseacre made! No man of the universe, only a man of the world could have said so!"

"You a librarian, and talk such rubbish!" I cried. "Plainly, you did not read many of the books in your charge!"

"Oh, yes! I went through all in your library—at the time, and came out at the other side not much the wiser. I was a bookworm then, but when I came to know it,

I woke among the butterflies. To be sure I have given up reading for a good many years—ever since I was made sexton.—There! I smell Grieg's Wedding March in the quiver of those rose-petals!"

I went to the rose-bush and listened hard, but could not hear the thinnest ghost of a sound; I only smelt something I had never before smelt in any rose. It was still rose-odour, but with a difference, caused, I suppose, by the Wedding March.

When I looked up, there was the bird by my side.

"Mr. Raven," I said, "forgive me for being so rude: I was irritated. Will you kindly show me my way home? I must go, for I have an appointment with my bailiff. One must not break faith with his servants!"

"You cannot break what was broken days ago!" he answered.

"Do show me the way," I pleaded.

"I cannot," he returned. "To go back, you must go through yourself, and that way no man can show another."

Entreaty was vain. I must accept my fate! But how was life to be lived in a world of which I had all the laws to learn? There would, however, be adventure! that held consolation; and whether I found my way home or not, I should at least have the rare advantage of knowing two worlds!

I had never yet done anything to justify my existence; my former world was nothing the better for my sojourn in it: here, however, I must earn, or in some way find, my bread! But I reasoned that, as I was not to blame in being here, I might expect to be taken care of here as well as there! I had had nothing to do with getting into the world I had just left, and in it I had found myself heir to a large property! If that world, as I now saw, had a claim upon me because I had eaten, and could eat again, upon this world I had a claim because I must eat—when it would in return have a claim on me!

"There is no hurry," said the raven, who stood regarding me; "we do not go much by the clock here. Still, the sooner one begins to do what has to be done, the better! I will take you to my wife."

"Thank you. Let us go!" I answered, and immediately he led the way.

CHAPTER V. THE OLD CHURCH

I followed him deep into the pine-forest. Neither of us said much while yet the sacred gloom of it closed us round. We came to larger and yet larger trees—older, and more individual, some of them grotesque with age. Then the forest grew thinner.

"You see that hawthorn?" said my guide at length, pointing with his beak.

I looked where the wood melted away on the edge of an open heath.

"I see a gnarled old man, with a great white head," I answered.

"Look again," he rejoined: "it is a hawthorn."

"It seems indeed an ancient hawthorn; but this is not the season for the hawthorn to blossom!" I objected.

"The season for the hawthorn to blossom," he replied, "is when the hawthorn blossoms. That tree is in the ruins of the church on your home-farm. You were going to give some directions to the bailiff about its churchyard, were you not, the morning of the thunder?"

"I was going to tell him I wanted it turned into a wilderness of rose-trees, and that the plough must never come within three yards of it."

"Listen!" said the raven, seeming to hold his breath.

I listened, and heard—was it the sighing of a far-off musical wind—or the ghost of a music that had once been glad? Or did I indeed hear anything?

"They go there still," said the raven.

"Who goes there? and where do they go?" I asked.

"Some of the people who used to pray there, go to the ruins still," he replied. "But they will not go much longer, I think."

"What makes them go now?"

"They need help from each other to get their thinking done, and their feelings hatched, so they talk and sing together; and then, they say, the big thought floats out of their hearts like a great ship out of the river at high water."

"Do they pray as well as sing?"

"No; they have found that each can best pray in his own silent heart.—Some people are always at their prayers.—Look! look! There goes one!"

He pointed right up into the air. A snow-white pigeon was mounting, with quick and yet quicker wing-flap, the unseen spiral of an ethereal stair. The sunshine flashed quivering from its wings.

"I see a pigeon!" I said.

"Of course you see a pigeon," rejoined the raven, "for there is the pigeon! I see a prayer on its way.—I wonder now what heart is that dove's mother! Some one may have come awake in my cemetery!"

"How can a pigeon be a prayer?" I said. "I understand, of course, how it should be a fit symbol or likeness for one; but a live pigeon to come out of a heart!"

"It MUST puzzle you! It cannot fail to do so!"

"A prayer is a thought, a thing spiritual!" I pursued.

"Very true! But if you understood any world besides your own, you would understand your own much better.—When a heart is really alive, then it is able to think live things. There is one heart all whose thoughts are strong, happy creatures, and whose very dreams are lives. When some pray, they lift heavy thoughts from the ground, only to drop them on it again; others send up their prayers in living shapes, this or that, the nearest likeness to each. All live things were thoughts to begin with, and are fit therefore to be used by those that think. When one says to the great Thinker:—'Here is one of thy thoughts: I am thinking it now!' that is a prayer—a word to the big heart from one of its own little hearts.—Look, there is another!"

This time the raven pointed his beak downward—to something at the foot of a block of granite. I looked, and saw a little flower. I had never seen one like it before, and cannot utter the feeling it woke in me by its gracious, trusting form, its colour, and its odour as of a new world that was yet the old. I can only say that it suggested an anemone, was of a pale rose-hue, and had a golden heart.

"That is a prayer-flower," said the raven.

"I never saw such a flower before!" I rejoined.

"There is no other such. Not one prayer-flower is ever quite like another," he returned.

"How do you know it a prayer-flower?" I asked.

"By the expression of it," he answered. "More than that I cannot tell you. If you know it, you know it; if you do not, you do not."

"Could you not teach me to know a prayer-flower when I see it?" I said.

"I could not. But if I could, what better would you be? you would not know it of YOURSELF and ITself! Why know the name of a thing when the thing itself you do not know? Whose work is it but your own to open your eyes? But indeed the business of the universe is to make such a fool of you that you will know yourself for one, and so begin to be wise!"

But I did see that the flower was different from any flower I had ever seen before; therefore I knew that I must be seeing a shadow of the prayer in it; and a great awe came over me to think of the heart listening to the flower.

CHAPTER VI. THE SEXTON'S COTTAGE

We had been for some time walking over a rocky moorland covered with dry plants and mosses, when I descried a little cottage in the farthest distance. The sun was not yet down, but he was wrapt in a gray cloud. The heath looked as if it had never been warm, and the wind blew strangely cold, as if from some region where it was always night.

"Here we are at last!" said the raven. "What a long way it is! In half the time I could have gone to Paradise and seen my cousin—him, you remember, who never came back to Noah! Dear! dear! it is almost winter!"

"Winter!" I cried; "it seems but half a day since we left home!"

"That is because we have travelled so fast," answered the raven. "In your world you cannot pull up the plumb-line you call gravitation, and let the world spin round under your feet! But here is my wife's house! She is very good to let me live with her, and call it the sexton's cottage!"

"But where is your churchyard—your cemetery—where you make your graves, I mean?" said I, seeing nothing but the flat heath.

The raven stretched his neck, held out his beak horizontally, turned it slowly round to all the points of the compass, and said nothing.

I followed the beak with my eyes, and lo, without church or graves, all was a churchyard! Wherever the dreary wind swept, there was the raven's cemetery! He was sexton of all he surveyed! lord of all that was laid aside! I stood in the burial-ground of the universe; its compass the unenclosed heath, its wall the gray horizon, low and starless! I had left spring and summer, autumn and sunshine behind me, and come to the winter that waited for me! I had set out in the prime of my youth, and here I was already!—But I mistook. The day might well be long in that region, for it contained the seasons. Winter slept there, the night through, in his winding-sheet of ice; with childlike smile, Spring came awake in the dawn; at noon, Summer

591

blazed abroad in her gorgeous beauty; with the slow-changing afternoon, old Autumn crept in, and died at the first breath of the vaporous, ghosty night.

As we drew near the cottage, the clouded sun was rushing down the steepest slope of the west, and he sank while we were yet a few yards from the door. The same instant I was assailed by a cold that seemed almost a material presence, and I struggled across the threshold as if from the clutches of an icy death. A wind swelled up on the moor, and rushed at the door as with difficulty I closed it behind me. Then all was still, and I looked about me.

A candle burned on a deal table in the middle of the room, and the first thing I saw was the lid of a coffin, as I thought, set up against the wall; but it opened, for it was a door, and a woman entered. She was all in white—as white as new-fallen snow; and her face was as white as her dress, but not like snow, for at once it suggested warmth. I thought her features were perfect, but her eyes made me forget them. The life of her face and her whole person was gathered and concentrated in her eyes, where it became light. It might have been coming death that made her face luminous, but the eyes had life in them for a nation—large, and dark with a darkness ever deepening as I gazed. A whole night-heaven lay condensed in each pupil; all the stars were in its blackness, and flashed; while round it for a horizon lay coiled an iris of the eternal twilight. What any eye IS, God only knows: her eyes must have been coming direct out of his own! the still face might be a primeval perfection; the live eyes were a continuous creation.

"Here is Mr. Vane, wife!" said the raven.

"He is welcome," she answered, in a low, rich, gentle voice. Treasures of immortal sound seemed to be buried in it.

I gazed, and could not speak.

"I knew you would be glad to see him!" added the raven.

She stood in front of the door by which she had entered, and did not come nearer.

"Will he sleep?" she asked.

"I fear not," he replied; "he is neither weary nor heavy laden."

"Why then have you brought him?"

"I have my fears it may prove precipitate."

"I do not quite understand you," I said, with an uneasy foreboding as to what she meant, but a vague hope of some escape. "Surely a man must do a day's work first!"

I gazed into the white face of the woman, and my heart fluttered. She returned my gaze in silence.

"Let me first go home," I resumed, "and come again after I have found or made, invented, or at least discovered something!"

"He has not yet learned that the day begins with sleep!" said the woman, turning to her husband. "Tell him he must rest before he can do anything!"

"Men," he answered, "think so much of having done, that they fall asleep upon it. They cannot empty an egg but they turn into the shell, and lie down!"

The words drew my eyes from the woman to the raven.

I saw no raven, but the librarian—the same slender elderly man, in a rusty black coat, large in the body and long in the tails. I had seen only his back before; now for the first time I saw his face. It was so thin that it showed the shape of the bones under it, suggesting the skulls his last-claimed profession must have made him familiar with. But in truth I had never before seen a face so alive, or a look so keen or so friendly as that in his pale blue eyes, which yet had a haze about them as if they had done much weeping.

"You knew I was not a raven!" he said with a smile.

"I knew you were Mr. Raven," I replied; "but somehow I thought you a bird too!"

"What made you think me a bird?"

"You looked a raven, and I saw you dig worms out of the earth with your beak."

"And then?"

"Toss them in the air." "And then?"

"They grew butterflies, and flew away."

"Did you ever see a raven do that? I told you I was a sexton!"

"Does a sexton toss worms in the air, and turn them into butterflies?"

"Yes."

"I never saw one do it!"

"You saw me do it!—But I am still librarian in your house, for I never was dismissed, and never gave up the office. Now I am librarian here as well."

"But you have just told me you were sexton here!"

"So I am. It is much the same profession. Except you are a true sexton, books are but dead bodies to you, and a library nothing but a catacomb!"

"You bewilder me!"

"That's all right!"

A few moments he stood silent. The woman, moveless as a statue, stood silent also by the coffin-door.

"Upon occasion," said the sexton at length, "it is more convenient to put one's bird-self in front. Every one, as you ought to know, has a beast-self—and a bird-self, and a stupid fish-self, ay, and a creeping serpent-self too—which it takes a deal of crushing to kill! In truth he has also a tree-self and a crystal-self, and I don't know how many selves more—all to get into harmony. You can tell what sort a man is by his creature that comes oftenest to the front."

He turned to his wife, and I considered him more closely. He was above the ordinary height, and stood more erect than when last I saw him. His face was, like his wife's, very pale; its nose handsomely encased the beak that had retired within it; its lips were very thin, and even they had no colour, but their curves were beautiful, and about them quivered a shadowy smile that had humour in it as well as love and pity.

"We are in want of something to eat and drink, wife," he said; "we have come a long way!"

"You know, husband," she answered, "we can give only to him that asks."

She turned her unchanging face and radiant eyes upon mine.

"Please give me something to eat, Mrs. Raven," I said, "and something—what you will—to quench my thirst."

"Your thirst must be greater before you can have what will quench it," she replied; "but what I can give you, I will gladly."

She went to a cupboard in the wall, brought from it bread and wine, and set them on the table.

We sat down to the perfect meal; and as I ate, the bread and wine seemed to go deeper than the hunger and thirst. Anxiety and discomfort vanished; expectation took their place.

I grew very sleepy, and now first felt weary.

"I have earned neither food nor sleep, Mrs. Raven," I said, "but you have given me the one freely, and now I hope you will give me the other, for I sorely need it."

"Sleep is too fine a thing ever to be earned," said the sexton; "it must be given and accepted, for it is a necessity. But it would be perilous to use this house as a half-way hostelry—for the repose of a night, that is, merely."

A wild-looking little black cat jumped on his knee as he spoke. He patted it as one pats a child to make it go to sleep: he seemed to me patting down the sod upon a grave—patting it lovingly, with an inward lullaby.

"Here is one of Mara's kittens!" he said to his wife: "will you give it something and put it out? she may want it!"

The woman took it from him gently, gave it a little piece of bread, and went out with it, closing the door behind her.

"How then am I to make use of your hospitality?" I asked.

"By accepting it to the full," he answered.

"I do not understand."

"In this house no one wakes of himself."

"Why?"

"Because no one anywhere ever wakes of himself. You can wake yourself no more than you can make yourself."

"Then perhaps you or Mrs. Raven would kindly call me!" I said, still nowise understanding, but feeling afresh that vague foreboding.

"We cannot."

"How dare I then go to sleep?" I cried.

"If you would have the rest of this house, you must not trouble yourself about waking. You must go to sleep heartily, altogether and outright." My soul sank within me.

The sexton sat looking me in the face. His eyes seemed to say, "Will you not trust me?" I returned his gaze, and answered,

"I will."

"Then come," he said; "I will show you your couch."

As we rose, the woman came in. She took up the candle, turned to the inner door, and led the way. I went close behind her, and the sexton followed.

CHAPTER VII. THE CEMETERY

The air as of an ice-house met me crossing the threshold. The door fell-to behind us. The sexton said something to his wife that made her turn toward us.—What a change had passed upon her! It was as if the splendour of her eyes had grown too much for them to hold, and, sinking into her countenance, made it flash with a loveliness like that of Beatrice in the white rose of the redeemed. Life itself, life eternal, immortal, streamed from it, an unbroken lightning. Even her hands shone with a white radiance, every "pearl-shell helmet" gleaming like a moonstone. Her beauty was overpowering; I was glad when she turned it from me.

But the light of the candle reached such a little way, that at first I could see nothing of the place. Presently, however, it fell on something that glimmered, a little raised from the floor. Was it a bed? Could live thing sleep in such a mortal cold? Then surely it was no wonder it should not wake of itself! Beyond that appeared a fainter shine; and then I thought I descried uncertain gleams on every side.

A few paces brought us to the first; it was a human form under a sheet, straight and still—whether of man or woman I could not tell, for the light seemed to avoid the face as we passed.

I soon perceived that we were walking along an aisle of couches, on almost every one of which, with its head to the passage, lay something asleep or dead, covered with a sheet white as snow. My soul grew silent with dread. Through aisle after aisle we went, among couches innumerable. I could see only a few of them at once, but they were on all sides, vanishing, as it seemed, in the infinite.—Was it here lay my choice of a bed? Must I go to sleep among the unwaking, with no one to rouse me? Was this the sexton's library? were these his books? Truly it was no half-way house, this chamber of the dead!

"One of the cellars I am placed to watch!" remarked Mr. Raven—in a low voice, as if fearing to disturb his silent guests. "Much wine is set here to ripen!—But it is dark for a stranger!" he added.

"The moon is rising; she will soon be here," said his wife, and her clear voice, low and sweet, sounded of ancient sorrow long bidden adieu.

Even as she spoke the moon looked in at an opening in the wall, and a thousand gleams of white responded to her shine. But not yet could I descry beginning or end of the couches. They stretched away and away, as if for all the disparted world to sleep upon. For along the far receding narrow ways, every couch stood by itself, and on each slept a lonely sleeper. I thought at first their sleep was death, but I soon saw it was something deeper still—a something I did not know.

The moon rose higher, and shone through other openings, but I could never see enough of the place at once to know its shape or character; now it would resemble a long cathedral nave, now a huge barn made into a dwelling of tombs. She looked colder than any moon in the frostiest night of the world, and where she shone direct upon them, cast a bluish, icy gleam on the white sheets and the pallid countenances—but it might be the faces that made the moon so cold!

Of such as I could see, all were alike in the brotherhood of death, all unlike in the character and history recorded upon them. Here lay a man who had died—for although this was not death, I have no other name to give it—in the prime of manly strength; his dark beard seemed to flow like a liberated stream from the glacier of his frozen countenance; his forehead was smooth as polished marble; a shadow of pain lingered about his lips, but only a shadow. On the next couch lay the form of a girl, passing lovely to behold. The sadness left on her face by parting was not yet absorbed in perfect peace, but absolute submission possessed the placid features, which bore no sign of wasting disease, of "killing care or grief of heart": if pain had been there, it was long charmed asleep, never again to wake. Many were the beautiful that there lay very still—some of them mere children; but I did not see one infant. The most beautiful of all was a lady whose white hair, and that alone, suggested her old when first she fell asleep. On her stately countenance rested—not submission, but a right noble acquiescence, an assurance, firm as the foundations of the universe, that all was as it should be. On some faces lingered the almost obliterated scars of strife, the marrings of hopeless loss, the fading shadows of sorrows that had seemed inconsolable: the aurora of the great morning had not yet quite melted them away; but those faces were few, and every one that bore such brand of pain seemed to plead, "Pardon me: I died only yesterday!" or, "Pardon me: I died but a century ago!" That some had been dead for ages I knew, not merely by their unutterable repose, but by something for which I have neither word nor symbol.

We came at last to three empty couches, immediately beyond which lay the form of a beautiful woman, a little past the prime of life. One of her arms was outside the sheet, and her hand lay with the palm upward, in its centre a dark spot. Next to her was the stalwart figure of a man of middle age. His arm too was outside the sheet, the strong hand almost closed, as if clenched on the grip of a sword. I thought he must be a king who had died fighting for the truth.

"Will you hold the candle nearer, wife?" whispered the sexton, bending down to examine the woman's hand.

"It heals well," he murmured to himself: "the nail found in her nothing to hurt!"

At last I ventured to speak.

"Are they not dead?" I asked softly.

"I cannot answer you," he replied in a subdued voice. "I almost forget what they mean by DEAD in the old world. If I said a person was dead, my wife would understand one thing, and you would imagine another.—This is but one of my treasure vaults," he went on, "and all my guests are not laid in vaults: out there on the moor they lie thick as the leaves of a forest after the first blast of your winter— thick, let me say rather, as if the great white rose of heaven had shed its petals over it. All night the moon reads their faces, and smiles."

"But why leave them in the corrupting moonlight?" I asked.

"Our moon," he answered, "is not like yours—the old cinder of a burnt-out world; her beams embalm the dead, not corrupt them. You observe that here the sexton lays his dead on the earth; he buries very few under it! In your world he lays huge stones on them, as if to keep them down; I watch for the hour to ring the resurrection-bell, and wake those that are still asleep. Your sexton looks at the clock to know when to ring the dead-alive to church; I hearken for the cock on the spire to crow; 'AWAKE, THOU THAT SLEEPEST, AND ARISE FROM THE DEAD!'"

I began to conclude that the self-styled sexton was in truth an insane parson: the whole thing was too mad! But how was I to get away from it? I was helpless! In this world of the dead, the raven and his wife were the only living I had yet seen: whither should I turn for help? I was lost in a space larger than imagination; for if here two things, or any parts of them, could occupy the same space, why not twenty or ten thousand?—But I dared not think further in that direction.

"You seem in your dead to see differences beyond my perception!" I ventured to remark.

"None of those you see," he answered, "are in truth quite dead yet, and some have but just begun to come alive and die. Others had begun to die, that is to come alive, long before they came to us; and when such are indeed dead, that instant they will wake and leave us. Almost every night some rise and go. But I will not say more, for I find my words only mislead you!—This is the couch that has been waiting for you," he ended, pointing to one of the three.

"Why just this?" I said, beginning to tremble, and anxious by parley to delay.

"For reasons which one day you will be glad to know," he answered.

"Why not know them now?"

"That also you will know when you wake."

"But these are all dead, and I am alive!" I objected, shuddering.

"Not much," rejoined the sexton with a smile, "—not nearly enough! Blessed be the true life that the pauses between its throbs are not death!"

"The place is too cold to let one sleep!" I said.

"Do these find it so?" he returned. "They sleep well—or will soon. Of cold they feel not a breath: it heals their wounds.—Do not be a coward, Mr. Vane. Turn your back on fear, and your face to whatever may come. Give yourself up to the night, and you will rest indeed. Harm will not come to you, but a good you cannot foreknow."

The sexton and I stood by the side of the couch, his wife, with the candle in her hand, at the foot of it. Her eyes were full of light, but her face was again of a still whiteness; it was no longer radiant.

"Would they have me make of a charnel-house my bed-chamber?" I cried aloud. "I will not. I will lie abroad on the heath; it cannot be colder there!"

"I have just told you that the dead are there also,
'Thick as autumnal leaves that strow the brooks
    In Vallombrosa,'"

said the librarian.

"I will NOT," I cried again; and in the compassing dark, the two gleamed out like spectres that waited on the dead; neither answered me; each stood still and sad, and looked at the other.

"Be of good comfort; we watch the flock of the great shepherd," said the sexton to his wife.

Then he turned to me.

"Didst thou not find the air of the place pure and sweet when thou enteredst it?" he asked.

"Yes; but oh, so cold!" I answered.

"Then know," he returned, and his voice was stern, "that thou who callest thyself alive, hast brought into this chamber the odours of death, and its air will not be wholesome for the sleepers until thou art gone from it!"

They went farther into the great chamber, and I was left alone in the moonlight with the dead.

I turned to escape.

What a long way I found it back through the dead! At first I was too angry to be afraid, but as I grew calm, the still shapes grew terrible. At last, with loud offence to the gracious silence, I ran, I fled wildly, and, bursting out, flung-to the door behind me. It closed with an awful silence.

I stood in pitch-darkness. Feeling about me, I found a door, opened it, and was aware of the dim light of a lamp. I stood in my library, with the handle of the masked door in my hand.

Had I come to myself out of a vision?—or lost myself by going back to one? Which was the real—what I now saw, or what I had just ceased to see? Could both be real, interpenetrating yet unmingling?

I threw myself on a couch, and fell asleep.

In the library was one small window to the east, through which, at this time of the year, the first rays of the sun shone upon a mirror whence they were reflected on the masked door: when I woke, there they shone, and thither they drew my eyes. With the feeling that behind it must lie the boundless chamber I had left by that door, I sprang to my feet, and opened it. The light, like an eager hound, shot before me into the closet, and pounced upon the gilded edges of a large book.

"What idiot," I cried, "has put that book in the shelf the wrong way?"

But the gilded edges, reflecting the light a second time, flung it on a nest of drawers in a dark corner, and I saw that one of them was half open.

"More meddling!" I cried, and went to close the drawer.

It contained old papers, and seemed more than full, for it would not close. Taking the topmost one out, I perceived that it was in my father's writing and of some length. The words on which first my eyes fell, at once made me eager to learn what it contained. I carried it to the library, sat down in one of the western windows, and read what follows.

CHAPTER VIII. MY FATHER'S MANUSCRIPT

I am filled with awe of what I have to write. The sun is shining golden above me; the sea lies blue beneath his gaze; the same world sends its growing things up to the sun, and its flying things into the air which I have breathed from my infancy; but I know the outspread splendour a passing show, and that at any moment it may, like the drop-scene of a stage, be lifted to reveal more wonderful things.

Shortly after my father's death, I was seated one morning in the library. I had been, somewhat listlessly, regarding the portrait that hangs among the books, which I knew only as that of a distant ancestor, and wishing I could learn something of its original. Then I had taken a book from the shelves and begun to read.

Glancing up from it, I saw coming toward me—not between me and the door, but between me and the portrait—a thin pale man in rusty black. He looked sharp and eager, and had a notable nose, at once reminding me of a certain jug my sisters used to call Mr. Crow.

"Finding myself in your vicinity, Mr. Vane, I have given myself the pleasure of calling," he said, in a peculiar but not disagreeable voice. "Your honoured grandfather treated me—I may say it without presumption—as a friend, having known me from childhood as his father's librarian."

It did not strike me at the time how old the man must be.

"May I ask where you live now, Mr. Crow?" I said.

He smiled an amused smile.

"You nearly hit my name," he rejoined, "which shows the family insight. You have seen me before, but only once, and could not then have heard it!"

"Where was that?"

"In this very room. You were quite a child, however!"

I could not be sure that I remembered him, but for a moment I fancied I did, and I begged him to set me right as to his name.

"There is such a thing as remembering without recognising the memory in it,"
he remarked. "For my name—which you have near enough—it used to be Raven."

I had heard the name, for marvellous tales had brought it me.

"It is very kind of you to come and see me," I said. "Will you not sit down?"

He seated himself at once.

"You knew my father, then, I presume?"

"I knew him," he answered with a curious smile, "but he did not care about my
acquaintance, and we never met.—That gentleman, however," he added, pointing
to the portrait,—"old Sir Up'ard, his people called him,—was in his day a friend of
mine yet more intimate than ever your grandfather became."

Then at length I began to think the interview a strange one. But in truth it was
hardly stranger that my visitor should remember Sir Upward, than that he should
have been my great-grandfather's librarian!

"I owe him much," he continued; "for, although I had read many more books
than he, yet, through the special direction of his studies, he was able to inform me
of a certain relation of modes which I should never have discovered of myself, and
could hardly have learned from any one else."

"Would you mind telling me all about that?" I said.

"By no means—as much at least as I am able: there are not such things as wilful
secrets," he answered—and went on.

"That closet held his library—a hundred manuscripts or so, for printing was
not then invented. One morning I sat there, working at a catalogue of them, when
he looked in at the door, and said, 'Come.' I laid down my pen and followed him
—across the great hall, down a steep rough descent, and along an underground
passage to a tower he had lately built, consisting of a stair and a room at the top of
it. The door of this room had a tremendous lock, which he undid with the smallest
key I ever saw. I had scarcely crossed the threshold after him, when, to my eyes,
he began to dwindle, and grew less and less. All at once my vision seemed to
come right, and I saw that he was moving swiftly away from me. In a minute
more he was the merest speck in the distance, with the tops of blue mountains
beyond him, clear against a sky of paler blue. I recognised the country, for I had
gone there and come again many a time, although I had never known this way
to it.

"Many years after, when the tower had long disappeared, I taught one of his
descendants what Sir Upward had taught me; and now and then to this day I use
your house when I want to go the nearest way home. I must indeed—without your
leave, for which I ask your pardon—have by this time well established a right of
way through it—not from front to back, but from bottom to top!"

"You would have me then understand, Mr. Raven," I said, "that you go through
my house into another world, heedless of disparting space?"

"That I go through it is an incontrovertible acknowledgement of space,"
returned the old librarian.

"Please do not quibble, Mr. Raven," I rejoined. "Please to take my question as
you know I mean it."

"There is in your house a door, one step through which carries me into a world
very much another than this."

"A better?"

"Not throughout; but so much another that most of its physical, and many of its mental laws are different from those of this world. As for moral laws, they must everywhere be fundamentally the same."

"You try my power of belief!" I said.

"You take me for a madman, probably?"

"You do not look like one."

"A liar then?"

"You give me no ground to think you such."

"Only you do not believe me?"

"I will go out of that door with you if you like: I believe in you enough to risk the attempt."

"The blunder all my children make!" he murmured. "The only door out is the door in!"

I began to think he must be crazy. He sat silent for a moment, his head resting on his hand, his elbow on the table, and his eyes on the books before him.

"A book," he said louder, "is a door in, and therefore a door out.—I see old Sir Up'ard," he went on, closing his eyes, "and my heart swells with love to him:—what world is he in?"

"The world of your heart!" I replied; "—that is, the idea of him is there."

"There is one world then at least on which your hall-door does not open?"

"I grant you so much; but the things in that world are not things to have and to hold."

"Think a little farther," he rejoined: "did anything ever become yours, except by getting into that world?—The thought is beyond you, however, at present!—I tell you there are more worlds, and more doors to them, than you will think of in many years!"

He rose, left the library, crossed the hall, and went straight up to the garret, familiar evidently with every turn. I followed, studying his back. His hair hung down long and dark, straight and glossy. His coat was wide and reached to his heels. His shoes seemed too large for him.

In the garret a light came through at the edges of the great roofing slabs, and showed us parts where was no flooring, and we must step from joist to joist: in the middle of one of these spaces rose a partition, with a door: through it I followed Mr. Raven into a small, obscure chamber, whose top contracted as it rose, and went slanting through the roof.

"That is the door I spoke of," he said, pointing to an oblong mirror that stood on the floor and leaned against the wall. I went in front of it, and saw our figures dimly reflected in its dusty face. There was something about it that made me uneasy. It looked old-fashioned and neglected, but, notwithstanding its ordinary seeming, the eagle, perched with outstretched wings on the top, appeared threatful.

"As a mirror," said the librarian, "it has grown dingy with age; but that is no matter: its clearness depends on the light."

"Light!" I rejoined; "there is no light here!"

He did not answer me, but began to pull at a little chain on the opposite wall. I heard a creaking: the top of the chamber was turning slowly round. He ceased pulling, looked at his watch, and began to pull again.

"We arrive almost to the moment!" he said; "it is on the very stroke of noon!"

The top went creaking and revolving for a minute or so. Then he pulled two other chains, now this, now that, and returned to the first. A moment more and the chamber grew much clearer: a patch of sunlight had fallen upon a mirror on the wall opposite that against which the other leaned, and on the dust I saw the path of the reflected rays to the mirror on the ground. But from the latter none were returned; they seemed to go clean through; there was nowhere in the chamber a second patch of light!

"Where are the sunrays gone?" I cried.

"That I cannot tell," returned Mr. Raven; "—back, perhaps, to where they came from first. They now belong, I fancy, to a sense not yet developed in us."

He then talked of the relations of mind to matter, and of senses to qualities, in a way I could only a little understand, whence he went on to yet stranger things which I could not at all comprehend. He spoke much about dimensions, telling me that there were many more than three, some of them concerned with powers which were indeed in us, but of which as yet we knew absolutely nothing. His words, however, I confess, took little more hold of me than the light did of the mirror, for I thought he hardly knew what he was saying.

Suddenly I was aware that our forms had gone from the mirror, which seemed full of a white mist. As I gazed I saw, growing gradually visible beyond the mist, the tops of a range of mountains, which became clearer and clearer. Soon the mist vanished entirely, uncovering the face of a wide heath, on which, at some distance, was the figure of a man moving swiftly away. I turned to address my companion; he was no longer by my side. I looked again at the form in the mirror, and recognised the wide coat flying, the black hair lifting in a wind that did not touch me. I rushed in terror from the place.

CHAPTER IX. I REPENT

I laid the manuscript down, consoled to find that my father had had a peep into that mysterious world, and that he knew Mr. Raven.

Then I remembered that I had never heard the cause or any circumstance of my father's death, and began to believe that he must at last have followed Mr. Raven, and not come back; whereupon I speedily grew ashamed of my flight. What wondrous facts might I not by this time have gathered concerning life and death, and wide regions beyond ordinary perception! Assuredly the Ravens were good people, and a night in their house would nowise have hurt me! They were doubtless strange, but it was faculty in which the one was peculiar, and beauty in which the other was marvellous! And I had not believed in them! had treated them as unworthy of my confidence, as harbouring a design against me! The more I thought of my behaviour to them, the more disgusted I became with myself. Why should I have feared such dead? To share their holy rest was an honour of which I had proved myself unworthy! What harm could that sleeping king, that lady with the wound in her palm, have done me? I fell a longing after the sweet and stately stillness of their two countenances, and wept. Weeping I threw myself on a couch, and suddenly fell asleep.

As suddenly I woke, feeling as if some one had called me. The house was still as an empty church. A blackbird was singing on the lawn. I said to myself, "I will go and tell them I am ashamed, and will do whatever they would have me do!" I rose, and went straight up the stairs to the garret.

The wooden chamber was just as when first I saw it, the mirror dimly reflecting everything before it. It was nearly noon, and the sun would be a little higher than when first I came: I must raise the hood a little, and adjust the mirrors accordingly! If I had but been in time to see Mr. Raven do it!

I pulled the chains, and let the light fall on the first mirror. I turned then to the other: there were the shapes of the former vision—distinguishable indeed, but tremulous like a landscape in a pool ruffled by "a small pipling wind!" I touched the glass; it was impermeable.

Suspecting polarisation as the thing required, I shifted and shifted the mirrors, changing their relation, until at last, in a great degree, so far as I was concerned, by chance, things came right between them, and I saw the mountains blue and steady and clear. I stepped forward, and my feet were among the heather.

All I knew of the way to the cottage was that we had gone through a pine-forest. I passed through many thickets and several small fir-woods, continually fancying afresh that I recognised something of the country; but I had come upon no forest, and now the sun was near the horizon, and the air had begun to grow chill with the coming winter, when, to my delight, I saw a little black object coming toward me: it was indeed the raven!

I hastened to meet him.

"I beg your pardon, sir, for my rudeness last night," I said. "Will you take me with you now? I heartily confess I do not deserve it."

"Ah!" he returned, and looked up. Then, after a brief pause, "My wife does not expect you to-night," he said. "She regrets that we at all encouraged your staying last week."

"Take me to her that I may tell her how sorry I am," I begged humbly.

"It is of no use," he answered. "Your night was not come then, or you would not have left us. It is not come now, and I cannot show you the way. The dead were rejoicing under their daisies—they all lie among the roots of the flowers of heaven —at the thought of your delight when the winter should be past, and the morning with its birds come: ere you left them, they shivered in their beds. When the spring of the universe arrives,—but that cannot be for ages yet! how many, I do not know —and do not care to know."

"Tell me one thing, I beg of you, Mr. Raven: is my father with you? Have you seen him since he left the world?"

"Yes; he is with us, fast asleep. That was he you saw with his arm on the coverlet, his hand half closed."

"Why did you not tell me? That I should have been so near him, and not know!"

"And turn your back on him!" corrected the raven.

"I would have lain down at once had I known!"

"I doubt it. Had you been ready to lie down, you would have known him!—Old Sir Up'ard," he went on, "and your twice great-grandfather, both are up and away long ago. Your great-grandfather has been with us for many a year; I think he will soon begin to stir. You saw him last night, though of course you did not know him."

"Why OF COURSE?"

"Because he is so much nearer waking than you. No one who will not sleep can ever wake."

"I do not at all understand you!"

"You turned away, and would not understand!" I held my peace.—But if I did not say something, he would go!

"And my grandfather—is he also with you?" I asked.

"No; he is still in the Evil Wood, fighting the dead."

"Where is the Evil Wood, that I may find him?"

"You will not find him; but you will hardly miss the wood. It is the place where those who will not sleep, wake up at night, to kill their dead and bury them."

"I cannot understand you!"

"Naturally not. Neither do I understand you; I can read neither your heart nor your face. When my wife and I do not understand our children, it is because there is not enough of them to be understood. God alone can understand foolishness."

"Then," I said, feeling naked and very worthless, "will you be so good as show me the nearest way home? There are more ways than one, I know, for I have gone by two already."

"There are indeed many ways."

"Tell me, please, how to recognise the nearest."

"I cannot," answered the raven; "you and I use the same words with different meanings. We are often unable to tell people what they NEED to know, because they WANT to know something else, and would therefore only misunderstand what we said. Home is ever so far away in the palm of your hand, and how to get there it is of no use to tell you. But you will get there; you must get there; you have to get there. Everybody who is not at home, has to go home. You thought you were at home where I found you: if that had been your home, you could not have left it. Nobody can leave home. And nobody ever was or ever will be at home without having gone there."

"Enigma treading on enigma!" I exclaimed. "I did not come here to be asked riddles."

"No; but you came, and found the riddles waiting for you! Indeed you are yourself the only riddle. What you call riddles are truths, and seem riddles because you are not true."

"Worse and worse!" I cried.

"And you MUST answer the riddles!" he continued. "They will go on asking themselves until you understand yourself. The universe is a riddle trying to get out, and you are holding your door hard against it."

"Will you not in pity tell me what I am to do—where I must go?"

"How should I tell YOUR to-do, or the way to it?"

"If I am not to go home, at least direct me to some of my kind."

"I do not know of any. The beings most like you are in that direction."

He pointed with his beak. I could see nothing but the setting sun, which blinded me.

"Well," I said bitterly, "I cannot help feeling hardly treated—taken from my home, abandoned in a strange world, and refused instruction as to where I am to go or what I am to do!"

"You forget," said the raven, "that, when I brought you and you declined my hospitality, you reached what you call home in safety: now you are come of yourself! Good night."

He turned and walked slowly away, with his beak toward the ground. I stood dazed. It was true I had come of myself, but had I not come with intent of atonement? My heart was sore, and in my brain was neither quest nor purpose, hope nor desire. I gazed after the raven, and would have followed him, but felt it useless.

All at once he pounced on a spot, throwing the whole weight of his body on his bill, and for some moments dug vigorously. Then with a flutter of his wings he threw back his head, and something shot from his bill, cast high in the air. That moment the sun set, and the air at once grew very dusk, but the something opened into a soft radiance, and came pulsing toward me like a fire-fly, but with a much larger and a yellower light. It flew over my head. I turned and followed it.

Here I interrupt my narrative to remark that it involves a constant struggle to say what cannot be said with even an approach to precision, the things recorded being, in their nature and in that of the creatures concerned in them, so inexpressibly different from any possible events of this economy, that I can present them only by giving, in the forms and language of life in this world, the modes in which they affected me—not the things themselves, but the feelings they woke in me. Even this much, however, I do with a continuous and abiding sense of failure, finding it impossible to present more than one phase of a multitudinously complicated significance, or one concentric sphere of a graduated embodiment. A single thing would sometimes seem to be and mean many things, with an uncertain identity at the heart of them, which kept constantly altering their look. I am indeed often driven to set down what I know to be but a clumsy and doubtful representation of the mere feeling aimed at, none of the communicating media of this world being fit to convey it, in its peculiar strangeness, with even an approach to clearness or certainty. Even to one who knew the region better than myself, I should have no assurance of transmitting the reality of my experience in it. While without a doubt, for instance, that I was actually regarding a scene of activity, I might be, at the same moment, in my consciousness aware that I was perusing a metaphysical argument.

CHAPTER X. THE BAD BURROW

As the air grew black and the winter closed swiftly around me, the fluttering fire blazed out more luminous, and arresting its flight, hovered waiting. So soon as I came under its radiance, it flew slowly on, lingering now and then above spots where the ground was rocky. Every time I looked up, it seemed to have grown larger, and at length gave me an attendant shadow. Plainly a bird-butterfly, it flew with a certain swallowy double. Its wings were very large, nearly square, and flashed all the colours of the rainbow. Wondering at their splendour, I became so absorbed in their beauty that I stumbled over a low rock, and lay stunned. When I came to myself, the creature was hovering over my head, radiating the whole chord of light, with multitudinous gradations and some kinds of colour I had never before seen. I rose and went on, but, unable to take my eyes off the shining thing to look to my steps, I struck my foot against a stone. Fearing then another fall, I sat down to watch the little glory, and a great longing awoke in me to have it in my hand. To my unspeakable delight, it began to sink toward me. Slowly at first, then swiftly it sank, growing larger as it came nearer. I felt as if the treasure of the universe were giving itself to me—put out my hand, and had it. But the instant I took it, its light went out; all was dark as pitch; a dead book with boards outspread lay cold and heavy in my hand. I threw it in the air—only to hear it fall among the heather. Burying my face in my hands, I sat in motionless misery.

But the cold grew so bitter that, fearing to be frozen, I got up. The moment I was on my feet, a faint sense of light awoke in me. "Is it coming to life?" I cried, and a great pang of hope shot through me. Alas, no! it was the edge of a moon peering up keen and sharp over a level horizon! She brought me light—but no guidance! SHE would not hover over me, would not wait on my faltering steps! She could but offer me an ignorant choice!

With a full face she rose, and I began to see a little about me. Westward of her, and not far from me, a range of low hills broke the horizon-line: I set out for it.

But what a night I had to pass ere I reached it! The moon seemed to know something, for she stared at me oddly. Her look was indeed icy-cold, but full of interest, or at least curiosity. She was not the same moon I had known on the earth; her face was strange to me, and her light yet stranger. Perhaps it came from an unknown sun! Every time I looked up, I found her staring at me with all her might! At first I was annoyed, as at the rudeness of a fellow creature; but soon I saw or fancied a certain wondering pity in her gaze: why was I out in her night? Then first I knew what an awful thing it was to be awake in the universe: I WAS, and could not help it!

As I walked, my feet lost the heather, and trod a bare spongy soil, something like dry, powdery peat. To my dismay it gave a momentary heave under me; then presently I saw what seemed the ripple of an earthquake running on before me, shadowy in the low moon. It passed into the distance; but, while yet I stared after it, a single wave rose up, and came slowly toward me. A yard or two away it burst, and from it, with a scramble and a bound, issued an animal like a tiger. About his mouth and ears hung clots of mould, and his eyes winked and flamed as he rushed at me, showing his white teeth in a soundless snarl. I stood fascinated, unconscious of either courage or fear. He turned his head to the ground, and plunged into it.

"That moon is affecting my brain," I said as I resumed my journey. "What life can be here but the phantasmic—the stuff of which dreams are made? I am indeed walking in a vain show!"

Thus I strove to keep my heart above the waters of fear, nor knew that she whom I distrusted was indeed my defence from the realities I took for phantoms: her light controlled the monsters, else had I scarce taken a second step on the hideous ground. "I will not be appalled by that which only seems!" I said to myself, yet felt it a terrible thing to walk on a sea where such fishes disported themselves below. With that, a step or two from me, the head of a worm began to come slowly out of the earth, as big as that of a polar bear and much resembling it, with a white mane to its red neck. The drawing wriggles with which its huge length extricated itself were horrible, yet I dared not turn my eyes from them. The moment its tail was free, it lay as if exhausted, wallowing in feeble effort to burrow again.

"Does it live on the dead," I wondered, "and is it unable to hurt the living? If they scent their prey and come out, why do they leave me unharmed?"

I know now it was that the moon paralysed them.

All the night through as I walked, hideous creatures, no two alike, threatened me. In some of them, beauty of colour enhanced loathliness of shape: one large serpent was covered from head to distant tail with feathers of glorious hues.

I became at length so accustomed to their hurtless menaces that I fell to beguiling the way with the invention of monstrosities, never suspecting that I owed each moment of life to the staring moon. Though hers was no primal radiance, it so hampered the evil things, that I walked in safety. For light is yet light, if but the last of a countless series of reflections! How swiftly would not my feet have carried me over the restless soil, had I known that, if still within their range when her lamp ceased to shine on the cursed spot, I should that moment be at the mercy of such as had no mercy, the centre of a writhing heap of hideousness, every individual of it as terrible as before it had but seemed! Fool of ignorance, I watched the descent of the weary, solemn, anxious moon down the widening vault above me, with no worse uneasiness than the dread of losing my way—where as yet I had indeed no way to lose.

I was drawing near the hills I had made my goal, and she was now not far from their sky-line, when the soundless wallowing ceased, and the burrow lay motionless and bare. Then I saw, slowly walking over the light soil, the form of a woman. A white mist floated about her, now assuming, now losing to reassume the shape of a garment, as it gathered to her or was blown from her by a wind that dogged her steps.

She was beautiful, but with such a pride at once and misery on her countenance that I could hardly believe what yet I saw. Up and down she walked, vainly endeavouring to lay hold of the mist and wrap it around her. The eyes in the beautiful face were dead, and on her left side was a dark spot, against which she would now and then press her hand, as if to stifle pain or sickness. Her hair hung nearly to her feet, and sometimes the wind would so mix it with the mist that I could not distinguish the one from the other; but when it fell gathering together again, it shone a pale gold in the moonlight.

Suddenly pressing both hands on her heart, she fell to the ground, and the mist rose from her and melted in the air. I ran to her. But she began to writhe in such torture that I stood aghast. A moment more and her legs, hurrying from her body, sped away serpents. From her shoulders fled her arms as in terror, serpents also. Then something flew up from her like a bat, and when I looked again, she was gone. The ground rose like the sea in a storm; terror laid hold upon me; I turned to the hills and ran.

I was already on the slope of their base, when the moon sank behind one of their summits, leaving me in its shadow. Behind me rose a waste and sickening cry, as of frustrate desire—the only sound I had heard since the fall of the dead butterfly; it made my heart shake like a flag in the wind. I turned, saw many dark objects bounding after me, and made for the crest of a ridge on which the moon still shone. She seemed to linger there that I might see to defend myself. Soon I came in sight of her, and climbed the faster.

Crossing the shadow of a rock, I heard the creatures panting at my heels. But just as the foremost threw himself upon me with a snarl of greedy hate, we rushed into the moon together. She flashed out an angry light, and he fell from me a bodiless blotch. Strength came to me, and I turned on the rest. But one by one as they darted into the light, they dropped with a howl; and I saw or fancied a strange smile on the round face above me.

I climbed to the top of the ridge: far away shone the moon, sinking to a low horizon. The air was pure and strong. I descended a little way, found it warmer, and sat down to wait the dawn.

The moon went below, and the world again was dark.

CHAPTER XI. THE EVIL WOOD

I fell fast asleep, and when I woke the sun was rising. I went to the top again, and looked back: the hollow I had crossed in the moonlight lay without sign of life. Could it be that the calm expanse before me swarmed with creatures of devouring greed?

I turned and looked over the land through which my way must lie. It seemed a wide desert, with a patch of a different colour in the distance that might be a forest. Sign of presence, human or animal, was none—smoke or dust or shadow of cultivation. Not a cloud floated in the clear heaven; no thinnest haze curtained any segment of its circling rim.

I descended, and set out for the imaginable forest: something alive might be there; on this side of it could not well be anything!

When I reached the plain, I found it, as far as my sight could go, of rock, here flat and channeled, there humped and pinnacled—evidently the wide bed of a vanished river, scored by innumerable water-runs, without a trace of moisture in them. Some of the channels bore a dry moss, and some of the rocks a few lichens almost as hard as themselves. The air, once "filled with pleasant noise of waters," was silent as death. It took me the whole day to reach the patch,—which I found indeed a forest—but not a rudiment of brook or runnel had I crossed! Yet through the glowing noon I seemed haunted by an aural mirage, hearing so plainly the voice of many waters that I could hardly believe the opposing testimony of my eyes.

The sun was approaching the horizon when I left the river-bed, and entered the forest. Sunk below the tree-tops, and sending his rays between their pillar-like boles, he revealed a world of blessed shadows waiting to receive me. I had expected a pine-wood, but here were trees of many sorts, some with strong resemblances to trees I knew, others with marvellous differences from any I had ever seen. I threw myself beneath the boughs of what seemed a eucalyptus in blossom:

its flowers had a hard calyx much resembling a skull, the top of which rose like a lid to let the froth-like bloom-brain overfoam its cup. From beneath the shadow of its falchion-leaves my eyes went wandering into deep after deep of the forest.

Soon, however, its doors and windows began to close, shutting up aisle and corridor and roomier glade. The night was about me, and instant and sharp the cold. Again what a night I found it! How shall I make my reader share with me its wild ghostiness?

The tree under which I lay rose high before it branched, but the boughs of it bent so low that they seemed ready to shut me in as I leaned against the smooth stem, and let my eyes wander through the brief twilight of the vanishing forest. Presently, to my listless roving gaze, the varied outlines of the clumpy foliage began to assume or imitate—say rather SUGGEST other shapes than their own. A light wind began to blow; it set the boughs of a neighbour tree rocking, and all their branches aswing, every twig and every leaf blending its individual motion with the sway of its branch and the rock of its bough. Among its leafy shapes was a pack of wolves that struggled to break from a wizard's leash: greyhounds would not have strained so savagely! I watched them with an interest that grew as the wind gathered force, and their motions life.

Another mass of foliage, larger and more compact, presented my fancy with a group of horses' heads and forequarters projecting caparisoned from their stalls. Their necks kept moving up and down, with an impatience that augmented as the growing wind broke their vertical rhythm with a wilder swaying from side to side. What heads they were! how gaunt, how strange!—several of them bare skulls—one with the skin tight on its bones! One had lost the under jaw and hung low, looking unutterably weary—but now and then hove high as if to ease the bit. Above them, at the end of a branch, floated erect the form of a woman, waving her arms in imperious gesture. The definiteness of these and other leaf masses first surprised and then discomposed me: what if they should overpower my brain with seeming reality? But the twilight became darkness; the wind ceased; every shape was shut up in the night; I fell asleep.

It was still dark when I began to be aware of a far-off, confused, rushing noise, mingled with faint cries. It grew and grew until a tumult as of gathering multitudes filled the wood. On all sides at once the sounds drew nearer; the spot where I lay seemed the centre of a commotion that extended throughout the forest. I scarce moved hand or foot lest I should betray my presence to hostile things.

The moon at length approached the forest, and came slowly into it: with her first gleam the noises increased to a deafening uproar, and I began to see dim shapes about me. As she ascended and grew brighter, the noises became yet louder, and the shapes clearer. A furious battle was raging around me. Wild cries and roars of rage, shock of onset, struggle prolonged, all mingled with words articulate, surged in my ears. Curses and credos, snarls and sneers, laughter and mockery, sacred names and howls of hate, came huddling in chaotic interpenetration. Skeletons and phantoms fought in maddest confusion. Swords swept through the phantoms: they only shivered. Maces crashed on the skeletons, shattering them hideously: not one fell or ceased to fight, so long as a single joint held two bones together. Bones of men and horses lay scattered and heaped; grinding and crunching them under foot fought the skeletons. Everywhere charged the bone-gaunt white steeds; everywhere on foot or on wind-blown misty battle-horses, raged and ravened and raved the indestructible spectres; weapons and hoofs clashed and crushed; while skeleton jaws and phantom-throats swelled the deafening tumult with the war-cry of every opinion, bad or good, that had bred strife, injustice, cruelty in any world. The holiest words went with the most hating blow. Lie-distorted truths flew hurtling in the wind of javelins and bones. Every moment some one would turn against his comrades, and fight more wildly than before, THE TRUTH! THE TRUTH! still his cry. One I noted who wheeled ever in a circle, and smote on all sides. Wearied out, a pair would sit for a minute side by side, then rise and renew the fierce combat. None stooped to comfort the fallen, or stepped wide to spare him.

The moon shone till the sun rose, and all the night long I had glimpses of a woman moving at her will above the strife-tormented multitude, now on this front now on that, one outstretched arm urging the fight, the other pressed against her side. "Ye are men: slay one another!" she shouted. I saw her dead eyes and her dark spot, and recalled what I had seen the night before.

Such was the battle of the dead, which I saw and heard as I lay under the tree.

Just before sunrise, a breeze went through the forest, and a voice cried, "Let the dead bury their dead!" At the word the contending thousands dropped noiseless, and when the sun looked in, he saw never a bone, but here and there a withered branch.

I rose and resumed my journey, through as quiet a wood as ever grew out of the quiet earth. For the wind of the morning had ceased when the sun appeared, and the trees were silent. Not a bird sang, not a squirrel, mouse, or weasel showed itself, not a belated moth flew athwart my path. But as I went I kept watch over myself, nor dared let my eyes rest on any forest-shape. All the time I seemed to hear faint sounds of mattock and spade and hurtling bones: any moment my eyes might open on things I would not see! Daylight prudence muttered that perhaps, to appear, ten thousand phantoms awaited only my consenting fancy.

In the middle of the afternoon I came out of the wood—to find before me a second net of dry water-courses. I thought at first that I had wandered from my attempted line, and reversed my direction; but I soon saw it was not so, and concluded presently that I had come to another branch of the same river-bed. I began at once to cross it, and was in the bottom of a wide channel when the sun set.

I sat down to await the moon, and growing sleepy, stretched myself on the moss. The moment my head was down, I heard the sounds of rushing streams—all sorts of sweet watery noises. The veiled melody of the molten music sang me into a dreamless sleep, and when I woke the sun was already up, and the wrinkled country widely visible. Covered with shadows it lay striped and mottled like the skin of some wild animal. As the sun rose the shadows diminished, and it seemed as if the rocks were re-absorbing the darkness that had oozed out of them during the night.

Hitherto I had loved my Arab mare and my books more, I fear, than live man or woman; now at length my soul was athirst for a human presence, and I longed even after those inhabitants of this alien world whom the raven had so vaguely described as nearest my sort. With heavy yet hoping heart, and mind haunted by a doubt whether I was going in any direction at all, I kept wearily travelling "north-west and by south."

CHAPTER XII. FRIENDS AND FOES

Coming, in one of the channels, upon what seemed a little shrub, the outlying picket, I trusted, of an army behind it, I knelt to look at it closer. It bore a small fruit, which, as I did not recognise it, I feared to gather and eat. Little I thought that I was watched from behind the rocks by hundreds of eyes eager with the question whether I would or would not take it.

I came to another plant somewhat bigger, then to another larger still, and at length to clumps of a like sort; by which time I saw that they were not shrubs but dwarf-trees. Before I reached the bank of this second branch of the river-bed, I found the channels so full of them that it was with difficulty I crossed such as I could not jump. In one I heard a great rush, as of a multitude of birds from an ivied wall, but saw nothing.

I came next to some large fruit-bearing trees, but what they bore looked coarse. They stood on the edge of a hollow, which evidently had once been the basin of a lake. From the left a forest seemed to flow into and fill it; but while the trees above were of many sorts, those in the hollow were almost entirely fruit-bearing.

I went a few yards down the slope of grass mingled with moss, and stretched myself upon it weary. A little farther down stood a tiny tree full of rosiest apples no bigger than small cherries, its top close to my hand; I pulled and ate one of them. Finding it delicious, I was in the act of taking another, when a sudden shouting of children, mingled with laughter clear and sweet as the music of a brook, startled me with delight.

"He likes our apples! He likes our apples! He's a good giant! He's a good giant!" cried many little voices.

"He's a giant!" objected one.

"He IS rather big," assented another, "but littleness isn't everything! It won't keep you from growing big and stupid except you take care!"

I rose on my elbow and stared. Above and about and below me stood a multitude of children, apparently of all ages, some just able to run alone, and some about twelve or thirteen. Three or four seemed older. They stood in a small knot, a little apart, and were less excited than the rest. The many were chattering in groups, declaiming and contradicting, like a crowd of grown people in a city, only with greater merriment, better manners, and more sense.

I gathered that, by the approach of my hand to a second apple, they knew that I liked the first; but how from that they argued me good, I did not see, nor wondered that one of them at least should suggest caution. I did not open my mouth, for I was afraid of frightening them, and sure I should learn more by listening than by asking questions. For I understood nearly all they said—at which I was not surprised: to understand is not more wonderful than to love.

There came a movement and slight dispersion among them, and presently a sweet, innocent-looking, lovingly roguish little fellow handed me a huge green apple. Silence fell on the noisy throng; all waited expectant.

"Eat, good giant," he said.

I sat up, took the apple, smiled thanks, and would have eaten; but the moment I bit into it, I flung it far away.

Again rose a shout of delight; they flung themselves upon me, so as nearly to smother me; they kissed my face and hands; they laid hold of my legs; they clambered about my arms and shoulders, embracing my head and neck. I came to the ground at last, overwhelmed with the lovely little goblins.

"Good, good giant!" they cried. "We knew you would come! Oh you dear, good, strong giant!"

The babble of their talk sprang up afresh, and ever the jubilant shout would rise anew from hundreds of clear little throats.

Again came a sudden silence. Those around me drew back; those atop of me got off and began trying to set me on my feet. Upon their sweet faces, concern had taken the place of merriment.

"Get up, good giant!" said a little girl. "Make haste! much haste! He saw you throw his apple away!"

Before she ended, I was on my feet. She stood pointing up the slope. On the brow of it was a clownish, bad-looking fellow, a few inches taller than myself. He looked hostile, but I saw no reason to fear him, for he had no weapon, and my little friends had vanished every one.

He began to descend, and I, in the hope of better footing and position, to go up. He growled like a beast as he turned toward me.

Reaching a more level spot, I stood and waited for him. As he came near, he held out his hand. I would have taken it in friendly fashion, but he drew it back, threatened a blow, and held it out again. Then I understood him to claim the apple I had flung away, whereupon I made a grimace of dislike and a gesture of rejection.

He answered with a howl of rage that seemed to say, "Do you dare tell me my apple was not fit to eat?"

"One bad apple may grow on the best tree," I said.

Whether he perceived my meaning I cannot tell, but he made a stride nearer, and I stood on my guard. He delayed his assault, however, until a second giant, much like him, who had been stealing up behind me, was close enough, when he rushed upon me. I met him with a good blow in the face, but the other struck me on the back of the head, and between them I was soon overpowered.

They dragged me into the wood above the valley, where their tribe lived—in wretched huts, built of fallen branches and a few stones. Into one of these they pushed me, there threw me on the ground, and kicked me. A woman was present, who looked on with indifference.

I may here mention that during my captivity I hardly learned to distinguish the women from the men, they differed so little. Often I wondered whether I had not come upon a sort of fungoid people, with just enough mind to give them motion and the expressions of anger and greed. Their food, which consisted of tubers, bulbs, and fruits, was to me inexpressibly disagreeable, but nothing offended them so much as to show dislike to it. I was cuffed by the women and kicked by the men because I would not swallow it.

I lay on the floor that night hardly able to move, but I slept a good deal, and woke a little refreshed. In the morning they dragged me to the valley, and tying my feet, with a long rope, to a tree, put a flat stone with a saw-like edge in my left hand. I shifted it to the right; they kicked me, and put it again in the left; gave me to understand that I was to scrape the bark off every branch that had no fruit on it; kicked me once more, and left me.

I set about the dreary work in the hope that by satisfying them I should be left very much to myself—to make my observations and choose my time for escape. Happily one of the dwarf-trees grew close by me, and every other minute I plucked and ate a small fruit, which wonderfully refreshed and strengthened me.

CHAPTER XIII. THE LITTLE ONES

I had been at work but a few moments, when I heard small voices near me, and presently the Little Ones, as I soon found they called themselves, came creeping out from among the tiny trees that like brushwood filled the spaces between the big ones. In a minute there were scores and scores about me. I made signs that the giants had but just left me, and were not far off; but they laughed, and told me the wind was quite clean.

"They are too blind to see us," they said, and laughed like a multitude of sheep-bells.

"Do you like that rope about your ankles?" asked one.

"I want them to think I cannot take it off," I replied.

"They can scarcely see their own feet!" he rejoined. "Walk with short steps and they will think the rope is all right."

As he spoke, he danced with merriment.

One of the bigger girls got down on her knees to untie the clumsy knot. I smiled, thinking those pretty fingers could do nothing with it, but in a moment it was loose.

They then made me sit down, and fed me with delicious little fruits; after which the smaller of them began to play with me in the wildest fashion, so that it was impossible for me to resume my work. When the first grew tired, others took their places, and this went on until the sun was setting, and heavy steps were heard approaching. The little people started from me, and I made haste to put the rope round my ankles.

"We must have a care," said the girl who had freed me; "a crush of one of their horrid stumpy feet might kill a very little one!"

"Can they not perceive you at all then?"

"They might see something move; and if the children were in a heap on the top of you, as they were a moment ago, it would be terrible; for they hate every live thing but themselves.—Not that they are much alive either!"

She whistled like a bird. The next instant not one of them was to be seen or heard, and the girl herself had disappeared.

It was my master, as doubtless he counted himself, come to take me home. He freed my ankles, and dragged me to the door of his hut; there he threw me on the ground, again tied my feet, gave me a kick, and left me.

Now I might at once have made my escape; but at length I had friends, and could not think of leaving them. They were so charming, so full of winsome ways, that I must see more of them! I must know them better! "To-morrow," I said to myself with delight, "I shall see them again!" But from the moment there was silence in the huts until I fell asleep, I heard them whispering all about me, and knew that I was lovingly watched by a multitude. After that, I think they hardly ever left me quite alone.

I did not come to know the giants at all, and I believe there was scarcely anything in them to know. They never became in the least friendly, but they were much too stupid to invent cruelties. Often I avoided a bad kick by catching the foot and giving its owner a fall, upon which he never, on that occasion, renewed his attempt.

But the little people were constantly doing and saying things that pleased, often things that surprised me. Every day I grew more loath to leave them. While I was at work, they would keep coming and going, amusing and delighting me, and taking all the misery, and much of the weariness out of my monotonous toil. Very soon I loved them more than I can tell. They did not know much, but they were very wise, and seemed capable of learning anything. I had no bed save the bare ground, but almost as often as I woke, it was in a nest of children—one or other of them in my arms, though which I seldom could tell until the light came, for they ordered the succession among themselves. When one crept into my bosom, unconsciously I clasped him there, and the rest lay close around me, the smaller nearer. It is hardly necessary to say that I did not suffer much from the nightly cold! The first thing they did in the morning, and the last before sunset, was to bring the good giant plenty to eat.

One morning I was surprised on waking to find myself alone. As I came to my senses, however, I heard subdued sounds of approach, and presently the girl already mentioned, the tallest and gravest of the community, and regarded by all as their mother, appeared from the wood, followed by the multitude in jubilation manifest—but silent lest they should rouse the sleeping giant at whose door I lay. She carried a boy-baby in her arms: hitherto a girl-baby, apparently about a year old, had been the youngest. Three of the bigger girls were her nurses, but they shared their treasure with all the rest. Among the Little Ones, dolls were unknown; the bigger had the smaller, and the smaller the still less, to tend and play with.

Lona came to me and laid the infant in my arms. The baby opened his eyes and looked at me, closed them again, and fell asleep.

"He loves you already!" said the girl.

"Where did you find him?" I asked.

"In the wood, of course," she answered, her eyes beaming with delight, "—where we always find them. Isn't he a beauty? We've been out all night looking for him. Sometimes it is not easy to find!"

"How do you know when there is one to find?" I asked.

"I cannot tell," she replied. "Every one makes haste to tell the other, but we never find out who told first. Sometimes I think one must have said it asleep, and another heard it half-awake. When there is a baby in the wood, no one can stop to ask questions; and when we have found it, then it is too late."

"Do more boy or girl babies come to the wood?"

"They don't come to the wood; we go to the wood and find them."

"Are there more boys or girls of you now?"

I had found that to ask precisely the same question twice, made them knit their brows.

"I do not know," she answered.

"You can count them, surely!"

"We never do that. We shouldn't like to be counted."

"Why?"

"It wouldn't be smooth. We would rather not know."

"Where do the babies come from first?"

"From the wood—always. There is no other place they can come from."

She knew where they came from last, and thought nothing else was to be known about their advent.

"How often do you find one?"

"Such a happy thing takes all the glad we've got, and we forget the last time. You too are glad to have him—are you not, good giant?"

"Yes, indeed, I am!" I answered. "But how do you feed him?"

"I will show you," she rejoined, and went away—to return directly with two or three ripe little plums. She put one to the baby's lips.

"He would open his mouth if he were awake," she said, and took him in her arms.

She squeezed a drop to the surface, and again held the fruit to the baby's lips. Without waking he began at once to suck it, and she went on slowly squeezing until nothing but skin and stone were left.

"There!" she cried, in a tone of gentle triumph. "A big-apple world it would be with nothing for the babies! We wouldn't stop in it—would we, darling? We would leave it to the bad giants!"

"But what if you let the stone into the baby's mouth when you were feeding him?" I said.

"No mother would do that," she replied. "I shouldn't be fit to have a baby!"

I thought what a lovely woman she would grow. But what became of them when they grew up? Where did they go? That brought me again to the question—where did they come from first?

"Will you tell me where you lived before?" I said.

"Here," she replied.

"Have you NEVER lived anywhere else?" I ventured.

"Never. We all came from the wood. Some think we dropped out of the trees."

"How is it there are so many of you quite little?"

"I don't understand. Some are less and some are bigger. I am very big."

"Baby will grow bigger, won't he?"

"Of course he will!"

"And will you grow bigger?"

"I don't think so. I hope not. I am the biggest. It frightens me sometimes."

"Why should it frighten you?"

She gave me no answer.

"How old are you?" I resumed.

"I do not know what you mean. We are all just that."

"How big will the baby grow?"

"I cannot tell.—Some," she added, with a trouble in her voice, "begin to grow after we think they have stopped.—That is a frightful thing. We don't talk about it!"

"What makes it frightful?"

She was silent for a moment, then answered,

"We fear they may be beginning to grow giants."

"Why should you fear that?"

"Because it is so terrible.—I don't want to talk about it!"

She pressed the baby to her bosom with such an anxious look that I dared not further question her.

Before long I began to perceive in two or three of the smaller children some traces of greed and selfishness, and noted that the bigger girls cast on these a not infrequent glance of anxiety.

None of them put a hand to my work: they would do nothing for the giants! But they never relaxed their loving ministrations to me. They would sing to me, one after another, for hours; climb the tree to reach my mouth and pop fruit into it with their dainty little fingers; and they kept constant watch against the approach of a giant.

Sometimes they would sit and tell me stories—mostly very childish, and often seeming to mean hardly anything. Now and then they would call a general assembly to amuse me. On one such occasion a moody little fellow sang me a strange crooning song, with a refrain so pathetic that, although unintelligible to me, it caused the tears to run down my face. This phenomenon made those who saw it regard me with much perplexity. Then first I bethought myself that I had not once, in that world, looked on water, falling or lying or running. Plenty there had been in some long vanished age—that was plain enough—but the Little Ones had never seen any before they saw my tears! They had, nevertheless, it seemed, some dim, instinctive perception of their origin; for a very small child went up to the singer, shook his clenched pud in his face, and said something like this: "'Ou skeeze ze juice out of ze good giant's seeberries! Bad giant!"

"How is it," I said one day to Lona, as she sat with the baby in her arms at the foot of my tree, "that I never see any children among the giants?"

She stared a little, as if looking in vain for some sense in the question, then replied,

"They are giants; there are no little ones."

"Have they never any children?" I asked.

"No; there are never any in the wood for them. They do not love them. If they saw ours, they would stamp them."

"Is there always the same number of the giants then? I thought, before I had time to know better, that they were your fathers and mothers."

She burst into the merriest laughter, and said,

"No, good giant; WE are THEIR firsters."

But as she said it, the merriment died out of her, and she looked scared.

I stopped working, and gazed at her, bewildered.

"How CAN that be?" I exclaimed.

"I do not say; I do not understand," she answered. "But we were here and they not. They go from us. I am sorry, but we cannot help it. THEY could have helped it."

"How long have you been here?" I asked, more and more puzzled—in the hope of some side-light on the matter.

"Always, I think," she replied. "I think somebody made us always."

I turned to my scraping.

She saw I did not understand.

"The giants were not made always," she resumed. "If a Little One doesn't care, he grows greedy, and then lazy, and then big, and then stupid, and then bad. The dull creatures don't know that they come from us. Very few of them believe we are anywhere. They say NONSENSE!—Look at little Blunty: he is eating one of their apples! He will be the next! Oh! oh! he will soon be big and bad and ugly, and not know it!"

The child stood by himself a little way off, eating an apple nearly as big as his head. I had often thought he did not look so good as the rest; now he looked disgusting.

"I will take the horrid thing from him!" I cried.

"It is no use," she answered sadly. "We have done all we can, and it is too late! We were afraid he was growing, for he would not believe anything told him; but when he refused to share his berries, and said he had gathered them for himself, then we knew it! He is a glutton, and there is no hope of him.—It makes me sick to see him eat!"

"Could not some of the boys watch him, and not let him touch the poisonous things?"

"He may have them if he will: it is all one—to eat the apples, and to be a boy that would eat them if he could. No; he must go to the giants! He belongs to them. You can see how much bigger he is than when first you came! He is bigger since yesterday."

"He is as like that hideous green lump in his hand as boy could look!"

"It suits what he is making himself."

"His head and it might change places!"

"Perhaps they do!"

"Does he want to be a giant?"

"He hates the giants, but he is making himself one all the same: he likes their apples! Oh baby, baby, he was just such a darling as you when we found him!"

"He will be very miserable when he finds himself a giant!"

"Oh, no; he will like it well enough! That is the worst of it."

"Will he hate the Little Ones?"

"He will be like the rest; he will not remember us—most likely will not believe there are Little Ones. He will not care; he will eat his apples."

"Do tell me how it will come about. I understand your world so little! I come from a world where everything is different."

"I do not know about WORLD. What is it? What more but a word in your beautiful big mouth?—That makes it something!"

"Never mind about the word; tell me what next will happen to Blunty."

"He will wake one morning and find himself a giant—not like you, good giant, but like any other bad giant. You will hardly know him, but I will tell you which. He will think he has been a giant always, and will not know you, or any of us. The giants have lost themselves, Peony says, and that is why they never smile. I wonder whether they are not glad because they are bad, or bad because they are not glad. But they can't be glad when they have no babies! I wonder what BAD means, good giant!"

"I wish I knew no more about it than you!" I returned. "But I try to be good, and mean to keep on trying."

"So do I—and that is how I know you are good."

A long pause followed.

"Then you do not know where the babies come from into the wood?" I said, making one attempt more.

"There is nothing to know there," she answered. "They are in the wood; they grow there."

"Then how is it you never find one before it is quite grown?" I asked.

She knitted her brows and was silent a moment:

"They're not there till they're finished," she said.

"It is a pity the little sillies can't speak till they've forgotten everything they had to tell!" I remarked.

"Little Tolma, the last before this baby, looked as if she had something to tell, when I found her under a beech-tree, sucking her thumb, but she hadn't. She only looked up at me—oh, so sweetly! SHE will never go bad and grow big! When they begin to grow big they care for nothing but bigness; and when they cannot grow any bigger, they try to grow fatter. The bad giants are very proud of being fat."

"So they are in my world," I said; "only they do not say FAT there, they say RICH."

"In one of their houses," continued Lona, "sits the biggest and fattest of them—so proud that nobody can see him; and the giants go to his house at certain times, and call out to him, and tell him how fat he is, and beg him to make them strong to eat more and grow fat like him."

The rumour at length reached my ears that Blunty had vanished. I saw a few grave faces among the bigger ones, but he did not seem to be much missed.

The next morning Lona came to me and whispered,

"Look! look there—by that quince-tree: that is the giant that was Blunty!—Would you have known him?"

"Never," I answered. "—But now you tell me, I could fancy it might be Blunty staring through a fog! He DOES look stupid!"

"He is for ever eating those apples now!" she said. "That is what comes of Little Ones that WON'T be little!"

"They call it growing-up in my world!" I said to myself. "If only she would teach me to grow the other way, and become a Little One!—Shall I ever be able to laugh like them?"

I had had the chance, and had flung it from me! Blunty and I were alike! He did not know his loss, and I had to be taught mine!

CHAPTER XIV. A CRISIS

For a time I had no desire save to spend my life with the Little Ones. But soon other thoughts and feelings began to influence me. First awoke the vague sense that I ought to be doing something; that I was not meant for the fattening of boors! Then it came to me that I was in a marvellous world, of which it was assuredly my business to discover the ways and laws; and that, if I would do anything in return for the children's goodness, I must learn more about them than they could tell me, and to that end must be free. Surely, I thought, no suppression of their growth can be essential to their loveliness and truth and purity! Not in any world could the possibility exist of such a discord between constitution and its natural outcome! Life and law cannot be so at variance that perfection must be gained by thwarting development! But the growth of the Little Ones WAS arrested! something interfered with it: what was it? Lona seemed the eldest of them, yet not more than fifteen, and had been long in charge of a multitude, in semblance and mostly in behaviour merest children, who regarded her as their mother! Were they growing at all? I doubted it. Of time they had scarcely the idea; of their own age they knew nothing! Lona herself thought she had lived always! Full of wisdom and empty of knowledge, she was at once their Love and their Law! But what seemed to me her ignorance might in truth be my own lack of insight! Her one anxiety plainly was, that her Little Ones should not grow, and change into bad giants! Their "good giant" was bound to do his best for them: without more knowledge of their nature, and some knowledge of their history, he could do nothing, and must therefore leave them! They would only be as they were before; they had in no way become dependent on me; they were still my protectors, I was not theirs; my presence but brought them more in danger of their idiotic neighbours! I longed to teach them many things: I must first understand more of those I would teach! Knowledge no doubt made bad people worse, but it must make good people better! I was convinced they would learn mathematics; and might they not be taught to write down the dainty melodies they murmured and forgot?

The conclusion was, that I must rise and continue my travels, in the hope of coming upon some elucidation of the fortunes and destiny of the bewitching little creatures.

My design, however, would not so soon have passed into action, but for what now occurred.

To prepare them for my temporary absence, I was one day telling them while at work that I would long ago have left the bad giants, but that I loved the Little Ones so much—when, as by one accord, they came rushing and crowding upon me; they scrambled over each other and up the tree and dropped on my head, until I was nearly smothered. With three very little ones in my arms, one on each shoulder clinging to my neck, one standing straight up on my head, four or five holding me fast by the legs, others grappling my body and arms, and a multitude climbing and descending upon these, I was helpless as one overwhelmed by lava. Absorbed in the merry struggle, not one of them saw my tyrant coming until he was almost upon me. With just one cry of "Take care, good giant!" they ran from me like mice, they dropped from me like hedgehogs, they flew from me up the tree like squirrels, and the same moment, sharp round the stem came the bad giant, and dealt me such a blow on the head with a stick that I fell to the ground. The children told me afterwards that they sent him "such a many bumps of big apples and stones" that he was frightened, and ran blundering home.

When I came to myself it was night. Above me were a few pale stars that expected the moon. I thought I was alone. My head ached badly, and I was terribly athirst.

I turned wearily on my side. The moment my ear touched the ground, I heard the gushing and gurgling of water, and the soft noises made me groan with longing. At once I was amid a multitude of silent children, and delicious little fruits began to visit my lips. They came and came until my thirst was gone.

Then I was aware of sounds I had never heard there before; the air was full of little sobs.

I tried to sit up. A pile of small bodies instantly heaped itself at my back. Then I struggled to my feet, with much pushing and pulling from the Little Ones, who were wonderfully strong for their size.

"You must go away, good giant," they said. "When the bad giants see you hurt, they will all trample on you."

"I think I must," I answered.

"Go and grow strong, and come again," they said.

"I will," I replied—and sat down.

"Indeed you must go at once!" whispered Lona, who had been supporting me, and now knelt beside me.

"I listened at his door," said one of the bigger boys, "and heard the bad giant say to his wife that he had found you idle, talking to a lot of moles and squirrels, and when he beat you, they tried to kill him. He said you were a wizard, and they must knock you, or they would have no peace."

"I will go at once," I said, "and come back as soon as I have found out what is wanted to make you bigger and stronger."

GEORGE MACDONALD

"We don't want to be bigger," they answered, looking very serious. "We WON'T grow bad giants!—We are strong now; you don't know how much strong!"

It was no use holding them out a prospect that had not any attraction for them! I said nothing more, but rose and moved slowly up the slope of the valley. At once they formed themselves into a long procession; some led the way, some walked with me helping me, and the rest followed. They kept feeding me as we went.

"You are broken," they said, "and much red juice has run out of you: put some in."

When we reached the edge of the valley, there was the moon just lifting her forehead over the rim of the horizon.

"She has come to take care of you, and show you the way," said Lona.

I questioned those about me as we walked, and learned there was a great place with a giant-girl for queen. When I asked if it was a city, they said they did not know. Neither could they tell how far off, or in what direction it was, or what was the giant-girl's name; all they knew was, that she hated the Little Ones, and would like to kill them, only she could not find them. I asked how they knew that; Lona answered that she had always known it. If the giant-girl came to look for them, they must hide hard, she said. When I told them I should go and ask her why she hated them, they cried out,

"No, no! she will kill you, good giant; she will kill you! She is an awful bad-giant witch!"

I asked them where I was to go then. They told me that, beyond the baby-forest, away where the moon came from, lay a smooth green country, pleasant to the feet, without rocks or trees. But when I asked how I was to set out for it.

"The moon will tell you, we think," they said.

They were taking me up the second branch of the river bed: when they saw that the moon had reached her height, they stopped to return.

"We have never gone so far from our trees before," they said. "Now mind you watch how you go, that you may see inside your eyes how to come back to us."

"And beware of the giant-woman that lives in the desert," said one of the bigger girls as they were turning, "I suppose you have heard of her!"

"No," I answered.

"Then take care not to go near her. She is called the Cat-woman. She is awfully ugly—AND SCRATCHES."

As soon as the bigger ones stopped, the smaller had begun to run back. The others now looked at me gravely for a moment, and then walked slowly away. Last to leave me, Lona held up the baby to be kissed, gazed in my eyes, whispered, "The Cat-woman will not hurt YOU," and went without another word. I stood a while, gazing after them through the moonlight, then turned and, with a heavy heart, began my solitary journey. Soon the laughter of the Little Ones overtook me, like sheep-bells innumerable, rippling the air, and echoing in the rocks about me. I turned again, and again gazed after them: they went gamboling along, with never a care in their sweet souls. But Lona walked apart with her baby.

Pondering as I went, I recalled many traits of my little friends.

Once when I suggested that they should leave the country of the bad giants, and go with me to find another, they answered, "But that would be to NOT ourselves!"—so strong in them was the love of place that their country seemed essential to their very being! Without ambition or fear, discomfort or greed, they had no motive to desire any change; they knew of nothing amiss; and, except their babies, they had never had a chance of helping any one but myself:—How were they to grow? But again, Why should they grow? In seeking to improve their conditions, might I not do them harm, and only harm? To enlarge their minds after the notions of my world—might it not be to distort and weaken them? Their fear of growth as a possible start for gianthood might be instinctive!

The part of philanthropist is indeed a dangerous one; and the man who would do his neighbour good must first study how not to do him evil, and must begin by pulling the beam out of his own eye.

CHAPTER XV. A STRANGE HOSTESS

I travelled on attended by the moon. As usual she was full—I had never seen her other—and to-night as she sank I thought I perceived something like a smile on her countenance.

When her under edge was a little below the horizon, there appeared in the middle of her disc, as if it had been painted upon it, a cottage, through the open door and window of which she shone; and with the sight came the conviction that I was expected there. Almost immediately the moon was gone, and the cottage had vanished; the night was rapidly growing dark, and my way being across a close succession of small ravines, I resolved to remain where I was and expect the morning. I stretched myself, therefore, in a sandy hollow, made my supper off the fruits the children had given me at parting, and was soon asleep.

I woke suddenly, saw above me constellations unknown to my former world, and had lain for a while gazing at them, when I became aware of a figure seated on the ground a little way from and above me. I was startled, as one is on discovering all at once that he is not alone. The figure was between me and the sky, so that I saw its outline well. From where I lay low in the hollow, it seemed larger than human.

It moved its head, and then first I saw that its back was toward me.

"Will you not come with me?" said a sweet, mellow voice, unmistakably a woman's.

Wishing to learn more of my hostess,

"I thank you," I replied, "but I am not uncomfortable here. Where would you have me go? I like sleeping in the open air."

"There is no hurt in the air," she returned; "but the creatures that roam the night in these parts are not such as a man would willingly have about him while he sleeps."

"I have not been disturbed," I said.

"No; I have been sitting by you ever since you lay down."

"That is very kind of you! How came you to know I was here? Why do you show me such favour?"

"I saw you," she answered, still with her back to me, "in the light of the moon, just as she went down. I see badly in the day, but at night perfectly. The shadow of my house would have hidden you, but both its doors were open. I was out on the waste, and saw you go into this hollow. You were asleep, however, before I could reach you, and I was not willing to disturb you. People are frightened if I come on them suddenly. They call me the Cat-woman. It is not my name."

I remembered what the children had told me—that she was very ugly, and scratched. But her voice was gentle, and its tone a little apologetic: she could not be a bad giantess!

"You shall not hear it from me," I answered, "Please tell me what I MAY call you!"

"When you know me, call me by the name that seems to you to fit me," she replied: "that will tell me what sort you are. People do not often give me the right one. It is well when they do."

"I suppose, madam, you live in the cottage I saw in the heart of the moon?"

"I do. I live there alone, except when I have visitors. It is a poor place, but I do what I can for my guests, and sometimes their sleep is sweet to them."

Her voice entered into me, and made me feel strangely still.

"I will go with you, madam," I said, rising.

She rose at once, and without a glance behind her led the way. I could see her just well enough to follow. She was taller than myself, but not so tall as I had thought her. That she never turned her face to me made me curious—nowise apprehensive, her voice rang so true. But how was I to fit her with a name who could not see her? I strove to get alongside of her, but failed: when I quickened my pace she quickened hers, and kept easily ahead of me. At length I did begin to grow a little afraid. Why was she so careful not to be seen? Extraordinary ugliness would account for it: she might fear terrifying me! Horror of an inconceivable monstrosity began to assail me: was I following through the dark an unheard of hideousness? Almost I repented of having accepted her hospitality.

Neither spoke, and the silence grew unbearable. I MUST break it!

"I want to find my way," I said, "to a place I have heard of, but whose name I have not yet learned. Perhaps you can tell it me!"

"Describe it, then, and I will direct you. The stupid Bags know nothing, and the careless little Lovers forget almost everything."

"Where do those live?"

"You are just come from them!"

"I never heard those names before!"

"You would not hear them. Neither people knows its own name!"

"Strange!"

"Perhaps so! but hardly any one anywhere knows his own name! It would make many a fine gentleman stare to hear himself addressed by what is really his name!"

I held my peace, beginning to wonder what my name might be.

"What now do you fancy yours?" she went on, as if aware of my thought. "But, pardon me, it is a matter of no consequence."

I had actually opened my mouth to answer her, when I discovered that my name was gone from me. I could not even recall the first letter of it! This was the second time I had been asked my name and could not tell it!

"Never mind," she said; "it is not wanted. Your real name, indeed, is written on your forehead, but at present it whirls about so irregularly that nobody can read it. I will do my part to steady it. Soon it will go slower, and, I hope, settle at last."

This startled me, and I was silent.

We had left the channels and walked a long time, but no sign of the cottage yet appeared.

"The Little Ones told me," I said at length, "of a smooth green country, pleasant to the feet!"

"Yes?" she returned.

"They told me too of a girl giantess that was queen somewhere: is that her country?"

"There is a city in that grassy land," she replied, "where a woman is princess. The city is called Bulika. But certainly the princess is not a girl! She is older than this world, and came to it from yours—with a terrible history, which is not over yet. She is an evil person, and prevails much with the Prince of the Power of the Air. The people of Bulika were formerly simple folk, tilling the ground and pasturing sheep. She came among them, and they received her hospitably. She taught them to dig for diamonds and opals and sell them to strangers, and made them give up tillage and pasturage and build a city. One day they found a huge snake and killed it; which so enraged her that she declared herself their princess, and became terrible to them. The name of the country at that time was THE LAND OF WATERS; for the dry channels, of which you have crossed so many, were then overflowing with live torrents; and the valley, where now the Bags and the Lovers have their fruit-trees, was a lake that received a great part of them. But the wicked princess gathered up in her lap what she could of the water over the whole country, closed it in an egg, and carried it away. Her lap, however, would not hold more than half of it; and the instant she was gone, what she had not yet taken fled away underground, leaving the country as dry and dusty as her own heart. Were it not for the waters under it, every living thing would long ago have perished from it. For where no water is, no rain falls; and where no rain falls, no springs rise. Ever since then, the princess has lived in Bulika, holding the inhabitants in constant terror, and doing what she can to keep them from multiplying. Yet they boast and believe themselves a prosperous, and certainly are a self-satisfied people—good at bargaining and buying, good at selling and cheating; holding well together for a common interest, and utterly treacherous where interests clash; proud of their princess and her power, and despising every one they get the better of; never doubting themselves the most honourable of all the nations, and each man counting himself better than any other. The depth of their worthlessness and height of their vainglory no one can understand who has not been there to see, who has not learned to know the miserable misgoverned and self-deceived creatures."

"I thank you, madam. And now, if you please, will you tell me something about the Little Ones—the Lovers? I long heartily to serve them. Who and what are they? and how do they come to be there? Those children are the greatest wonder I have found in this world of wonders."

"In Bulika you may, perhaps, get some light on those matters. There is an ancient poem in the library of the palace, I am told, which of course no one there

LILITH

can read, but in which it is plainly written that after the Lovers have gone through great troubles and learned their own name, they will fill the land, and make the giants their slaves."

"By that time they will have grown a little, will they not?" I said.

"Yes, they will have grown; yet I think too they will not have grown. It is possible to grow and not to grow, to grow less and to grow bigger, both at once— yes, even to grow by means of not growing!"

"Your words are strange, madam!" I rejoined. "But I have heard it said that some words, because they mean more, appear to mean less!"

"That is true, and such words HAVE to be understood. It were well for the princess of Bulika if she heard what the very silence of the land is shouting in her ears all day long! But she is far too clever to understand anything."

"Then I suppose, when the little Lovers are grown, their land will have water again?"

"Not exactly so: when they are thirsty enough, they will have water, and when they have water, they will grow. To grow, they must have water. And, beneath, it is flowing still."

"I have heard that water twice," I said; "—once when I lay down to wait for the moon—and when I woke the sun was shining! and once when I fell, all but killed by the bad giant. Both times came the voices of the water, and healed me."

The woman never turned her head, and kept always a little before me, but I could hear every word that left her lips, and her voice much reminded me of the woman's in the house of death. Much of what she said, I did not understand, and therefore cannot remember. But I forgot that I had ever been afraid of her.

We went on and on, and crossed yet a wide tract of sand before reaching the cottage. Its foundation stood in deep sand, but I could see that it was a rock. In character the cottage resembled the sexton's, but had thicker walls. The door, which was heavy and strong, opened immediately into a large bare room, which had two little windows opposite each other, without glass. My hostess walked in at the open door out of which the moon had looked, and going straight to the farthest corner, took a long white cloth from the floor, and wound it about her head and face. Then she closed the other door, in at which the moon had looked, trimmed a small horn lantern that stood on the hearth, and turned to receive me.

"You are very welcome, Mr. Vane!" she said, calling me by the name I had forgotten. "Your entertainment will be scanty, but, as the night is not far spent, and the day not at hand, it is better you should be indoors. Here you will be safe, and a little lack is not a great misery."

"I thank you heartily, madam," I replied. "But, seeing you know the name I could not tell you, may I not now know yours?"

"My name is Mara," she answered.

Then I remembered the sexton and the little black cat.

"Some people," she went on, "take me for Lot's wife, lamenting over Sodom; and some think I am Rachel, weeping for her children; but I am neither of those."

"I thank you again, Mara," I said. "—May I lie here on your floor till the morning?"

"At the top of that stair," she answered, "you will find a bed—on which some have slept better than they expected, and some have waked all the night and slept all the next day. It is not a very soft one, but it is better than the sand—and there are no hyenas sniffing about it!"

The stair, narrow and steep, led straight up from the room to an unceiled and unpartitioned garret, with one wide, low dormer window. Close under the sloping roof stood a narrow bed, the sight of which with its white coverlet made me shiver, so vividly it recalled the couches in the chamber of death. On the table was a dry loaf, and beside it a cup of cold water. To me, who had tasted nothing but fruit for months, they were a feast.

"I must leave you in the dark," my hostess called from the bottom of the stair. "This lantern is all the light I have, and there are things to do to-night."

"It is of no consequence, thank you, madam," I returned. "To eat and drink, to lie down and sleep, are things that can be done in the dark."

"Rest in peace," she said.

I ate up the loaf, drank the water every drop, and laid myself down. The bed was hard, the covering thin and scanty, and the night cold: I dreamed that I lay in the chamber of death, between the warrior and the lady with the healing wound.

I woke in the middle of the night, thinking I heard low noises of wild animals.

"Creatures of the desert scenting after me, I suppose!" I said to myself, and, knowing I was safe, would have gone to sleep again. But that instant a rough purring rose to a howl under my window, and I sprang from my bed to see what sort of beast uttered it.

Before the door of the cottage, in the full radiance of the moon, a tall woman stood, clothed in white, with her back toward me. She was stooping over a large white animal like a panther, patting and stroking it with one hand, while with the other she pointed to the moon half-way up the heaven, then drew a perpendicular line to the horizon. Instantly the creature darted off with amazing swiftness in the direction indicated. For a moment my eyes followed it, then sought the woman; but she was gone, and not yet had I seen her face! Again I looked after the animal, but whether I saw or only fancied a white speck in the distance, I could not tell.—What did it mean? What was the monster-cat sent off to do? I shuddered, and went back to my bed. Then I remembered that, when I lay down in the sandy hollow outside, the moon was setting; yet here she was, a few hours after, shining in all her glory! "Everything is uncertain here," I said to myself, "—even the motions of the heavenly bodies!"

I learned afterward that there were several moons in the service of this world, but the laws that ruled their times and different orbits I failed to discover.

Again I fell asleep, and slept undisturbed.

When I went down in the morning, I found bread and water waiting me, the loaf so large that I ate only half of it. My hostess sat muffled beside me while I broke my fast, and except to greet me when I entered, never opened her mouth until I asked her to instruct me how to arrive at Bulika. She then told me to go up the bank of the river-bed until it disappeared; then verge to the right until I came to a forest—in which I might spend a night, but which I must leave with my face to the rising moon. Keeping in the same direction, she said, until I reached a running stream, I must cross that at right angles, and go straight on until I saw the city on the horizon.

I thanked her, and ventured the remark that, looking out of the window in the night, I was astonished to see her messenger understand her so well, and go so straight and so fast in the direction she had indicated.

"If I had but that animal of yours to guide me—" I went on, hoping to learn something of its mission, but she interrupted me, saying,

"It was to Bulika she went—the shortest way."

"How wonderfully intelligent she looked!"

"Astarte knows her work well enough to be sent to do it," she answered.

"Have you many messengers like her?"

"As many as I require."

"Are they hard to teach?"

"They need no teaching. They are all of a certain breed, but not one of the breed is like another. Their origin is so natural it would seem to you incredible."

"May I not know it?"

"A new one came to me last night—from your head while you slept."

I laughed.

"All in this world seem to love mystery!" I said to myself. "Some chance word of mine suggested an idea—and in this form she embodies the small fact!"

"Then the creature is mine!" I cried.

"Not at all!" she answered. "That only can be ours in whose existence our will is a factor."

"Ha! a metaphysician too!" I remarked inside, and was silent.

"May I take what is left of the loaf?" I asked presently.

"You will want no more to-day," she replied.

"To-morrow I may!" I rejoined.

She rose and went to the door, saying as she went,

"It has nothing to do with to-morrow—but you may take it if you will."

She opened the door, and stood holding it. I rose, taking up the bread—but lingered, much desiring to see her face.

"Must I go, then?" I asked.

"No one sleeps in my house two nights together!" she answered.

"I thank you, then, for your hospitality, and bid you farewell!" I said, and turned to go.

"The time will come when you must house with me many days and many nights," she murmured sadly through her muffling.

"Willingly," I replied.

"Nay, NOT willingly!" she answered.

I said to myself that she was right—I would not willingly be her guest a second time! but immediately my heart rebuked me, and I had scarce crossed the threshold when I turned again.

She stood in the middle of the room; her white garments lay like foamy waves at her feet, and among them the swathings of her face: it was lovely as a night of stars. Her great gray eyes looked up to heaven; tears were flowing down her pale cheeks. She reminded me not a little of the sexton's wife, although the one looked as if she had not wept for thousands of years, and the other as if she wept constantly behind the wrappings of her beautiful head. Yet something in the very eyes that wept seemed to say, "Weeping may endure for a night, but joy cometh in the morning."

I had bowed my head for a moment, about to kneel and beg her forgiveness, when, looking up in the act, I found myself outside a doorless house. I went round and round it, but could find no entrance.

I had stopped under one of the windows, on the point of calling aloud my repentant confession, when a sudden wailing, howling scream invaded my ears, and my heart stood still. Something sprang from the window above my head, and lighted beyond me. I turned, and saw a large gray cat, its hair on end, shooting toward the river-bed. I fell with my face in the sand, and seemed to hear within the house the gentle sobbing of one who suffered but did not repent.

CHAPTER XVI. A GRUESOME DANCE

I rose to resume my journey, and walked many a desert mile. How I longed for a mountain, or even a tall rock, from whose summit I might see across the dismal plain or the dried-up channels to some bordering hope! Yet what could such fore-sight have availed me? That which is within a man, not that which lies beyond his vision, is the main factor in what is about to befall him: the operation upon him is the event. Foreseeing is not understanding, else surely the prophecy latent in man would come oftener to the surface!

The sun was half-way to the horizon when I saw before me a rugged rocky ascent; but ere I reached it my desire to climb was over, and I longed to lie down. By that time the sun was almost set, and the air had begun to grow dark. At my feet lay a carpet of softest, greenest moss, couch for a king: I threw myself upon it, and weariness at once began to ebb, for, the moment my head was down, the third time I heard below me many waters, playing broken airs and ethereal harmonies with the stones of their buried channels. Loveliest chaos of music-stuff the harp aquarian kept sending up to my ears! What might not a Händel have done with that ever-recurring gurgle and bell-like drip, to the mingling and mutually destructive melodies their common refrain!

As I lay listening, my eyes went wandering up and down the rocky slope abrupt above me, reading on its face the record that down there, ages ago, rushed a cataract, filling the channels that had led me to its foot. My heart swelled at the thought of the splendid tumult, where the waves danced revelling in helpless fall, to mass their music in one organ-roar below. But soon the hidden brooks lulled me to sleep, and their lullabies mingled with my dreams.

I woke before the sun, and eagerly climbed to see what lay beyond. Alas, nothing but a desert of finest sand! Not a trace was left of the river that had plunged adown the rocks! The powdery drift had filled its course to the level of the dreary expanse! As I looked back I saw that the river had divided into two branches as it fell, that whose bank I had now followed to the foot of the rocky scaur, and that which first I crossed to the Evil Wood. The wood I descried between the two on the far horizon. Before me and to the left, the desert stretched beyond my vision, but far to the right I could see a lift in the sky-line, giving hope of the forest to which my hostess had directed me.

I sat down, and sought in my pocket the half-loaf I had brought with me—then first to understand what my hostess had meant concerning it. Verily the bread was not for the morrow: it had shrunk and hardened to a stone! I threw it away, and set out again.

About noon I came to a few tamarisk and juniper trees, and then to a few stunted firs. As I went on, closer thickets and larger firs met me, and at length I was in just such a forest of pines and other trees as that in which the Little Ones found their babies, and believed I had returned upon a farther portion of the same. But what mattered WHERE while EVERYWHERE was the same as NOWHERE! I had not yet, by doing something in it, made ANYWHERE into a place! I was not yet alive; I was only dreaming I lived! I was but a consciousness with an outlook! Truly I had been nothing else in the world I had left, but now I knew the fact! I said to myself that if in this forest I should catch the faint gleam of the mirror, I would turn far aside lest it should entrap me unawares, and give me back to my old existence: here I might learn to be something by doing something! I could not endure the thought of going back, with so many beginnings and not an end achieved. The Little Ones would meet what fate was appointed them; the awful witch I should never meet; the dead would ripen and arise without me; I should but wake to know that I had dreamed, and that all my going was nowhither! I would rather go on and on than come to such a close!

I went deeper into the wood: I was weary, and would rest in it.

The trees were now large, and stood in regular, almost geometric, fashion, with roomy spaces between. There was little undergrowth, and I could see a long way in every direction. The forest was like a great church, solemn and silent and empty, for I met nothing on two feet or four that day. Now and then, it is true, some swift thing, and again some slow thing, would cross the space on which my eye happened that moment to settle; but it was always at some distance, and only enhanced the sense of wideness and vacancy. I heard a few birds, and saw plenty of butterflies, some of marvellously gorgeous colouring and combinations of colour, some of a pure and dazzling whiteness.

Coming to a spot where the pines stood farther apart and gave room for flowering shrubs, and hoping it a sign of some dwelling near, I took the direction where yet more and more roses grew, for I was hungry after the voice and face of my kind —after any live soul, indeed, human or not, which I might in some measure understand. What a hell of horror, I thought, to wander alone, a bare existence never going out of itself, never widening its life in another life, but, bound with the cords of its poor peculiarities, lying an eternal prisoner in the dungeon of its own being! I began to learn that it was impossible to live for oneself even, save in the presence of others—then, alas, fearfully possible! evil was only through good! selfishness but a parasite on the tree of life! In my own world I had the habit of solitary song; here not a crooning murmur ever parted my lips! There I sang without thinking; here I thought without singing! there I had never had a bosom-friend; here the affection of an idiot would be divinely welcome! "If only I had a dog to love!" I sighed—and regarded with wonder my past self, which preferred the company of book or pen to that of man or woman; which, if the author of a tale I was enjoying appeared, would wish him away that I might return to his story. I had chosen the dead rather than the living, the thing thought rather than the thing thinking! "Any man," I said now, "is more than the greatest of books!" I had not cared for my live brothers and sisters, and now I was left without even the dead to comfort me!

The wood thinned yet more, and the pines grew yet larger, sending up huge stems, like columns eager to support the heavens. More trees of other kinds appeared; the forest was growing richer! The roses wore now trees, and their flowers of astonishing splendour.

Suddenly I spied what seemed a great house or castle; but its forms were so strangely indistinct, that I could not be certain it was more than a chance combination of tree-shapes. As I drew nearer, its lines yet held together, but neither they nor the body of it grew at all more definite; and when at length I stood in front of it, I remained as doubtful of its nature as before. House or castle habitable, it certainly was not; it might be a ruin overgrown with ivy and roses! Yet of building hid in the foliage, not the poorest wall-remnant could I discern. Again and again I seemed to descry what must be building, but it always vanished before closer inspection. Could it be, I pondered, that the ivy had embraced a huge edifice and consumed it, and its interlaced branches retained the shapes of the walls it had assimilated?—I could be sure of nothing concerning the appearance.

Before me was a rectangular vacancy—the ghost of a doorway without a door: I stepped through it, and found myself in an open space like a great hall, its floor covered with grass and flowers, its walls and roof of ivy and vine, mingled with roses.

There could be no better place in which to pass the night! I gathered a quantity of withered leaves, laid them in a corner, and threw myself upon them. A red sunset filled the hall, the night was warm, and my couch restful; I lay gazing up at the live ceiling, with its tracery of branches and twigs, its clouds of foliage, and peeping patches of loftier roof. My eyes went wading about as if tangled in it, until the sun was down, and the sky beginning to grow dark. Then the red roses turned black, and soon the yellow and white alone were visible. When they vanished, the stars came instead, hanging in the leaves like live topazes, throbbing and sparkling and flashing many colours: I was canopied with a tree from Aladdin's cave!

Then I discovered that it was full of nests, whence tiny heads, nearly indistinguishable, kept popping out with a chirp or two, and disappearing again. For a while there were rustlings and stirrings and little prayers; but as the darkness grew, the small heads became still, and at last every feathered mother had her brood quiet under her wings, the talk in the little beds was over, and God's bird-nursery at rest beneath the waves of sleep. Once more a few flutterings made me look up: an owl went sailing across. I had only a glimpse of him, but several times felt the cool wafture of his silent wings. The mother birds did not move again; they saw that he was looking for mice, not children.

About midnight I came wide awake, roused by a revelry, whose noises were yet not loud. Neither were they distant; they were close to me, but attenuate. My eyes were so dazzled, however, that for a while I could see nothing; at last they came to themselves.

I was lying on my withered leaves in the corner of a splendid hall. Before me was a crowd of gorgeously dressed men and gracefully robed women, none of whom seemed to see me. In dance after dance they vaguely embodied the story of life, its meetings, its passions, its partings. A student of Shakspere, I had learned something of every dance alluded to in his plays, and hence partially understood several of those I now saw—the minuet, the pavin, the hey, the coranto, the lavolta. The dancers were attired in fashion as ancient as their dances.

A moon had risen while I slept, and was shining through the countless-windowed roof; but her light was crossed by so many shadows that at first I could distinguish almost nothing of the faces of the multitude; I could not fail, however, to perceive that there was something odd about them: I sat up to see them better.—Heavens! could I call them faces? They were skull fronts!—hard, gleaming bone, bare jaws, truncated noses, lipless teeth which could no more take part in any smile! Of these, some flashed set and white and murderous; others were clouded with decay, broken and gapped, coloured of the earth in which they seemed so long to have lain! Fearfuller yet, the eye-sockets were not empty; in each was a lidless living eye! In those wrecks of faces, glowed or flashed or sparkled eyes of every colour, shape, and expression. The beautiful, proud eye, dark and lustrous, condescending to whatever it rested upon, was the more terrible; the lovely, languishing eye, the more repulsive; while the dim, sad eyes, less at variance with their setting, were sad exceedingly, and drew the heart in spite of the horror out of which they gazed.

I rose and went among the apparitions, eager to understand something of their being and belongings. Were they souls, or were they and their rhythmic motions but phantasms of what had been? By look nor by gesture, not by slightest break in the measure, did they show themselves aware of me; I was not present to them: how much were they in relation to each other? Surely they saw their companions as I saw them! Or was each only dreaming itself and the rest? Did they know each how they appeared to the others—a death with living eyes? Had they used their faces, not for communication, not to utter thought and feeling, not to share existence with their neighbours, but to appear what they wished to appear, and conceal what they were? and, having made their faces masks, were they therefore deprived of those masks, and condemned to go without faces until they repented?

"How long must they flaunt their facelessness in faceless eyes?" I wondered. "How long will the frightful punition endure? Have they at length begun to love and be wise? Have they yet yielded to the shame that has found them?"

I heard not a word, saw not a movement of one naked mouth. Were they because of lying bereft of speech? With their eyes they spoke as if longing to be understood: was it truth or was it falsehood that spoke in their eyes? They seemed to know one another: did they see one skull beautiful, and another plain? Difference must be there, and they had had long study of skulls!

My body was to theirs no obstacle: was I a body, and were they but forms? or was I but a form, and were they bodies? The moment one of the dancers came close against me, that moment he or she was on the other side of me, and I could tell, without seeing, which, whether man or woman, had passed through my house.

On many of the skulls the hair held its place, and however dressed, or in itself however beautiful, to my eyes looked frightful on the bones of the forehead and temples. In such case, the outer ear often remained also, and at its tip, the jewel of the ear as Sidney calls it, would hang, glimmering, gleaming, or sparkling, pearl or opal or diamond—under the night of brown or of raven locks, the sunrise of golden ripples, or the moonshine of pale, interclouded, fluffy cirri—lichenous all on the ivory-white or damp-yellow naked bone. I looked down and saw the daintily domed instep; I looked up and saw the plump shoulders basing the spring of the round full neck—which withered at half-height to the fluted shaft of a gibbose cranium.

The music became wilder, the dance faster and faster; eyes flared and flashed, jewels twinkled and glittered, casting colour and fire on the pallid grins that glode through the hall, weaving a ghastly rhythmic woof in intricate maze of multitudinous motion, when sudden came a pause, and every eye turned to the same spot:— in the doorway stood a woman, perfect in form, in holding, and in hue, regarding the company as from the pedestal of a goddess, while the dancers stood "like one forbid," frozen to a new death by the vision of a life that killed. "Dead things, I live!" said her scornful glance. Then, at once, like leaves in which an instant wind awakes, they turned each to another, and broke afresh into melodious consorted motion, a new expression in their eyes, late solitary, now filled with the interchange of a common triumph. "Thou also," they seemed to say, "wilt soon become weak as we! thou wilt soon become like unto us!" I turned mine again to the woman—and saw upon her side a small dark shadow.

She had seen the change in the dead stare; she looked down; she understood the talking eyes; she pressed both her lovely hands on the shadow, gave a smothered cry, and fled. The birds moved rustling in their nests, and a flash of joy lit up the eyes of the dancers, when suddenly a warm wind, growing in strength as it swept through the place, blew out every light. But the low moon yet glimmered on the horizon with "sick assay" to shine, and a turbid radiance yet gleamed from so many eyes, that I saw well enough what followed. As if each shape had been but a snow-image, it began to fall to pieces, ruining in the warm wind. In papery flakes the flesh peeled from its bones, dropping like soiled snow from under its garments; these fell fluttering in rags and strips, and the whole white skeleton, emerging from garment and flesh together, stood bare and lank amid the decay that littered the floor. A faint rattling shiver went through the naked company; pair after pair the lamping eyes went out; and the darkness grew round me with the loneliness. For a moment the leaves were still swept fluttering all one way; then the wind ceased, and the owl floated silent through the silent night.

Not for a moment had I been afraid. It is true that whoever would cross the threshold of any world, must leave fear behind him; but, for myself, I could claim no part in its absence. No conscious courage was operant in me; simply, I was not afraid. I neither knew why I was not afraid, nor wherefore I might have been afraid. I feared not even fear—which of all dangers is the most dangerous.

I went out into the wood, at once to resume my journey. Another moon was rising, and I turned my face toward it.

CHAPTER XVII. A GROTESQUE TRAGEDY

I had not gone ten paces when I caught sight of a strange-looking object, and went nearer to know what it might be. I found it a mouldering carriage of ancient form, ruinous but still upright on its heavy wheels. On each side of the pole, still in its place, lay the skeleton of a horse; from their two grim white heads ascended the shrivelled reins to the hand of the skeleton-coachman seated on his tattered hammer-cloth; both doors had fallen away; within sat two skeletons, each leaning back in its corner.

Even as I looked, they started awake, and with a cracking rattle of bones, each leaped from the door next it. One fell and lay; the other stood a moment, its structure shaking perilously; then with difficulty, for its joints were stiff, crept, holding by the back of the carriage, to the opposite side, the thin leg-bones seeming hardly strong enough to carry its weight, where, kneeling by the other, it sought to raise it, almost falling itself again in the endeavour.

The prostrate one rose at length, as by a sudden effort, to the sitting posture. For a few moments it turned its yellowish skull to this side and that; then, heedless of its neighbour, got upon its feet by grasping the spokes of the hind wheel. Half erected thus, it stood with its back to the other, both hands holding one of its knee-joints. With little less difficulty and not a few contortions, the kneeling one rose next, and addressed its companion.

"Have you hurt yourself, my lord?" it said, in a voice that sounded far-off, and ill-articulated as if blown aside by some spectral wind.

"Yes, I have," answered the other, in like but rougher tone. "You would do nothing to help me, and this cursed knee is out!"

"I did my best, my lord."

"No doubt, my lady, for it was bad! I thought I should never find my feet again! —But, bless my soul, madam! are you out in your bones?"

She cast a look at herself.

"I have nothing else to be out in," she returned; "—and YOU at least cannot complain! But what on earth does it mean? Am I dreaming?"

"YOU may be dreaming, madam—I cannot tell; but this knee of mine forbids me the grateful illusion.—Ha! I too, I perceive, have nothing to walk in but bones! —Not so unbecoming to a man, however! I trust to goodness they are not MY bones! every one aches worse than another, and this loose knee worst of all! The bed must have been damp—and I too drunk to know it!"

"Probably, my lord of Cokayne!"

"What! what!—You make me think I too am dreaming—aches and all! How do YOU know the title my roistering bullies give me? I don't remember you!— Anyhow, you have no right to take liberties! My name is—I am lord——tut, tut! What do you call me when I'm—I mean when you are sober? I cannot—at the moment,—Why, what IS my name?—I must have been VERY drunk when I went to bed! I often am!"

"You come so seldom to mine, that I do not know, my lord; but I may take your word for THAT!"

"I hope so!"

"—if for nothing else!" "Hoity toity! I never told you a lie in my life!"

"You never told me anything but lies."

"Upon my honour!—Why, I never saw the woman before!"

"You knew me well enough to lie to, my lord!"

"I do seem to begin to dream I have met you before, but, upon my oath, there is nothing to know you by! Out of your clothes, who is to tell who you may not be?— One thing I MAY swear—that I never saw you so much undressed before!—By heaven, I have no recollection of you!"

"I am glad to hear it: my recollections of you are the less distasteful!—Good morning, my lord!"

She turned away, hobbled, clacking, a few paces, and stood again.

"You are just as heartless as—as—any other woman, madam!—Where in this hell of a place shall I find my valet?—What was the cursed name I used to call the fool?"

He turned his bare noddle this way and that on its creaking pivot, still holding his knee with both hands.

"I will be your valet for once, my lord," said the lady, turning once more to him. "—What can I do for you? It is not easy to tell!"

"Tie my leg on, of course, you fool! Can't you see it is all but off? Heigho, my dancing days!"

She looked about with her eyeless sockets and found a piece of fibrous grass, with which she proceeded to bind together the adjoining parts that had formed the knee. When she had done, he gave one or two carefully tentative stamps.

"You used to stamp rather differently, my lord!" she said, as she rose from her knees.

"Eh? what!—Now I look at you again, it seems to me I used to hate you!—Eh?"

"Naturally, my lord! You hated a good many people!—your wife, of course, among the rest!"

"Ah, I begin, I be-gin—— But—I must have been a long time somewhere! I really forget!—There! your damned, miserable bit of grass is breaking!—We used to get on PRETTY well together—eh?"

"Not that I remember, my lord. The only happy moments I had in your company were scattered over the first week of our marriage."

"Was that the way of it? Ha! ha!—Well, it's over now, thank goodness!"

"I wish I could believe it! Why were we sitting there in that carriage together? It wakes apprehension!"

"I think we were divorced, my lady!"

"Hardly enough: we are still together!"

"A sad truth, but capable of remedy: the forest seems of some extent!"

"I doubt! I doubt!"

"I am sorry I cannot think of a compliment to pay you—without lying, that is. To judge by your figure and complexion you have lived hard since I saw you last! I cannot surely be QUITE so naked as your ladyship!—I beg your pardon, madam! I trust you will take it I am but jesting in a dream! It is of no consequence, however; dreaming or waking, all's one—all merest appearance! You can't be certain of anything, and that's as good as knowing there is nothing! Life may teach any fool that!"

"It has taught me the fool I was to love you!"

"You were not the only fool to do that! Women had a trick of falling in love with me:—I had forgotten that you were one of them!" "I did love you, my lord—a little —at one time!"

"Ah, there was your mistake, my lady! You should have loved me much, loved me devotedly, loved me savagely—loved me eternally! Then I should have tired of you the sooner, and not hated you so much afterward!—But let bygones be bygones!—WHERE are we? Locality is the question! To be or not to be, is NOT the question!"

"We are in the other world, I presume!"

"Granted!—but in which or what sort of other world? This can't be hell!"

"It must: there's marriage in it! You and I are damned in each other."

"Then I'm not like Othello, damned in a fair wife!—Oh, I remember my Shakspeare, madam!"

She picked up a broken branch that had fallen into a bush, and steadying herself with it, walked away, tossing her little skull.

"Give that stick to me," cried her late husband; "I want it more than you."

She returned him no answer.

"You mean to make me beg for it?"

"Not at all, my lord. I mean to keep it," she replied, continuing her slow departure.

"Give it me at once; I mean to have it! I require it."

"Unfortunately, I think I require it myself!" returned the lady, walking a little quicker, with a sharper cracking of her joints and clinking of her bones.

He started to follow her, but nearly fell: his knee-grass had burst, and with an oath he stopped, grasping his leg again.

"Come and tie it up properly!" he would have thundered, but he only piped and whistled!

She turned and looked at him.

"Come and tie it up instantly!" he repeated.

She walked a step or two farther from him.

"I swear I will not touch you!" he cried.

"Swear on, my lord! there is no one here to believe you. But, pray, do not lose your temper, or you will shake yourself to pieces, and where to find string enough to tie up all your crazy joints, is more than I can tell."

She came back, and knelt once more at his side—first, however, laying the stick in dispute beyond his reach and within her own.

The instant she had finished retying the joint, he made a grab at her, thinking, apparently, to seize her by the hair; but his hard fingers slipped on the smooth poll.

"Disgusting!" he muttered, and laid hold of her upper arm-bone.

"You will break it!" she said, looking up from her knees.

"I will, then!" he answered, and began to strain at it.

"I shall not tie your leg again the next time it comes loose!" she threatened.

He gave her arm a vicious twist, but happily her bones were in better condition than his. She stretched her other hand toward the broken branch.

"That's right: reach me the stick!" he grinned.

She brought it round with such a swing that one of the bones of the sounder leg snapped. He fell, choking with curses. The lady laughed.

"Now you will have to wear splints always!" she said; "such dry bones never mend!"

"You devil!" he cried.

"At your service, my lord! Shall I fetch you a couple of wheel-spokes? Neat— but heavy, I fear!"

He turned his bone-face aside, and did not answer, but lay and groaned. I marvelled he had not gone to pieces when he fell. The lady rose and walked away —not all ungracefully, I thought.

"What can come of it?" I said to myself. "These are too wretched for any world, and this cannot be hell, for the Little Ones are in it, and the sleepers too! What can it all mean? Can things ever come right for skeletons?"

"There are words too big for you and me: ALL is one of them, and EVER is another," said a voice near me which I knew.

I looked about, but could not see the speaker.

"You are not in hell," it resumed. "Neither am I in hell. But those skeletons are in hell!"

Ere he ended I caught sight of the raven on the bough of a beech, right over my head. The same moment he left it, and alighting on the ground, stood there, the thin old man of the library, with long nose and long coat.

"The male was never a gentleman," he went on, "and in the bony stage of retrogression, with his skeleton through his skin, and his character outside his manners, does not look like one. The female is less vulgar, and has a little heart. But, the restraints of society removed, you see them now just as they are and always were!"

"Tell me, Mr. Raven, what will become of them," I said.

"We shall see," he replied. "In their day they were the handsomest couple at court; and now, even in their dry bones, they seem to regard their former repute as an inalienable possession; to see their faces, however, may yet do something for them! They felt themselves rich too while they had pockets, but they have already begun to feel rather pinched! My lord used to regard my lady as a worthless encumbrance, for he was tired of her beauty and had spent her money; now he needs her to cobble his joints for him! These changes have roots of hope in them. Besides, they cannot now get far away from each other, and they see none else of their own kind: they must at last grow weary of their mutual repugnance, and begin to love one another! for love, not hate, is deepest in what Love 'loved into being.'"

"I saw many more of their kind an hour ago, in the hall close by!" I said.

"Of their kind, but not of their sort," he answered. "For many years these will see none such as you saw last night. Those are centuries in advance of these. You saw that those could even dress themselves a little! It is true they cannot yet retain their clothes so long as they would—only, at present, for a part of the night; but they are pretty steadily growing more capable, and will by and by develop faces; for every grain of truthfulness adds a fibre to the show of their humanity. Nothing but truth can appear; and whatever is must seem."

"Are they upheld by this hope?" I asked.

"They are upheld by hope, but they do not in the least know their hope; to understand it, is yet immeasurably beyond them," answered Mr. Raven.

His unexpected appearance had caused me no astonishment. I was like a child, constantly wondering, and surprised at nothing.

"Did you come to find me, sir?" I asked.

"Not at all," he replied. "I have no anxiety about you. Such as you always come back to us."

"Tell me, please, who am I such as?" I said.

"I cannot make my friend the subject of conversation," he answered, with a smile.

"But when that friend is present!" I urged.

"I decline the more strongly," he rejoined.

"But when that friend asks you!" I persisted.

"Then most positively I refuse," he returned.

"Why?"

"Because he and I would be talking of two persons as if they were one and the same. Your consciousness of yourself and my knowledge of you are far apart!"

The lapels of his coat flew out, and the lappets lifted, and I thought the metamorphosis of HOMO to CORVUS was about to take place before my eyes. But the coat closed again in front of him, and he added, with seeming inconsequence,

"In this world never trust a person who has once deceived you. Above all, never do anything such a one may ask you to do."

"I will try to remember," I answered; "—but I may forget!"

"Then some evil that is good for you will follow."

"And if I remember?"

"Some evil that is not good for you, will not follow."

The old man seemed to sink to the ground, and immediately I saw the raven several yards from me, flying low and fast.

CHAPTER XVIII. DEAD OR ALIVE?

I went walking on, still facing the moon, who, not yet high, was staring straight into the forest. I did not know what ailed her, but she was dark and dented, like a battered disc of old copper, and looked dispirited and weary. Not a cloud was nigh to keep her company, and the stars were too bright for her. "Is this going to last for ever?" she seemed to say. She was going one way and I was going the other, yet through the wood we went a long way together. We did not commune much, for my eyes were on the ground; but her disconsolate look was fixed on me: I felt without seeing it. A long time we were together, I and the moon, walking side by side, she the dull shine, and I the live shadow.

Something on the ground, under a spreading tree, caught my eye with its whiteness, and I turned toward it. Vague as it was in the shadow of the foliage, it suggested, as I drew nearer, a human body. "Another skeleton!" I said to myself, kneeling and laying my hand upon it. A body it was, however, and no skeleton, though as nearly one as body could well be. It lay on its side, and was very cold— not cold like a stone, but cold like that which was once alive, and is alive no more. The closer I looked at it, the oftener I touched it, the less it seemed possible it should be other than dead. For one bewildered moment, I fancied it one of the wild dancers, a ghostly Cinderella, perhaps, that had lost her way home, and perished in the strange night of an out-of-door world! It was quite naked, and so worn that, even in the shadow, I could, peering close, have counted without touching them, every rib in its side. All its bones, indeed, were as visible as if tight-covered with only a thin elastic leather. Its beautiful yet terrible teeth, unseemly disclosed by the retracted lips, gleamed ghastly through the dark. Its hair was longer than itself, thick and very fine to the touch, and black as night.

It was the body of a tall, probably graceful woman.—How had she come there? Not of herself, and already in such wasted condition, surely! Her strength must have failed her; she had fallen, and lain there until she died of hunger! But how,

643

even so, could she be thus emaciated? And how came she to be naked? Where were the savages to strip and leave her? or what wild beasts would have taken her garments? That her body should have been left was not wonderful!

I rose to my feet, stood, and considered. I must not, could not let her lie exposed and forsaken! Natural reverence forbade it. Even the garment of a woman claims respect; her body it were impossible to leave uncovered! Irreverent eyes might look on it! Brutal claws might toss it about! Years would pass ere the friendly rains washed it into the soil!—But the ground was hard, almost solid with interlacing roots, and I had but my bare hands!

At first it seemed plain that she had not long been dead: there was not a sign of decay about her! But then what had the slow wasting of life left of her to decay?

Could she be still alive? Might she not? What if she were! Things went very strangely in this strange world! Even then there would be little chance of bringing her back, but I must know she was dead before I buried her!

As I left the forest-hall, I had spied in the doorway a bunch of ripe grapes, and brought it with me, eating as I came: a few were yet left on the stalk, and their juice might possibly revive her! Anyhow it was all I had with which to attempt her rescue! The mouth was happily a little open; but the head was in such an awkward position that, to move the body, I passed my arm under the shoulder on which it lay, when I found the pine-needles beneath it warm: she could not have been any time dead, and MIGHT still be alive, though I could discern no motion of the heart, or any indication that she breathed! One of her hands was clenched hard, apparently inclosing something small. I squeezed a grape into her mouth, but no swallowing followed.

To do for her all I could, I spread a thick layer of pine-needles and dry leaves, laid one of my garments over it, warm from my body, lifted her upon it, and covered her with my clothes and a great heap of leaves: I would save the little warmth left in her, hoping an increase to it when the sun came back. Then I tried another grape, but could perceive no slightest movement of mouth or throat.

"Doubt," I said to myself, "may be a poor encouragement to do anything, but it is a bad reason for doing nothing." So tight was the skin upon her bones that I dared not use friction.

I crept into the heap of leaves, got as close to her as I could, and took her in my arms. I had not much heat left in me, but what I had I would share with her! Thus I spent what remained of the night, sleepless, and longing for the sun. Her cold seemed to radiate into me, but no heat to pass from me to her.

Had I fled from the beautiful sleepers, I thought, each on her "dim, straight" silver couch, to lie alone with such a bedfellow! I had refused a lovely privilege: I was given over to an awful duty! Beneath the sad, slow-setting moon, I lay with the dead, and watched for the dawn.

The darkness had given way, and the eastern horizon was growing dimly clearer, when I caught sight of a motion rather than of anything that moved—not far from me, and close to the ground. It was the low undulating of a large snake, which passed me in an unswerving line. Presently appeared, making as it seemed for the same point, what I took for a roebuck-doe and her calf. Again a while, and two creatures like bear-cubs came, with three or four smaller ones behind them. The light was now growing so rapidly that when, a few minutes after, a troop of horses went trotting past, I could see that, although the largest of them were no bigger than the smallest Shetland pony, they must yet be full-grown, so perfect were they in form, and so much had they all the ways and action of great horses. They were of many breeds. Some seemed models of cart-horses, others of chargers, hunters, racers. Dwarf cattle and small elephants followed.

"Why are the children not here!" I said to myself. "The moment I am free of this poor woman, I must go back and fetch them!"

Where were the creatures going? What drew them? Was this an exodus, or a morning habit? I must wait for the sun! Till he came I must not leave the woman! I laid my hand on the body, and could not help thinking it felt a trifle warmer. It might have gained a little of the heat I had lost! it could hardly have generated any! What reason for hope there was had not grown less!

The forehead of the day began to glow, and soon the sun came peering up, as if to see for the first time what all this stir of a new world was about. At sight of his great innocent splendour, I rose full of life, strong against death. Removing the handkerchief I had put to protect the mouth and eyes from the pine-needles, I looked anxiously to see whether I had found a priceless jewel, or but its empty case.

The body lay motionless as when I found it. Then first, in the morning light, I saw how drawn and hollow was the face, how sharp were the bones under the skin, how every tooth shaped itself through the lips. The human garment was indeed worn to its threads, but the bird of heaven might yet be nestling within, might yet awake to motion and song!

But the sun was shining on her face! I re-arranged the handkerchief, laid a few leaves lightly over it, and set out to follow the creatures. Their main track was well beaten, and must have long been used—likewise many of the tracks that, joining it from both sides, merged in, and broadened it. The trees retreated as I went, and the grass grew thicker. Presently the forest was gone, and a wide expanse of loveliest green stretched away to the horizon. Through it, along the edge of the forest, flowed a small river, and to this the track led. At sight of the water a new though undefined hope sprang up in me. The stream looked everywhere deep, and was full to the brim, but nowhere more than a few yards wide. A bluish mist rose from it, vanishing as it rose. On the opposite side, in the plentiful grass, many small animals were feeding. Apparently they slept in the forest, and in the morning sought the plain, swimming the river to reach it. I knelt and would have drunk, but the water was hot, and had a strange metallic taste.

I leapt to my feet: here was the warmth I sought—the first necessity of life! I sped back to my helpless charge.

Without well considering my solitude, no one will understand what seemed to lie for me in the redemption of this woman from death. "Prove what she may," I thought with myself, "I shall at least be lonely no more!" I had found myself such poor company that now first I seemed to know what hope was. This blessed water would expel the cold death, and drown my desolation!

I bore her to the stream. Tall as she was, I found her marvellously light, her bones were so delicate, and so little covered them. I grew yet more hopeful when I found her so far from stiff that I could carry her on one arm, like a sleeping child, leaning against my shoulder. I went softly, dreading even the wind of my motion, and glad there was no other.

The water was too hot to lay her at once in it: the shock might scare from her the yet fluttering life! I laid her on the bank, and dipping one of my garments, began to

bathe the pitiful form. So wasted was it that, save from the plentifulness and blackness of the hair, it was impossible even to conjecture whether she was young or old.
Her eyelids were just not shut, which made her look dead the more: there was a
crack in the clouds of her night, at which no sun shone through!

The longer I went on bathing the poor bones, the less grew my hope that they
would ever again be clothed with strength, that ever those eyelids would lift, and a
soul look out; still I kept bathing continuously, allowing no part time to grow cold
while I bathed another; and gradually the body became so much warmer, that at
last I ventured to submerge it: I got into the stream and drew it in, holding the face
above the water, and letting the swift, steady current flow all about the rest. I noted,
but was able to conclude nothing from the fact, that, for all the heat, the shut hand
never relaxed its hold.

After about ten minutes, I lifted it out and laid it again on the bank, dried it, and
covered it as well as I could, then ran to the forest for leaves.

The grass and soil were dry and warm; and when I returned I thought it had
scarcely lost any of the heat the water had given it. I spread the leaves upon it, and
ran for more—then for a third and a fourth freight.

I could now leave it and go to explore, in the hope of discovering some shelter. I
ran up the stream toward some rocky hills I saw in that direction, which were not
far off.

When I reached them, I found the river issuing full grown from a rock at the
bottom of one of them. To my fancy it seemed to have run down a stair inside, an
eager cataract, at every landing wild to get out, but only at the foot finding a door
of escape.

It did not fill the opening whence it rushed, and I crept through into a little cave,
where I learned that, instead of hurrying tumultuously down a stair, it rose quietly
from the ground at the back like the base of a large column, and ran along one side,
nearly filling a deep, rather narrow channel. I considered the place, and saw that, if
I could find a few fallen boughs long enough to lie across the channel, and large
enough to bear a little weight without bending much, I might, with smaller
branches and plenty of leaves, make upon them a comfortable couch, which the
stream under would keep constantly warm. Then I ran back to see how my charge
fared.

She was lying as I had left her. The heat had not brought her to life, but neither
had it developed anything to check farther hope. I got a few boulders out of the
channel, and arranged them at her feet and on both sides of her.

Running again to the wood, I had not to search long ere I found some small
boughs fit for my purpose—mostly of beech, their dry yellow leaves yet clinging to
them. With these I had soon laid the floor of a bridge-bed over the torrent. I crossed
the boughs with smaller branches, interlaced these with twigs, and buried all deep
in leaves and dry moss.

When thus at length, after not a few journeys to the forest, I had completed a
warm, dry, soft couch, I took the body once more, and set out with it for the cave. It
was so light that now and then as I went I almost feared lest, when I laid it down, I
should find it a skeleton after all; and when at last I did lay it gently on the pathless
bridge, it was a greater relief to part with that fancy than with the weight. Once
more I covered the body with a thick layer of leaves; and trying again to feed her
with a grape, found to my joy that I could open the mouth a little farther. The

grape, indeed, lay in it unheeded, but I hoped some of the juice might find its way down.

After an hour or two on the couch, she was no longer cold. The warmth of the brook had interpenetrated her frame—truly it was but a frame!—and she was warm to the touch;—not, probably, with the warmth of life, but with a warmth which rendered it more possible, if she were alive, that she might live. I had read of one in a trance lying motionless for weeks!

In that cave, day after day, night after night, seven long days and nights, I sat or lay, now waking now sleeping, but always watching. Every morning I went out and bathed in the hot stream, and every morning felt thereupon as if I had eaten and drunk—which experience gave me courage to lay her in it also every day. Once as I did so, a shadow of discoloration on her left side gave me a terrible shock, but the next morning it had vanished, and I continued the treatment—every morning, after her bath, putting a fresh grape in her mouth.

I too ate of the grapes and other berries I found in the forest; but I believed that, with my daily bath in that river, I could have done very well without eating at all.

Every time I slept, I dreamed of finding a wounded angel, who, unable to fly, remained with me until at last she loved me and would not leave me; and every time I woke, it was to see, instead of an angel-visage with lustrous eyes, the white, motionless, wasted face upon the couch. But Adam himself, when first he saw her asleep, could not have looked more anxiously for Eve's awaking than I watched for this woman's. Adam knew nothing of himself, perhaps nothing of his need of another self; I, an alien from my fellows, had learned to love what I had lost! Were this one wasted shred of womanhood to disappear, I should have nothing in me but a consuming hunger after life! I forgot even the Little Ones: things were not amiss with them! here lay what might wake and be a woman! might actually open eyes, and look out of them upon me!

Now first I knew what solitude meant—now that I gazed on one who neither saw nor heard, neither moved nor spoke. I saw now that a man alone is but a being that may become a man—that he is but a need, and therefore a possibility. To be enough for himself, a being must be an eternal, self-existent worm! So superbly constituted, so simply complicate is man; he rises from and stands upon such a pedestal of lower physical organisms and spiritual structures, that no atmosphere will comfort or nourish his life, less divine than that offered by other souls; nowhere but in other lives can he breathe. Only by the reflex of other lives can he ripen his specialty, develop the idea of himself, the individuality that distinguishes him from every other. Were all men alike, each would still have an individuality, secured by his personal consciousness, but there would be small reason why there should be more than two or three such; while, for the development of the differences which make a large and lofty unity possible, and which alone can make millions into a church, an endless and measureless influence and reaction are indispensable. A man to be perfect—complete, that is, in having reached the spiritual condition of persistent and universal growth, which is the mode wherein he inherits the infinitude of his Father—must have the education of a world of fellowmen. Save for the hope of the dawn of life in the form beside me, I should have fled for fellowship to the beasts that grazed and did not speak. Better to go about with them—infinitely better—than to live alone! But with the faintest prospect of a woman to my friend, I, poorest of creatures, was yet a possible man!

CHAPTER XIX. THE WHITE LEECH

I woke one morning from a profound sleep, with one of my hands very painful. The back of it was much swollen, and in the centre of the swelling was a triangular wound, like the bite of a leech. As the day went on, the swelling subsided, and by the evening the hurt was all but healed. I searched the cave, turning over every stone of any size, but discovered nothing I could imagine capable of injuring me.

Slowly the days passed, and still the body never moved, never opened its eyes. It could not be dead, for assuredly it manifested no sign of decay, and the air about it was quite pure. Moreover, I could imagine that the sharpest angles of the bones had begun to disappear, that the form was everywhere a little rounder, and the skin had less of the parchment-look: if such change was indeed there, life must be there! the tide which had ebbed so far toward the infinite, must have begun again to flow! Oh joy to me, if the rising ripples of life's ocean were indeed burying under lovely shape the bones it had all but forsaken! Twenty times a day I looked for evidence of progress, and twenty times a day I doubted—sometimes even despaired; but the moment I recalled the mental picture of her as I found her, hope revived.

Several weeks had passed thus, when one night, after lying a long time awake, I rose, thinking to go out and breathe the cooler air; for, although from the running of the stream it was always fresh in the cave, the heat was not seldom a little oppressive. The moon outside was full, the air within shadowy clear, and naturally I cast a lingering look on my treasure ere I went. "Bliss eternal!" I cried aloud, "do I see her eyes?" Great orbs, dark as if cut from the sphere of a starless night, and luminous by excess of darkness, seemed to shine amid the glimmering whiteness of her face. I stole nearer, my heart beating so that I feared the noise of it startling her. I bent over her. Alas, her eyelids were close shut! Hope and Imagination had wrought mutual illusion! my heart's desire would never be! I turned away, threw myself on the floor of the cave, and wept. Then I bethought me that her eyes had been a little open, and that now the awful chink out of which nothingness had peered, was gone: it might be that she had opened them for a moment, and was again asleep!—it might be she was awake and holding them close! In either case, life, less or more, must have shut them! I was comforted, and fell fast asleep.

That night I was again bitten, and awoke with a burning thirst.

In the morning I searched yet more thoroughly, but again in vain. The wound was of the same character, and, as before, was nearly well by the evening. I concluded that some large creature of the leech kind came occasionally from the hot stream. "But, if blood be its object," I said to myself, "so long as I am there, I need hardly fear for my treasure!"

That same morning, when, having peeled a grape as usual and taken away the seeds, I put it in her mouth, her lips made a slight movement of reception, and I KNEW she lived!

My hope was now so much stronger that I began to think of some attire for her: she must be able to rise the moment she wished! I betook myself therefore to the forest, to investigate what material it might afford, and had hardly begun to look when fibrous skeletons, like those of the leaves of the prickly pear, suggested themselves as fit for the purpose. I gathered a stock of them, laid them to dry in the sun, pulled apart the reticulated layers, and of these had soon begun to fashion two loose garments, one to hang from her waist, the other from her shoulders. With the stiletto-point of an aloe-leaf and various filaments, I sewed together three thicknesses of the tissue.

During the week that followed, there was no farther sign except that she more evidently took the grapes. But indeed all the signs became surer: plainly she was growing plumper, and her skin fairer. Still she did not open her eyes; and the horrid fear would at times invade me, that her growth was of some hideous fungoid nature, the few grapes being nowise sufficient to account for it.

Again I was bitten; and now the thing, whatever it was, began to pay me regular visits at intervals of three days. It now generally bit me in the neck or the arm, invariably with but one bite, always while I slept, and never, even when I slept, in the daytime. Hour after hour would I lie awake on the watch, but never heard it coming, or saw sign of its approach. Neither, I believe, did I ever feel it bite me. At length I became so hopeless of catching it, that I no longer troubled myself either to look for it by day, or lie in wait for it at night. I knew from my growing weakness that I was losing blood at a dangerous rate, but I cared little for that: in sight of my eyes death was yielding to life; a soul was gathering strength to save me from loneliness; we would go away together, and I should speedily recover!

The garments were at length finished, and, contemplating my handiwork with no small satisfaction, I proceeded to mat layers of the fibre into sandals.

One night I woke suddenly, breathless and faint, and longing after air, and had risen to crawl from the cave, when a slight rustle in the leaves of the couch set me listening motionless.

"I caught the vile thing," said a feeble voice, in my mother-tongue; "I caught it in the very act!"

She was alive! she spoke! I dared not yield to my transport lest I should terrify her.

"What creature?" I breathed, rather than said.

"The creature," she answered, "that was biting you."

"What was it?"

"A great white leech."

"How big?" I pursued, forcing myself to be calm.

"Not far from six feet long, I should think," she answered.

"You have saved my life, perhaps!—But how could you touch the horrid thing! How brave of you!" I cried.

"I did!" was all her answer, and I thought she shuddered.

"Where is it? What could you do with such a monster?"

"I threw it in the river."

"Then it will come again, I fear!"

"I do not think I could have killed it, even had I known how!—I heard you moaning, and got up to see what disturbed you; saw the frightful thing at your neck, and pulled it away. But I could not hold it, and was hardly able to throw it from me. I only heard it splash in the water!"

"We'll kill it next time!" I said; but with that I turned faint, sought the open air, but fell.

When I came to myself the sun was up. The lady stood a little way off, looking, even in the clumsy attire I had fashioned for her, at once grand and graceful. I HAD seen those glorious eyes! Through the night they had shone! Dark as the darkness primeval, they now outshone the day! She stood erect as a column, regarding me. Her pale cheek indicated no emotion, only question. I rose.

"We must be going!" I said. "The white leech——"

I stopped: a strange smile had flickered over her beautiful face.

"Did you find me there?" she asked, pointing to the cave.

"No; I brought you there," I replied.

"You brought me?"

"Yes."

"From where?"

"From the forest."

"What have you done with my clothes—and my jewels?"

"You had none when I found you."

"Then why did you not leave me?"

"Because I hoped you were not dead."

"Why should you have cared?"

"Because I was very lonely, and wanted you to live."

"You would have kept me enchanted for my beauty!" she said, with proud scorn.

Her words and her look roused my indignation.

"There was no beauty left in you," I said.

"Why, then, again, did you not let me alone?"

"Because you were of my own kind."

"Of YOUR kind?" she cried, in a tone of utter contempt.

"I thought so, but find I was mistaken!"

"Doubtless you pitied me!"

"Never had woman more claim on pity, or less on any other feeling!"

With an expression of pain, mortification, and anger unutterable, she turned from me and stood silent. Starless night lay profound in the gulfs of her eyes: hate of him who brought it back had slain their splendour. The light of life was gone from them.

"Had you failed to rouse me, what would you have done?" she asked suddenly without moving.

"I would have buried it."

"It! What?—You would have buried THIS?" she exclaimed, flashing round upon me in a white fury, her arms thrown out, and her eyes darting forks of cold lightning.

"Nay; that I saw not! That, weary weeks of watching and tending have brought back to you," I answered—for with such a woman I must be plain! "Had I seen the smallest sign of decay, I would at once have buried you."

"Dog of a fool!" she cried, "I was but in a trance—Samoil! what a fate!—Go and fetch the she-savage from whom you borrowed this hideous disguise."

"I made it for you. It is hideous, but I did my best."

She drew herself up to her tall height.

"How long have I been insensible?" she demanded. "A woman could not have made that dress in a day!"

"Not in twenty days," I rejoined, "hardly in thirty!"

"Ha! How long do you pretend I have lain unconscious?—Answer me at once."

"I cannot tell how long you had lain when I found you, but there was nothing left of you save skin and bone: that is more than three months ago.—Your hair was beautiful, nothing else! I have done for it what I could."

"My poor hair!" she said, and brought a great armful of it round from behind her; "—it will be more than a three-months' care to bring YOU to life again!—I suppose I must thank you, although I cannot say I am grateful!"

"There is no need, madam: I would have done the same for any woman—yes, or for any man either!"

"How is it my hair is not tangled?" she said, fondling it.

"It always drifted in the current."

"How?—What do you mean?"

"I could not have brought you to life but by bathing you in the hot river every morning."

She gave a shudder of disgust, and stood for a while with her gaze fixed on the hurrying water. Then she turned to me:

"We must understand each other!" she said. "—You have done me the two worst of wrongs—compelled me to live, and put me to shame: neither of them can I pardon!"

She raised her left hand, and flung it out as if repelling me. Something ice-cold struck me on the forehead. When I came to myself, I was on the ground, wet and shivering.

CHAPTER XX. GONE!—BUT HOW?

I rose, and looked around me, dazed at heart. For a moment I could not see her: she was gone, and loneliness had returned like the cloud after the rain! She whom I brought back from the brink of the grave, had fled from me, and left me with desolation! I dared not one moment remain thus hideously alone. Had I indeed done her a wrong? I must devote my life to sharing the burden I had compelled her to resume!

I descried her walking swiftly over the grass, away from the river, took one plunge for a farewell restorative, and set out to follow her. The last visit of the white leech, and the blow of the woman, had enfeebled me, but already my strength was reviving, and I kept her in sight without difficulty.

"Is this, then, the end?" I said as I went, and my heart brooded a sad song. Her angry, hating eyes haunted me. I could understand her resentment at my having forced life upon her, but how had I further injured her? Why should she loathe me? Could modesty itself be indignant with true service? How should the proudest woman, conscious of my every action, cherish against me the least sense of disgracing wrong? How reverently had I not touched her! As a father his motherless child, I had borne and tended her! Had all my labour, all my despairing hope gone to redeem only ingratitude? "No," I answered myself; "beauty must have a heart! However profoundly hidden, it must be there! The deeper buried, the stronger and truer will it wake at last in its beautiful grave! To rouse that heart were a better gift to her than the happiest life! It would be to give her a nobler, a higher life!"

She was ascending a gentle slope before me, walking straight and steady as one that knew whither, when I became aware that she was increasing the distance between us. I summoned my strength, and it came in full tide. My veins filled with fresh life! My body seemed to become ethereal, and, following like an easy wind, I rapidly overtook her.

Not once had she looked behind. Swiftly she moved, like a Greek goddess to rescue, but without haste. I was within three yards of her, when she turned sharply, yet with grace unbroken, and stood. Fatigue or heat she showed none. Her paleness was not a pallor, but a pure whiteness; her breathing was slow and deep. Her eyes seemed to fill the heavens, and give light to the world. It was nearly noon, but the sense was upon me as of a great night in which an invisible dew makes the stars look large.

"Why do you follow me?" she asked, quietly but rather sternly, as if she had never before seen me.

"I have lived so long," I answered, "on the mere hope of your eyes, that I must want to see them again!"

"You WILL not be spared!" she said coldly. "I command you to stop where you stand."

"Not until I see you in a place of safety will I leave you," I replied.

"Then take the consequences," she said, and resumed her swift-gliding walk.

But as she turned she cast on me a glance, and I stood as if run through with a spear. Her scorn had failed: she would kill me with her beauty!

Despair restored my volition; the spell broke; I ran, and overtook her.

"Have pity upon me!" I cried.

She gave no heed. I followed her like a child whose mother pretends to abandon him. "I will be your slave!" I said, and laid my hand on her arm.

She turned as if a serpent had bit her. I cowered before the blaze of her eyes, but could not avert my own.

"Pity me," I cried again.

She resumed her walking.

The whole day I followed her. The sun climbed the sky, seemed to pause on its summit, went down the other side. Not a moment did she pause, not a moment did I cease to follow. She never turned her head, never relaxed her pace.

The sun went below, and the night came up. I kept close to her: if I lost sight of her for a moment, it would be for ever!

All day long we had been walking over thick soft grass: abruptly she stopped, and threw herself upon it. There was yet light enough to show that she was utterly weary. I stood behind her, and gazed down on her for a moment.

Did I love her? I knew she was not good! Did I hate her? I could not leave her! I knelt beside her.

"Begone! Do not dare touch me," she cried.

Her arms lay on the grass by her sides as if paralyzed.

Suddenly they closed about my neck, rigid as those of the torture-maiden. She drew down my face to hers, and her lips clung to my cheek. A sting of pain shot somewhere through me, and pulsed. I could not stir a hair's breadth. Gradually the pain ceased. A slumberous weariness, a dreamy pleasure stole over me, and then I knew nothing.

All at once I came to myself. The moon was a little way above the horizon, but spread no radiance; she was but a bright thing set in blackness. My cheek smarted; I put my hand to it, and found a wet spot. My neck ached: there again was a wet spot! I sighed heavily, and felt very tired. I turned my eyes listlessly around me— and saw what had become of the light of the moon: it was gathered about the lady! she stood in a shimmering nimbus! I rose and staggered toward her.

"Down!" she cried imperiously, as to a rebellious dog. "Follow me a step if you dare!"

"I will!" I murmured, with an agonised effort.

"Set foot within the gates of my city, and my people will stone you: they do not love beggars!"

I was deaf to her words. Weak as water, and half awake, I did not know that I moved, but the distance grew less between us. She took one step back, raised her left arm, and with the clenched hand seemed to strike me on the forehead. I received as it were a blow from an iron hammer, and fell.

I sprang to my feet, cold and wet, but clear-headed and strong. Had the blow revived me? it had left neither wound nor pain!—But how came I wet?—I could not have lain long, for the moon was no higher!

The lady stood some yards away, her back toward me. She was doing something, I could not distinguish what. Then by her sudden gleam I knew she had thrown off her garments, and stood white in the dazed moon. One moment she stood—and fell forward.

A streak of white shot away in a swift-drawn line. The same instant the moon recovered herself, shining out with a full flash, and I saw that the streak was a long-bodied thing, rushing in great, low-curved bounds over the grass. Dark spots seemed to run like a stream adown its back, as if it had been fleeting along under the edge of a wood, and catching the shadows of the leaves.

"God of mercy!" I cried, "is the terrible creature speeding to the night-infolded city?" and I seemed to hear from afar the sudden burst and spread of outcrying terror, as the pale savage bounded from house to house, rending and slaying.

While I gazed after it fear-stricken, past me from behind, like a swift, all but noiseless arrow, shot a second large creature, pure white. Its path was straight for the spot where the lady had fallen, and, as I thought, lay. My tongue clave to the roof of my mouth. I sprang forward pursuing the beast. But in a moment the spot I made for was far behind it.

"It was well," I thought, "that I could not cry out: if she had risen, the monster would have been upon her!"

But when I reached the place, no lady was there; only the garments she had dropped lay dusk in the moonlight.

I stood staring after the second beast. It tore over the ground with yet greater swiftness than the former—in long, level, skimming leaps, the very embodiment of wasteless speed. It followed the line the other had taken, and I watched it grow smaller and smaller, until it disappeared in the uncertain distance.

But where was the lady? Had the first beast surprised her, creeping upon her noiselessly? I had heard no shriek! and there had not been time to devour her! Could it have caught her up as it ran, and borne her away to its den? So laden it could not have run so fast! and I should have seen that it carried something!

Horrible doubts began to wake in me. After a thorough but fruitless search, I set out in the track of the two animals.

CHAPTER XXI. THE FUGITIVE MOTHER

As I hastened along, a cloud came over the moon, and from the gray dark suddenly emerged a white figure, clasping a child to her bosom, and stooping as she ran. She was on a line parallel with my own, but did not perceive me as she hurried along, terror and anxiety in every movement of her driven speed.

"She is chased!" I said to myself. "Some prowler of this terrible night is after her!"

To follow would have added to her fright: I stepped into her track to stop her pursuer.

As I stood for a moment looking after her through the dusk, behind me came a swift, soft-footed rush, and ere I could turn, something sprang over my head, struck me sharply on the forehead, and knocked me down. I was up in an instant, but all I saw of my assailant was a vanishing whiteness. I ran after the beast, with the blood trickling from my forehead; but had run only a few steps, when a shriek of despair tore the quivering night. I ran the faster, though I could not but fear it must already be too late.

In a minute or two I spied a low white shape approaching me through the vapour-dusted moonlight. It must be another beast, I thought at first, for it came slowly, almost crawling, with strange, floundering leaps, as of a creature in agony! I drew aside from its path, and waited. As it neared me, I saw it was going on three legs, carrying its left fore-paw high from the ground. It had many dark, oval spots on a shining white skin, and was attended by a low rushing sound, as of water falling upon grass. As it went by me, I saw something streaming from the lifted paw.

"It is blood!" I said to myself, "some readier champion than I has wounded the beast!" But, strange to tell, such a pity seized me at sight of the suffering creature, that, though an axe had been in my hand I could not have struck at it. In a broken succession of hobbling leaps it went out of sight, its blood, as it seemed, still issuing in a small torrent, which kept flowing back softly through the grass beside me. "If it go on bleeding like that," I thought, "it will soon be hurtless!"

I went on, for I might yet be useful to the woman, and hoped also to see her deliverer.

I descried her a little way off, seated on the grass, with her child in her lap.

"Can I do anything for you?" I asked.

At the sound of my voice she started violently, and would have risen. I threw myself on the ground.

"You need not be frightened," I said. "I was following the beast when happily you found a nearer protector! It passed me now with its foot bleeding so much that by this time it must be all but dead!"

"There is little hope of that!" she answered, trembling. "Do you not know whose beast she is?"

Now I had certain strange suspicions, but I answered that I knew nothing of the brute, and asked what had become of her champion.

"What champion?" she rejoined. "I have seen no one."

"Then how came the monster to grief?"

"I pounded her foot with a stone—as hard as I could strike. Did you not hear her cry?"

"Well, you are a brave woman!" I answered. "I thought it was you gave the cry!"

"It was the leopardess."

"I never heard such a sound from the throat of an animal! it was like the scream of a woman in torture!"

"My voice was gone; I could not have shrieked to save my baby! When I saw the horrid mouth at my darling's little white neck, I caught up a stone and mashed her lame foot."

"Tell me about the creature," I said; "I am a stranger in these parts."

"You will soon know about her if you are going to Bulika!" she answered. "Now, I must never go back there!"

"Yes, I am going to Bulika," I said, "—to see the princess."

"Have a care; you had better not go!—But perhaps you are—! The princess is a very good, kind woman!"

I heard a little movement. Clouds had by this time gathered so thick over the moon that I could scarcely see my companion: I feared she was rising to run from me.

"You are in no danger of any sort from me," I said. "What oath would you like me to take?"

"I know by your speech that you are not of the people of Bulika," she replied; "I will trust you!—I am not of them, either, else I should not be able: they never trust any one—If only I could see you! But I like your voice!—There, my darling is asleep! The foul beast has not hurt her!—Yes: it was my baby she was after!" she went on, caressing the child. "And then she would have torn her mother to pieces for carrying her off!—Some say the princess has two white leopardesses," she continued: "I know only one—with spots. Everybody knows HER! If the princess hear of a baby, she sends her immediately to suck its blood, and then it either dies or grows up an idiot. I would have gone away with my baby, but the princess was from home, and I thought I might wait until I was a little stronger. But she must have taken the beast with her, and been on her way home when I left, and come across my track. I heard the SNIFF-SNUFF of the leopardess behind me, and ran;—oh, how I ran!—But my darling will not die! There is no mark on her!"

"Where are you taking her?"

"Where no one ever tells!"

"Why is the princess so cruel?"

"There is an old prophecy that a child will be the death of her. That is why she will listen to no offer of marriage, they say."

"But what will become of her country if she kill all the babies?"

"She does not care about her country. She sends witches around to teach the women spells that keep babies away, and give them horrible things to eat. Some say she is in league with the Shadows to put an end to the race. At night we hear the questing beast, and lie awake and shiver. She can tell at once the house where a baby is coming, and lies down at the door, watching to get in. There are words that have power to shoo her away, only they do not always work—But here I sit talking, and the beast may by this time have got home, and her mistress be sending the other after us!"

As thus she ended, she rose in haste.

"I do not think she will ever get home.—Let me carry the baby for you!" I said, as I rose also.

She returned me no answer, and when I would have taken it, only clasped it the closer.

"I cannot think," I said, walking by her side, "how the brute could be bleeding so much!"

"Take my advice, and don't go near the palace," she answered. "There are sounds in it at night as if the dead were trying to shriek, but could not open their mouths!"

She bade me an abrupt farewell. Plainly she did not want more of my company; so I stood still, and heard her footsteps die away on the grass.

CHAPTER XXII. BULIKA

I had lost all notion of my position, and was walking about in pure, helpless impatience, when suddenly I found myself in the path of the leopardess, wading in the blood from her paw. It ran against my ankles with the force of a small brook, and I got out of it the more quickly because of an unshaped suspicion in my mind as to whose blood it might be. But I kept close to the sound of it, walking up the side of the stream, for it would guide me in the direction of Bulika.

I soon began to reflect, however, that no leopardess, no elephant, no hugest animal that in our world preceded man, could keep such a torrent flowing, except every artery in its body were open, and its huge system went on filling its vessels from fields and lakes and forests as fast as they emptied themselves: it could not be blood! I dipped a finger in it, and at once satisfied myself that it was not. In truth, however it might have come there, it was a softly murmuring rivulet of water that ran, without channel, over the grass! But sweet as was its song, I dared not drink of it; I kept walking on, hoping after the light, and listening to the familiar sound so long unheard—for that of the hot stream was very different. The mere wetting of my feet in it, however, had so refreshed me, that I went on without fatigue till the darkness began to grow thinner, and I knew the sun was drawing nigh. A few minutes more, and I could discern, against the pale aurora, the wall-towers of a city —seemingly old as time itself. Then I looked down to get a sight of the brook.

It was gone. I had indeed for a long time noted its sound growing fainter, but at last had ceased to attend to it. I looked back: the grass in its course lay bent as it had flowed, and here and there glimmered a small pool. Toward the city, there was no trace of it. Near where I stood, the flow of its fountain must at least have paused!

Around the city were gardens, growing many sorts of vegetables, hardly one of which I recognised. I saw no water, no flowers, no sign of animals. The gardens came very near the walls, but were separated from them by huge heaps of gravel and refuse thrown from the battlements.

I went up to the nearest gate, and found it but half-closed, nowise secured, and without guard or sentinel. To judge by its hinges, it could not be farther opened or shut closer. Passing through, I looked down a long ancient street. It was utterly silent, and with scarce an indication in it of life present. Had I come upon a dead city? I turned and went out again, toiled a long way over the dust-heaps, and crossed several roads, each leading up to a gate: I would not re-enter until some of the inhabitants should be stirring.

What was I there for? what did I expect or hope to find? what did I mean to do?

I must see, if but once more, the woman I had brought to life! I did not desire her society: she had waked in me frightful suspicions; and friendship, not to say love, was wildly impossible between us! But her presence had had a strange influence upon me, and in her presence I must resist, and at the same time analyse that influence! The seemingly inscrutable in her I would fain penetrate: to understand something of her mode of being would be to look into marvels such as imagination could never have suggested! In this I was too daring: a man must not, for knowledge, of his own will encounter temptation! On the other hand, I had reinstated an evil force about to perish, and was, to the extent of my opposing faculty, accountable for what mischief might ensue! I had learned that she was the enemy of children: the Little Ones might be in her danger! It was in the hope of finding out something of their history that I had left them; on that I had received a little light: I must have more; I must learn how to protect them!

Hearing at length a little stir in the place, I walked through the next gate, and thence along a narrow street of tall houses to a little square, where I sat down on the base of a pillar with a hideous bat-like creature atop. Ere long, several of the inhabitants came sauntering past. I spoke to one: he gave me a rude stare and ruder word, and went on.

I got up and went through one narrow street after another, gradually filling with idlers, and was not surprised to see no children. By and by, near one of the gates, I encountered a group of young men who reminded me not a little of the bad giants. They came about me staring, and presently began to push and hustle me, then to throw things at me. I bore it as well as I could, wishing not to provoke enmity where wanted to remain for a while. Oftener than once or twice I appealed to passers-by whom I fancied more benevolent-looking, but none would halt a moment to listen to me. I looked poor, and that was enough: to the citizens of Bulika, as to house-dogs, poverty was an offence! Deformity and sickness were taxed; and no legislation of their princess was more heartily approved of than what tended to make poverty subserve wealth.

I took to my heels at last, and no one followed me beyond the gate. A lumbering fellow, however, who sat by it eating a hunch of bread, picked up a stone to throw after me, and happily, in his stupid eagerness, threw, not the stone but the bread. I took it, and he did not dare follow to reclaim it: beyond the walls they were cowards every one. I went off a few hundred yards, threw myself down, ate the bread, fell asleep, and slept soundly in the grass, where the hot sunlight renewed my strength.

It was night when I woke. The moon looked down on me in friendly fashion, seeming to claim with me old acquaintance. She was very bright, and the same moon, I thought, that saw me through the terrors of my first night in that strange world. A cold wind blew from the gate, bringing with it an evil odour; but it did not chill me, for the sun had plenished me with warmth. I crept again into the city. There I found the few that were still in the open air crouched in corners to escape the shivering blast.

I was walking slowly through the long narrow street, when, just before me, a huge white thing bounded across it, with a single flash in the moonlight, and disappeared. I turned down the next opening, eager to get sight of it again.

It was a narrow lane, almost too narrow to pass through, but it led me into a wider street. The moment I entered the latter, I saw on the opposite side, in the shadow, the creature I had followed, itself following like a dog what I took for a man. Over his shoulder, every other moment, he glanced at the animal behind him, but neither spoke to it, nor attempted to drive it away. At a place where he had to cross a patch of moonlight, I saw that he cast no shadow, and was himself but a flat superficial shadow, of two dimensions. He was, nevertheless, an opaque shadow, for he not merely darkened any object on the other side of him, but rendered it, in fact, invisible. In the shadow he was blacker than the shadow; in the moonlight he looked like one who had drawn his shadow up about him, for not a suspicion of it moved beside or under him; while the gleaming animal, which followed so close at his heels as to seem the white shadow of his blackness, and which I now saw to be a leopardess, drew her own gliding shadow black over the ground by her side. When they passed together from the shadow into the moonlight, the Shadow deepened in blackness, the animal flashed into radiance. I was at the moment walking abreast of them on the opposite side, my bare feet sounding on the flat stones: the leopardess never turned head or twitched ear; the shadow seemed once to look at me, for I lost his profile, and saw for a second only a sharp upright line. That instant the wind found me and blew through me: I shuddered from head to foot, and my heart went from wall to wall of my bosom, like a pebble in a child's rattle.

CHAPTER XXIII. A WOMAN OF BULIKA

I turned aside into an alley, and sought shelter in a small archway. In the mouth of it I stopped, and looked out at the moonlight which filled the alley. The same instant a woman came gliding in after me, turned, trembling, and looked out also. A few seconds passed; then a huge leopard, its white skin dappled with many blots, darted across the archway. The woman pressed close to me, and my heart filled with pity. I put my arm round her.

"If the brute come here, I will lay hold of it," I said, "and you must run."

"Thank you!" she murmured.

"Have you ever seen it before?" I asked.

"Several times," she answered, still trembling. "She is a pet of the princess's. You are a stranger, or you would know her!"

"I am a stranger," I answered. "But is she, then, allowed to run loose?"

"She is kept in a cage, her mouth muzzled, and her feet in gloves of crocodile leather. Chained she is too; but she gets out often, and sucks the blood of any child she can lay hold of. Happily there are not many mothers in Bulika!"

Here she burst into tears.

"I wish I were at home!" she sobbed. "The princess returned only last night, and there is the leopardess out already! How am I to get into the house? It is me she is after, I know! She will be lying at my own door, watching for me!—But I am a fool to talk to a stranger!"

"All strangers are not bad!" I said. "The beast shall not touch you till she has done with me, and by that time you will be in. You are happy to have a house to go to! What a terrible wind it is!"

"Take me home safe, and I will give you shelter from it," she rejoined. "But we must wait a little!"

I asked her many questions. She told me the people never did anything except dig for precious stones in their cellars. They were rich, and had everything made for them in other towns.

"Why?" I asked.

"Because it is a disgrace to work," she answered. "Everybody in Bulika knows that!"

I asked how they were rich if none of them earned money. She replied that their ancestors had saved for them, and they never spent. When they wanted money they sold a few of their gems.

"But there must be some poor!" I said.

"I suppose there must be, but we never think of such people. When one goes poor, we forget him. That is how we keep rich. We mean to be rich always."

"But when you have dug up all your precious stones and sold them, you will have to spend your money, and one day you will have none left!"

"We have so many, and there are so many still in the ground, that that day will never come," she replied.

"Suppose a strange people were to fall upon you, and take everything you have!"

"No strange people will dare; they are all horribly afraid of our princess. She it is who keeps us safe and free and rich!"

Every now and then as she spoke, she would stop and look behind her.

I asked why her people had such a hatred of strangers. She answered that the presence of a stranger defiled the city.

"How is that?" I said.

"Because we are more ancient and noble than any other nation.—Therefore," she added, "we always turn strangers out before night."

"How, then, can you take me into your house?" I asked.

"I will make an exception of you," she replied.

"Is there no place in the city for the taking in of strangers?"

"Such a place would be pulled down, and its owner burned. How is purity to be preserved except by keeping low people at a proper distance? Dignity is such a delicate thing!"

She told me that their princess had reigned for thousands of years; that she had power over the air and the water as well as the earth—and, she believed, over the fire too; that she could do what she pleased, and was answerable to nobody.

When at length she was willing to risk the attempt, we took our way through lanes and narrow passages, and reached her door without having met a single live creature. It was in a wider street, between two tall houses, at the top of a narrow, steep stair, up which she climbed slowly, and I followed. Ere we reached the top, however, she seemed to take fright, and darted up the rest of the steps: I arrived just in time to have the door closed in my face, and stood confounded on the landing, where was about length enough, between the opposite doors of the two houses, for a man to lie down.

Weary, and not scrupling to defile Bulika with my presence, I took advantage of the shelter, poor as it was.

CHAPTER XXIV. THE WHITE LEOPARDESS

At the foot of the stair lay the moonlit street, and I could hear the unwholesome, inhospitable wind blowing about below. But not a breath of it entered my retreat, and I was composing myself to rest, when suddenly my eyes opened, and there was the head of the shining creature I had seen following the Shadow, just rising above the uppermost step! The moment she caught sight of my eyes, she stopped and began to retire, tail foremost. I sprang up; whereupon, having no room to turn, she threw herself backward, head over tail, scrambled to her feet, and in a moment was down the stair and gone. I followed her to the bottom, and looked all up and down the street. Not seeing her, I went back to my hard couch.

There were, then, two evil creatures prowling about the city, one with, and one without spots! I was not inclined to risk much for man or woman in Bulika, but the life of a child might well be worth such a poor one as mine, and I resolved to keep watch at that door the rest of the night.

Presently I heard the latch move, slow, slow: I looked up, and seeing the door half-open, rose and slid softly in. Behind it stood, not the woman I had befriended, but the muffled woman of the desert. Without a word she led me a few steps to an empty stone-paved chamber, and pointed to a rug on the floor. I wrapped myself in it, and once more lay down. She shut the door of the room, and I heard the outer door open and close again. There was no light save what came from the moonlit air.

As I lay sleepless, I began to hear a stifled moaning. It went on for a good while, and then came the cry of a child, followed by a terrible shriek. I sprang up and darted into the passage: from another door in it came the white leopardess with a new-born baby in her mouth, carrying it like a cub of her own. I threw myself upon her, and compelled her to drop the infant, which fell on the stone slabs with a piteous wail.

At the cry appeared the muffled woman. She stepped over us, the beast and myself, where we lay struggling in the narrow passage, took up the child, and carried it away. Returning, she lifted me off the animal, opened the door, and pushed me gently out. At my heels followed the leopardess.

"She too has failed me!" thought I; "—given me up to the beast to be settled with at her leisure! But we shall have a tussle for it!"

I ran down the stair, fearing she would spring on my back, but she followed me quietly. At the foot I turned to lay hold of her, but she sprang over my head; and when again I turned to face her, she was crouching at my feet! I stooped and stroked her lovely white skin; she responded by licking my bare feet with her hard dry tongue. Then I patted and fondled her, a well of tenderness overflowing in my heart: she might be treacherous too, but if I turned from every show of love lest it should be feigned, how was I ever to find the real love which must be somewhere in every world?

I stood up; she rose, and stood beside me.

A bulky object fell with a heavy squelch in the middle of the street, a few yards from us. I ran to it, and found a pulpy mass, with just form enough left to show it the body of a woman. It must have been thrown from some neighbouring window! I looked around me: the Shadow was walking along the other side of the way, with the white leopardess again at his heel!

I followed and gained upon them, urging in my heart for the leopardess that probably she was not a free agent. When I got near them, however, she turned and flew at me with such a hideous snarl, that instinctively I drew back: instantly she resumed her place behind the Shadow. Again I drew near; again she flew at me, her eyes flaming like live emeralds. Once more I made the experiment: she snapped at me like a dog, and bit me. My heart gave way, and I uttered a cry; whereupon the creature looked round with a glance that plainly meant—"Why WOULD you make me do it?"

I turned away angry with myself: I had been losing my time ever since I entered the place! night as it was I would go straight to the palace! From the square I had seen it—high above the heart of the city, compassed with many defences, more a fortress than a palace!

But I found its fortifications, like those of the city, much neglected, and partly ruinous. For centuries, clearly, they had been of no account! It had great and strong gates, with something like a drawbridge to them over a rocky chasm; but they stood open, and it was hard to believe that water had ever occupied the hollow before them. All was so still that sleep seemed to interpenetrate the structure, causing the very moonlight to look discordantly awake. I must either enter like a thief, or break a silence that rendered frightful the mere thought of a sound!

Like an outcast dog I was walking about the walls, when I came to a little recess with a stone bench: I took refuge in it from the wind, lay down, and in spite of the cold fell fast asleep.

I was wakened by something leaping upon me, and licking my face with the rough tongue of a feline animal. "It is the white leopardess!" I thought. "She is come to suck my blood!—and why should she not have it?—it would cost me more to defend than to yield it!" So I lay still, expecting a shoot of pain. But the pang did not arrive; a pleasant warmth instead began to diffuse itself through me. Stretched at my back, she lay as close to me as she could lie, the heat of her body slowly pene-trating mine, and her breath, which had nothing of the wild beast in it, swathing my head and face in a genial atmosphere. A full conviction that her intention toward me was good, gained possession of me. I turned like a sleepy boy, threw my arm over her, and sank into profound unconsciousness.

When I began to come to myself, I fancied I lay warm and soft in my own bed. "Is it possible I am at home?" I thought. The well-known scents of the garden seemed to come crowding in. I rubbed my eyes, and looked out: I lay on a bare stone, in the heart of a hateful city!

I sprang from the bench. Had I indeed had a leopardess for my bedfellow, or had I but dreamed it? She had but just left me, for the warmth of her body was with me yet!

I left the recess with a new hope, as strong as it was shapeless. One thing only was clear to me: I must find the princess! Surely I had some power with her, if not over her! Had I not saved her life, and had she not prolonged it at the expense of my vitality? The reflection gave me courage to encounter her, be she what she might.

CHAPTER XXV. THE PRINCESS

Making a circuit of the castle, I came again to the open gates, crossed the ravine-like moat, and found myself in a paved court, planted at regular intervals with towering trees like poplars. In the centre was one taller than the rest, whose branches, near the top, spread a little and gave it some resemblance to a palm. Between their great stems I got glimpses of the palace, which was of a style strange to me, but suggested Indian origin. It was long and low, with lofty towers at the corners, and one huge dome in the middle, rising from the roof to half the height of the towers. The main entrance was in the centre of the front—a low arch that seemed half an ellipse. No one was visible, the doors stood wide open, and I went unchallenged into a large hall, in the form of a longish ellipse. Toward one side stood a cage, in which couched, its head on its paws, a huge leopardess, chained by a steel collar, with its mouth muzzled and its paws muffled. It was white with dark oval spots, and lay staring out of wide-open eyes, with canoe-shaped pupils, and great green irids. It appeared to watch me, but not an eyeball, not a foot, not a whisker moved, and its tail stretched out behind it rigid as an iron bar. I could not tell whether it was a live thing or not.

From this vestibule two low passages led; I took one of them, and found it branch into many, all narrow and irregular. At a spot where was scarce room for two to pass, a page ran against me. He started back in terror, but having scanned me, gathered impudence, puffed himself out, and asked my business.

"To see the princess," I answered.

"A likely thing!" he returned. "I have not seen her highness this morning myself!"

I caught him by the back of the neck, shook him, and said, "Take me to her at once, or I will drag you with me till I find her. She shall know how her servants receive her visitors."

He gave a look at me, and began to pull like a blind man's dog, leading me thus to a large kitchen, where were many servants, feebly busy, and hardly awake. I expected them to fall upon me and drive me out, but they stared instead, with wide eyes—not at me, but at something behind me, and grew more ghastly as they stared. I turned my head, and saw the white leopardess, regarding them in a way that might have feared stouter hearts.

Presently, however, one of them, seeing, I suppose, that attack was not imminent, began to recover himself; I turned to him, and let the boy go.

"Take me to the princess," I said.

"She has not yet left her room, your lordship," he replied.

"Let her know that I am here, waiting audience of her."

"Will your lordship please to give me your name?"

"Tell her that one who knows the white leech desires to see her."

"She will kill me if I take such a message: I must not. I dare not."

"You refuse?"

He cast a glance at my attendant, and went.

The others continued staring—too much afraid of her to take their eyes off her. I turned to the graceful creature, where she stood, her muzzle dropped to my heel, white as milk, a warm splendour in the gloomy place, and stooped and patted her. She looked up at me; the mere movement of her head was enough to scatter them in all directions. She rose on her hind legs, and put her paws on my shoulders; I threw my arms round her. She pricked her ears, broke from me, and was out of sight in a moment.

The man I had sent to the princess entered.

"Please to come this way, my lord," he said.

My heart gave a throb, as if bracing itself to the encounter. I followed him through many passages, and was at last shown into a room so large and so dark that its walls were invisible. A single spot on the floor reflected a little light, but around that spot all was black. I looked up, and saw at a great height an oval aperture in the roof, on the periphery of which appeared the joints between blocks of black marble. The light on the floor showed close fitting slabs of the same material. I found afterward that the elliptical wall as well was of black marble, absorbing the little light that reached it. The roof was the long half of an ellipsoid, and the opening in it was over one of the foci of the ellipse of the floor. I fancied I caught sight of reddish lines, but when I would have examined them, they were gone.

All at once, a radiant form stood in the centre of the darkness, flashing a splendour on every side. Over a robe of soft white, her hair streamed in a cataract, black as the marble on which it fell. Her eyes were a luminous blackness; her arms and feet like warm ivory. She greeted me with the innocent smile of a girl—and in face, figure, and motion seemed but now to have stepped over the threshold of womanhood. "Alas," thought I, "ill did I reckon my danger! Can this be the woman I rescued—she who struck me, scorned me, left me?" I stood gazing at her out of the darkness; she stood gazing into it, as if searching for me.

She disappeared. "She will not acknowledge me!" I thought. But the next instant her eyes flashed out of the dark straight into mine. She had descried me and come to me!

"You have found me at last!" she said, laying her hand on my shoulder. "I knew you would!"

My frame quivered with conflicting consciousnesses, to analyse which I had no power. I was simultaneously attracted and repelled: each sensation seemed either.

"You shiver!" she said. "This place is cold for you! Come."

I stood silent: she had struck me dumb with beauty; she held me dumb with sweetness.

Taking me by the hand, she drew me to the spot of light, and again flashed upon me. An instant she stood there.

"You have grown brown since last I saw you," she said.

"This is almost the first roof I have been under since you left me," I replied.

"Whose was the other?" she rejoined.

"I do not know the woman's name."

"I would gladly learn it! The instinct of hospitality is not strong in my people!" She took me again by the hand, and led me through the darkness many steps to a curtain of black. Beyond it was a white stair, up which she conducted me to a beautiful chamber.

"How you must miss the hot flowing river!" she said. "But there is a bath in the corner with no white leeches in it! At the foot of your couch you will find a garment. When you come down, I shall be in the room to your left at the foot of the stair."

I stood as she left me, accusing my presumption: how was I to treat this lovely woman as a thing of evil, who behaved to me like a sister?—Whence the marvellous change in her? She left me with a blow; she received me almost with an embrace! She had reviled me; she said she knew I would follow and find her! Did she know my doubts concerning her—how much I should want explained? COULD she explain all? Could I believe her if she did? As to her hospitality, I had surely earned and might accept that—at least until I came to a definite judgment concerning her!

Could such beauty as I saw, and such wickedness as I suspected, exist in the same person? If they could, HOW was it possible? Unable to answer the former question, I must let the latter wait!

Clear as crystal, the water in the great white bath sent a sparkling flash from the corner where it lay sunk in the marble floor, and seemed to invite me to its embrace. Except the hot stream, two draughts in the cottage of the veiled woman, and the pools in the track of the wounded leopardess, I had not seen water since leaving home: it looked a thing celestial. I plunged in.

Immediately my brain was filled with an odour strange and delicate, which yet I did not altogether like. It made me doubt the princess afresh: had she medicated it? had she enchanted it? was she in any way working on me unlawfully? And how was there water in the palace, and not a drop in the city? I remembered the crushed paw of the leopardess, and sprang from the bath.

What had I been bathing in? Again I saw the fleeing mother, again I heard the howl, again I saw the limping beast. But what matter whence it flowed? was not the water sweet? Was it not very water the pitcher-plant secreted from its heart, and stored for the weary traveller? Water came from heaven: what mattered the well where it gathered, or the spring whence it burst? But I did not re-enter the bath.

I put on the robe of white wool, embroidered on the neck and hem, that lay ready for me, and went down the stair to the room whither my hostess had directed me. It was round, all of alabaster, and without a single window: the light came through everywhere, a soft, pearly shimmer rather than shine. Vague shadowy forms went flitting about over the walls and low dome, like loose rain-clouds over a grey-blue sky.

The princess stood waiting me, in a robe embroidered with argentine rings and discs, rectangles and lozenges, close together—a silver mail. It fell unbroken from her neck and hid her feet, but its long open sleeves left her arms bare.

In the room was a table of ivory, bearing cakes and fruit, an ivory jug of milk, a crystal jug of wine of a pale rose-colour, and a white loaf.

"Here we do not kill to eat," she said; "but I think you will like what I can give you."

I told her I could desire nothing better than what I saw. She seated herself on a couch by the table, and made me a sign to sit by her.

She poured me out a bowlful of milk, and, handing me the loaf, begged me to break from it such a piece as I liked. Then she filled from the wine-jug two silver goblets of grotesquely graceful workmanship.

"You have never drunk wine like this!" she said.

I drank, and wondered: every flower of Hybla and Hymettus must have sent its ghost to swell the soul of that wine!

"And now that you will be able to listen," she went on, "I must do what I can to make myself intelligible to you. Our natures, however, are so different, that this may not be easy. Men and women live but to die; we, that is such as I—we are but a few—live to live on. Old age is to you a horror; to me it is a dear desire: the older we grow, the nearer we are to our perfection. Your perfection is a poor thing, comes soon, and lasts but a little while; ours is a ceaseless ripening. I am not yet ripe, and have lived thousands of your years—how many, I never cared to note. The ever-lasting will not be measured.

"Many lovers have sought me; I have loved none of them: they sought but to enslave me; they sought me but as the men of my city seek gems of price.—When you found me, I found a man! I put you to the test; you stood it; your love was genuine!—It was, however, far from ideal—far from such love as I would have. You loved me truly, but not with true love. Pity has, but is not love. What woman of any world would return love for pity? Such love as yours was then, is hateful to me. I knew that, if you saw me as I am, you would love me—like the rest of them—to have and to hold: I would none of that either! I would be otherwise loved! I would have a love that outlived hopelessness, outmeasured indifference, hate, scorn! Therefore did I put on cruelty, despite, ingratitude. When I left you, I had shown myself such as you could at least no longer follow from pity: I was no longer in need of you! But you must satisfy my desire or set me free—prove yourself price-less or worthless! To satisfy the hunger of my love, you must follow me, looking for nothing, not gratitude, not even pity in return!—follow and find me, and be content with merest presence, with scantest forbearance!—I, not you, have failed; I yield the contest."

She looked at me tenderly, and hid her face in her hands. But I had caught a flash and a sparkle behind the tenderness, and did not believe her. She laid herself out to secure and enslave me; she only fascinated me!

"Beautiful princess," I said, "let me understand how you came to be found in such evil plight."

"There are things I cannot explain," she replied, "until you have become capable of understanding them—which can only be when love is grown perfect. There are many things so hidden from you that you cannot even wish to know them; but any question you can put, I can in some measure answer.

"I had set out to visit a part of my dominions occupied by a savage dwarf-people, strong and fierce, enemies to law and order, opposed to every kind of progress—an evil race. I went alone, fearing nothing, unaware of the least necessity for precaution. I did not know that upon the hot stream beside which you found me, a certain woman, by no means so powerful as myself, not being immortal, had cast what you call a spell—which is merely the setting in motion of a force as natural as any other, but operating primarily in a region beyond the ken of the mortal who makes use of the force.

"I set out on my journey, reached the stream, bounded across it,——"

A shadow of embarrassment darkened her cheek: I understood it, but showed no sign. Checked for the merest moment, she went on:

"—you know what a step it is in parts!—But in the very act, an indescribable cold invaded me. I recognised at once the nature of the assault, and knew it could affect me but temporarily. By sheer force of will I dragged myself to the wood—nor knew anything more until I saw you asleep, and the horrible worm at your neck. I crept out, dragged the monster from you, and laid my lips to the wound. You began to wake; I buried myself among the leaves."

She rose, her eyes flashing as never human eyes flashed, and threw her arms high over her head.

"What you have made me is yours!" she cried. "I will repay you as never yet did woman! My power, my beauty, my love are your own: take them."

She dropt kneeling beside me, laid her arms across my knees, and looked up in my face.

Then first I noted on her left hand a large clumsy glove. In my mind's eye I saw hair and claws under it, but I knew it was a hand shut hard—perhaps badly bruised. I glanced at the other: it was lovely as hand could be, and I felt that, if I did less than loathe her, I should love her. Not to dally with usurping emotions, I turned my eyes aside.

She started to her feet. I sat motionless, looking down.

"To me she may be true!" said my vanity. For a moment I was tempted to love a lie.

An odour, rather than the gentlest of airy pulses, was fanning me. I glanced up. She stood erect before me, waving her lovely arms in seemingly mystic fashion.

A frightful roar made my heart rebound against the walls of its cage. The alabaster trembled as if it would shake into shivers. The princess shuddered visibly.

"My wine was too strong for you!" she said, in a quavering voice; "I ought not to have let you take a full draught! Go and sleep now, and when you wake ask me what you please.—I will go with you: come."

As she preceded me up the stair,—

"I do not wonder that roar startled you!" she said. "It startled me, I confess: for a moment I feared she had escaped. But that is impossible."

The roar seemed to me, however—I could not tell why—to come from the WHITE leopardess, and to be meant for me, not the princess.

With a smile she left me at the door of my room, but as she turned I read anxiety on her beautiful face.

CHAPTER XXVI. A BATTLE ROYAL

I threw myself on the bed, and began to turn over in my mind the tale she had told me. She had forgotten herself, and, by a single incautious word, removed one perplexity as to the condition in which I found her in the forest! The leopardess BOUNDED over; the princess lay prostrate on the bank: the running stream had dissolved her self-enchantment! Her own account of the object of her journey revealed the danger of the Little Ones then imminent: I had saved the life of their one fearful enemy!

I had but reached this conclusion when I fell asleep. The lovely wine may not have been quite innocent.

When I opened my eyes, it was night. A lamp, suspended from the ceiling, cast a clear, although soft light through the chamber. A delicious languor infolded me. I seemed floating, far from land, upon the bosom of a twilight sea. Existence was in itself pleasure. I had no pain. Surely I was dying!

No pain!—ah, what a shoot of mortal pain was that! what a sickening sting! It went right through my heart! Again! That was sharpness itself!—and so sickening! I could not move my hand to lay it on my heart; something kept it down!

The pain was dying away, but my whole body seemed paralysed. Some evil thing was upon me!—something hateful! I would have struggled, but could not reach a struggle. My will agonised, but in vain, to assert itself. I desisted, and lay passive. Then I became aware of a soft hand on my face, pressing my head into the pillow, and of a heavy weight lying across me.

I began to breathe more freely; the weight was gone from my chest; I opened my eyes.

The princess was standing above me on the bed, looking out into the room, with the air of one who dreamed. Her great eyes were clear and calm. Her mouth wore a look of satisfied passion; she wiped from it a streak of red.

She caught my gaze, bent down, and struck me on the eyes with the handkerchief in her hand: it was like drawing the edge of a knife across them, and for a moment or two I was blind.

I heard a dull heavy sound, as of a large soft-footed animal alighting from a little jump. I opened my eyes, and saw the great swing of a long tail as it disappeared through the half-open doorway. I sprang after it.

The creature had vanished quite. I shot down the stair, and into the hall of alabaster. The moon was high, and the place like the inside of a faint, sun-blanched moon. The princess was not there. I must find her: in her presence I might protect myself; out of it I could not! I was a tame animal for her to feed upon; a human fountain for a thirst demoniac! She showed me favour the more easily to use me! My waking eyes did not fear her, but they would close, and she would come! Not seeing her, I felt her everywhere, for she might be anywhere—might even now be waiting me in some secret cavern of sleep! Only with my eyes upon her could I feel safe from her!

Outside the alabaster hall it was pitch-dark, and I had to grope my way along with hands and feet. At last I felt a curtain, put it aside, and entered the black hall. There I found a great silent assembly. How it was visible I neither saw nor could imagine, for the walls, the floor, the roof, were shrouded in what seemed an infinite blackness, blacker than the blackest of moonless, starless nights; yet my eyes could separate, although vaguely, not a few of the individuals in the mass interpenetrated and divided, as well as surrounded, by the darkness. It seemed as if my eyes would never come quite to themselves. I pressed their balls and looked and looked again, but what I saw would not grow distinct. Blackness mingled with form, silence and undefined motion possessed the wide space. All was a dim, confused dance, filled with recurrent glimpses of shapes not unknown to me. Now appeared a woman, with glorious eyes looking out of a skull; now an armed figure on a skeleton horse; now one now another of the hideous burrowing phantasms. I could trace no order and little relation in the mingling and crossing currents and eddies. If I seemed to catch the shape and rhythm of a dance, it was but to see it break, and confusion prevail. With the shifting colours of the seemingly more solid shapes, mingled a multitude of shadows, independent apparently of originals, each moving after its own free shadow-will. I looked everywhere for the princess, but throughout the wildly changing kaleidoscopic scene, could not see her nor discover indication of her presence. Where was she? What might she not be doing? No one took the least notice of me as I wandered hither and thither seeking her. At length losing hope, I turned away to look elsewhere. Finding the wall, and keeping to it with my hand, for even then I could not see it, I came, groping along, to a curtained opening into the vestibule.

Dimly moonlighted, the cage of the leopardess was the arena of what seemed a desperate although silent struggle. Two vastly differing forms, human and bestial, with entangled confusion of mingling bodies and limbs, writhed and wrestled in closest embrace. It had lasted but an instant when I saw the leopardess out of the cage, walking quietly to the open door. As I hastened after her I threw a glance behind me: there was the leopardess in the cage, couching motionless as when I saw her first.

The moon, half-way up the sky, was shining round and clear; the bodiless shadow I had seen the night before, was walking through the trees toward the gate; and after him went the leopardess, swinging her tail. I followed, a little way off, as silently as they, and neither of them once looked round. Through the open gate we went down to the city, lying quiet as the moonshine upon it. The face of the moon was very still, and its stillness looked like that of expectation.

The Shadow took his way straight to the stair at the top of which I had lain the night before. Without a pause he went up, and the leopardess followed. I quickened my pace, but, a moment after, heard a cry of horror. Then came the fall of something soft and heavy between me and the stair, and at my feet lay a body, frightfully blackened and crushed, but still recognisable as that of the woman who had led me home and shut me out. As I stood petrified, the spotted leopardess came bounding down the stair with a baby in her mouth. I darted to seize her ere she could turn at the foot; but that instant, from behind me, the white leopardess, like a great bar of glowing silver, shot through the moonlight, and had her by the neck. She dropped the child; I caught it up, and stood to watch the battle between them.

What a sight it was—now the one, now the other uppermost, both too intent for any noise beyond a low growl, a whimpered cry, or a snarl of hate—followed by a quicker scrambling of claws, as each, worrying and pushing and dragging, struggled for foothold on the pavement! The spotted leopardess was larger than the white, and I was anxious for my friend; but I soon saw that, though neither stronger nor more active, the white leopardess had the greater endurance. Not once did she lose her hold on the neck of the other. From the spotted throat at length issued a howl of agony, changing, by swift-crowded gradations, into the long-drawn CRESCENDO of a woman's uttermost wail. The white one relaxed her jaws; the spotted one drew herself away, and rose on her hind legs. Erect in the moonlight stood the princess, a confused rush of shadows careering over her whiteness—the spots of the leopard crowding, hurrying, fleeing to the refuge of her eyes, where merging they vanished. The last few, outsped and belated, mingled with the cloud of her streamy hair, leaving her radiant as the moon when a legion of little vapours has flown, wind-hunted, off her silvery disc—save that, adown the white column of her throat, a thread of blood still trickled from every wound of her adversary's terrible teeth. She turned away, took a few steps with the gait of a Hecate, fell, covered afresh with her spots, and fled at a long, stretching gallop.

The white leopardess turned also, sprang upon me, pulled my arms asunder, caught the baby as it fell, and flew with it along the street toward the gate.

CHAPTER XXVII. THE SILENT FOUNTAIN

I turned and followed the spotted leopardess, catching but one glimpse of her as she tore up the brow of the hill to the gate of the palace. When I reached the entrance-hall, the princess was just throwing the robe around her which she had left on the floor. The blood had ceased to flow from her wounds, and had dried in the wind of her flight.

When she saw me, a flash of anger crossed her face, and she turned her head aside. Then, with an attempted smile, she looked at me, and said,

"I have met with a small accident! Happening to hear that the cat-woman was again in the city, I went down to send her away. But she had one of her horrid creatures with her: it sprang upon me, and had its claws in my neck before I could strike it!"

She gave a shiver, and I could not help pitying her, although I knew she lied, for her wounds were real, and her face reminded me of how she looked in the cave. My heart began to reproach me that I had let her fight unaided, and I suppose I looked the compassion I felt.

"Child of folly!" she said, with another attempted smile, "—not crying, surely! —Wait for me here; I am going into the black hall for a moment. I want you to get me something for my scratches."

But I followed her close. Out of my sight I feared her.

The instant the princess entered, I heard a buzzing sound as of many low voices, and, one portion after another, the assembly began to be shiftingly illuminated, as by a ray that went travelling from spot to spot. Group after group would shine out for a space, then sink back into the general vagueness, while another part of the vast company would grow momently bright.

Some of the actions going on when thus illuminated, were not unknown to me; I had been in them, or had looked on them, and so had the princess: present with every one of them I now saw her. The skull-headed dancers footed the grass in the forest-hall: there was the princess looking in at the door! The fight went on in the Evil Wood: there was the princess urging it! Yet I was close behind her all the time, she standing motionless, her head sunk on her bosom. The confused murmur continued, the confused commotion of colours and shapes; and still the ray went shifting and showing. It settled at last on the hollow in the heath, and there was the princess, walking up and down, and trying in vain to wrap the vapour around her! Then first I was startled at what I saw: the old librarian walked up to her, and stood for a moment regarding her; she fell; her limbs forsook her and fled; her body vanished.

A wild shriek rang through the echoing place, and with the fall of her eidolon, the princess herself, till then standing like a statue in front of me, fell heavily, and lay still. I turned at once and went out: not again would I seek to restore her! As I stood trembling beside the cage, I knew that in the black ellipsoid I had been in the brain of the princess!—I saw the tail of the leopardess quiver once.

While still endeavouring to compose myself, I heard the voice of the princess beside me.

"Come now," she said; "I will show you what I want you to do for me."

She led the way into the court. I followed in dazed compliance.

The moon was near the zenith, and her present silver seemed brighter than the gold of the absent sun. She brought me through the trees to the tallest of them, the one in the centre. It was not quite like the rest, for its branches, drawing their ends together at the top, made a clump that looked from beneath like a fir-cone. The princess stood close under it, gazing up, and said, as if talking to herself,

"On the summit of that tree grows a tiny blossom which would at once heal my scratches! I might be a dove for a moment and fetch it, but I see a little snake in the leaves whose bite would be worse to a dove than the bite of a tiger to me!—How I hate that cat-woman!"

She turned to me quickly, saying with one of her sweetest smiles,

"Can you climb?"

The smile vanished with the brief question, and her face changed to a look of sadness and suffering. I ought to have left her to suffer, but the way she put her hand to her wounded neck went to my heart.

I considered the tree. All the way up to the branches, were projections on the stem like the remnants on a palm of its fallen leaves.

"I can climb that tree," I answered.

"Not with bare feet!" she returned.

In my haste to follow the leopardess disappearing, I had left my sandals in my room.

"It is no matter," I said; "I have long gone barefoot!"

Again I looked at the tree, and my eyes went wandering up the stem until my sight lost itself in the branches. The moon shone like silvery foam here and there on the rugged bole, and a little rush of wind went through the top with a murmurous sound as of water falling softly into water. I approached the tree to begin my ascent of it. The princess stopped me.

"I cannot let you attempt it with your feet bare!" she insisted. "A fall from the top would kill you!"

"So would a bite from the snake!" I answered—not believing, I confess, that there was any snake.

"It would not hurt YOU!" she replied. "—Wait a moment."

She tore from her garment the two wide borders that met in front, and kneeling on one knee, made me put first my left foot, then my right on the other, and bound them about with the thick embroidered strips.

"You have left the ends hanging, princess!" I said.

"I have nothing to cut them off with; but they are not long enough to get entangled," she replied.

I turned to the tree, and began to climb.

Now in Bulika the cold after sundown was not so great as in certain other parts of the country—especially about the sexton's cottage; yet when I had climbed a little way, I began to feel very cold, grew still colder as I ascended, and became coldest of all when I got among the branches. Then I shivered, and seemed to have lost my hands and feet.

There was hardly any wind, and the branches did not sway in the least, yet, as I approached the summit, I became aware of a peculiar unsteadiness: every branch on which I placed foot or laid hold, seemed on the point of giving way. When my head rose above the branches near the top, and in the open moonlight I began to look about for the blossom, that instant I found myself drenched from head to foot. The next, as if plunged in a stormy water, I was flung about wildly, and felt myself sinking. Tossed up and down, tossed this way and tossed that way, rolled over and over, checked, rolled the other way and tossed up again, I was sinking lower and lower. Gasping and gurgling and choking, I fell at last upon a solid bottom.

"I told you so!" croaked a voice in my ear.

CHAPTER XXVIII. I AM SILENCED

I rubbed the water out of my eyes, and saw the raven on the edge of a huge stone basin. With the cold light of the dawn reflected from his glossy plumage, he stood calmly looking down upon me. I lay on my back in water, above which, leaning on my elbows, I just lifted my face. I was in the basin of the large fountain constructed by my father in the middle of the lawn. High over me glimmered the thick, steel-shiny stalk, shooting, with a torrent uprush, a hundred feet into the air, to spread in a blossom of foam.

Nettled at the coolness of the raven's remark,

"You told me nothing!" I said.

"I told you to do nothing any one you distrusted asked you!"

"Tut! how was mortal to remember that?"

"You will not forget the consequences of having forgotten it!" replied Mr. Raven, who stood leaning over the margin of the basin, and stretched his hand across to me.

I took it, and was immediately beside him on the lawn, dripping and streaming.

"You must change your clothes at once!" he said. "A wetting does not signify where you come from—though at present such an accident is unusual; here it has its inconveniences!"

He was again a raven, walking, with something stately in his step, toward the house, the door of which stood open.

"I have not much to change!" I laughed; for I had flung aside my robe to climb the tree.

"It is a long time since I moulted a feather!" said the raven.

In the house no one seemed awake. I went to my room, found a dressing-gown, and descended to the library.

As I entered, the librarian came from the closet. I threw myself on a couch. Mr.

Raven drew a chair to my side and sat down. For a minute or two neither spoke. I was the first to break the silence.

"What does it all mean?" I said.

"A good question!" he rejoined: "nobody knows what anything is; a man can learn only what a thing means! Whether he do, depends on the use he is making of it."

"I have made no use of anything yet!"

"Not much; but you know the fact, and that is something! Most people take more than a lifetime to learn that they have learned nothing, and done less! At least you have not been without the desire to be of use!"

"I did want to do something for the children—the precious Little Ones, I mean."

"I know you did—and started the wrong way!"

"I did not know the right way."

"That is true also—but you are to blame that you did not."

"I am ready to believe whatever you tell me—as soon as I understand what it means."

"Had you accepted our invitation, you would have known the right way. When a man will not act where he is, he must go far to find his work."

"Indeed I have gone far, and got nowhere, for I have not found my work! I left the children to learn how to serve them, and have only learned the danger they are in."

"When you were with them, you were where you could help them: you left your work to look for it! It takes a wise man to know when to go away; a fool may learn to go back at once!"

"Do you mean, sir, I could have done something for the Little Ones by staying with them?"

"Could you teach them anything by leaving them?"

"No; but how could I teach them? I did not know how to begin. Besides, they were far ahead of me!"

"That is true. But you were not a rod to measure them with! Certainly, if they knew what you know, not to say what you might have known, they would be ahead of you—out of sight ahead! but you saw they were not growing—or growing so slowly that they had not yet developed the idea of growing! they were even afraid of growing!—You had never seen children remain children!"

"But surely I had no power to make them grow!"

"You might have removed some of the hindrances to their growing!"

"What are they? I do not know them. I did think perhaps it was the want of water!"

"Of course it is! they have none to cry with!"

"I would gladly have kept them from requiring any for that purpose!"

"No doubt you would—the aim of all stupid philanthropists! Why, Mr. Vane, but for the weeping in it, your world would never have become worth saving! You confess you thought it might be water they wanted: why did not you dig them a well or two?"

"That never entered my mind!"

"Not when the sounds of the waters under the earth entered your ears?"

"I believe it did once. But I was afraid of the giants for them. That was what made me bear so much from the brutes myself!"

"Indeed you almost taught the noble little creatures to be afraid of the stupid Bags! While they fed and comforted and worshipped you, all the time you submitted to be the slave of bestial men! You gave the darlings a seeming coward for their hero! A worse wrong you could hardly have done them. They gave you their hearts; you owed them your soul!—You might by this time have made the Bags hewers of wood and drawers of water to the Little Ones!"

"I fear what you say is true, Mr. Raven! But indeed I was afraid that more knowledge might prove an injury to them—render them less innocent, less lovely."

"They had given you no reason to harbour such a fear!"

"Is not a little knowledge a dangerous thing?"

"That is one of the pet falsehoods of your world! Is man's greatest knowledge more than a little? or is it therefore dangerous? The fancy that knowledge is in itself a great thing, would make any degree of knowledge more dangerous than any amount of ignorance. To know all things would not be greatness."

"At least it was for love of them, not from cowardice that I served the giants!"

"Granted. But you ought to have served the Little Ones, not the giants! You ought to have given the Little Ones water; then they would soon have taught the giants their true position. In the meantime you could yourself have made the giants cut down two-thirds of their coarse fruit-trees to give room to the little delicate ones! You lost your chance with the Lovers, Mr. Vane! You speculated about them instead of helping them!"

CHAPTER XXIX. THE PERSIAN CAT

I sat in silence and shame. What he said was true: I had not been a wise neighbour to the Little Ones!

Mr. Raven resumed:

"You wronged at the same time the stupid creatures themselves. For them slavery would have been progress. To them a few such lessons as you could have given them with a stick from one of their own trees, would have been invaluable."

"I did not know they were cowards!"

"What difference does that make? The man who grounds his action on another's cowardice, is essentially a coward himself.—I fear worse will come of it! By this time the Little Ones might have been able to protect themselves from the princess, not to say the giants—they were always fit enough for that; as it was they laughed at them! but now, through your relations with her,——"

"I hate her!" I cried.

"Did you let her know you hated her?"

Again I was silent.

"Not even to her have you been faithful!—But hush! we were followed from the fountain, I fear!"

"No living creature did I see!—except a disreputable-looking cat that bolted into the shrubbery."

"It was a magnificent Persian—so wet and draggled, though, as to look what she was—worse than disreputable!"

"What do you mean, Mr. Raven?" I cried, a fresh horror taking me by the throat. "—There was a beautiful blue Persian about the house, but she fled at the very sound of water!—Could she have been after the goldfish?"

"We shall see!" returned the librarian. "I know a little about cats of several sorts, and there is that in the room which will unmask this one, or I am mistaken in her."

He rose, went to the door of the closet, brought from it the mutilated volume, and sat down again beside me. I stared at the book in his hand: it was a whole book, entire and sound!

"Where was the other half of it?" I gasped.

"Sticking through into my library," he answered.

I held my peace. A single question more would have been a plunge into a bottomless sea, and there might be no time!

"Listen," he said: "I am going to read a stanza or two. There is one present who, I imagine, will hardly enjoy the reading!"

He opened the vellum cover, and turned a leaf or two. The parchment was discoloured with age, and one leaf showed a dark stain over two-thirds of it. He slowly turned this also, and seemed looking for a certain passage in what appeared a continuous poem. Somewhere about the middle of the book he began to read.

But what follows represents—not what he read, only the impression it made upon me. The poem seemed in a language I had never before heard, which yet I understood perfectly, although I could not write the words, or give their meaning save in poor approximation. These fragments, then, are the shapes which those he read have finally taken in passing again through my brain:—

"But if I found a man that could believe
      In what he saw not, felt not, and yet knew,
   From him I should take substance, and receive
      Firmness and form relate to touch and view;
      Then should I clothe me in the likeness true
   Of that idea where his soul did cleave!"

He turned a leaf and read again:—
   "In me was every woman. I had power
      Over the soul of every living man,
   Such as no woman ever had in dower—
      Could what no woman ever could, or can;
      All women, I, the woman, still outran,
   Outsoared, outsank, outreigned, in hall or bower.

   "For I, though me he neither saw nor heard,
      Nor with his hand could touch finger of mine,
   Although not once my breath had ever stirred
      A hair of him, could trammel brain and spine
      With rooted bonds which Death could not untwine—
   Or life, though hope were evermore deferred."

Again he paused, again turned a leaf, and again began:—

"For by his side I lay, a bodiless thing;

I breathed not, saw not, felt not, only thought,
And made him love me—with a hungering
    After he knew not what—if it was aught
    Or but a nameless something that was wrought
By him out of himself; for I did sing

"A song that had no sound into his soul;
    I lay a heartless thing against his heart,
Giving him nothing where he gave his whole
    Being to clothe me human, every part:
    That I at last into his sense might dart,
Thus first into his living mind I stole.

"Ah, who was ever conquering Love but I!
    Who else did ever throne in heart of man!
To visible being, with a gladsome cry
    Waking, life's tremor through me throbbing ran!"

A strange, repulsive feline wail arose somewhere in the room. I started up on my elbow and stared about me, but could see nothing.

Mr. Raven turned several leaves, and went on:—

"Sudden I woke, nor knew the ghastly fear
    That held me—not like serpent coiled about,
But like a vapour moist, corrupt, and drear,
    Filling heart, soul, and breast and brain throughout;
    My being lay motionless in sickening doubt,
Nor dared to ask how came the horror here.

"My past entire I knew, but not my now;
    I understood nor what I was, nor where;
I knew what I had been: still on my brow
    I felt the touch of what no more was there!
    I was a fainting, dead, yet live Despair;
A life that flouted life with mop and mow!

"That I was a queen I knew right well,
    And sometimes wore a splendour on my head
Whose flashing even dead darkness could not quell—
    The like on neck and arms and girdle-stead;
    And men declared a light my closed eyes shed
That killed the diamond in its silver cell."

Again I heard the ugly cry of feline pain. Again I looked, but saw neither shape nor motion. Mr. Raven seemed to listen a moment, but again turned several pages, and resumed:—

"Hideously wet, my hair of golden hue
    Fouled my fair hands: to have it swiftly shorn
  I had given my rubies, all for me dug new—
    No eyes had seen, and such no waist had worn!
    For a draught of water from a drinking horn,
  For one blue breath, I had given my sapphires blue!

  "Nay, I had given my opals for a smock,
    A peasant-maiden's garment, coarse and clean:
  My shroud was rotting! Once I heard a cock
    Lustily crow upon the hillock green
    Over my coffin. Dulled by space between,
  Came back an answer like a ghostly mock."

Once more arose the bestial wail.
   "I thought some foul thing was in the room!" said the librarian, casting a glance around him; but instantly he turned a leaf or two, and again read:—

"For I had bathed in milk and honey-dew,
    In rain from roses shook, that ne'er touched earth,
  And ointed me with nard of amber hue;
    Never had spot me spotted from my birth,
    Or mole, or scar of hurt, or fret of dearth;
  Never one hair superfluous on me grew.

  "Fleeing cold whiteness, I would sit alone—
    Not in the sun—I feared his bronzing light,
  But in his radiance back around me thrown
    By fulgent mirrors tempering his might;
    Thus bathing in a moon-bath not too bright,
  My skin I tinted slow to ivory tone.

  "But now, all round was dark, dark all within!
    My eyes not even gave out a phantom-flash;
  My fingers sank in pulp through pulpy skin;
    My body lay death-weltered in a mash

Of slimy horrors———"

With a fearsome yell, her clammy fur staring in clumps, her tail thick as a cable, her eyes flashing green as a chrysoprase, her distended claws entangling themselves so that she floundered across the carpet, a huge white cat rushed from somewhere, and made for the chimney. Quick as thought the librarian threw the manuscript between her and the hearth. She crouched instantly, her eyes fixed on the book. But his voice went on as if still he read, and his eyes seemed also fixed on the book:—

"Ah, the two worlds! so strangely are they one,
    And yet so measurelessly wide apart!
  Oh, had I lived the bodiless alone
    And from defiling sense held safe my heart,
    Then had I scaped the canker and the smart,
  Scaped life-in-death, scaped misery's endless moan!"

At these words such a howling, such a prolonged yell of agony burst from the cat, that we both stopped our ears. When it ceased, Mr. Raven walked to the fire-place, took up the book, and, standing between the creature and the chimney, pointed his finger at her for a moment. She lay perfectly still. He took a half-burnt stick from the hearth, drew with it some sign on the floor, put the manuscript back in its place, with a look that seemed to say, "Now we have her, I think!" and, returning to the cat, stood over her and said, in a still, solemn voice:—

"Lilith, when you came here on the way to your evil will, you little thought into whose hands you were delivering yourself!—Mr. Vane, when God created me,—not out of Nothing, as say the unwise, but out of His own endless glory—He brought me an angelic splendour to be my wife: there she lies! For her first thought was POWER; she counted it slavery to be one with me, and bear children for Him who gave her being. One child, indeed, she bore; then, puffed with the fancy that she had created her, would have me fall down and worship her! Finding, however, that I would but love and honour, never obey and worship her, she poured out her blood to escape me, fled to the army of the aliens, and soon had so ensnared the heart of the great Shadow, that he became her slave, wrought her will, and made her queen of Hell. How it is with her now, she best knows, but I know also. The one child of her body she fears and hates, and would kill, asserting a right, which is a lie, over what God sent through her into His new world. Of creating, she knows no more than the crystal that takes its allotted shape, or the worm that makes two worms when it is cloven asunder. Vilest of God's creatures, she lives by the blood and lives and souls of men. She consumes and slays, but is powerless to destroy as to create."

The animal lay motionless, its beryl eyes fixed flaming on the man: his eyes on hers held them fixed that they could not move from his.

"Then God gave me another wife—not an angel but a woman—who is to this as light is to darkness."

The cat gave a horrible screech, and began to grow bigger. She went on growing and growing. At last the spotted leopardess uttered a roar that made the house tremble. I sprang to my feet. I do not think Mr. Raven started even with his eyelids.

"It is but her jealousy that speaks," he said, "jealousy self-kindled, foiled and fruitless; for here I am, her master now whom she, would not have for her husband! while my beautiful Eve yet lives, hoping immortally! Her hated daughter lives also, but beyond her evil ken, one day to be what she counts her destruction—for even Lilith shall be saved by her childbearing. Meanwhile she exults that my human wife plunged herself and me in despair, and has borne me a countless race of miserables; but my Eve repented, and is now beautiful as never was woman or angel, while her groaning, travailing world is the nursery of our Father's children. I too have repented, and am blessed.—Thou, Lilith, hast not yet repented; but thou must.—Tell me, is the great Shadow beautiful? Knowest thou how long thou wilt thyself remain beautiful?—Answer me, if thou knowest."

Then at last I understood that Mr. Raven was indeed Adam, the old and the new man; and that his wife, ministering in the house of the dead, was Eve, the mother of us all, the lady of the New Jerusalem.

The leopardess reared; the flickering and fleeing of her spots began; the princess at length stood radiant in her perfect shape.

"I AM beautiful—and immortal!" she said—and she looked the goddess she would be.

"As a bush that burns, and is consumed," answered he who had been her husband. "—What is that under thy right hand?"

For her arm lay across her bosom, and her hand was pressed to her side.

A swift pang contorted her beautiful face, and passed.

"It is but a leopard-spot that lingers! it will quickly follow those I have dismissed," she answered.

"Thou art beautiful because God created thee, but thou art the slave of sin: take thy hand from thy side."

Her hand sank away, and as it dropt she looked him in the eyes with a quailing fierceness that had in it no surrender.

He gazed a moment at the spot.

"It is not on the leopard; it is in the woman!" he said. "Nor will it leave thee until it hath eaten to thy heart, and thy beauty hath flowed from thee through the open wound!"

She gave a glance downward, and shivered.

"Lilith," said Adam, and his tone had changed to a tender beseeching, "hear me, and repent, and He who made thee will cleanse thee!"

Her hand returned quivering to her side. Her face grew dark. She gave the cry of one from whom hope is vanishing. The cry passed into a howl. She lay writhing on the floor, a leopardess covered with spots.

"The evil thou meditatest," Adam resumed, "thou shalt never compass, Lilith, for Good and not Evil is the Universe. The battle between them may last for count-less ages, but it must end: how will it fare with thee when Time hath vanished in the dawn of the eternal morn? Repent, I beseech thee; repent, and be again an angel of God!"

She rose, she stood upright, a woman once more, and said,

"I will not repent. I will drink the blood of thy child." My eyes were fastened on the princess; but when Adam spoke, I turned to him: he stood towering above her; the form of his visage was altered, and his voice was terrible.

"Down!" he cried; "or by the power given me I will melt thy very bones."

She flung herself on the floor, dwindled and dwindled, and was again a gray cat. Adam caught her up by the skin of her neck, bore her to the closet, and threw her in. He described a strange figure on the threshold, and closing the door, locked it.

Then he returned to my side the old librarian, looking sad and worn, and furtively wiping tears from his eyes.

CHAPTER XXX. ADAM EXPLAINS

"We must be on our guard," he said, "or she will again outwit us. She would befool the very elect!"

"How are we to be on our guard?" I asked.

"Every way," he answered. "She fears, therefore hates her child, and is in this house on her way to destroy her. The birth of children is in her eyes the death of their parents, and every new generation the enemy of the last. Her daughter appears to her an open channel through which her immortality—which yet she counts self-inherent—is flowing fast away: to fill it up, almost from her birth she has pursued her with an utter enmity. But the result of her machinations hitherto is, that in the region she claims as her own, has appeared a colony of children, to which that daughter is heart and head and sheltering wings. My Eve longed after the child, and would have been to her as a mother to her first-born, but we were then unfit to train her: she was carried into the wilderness, and for ages we knew nothing of her fate. But she was divinely fostered, and had young angels for her playmates; nor did she ever know care until she found a baby in the wood, and the mother-heart in her awoke. One by one she has found many children since, and that heart is not yet full. Her family is her absorbing charge, and never children were better mothered. Her authority over them is without appeal, but it is unknown to herself, and never comes to the surface except in watchfulness and service. She has forgotten the time when she lived without them, and thinks she came herself from the wood, the first of the family.

"You have saved the life of her and their enemy; therefore your life belongs to her and them. The princess was on her way to destroy them, but as she crossed that stream, vengeance overtook her, and she would have died had you not come to her aid. You did; and ere now she would have been raging among the Little Ones, had she dared again cross the stream. But there was yet a way to the blessed little colony through the world of the three dimensions; only, from that, by the slaying of her former body, she had excluded herself, and except in personal contact with one belonging to it, could not re-enter it. You provided the opportunity: never, in all her long years, had she had one before. Her hand, with lightest touch, was on one or other of your muffled feet, every step as you climbed. In that little chamber, she is now watching to leave it as soon as ever she may."

"She cannot know anything about the door!—she cannot at least know how to open it!" I said; but my heart was not so confident as my words.

"Hush, hush!" whispered the librarian, with uplifted hand; "she can hear through anything!—You must go at once, and make your way to my wife's cottage. I will remain to keep guard over her."

"Let me go to the Little Ones!" I cried.

"Beware of that, Mr. Vane. Go to my wife, and do as she tells you."

His advice did not recommend itself: why haste to encounter measureless delay? If not to protect the children, why go at all? Alas, even now I believed him only enough to ask him questions, not to obey him!

"Tell me first, Mr. Raven," I said, "why, of all places, you have shut her up there! The night I ran from your house, it was immediately into that closet!"

"The closet is no nearer our cottage, and no farther from it, than any or every other place."

"But," I returned, hard to persuade where I could not understand, "how is it then that, when you please, you take from that same door a whole book where I saw and felt only a part of one? The other part, you have just told me, stuck through into your library: when you put it again on the shelf, will it not again stick through into that? Must not then the two places, in which parts of the same volume can at the same moment exist, lie close together? Or can one part of the book be in space, or SOMEWHERE, and the other out of space, or NOWHERE?"

"I am sorry I cannot explain the thing to you," he answered; "but there is no provision in you for understanding it. Not merely, therefore, is the phenomenon inexplicable to you, but the very nature of it is inapprehensible by you. Indeed I but partially apprehend it myself. At the same time you are constantly experiencing things which you not only do not, but cannot understand. You think you understand them, but your understanding of them is only your being used to them, and therefore not surprised at them. You accept them, not because you understand them, but because you must accept them: they are there, and have unavoidable relations with you! The fact is, no man understands anything; when he knows he does not understand, that is his first tottering step—not toward understanding, but toward the capability of one day understanding. To such things as these you are not used, therefore you do not fancy you understand them. Neither I nor any man can here help you to understand; but I may, perhaps, help you a little to believe!"

He went to the door of the closet, gave a low whistle, and stood listening. A moment after, I heard, or seemed to hear, a soft whir of wings, and, looking up, saw a white dove perch for an instant on the top of the shelves over the portrait, thence drop to Mr. Raven's shoulder, and lay her head against his cheek. Only by the motions of their two heads could I tell that they were talking together; I heard nothing. Neither had I moved my eyes from them, when suddenly she was not there, and Mr. Raven came back to his seat.

"Why did you whistle?" I asked. "Surely sound here is not sound there!"

"You are right," he answered. "I whistled that you might know I called her. Not the whistle, but what the whistle meant reached her.—There is not a minute to lose: you must go!"

"I will at once!" I replied, and moved for the door.

"You will sleep to-night at my hostelry!" he said—not as a question, but in a tone of mild authority.

"My heart is with the children," I replied. "But if you insist——"

"I do insist. You can otherwise effect nothing.—I will go with you as far as the mirror, and see you off."

He rose. There came a sudden shock in the closet. Apparently the leopardess had flung herself against the heavy door. I looked at my companion.

"Come; come!" he said.

Ere we reached the door of the library, a howling yell came after us, mingled with the noise of claws that scored at the hard oak. I hesitated, and half turned.

"To think of her lying there alone," I murmured, "—with that terrible wound!"

"Nothing will ever close that wound," he answered, with a sigh. "It must eat into her heart! Annihilation itself is no death to evil. Only good where evil was, is evil dead. An evil thing must live with its evil until it chooses to be good. That alone is the slaying of evil."

I held my peace until a sound I did not understand overtook us.

"If she should break loose!" I cried.

"Make haste!" he rejoined. "I shall hurry down the moment you are gone, and I have disarranged the mirrors."

We ran, and reached the wooden chamber breathless. Mr. Raven seized the chains and adjusted the hood. Then he set the mirrors in their proper relation, and came beside me in front of the standing one. Already I saw the mountain range emerging from the mist.

Between us, wedging us asunder, darted, with the yell of a demon, the huge bulk of the spotted leopardess. She leaped through the mirror as through an open window, and settled at once into a low, even, swift gallop.

I cast a look of dismay at my companion, and sprang through to follow her. He came after me leisurely.

"You need not run," he called; "you cannot overtake her. This is our way."

As he spoke he turned in the opposite direction.

"She has more magic at her finger-tips than I care to know!" he added quietly.

"We must do what we can!" I said, and ran on, but sickening as I saw her dwindle in the distance, stopped, and went back to him.

"Doubtless we must," he answered. "But my wife has warned Mara, and she will do her part; you must sleep first: you have given me your word!"

"Nor do I mean to break it. But surely sleep is not the first thing! Surely, surely, action takes precedence of repose!"

"A man can do nothing he is not fit to do.—See! did I not tell you Mara would do her part?"

I looked whither he pointed, and saw a white spot moving at an acute angle with the line taken by the leopardess.

"There she is!" he cried. "The spotted leopardess is strong, but the white is stronger!"

"I have seen them fight: the combat did not appear decisive as to that."

"How should such eyes tell which have never slept? The princess did not confess herself beaten—that she never does—but she fled! When she confesses her last hope gone, that it is indeed hard to kick against the goad, then will her day begin to dawn! Come; come! He who cannot act must make haste to sleep!"

CHAPTER XXXI. THE SEXTON'S OLD HORSE

I stood and watched the last gleam of the white leopardess melt away, then turned to follow my guide—but reluctantly. What had I to do with sleep? Surely reason was the same in every world, and what reason could there be in going to sleep with the dead, when the hour was calling the live man? Besides, no one would wake me, and how could I be certain of waking early—of waking at all?—the sleepers in that house let morning glide into noon, and noon into night, nor ever stirred! I murmured, but followed, for I knew not what else to do.

The librarian walked on in silence, and I walked silent as he. Time and space glided past us. The sun set; it began to grow dark, and I felt in the air the spreading cold of the chamber of death. My heart sank lower and lower. I began to lose sight of the lean, long-coated figure, and at length could no more hear his swishing stride through the heather. But then I heard instead the slow-flapping wings of the raven; and, at intervals, now a firefly, now a gleaming butterfly rose into the rayless air.

By and by the moon appeared, slow crossing the far horizon.

"You are tired, are you not, Mr. Vane?" said the raven, alighting on a stone. "You must make acquaintance with the horse that will carry you in the morning!"

He gave a strange whistle through his long black beak. A spot appeared on the face of the half-risen moon. To my ears came presently the drumming of swift, soft-galloping hoofs, and in a minute or two, out of the very disc of the moon, low-thundered the terrible horse. His mane flowed away behind him like the crest of a wind-fighting wave, torn seaward in hoary spray, and the whisk of his tail kept blinding the eye of the moon. Nineteen hands he seemed, huge of bone, tight of skin, hard of muscle—a steed the holy Death himself might choose on which to ride abroad and slay! The moon seemed to regard him with awe; in her scary light he looked a very skeleton, loosely roped together. Terrifically large, he moved with the lightness of a winged insect. As he drew near, his speed slackened, and his mane and tail drifted about him settling.

Now I was not merely a lover of horses, but I loved every horse I saw. I had never spent money except upon horses, and had never sold a horse. The sight of this mighty one, terrible to look at, woke in me longing to possess him. It was pure greed, nay, rank covetousness, an evil thing in all the worlds. I do not mean that I could have stolen him, but that, regardless of his proper place, I would have bought him if I could. I laid my hands on him, and stroked the protuberant bones that humped a hide smooth and thin, and shiny as satin—so shiny that the very shape of the moon was reflected in it; I fondled his sharp-pointed ears, whispered words in them, and breathed into his red nostrils the breath of a man's life. He in return breathed into mine the breath of a horse's life, and we loved one another. What eyes he had! Blue-filmy like the eyes of the dead, behind each was a glowing coal! The raven, with wings half extended, looked on pleased at my love-making to his magnificent horse.

"That is well! be friends with him," he said: "he will carry you all the better to-morrow!—Now we must hurry home!"

My desire to ride the horse had grown passionate.

"May I not mount him at once, Mr. Raven?" I cried.

"By all means!" he answered. "Mount, and ride him home."

The horse bent his head over my shoulder lovingly. I twisted my hands in his mane and scrambled onto his back, not without aid from certain protuberant bones.

"He would outspeed any leopard in creation!" I cried.

"Not that way at night," answered the raven; "the road is difficult.—But come; loss now will be gain then! To wait is harder than to run, and its meed is the fuller. Go on, my son—straight to the cottage. I shall be there as soon as you. It will rejoice my wife's heart to see son of hers on that horse!"

I sat silent. The horse stood like a block of marble.

"Why do you linger?" asked the raven.

"I long so much to ride after the leopardess," I answered, "that I can scarce restrain myself!"

"You have promised!"

"My debt to the Little Ones appears, I confess, a greater thing than my bond to you."

"Yield to the temptation and you will bring mischief upon them—and on your-self also."

"What matters it for me? I love them; and love works no evil. I will go."

But the truth was, I forgot the children, infatuate with the horse.

Eyes flashed through the darkness, and I knew that Adam stood in his own shape beside me. I knew also by his voice that he repressed an indignation almost too strong for him.

"Mr. Vane," he said, "do you not know why you have not yet done anything worth doing?"

"Because I have been a fool," I answered.

"Wherein?"

"In everything."

"Which do you count your most indiscreet action?"

"Bringing the princess to life: I ought to have left her to her just fate."

"Nay, now you talk foolishly! You could not have done otherwise than you did, not knowing she was evil!—But you never brought any one to life! How could you, yourself dead?"

"I dead?" I cried.

"Yes," he answered; "and you will be dead, so long as you refuse to die."

"Back to the old riddling!" I returned scornfully.

"Be persuaded, and go home with me," he continued gently. "The most—nearly the only foolish thing you ever did, was to run from our dead."

I pressed the horse's ribs, and he was off like a sudden wind. I gave him a pat on the side of the neck, and he went about in a sharp-driven curve, "close to the ground, like a cat when scratchingly she wheels about after a mouse," leaning sideways till his mane swept the tops of the heather.

Through the dark I heard the wings of the raven. Five quick flaps I heard, and he perched on the horse's head. The horse checked himself instantly, ploughing up the ground with his feet.

"Mr. Vane," croaked the raven, "think what you are doing! Twice already has evil befallen you—once from fear, and once from heedlessness: breach of word is far worse; it is a crime."

"The Little Ones are in frightful peril, and I brought it upon them!" I cried. "—But indeed I will not break my word to you. I will return, and spend in your house what nights—what days—what years you please."

"I tell you once more you will do them other than good if you go to-night," he insisted.

But a false sense of power, a sense which had no root and was merely vibrated into me from the strength of the horse, had, alas, rendered me too stupid to listen to anything he said!

"Would you take from me my last chance of reparation?" I cried. "This time there shall be no shirking! It is my duty, and I will go—if I perish for it!"

"Go, then, foolish boy!" he returned, with anger in his croak. "Take the horse, and ride to failure! May it be to humility!"

He spread his wings and flew. Again I pressed the lean ribs under me.

"After the spotted leopardess!" I whispered in his ear.

He turned his head this way and that, snuffing the air; then started, and went a few paces in a slow, undecided walk. Suddenly he quickened his walk; broke into a trot; began to gallop, and in a few moments his speed was tremendous. He seemed to see in the dark; never stumbled, not once faltered, not once hesitated. I sat as on the ridge of a wave. I felt under me the play of each individual muscle: his joints were so elastic, and his every movement glided so into the next, that not once did he jar me. His growing swiftness bore him along until he flew rather than ran. The wind met and passed us like a tornado.

Across the evil hollow we sped like a bolt from an arblast. No monster lifted its neck; all knew the hoofs that thundered over their heads! We rushed up the hills, we shot down their farther slopes; from the rocky chasms of the river-bed he did not swerve; he held on over them his fierce, terrible gallop. The moon, half-way up the heaven, gazed with a solemn trouble in her pale countenance. Rejoicing in the power of my steed and in the pride of my life, I sat like a king and rode.

We were near the middle of the many channels, my horse every other moment clearing one, sometimes two in his stride, and now and then gathering himself for a great bounding leap, when the moon reached the key-stone of her arch. Then came a wonder and a terror: she began to descend rolling like the nave of Fortune's wheel bowled by the gods, and went faster and faster. Like our own moon, this one had a human face, and now the broad forehead now the chin was uppermost as she rolled. I gazed aghast.

Across the ravines came the howling of wolves. An ugly fear began to invade the hollow places of my heart; my confidence was on the wane! The horse maintained his headlong swiftness, with ears pricked forward, and thirsty nostrils exulting in the wind his career created. But there was the moon jolting like an old chariot-wheel down the hill of heaven, with awful boding! She rolled at last over the horizon-edge and disappeared, carrying all her light with her.

The mighty steed was in the act of clearing a wide shallow channel when we were caught in the net of the darkness. His head dropped; its impetus carried his helpless bulk across, but he fell in a heap on the margin, and where he fell he lay. I got up, kneeled beside him, and felt him all over. Not a bone could I find broken, but he was a horse no more. I sat down on the body, and buried my face in my hands.

CHAPTER XXXII. THE LOVERS AND THE BAGS

Bitterly cold grew the night. The body froze under me. The cry of the wolves came nearer; I heard their feet soft-padding on the rocky ground; their quick panting filled the air. Through the darkness I saw the many glowing eyes; their half-circle contracted around me. My time was come! I sprang to my feet.—Alas, I had not even a stick!

They came in a rush, their eyes flashing with fury of greed, their black throats agape to devour me. I stood hopelessly waiting them. One moment they halted over the horse—then came at me.

With a sound of swiftness all but silence, a cloud of green eyes came down on their flank. The heads that bore them flew at the wolves with a cry feebler yet fiercer than their howling snarl, and by the cry I knew them: they were cats, led by a huge gray one. I could see nothing of him but his eyes, yet I knew him—and so knew his colour and bigness. A terrific battle followed, whose tale alone came to me through the night. I would have fled, for surely it was but a fight which should have me!—only where was the use? my first step would be a fall! and my foes of either kind could both see and scent me in the dark!

All at once I missed the howling, and the caterwauling grew wilder. Then came the soft padding, and I knew it meant flight: the cats had defeated the wolves! In a moment the sharpest of sharp teeth were in my legs; a moment more and the cats were all over me in a live cataract, biting wherever they could bite, furiously scratching me anywhere and everywhere. A multitude clung to my body; I could not flee. Madly I fell on the hateful swarm, every finger instinct with destruction. I tore them off me, I throttled at them in vain: when I would have flung them from me, they clung to my hands like limpets. I trampled them under my feet, thrust my fingers in their eyes, caught them in jaws stronger than theirs, but could not rid myself of one. Without cease they kept discovering upon me space for fresh mouthfuls; they hauled at my skin with the widespread, horribly curved pincers of clutching claws; they hissed and spat in my face—but never touched it until, in my despair, I threw myself on the ground, when they forsook my body, and darted at my face. I rose, and immediately they left it, the more to occupy themselves with my legs. In an agony I broke from them and ran, careless whither, cleaving the solid dark. They accompanied me in a surrounding torrent, now rubbing, now leaping up against me, but tormenting me no more. When I fell, which was often, they gave me time to rise; when from fear of falling I slackened my pace, they flew afresh at my legs. All that miserable night they kept me running—but they drove me by a comparatively smooth path, for I tumbled into no gully, and passing the Evil Wood without seeing it, left it behind in the dark. When at length the morning appeared, I was beyond the channels, and on the verge of the orchard valley. In my joy I would have made friends with my persecutors, but not a cat was to be seen. I threw myself on the moss, and fell fast asleep.

I was waked by a kick, to find myself bound hand and foot, once more the thrall of the giants!

"What fitter?" I said to myself; "to whom else should I belong?" and I laughed in the triumph of self-disgust. A second kick stopped my false merriment; and thus recurrently assisted by my captors, I succeeded at length in rising to my feet.

Six of them were about me. They undid the rope that tied my legs together, attached a rope to each of them, and dragged me away. I walked as well as I could, but, as they frequently pulled both ropes at once, I fell repeatedly, whereupon they always kicked me up again. Straight to my old labour they took me, tied my leg-ropes to a tree, undid my arms, and put the hateful flint in my left hand. Then they lay down and pelted me with fallen fruit and stones, but seldom hit me. If I could have freed my legs, and got hold of a stick I spied a couple of yards from me, I would have fallen upon all six of them! "But the Little Ones will come at night!" I said to myself, and was comforted.

All day I worked hard. When the darkness came, they tied my hands, and left me fast to the tree. I slept a good deal, but woke often, and every time from a dream of lying in the heart of a heap of children. With the morning my enemies reappeared, bringing their kicks and their bestial company.

It was about noon, and I was nearly failing from fatigue and hunger, when I heard a sudden commotion in the brushwood, followed by a burst of the bell-like laughter so dear to my heart. I gave a loud cry of delight and welcome. Immediately rose a trumpeting as of baby-elephants, a neighing as of foals, and a bellowing as of calves, and through the bushes came a crowd of Little Ones, on diminutive horses, on small elephants, on little bears; but the noises came from the riders, not the animals. Mingled with the mounted ones walked the bigger of the boys and girls, among the latter a woman with a baby crowing in her arms. The giants sprang to their lumbering feet, but were instantly saluted with a storm of sharp stones; the horses charged their legs; the bears rose and hugged them at the waist; the elephants threw their trunks round their necks, pulled them down, and gave them such a trampling as they had sometimes given, but never received before. In a moment my ropes were undone, and I was in the arms, seemingly innumerable, of the Little Ones. For some time I saw no more of the giants.

They made me sit down, and my Lona came, and without a word began to feed me with the loveliest red and yellow fruits. I sat and ate, the whole colony mounting guard until I had done. Then they brought up two of the largest of their elephants, and having placed them side by side, hooked their trunks and tied their tails together. The docile creatures could have untied their tails with a single shake, and unhooked their trunks by forgetting them; but tails and trunks remained as their little masters had arranged them, and it was clear the elephants understood that they must keep their bodies parallel. I got up, and laid myself in the hollow between their two backs; when the wise animals, counteracting the weight that pushed them apart, leaned against each other, and made for me a most comfortable litter. My feet, it is true, projected beyond their tails, but my head lay pillowed on an ear of each. Then some of the smaller children, mounting for a bodyguard, ranged themselves in a row along the back of each of my bearers; the whole assembly formed itself in train; and the procession began to move.

Whither they were carrying me, I did not try to conjecture; I yielded myself to their pleasure, almost as happy as they. Chattering and laughing and playing glad tricks innumerable at first, the moment they saw I was going to sleep, they became still as judges.

I woke: a sudden musical uproar greeted the opening of my eyes.

We were travelling through the forest in which they found the babies, and which, as I had suspected, stretched all the way from the valley to the hot stream.

A tiny girl sat with her little feet close to my face, and looked down at me coaxingly for a while, then spoke, the rest seeming to hang on her words.

"We make a petisson to king," she said.

"What is it, my darling?" I asked.

"Shut eyes one minute," she answered.

"Certainly I will! Here goes!" I replied, and shut my eyes close.

"No, no! not fore I tell oo!" she cried.

I opened them again, and we talked and laughed together for quite another hour.

"Close eyes!" she said suddenly.

I closed my eyes, and kept them close. The elephants stood still. I heard a soft scurry, a little rustle, and then a silence—for in that world SOME silences ARE heard.

"Open eyes!" twenty voices a little way off shouted at once; but when I obeyed, not a creature was visible except the elephants that bore me. I knew the children marvellously quick in getting out of the way—the giants had taught them that; but when I raised myself, and looking about in the open shrubless forest, could descry neither hand nor heel, I stared in "blank astonishment."

The sun was set, and it was fast getting dark, yet presently a multitude of birds began to sing. I lay down to listen, pretty sure that, if I left them alone, the hiders would soon come out again.

The singing grew to a little storm of bird-voices. "Surely the children must have something to do with it!—And yet how could they set the birds singing?" I said to myself as I lay and listened. Soon, however, happening to look up into the tree under which my elephants stood, I thought I spied a little motion among the leaves, and looked more keenly. Sudden white spots appeared in the dark foliage, the music died down, a gale of childish laughter rippled the air, and white spots came out in every direction: the trees were full of children! In the wildest merriment they began to descend, some dropping from bough to bough so rapidly that I could scarce believe they had not fallen. I left my litter, and was instantly surrounded—a mark for all the artillery of their jubilant fun. With stately composure the elephants walked away to bed.

"But," said I, when their uproarious gladness had had scope for a while, "how is it that I never before heard you sing like the birds? Even when I thought it must be you, I could hardly believe it!"

"Ah," said one of the wildest, "but we were not birds then! We were run-creatures, not fly-creatures! We had our hide-places in the bushes then; but when we came to no-bushes, only trees, we had to build nests! When we built nests, we grew birds, and when we were birds, we had to do birds! We asked them to teach us their noises, and they taught us, and now we are real birds!—Come and see my nest. It's not big enough for king, but it's big enough for king to see me in it!"

I told him I could not get up a tree without the sun to show me the way; when he came, I would try.

"Kings seldom have wings!" I added.

"King! king!" cried one, "oo knows none of us hasn't no wings—foolis feddery tings! Arms and legs is better."

"That is true. I can get up without wings—and carry straws in my mouth too, to build my nest with!"

"Oo knows!" he answered, and went away sucking his thumb.

A moment after, I heard him calling out of his nest, a great way up a walnut tree of enormous size,

"Up adain, king! Dood night! I seepy!"

And I heard no more of him till he woke me in the morning.

CHAPTER XXXIII. LONA'S NARRATIVE

I lay down by a tree, and one and one or in little groups, the children left me and climbed to their nests. They were always so tired at night and so rested in the morning, that they were equally glad to go to sleep and to get up again. I, although tired also, lay awake: Lona had not bid me good night, and I was sure she would come.

I had been struck, the moment I saw her again, with her resemblance to the princess, and could not doubt her the daughter of whom Adam had told me; but in Lona the dazzling beauty of Lilith was softened by childlikeness, and deepened by the sense of motherhood. "She is occupied probably," I said to myself, "with the child of the woman I met fleeing!" who, she had already told me, was not half mother enough.

She came at length, sat down beside me, and after a few moments of silent delight, expressed mainly by stroking my face and hands, began to tell me everything that had befallen since I went. The moon appeared as we talked, and now and then, through the leaves, lighted for a quivering moment her beautiful face—full of thought, and a care whose love redeemed and glorified it. How such a child should have been born of such a mother—such a woman of such a princess, was hard to understand; but then, happily, she had two parents—say rather, three! She drew my heart by what in me was likest herself, and I loved her as one who, grow to what perfection she might, could only become the more a child. I knew now that I loved her when I left her, and that the hope of seeing her again had been my main comfort. Every word she spoke seemed to go straight to my heart, and, like the truth itself, make it purer.

She told me that after I left the orchard valley, the giants began to believe a little more in the actual existence of their neighbours, and became in consequence more hostile to them. Sometimes the Little Ones would see them trampling furiously, perceiving or imagining some indication of their presence, while they indeed stood beside, and laughed at their foolish rage. By and by, however, their animosity assumed a more practical shape: they began to destroy the trees on whose fruit the Little Ones lived. This drove the mother of them all to meditate counteraction. Setting the sharpest of them to listen at night, she learned that the giants thought I was hidden somewhere near, intending, as soon as I recovered my strength, to come in the dark and kill them sleeping. Thereupon she concluded that the only way to stop the destruction was to give them ground for believing that they had abandoned the place. The Little Ones must remove into the forest—beyond the range of the giants, but within reach of their own trees, which they must visit by night! The main objection to the plan was, that the forest had little or no under-growth to shelter—or conceal them if necessary.

But she reflected that where birds, there the Little Ones could find habitation. They had eager sympathies with all modes of life, and could learn of the wildest creatures: why should they not take refuge from the cold and their enemies in the tree-tops? why not, having lain in the low brushwood, seek now the lofty foliage? why not build nests where it would not serve to scoop hollows? All that the birds could do, the Little Ones could learn—except, indeed, to fly!

She spoke to them on the subject, and they heard with approval. They could already climb the trees, and they had often watched the birds building their nests! The trees of the forest, although large, did not look bad! They went up much nearer the sky than those of the giants, and spread out their arms—some even stretched them down—as if inviting them to come and live with them! Perhaps, in the top of the tallest, they might find that bird that laid the baby-eggs, and sat upon them till they were ripe, then tumbled them down to let the little ones out! Yes; they would build sleep-houses in the trees, where no giant would see them, for never by any chance did one throw back his dull head to look up! Then the bad giants would be sure they had left the country, and the Little Ones would gather their own apples and pears and figs and mesples and peaches when they were asleep!

Thus reasoned the Lovers, and eagerly adopted Lona's suggestion—with the result that they were soon as much at home in the tree-tops as the birds themselves, and that the giants came ere long to the conclusion that they had frightened them out of the country—whereupon they forgot their trees, and again almost ceased to believe in the existence of their small neighbours.

Lona asked me whether I had not observed that many of the children were grown. I answered I had not, but could readily believe it. She assured me it was so, but said the certain evidence that their minds too had grown since their migration upward, had gone far in mitigation of the alarm the discovery had occasioned her.

In the last of the short twilight, and later when the moon was shining, they went down to the valley, and gathered fruit enough to serve them the next day; for the giants never went out in the twilight: that to them was darkness; and they hated the moon: had they been able, they would have extinguished her. But soon the Little Ones found that fruit gathered in the night was not altogether good the next day; so the question arose whether it would not be better, instead of pretending to have left the country, to make the bad giants themselves leave it.

They had already, she said, in exploring the forest, made acquaintance with the animals in it, and with most of them personally. Knowing therefore how strong as well as wise and docile some of them were, and how swift as well as manageable many others, they now set themselves to secure their aid against the giants, and with loving, playful approaches, had soon made more than friends of most of them, from the first addressing horse or elephant as Brother or Sister Elephant, Brother or Sister Horse, until before long they had an individual name for each. It was some little time longer before they said Brother or Sister Bear, but that came next, and the other day she had heard one little fellow cry, "Ah, Sister Serpent!" to a snake that bit him as he played with it too roughly. Most of them would have nothing to do with a caterpillar, except watch it through its changes; but when at length it came from its retirement with wings, all would immediately address it as Sister Butterfly, congratulating it on its metamorphosis—for which they used a word that meant something like REPENTANCE—and evidently regarding it as something sacred.

One moonlit evening, as they were going to gather their fruit, they came upon a woman seated on the ground with a baby in lap—the woman I had met on my way to Bulika. They took her for a giantess that had stolen one of their babies, for they regarded all babies as their property. Filled with anger they fell upon her multitudinously, beating her after a childish, yet sufficiently bewildering fashion. She would have fled, but a boy threw himself down and held her by the feet. Recovering her wits, she recognised in her assailants the children whose hospitality she sought, and at once yielded the baby. Lona appeared, and carried it away in her bosom.

But while the woman noted that in striking her they were careful not to hurt the child, the Little Ones noted that, as she surrendered her, she hugged and kissed her just as they wanted to do, and came to the conclusion that she must be a giantess of the same kind as the good giant. The moment Lona had the baby, therefore, they brought the mother fruit, and began to show her every sort of childish attention.

Now the woman had been in perplexity whither to betake herself, not daring to go back to the city, because the princess was certain to find out who had lamed her leopardess: delighted with the friendliness of the little people, she resolved to remain with them for the present: she would have no trouble with her infant, and might find some way of returning to her husband, who was rich in money and gems, and very seldom unkind to her.

Here I must supplement, partly from conjecture, what Lona told me about the woman. With the rest of the inhabitants of Bulika, she was aware of the tradition that the princess lived in terror of the birth of an infant destined to her destruction. They were all unacquainted, however, with the frightful means by which she preserved her youth and beauty; and her deteriorating physical condition requiring a larger use of those means, they took the apparent increase of her hostility to children for a sign that she saw her doom approaching. This, although no one dreamed of any attempt against her, nourished in them hopes of change.

Now arose in the mind of the woman the idea of furthering the fulfilment of the shadowy prediction, or of using the myth at least for her own restoration to her husband. For what seemed more probable than that the fate foretold lay with these very children? They were marvellously brave, and the Bulikans cowards, in abject terror of animals! If she could rouse in the Little Ones the ambition of taking the city, then in the confusion of the attack, she would escape from the little army, reach her house unrecognised, and there lying hidden, await the result!

Should the children now succeed in expelling the giants, she would begin at once, while they were yet flushed with victory, to suggest the loftier aim! By disposition, indeed, they were unfit for warfare; they hardly ever quarrelled, and never fought; loved every live thing, and hated either to hurt or to suffer. Still, they were easily influenced, and could certainly be taught any exercise within their strength! —At once she set some of the smaller ones throwing stones at a mark; and soon they were all engrossed with the new game, and growing skilful in it.

The first practical result was their use of stones in my rescue. While gathering fruit, they found me asleep, went home, held a council, came the next day with their elephants and horses, overwhelmed the few giants watching me, and carried me off. Jubilant over their victory, the smaller boys were childishly boastful, the bigger boys less ostentatious, while the girls, although their eyes flashed more, were not so talkative as usual. The woman of Bulika no doubt felt encouraged.

We talked the greater part of the night, chiefly about the growth of the children, and what it might indicate. With Lona's power of recognising truth I had long been familiar; now I began to be astonished at her practical wisdom. Probably, had I been more of a child myself, I should have wondered less.

It was yet far from morning when I became aware of a slight fluttering and scrambling. I rose on my elbow, and looking about me, saw many Little Ones descend from their nests. They disappeared, and in a few moments all was again still.

"What are they doing?" I asked.

"They think," answered Lona, "that, stupid as they are, the giants will search the wood, and they are gone to gather stones with which to receive them. Stones are not plentiful in the forest, and they have to scatter far to find enow. They will carry them to their nests, and from the trees attack the giants as they come within reach. Knowing their habits, they do not expect them before the morning. If they do come, it will be the opening of a war of expulsion: one or the other people must go. The result, however, is hardly doubtful. We do not mean to kill them; indeed, their skulls are so thick that I do not think we could!—not that killing would do them much harm; they are so little alive! If one were killed, his giantess would not remember him beyond three days!"

"Do the children then throw so well that the thing MIGHT happen?" I asked.

"Wait till you see them!" she answered, with a touch of pride. "—But I have not yet told you," she went on, "of a strange thing that happened the night before last! —We had come home from gathering our fruit, and were asleep in our nests, when we were roused by the horrid noises of beasts fighting. The moon was bright, and in a moment our trees glittered with staring little eyes, watching two huge leopardesses, one perfectly white, the other covered with black spots, which worried and tore each other with I do not know how many teeth and claws. To judge by her back, the spotted creature must have been climbing a tree when the other sprang upon her. When first I saw them, they were just under my own tree, rolling over and over each other. I got down on the lowest branch, and saw them perfectly. The children enjoyed the spectacle, siding some with this one, some with that, for we had never seen such beasts before, and thought they were only at play. But by degrees their roaring and growling almost ceased, and I saw that they were in deadly earnest, and heartily wished neither might be left able to climb a tree. But when the children saw the blood pouring from their flanks and throats, what do you think they did? They scurried down to comfort them, and gathering in a great crowd about the terrible creatures, began to pat and stroke them. Then I got down as well, for they were much too absorbed to heed my calling to them; but before I could reach them, the white one stopped fighting, and sprang among them with such a hideous yell that they flew up into the trees like birds. Before I got back into mine, the wicked beasts were at it again tooth and claw. Then Whitey had the best of it; Spotty ran away as fast as she could run, and Whitey came and lay down at the foot of my tree. But in a minute or two she was up again, and walking about as if she thought Spotty might be lurking somewhere. I waked often, and every time I looked out, I saw her. In the morning she went away."

"I know both the beasts," I said. "Spotty is a bad beast. She hates the children, and would kill every one of them. But Whitey loves them. She ran at them only to frighten them away, lest Spotty should get hold of any of them. No one needs be afraid of Whitey!"

By this time the Little Ones were coming back, and with much noise, for they had no care to keep quiet now that they were at open war with the giants, and laden with good stones. They mounted to their nests again, though with difficulty because of their burdens, and in a minute were fast asleep. Lona retired to her tree. I lay where I was, and slept the better that I thought most likely the white leopardess was still somewhere in the wood.

I woke soon after the sun, and lay pondering. Two hours passed, and then in truth the giants began to appear, in straggling companies of three and four, until I counted over a hundred of them. The children were still asleep, and to call them would draw the attention of the giants: I would keep quiet so long as they did not discover me. But by and by one came blundering upon me, stumbled, fell, and rose again. I thought he would pass heedless, but he began to search about. I sprang to my feet, and struck him in the middle of his huge body. The roar he gave roused the children, and a storm as of hail instantly came on, of which not a stone struck me, and not one missed the giant. He fell and lay. Others drew near, and the storm extended, each purblind creature becoming, as he entered the range of a garrisoned tree, a target for converging stones. In a short time almost every giant was prostrate, and a jubilant pæan of bird-song rose from the tops of fifty trees.

Many elephants came hurrying up, and the children descending the trees like monkeys, in a moment every elephant had three or four of them on his back, and thus loaded, began to walk over the giants, who lay and roared. Losing patience at length with their noise, the elephants gave them a few blows of their trunks, and left them.

Until night the bad giants remained where they had fallen, silent and motionless. The next morning they had disappeared every one, and the children saw no more of them. They removed to the other end of the orchard valley, and never after ventured into the forest.

CHAPTER XXXIV. PREPARATION

Victory thus gained, the woman of Bulika began to speak about the city, and talked much of its defenceless condition, of the wickedness of its princess, of the cowardice of its inhabitants. In a few days the children chattered of nothing but Bulika, although indeed they had not the least notion of what a city was. Then first I became aware of the design of the woman, although not yet of its motive.

The idea of taking possession of the place, recommended itself greatly to Lona— and to me also. The children were now so rapidly developing faculty, that I could see no serious obstacle to the success of the enterprise. For the terrible Lilith— woman or leopardess, I knew her one vulnerable point, her doom through her daughter, and the influence the ancient prophecy had upon the citizens: surely whatever in the enterprise could be called risk, was worth taking! Successful,—and who could doubt their success?—must not the Little Ones, from a crowd of children, speedily become a youthful people, whose government and influence would be all for righteousness? Ruling the wicked with a rod of iron, would they not be the redemption of the nation?

At the same time, I have to confess that I was not without views of personal advantage, not without ambition in the undertaking. It was just, it seemed to me, that Lona should take her seat on the throne that had been her mother's, and natural that she should make of me her consort and minister. For me, I would spend my life in her service; and between us, what might we not do, with such a core to it as the Little Ones, for the development of a noble state?

I confess also to an altogether foolish dream of opening a commerce in gems between the two worlds—happily impossible, for it could have done nothing but harm to both.

Calling to mind the appeal of Adam, I suggested to Lona that to find them water might perhaps expedite the growth of the Little Ones. She judged it prudent, however, to leave that alone for the present, as we did not know what its first consequences might be; while, in the course of time, it would almost certainly subject them to a new necessity.

"They are what they are without it!" she said: "when we have the city, we will search for water!"

We began, therefore, and pushed forward our preparations, constantly reviewing the merry troops and companies. Lona gave her attention chiefly to the commissariat, while I drilled the little soldiers, exercised them in stone-throwing, taught them the use of some other weapons, and did all I could to make warriors of them. The main difficulty was to get them to rally to their flag the instant the call was sounded. Most of them were armed with slings, some of the bigger boys with bows and arrows. The bigger girls carried aloe-spikes, strong as steel and sharp as needles, fitted to longish shafts—rather formidable weapons. Their sole duty was the charge of such as were too small to fight.

Lona had herself grown a good deal, but did not seem aware of it: she had always been, as she still was, the tallest! Her hair was much longer, and she was become almost a woman, but not one beauty of childhood had she outgrown. When first we met after our long separation, she laid down her infant, put her arms round my neck, and clung to me silent, her face glowing with gladness: the child whimpered; she sprang to him, and had him in her bosom instantly. To see her with any thoughtless, obstinate, or irritable little one, was to think of a tender grand-mother. I seemed to have known her for ages—for always—from before time began! I hardly remembered my mother, but in my mind's eye she now looked like Lona; and if I imagined sister or child, invariably she had the face of Lona! My every imagination flew to her; she was my heart's wife! She hardly ever sought me, but was almost always within sound of my voice. What I did or thought, I referred constantly to her, and rejoiced to believe that, while doing her work in absolute independence, she was most at home by my side. Never for me did she neglect the smallest child, and my love only quickened my sense of duty. To love her and to do my duty, seemed, not indeed one, but inseparable. She might suggest something I should do; she might ask me what she ought to do; but she never seemed to suppose that I, any more than she, would like to do, or could care about anything except what must be done. Her love overflowed upon me—not in caresses, but in a closeness of recognition which I can compare to nothing but the devotion of a divine animal.

I never told her anything about her mother.

The wood was full of birds, the splendour of whose plumage, while it took nothing from their song, seemed almost to make up for the lack of flowers—which, apparently, could not grow without water. Their glorious feathers being every-where about in the forest, it came into my heart to make from them a garment for Lona. While I gathered, and bound them in overlapping rows, she watched me with evident appreciation of my choice and arrangement, never asking what I was fashioning, but evidently waiting expectant the result of my work. In a week or two it was finished—a long loose mantle, to fasten at the throat and waist, with open-ings for the arms.

I rose and put it on her. She rose, took it off, and laid it at my feet—I imagine from a sense of propriety. I put it again on her shoulders, and showed her where to put her arms through. She smiled, looked at the feathers a little and stroked them—again took it off and laid it down, this time by her side. When she left me, she carried it with her, and I saw no more of it for some days. At length she came to me one morning wearing it, and carrying another garment which she had fashioned similarly, but of the dried leaves of a tough evergreen. It had the strength almost of leather, and the appearance of scale-armour. I put it on at once, and we always thereafter wore those garments when on horseback.

For, on the outskirts of the forest, had appeared one day a troop of full-grown horses, with which, as they were nowise alarmed at creatures of a shape so different from their own, I had soon made friends, and two of the finest I had trained for Lona and myself. Already accustomed to ride a small one, her delight was great when first she looked down from the back of an animal of the giant kind; and the horse showed himself proud of the burden he bore. We exercised them every day until they had such confidence in us as to obey instantly and fear nothing; after which we always rode them at parade and on the march.

The undertaking did indeed at times appear to me a foolhardy one, but the confidence of the woman of Bulika, real or simulated, always overcame my hesitancy. The princess's magic, she insisted, would prove powerless against the children; and as to any force she might muster, our animal-allies alone would assure our superiority: she was herself, she said, ready, with a good stick, to encounter any two men of Bulika. She confessed to not a little fear of the leopardess, but I was myself ready for her. I shrank, however, from carrying ALL the children with us.

"Would it not be better," I said, "that you remained in the forest with your baby and the smallest of the Little Ones?"

She answered that she greatly relied on the impression the sight of them would make on the women, especially the mothers.

"When they see the darlings," she said, "their hearts will be taken by storm; and I must be there encouraging them to make a stand! If there be a remnant of hardihood in the place, it will be found among the women!"

"YOU must not encumber yourself," I said to Lona, "with any of the children; you will be wanted everywhere!"

For there were two babies besides the woman's, and even on horseback she had almost always one in her arms.

"I do not remember ever being without a child to take care of," she answered; "but when we reach the city, it shall be as you wish!"

Her confidence in one who had failed so unworthily, shamed me. But neither had I initiated the movement, nor had I any ground for opposing it; I had no choice, but must give it the best help I could! For myself, I was ready to live or die with Lona. Her humility as well as her trust humbled me, and I gave myself heartily to her purposes.

Our way lying across a grassy plain, there was no need to take food for the horses, or the two cows which would accompany us for the infants; but the elephants had to be provided for. True, the grass was as good for them as for those other animals, but it was short, and with their one-fingered long noses, they could not pick enough for a single meal. We had, therefore, set the whole colony to gather grass and make hay, of which the elephants themselves could carry a quantity sufficient to last them several days, with the supplement of what we would gather fresh every time we halted. For the bears we stored nuts, and for ourselves dried plenty of fruits. We had caught and tamed several more of the big horses, and now having loaded them and the elephants with these provisions, we were prepared to set out.

Then Lona and I held a general review, and I made them a little speech. I began by telling them that I had learned a good deal about them, and knew now where they came from. "We did not come from anywhere," they cried, interrupting me; "we are here!"

I told them that every one of them had a mother of his own, like the mother of the last baby; that I believed they had all been brought from Bulika when they were so small that they could not now remember it; that the wicked princess there was so afraid of babies, and so determined to destroy them, that their mothers had to carry them away and leave them where she could not find them; and that now we were going to Bulika, to find their mothers, and deliver them from the bad giantess.

"But I must tell you," I continued, "that there is danger before us, for, as you know, we may have to fight hard to take the city."

"We can fight! we are ready!" cried the boys.

"Yes, you can," I returned, "and I know you will: mothers are worth fighting for! Only mind, you must all keep together."

"Yes, yes; we'll take care of each other," they answered. "Nobody shall touch one of us but his own mother!"

"You must mind, every one, to do immediately what your officers tell you!"

"We will, we will!—Now we're quite ready! Let us go!"

"Another thing you must not forget," I went on: "when you strike, be sure you make it a downright swinging blow; when you shoot an arrow, draw it to the head; when you sling a stone, sling it strong and straight."

"That we will!" they cried with jubilant, fearless shout.

"Perhaps you will be hurt!"

"We don't mind that!—Do we, boys?"

"Not a bit!"

"Some of you may very possibly be killed!" I said.

"I don't mind being killed!" cried one of the finest of the smaller boys: he rode a beautiful little bull, which galloped and jumped like a horse.

"I don't either! I don't either!" came from all sides.

Then Lona, queen and mother and sister of them all, spoke from her big horse by my side:

"I would give my life," she said, "to have my mother! She might kill me if she liked! I should just kiss her and die!"

"Come along, boys!" cried a girl. "We're going to our mothers!"

A pang went through my heart.—But I could not draw back; it would be moral ruin to the Little Ones!

CHAPTER XXXV. THE LITTLE ONES IN BULIKA

It was early in the morning when we set out, making, between the blue sky and the green grass, a gallant show on the wide plain. We would travel all the morning, and rest the afternoon; then go on at night, rest the next day, and start again in the short twilight. The latter part of our journey we would endeavour so to divide as to arrive at the city with the first of the morning, and be already inside the gates when discovered.

It seemed as if all the inhabitants of the forest would migrate with us. A multitude of birds flew in front, imagining themselves, no doubt, the leading division; great companies of butterflies and other insects played about our heads; and a crowd of four-footed creatures followed us. These last, when night came, left us almost all; but the birds and the butterflies, the wasps and the dragon-flies, went with us to the very gates of the city.

We halted and slept soundly through the afternoon: it was our first real march, but none were tired. In the night we went faster, because it was cold. Many fell asleep on the backs of their beasts, and woke in the morning quite fresh. None tumbled off. Some rode shaggy, shambling bears, which yet made speed enough, going as fast as the elephants. Others were mounted on different kinds of deer, and would have been racing all the way had I not prevented it. Those atop of the hay on the elephants, unable to see the animals below them, would keep talking to them as long as they were awake. Once, when we had halted to feed, I heard a little fellow, as he drew out the hay to give him, commune thus with his "darling beast":

"Nosy dear, I am digging you out of the mountain, and shall soon get down to you: be patient; I'm a coming! Very soon now you'll send up your nose to look for me, and then we'll kiss like good elephants, we will!"

The same night there burst out such a tumult of elephant-trumpeting, horse-neighing, and child-imitation, ringing far over the silent levels, that, uncertain how

708

near the city might not be, I quickly stilled the uproar lest it should give warning of our approach.

Suddenly, one morning, the sun and the city rose, as it seemed, together. To the children the walls appeared only a great mass of rock, but when I told them the inside was full of nests of stone, I saw apprehension and dislike at once invade their hearts: for the first time in their lives, I believe—many of them long little lives—they knew fear. The place looked to them bad: how were they to find mothers in such a place? But they went on bravely, for they had confidence in Lona—and in me too, little as I deserved it.

We rode through the sounding archway. Sure never had such a drumming of hoofs, such a padding of paws and feet been heard on its old pavement! The horses started and looked scared at the echo of their own steps; some halted a moment, some plunged wildly and wheeled about; but they were soon quieted, and went on. Some of the Little Ones shivered, and all were still as death. The three girls held closer the infants they carried. All except the bears and butterflies manifested fear.

On the countenance of the woman lay a dark anxiety; nor was I myself unaffected by the general dread, for the whole army was on my hands and on my conscience: I had brought it up to the danger whose shadow was now making itself felt! But I was supported by the thought of the coming kingdom of the Little Ones, with the bad giants its slaves, and the animals its loving, obedient friends! Alas, I who dreamed thus, had not myself learned to obey! Untrusting, unfaithful obstinacy had set me at the head of that army of innocents! I was myself but a slave, like any king in the world I had left who does or would do only what pleases him! But Lona rode beside me a child indeed, therefore a free woman—calm, silent, watchful, not a whit afraid!

We were nearly in the heart of the city before any of its inhabitants became aware of our presence. But now windows began to open, and sleepy heads to look out. Every face wore at first a dull stare of wonderless astonishment, which, as soon as the starers perceived the animals, changed to one of consternation. In spite of their fear, however, when they saw that their invaders were almost all children, the women came running into the streets, and the men followed. But for a time all of them kept close to the houses, leaving open the middle of the way, for they durst not approach the animals.

At length a boy, who looked about five years old, and was full of the idea of his mother, spying in the crowd a woman whose face attracted him, threw himself upon her from his antelope, and clung about her neck; nor was she slow to return his embrace and kisses. But the hand of a man came over her shoulder, and seized him by the neck. Instantly a girl ran her sharp spear into the fellow's arm. He sent forth a savage howl, and immediately stabbed by two or three more, fled yelling.

"They are just bad giants!" said Lona, her eyes flashing as she drove her horse against one of unusual height who, having stirred up the little manhood in him, stood barring her way with a club. He dared not abide the shock, but slunk aside, and the next moment went down, struck by several stones. Another huge fellow, avoiding my charger, stepped suddenly, with a speech whose rudeness alone was intelligible, between me and the boy who rode behind me. The boy told him to address the king; the giant struck his little horse on the head with a hammer, and he fell. Before the brute could strike again, however, one of the elephants behind laid him prostrate, and trampled on him so that he did not attempt to get up until hundreds of feet had walked over him, and the army was gone by.

But at sight of the women what a dismay clouded the face of Lona! Hardly one of them was even pleasant to look upon! Were her darlings to find mothers among such as these?

Hardly had we halted in the central square, when two girls rode up in anxious haste, with the tidings that two of the boys had been hurried away by some women. We turned at once, and then first discovered that the woman we befriended had disappeared with her baby.

But at the same moment we descried a white leopardess come bounding toward us down a narrow lane that led from the square to the palace. The Little Ones had not forgotten the fight of the two leopardesses in the forest: some of them looked terrified, and their ranks began to waver; but they remembered the order I had just given them, and stood fast.

We stopped to see the result; when suddenly a small boy, called Odu, remarkable for his speed and courage, who had heard me speak of the goodness of the white leopardess, leaped from the back of his bear, which went shambling after him, and ran to meet her. The leopardess, to avoid knocking him down, pulled herself up so suddenly that she went rolling over and over: when she recovered her feet she found the child on her back. Who could doubt the subjugation of a people which saw an urchin of the enemy bestride an animal of which they lived in daily terror? Confident of the effect on the whole army, we rode on.

As we stopped at the house to which our guides led us, we heard a scream; I sprang down, and thundered at the door. My horse came and pushed me away with his nose, turned about, and had begun to batter the door with his heels, when up came little Odu on the leopardess, and at sight of her he stood still, trembling. But she too had heard the cry, and forgetting the child on her back, threw herself at the door; the boy was dashed against it, and fell senseless. Before I could reach him, Lona had him in her arms, and as soon as he came to himself, set him on the back of his bear, which had still followed him.

When the leopardess threw herself the third time against the door, it gave way, and she darted in. We followed, but she had already vanished. We sprang up a stair, and went all over the house, to find no one. Darting down again, we spied a door under the stair, and got into a labyrinth of excavations. We had not gone far, however, when we met the leopardess with the child we sought across her back.

He told us that the woman he took for his mother threw him into a hole, saying she would give him to the leopardess. But the leopardess was a good one, and took him out.

Following in search of the other boy, we got into the next house more easily, but to find, alas, that we were too late: one of the savages had just killed the little captive! It consoled Lona, however, to learn which he was, for she had been expecting him to grow a bad giant, from which worst of fates death had saved him. The leopardess sprang upon his murderer, took him by the throat, dragged him into the street, and followed Lona with him, like a cat with a great rat in her jaws.

"Let us leave the horrible place," said Lona; "there are no mothers here! This people is not worth delivering."

The leopardess dropped her burden, and charged into the crowd, this way and that, wherever it was thickest. The slaves cried out and ran, tumbling over each other in heaps.

When we got back to the army, we found it as we had left it, standing in order and ready.

But I was far from easy: the princess gave no sign, and what she might be plotting we did not know! Watch and ward must be kept the night through!

The Little Ones were such hardy creatures that they could repose anywhere: we told them to lie down with their animals where they were, and sleep till they were called. In one moment they were down, and in another lapt in the music of their sleep, a sound as of water over grass, or a soft wind among leaves. Their animals slept more lightly, ever on the edge of waking. The bigger boys and girls walked softly hither and thither among the dreaming multitude. All was still; the whole wicked place appeared at rest.

CHAPTER XXXVI. MOTHER AND DAUGHTER

Lona was so disgusted with the people, and especially with the women, that she wished to abandon the place as soon as possible; I, on the contrary, felt very strongly that to do so would be to fail wilfully where success was possible; and, far worse, to weaken the hearts of the Little Ones, and so bring them into much greater danger. If we retreated, it was certain the princess would not leave us unassailed! if we encountered her, the hope of the prophecy went with us! Mother and daughter must meet: it might be that Lona's loveliness would take Lilith's heart by storm! if she threatened violence, I should be there between them! If I found that I had no other power over her, I was ready, for the sake of my Lona, to strike her pitilessly on the closed hand! I knew she was doomed: most likely it was decreed that her doom should now be brought to pass through us!

Still without hint of the relation in which she stood to the princess, I stated the case to Lona as it appeared to me. At once she agreed to accompany me to the palace.

From the top of one of its great towers, the princess had, in the early morning, while the city yet slept, descried the approach of the army of the Little Ones. The sight awoke in her an over-mastering terror: she had failed in her endeavour to destroy them, and they were upon her! The prophecy was about to be fulfilled!

When she came to herself, she descended to the black hall, and seated herself in the north focus of the ellipse, under the opening in the roof.

For she must think! Now what she called THINKING required a clear consciousness of herself, not as she was, but as she chose to believe herself; and to aid her in the realisation of this consciousness, she had suspended, a little way from and above her, itself invisible in the darkness of the hall, a mirror to receive the full sunlight reflected from her person. For the resulting vision of herself in the splendour of her beauty, she sat waiting the meridional sun.

Many a shadow moved about her in the darkness, but as often as, with a certain inner eye which she had, she caught sight of one, she refused to regard it. Close under the mirror stood the Shadow which attended her walks, but, self-occupied, him she did not see.

The city was taken; the inhabitants were cowering in terror; the Little Ones and their strange cavalry were encamped in the square; the sun shone upon the princess, and for a few minutes she saw herself glorious. The vision passed, but she sat on. The night was now come, and darkness clothed and filled the glass, yet she did not move. A gloom that swarmed with shadows, wallowed in the palace; the servants shivered and shook, but dared not leave it because of the beasts of the Little Ones; all night long the princess sat motionless: she must see her beauty again! she must try again to think! But courage and will had grown weary of her, and would dwell with her no more!

In the morning we chose twelve of the tallest and bravest of the boys to go with us to the palace. We rode our great horses, and they small horses and elephants.

The princess sat waiting the sun to give her the joy of her own presence. The tide of the light was creeping up the shore of the sky, but until the sun stood overhead, not a ray could enter the black hall.

He rose to our eyes, and swiftly ascended. As we climbed the steep way to the palace, he climbed the dome of its great hall. He looked in at the eye of it—and with sudden radiance the princess flashed upon her own sight. But she sprang to her feet with a cry of despair: alas her whiteness! the spot covered half her side, and was black as the marble around her! She clutched her robe, and fell back in her chair. The Shadow glided out, and she saw him go.

We found the gate open as usual, passed through the paved grove up to the palace door, and entered the vestibule. There in her cage lay the spotted leopardess, apparently asleep or lifeless. The Little Ones paused a moment to look at her. She leaped up rampant against the cage. The horses reared and plunged; the elephants retreated a step. The next instant she fell supine, writhed in quivering spasms, and lay motionless. We rode into the great hall.

The princess yet leaned back in her chair in the shaft of sunlight, when from the stones of the court came to her ears the noise of the horses' hoofs. She started, listened, and shook: never had such sound been heard in her palace! She pressed her hand to her side, and gasped. The trampling came nearer and nearer; it entered the hall itself; moving figures that were not shadows approached her through the darkness!

For us, we saw a splendour, a glorious woman centring the dark. Lona sprang from her horse, and bounded to her. I sprang from mine, and followed Lona.

"Mother! mother!" she cried, and her clear, lovely voice echoed in the dome.

The princess shivered; her face grew almost black with hate, her eyebrows met on her forehead. She rose to her feet, and stood.

"Mother! mother!" cried Lona again, as she leaped on the daïs, and flung her arms around the princess.

An instant more and I should have reached them!—in that instant I saw Lona lifted high, and dashed on the marble floor. Oh, the horrible sound of her fall! At my feet she fell, and lay still. The princess sat down with the smile of a demoness.

I dropped on my knees beside Lona, raised her from the stones, and pressed her to my bosom. With indignant hate I glanced at the princess; she answered me with her sweetest smile. I would have sprung upon her, taken her by the throat, and strangled her, but love of the child was stronger than hate of the mother, and I clasped closer my precious burden. Her arms hung helpless; her blood trickled over my hands, and fell on the floor with soft, slow little plashes.

The horses scented it—mine first, then the small ones. Mine reared, shivering and wild-eyed, went about, and thundered blindly down the dark hall, with the little horses after him. Lona's stood gazing down at his mistress, and trembling all over. The boys flung themselves from their horses' backs, and they, not seeing the black wall before them, dashed themselves, with mine, to pieces against it. The elephants came on to the foot of the daïs, and stopped, wildly trumpeting; the Little Ones sprang upon it, and stood horrified; the princess lay back in her seat, her face that of a corpse, her eyes alone alive, wickedly flaming. She was again withered and wasted to what I found in the wood, and her side was as if a great branding hand had been laid upon it. But Lona saw nothing, and I saw but Lona.

"Mother! mother!" she sighed, and her breathing ceased.

I carried her into the court: the sun shone upon a white face, and the pitiful shadow of a ghostly smile. Her head hung back. She was "dead as earth."

I forgot the Little Ones, forgot the murdering princess, forgot the body in my arms, and wandered away, looking for my Lona. The doors and windows were crowded with brute-faces jeering at me, but not daring to speak, for they saw the white leopardess behind me, hanging her head close at my heel. I spurned her with my foot. She held back a moment, and followed me again.

I reached the square: the little army was gone! Its emptiness roused me. Where were the Little Ones, HER Little Ones? I had lost her children! I stared helpless about me, staggered to the pillar, and sank upon its base.

But as I sat gazing on the still countenance, it seemed to smile a live momentary smile. I never doubted it an illusion, yet believed what it said: I should yet see her alive! It was not she, it was I who was lost, and she would find me!

I rose to go after the Little Ones, and instinctively sought the gate by which we had entered. I looked around me, but saw nothing of the leopardess.

The street was rapidly filling with a fierce crowd. They saw me encumbered with my dead, but for a time dared not assail me. Ere I reached the gate, however, they had gathered courage. The women began to hustle me; I held on heedless. A man pushed against my sacred burden: with a kick I sent him away howling. But the crowd pressed upon me, and fearing for the dead that was beyond hurt, I clasped my treasure closer, and freed my right arm. That instant, however, a commotion arose in the street behind me; the crowd broke; and through it came the Little Ones I had left in the palace. Ten of them were upon four of the elephants; on the two other elephants lay the princess, bound hand and foot, and quite still, save that her eyes rolled in their ghastly sockets. The two other Little Ones rode behind her on Lona's horse. Every now and then the wise creatures that bore her threw their trunks behind and felt her cords.

I walked on in front, and out of the city. What an end to the hopes with which I entered the evil place! We had captured the bad princess, and lost our all-beloved queen! My life was bare! my heart was empty!

CHAPTER XXXVII. THE SHADOW

A murmur of pleasure from my companions roused me: they had caught sight of their fellows in the distance! The two on Lona's horse rode on to join them. They were greeted with a wavering shout—which immediately died away. As we drew near, the sound of their sobs reached us like the breaking of tiny billows.

When I came among them, I saw that something dire had befallen them: on their childish faces was the haggard look left by some strange terror. No possible grief could have wrought the change. A few of them came slowly round me, and held out their arms to take my burden. I yielded it; the tender hopelessness of the smile with which they received it, made my heart swell with pity in the midst of its own desolation. In vain were their sobs over their mother-queen; in vain they sought to entice from her some recognition of their love; in vain they kissed and fondled her as they bore her away: she would not wake! On each side one carried an arm, gently stroking it; as many as could get near, put their arms under her body; those who could not, crowded around the bearers. On a spot where the grass grew thicker and softer they laid her down, and there all the Little Ones gathered sobbing.

Outside the crowd stood the elephants, and I near them, gazing at my Lona over the many little heads between. Those next me caught sight of the princess, and stared trembling. Odu was the first to speak.

"I have seen that woman before!" he whispered to his next neighbour. "It was she who fought the white leopardess, the night they woke us with their yelling!"

"Silly!" returned his companion. "That was a wild beast, with spots!"

"Look at her eyes!" insisted Odu. "I know she is a bad giantess, but she is a wild beast all the same. I know she is the spotted one!"

The other took a step nearer; Odu drew him back with a sharp pull.

"Don't look at her!" he cried, shrinking away, yet fascinated by the hate-filled longing in her eyes. "She would eat you up in a moment! It was HER shadow! She is the wicked princess!"

"That cannot be! they said she was beautiful!"

"Indeed it is the princess!" I interposed. "Wickedness has made her ugly!"

She heard, and what a look was hers!

"It was very wrong of me to run away!" said Odu thoughtfully.

"What made you run away?" I asked. "I expected to find you where I left you!"

He did not reply at once.

"I don't know what made me run," answered another. "I was frightened!"

"It was a man that came down the hill from the palace," said a third.

"How did he frighten you?"

"I don't know."

"He wasn't a man," said Odu; "he was a shadow; he had no thick to him!"

"Tell me more about him."

"He came down the hill very black, walking like a bad giant, but spread flat. He was nothing but blackness. We were frightened the moment we saw him, but we did not run away; we stood and watched him. He came on as if he would walk over us. But before he reached us, he began to spread and spread, and grew bigger end bigger, till at last he was so big that he went out of our sight, and we saw him no more, and then he was upon us!"

"What do you mean by that?"

"He was all black through between us, and we could not see one another; and then he was inside us."

"How did you know he was inside you?"

"He did me quite different. I felt like bad. I was not Odu any more—not the Odu I knew. I wanted to tear Sozo to pieces—not really, but like!"

He turned and hugged Sozo.

"It wasn't me, Sozo," he sobbed. "Really, deep down, it was Odu, loving you always! And Odu came up, and knocked Naughty away. I grew sick, and thought I must kill myself to get out of the black. Then came a horrible laugh that had heard my think, and it set the air trembling about me. And then I suppose I ran away, but I did not know I had run away until I found myself running, fast as could, and all the rest running too. I would have stopped, but I never thought of it until I was out of the gate among the grass. Then I knew that I had run away from a shadow that wanted to be me and wasn't, and that I was the Odu that loved Sozo. It was the shadow that got into me, and hated him from inside me; it was not my own self me! And now I know that I ought not to have run away! But indeed I did not quite know what I was doing until it was done! My legs did it, I think: they grew frightened, and forgot me, and ran away! Naughty legs! There! and there!"

Thus ended Odu, with a kick to each of his naughty legs.

"What became of the shadow?" I asked.

"I do not know," he answered. "I suppose he went home into the night where there is no moon."

I fell a wondering where Lona was gone, and dropping on the grass, took the dead thing in my lap, and whispered in its ear, "Where are you, Lona? I love you!" But its lips gave no answer. I kissed them, not quite cold, laid the body down again, and appointing a guard over it, rose to provide for the safety of Lona's people during the night.

Before the sun went down, I had set a watch over the princess outside the camp, and sentinels round it: intending to walk about it myself all night long, I told the rest of the army to go to sleep. They threw themselves on the grass and were asleep in a moment.

When the moon rose I caught a glimpse of something white; it was the leopardess. She swept silently round the sleeping camp, and I saw her pass three times between the princess and the Little Ones. Thereupon I made the watch lie down with the others, and stretched myself beside the body of Lona.

CHAPTER XXXVIII. TO THE HOUSE OF BITTERNESS

In the morning we set out, and made for the forest as fast as we could. I rode Lona's horse, and carried her body. I would take it to her father: he would give it a couch in the chamber of his dead! or, if he would not, seeing she had not come of herself, I would watch it in the desert until it mouldered away! But I believed he would, for surely she had died long ago! Alas, how bitterly must I not humble myself before him!

To Adam I must take Lilith also. I had no power to make her repent! I had hardly a right to slay her—much less a right to let her loose in the world! and surely I scarce merited being made for ever her gaoler!

Again and again, on the way, I offered her food; but she answered only with a look of hungering hate. Her fiery eyes kept rolling to and fro, nor ever closed, I believe, until we reached the other side of the hot stream. After that they never opened until we came to the House of Bitterness.

One evening, as we were camping for the night, I saw a little girl go up to her, and ran to prevent mischief. But ere I could reach them, the child had put something to the lips of the princess, and given a scream of pain.

"Please, king," she whimpered, "suck finger. Bad giantess make hole in it!"

I sucked the tiny finger.

"Well now!" she cried, and a minute after was holding a second fruit to a mouth greedy of other fare. But this time she snatched her hand quickly away, and the fruit fell to the ground. The child's name was Luva.

The next day we crossed the hot stream. Again on their own ground, the Little Ones were jubilant. But their nests were still at a great distance, and that day we went no farther than the ivy-hall, where, because of its grapes, I had resolved to spend the night. When they saw the great clusters, at once they knew them good, rushed upon them, ate eagerly, and in a few minutes were all fast asleep on the green floor and in the forest around the hall. Hoping again to see the dance, and expecting the Little Ones to sleep through it, I had made them leave a wide space in the middle. I lay down among them, with Lona by my side, but did not sleep.

The night came, and suddenly the company was there. I was wondering with myself whether, night after night, they would thus go on dancing to all eternity, and whether I should not one day have to join them because of my stiff-neckedness, when the eyes of the children came open, and they sprang to their feet, wide awake. Immediately every one caught hold of a dancer, and away they went, bounding and skipping. The spectres seemed to see and welcome them: perhaps they knew all about the Little Ones, for they had themselves long been on their way back to childhood! Anyhow, their innocent gambols must, I thought, bring refreshment to weary souls who, their present taken from them and their future dark, had no life save the shadow of their vanished past. Many a merry but never a rude prank did the children play; and if they did at times cause a momentary jar in the rhythm of the dance, the poor spectres, who had nothing to smile withal, at least manifested no annoyance.

Just ere the morning began to break, I started to see the skeleton-princess in the doorway, her eyes open and glowing, the fearful spot black on her side. She stood for a moment, then came gliding in, as if she would join the dance. I sprang to my feet. A cry of repugnant fear broke from the children, and the lights vanished. But the low moon looked in, and I saw them clinging to each other. The ghosts were gone—at least they were no longer visible. The princess too had disappeared. I darted to the spot where I had left her: she lay with her eyes closed, as if she had never moved. I returned to the hall. The Little Ones were already on the floor, composing themselves to sleep.

The next morning, as we started, we spied, a little way from us, two skeletons moving about in a thicket. The Little Ones broke their ranks, and ran to them. I followed; and, although now walking at ease, without splint or ligature, I was able to recognise the pair I had before seen in that neighbourhood. The children at once made friends with them, laying hold of their arms, and stroking the bones of their long fingers; and it was plain the poor creatures took their attentions kindly. The two seemed on excellent terms with each other. Their common deprivation had drawn them together! the loss of everything had been the beginning of a new life to them!

Perceiving that they had gathered handfuls of herbs, and were looking for more —presumably to rub their bones with, for in what other way could nourishment reach their system so rudimentary?—the Little Ones, having keenly examined those they held, gathered of the same sorts, and filled the hands the skeletons held out to receive them. Then they bid them goodbye, promising to come and see them again, and resumed their journey, saying to each other they had not known there were such nice people living in the same forest.

When we came to the nest-village, I remained there a night with them, to see them resettled; for Lona still looked like one just dead, and there seemed no need of haste.

The princess had eaten nothing, and her eyes remained shut: fearing she might die ere we reached the end of our journey, I went to her in the night, and laid my bare arm upon her lips. She bit into it so fiercely that I cried out. How I got away from her I do not know, but I came to myself lying beyond her reach. It was then morning, and immediately I set about our departure.

719

Choosing twelve Little Ones, not of the biggest and strongest, but of the sweetest and merriest, I mounted them on six elephants, and took two more of the wise CLUMSIES, as the children called them, to bear the princess. I still rode Lona's horse, and carried her body wrapt in her cloak before me. As nearly as I could judge I took the direct way, across the left branch of the river-bed, to the House of Bitterness, where I hoped to learn how best to cross the broader and rougher branch, and how to avoid the basin of monsters: I dreaded the former for the elephants, the latter for the children.

I had one terrible night on the way—the third, passed in the desert between the two branches of the dead river.

We had stopped the elephants in a sheltered place, and there let the princess slip down between them, to lie on the sand until the morning. She seemed quite dead, but I did not think she was. I laid myself a little way from her, with the body of Lona by my other side, thus to keep watch at once over the dead and the danger-ous. The moon was half-way down the west, a pale, thoughtful moon, mottling the desert with shadows. Of a sudden she was eclipsed, remaining visible, but sending forth no light: a thick, diaphanous film covered her patient beauty, and she looked troubled. The film swept a little aside, and I saw the edge of it against her clearness —the jagged outline of a bat-like wing, torn and hooked. Came a cold wind with a burning sting—and Lilith was upon me. Her hands were still bound, but with her teeth she pulled from my shoulder the cloak Lona made for me, and fixed them in my flesh. I lay as one paralysed.

Already the very life seemed flowing from me into her, when I remembered, and struck her on the hand. She raised her head with a gurgling shriek, and I felt her shiver. I flung her from me, and sprang to my feet.

She was on her knees, and rocked herself to and fro. A second blast of hot-stinging cold enveloped us; the moon shone out clear, and I saw her face—gaunt and ghastly, besmeared with red.

"Down, devil!" I cried.

"Where are you taking me?" she asked, with the voice of a dull echo from a sepulchre.

"To your first husband," I answered.

"He will kill me!" she moaned.

"At least he will take you off my hands!"

"Give me my daughter," she suddenly screamed, grinding her teeth.

"Never! Your doom is upon you at last!"

"Loose my hands for pity's sake!" she groaned. "I am in torture. The cords are sunk in my flesh."

"I dare not. Lie down!" I said.

She threw herself on the ground like a log.

The rest of the night passed in peace, and in the morning she again seemed dead.

Before evening we came in sight of the House of Bitterness, and the next moment one of the elephants came alongside of my horse.

"Please, king, you are not going to that place?" whispered the Little One who rode on his neck.

"Indeed I am! We are going to stay the night there," I answered.

"Oh, please, don't! That must be where the cat-woman lives!"

"If you had ever seen her, you would not call her by that name!"

"Nobody ever sees her: she has lost her face! Her head is back and side all round."

"She hides her face from dull, discontented people!—Who taught you to call her the cat-woman?"

"I heard the bad giants call her so."

"What did they say about her?"

"That she had claws to her toes."

"It is not true. I know the lady. I spent a night at her house."

"But she MAY have claws to her toes! You might see her feet, and her claws be folded up inside their cushions!"

"Then perhaps you think that I have claws to my toes?"

"Oh, no; that can't be! you are good!"

"The giants might have told you so!" I pursued.

"We shouldn't believe them about you!"

"Are the giants good?"

"No; they love lying."

"Then why do you believe them about her? I know the lady is good; she cannot have claws."

"Please how do you know she is good?"

"How do you know I am good?"

I rode on, while he waited for his companions, and told them what I had said.

They hastened after me, and when they came up,—

"I would not take you to her house if I did not believe her good," I said.

"We know you would not," they answered.

"If I were to do something that frightened you—what would you say?"

"The beasts frightened us sometimes at first, but they never hurt us!" answered one.

"That was before we knew them!" added another.

"Just so!" I answered. "When you see the woman in that cottage, you will know that she is good. You may wonder at what she does, but she will always be good. I know her better than you know me. She will not hurt you,—or if she does,——"

"Ah, you are not sure about it, king dear! You think she MAY hurt us!"

"I am sure she will never be unkind to you, even if she do hurt you!"

They were silent for a while.

"I'm not afraid of being hurt—a little!—a good deal!" cried Odu. "But I should not like scratches in the dark! The giants say the cat-woman has claw-feet all over her house!"

"I am taking the princess to her," I said.

"Why?"

"Because she is her friend."

"How can she be good then?"

"Little Tumbledown is a friend of the princess," I answered; "so is Luva: I saw them both, more than once, trying to feed her with grapes!"

"Little Tumbledown is good! Luva is very good!"

"That is why they are her friends."

"Will the cat-woman—I mean the woman that isn't the cat-woman, and has no claws to her toes—give her grapes?"

"She is more likely to give her scratches!"

"Why?—You say she is her friend!"

"That is just why.—A friend is one who gives us what we need, and the princess is sorely in need of a terrible scratching."

They were silent again.

"If any of you are afraid," I said, "you may go home; I shall not prevent you. But I cannot take one with me who believes the giants rather than me, or one who will call a good lady the cat-woman!"

"Please, king," said one, "I'm so afraid of being afraid!"

"My boy," I answered, "there is no harm in being afraid. The only harm is in doing what Fear tells you. Fear is not your master! Laugh in his face and he will run away."

"There she is—in the door waiting for us!" cried one, and put his hands over his eyes.

"How ugly she is!" cried another, and did the same.

"You do not see her," I said; "her face is covered!"

"She has no face!" they answered.

"She has a very beautiful face. I saw it once.—It is indeed as beautiful as Lona's!" I added with a sigh.

"Then what makes her hide it?"

"I think I know:—anyhow, she has some good reason for it!"

"I don't like the cat-woman! she is frightful!"

"You cannot like, and you ought not to dislike what you have never seen.— Once more, you must not call her the cat-woman!"

"What are we to call her then, please?"

"Lady Mara."

"That is a pretty name!" said a girl; "I will call her 'lady Mara'; then perhaps she will show me her beautiful face!"

Mara, drest and muffled in white, was indeed standing in the doorway to receive us.

"At last!" she said. "Lilith's hour has been long on the way, but it is come! Everything comes. Thousands of years have I waited—and not in vain!"

She came to me, took my treasure from my arms, carried it into the house, and returning, took the princess. Lilith shuddered, but made no resistance. The beasts lay down by the door. We followed our hostess, the Little Ones looking very grave. She laid the princess on a rough settle at one side of the room, unbound her, and turned to us.

"Mr. Vane," she said, "and you, Little Ones, I thank you! This woman would not yield to gentler measures; harder must have their turn. I must do what I can to make her repent!"

The pitiful-hearted Little Ones began to sob sorely.

"Will you hurt her very much, lady Mara?" said the girl I have just mentioned, putting her warm little hand in mine.

"Yes; I am afraid I must! I fear she will make me!" answered Mara. "It would be cruel to hurt her too little. It would have all to be done again, only worse."

"May I stop with her?"

"No, my child. She loves no one, therefore she cannot be WITH any one. There is One who will be with her, but she will not be with Him."

"Will the shadow that came down the hill be with her?"

"The great Shadow will be in her, I fear, but he cannot be WITH her, or with any one. She will know I am beside her, but that will not comfort her."

"Will you scratch her very deep?" asked Odu, going near, and putting his hand in hers. "Please, don't make the red juice come!"

She caught him up, turned her back to the rest of us, drew the muffling down from her face, and held him at arms' length that he might see her.

As if his face had been a mirror, I saw in it what he saw. For one moment he stared, his little mouth open; then a divine wonder arose in his countenance, and swiftly changed to intense delight. For a minute he gazed entranced, then she set him down. Yet a moment he stood looking up at her, lost in contemplation—then ran to us with the face of a prophet that knows a bliss he cannot tell. Mara rearranged her mufflings, and turned to the other children.

"You must eat and drink before you go to sleep," she said; "you have had a long journey!"

She set the bread of her house before them, and a jug of cold water. They had never seen bread before, and this was hard and dry, but they ate it without sign of distaste. They had never seen water before, but they drank without demur, one after the other looking up from the draught with a face of glad astonishment. Then she led away the smallest, and the rest went trooping after her. With her own gentle hands, they told me, she put them to bed on the floor of the garret.

CHAPTER XXXIX. THAT NIGHT

Their night was a troubled one, and they brought a strange report of it into the day. Whether the fear of their sleep came out into their waking, or their waking fear sank with them into their dreams, awake or asleep they were never at rest from it. All night something seemed going on in the house—something silent, something terrible, something they were not to know. Never a sound awoke; the darkness was one with the silence, and the silence was the terror.

Once, a frightful wind filled the house, and shook its inside, they said, so that it quivered and trembled like a horse shaking himself; but it was a silent wind that made not even a moan in their chamber, and passed away like a soundless sob.

They fell asleep. But they woke again with a great start. They thought the house was filling with water such as they had been drinking. It came from below, and swelled up until the garret was full of it to the very roof. But it made no more sound than the wind, and when it sank away, they fell asleep dry and warm.

The next time they woke, all the air, they said, inside and out, was full of cats. They swarmed—up and down, along and across, everywhere about the room. They felt their claws trying to get through the night-gowns lady Mara had put on them, but they could not; and in the morning not one of them had a scratch. Through the dark suddenly, came the only sound they heard the night long—the far-off howl of the huge great-grandmother-cat in the desert: she must have been calling her little ones, they thought, for that instant the cats stopped, and all was still. Once more they fell fast asleep, and did not wake till the sun was rising.

Such was the account the children gave of their experiences. But I was with the veiled woman and the princess all through the night: something of what took place I saw; much I only felt; and there was more which eye could not see, and heart only could in a measure understand.

As soon as Mara left the room with the children, my eyes fell on the white leopardess: I thought we had left her behind us, but there she was, cowering in a corner.

Apparently she was in mortal terror of what she might see. A lamp stood on the high chimney-piece, and sometimes the room seemed full of lamp-shadows, sometimes of cloudy forms. The princess lay on the settle by the wall, and seemed never to have moved hand or foot. It was a fearsome waiting.

When Mara returned, she drew the settle with Lilith upon it to the middle of the room, then sat down opposite me, at the other side of the hearth. Between us burned a small fire.

Something terrible was on its way! The cloudy presences flickered and shook. A silvery creature like a slowworm came crawling out from among them, slowly crossed the clay floor, and crept into the fire. We sat motionless. The something came nearer.

But the hours passed, midnight drew nigh, and there was no change. The night was very still. Not a sound broke the silence, not a rustle from the fire, not a crack from board or beam. Now and again I felt a sort of heave, but whether in the earth or in the air or in the waters under the earth, whether in my own body or in my soul—whether it was anywhere, I could not tell. A dread sense of judgment was upon me. But I was not afraid, for I had ceased to care for aught save the thing that must be done.

Suddenly it was midnight. The muffled woman rose, turned toward the settle, and slowly unwound the long swathes that hid her face: they dropped on the ground, and she stepped over them. The feet of the princess were toward the hearth; Mara went to her head, and turning, stood behind it. Then I saw her face. It was lovely beyond speech—white and sad, heart-and-soul sad, but not unhappy, and I knew it never could be unhappy. Great tears were running down her cheeks: she wiped them away with her robe; her countenance grew very still, and she wept no more. But for the pity in every line of her expression, she would have seemed severe. She laid her hand on the head of the princess—on the hair that grew low on the forehead, and stooping, breathed on the sallow brow. The body shuddered.

"Will you turn away from the wicked things you have been doing so long?" said Mara gently.

The princess did not answer. Mara put the question again, in the same soft, inviting tone.

Still there was no sign of hearing. She spoke the words a third time.

Then the seeming corpse opened its mouth and answered, its words appearing to frame themselves of something else than sound.—I cannot shape the thing further: sounds they were not, yet they were words to me.

"I will not," she said. "I will be myself and not another!"

"Alas, you are another now, not yourself! Will you not be your real self?"

"I will be what I mean myself now."

"If you were restored, would you not make what amends you could for the misery you have caused?"

"I would do after my nature."

"You do not know it: your nature is good, and you do evil!"

"I will do as my Self pleases—as my Self desires."

"You will do as the Shadow, overshadowing your Self inclines you?"

"I will do what I will to do."

"You have killed your daughter, Lilith!"

"I have killed thousands. She is my own!"

725

"She was never yours as you are another's."

"I am not another's; I am my own, and my daughter is mine."

"Then, alas, your hour is come!"

"I care not. I am what I am; no one can take from me myself!"

"You are not the Self you imagine."

"So long as I feel myself what it pleases me to think myself, I care not. I am content to be to myself what I would be. What I choose to seem to myself makes me what I am. My own thought makes me me; my own thought of myself is me. Another shall not make me!"

"But another has made you, and can compel you to see what you have made yourself. You will not be able much longer to look to yourself anything but what he sees you! You will not much longer have satisfaction in the thought of yourself. At this moment you are aware of the coming change!"

"No one ever made me. I defy that Power to unmake me from a free woman! You are his slave, and I defy you! You may be able to torture me—I do not know, but you shall not compel me to anything against my will!"

"Such a compulsion would be without value. But there is a light that goes deeper than the will, a light that lights up the darkness behind it: that light can change your will, can make it truly yours and not another's—not the Shadow's. Into the created can pour itself the creating will, and so redeem it!"

"That light shall not enter me: I hate it!—Begone, slave!"

"I am no slave, for I love that light, and will with the deeper will which created mine. There is no slave but the creature that wills against its creator. Who is a slave but her who cries, 'I am free,' yet cannot cease to exist!"

"You speak foolishness from a cowering heart! You imagine me given over to you: I defy you! I hold myself against you! What I choose to be, you cannot change. I will not be what you think me—what you say I am!"

"I am sorry: you must suffer!"

"But be free!"

"She alone is free who would make free; she loves not freedom who would enslave: she is herself a slave. Every life, every will, every heart that came within your ken, you have sought to subdue: you are the slave of every slave you have made—such a slave that you do not know it!—See your own self!"

She took her hand from the head of the princess, and went two backward paces from her.

A soundless presence as of roaring flame possessed the house—the same, I presume, that was to the children a silent wind. Involuntarily I turned to the hearth: its fire was a still small moveless glow. But I saw the worm-thing come creeping out, white-hot, vivid as incandescent silver, the live heart of essential fire. Along the floor it crawled toward the settle, going very slow. Yet more slowly it crept up on it, and laid itself, as unwilling to go further, at the feet of the princess. I rose and stole nearer. Mara stood motionless, as one that waits an event foreknown. The shining thing crawled on to a bare bony foot: it showed no suffering, neither was the settle scorched where the worm had lain. Slowly, very slowly, it crept along her robe until it reached her bosom, where it disappeared among the folds.

The face of the princess lay stonily calm, the eyelids closed as over dead eyes; and for some minutes nothing followed. At length, on the dry, parchment-like skin, began to appear drops as of the finest dew: in a moment they were as large as seed-pearls, ran together, and began to pour down in streams. I darted forward to snatch the worm from the poor withered bosom, and crush it with my foot. But Mara, Mother of Sorrow, stepped between, and drew aside the closed edges of the robe: no serpent was there—no searing trail; the creature had passed in by the centre of the black spot, and was piercing through the joints and marrow to the thoughts and intents of the heart. The princess gave one writhing, contorted shudder, and I knew the worm was in her secret chamber.

"She is seeing herself!" said Mara; and laying her hand on my arm, she drew me three paces from the settle.

Of a sudden the princess bent her body upward in an arch, then sprang to the floor, and stood erect. The horror in her face made me tremble lest her eyes should open, and the sight of them overwhelm me. Her bosom heaved and sank, but no breath issued. Her hair hung and dripped; then it stood out from her head and emitted sparks; again hung down, and poured the sweat of her torture on the floor.

I would have thrown my arms about her, but Mara stopped me.

"You cannot go near her," she said. "She is far away from us, afar in the hell of her self-consciousness. The central fire of the universe is radiating into her the knowledge of good and evil, the knowledge of what she is. She sees at last the good she is not, the evil she is. She knows that she is herself the fire in which she is burning, but she does not know that the Light of Life is the heart of that fire. Her torment is that she is what she is. Do not fear for her; she is not forsaken. No gentler way to help her was left. Wait and watch."

It may have been five minutes or five years that she stood thus—I cannot tell; but at last she flung herself on her face.

Mara went to her, and stood looking down upon her. Large tears fell from her eyes on the woman who had never wept, and would not weep.

"Will you change your way?" she said at length.

"Why did he make me such?" gasped Lilith. "I would have made myself—oh, so different! I am glad it was he that made me and not I myself! He alone is to blame for what I am! Never would I have made such a worthless thing! He meant me such that I might know it and be miserable! I will not be made any longer!"

"Unmake yourself, then," said Mara.

"Alas, I cannot! You know it, and mock me! How often have I not agonised to cease, but the tyrant keeps me being! I curse him!—Now let him kill me!"

The words came in jets as from a dying fountain.

"Had he not made you," said Mara, gently and slowly, "you could not even hate him. But he did not make you such. You have made yourself what you are.—Be of better cheer: he can remake you."

"I will not be remade!"

"He will not change you; he will only restore you to what you were."

"I will not be aught of his making."

"Are you not willing to have that set right which you have set wrong?"

She lay silent; her suffering seemed abated.

"If you are willing, put yourself again on the settle."

"I will not," she answered, forcing the words through her clenched teeth.

A wind seemed to wake inside the house, blowing without sound or impact; and a water began to rise that had no lap in its ripples, no sob in its swell. It was cold, but it did not benumb. Unseen and noiseless it came. It smote no sense in me, yet I knew it rising. I saw it lift at last and float her. Gently it bore her, unable to resist, and left rather than laid her on the settle. Then it sank swiftly away.

The strife of thought, accusing and excusing, began afresh, and gathered fierceness. The soul of Lilith lay naked to the torture of pure interpenetrating inward light. She began to moan, and sigh deep sighs, then murmur as holding colloquy with a dividual self: her queendom was no longer whole; it was divided against itself. One moment she would exult as over her worst enemy, and weep; the next she would writhe as in the embrace of a friend whom her soul hated, and laugh like a demon. At length she began what seemed a tale about herself, in a language so strange, and in forms so shadowy, that I could but here and there understand a little. Yet the language seemed the primeval shape of one I knew well, and the forms to belong to dreams which had once been mine, but refused to be recalled. The tale appeared now and then to touch upon things that Adam had read from the disparted manuscript, and often to make allusion to influences and forces—vices too, I could not help suspecting—with which I was unacquainted.

She ceased, and again came the horror in her hair, the sparkling and flowing alternate. I sent a beseeching look to Mara.

"Those, alas, are not the tears of repentance!" she said. "The true tears gather in the eyes. Those are far more bitter, and not so good. Self-loathing is not sorrow. Yet it is good, for it marks a step in the way home, and in the father's arms the prodigal forgets the self he abominates. Once with his father, he is to himself of no more account. It will be so with her."

She went nearer and said,

"Will you restore that which you have wrongfully taken?"

"I have taken nothing," answered the princess, forcing out the words in spite of pain, "that I had not the right to take. My power to take manifested my right."

Mara left her.

Gradually my soul grew aware of an invisible darkness, a something more terrible than aught that had yet made itself felt. A horrible Nothingness, a Negation positive infolded her; the border of its being that was yet no being, touched me, and for one ghastly instant I seemed alone with Death Absolute! It was not the absence of everything I felt, but the presence of Nothing. The princess dashed herself from the settle to the floor with an exceeding great and bitter cry. It was the recoil of Being from Annihilation.

"For pity's sake," she shrieked, "tear my heart out, but let me live!"

With that there fell upon her, and upon us also who watched with her, the perfect calm as of a summer night. Suffering had all but reached the brim of her life's cup, and a hand had emptied it! She raised her head, half rose, and looked around her. A moment more, and she stood erect, with the air of a conqueror: she had won the battle! Dareful she had met her spiritual foes; they had withdrawn defeated! She raised her withered arm above her head, a pæan of unholy triumph in her throat—when suddenly her eyes fixed in a ghastly stare.—What was she seeing?

I looked, and saw: before her, cast from unseen heavenly mirror, stood the reflection of herself, and beside it a form of splendent beauty. She trembled, and sank again on the floor helpless. She knew the one what God had intended her to be, the other what she had made herself.

The rest of the night she lay motionless altogether.

With the gray dawn growing in the room, she rose, turned to Mara, and said, in prideful humility, "You have conquered. Let me go into the wilderness and bewail myself."

Mara saw that her submission was not feigned, neither was it real. She looked at her a moment, and returned:

"Begin, then, and set right in the place of wrong."

"I know not how," she replied—with the look of one who foresaw and feared the answer.

"Open thy hand, and let that which is in it go."

A fierce refusal seemed to struggle for passage, but she kept it prisoned.

"I cannot," she said. "I have no longer the power. Open it for me."

She held out the offending hand. It was more a paw than a hand. It seemed to me plain that she could not open it.

Mara did not even look at it.

"You must open it yourself," she said quietly.

"I have told you I cannot!"

"You can if you will—not indeed at once, but by persistent effort. What you have done, you do not yet wish undone—do not yet intend to undo!"

"You think so, I dare say," rejoined the princess with a flash of insolence, "but I KNOW that I cannot open my hand!"

"I know you better than you know yourself, and I know you can. You have often opened it a little way. Without trouble and pain you cannot open it quite, but you CAN open it. At worst you could beat it open! I pray you, gather your strength, and open it wide."

"I will not try what I know impossible. It would be the part of a fool!"

"Which you have been playing all your life! Oh, you are hard to teach!"

Defiance reappeared on the face of the princess. She turned her back on Mara, saying, "I know what you have been tormenting me for! You have not succeeded, nor shall you succeed! You shall yet find me stronger than you think! I will yet be mistress of myself! I am still what I have always known myself—queen of Hell, and mistress of the worlds!"

Then came the most fearful thing of all. I did not know what it was; I knew myself unable to imagine it; I knew only that if it came near me I should die of terror! I now know that it was LIFE IN DEATH—life dead, yet existent; and I knew that Lilith had had glimpses, but only glimpses of it before: it had never been with her until now.

She stood as she had turned. Mara went and sat down by the fire. Fearing to stand alone with the princess, I went also and sat again by the hearth. Something began to depart from me. A sense of cold, yet not what we call cold, crept, not into, but out of my being, and pervaded it. The lamp of life and the eternal fire seemed dying together, and I about to be left with naught but the consciousness that I had been alive. Mercifully, bereavement did not go so far, and my thought went back to Lilith.

Something was taking place in her which we did not know. We knew we did not feel what she felt, but we knew we felt something of the misery it caused her. The thing itself was in her, not in us; its reflex, her misery, reached us, and was again reflected in us: she was in the outer darkness, we present with her who was in it! We were not in the outer darkness; had we been, we could not have been WITH her; we should have been timelessly, spacelessly, absolutely apart. The darkness knows neither the light nor itself; only the light knows itself and the darkness also. None but God hates evil and understands it.

Something was gone from her, which then first, by its absence, she knew to have been with her every moment of her wicked years. The source of life had withdrawn itself; all that was left her of conscious being was the dregs of her dead and corrupted life.

She stood rigid. Mara buried her head in her hands. I gazed on the face of one who knew existence but not love—knew nor life, nor joy, nor good; with my eyes I saw the face of a live death! She knew life only to know that it was dead, and that, in her, death lived. It was not merely that life had ceased in her, but that she was consciously a dead thing. She had killed her life, and was dead—and knew it. She must DEATH IT for ever and ever! She had tried her hardest to unmake herself, and could not! she was a dead life! she could not cease! she must BE! In her face I saw and read beyond its misery—saw in its dismay that the dismay behind it was more than it could manifest. It sent out a livid gloom; the light that was in her was darkness, and after its kind it shone. She was what God could not have created. She had usurped beyond her share in self-creation, and her part had undone His! She saw now what she had made, and behold, it was not good! She was as a conscious corpse, whose coffin would never come to pieces, never set her free! Her bodily eyes stood wide open, as if gazing into the heart of horror essential—her own indestructible evil. Her right hand also was now clenched—upon existent Nothing—her inheritance!

But with God all things are possible: He can save even the rich!

Without change of look, without sign of purpose, Lilith walked toward Mara. She felt her coming, and rose to meet her.

"I yield," said the princess. "I cannot hold out. I am defeated.—Not the less, I cannot open my hand."

"Have you tried?"

"I am trying now with all my might."

"I will take you to my father. You have wronged him worst of the created, therefore he best of the created can help you."

"How can HE help me?"

"He will forgive you."

"Ah, if he would but help me to cease! Not even that am I capable of! I have no power over myself; I am a slave! I acknowledge it. Let me die."

"A slave thou art that shall one day be a child!" answered Mara.—"Verily, thou shalt die, but not as thou thinkest. Thou shalt die out of death into life. Now is the Life for, that never was against thee!"

Like her mother, in whom lay the motherhood of all the world, Mara put her arms around Lilith, and kissed her on the forehead. The fiery-cold misery went out of her eyes, and their fountains filled. She lifted, and bore her to her own bed in a corner of the room, laid her softly upon it, and closed her eyes with caressing hands.

Lilith lay and wept. The Lady of Sorrow went to the door and opened it.

Morn, with the Spring in her arms, waited outside. Softly they stole in at the opened door, with a gentle wind in the skirts of their garments. It flowed and flowed about Lilith, rippling the unknown, upwaking sea of her life eternal;

rippling and to ripple it, until at length she who had been but as a weed cast on the dry sandy shore to wither, should know herself an inlet of the everlasting ocean, henceforth to flow into her for ever, and ebb no more. She answered the morning wind with reviving breath, and began to listen. For in the skirts of the wind had come the rain—the soft rain that heals the mown, the many-wounded grass— soothing it with the sweetness of all music, the hush that lives between music and silence. It bedewed the desert places around the cottage, and the sands of Lilith's heart heard it, and drank it in. When Mara returned to sit by her bed, her tears were flowing softer than the rain, and soon she was fast asleep.

CHAPTER XL. THE HOUSE OF DEATH

The Mother of Sorrows rose, muffled her face, and went to call the Little Ones. They slept as if all the night they had not moved, but the moment she spoke they sprang to their feet, fresh as if new-made. Merrily down the stair they followed her, and she brought them where the princess lay, her tears yet flowing as she slept. Their glad faces grew grave. They looked from the princess out on the rain, then back at the princess.

"The sky is falling!" said one.

"The white juice is running out of the princess!" cried another, with an awed look.

"Is it rivers?" asked Odu, gazing at the little streams that flowed adown her hollow cheeks.

"Yes," answered Mara, "—the most wonderful of all rivers."

"I thought rivers was bigger, and rushed, like a lot of Little Ones, making loud noises!" he returned, looking at me, from whom alone he had heard of rivers.

"Look at the rivers of the sky!" said Mara. "See how they come down to wake up the waters under the earth! Soon will the rivers be flowing everywhere, merry and loud, like thousands and thousands of happy children. Oh, how glad they will make you, Little Ones! You have never seen any, and do not know how lovely is the water!"

"That will be the glad of the ground that the princess is grown good," said Odu. "See the glad of the sky!"

"Are the rivers the glad of the princess?" asked Luva. "They are not her juice, for they are not red!"

"They are the juice inside the juice," answered Mara.

Odu put one finger to his eye, looked at it, and shook his head.

"Princess will not bite now!" said Luva.

"No; she will never do that again," replied Mara. "—But now we must take her nearer home."

"Is that a nest?" asked Sozo.

"Yes; a very big nest. But we must take her to another place first."

"What is that?"

"It is the biggest room in all this world.—But I think it is going to be pulled down: it will soon be too full of little nests.—Go and get your clumsies."

"Please are there any cats in it?"

"Not one. The nests are too full of lovely dreams for one cat to get in."

"We shall be ready in a minute," said Odu, and ran out, followed by all except Luva.

Lilith was now awake, and listening with a sad smile.

"But her rivers are running so fast!" said Luva, who stood by her side and seemed unable to take her eyes from her face. "Her robe is all—I don't know what. Clumsies won't like it!"

"They won't mind it," answered Mara. "Those rivers are so clean that they make the whole world clean."

I had fallen asleep by the fire, but for some time had been awake and listening, and now rose.

"It is time to mount, Mr. Vane," said our hostess.

"Tell me, please," I said, "is there not a way by which to avoid the channels and the den of monsters?"

"There is an easy way across the river-bed, which I will show you," she answered; "but you must pass once more through the monsters."

"I fear for the children," I said.

"Fear will not once come nigh them," she rejoined.

We left the cottage. The beasts stood waiting about the door. Odu was already on the neck of one of the two that were to carry the princess. I mounted Lona's horse; Mara brought her body, and gave it me in my arms. When she came out again with the princess, a cry of delight arose from the children: she was no longer muffled! Gazing at her, and entranced with her loveliness, the boys forgot to receive the princess from her; but the elephants took Lilith tenderly with their trunks, one round her body and one round her knees, and, Mara helping, laid her along between them.

"Why does the princess want to go?" asked a small boy. "She would keep good if she staid here!"

"She wants to go, and she does not want to go: we are helping her," answered Mara. "She will not keep good here."

"What are you helping her to do?" he went on.

"To go where she will get more help—help to open her hand, which has been closed for a thousand years."

"So long? Then she has learned to do without it: why should she open it now?"

"Because it is shut upon something that is not hers."

"Please, lady Mara, may we have some of your very dry bread before we go?" said Luva.

Mara smiled, and brought them four loaves and a great jug of water.

"We will eat as we go," they said. But they drank the water with delight.

"I think," remarked one of them, "it must be elephant-juice! It makes me so strong!"

We set out, the Lady of Sorrow walking with us, more beautiful than the sun, and the white leopardess following her. I thought she meant but to put us in the path across the channels, but I soon found she was going with us all the way. Then I would have dismounted that she might ride, but she would not let me.

"I have no burden to carry," she said. "The children and I will walk together."

It was the loveliest of mornings; the sun shone his brightest, and the wind blew his sweetest, but they did not comfort the desert, for it had no water.

We crossed the channels without difficulty, the children gamboling about Mara all the way, but did not reach the top of the ridge over the bad burrow until the sun was already in the act of disappearing. Then I made the Little Ones mount their elephants, for the moon might be late, and I could not help some anxiety about them.

The Lady of Sorrow now led the way by my side; the elephants followed—the two that bore the princess in the centre; the leopardess brought up the rear; and just as we reached the frightful margin, the moon looked up and showed the shallow basin lying before us untroubled. Mara stepped into it; not a movement answered her tread or the feet of my horse. But the moment that the elephants carrying the princess touched it, the seemingly solid earth began to heave and boil, and the whole dread brood of the hellish nest was commoved. Monsters uprose on all sides, every neck at full length, every beak and claw outstretched, every mouth agape. Long-billed heads, horribly jawed faces, knotty tentacles innumerable, went out after Lilith. She lay in an agony of fear, nor dared stir a finger. Whether the hideous things even saw the children, I doubt; certainly not one of them touched a child; not one loathly member passed the live rampart of her body-guard, to lay hold of her.

"Little Ones," I cried, "keep your elephants close about the princess. Be brave; they will not touch you."

"What will not touch us? We don't know what to be brave at!" they answered; and I perceived they were unaware of one of the deformities around them.

"Never mind then," I returned; "only keep close."

They were panoplied in their blindness! Incapacity to see was their safety. What they could nowise be aware of, could not hurt them.

But the hideous forms I saw that night! Mara was a few paces in front of me when a solitary, bodiless head bounced on the path between us. The leopardess came rushing under the elephants from behind, and would have seized it, but, with frightful contortions of visage and a loathsome howl, it gave itself a rapid rotatory twist, sprang from her, and buried itself in the ground. The death in my arms assoiling me from fear, I regarded them all unmoved, although never, sure, was elsewhere beheld such a crew accursed!

Mara still went in front of me, and the leopardess now walked close behind her, shivering often, for it was very cold, when suddenly the ground before me to my left began to heave, and a low wave of earth came slinking toward us. It rose higher as it drew hear; out of it slouched a dreadful head with fleshy tubes for hair, and opening a great oval mouth, snapped at me. The leopardess sprang, but fell baffled beyond it.

Almost under our feet, shot up the head of an enormous snake, with a lamping wallowing glare in its eyes. Again the leopardess rushed to the attack, but found nothing. At a third monster she darted with like fury, and like failure—then sullenly ceased to heed the phantom-horde. But I understood the peril and hastened the crossing—the rather that the moon was carrying herself strangely. Even as she rose she seemed ready to drop and give up the attempt as hopeless; and since, I saw her sink back once fully her own breadth. The arc she made was very low, and now she had begun to descend rapidly.

We were almost over, when, between us and the border of the basin, arose a long neck, on the top of which, like the blossom of some Stygian lily, sat what seemed the head of a corpse, its mouth half open, and full of canine teeth. I went on; it retreated, then drew aside. The lady stepped on the firm land, but the leopardess between us, roused once more, turned, and flew at the throat of the terror. I remained where I was to see the elephants, with the princess and the children, safe on the bank. Then I turned to look after the leopardess. That moment the moon went down, For an instant I saw the leopardess and the snake-monster convolved in a cloud of dust; then darkness hid them. Trembling with fright, my horse wheeled, and in three bounds overtook the elephants.

As we came up with them, a shapeless jelly dropped on the princess. A white dove dropped immediately on the jelly, stabbing it with its beak. It made a squelching, sucking sound, and fell off. Then I heard the voice of a woman talking with Mara, and I knew the voice.

"I fear she is dead!" said Mara.

"I will send and find her," answered the mother. "But why, Mara, shouldst thou at all fear for her or for any one? Death cannot hurt her who dies doing the work given her to do."

"I shall miss her sorely; she is good and wise. Yet I would not have her live beyond her hour!"

"She has gone down with the wicked; she will rise with the righteous. We shall see her again ere very long."

"Mother," I said, although I did not see her, "we come to you many, but most of us are Little Ones. Will you be able to receive us all?"

"You are welcome every one," she answered. "Sooner or later all will be little ones, for all must sleep in my house! It is well with those that go to sleep young and willing!—My husband is even now preparing her couch for Lilith. She is neither young nor quite willing, but it is well indeed that she is come."

I heard no more. Mother and daughter had gone away together through the dark. But we saw a light in the distance, and toward it we went stumbling over the moor.

Adam stood in the door, holding the candle to guide us, and talking with his wife, who, behind him, laid bread and wine on the table within.

"Happy children," I heard her say, "to have looked already on the face of my daughter! Surely it is the loveliest in the great world!"

When we reached the door, Adam welcomed us almost merrily. He set the candle on the threshold, and going to the elephants, would have taken the princess to carry her in; but she repulsed him, and pushing her elephants asunder, stood erect between them. They walked from beside her, and left her with him who had been her husband—ashamed indeed of her gaunt uncomeliness, but unsubmissive. He stood with a welcome in his eyes that shone through their severity.

"We have long waited for thee, Lilith!" he said.

She returned him no answer.

Eve and her daughter came to the door.

"The mortal foe of my children!" murmured Eve, standing radiant in her beauty.

"Your children are no longer in her danger," said Mara; "she has turned from evil."

"Trust her not hastily, Mara," answered her mother; "she has deceived a multitude!"

"But you will open to her the mirror of the Law of Liberty, mother, that she may go into it, and abide in it! She consents to open her hand and restore: will not the great Father restore her to inheritance with His other children?"

"I do not know Him!" murmured Lilith, in a voice of fear and doubt.

"Therefore it is that thou art miserable," said Adam.

"I will go back whence I came!" she cried, and turned, wringing her hands, to depart.

"That is indeed what I would have thee do, where I would have thee go—to Him from whom thou camest! In thy agony didst thou not cry out for Him?"

"I cried out for Death—to escape Him and thee!"

"Death is even now on his way to lead thee to Him. Thou knowest neither Death nor the Life that dwells in Death! Both befriend thee. I am dead, and would see thee dead, for I live and love thee. Thou art weary and heavy-laden: art thou not ashamed? Is not the being thou hast corrupted become to thee at length an evil thing? Wouldst thou yet live on in disgrace eternal? Cease thou canst not: wilt thou not be restored and BE?"

She stood silent with bowed head.

"Father," said Mara, "take her in thine arms, and carry her to her couch. There she will open her hand, and die into life."

"I will walk," said the princess.

Adam turned and led the way. The princess walked feebly after him into the cottage.

Then Eve came out to me where I sat with Lona in my bosom. She reached up her arms, took her from me, and carried her in. I dismounted, and the children also. The horse and the elephants stood shivering; Mara patted and stroked them every one; they lay down and fell asleep. She led us into the cottage, and gave the Little Ones of the bread and wine on the table. Adam and Lilith were standing there together, but silent both.

Eve came from the chamber of death, where she had laid Lona down, and offered of the bread and wine to the princess.

"Thy beauty slays me! It is death I would have, not food!" said Lilith, and turned from her.

"This food will help thee to die," answered Eve.

But Lilith would not taste of it.

"If thou wilt nor eat nor drink, Lilith," said Adam, "come and see the place where thou shalt lie in peace."

He led the way through the door of death, and she followed submissive. But when her foot crossed the threshold she drew it back, and pressed her hand to her bosom, struck through with the cold immortal.

A wild blast fell roaring on the roof, and died away in a moan. She stood ghastly with terror.

"It is he!" said her voiceless lips: I read their motion.

"Who, princess!" I whispered.

"The great Shadow," she murmured.

"Here he cannot enter," said Adam. "Here he can hurt no one. Over him also is power given me."

"Are the children in the house?" asked Lilith, and at the word the heart of Eve began to love her.

"He never dared touch a child," she said. "Nor have you either ever hurt a child. Your own daughter you have but sent into the loveliest sleep, for she was already a long time dead when you slew her. And now Death shall be the atone-maker; you shall sleep together."

"Wife," said Adam, "let us first put the children to bed, that she may see them safe!"

He came back to fetch them. As soon as he was gone, the princess knelt to Eve, clasped her knees, and said,

"Beautiful Eve, persuade your husband to kill me: to you he will listen! Indeed I would but cannot open my hand."

"You cannot die without opening it. To kill you would not serve you," answered Eve. "But indeed he cannot! no one can kill you but the Shadow; and whom he kills never knows she is dead, but lives to do his will, and thinks she is doing her own."

"Show me then to my grave; I am so weary I can live no longer. I must go to the Shadow—yet I would not!"

She did not, could not understand!

She struggled to rise, but fell at the feet of Eve. The Mother lifted, and carried her inward.

I followed Adam and Mara and the children into the chamber of death. We passed Eve with Lilith in her arms, and went farther in.

"You shall not go to the Shadow," I heard Eve say, as we passed them. "Even now is his head under my heel!"

The dim light in Adam's hand glimmered on the sleeping faces, and as he went on, the darkness closed over them. The very air seemed dead: was it because none of the sleepers breathed it? Profoundest sleep filled the wide place. It was as if not one had waked since last I was there, for the forms I had then noted lay there still. My father was just as I had left him, save that he seemed yet nearer to a perfect peace. The woman beside him looked younger.

The darkness, the cold, the silence, the still air, the faces of the lovely dead, made the hearts of the children beat softly, but their little tongues would talk—with low, hushed voices.

"What a curious place to sleep in!" said one, "I would rather be in my nest!" "It is SO cold!" said another.

"Yes, it is cold," answered our host; "but you will not be cold in your sleep."

"Where are our nests?" asked more than one, looking round and seeing no couch unoccupied.

"Find places, and sleep where you choose," replied Adam.

Instantly they scattered, advancing fearlessly beyond the light, but we still heard their gentle voices, and it was plain they saw where I could not.

"Oh," cried one, "here is such a beautiful lady!—may I sleep beside her? I will creep in quietly, and not wake her."

"Yes, you may," answered the voice of Eve behind us; and we came to the couch while the little fellow was yet creeping slowly and softly under the sheet. He laid his head beside the lady's, looked up at us, and was still. His eyelids fell; he was asleep.

We went a little farther, and there was another who had climbed up on the couch of a woman.

"Mother! mother!" he cried, kneeling over her, his face close to hers. "—She's so cold she can't speak," he said, looking up to us; "but I will soon make her warm!"

He lay down, and pressing close to her, put his little arm over her. In an instant he too was asleep, smiling an absolute content.

We came to a third Little One; it was Luva. She stood on tiptoe, leaning over the edge of a couch.

"My own mother wouldn't have me," she said softly: "will you?"

Receiving no reply, she looked up at Eve. The great mother lifted her to the couch, and she got at once under the snowy covering.

Each of the Little Ones had by this time, except three of the boys, found at least an unobjecting bedfellow, and lay still and white beside a still, white woman. The little orphans had adopted mothers! One tiny girl had chosen a father to sleep with, and that was mine. A boy lay by the side of the beautiful matron with the slow-healing hand. On the middle one of the three couches hitherto unoccupied, lay Lona.

Eve set Lilith down beside it. Adam pointed to the vacant couch on Lona's right hand, and said,

"There, Lilith, is the bed I have prepared for you!"

She glanced at her daughter lying before her like a statue carved in semi-transparent alabaster, and shuddered from head to foot. "How cold it is!" she murmured.

"You will soon begin to find comfort in the cold," answered Adam.

"Promises to the dying are easy!" she said.

"But I know it: I too have slept. I am dead!"

"I believed you dead long ago; but I see you alive!"

"More alive than you know, or are able to understand. I was scarce alive when first you knew me. Now I have slept, and am awake; I am dead, and live indeed!"

"I fear that child," she said, pointing to Lona: "she will rise and terrify me!"

"She is dreaming love to you."

"But the Shadow!" she moaned; "I fear the Shadow! he will be wroth with me!"

"He at sight of whom the horses of heaven start and rear, dares not disturb one dream in this quiet chamber!"

"I shall dream then?"

"You will dream."

"What dreams?"

"That I cannot tell, but none HE can enter into. When the Shadow comes here, it will be to lie down and sleep also.—His hour will come, and he knows it will."

"How long shall I sleep?"

"You and he will be the last to wake in the morning of the universe."

The princess lay down, drew the sheet over her, stretched herself out straight, and lay still with open eyes.

Adam turned to his daughter. She drew near.

"Lilith," said Mara, "you will not sleep, if you lie there a thousand years, until you have opened your hand, and yielded that which is not yours to give or to withhold."

"I cannot," she answered. "I would if I could, and gladly, for I am weary, and the shadows of death are gathering about me."

"They will gather and gather, but they cannot infold you while yet your hand remains unopened. You may think you are dead, but it will be only a dream; you may think you have come awake, but it will still be only a dream. Open your hand, and you will sleep indeed—then wake indeed."

"I am trying hard, but the fingers have grown together and into the palm."

"I pray you put forth the strength of your will. For the love of life, draw together your forces and break its bonds!"

"I have struggled in vain; I can do no more. I am very weary, and sleep lies heavy upon my lids."

"The moment you open your hand, you will sleep. Open it, and make an end."

A tinge of colour arose in the parchment-like face; the contorted hand trembled with agonised effort. Mara took it, and sought to aid her.

"Hold, Mara!" cried her father. "There is danger!"

The princess turned her eyes upon Eve, beseechingly.

"There was a sword I once saw in your husband's hands," she murmured. "I fled when I saw it. I heard him who bore it say it would divide whatever was not one and indivisible!"

"I have the sword," said Adam. "The angel gave it me when he left the gate."

"Bring it, Adam," pleaded Lilith, "and cut me off this hand that I may sleep."

"I will," he answered.

He gave the candle to Eve, and went. The princess closed her eyes.

In a few minutes Adam returned with an ancient weapon in his hand. The scabbard looked like vellum grown dark with years, but the hilt shone like gold that nothing could tarnish. He drew out the blade. It flashed like a pale blue northern streamer, and the light of it made the princess open her eyes. She saw the sword, shuddered, and held out her hand. Adam took it. The sword gleamed once, there was one little gush of blood, and he laid the severed hand in Mara's lap. Lilith had given one moan, and was already fast asleep. Mara covered the arm with the sheet, and the three turned away.

"Will you not dress the wound?" I said.

"A wound from that sword," answered Adam, "needs no dressing. It is healing and not hurt."

"Poor lady!" I said, "she will wake with but one hand!"

"Where the dead deformity clung," replied Mara, "the true, lovely hand is already growing."

We heard a childish voice behind us, and turned again. The candle in Eve's hand shone on the sleeping face of Lilith, and the waking faces of the three Little Ones, grouped on the other side of her couch. "How beautiful she is grown!" said one of them.

"Poor princess!" said another; "I will sleep with her. She will not bite any more!"

As he spoke he climbed into her bed, and was immediately fast asleep. Eve covered him with the sheet.

"I will go on her other side," said the third. "She shall have two to kiss her when she wakes!"

"And I am left alone!" said the first mournfully.

"I will put you to bed," said Eve.

She gave the candle to her husband, and led the child away.

We turned once more to go back to the cottage. I was very sad, for no one had offered me a place in the house of the dead. Eve joined us as we went, and walked on before with her husband. Mara by my side carried the hand of Lilith in the lap of her robe.

"Ah, you have found her!" we heard Eve say as we stepped into the cottage.

The door stood open; two elephant-trunks came through it out of the night beyond.

"I sent them with the lantern," she went on to her husband, "to look for Mara's leopardess: they have brought her."

I followed Adam to the door, and between us we took the white creature from the elephants, and carried her to the chamber we had just left, the women preceding us, Eve with the light, and Mara still carrying the hand. There we laid the beauty across the feet of the princess, her fore-paws outstretched, and her head couching between them.

CHAPTER XLI. I AM SENT

Then I turned and said to Eve,

"Mother, one couch next to Lona is empty: I know I am unworthy, but may I not sleep this night in your chamber with my dead? Will you not pardon both my cowardice and my self-confidence, and take me in? I give me up. I am sick of myself, and would fain sleep the sleep!"

"The couch next to Lona is the one already prepared for you," she answered; "but something waits to be done ere you sleep."

"I am ready," I replied.

"How do you know you can do it?" she asked with a smile.

"Because you require it," I answered. "What is it?"

She turned to Adam:

"Is he forgiven, husband?"

"From my heart."

"Then tell him what he has to do."

Adam turned to his daughter.

"Give me that hand, Mara, my child."

She held it out to him in her lap. He took it tenderly.

"Let us go to the cottage," he said to me; "there I will instruct you."

As we went, again arose a sudden stormful blast, mingled with a great flapping on the roof, but it died away as before in a deep moan.

When the door of the death-chamber was closed behind us, Adam seated himself, and I stood before him.

"You will remember," he said, "how, after leaving my daughter's house, you came to a dry rock, bearing the marks of an ancient cataract; you climbed that rock, and found a sandy desert: go to that rock now, and from its summit walk deep into the desert. But go not many steps ere you lie down, and listen with your head on the sand. If you hear the murmur of water beneath, go a little farther, and listen again. If you still hear the sound, you are in the right direction. Every few yards you must stop, lie down, and hearken. If, listening thus, at any time you hear no sound of water, you are out of the way, and must hearken in every direction until you hear it again. Keeping with the sound, and careful not to retrace your steps, you will soon hear it louder, and the growing sound will lead you to where it is loudest: that is the spot you seek. There dig with the spade I will give you, and dig until you come to moisture: in it lay the hand, cover it to the level of the desert, and come home.—But give good heed, and carry the hand with care. Never lay it down, in what place of seeming safety soever; let nothing touch it; stop nor turn aside for any attempt to bar your way; never look behind you; speak to no one, answer no one, walk straight on.—It is yet dark, and the morning is far distant, but you must set out at once."

He gave me the hand, and brought me a spade.

"This is my gardening spade," he said; "with it I have brought many a lovely thing to the sun."

I took it, and went out into the night.

It was very cold, and pitch-dark. To fall would be a dread thing, and the way I had to go was a difficult one even in the broad sunlight! But I had not set myself the task, and the minute I started I learned that I was left to no chance: a pale light broke from the ground at every step, and showed me where next to set my foot. Through the heather and the low rocks I walked without once even stumbling. I found the bad burrow quite still; not a wave arose, not a head appeared as I crossed it.

A moon came, and herself showed me the easy way: toward morning I was almost over the dry channels of the first branch of the river-bed, and not far, I judged, from Mara's cottage.

The moon was very low, and the sun not yet up, when I saw before me in the path, here narrowed by rocks, a figure covered from head to foot as with a veil of moonlit mist. I kept on my way as if I saw nothing. The figure threw aside its veil.

"Have you forgotten me already?" said the princess—or what seemed she.

I neither hesitated nor answered; I walked straight on.

"You meant then to leave me in that horrible sepulchre! Do you not yet understand that where I please to be, there I am? Take my hand: I am alive as you!"

I was on the point of saying, "Give me your left hand," but bethought myself, held my peace, and steadily advanced.

"Give me my hand," she suddenly shrieked, "or I will tear you in pieces: you are mine!"

She flung herself upon me. I shuddered, but did not falter. Nothing touched me, and I saw her no more.

With measured tread along the path, filling it for some distance, came a body of armed men. I walked through them—nor know whether they gave way to me, or were bodiless things. But they turned and followed me; I heard and felt their march at my very heels; but I cast no look behind, and the sound of their steps and the clash of their armour died away.

A little farther on, the moon being now close to the horizon and the way in deep shadow, I descried, seated where the path was so narrow that I could not pass her, a woman with muffled face.

"Ah," she said, "you are come at last! I have waited here for you an hour or more! You have done well! Your trial is over. My father sent me to meet you that you might have a little rest on the way. Give me your charge, and lay your head in my lap; I will take good care of both until the sun is well risen. I am not bitterness always, neither to all men!"

Her words were terrible with temptation, for I was very weary. And what more likely to be true! If I were, through slavish obedience to the letter of the command and lack of pure insight, to trample under my feet the very person of the Lady of Sorrow! My heart grew faint at the thought, then beat as if it would burst my bosom.

Nevertheless my will hardened itself against my heart, and my step did not falter. I took my tongue between my teeth lest I should unawares answer, and kept on my way. If Adam had sent her, he could not complain that I would not heed her! Nor would the Lady of Sorrow love me the less that even she had not been able to turn me aside!

Just ere I reached the phantom, she pulled the covering from her face: great indeed was her loveliness, but those were not Mara's eyes! no lie could truly or for long imitate them! I advanced as if the thing were not there, and my foot found empty room.

I had almost reached the other side when a Shadow—I think it was The Shadow, barred my way. He seemed to have a helmet upon his head, but as I drew closer I perceived it was the head itself I saw—so distorted as to bear but a doubtful resemblance to the human. A cold wind smote me, dank and sickening—repulsive as the air of a charnel-house; firmness forsook my joints, and my limbs trembled as if they would drop in a helpless heap. I seemed to pass through him, but I think now that he passed through me: for a moment I was as one of the damned. Then a soft wind like the first breath of a new-born spring greeted me, and before me arose the dawn.

My way now led me past the door of Mara's cottage. It stood wide open, and upon the table I saw a loaf of bread and a pitcher of water. In or around the cottage was neither howl nor wail.

I came to the precipice that testified to the vanished river. I climbed its worn face, and went on into the desert. There at last, after much listening to and fro, I determined the spot where the hidden water was loudest, hung Lilith's hand about my neck, and began to dig. It was a long labour, for I had to make a large hole because of the looseness of the sand; but at length I threw up a damp spadeful. I flung the sexton-tool on the verge, and laid down the hand. A little water was already oozing from under its fingers. I sprang out, and made haste to fill the grave. Then, utterly fatigued, I dropped beside it, and fell asleep.

CHAPTER XLII. I SLEEP THE SLEEP

When I woke, the ground was moist about me, and my track to the grave was growing a quicksand. In its ancient course the river was swelling, and had begun to shove at its burden. Soon it would be roaring down the precipice, and, divided in its fall, rushing with one branch to resubmerge the orchard valley, with the other to drown perhaps the monster horde, and between them to isle the Evil Wood. I set out at once on my return to those who sent me.

When I came to the precipice, I took my way betwixt the branches, for I would pass again by the cottage of Mara, lest she should have returned: I longed to see her once more ere I went to sleep; and now I knew where to cross the channels, even if the river should have overtaken me and filled them. But when I reached it, the door stood open still; the bread and the water were still on the table; and deep silence was within and around it. I stopped and called aloud at the door, but no voice replied, and I went my way.

A little farther, I came where sat a grayheaded man on the sand, weeping.

"What ails you, sir?" I asked. "Are you forsaken?"

"I weep," he answered, "because they will not let me die. I have been to the house of death, and its mistress, notwithstanding my years, refuses me. Intercede for me, sir, if you know her, I pray you."

"Nay, sir," I replied, "that I cannot; for she refuses none whom it is lawful for her to receive."

"How know you this of her? You have never sought death! you are much too young to desire it!"

"I fear your words may indicate that, were you young again, neither would you desire it."

"Indeed, young sir, I would not! and certain I am that you cannot."

"I may not be old enough to desire to die, but I am young enough to desire to live indeed! Therefore I go now to learn if she will at length take me in. You wish to

744

die because you do not care to live: she will not open her door to you, for no one can die who does not long to live."

"It ill becomes your youth to mock a friendless old man. Pray, cease your riddles!"

"Did not then the Mother tell you something of the same sort?"

"In truth I believe she did; but I gave little heed to her excuses."

"Ah, then, sir," I rejoined, "it is but too plain you have not yet learned to die, and I am heartily grieved for you. Such had I too been but for the Lady of Sorrow. I am indeed young, but I have wept many tears; pardon me, therefore, if I presume to offer counsel:—Go to the Lady of Sorrow, and 'take with both hands' * what she will give you. Yonder lies her cottage. She is not in it now, but her door stands open, and there is bread and water on her table. Go in; sit down; eat of the bread; drink of the water; and wait there until she appear. Then ask counsel of her, for she is true, and her wisdom is great."

He fell to weeping afresh, and I left him weeping. What I said, I fear he did not heed. But Mara would find him!

The sun was down, and the moon unrisen, when I reached the abode of the monsters, but it was still as a stone till I passed over. Then I heard a noise of many waters, and a great cry behind me, but I did not turn my head.

Ere I reached the house of death, the cold was bitter and the darkness dense; and the cold and the darkness were one, and entered into my bones together. But the candle of Eve, shining from the window, guided me, and kept both frost and murk from my heart.

The door stood open, and the cottage lay empty. I sat down disconsolate.

And as I sat, there grew in me such a sense of loneliness as never yet in my wanderings had I felt. Thousands were near me, not one was with me! True, it was I who was dead, not they; but, whether by their life or by my death, we were divided! They were alive, but I was not dead enough even to know them alive: doubt WOULD come. They were, at best, far from me, and helpers I had none to lay me beside them!

Never before had I known, or truly imagined desolation! In vain I took myself to task, saying the solitude was but a seeming: I was awake, and they slept—that was all! it was only that they lay so still and did not speak! they were with me now, and soon, soon I should be with them!

I dropped Adam's old spade, and the dull sound of its fall on the clay floor seemed reverberated from the chamber beyond: a childish terror seized me; I sat and stared at the coffin-door.—But father Adam, mother Eve, sister Mara would soon come to me, and then—welcome the cold world and the white neighbours! I forgot my fears, lived a little, and loved my dead.

Something did move in the chamber of the dead! There came from it what was LIKE a dim, far-off sound, yet was not what I knew as sound. My soul sprang into my ears. Was it a mere thrill of the dead air, too slight to be heard, but quivering in every spiritual sense? I KNEW without hearing, without feeling it!

The something was coming! it drew nearer! In the bosom of my desertion awoke an infant hope. The noiseless thrill reached the coffin-door—became sound, and smote on my ear.

The door began to move—with a low, soft creaking of its hinges. It was opening! I ceased to listen, and stared expectant.

It opened a little way, and a face came into the opening. It was Lona's. Its eyes were closed, but the face itself was upon me, and seemed to see me. It was white as Eve's, white as Mara's, but did not shine like their faces. She spoke, and her voice was like a sleepy night-wind in the grass.

"Are you coming, king?" it said. "I cannot rest until you are with me, gliding down the river to the great sea, and the beautiful dream-land. The sleepiness is full of lovely things: come and see them."

"Ah, my darling!" I cried. "Had I but known!—I thought you were dead!"

She lay on my bosom—cold as ice frozen to marble. She threw her arms, so white, feebly about me, and sighed—

"Carry me back to my bed, king. I want to sleep."

I bore her to the death-chamber, holding her tight lest she should dissolve out of my arms. Unaware that I saw, I carried her straight to her couch.

"Lay me down," she said, "and cover me from the warm air; it hurts—a little. Your bed is there, next to mine. I shall see you when I wake."

She was already asleep. I threw myself on my couch—blessed as never was man on the eve of his wedding.

"Come, sweet cold," I said, "and still my heart speedily."

But there came instead a glimmer of light in the chamber, and I saw the face of Adam approaching. He had not the candle, yet I saw him. At the side of Lona's couch, he looked down on her with a questioning smile, and then greeted me across it.

"We have been to the top of the hill to hear the waters on their way," he said. "They will be in the den of the monsters to-night.—But why did you not await our return?"

"My child could not sleep!" I answered.

"She is fast asleep!" he rejoined.

"Yes, now!" I said; "but she was awake when I laid her down."

"She was asleep all the time!" he insisted. "She was perhaps dreaming about you—and came to you?"

"She did."

"And did you not see that her eyes were closed?"

"Now I think of it, I did."

"If you had looked ere you laid her down, you would have seen her asleep on the couch."

"That would have been terrible!"

"You would only have found that she was no longer in your arms."

"That would have been worse!"

"It is, perhaps, to think of; but to see it would not have troubled you."

"Dear father," I said, "how is it that I am not sleepy? I thought I should go to sleep like the Little Ones the moment I laid my head down!"

"Your hour is not quite come. You must have food ere you sleep."

"Ah, I ought not to have lain down without your leave, for I cannot sleep without your help! I will get up at once!"

But I found my own weight more than I could move.

"There is no need: we will serve you here," he answered. "—You do not feel cold, do you?"

"Not too cold to lie still, but perhaps too cold to eat!"

He came to the side of my couch, bent over me, and breathed on my heart. At once I was warm.

As he left me, I heard a voice, and knew it was the Mother's. She was singing, and her song was sweet and soft and low, and I thought she sat by my bed in the dark; but ere it ceased, her song soared aloft, and seemed to come from the throat of a woman-angel, high above all the region of larks, higher than man had ever yet lifted up his heart. I heard every word she sang, but could keep only this:—

"Many a wrong, and its curing song;
    Many a road, and many an inn;
    Room to roam, but only one home
    For all the world to win!"

and I thought I had heard the song before.

Then the three came to my couch together, bringing me bread and wine, and I sat up to partake of it. Adam stood on one side of me, Eve and Mara on the other.

"You are good indeed, father Adam, mother Eve, sister Mara," I said, "to receive me! In my soul I am ashamed and sorry!"

"We knew you would come again!" answered Eve.

"How could you know it?" I returned.

"Because here was I, born to look after my brothers and sisters!" answered Mara with a smile.

"Every creature must one night yield himself and lie down," answered Adam: "he was made for liberty, and must not be left a slave!"

"It will be late, I fear, ere all have lain down!" I said.

"There is no early or late here," he rejoined. "For him the true time then first begins who lays himself down. Men are not coming home fast; women are coming faster. A desert, wide and dreary, parts him who lies down to die from him who lies down to live. The former may well make haste, but here is no haste."

"To our eyes," said Eve, "you were coming all the time: we knew Mara would find you, and you must come!"

"How long is it since my father lay down?" I asked.

"I have told you that years are of no consequence in this house," answered Adam; "we do not heed them. Your father will wake when his morning comes. Your mother, next to whom you are lying,——"

"Ah, then, it IS my mother!" I exclaimed.

"Yes—she with the wounded hand," he assented; "—she will be up and away long ere your morning is ripe."

"I am sorry."

"Rather be glad."

"It must be a sight for God Himself to see such a woman come awake!"

"It is indeed a sight for God, a sight that makes her Maker glad! He sees of the travail of His soul, and is satisfied!—Look at her once more, and sleep."

He let the rays of his candle fall on her beautiful face.

"She looks much younger!" I said.

"She IS much younger," he replied. "Even Lilith already begins to look younger!"

I lay down, blissfully drowsy.

"But when you see your mother again," he continued, "you will not at first know her. She will go on steadily growing younger until she reaches the perfection of her womanhood—a splendour beyond foresight. Then she will open her eyes, behold on one side her husband, on the other her son—and rise and leave them to go to a father and a brother more to her than they."

I heard as one in a dream. I was very cold, but already the cold caused me no suffering. I felt them put on me the white garment of the dead. Then I forgot everything. The night about me was pale with sleeping faces, but I was asleep also, nor knew that I slept.

CHAPTER XLIII. THE DREAMS THAT CAME

I grew aware of existence, aware also of the profound, the infinite cold. I was intensely blessed—more blessed, I know, than my heart, imagining, can now recall. I could not think of warmth with the least suggestion of pleasure. I knew that I had enjoyed it, but could not remember how. The cold had soothed every care, dissolved every pain, comforted every sorrow. COMFORTED? Nay; sorrow was swallowed up in the life drawing nigh to restore every good and lovely thing a hundredfold! I lay at peace, full of the quietest expectation, breathing the damp odours of Earth's bountiful bosom, aware of the souls of primroses, daisies and snowdrops, patiently waiting in it for the Spring.

How convey the delight of that frozen, yet conscious sleep! I had no more to stand up! had only to lie stretched out and still! How cold I was, words cannot tell; yet I grew colder and colder—and welcomed the cold yet more and more. I grew continuously less conscious of myself, continuously more conscious of bliss, unimaginable yet felt. I had neither made it nor prayed for it: it was mine in virtue of existence! and existence was mine in virtue of a Will that dwelt in mine.

Then the dreams began to arrive—and came crowding.—I lay naked on a snowy peak. The white mist heaved below me like a billowy sea. The cold moon was in the air with me, and above the moon and me the colder sky, in which the moon and I dwelt. I was Adam, waiting for God to breathe into my nostrils the breath of life.—I was not Adam, but a child in the bosom of a mother white with a radiant whiteness. I was a youth on a white horse, leaping from cloud to cloud of a blue heaven, hasting calmly to some blessed goal. For centuries I dreamed—or was it chiliads? or only one long night?—But why ask? for time had nothing to do with me; I was in the land of thought—farther in, higher up than the seven dimensions, the ten senses: I think I was where I am—in the heart of God.—I dreamed away dim cycles in the centre of a melting glacier, the spectral moon drawing nearer and nearer, the wind and the welter of a torrent growing in my ears. I lay and heard them: the wind and the water and the moon sang a peaceful waiting for a redemption drawing nigh. I dreamed cycles, I say, but, for aught I knew or can tell, they were the solemn, æonian march of a second, pregnant with eternity.

Then, of a sudden, but not once troubling my conscious bliss, all the wrongs I had ever done, from far beyond my earthly memory down to the present moment, were with me. Fully in every wrong lived the conscious I, confessing, abjuring, lamenting the dead, making atonement with each person I had injured, hurt, or offended. Every human soul to which I had caused a troubled thought, was now grown unspeakably dear to me, and I humbled myself before it, agonising to cast from between us the clinging offence. I wept at the feet of the mother whose commands I had slighted; with bitter shame I confessed to my father that I had told him two lies, and long forgotten them: now for long had remembered them, and kept them in memory to crush at last at his feet. I was the eager slave of all whom I had thus or anyhow wronged. Countless services I devised to render them! For this one I would build such a house as had never grown from the ground! for that one I would train such horses as had never yet been seen in any world! For a third I would make such a garden as had never bloomed, haunted with still pools, and alive with running waters! I would write songs to make their hearts swell, and tales to make them glow! I would turn the forces of the world into such channels of invention as to make them laugh with the joy of wonder! Love possessed me! Love was my life! Love was to me, as to him that made me, all in all!

Suddenly I found myself in a solid blackness, upon which the ghost of light that dwells in the caverns of the eyes could not cast one fancied glimmer. But my heart, which feared nothing and hoped infinitely, was full of peace. I lay imagining what the light would be when it came, and what new creation it would bring with it—when, suddenly, without conscious volition, I sat up and stared about me.

The moon was looking in at the lowest, horizontal, crypt-like windows of the death-chamber, her long light slanting, I thought, across the fallen, but still ripening sheaves of the harvest of the great husbandman.—But no; that harvest was gone! Gathered in, or swept away by chaotic storm, not a sacred sheaf was there! My dead were gone! I was alone!—In desolation dread lay depths yet deeper than I had hitherto known!—Had there never been any ripening dead? Had I but dreamed them and their loveliness? Why then these walls? why the empty couches? No; they were all up! they were all abroad in the new eternal day, and had forgotten me! They had left me behind, and alone! Tenfold more terrible was the tomb its inhabitants away! The quiet ones had made me quiet with their presence—had pervaded my mind with their blissful peace; now I had no friend, and my lovers were far from me! A moment I sat and stared horror-stricken. I had been alone with the moon on a mountain top in the sky; now I was alone with her in a huge cenotaph: she too was staring about, seeking her dead with ghastly gaze! I sprang to my feet, and staggered from the fearful place.

The cottage was empty. I ran out into the night.

No moon was there! Even as I left the chamber, a cloudy rampart had risen and covered her. But a broad shimmer came from far over the heath, mingled with a ghostly murmuring music, as if the moon were raining a light that plashed as it fell. I ran stumbling across the moor, and found a lovely lake, margined with reeds and rushes: the moon behind the cloud was gazing upon the monsters' den, full of clearest, brightest water, and very still.—But the musical murmur went on, filling the quiet air, and drawing me after it.

I walked round the border of the little mere, and climbed the range of hills. What a sight rose to my eyes! The whole expanse where, with hot, aching feet, I had crossed and recrossed the deep-scored channels and ravines of the dry river-bed, was alive with streams, with torrents, with still pools—"a river deep and wide"! How the moon flashed on the water! how the water answered the moon with flashes of its own—white flashes breaking everywhere from its rock-encountered flow! And a great jubilant song arose from its bosom, the song of new-born liberty. I stood a moment gazing, and my heart also began to exult: my life was not all a failure! I had helped to set this river free!—My dead were not lost! I had but to go after and find them! I would follow and follow until I came whither they had gone! Our meeting might be thousands of years away, but at last—AT LAST I should hold them! Wherefore else did the floods clap their hands?

I hurried down the hill: my pilgrimage was begun! In what direction to turn my steps I knew not, but I must go and go till I found my living dead! A torrent ran swift and wide at the foot of the range: I rushed in, it laid no hold upon me; I waded through it. The next I sprang across; the third I swam; the next I waded again.

I stopped to gaze on the wondrous loveliness of the ceaseless flash and flow, and to hearken to the multitudinous broken music. Every now and then some incipient air would seem about to draw itself clear of the dulcet confusion, only to merge again in the consorted roar. At moments the world of waters would invade as if to overwhelm me—not with the force of its seaward rush, or the shouting of its liberated throng, but with the greatness of the silence wandering into sound.

As I stood lost in delight, a hand was laid on my shoulder. I turned, and saw a man in the prime of strength, beautiful as if fresh from the heart of the glad creator, young like him who cannot grow old. I looked: it was Adam. He stood large and grand, clothed in a white robe, with the moon in his hair.

"Father," I cried, "where is she? Where are the dead? Is the great resurrection come and gone? The terror of my loneliness was upon me; I could not sleep without my dead; I ran from the desolate chamber.—Whither shall I go to find them?"

"You mistake, my son," he answered, in a voice whose very breath was consolation. "You are still in the chamber of death, still upon your couch, asleep and dreaming, with the dead around you."

"Alas! when I but dream how am I to know it? The dream best dreamed is the likest to the waking truth!"

"When you are quite dead, you will dream no false dream. The soul that is true can generate nothing that is not true, neither can the false enter it."

"But, sir," I faltered, "how am I to distinguish betwixt the true and the false where both alike seem real?"

"Do you not understand?" he returned, with a smile that might have slain all the sorrows of all his children. "You CANNOT perfectly distinguish between the true and the false while you are not yet quite dead; neither indeed will you when you are quite dead—that is, quite alive, for then the false will never present itself. At this moment, believe me, you are on your bed in the house of death."

"I am trying hard to believe you, father. I do indeed believe you, although I can neither see nor feel the truth of what you say."

"You are not to blame that you cannot. And because even in a dream you believe me, I will help you.—Put forth your left hand open, and close it gently: it will clasp the hand of your Lona, who lies asleep where you lie dreaming you are awake."

I put forth my hand: it closed on the hand of Lona, firm and soft and deathless.

"But, father," I cried, "she is warm!"

"Your hand is as warm to hers. Cold is a thing unknown in our country. Neither she nor you are yet in the fields of home, but each to each is alive and warm and healthful."

Then my heart was glad. But immediately supervened a sharp-stinging doubt.

"Father," I said, "forgive me, but how am I to know surely that this also is not a part of the lovely dream in which I am now walking with thyself?"

"Thou doubtest because thou lovest the truth. Some would willingly believe life but a phantasm, if only it might for ever afford them a world of pleasant dreams: thou art not of such! Be content for a while not to know surely. The hour will come, and that ere long, when, being true, thou shalt behold the very truth, and doubt will be for ever dead. Scarce, then, wilt thou be able to recall the features of the phantom. Thou wilt then know that which thou canst not now dream. Thou hast not yet looked the Truth in the face, hast as yet at best but seen him through a cloud. That which thou seest not, and never didst see save in a glass darkly—that which, indeed, never can be known save by its innate splendour shining straight into pure eyes—that thou canst not but doubt, and art blameless in doubting until thou seest it face to face, when thou wilt no longer be able to doubt it. But to him who has once seen even a shadow only of the truth, and, even but hoping he has seen it when it is present no longer, tries to obey it—to him the real vision, the Truth himself, will come, and depart no more, but abide with him for ever."

"I think I see, father," I said; "I think I understand."

"Then remember, and recall. Trials yet await thee, heavy, of a nature thou knowest not now. Remember the things thou hast seen. Truly thou knowest not those things, but thou knowest what they have seemed, what they have meant to thee! Remember also the things thou shalt yet see. Truth is all in all; and the truth of things lies, at once hid and revealed, in their seeming."

"How can that be, father?" I said, and raised my eyes with the question; for I had been listening with downbent head, aware of nothing but the voice of Adam.

He was gone; in my ears was nought but the sounding silence of the swift-flowing waters. I stretched forth my hands to find him, but no answering touch met their seeking. I was alone—alone in the land of dreams! To myself I seemed wide awake, but I believed I was in a dream, because he had told me so.

Even in a dream, however, the dreamer must do something! he cannot sit down and refuse to stir until the dream grow weary of him and depart: I took up my wandering, and went on.

Many channels I crossed, and came to a wider space of rock; there, dreaming I was weary, I laid myself down, and longed to be awake.

I was about to rise and resume my journey, when I discovered that I lay beside a pit in the rock, whose mouth was like that of a grave. It was deep and dark; I could see no bottom.

Now in the dreams of my childhood I had found that a fall invariably woke me, and would, therefore, when desiring to discontinue a dream, seek some eminence whence to cast myself down that I might wake: with one glance at the peaceful heavens, and one at the rushing waters, I rolled myself over the edge of the pit.

For a moment consciousness left me. When it returned, I stood in the garret of my own house, in the little wooden chamber of the cowl and the mirror.

Unspeakable despair, hopelessness blank and dreary, invaded me with the knowledge: between me and my Lona lay an abyss impassable! stretched a distance no chain could measure! Space and Time and Mode of Being, as with walls of adamant unscalable, impenetrable, shut me in from that gulf! True, it might yet be in my power to pass again through the door of light, and journey back to the chamber of the dead; and if so, I was parted from that chamber only by a wide heath, and by the pale, starry night betwixt me and the sun, which alone could open for me the mirror-door, and was now far away on the other side of the world! but an immeasurably wider gulf sank between us in this—that she was asleep and I was awake! that I was no longer worthy to share with her that sleep, and could no longer hope to awake from it with her! For truly I was much to blame: I had fled from my dream! The dream was not of my making, any more than was my life: I ought to have seen it to the end! and in fleeing from it, I had left the holy sleep itself behind me!—I would go back to Adam, tell him the truth, and bow to his decree!

I crept to my chamber, threw myself on my bed, and passed a dreamless night.

I rose, and listlessly sought the library. On the way I met no one; the house seemed dead. I sat down with a book to await the noontide: not a sentence could I understand! The mutilated manuscript offered itself from the masked door: the sight of it sickened me; what to me was the princess with her devilry!

I rose and looked out of a window. It was a brilliant morning. With a great rush the fountain shot high, and fell roaring back. The sun sat in its feathery top. Not a bird sang, not a creature was to be seen. Raven nor librarian came near me. The world was dead about me. I took another book, sat down again, and went on waiting.

Noon was near. I went up the stairs to the dumb, shadowy roof. I closed behind me the door into the wooden chamber, and turned to open the door out of a dreary world.

I left the chamber with a heart of stone. Do what I might, all was fruitless. I pulled the chains; adjusted and re-adjusted the hood; arranged and re-arranged the mirrors; no result followed. I waited and waited to give the vision time; it would not come; the mirror stood blank; nothing lay in its dim old depth but the mirror opposite and my haggard face.

I went back to the library. There the books were hateful to me—for I had once loved them.

That night I lay awake from down-lying to uprising, and the next day renewed my endeavours with the mystic door. But all was yet in vain. How the hours went I cannot think. No one came nigh me; not a sound from the house below entered my ears. Not once did I feel weary—only desolate, drearily desolate.

I passed a second sleepless night. In the morning I went for the last time to the chamber in the roof, and for the last time sought an open door: there was none. My heart died within me. I had lost my Lona!

Was she anywhere? had she ever been, save in the mouldering cells of my brain? "I must die one day," I thought, "and then, straight from my death-bed, I will set out to find her! If she is not, I will go to the Father and say—'Even thou canst not help me: let me cease, I pray thee!'"

CHAPTER XLIV. THE WAKING

The fourth night I seemed to fall asleep, and that night woke indeed. I opened my eyes and knew, although all was dark around me, that I lay in the house of death, and that every moment since there I fell asleep I had been dreaming, and now first was awake. "At last!" I said to my heart, and it leaped for joy. I turned my eyes; Lona stood by my couch, waiting for me! I had never lost her!—only for a little time lost the sight of her! Truly I needed not have lamented her so sorely!

It was dark, as I say, but I saw her: SHE was not dark! Her eyes shone with the radiance of the Mother's, and the same light issued from her face—nor from her face only, for her death-dress, filled with the light of her body now tenfold awake in the power of its resurrection, was white as snow and glistering. She fell asleep a girl; she awoke a woman, ripe with the loveliness of the life essential. I folded her in my arms, and knew that I lived indeed.

"I woke first!" she said, with a wondering smile.

"You did, my love, and woke me!"

"I only looked at you and waited," she answered.

The candle came floating toward us through the dark, and in a few moments Adam and Eve and Mara were with us. They greeted us with a quiet good-morning and a smile: they were used to such wakings!

"I hope you have had a pleasant darkness!" said the Mother.

"Not very," I answered, "but the waking from it is heavenly."

"It is but begun," she rejoined; "you are hardly yet awake!"

"He is at least clothed-upon with Death, which is the radiant garment of Life," said Adam.

He embraced Lona his child, put an arm around me, looked a moment or two inquiringly at the princess, and patted the head of the leopardess.

"I think we shall meet you two again before long," he said, looking first at Lona, then at me.

"Have we to die again?" I asked.

"No," he answered, with a smile like the Mother's; "you have died into life, and will die no more; you have only to keep dead. Once dying as we die here, all the dying is over. Now you have only to live, and that you must, with all your blessed might. The more you live, the stronger you become to live."

"But shall I not grow weary with living so strong?" I said. "What if I cease to live with all my might?"

"It needs but the will, and the strength is there!" said the Mother. "Pure life has no weakness to grow weary withal. THE Life keeps generating ours.—Those who will not die, die many times, die constantly, keep dying deeper, never have done dying; here all is upwardness and love and gladness."

She ceased with a smile and a look that seemed to say, "We are mother and son; we understand each other! Between us no farewell is possible."

Mara kissed me on the forehead, and said, gayly,

"I told you, brother, all would be well!—When next you would comfort, say, 'What will be well, is even now well.'"

She gave a little sigh, and I thought it meant, "But they will not believe you!"

"—You know me now!" she ended, with a smile like her mother's.

"I know you!" I answered: "you are the voice that cried in the wilderness before ever the Baptist came! you are the shepherd whose wolves hunt the wandering sheep home ere the shadow rise and the night grow dark!"

"My work will one day be over," she said, "and then I shall be glad with the gladness of the great shepherd who sent me."

"All the night long the morning is at hand," said Adam.

"What is that flapping of wings I hear?" I asked.

"The Shadow is hovering," replied Adam: "there is one here whom he counts his own! But ours once, never more can she be his!"

I turned to look on the faces of my father and mother, and kiss them ere we went: their couches were empty save of the Little Ones who had with love's boldness appropriated their hospitality! For an instant that awful dream of desolation overshadowed me, and I turned aside.

"What is it, my heart?" said Lona.

"Their empty places frightened me," I answered.

"They are up and away long ago," said Adam. "They kissed you ere they went, and whispered, 'Come soon.'"

"And I neither to feel nor hear them!" I murmured.

"How could you—far away in your dreary old house! You thought the dreadful place had you once more! Now go and find them.—Your parents, my child," he added, turning to Lona, "must come and find you!"

The hour of our departure was at hand. Lona went to the couch of the mother who had slain her, and kissed her tenderly—then laid herself in her father's arms.

"That kiss will draw her homeward, my Lona!" said Adam.

"Who were her parents?" asked Lona.

"My father," answered Adam, "is her father also."

She turned and laid her hand in mine.

I kneeled and humbly thanked the three for helping me to die. Lona knelt beside me, and they all breathed upon us.

"Hark! I hear the sun," said Adam.

I listened: he was coming with the rush as of a thousand times ten thousand far-off wings, with the roar of a molten and flaming world millions upon millions of miles away. His approach was a crescendo chord of a hundred harmonies.

The three looked at each other and smiled, and that smile went floating heavenward a three-petaled flower, the family's morning thanksgiving. From their mouths and their faces it spread over their bodies and shone through their garments. Ere I could say, "Lo, they change!" Adam and Eve stood before me the angels of the resurrection, and Mara was the Magdalene with them at the sepulchre. The countenance of Adam was like lightning, and Eve held a napkin that flung flakes of splendour about the place.

A wind began to moan in pulsing gusts.

"You hear his wings now!" said Adam; and I knew he did not mean the wings of the morning.

"It is the great Shadow stirring to depart," he went on. "Wretched creature, he has himself within him, and cannot rest!"

"But is there not in him something deeper yet?" I asked.

"Without a substance," he answered, "a shadow cannot be—yea, or without a light behind the substance!"

He listened for a moment, then called out, with a glad smile, "Hark to the golden cock! Silent and motionless for millions of years has he stood on the clock of the universe; now at last he is flapping his wings! now will he begin to crow! and at intervals will men hear him until the dawn of the day eternal."

I listened. Far away—as in the heart of an æonian silence, I heard the clear jubilant outcry of the golden throat. It hurled defiance at death and the dark; sang infinite hope, and coming calm. It was the "expectation of the creature" finding at last a voice; the cry of a chaos that would be a kingdom!

Then I heard a great flapping.

"The black bat is flown!" said Mara.

"Amen, golden cock, bird of God!" cried Adam, and the words rang through the house of silence, and went up into the airy regions.

At his AMEN—like doves arising on wings of silver from among the potsherds, up sprang the Little Ones to their knees on their beds, calling aloud,

"Crow! crow again, golden cock!"—as if they had both seen and heard him in their dreams.

Then each turned and looked at the sleeping bedfellow, gazed a moment with loving eyes, kissed the silent companion of the night, and sprang from the couch. The Little Ones who had lain down beside my father and mother gazed blank and sad for a moment at their empty places, then slid slowly to the floor. There they fell each into the other's arms, as if then first, each by the other's eyes, assured they were alive and awake. Suddenly spying Lona, they came running, radiant with bliss, to embrace her. Odu, catching sight of the leopardess on the feet of the princess, bounded to her next, and throwing an arm over the great sleeping head, fondled and kissed it.

"Wake up, wake up, darling!" he cried; "it is time to wake!"

The leopardess did not move.

"She has slept herself cold!" he said to Mara, with an upcast look of appealing consternation.

"She is waiting for the princess to wake, my child," said Mara.

Odu looked at the princess, and saw beside her, still asleep, two of his companions. He flew at them.

"Wake up! wake up!" he cried, and pushed and pulled, now this one, now that. But soon he began to look troubled, and turned to me with misty eyes.

"They will not wake!" he said. "And why are they so cold?"

"They too are waiting for the princess," I answered.

He stretched across, and laid his hand on her face.

"She is cold too! What is it?" he cried—and looked round in wondering dismay. Adam went to him.

"Her wake is not ripe yet," he said: "she is busy forgetting. When she has forgotten enough to remember enough, then she will soon be ripe, and wake."

"And remember?"

"Yes—but not too much at once though."

"But the golden cock has crown!" argued the child, and fell again upon his companions.

"Peter! Peter! Crispy!" he cried. "Wake up, Peter! wake up, Crispy! We are all awake but you two! The gold cock has crown SO loud! The sun is awake and coming! Oh, why WON'T you wake?"

But Peter would not wake, neither would Crispy, and Odu wept outright at last.

"Let them sleep, darling!" said Adam. "You would not like the princess to wake and find nobody? They are quite happy. So is the leopardess."

He was comforted, and wiped his eyes as if he had been all his life used to weeping and wiping, though now first he had tears wherewith to weep—soon to be wiped altogether away.

We followed Eve to the cottage. There she offered us neither bread nor wine, but stood radiantly desiring our departure. So, with never a word of farewell, we went out. The horse and the elephants were at the door, waiting for us. We were too happy to mount them, and they followed us.

CHAPTER XLV. THE JOURNEY HOME

It had ceased to be dark; we walked in a dim twilight, breathing through the dimness the breath of the spring. A wondrous change had passed upon the world— or was it not rather that a change more marvellous had taken place in us? Without light enough in the sky or the air to reveal anything, every heather-bush, every small shrub, every blade of grass was perfectly visible—either by light that went out from it, as fire from the bush Moses saw in the desert, or by light that went out of our eyes. Nothing cast a shadow; all things interchanged a little light. Every growing thing showed me, by its shape and colour, its indwelling idea—the informing thought, that is, which was its being, and sent it out. My bare feet seemed to love every plant they trod upon. The world and my being, its life and mine, were one. The microcosm and macrocosm were at length atoned, at length in harmony! I lived in everything; everything entered and lived in me. To be aware of a thing, was to know its life at once and mine, to know whence we came, and where we were at home—was to know that we are all what we are, because Another is what he is! Sense after sense, hitherto asleep, awoke in me—sense after sense indescribable, because no correspondent words, no likenesses or imaginations exist, wherewithal to describe them. Full indeed—yet ever expanding, ever making room to receive—was the conscious being where things kept entering by so many open doors! When a little breeze brushing a bush of heather set its purple bells a ringing, I was myself in the joy of the bells, myself in the joy of the breeze to which responded their sweet TIN-TINNING**, myself in the joy of the sense, and of the soul that received all the joys together. To everything glad I lent the hall of my being wherein to revel. I was a peaceful ocean upon which the ground-swell of a living joy was continually lifting new waves; yet was the joy ever the same joy, the eternal joy, with tens of thousands of changing forms. Life was a cosmic holiday.

Now I knew that life and truth were one; that life mere and pure is in itself bliss; that where being is not bliss, it is not life, but life-in-death. Every inspiration of the dark wind that blew where it listed, went out a sigh of thanksgiving. At last I was! I lived, and nothing could touch my life! My darling walked beside me, and we were on our way home to the Father!

So much was ours ere ever the first sun rose upon our freedom: what must not the eternal day bring with it!

We came to the fearful hollow where once had wallowed the monsters of the earth: it was indeed, as I had beheld it in my dream, a lovely lake. I gazed into its pellucid depths. A whirlpool had swept out the soil in which the abortions burrowed, and at the bottom lay visible the whole horrid brood: a dim greenish light pervaded the crystalline water, and revealed every hideous form beneath it. Coiled in spires, folded in layers, knotted on themselves, or "extended long and large," they weltered in motionless heaps—shapes more fantastic in ghoulish, blasting dismay, than ever wine-sodden brain of exhausted poet fevered into misbeing. He who dived in the swirling Maelstrom saw none to compare with them in horror: tentacular convolutions, tumid bulges, glaring orbs of sepian deformity, would have looked to him innocence beside such incarnations of hatefulness—every head the wicked flower that, bursting from an abominable stalk, perfected its evil significance.

Not one of them moved as we passed. But they were not dead. So long as exist men and women of unwholesome mind, that lake will still be peopled with loathsomenesses.

But hark the herald of the sun, the auroral wind, softly trumpeting his approach! The master-minister of the human tabernacle is at hand! Heaping before his prow a huge ripple-fretted wave of crimson and gold, he rushes aloft, as if new launched from the urging hand of his maker into the upper sea—pauses, and looks down on the world. White-raving storm of molten metals, he is but a coal from the altar of the Father's never-ending sacrifice to his children. See every little flower straighten its stalk, lift up its neck, and with outstretched head stand expectant: something more than the sun, greater than the light, is coming, is coming—none the less surely coming that it is long upon the road! What matters to-day, or to-morrow, or ten thousand years to Life himself, to Love himself! He is coming, is coming, and the necks of all humanity are stretched out to see him come! Every morning will they thus outstretch themselves, every evening will they droop and wait—until he comes.—Is this but an air-drawn vision? When he comes, will he indeed find them watching thus?

It was a glorious resurrection-morning. The night had been spent in preparing it!

The children went gamboling before, and the beasts came after us. Fluttering butterflies, darting dragon-flies hovered or shot hither and thither about our heads, a cloud of colours and flashes, now descending upon us like a snow-storm of rainbow flakes, now rising into the humid air like a rolling vapour of embodied odours. It was a summer-day more like itself, that is, more ideal, than ever man that had not died found summer-day in any world. I walked on the new earth, under the new heaven, and found them the same as the old, save that now they opened their minds to me, and I saw into them. Now, the soul of everything I met came out to greet me and make friends with me, telling me we came from the same, and meant the same. I was going to him, they said, with whom they always were, and whom they always meant; they were, they said, lightnings that took shape as they flashed from him to his. The dark rocks drank like sponges the rays that showered upon them; the great world soaked up the light, and sent out the living. Two joy-fires were Lona and I. Earth breathed heavenward her sweet-savoured smoke; we breathed homeward our longing desires. For thanksgiving, our very consciousness was that.

We came to the channels, once so dry and wearyful: they ran and flashed and foamed with living water that shouted in its gladness! Far as the eye could see, all was a rushing, roaring, dashing river of water made vocal by its rocks.

We did not cross it, but "walked in glory and in joy" up its right bank, until we reached the great cataract at the foot of the sandy desert, where, roaring and swirling and dropping sheer, the river divided into its two branches. There we climbed the height—and found no desert: through grassy plains, between grassy banks, flowed the deep, wide, silent river full to the brim. Then first to the Little Ones was revealed the glory of God in the limpid flow of water. Instinctively they plunged and swam, and the beasts followed them.

The desert rejoiced and blossomed as the rose. Wide forests had sprung up, their whole undergrowth flowering shrubs peopled with song-birds. Every thicket gave birth to a rivulet, and every rivulet to its water-song.

The place of the buried hand gave no sign. Beyond and still beyond, the river came in full volume from afar. Up and up we went, now along grassy margin, and now through forest of gracious trees. The grass grew sweeter and its flowers more lovely and various as we went; the trees grew larger, and the wind fuller of messages.

We came at length to a forest whose trees were greater, grander, and more beau-tiful than any we had yet seen. Their live pillars upheaved a thick embowed roof, betwixt whose leaves and blossoms hardly a sunbeam filtered. Into the rafters of this aerial vault the children climbed, and through them went scrambling and leaping in a land of bloom, shouting to the unseen elephants below, and hearing them trumpet their replies. The conversations between them Lona understood while I but guessed at them blunderingly. The Little Ones chased the squirrels, and the squirrels, frolicking, drew them on—always at length allowing themselves to be caught and petted. Often would some bird, lovely in plumage and form, light upon one of them, sing a song of what was coming, and fly away. Not one monkey of any sort could they see.

CHAPTER XLVI. THE CITY

Lona and I, who walked below, heard at last a great shout overhead, and in a moment or two the Little Ones began to come dropping down from the foliage with the news that, climbing to the top of a tree yet taller than the rest, they had descried, far across the plain, a curious something on the side of a solitary mountain—which mountain, they said, rose and rose, until the sky gathered thick to keep it down, and knocked its top off.

"It may be a city," they said, "but it is not at all like Bulika."

I went up to look, and saw a great city, ascending into blue clouds, where I could not distinguish mountain from sky and cloud, or rocks from dwellings. Cloud and mountain and sky, palace and precipice mingled in a seeming chaos of broken shadow and shine.

I descended, the Little Ones came with me, and together we sped on faster. They grew yet merrier as they went, leading the way, and never looking behind them. The river grew lovelier and lovelier, until I knew that never before had I seen real water. Nothing in this world is more than LIKE it.

By and by we could from the plain see the city among the blue clouds. But other clouds were gathering around a lofty tower—or was it a rock?—that stood above the city, nearer the crest of the mountain. Gray, and dark gray, and purple, they writhed in confused, contrariant motions, and tossed up a vaporous foam, while spots in them gyrated like whirlpools. At length issued a dazzling flash, which seemed for a moment to play about the Little Ones in front of us. Blinding darkness followed, but through it we heard their voices, low with delight.

"Did you see?"

"I saw."

"What did you see?"

"The beautifullest man."

"I heard him speak!"

762

"I didn't: what did he say?"

Here answered the smallest and most childish of the voices—that of Luva:—

"He said, ''Ou's all mine's, 'ickle ones: come along!'"

I had seen the lightning, but heard no words; Lona saw and heard with the children. A second flash came, and my eyes, though not my ears, were opened. The great quivering light was compact of angel-faces. They lamped themselves visible, and vanished.

A third flash came; its substance and radiance were human.

"I see my mother!" I cried.

"I see lots o' mothers!" said Luva.

Once more the cloud flashed—all kinds of creatures—horses and elephants, lions and dogs—oh, such beasts! And such birds!—great birds whose wings gleamed singly every colour gathered in sunset or rainbow! little birds whose feathers sparkled as with all the precious stones of the hoarding earth!—silvery cranes; red flamingoes; opal pigeons; peacocks gorgeous in gold and green and blue; jewelly humming birds!—great-winged butterflies; lithe-volumed creeping things—all in one heavenly flash!

"I see that serpents grow birds here, as caterpillars used to grow butterflies!" remarked Lona.

"I saw my white pony, that died when I was a child.—I needn't have been so sorry; I should just have waited!" I said.

Thunder, clap or roll, there had been none. And now came a sweet rain, filling the atmosphere with a caressing coolness. We breathed deep, and stepped out with stronger strides. The falling drops flashed the colours of all the waked up gems of the earth, and a mighty rainbow spanned the city.

The blue clouds gathered thicker; the rain fell in torrents; the children exulted and ran; it was all we could do to keep them in sight.

With silent, radiant roll, the river swept onward, filling to the margin its smooth, soft, yielding channel. For, instead of rock or shingle or sand, it flowed over grass in which grew primroses and daisies, crocuses and narcissi, pimpernels and anemones, a starry multitude, large and bright through the brilliant water. The river had gathered no turbid cloudiness from the rain, not even a tinge of yellow or brown; the delicate mass shone with the pale berylline gleam that ascended from its deep, dainty bed.

Drawing nearer to the mountain, we saw that the river came from its very peak, and rushed in full volume through the main street of the city. It descended to the gate by a stair of deep and wide steps, mingled of porphyry and serpentine, which continued to the foot of the mountain. There arriving we found shallower steps on both banks, leading up to the gate, and along the ascending street. Without the briefest halt, the Little Ones ran straight up the stair to the gate, which stood open.

Outside, on the landing, sat the portress, a woman-angel of dark visage, leaning her shadowed brow on her idle hand. The children rushed upon her, covering her with caresses, and ere she understood, they had taken heaven by surprise, and were already in the city, still mounting the stair by the side of the descending torrent. A great angel, attended by a company of shining ones, came down to meet and receive them, but merrily evading them all, up still they ran. In merry dance, however, a group of woman-angels descended upon them, and in a moment they were fettered in heavenly arms. The radiants carried them away, and I saw them no more.

"Ah!" said the mighty angel, continuing his descent to meet us who were now almost at the gate and within hearing of his words, "this is well! these are soldiers to take heaven itself by storm!—I hear of a horde of black bats on the frontiers: these will make short work with such!"

Seeing the horse and the elephants clambering up behind us—

"Take those animals to the royal stables," he added; "there tend them; then turn them into the king's forest."

"Welcome home!" he said to us, bending low with the sweetest smile.

Immediately he turned and led the way higher. The scales of his armour flashed like flakes of lightning.

Thought cannot form itself to tell what I felt, thus received by the officers of heaven***. All I wanted and knew not, must be on its way to me!

We stood for a moment at the gate whence issued roaring the radiant river. I know not whence came the stones that fashioned it, but among them I saw the prototypes of all the gems I had loved on earth—far more beautiful than they, for these were living stones—such in which I saw, not the intent alone, but the intender too; not the idea alone, but the imbodier present, the operant outsender: nothing in this kingdom was dead; nothing was mere; nothing only a thing.

We went up through the city and passed out. There was no wall on the upper side, but a huge pile of broken rocks, upsloping like the moraine of an eternal glacier; and through the openings between the rocks, the river came billowing out. On their top I could dimly discern what seemed three or four great steps of a stair, disappearing in a cloud white as snow; and above the steps I saw, but with my mind's eye only, as it were a grand old chair, the throne of the Ancient of Days. Over and under and between those steps issued, plenteously, unceasingly new-born, the river of the water of life.

The great angel could guide us no farther: those rocks we must ascend alone!

My heart beating with hope and desire, I held faster the hand of my Lona, and we began to climb; but soon we let each other go, to use hands as well as feet in the toilsome ascent of the huge stones. At length we drew near the cloud, which hung down the steps like the borders of a garment, passed through the fringe, and entered the deep folds. A hand, warm and strong, laid hold of mine, and drew me to a little door with a golden lock. The door opened; the hand let mine go, and pushed me gently through. I turned quickly, and saw the board of a large book in the act of closing behind me. I stood alone in my library.

CHAPTER XLVII. THE "ENDLESS ENDING"

As yet I have not found Lona, but Mara is much with me. She has taught me many things, and is teaching me more.

Can it be that that last waking also was in the dream? that I am still in the chamber of death, asleep and dreaming, not yet ripe enough to wake? Or can it be that I did not go to sleep outright and heartily, and so have come awake too soon? If that waking was itself but a dream, surely it was a dream of a better waking yet to come, and I have not been the sport of a false vision! Such a dream must have yet lovelier truth at the heart of its dreaming!

In moments of doubt I cry,

"Could God Himself create such lovely things as I dreamed?"

"Whence then came thy dream?" answers Hope.

"Out of my dark self, into the light of my consciousness."

"But whence first into thy dark self?" rejoins Hope.

"My brain was its mother, and the fever in my blood its father."

"Say rather," suggests Hope, "thy brain was the violin whence it issued, and the fever in thy blood the bow that drew it forth.—But who made the violin? and who guided the bow across its strings? Say rather, again—who set the song birds each on its bough in the tree of life, and startled each in its order from its perch? Whence came the fantasia? and whence the life that danced thereto? Didst THOU say, in the dark of thy own unconscious self, 'Let beauty be; let truth seem!' and straightway beauty was, and truth but seemed?"

Man dreams and desires; God broods and wills and quickens.

When a man dreams his own dream, he is the sport of his dream; when Another gives it him, that Other is able to fulfil it.

I have never again sought the mirror. The hand sent me back: I will not go out again by that door! "All the days of my appointed time will I wait till my change come."

Now and then, when I look round on my books, they seem to waver as if a wind rippled their solid mass, and another world were about to break through. Sometimes when I am abroad, a like thing takes place; the heavens and the earth, the trees and the grass appear for a moment to shake as if about to pass away; then, lo, they have settled again into the old familiar face! At times I seem to hear whisperings around me, as if some that loved me were talking of me; but when I would distinguish the words, they cease, and all is very still. I know not whether these things rise in my brain, or enter it from without. I do not seek them; they come, and I let them go.

Strange dim memories, which will not abide identification, often, through misty windows of the past, look out upon me in the broad daylight, but I never dream now. It may be, notwithstanding, that, when most awake, I am only dreaming the more! But when I wake at last into that life which, as a mother her child, carries this life in its bosom, I shall know that I wake, and shall doubt no more.

I wait; asleep or awake, I wait.

Novalis says, "Our life is no dream, but it should and will perhaps become one."

*Chapter 42: William Law.

**Chapter 45: Tin tin sonando con sì dolce nota
Che 'l ben disposto spirito d' amor turge.
DEL PARADISO, x. 142.

***Chapter 46: Oma' vedrai di sì fatti uficiali.
Del Purgatorio, ii. 30.

Made in the USA
Las Vegas, NV
24 October 2023

79657609R00430